MICHAEL MALONE is hailed as one of the South's – if not America's – greatest writers, and has been awarded the O. Henry award, the Writers Guild award, the Edgar and the Emmy. He has written five previous novels, many short stories, and scripts for television series. He lives in Hillsborough in his native North Carolina with his wife.

'A complex and satisfying plot, a rich panorama ... a moral vision ... magnificent.'

New York Times Book Review

'A finely populated detection thriller.'

The Sunday Times

'Perhaps the best novelist of the New South ... and one of the most distinctive talents to emerge in crime fiction.'

Guardian

'Marvellously engaging ... splendid ... hilarious.'

Kirkus Review

Other books by the same author

First Lady
Uncivil Seasons

Michael
Malone
TIME'S WITNESS

ROBINSON
London

Constable & Robinson Ltd
3 The Lanchesters
162 Fulham Palace Road
London W6 9ER
www.constablerobinson.com

First published in the UK by Chatto & Windus Ltd, 1989
Published in Abacus by Sphere Books Ltd, 1991

This edition published in the UK by Robinson,
an imprint of Constable & Robinson Ltd, 2002

A copy of the British Library Cataloguing in
Publication data is available from the British Library.

ISBN 1–84119–522–7

Printed and bound in the EU

10 9 8 7 6 5 4 3 2 1

Acknowledgments

For their kind willingness to answer a long stream of questions about criminal jurisprudence, my gratitude to Carl Fox, District Attorney of Orange County, North Carolina, to lawyers Dan Reed and Maria Mangano, and to Professor Daniel Pollitt at the Law School of the University of North Carolina in Chapel Hill. For their help in gathering information, special thanks to Virginia Hill, and to Sheila Waller, who also patiently drove me from police station to courthouse throughout the Piedmont.

Patricia Conners, trial counsel in Boston, Massachusetts, was good enough to cast a trained eye over *Time's Witness*, and I appreciate her generous interest in reading the manuscript for me.

Material provided by Klanwatch at the Southern Poverty Law Center was invaluable, as was the knowledgeable and very moving work done on death row prisoners by Katheryn Watterson Buckhart.

The characters and events portrayed in *Time's Witness* are fictitious. The setting is the state of North Carolina, and certain public institutions and public offices are mentioned, but the characters involved in them are entirely imaginary. Any similarities to real persons, living or dead, is purely coincidental and not intended by the author.

Specific settings are also fictional: 'Dollard Prison' is in no way a portrait of any actual prison. Nor have I attempted to follow with absolute legal accuracy the current courtroom and criminal policies of any given region: For example, in North Carolina now, prisoners are executed by lethal injection, whereas in this novel, the state still uses the gas chamber.

In memory of my mother

FAYLENE JONES MALONE

a Southern schoolteacher,

who taught that justice is everyone's right
and everyone's responsibility

Prologue

Of charity, what kin are you to me?

– *Twelfth Night*

I don't know about Will Rogers, but I grew up deciding the world was nothing but a sad, dangerous junk pile heaped with shabby geegaws, the bullies who peddled them, and the broken-up human beings who worked the line. Some good people came along, and they softened my opinion. So I'm open to any evidence they can show me that God's not asleep at the wheel, barrelling blind down the highway with all us dumb scared creatures screaming in the back seat.

My name's Cuddy Mangum. I don't much like it. Short for Cudberth, by which I suspect my mother meant Cuthbert, though I never called it to her attention. Everybody's always known me as Cuddy. Cudberth would have been worse. Or Cud.

A few years back, at the start of the eighties, I was made police chief here in Hillston, North Carolina. If you ever read a story by Justin Savile, you know that, but chances are you've got too cute a notion of who I am. Justin's loved me for years without a clue to my meaning. He sees things personally. Me, I look at the package, and the programme. According to Justin, I'm somewhere between young Abe Lincoln in cracker country and the mop-up man on 'Hee Haw.' A kind of Carolina Will Rogers without the rope tricks. And Justin's always adding to his portrait. He never read a book without looking for everybody he knows in it, and it didn't take him long to find me chasing after a dream like Gatsby, wearing

1

some buckskin moral outfit Natty Bumpo left behind. I'm not saying his views aren't flattering. But if my arms had had the stretch of Justin's imagination, I could have bounced through the state university free, playing basketball, instead of slapping concrete on the new sports arena for four years to pay my way.

Justin and I are natives of the same tobacco and textiles city in the North Carolina Piedmont. But his folks shipped him out of Hillston early, off to some woodsy New England prep school, then to Harvard, where his imagination got away from him for a while, and they had to lock him up in a sanatorium near Asheville. I saw it once; it looked like Monte Carlo. Afterwards, they smuggled him into law school in Virginia, but he ran home to Hillston and threw them into a hissie by joining the police. I've heard his reasons. They're all personal.

I didn't have near enough the imagination for the first place I was shipped after college, and after too long a while slithering through rice paddies in the Mekong Delta, I crawled back to Hillston as fast as my psychic state allowed. I wanted a master's degree from Haver University, and I wanted to get to know my wife, Cheryl. It turned out she'd made other plans with a fellow I used to like. She was my last living family, if you want to call her that. My folks are dead. A long time ago, my sister Vivian's boyfriend, going drunk into a curve at eighty miles an hour, smashed them both through a steel rail on Route 28. He survived, and died in a motorcycle accident three months after he got out of traction. His parents still owed University Hospital over twelve thousand dollars. For his personal motto in the Hillston High yearbook, this boy had them write, 'I want to live fast, love hard, die young, and leave a beautiful memory.' That year, six different East Hillston guys had this same motto. Vivian's boyfriend was the second to get his wish.

In 1931 my daddy walked into Hillston barefooted. The first big building he saw was Cadmean Textile Mills, so he took a job there sweeping floors. His folks worked a farm fifteen miles outside the town. They didn't own it, and they couldn't feed him. After forty-two years on the Cadmean line, he didn't own the house he died in. He did own a long series of large cheap cars loaded with chrome that he buffed with a shammy rag on Sunday afternoons. I don't know if there was anything else he loved. Any dreams he kept, he kept private. Mama never learned to drive the cars. She had bad teeth and a purplish birthmark across her right cheek that she covered with the palm of her hand, and she

2

was shy about going anyplace except the East Hillston A&P and the Baptist Church of the Kingdom of Christ. By third grade, I'd stopped asking her for help with my homework. Her tongue would stutter struggling to decipher the big printed letters, and a thin line of sweat would rise just above her lips, and her birth-mark would blush purple.

I didn't have the best thing, which is class. Here in the South that means an old family tree, with all its early rough graspy roots buried deep down in the past where nobody has to look at them. And I didn't have the second-best thing, which is looks – because the hard fact is, resembling young Abe Lincoln is no asset at a high-school sock hop. But I had the third thing, which is brains. So I was lucky enough to learn how to see where the light was, and where to look around for the switch. I don't mean moving out of East Hillston, but I mean that too. I've got a job that makes some use of my brain, and is some use to other people. I've got eight walls of books. I've got a new white Oldsmobile my daddy would have just admired. I own a condo-minium in River Rise, west of town, so big I haven't had time to furnish half of it. It's big enough for love to have some space, because let me tell you, love likes a lot of room; it's hate that does fine when it's cramped. I've got so many former neighbours to prove that fact, it comes close to breaking my heart.

Justin Bartholomew Savile V is a Liberal Democrat, a group just about abandoned by everybody except the upper classes. Justin's father (J.B.S. IV) was the kind of Virginian who'd name his son J.B.S. V; his hobby was running Haver University Medical School. Justin's mother is a Dollard. Well now, Dollards. For a couple of centuries they've sat slicing up the pie of the Carolina Piedmont and passing the pieces around to each other with polite little nods. 'Why I don't mind if I do, thank you so much.' Justin's great-great-grandfather Eustace Dollard was one of the state's best-remembered governors (mostly because his daddy had led a charge into the Wilderness against the Yankees without bothering to see if anybody was behind him), but also because Eustace had chiselled his name into a hundred large-sized public buildings, including the state penitentiary. From what I've read about the governor, Dollard State Prison's a fitting memorial.

Like I say, Justin loves me. Once he even came real close to getting himself killed, leaping between me and a bullet. He didn't think, his genes just jumped forward like they thought they were back in the Wilderness. So I keep that in mind, his body stretched over me, soaking my hair with blood, when I think about another time, the day I came to see him in the hospital. It was the look in his eyes when I told him the Hillston City Council had just made me chief of police, and consequently his superior. That look was there for just a blink before pleasure took it over. Oh, it wasn't envy or jealousy or distaste. It was a look of pure unvarnished surprise. See, it hadn't – it couldn't occur to Justin that some East Hillston wisecracking white trash, with a mama so ignorant she'd named him Cudberth by mistake, could walk so far off the line as to embody the Law. Lord knows what innocent notions Justin has of Abe Lincoln's political savvy. Now, personally, he was happy for me, and proud of me. He loved it when I taped my poster of Elvis up behind my desk. If I'd called him on that blink of surprise, he wouldn't have had a clue to my meaning. And the God's truth is, Justin Savile's the kindest man I ever met.

My friend Justin's blink is sad proof of the power of the package and the programme, the same ones that are walking a black man named George Hall into the gas chamber at Dollard State Prison on Saturday unless the governor changes his mind. So me, I'm for a new program, not to mention a new governor. Like George Hall, I can't rely on kindness.

Part One

A Common Recreation

Chapter 1

I was over in Vietnam trying hard not to get killed when the death penalty went out of fashion back home. That was 1967. At the time some kind folks thought we had us a moral revolution going that couldn't slip back; it was racing along the road to glory, chucking war and racism and sexism out the windows like roadside trash. These sweet Americans could no more imagine a backward slide than Romans could imagine their Forum was going to end up a cow pasture in something called the Dark Ages, much less a big litter box for stray cats tiptoeing through the condoms and cigarette butts.

So when I joined the Hillston police, everybody figured the death penalty was gone for good, like racks and thumbscrews. Turned out it was only gone for nine years, seven months, and fourteen days. Then a Death Row huckster told the state of Utah he wanted them to shoot him, and Utah had to fight off the volunteers eager to oblige, and the United States was back in the habit of killing people to stop people from killing people.

Nobody'd heard a word from the governor, so my state was still planning to kill George Hall at nine o'clock Saturday night. It used to be, before the moratorium, executions at Dollard State Prison were scheduled early in the morning. Then, after the Supreme Court changed its mind and told the state that capital punishment wasn't cruel and unusual after all, somebody over in the Raleigh legislature decided that on the other hand, it was cruel to make condemned prisoners sit up all night waiting to die at dawn, since studies showed that not too many of them could sleep. So they changed the time of death to midnight. But given the fact that our Haver County DA, Mitchell Bazemore, held the national record for death penalty convictions (forty-four, so far, and still counting), before long the staff at Dollard starting protesting about the late hours – the doctor on call at the gas chamber had a daytime job in a clinic at Haver Power and Light – and eventually they scheduled executions for nine P.M., or as close to it as they could manage.

George Hall was the first man I ever arrested in a homicide case. He was young, black, unemployed, and he shot an off-duty cop outside a bar in East Hillston. With the officer's own pistol. George was sitting on the sidewalk beside the gun when I happened to drive by. 'I'm not running, just don't shoot!' was the first thing he said to me. His nose was still bleeding from where this particular off-duty cop had stuck his pistol in it. At the time, a fidgety toady named Van Fulcher was chief of police; he showed up fast, and relieved me of the case even faster – not because he was wild about either justice or Bobby Pym, the dead cop, but because whenever a case looked likely to interest anybody with a camera (and a black man shooting a white policeman was about as likely as you could get in the Piedmont Carolinas), Captain Fulcher suddenly felt the urge to take a personal interest: 'Go hands on' was how he put it. So Fulcher went 'hands on' in the Hall investigation, which was a short one. So was the trial. George had a court-appointed lawyer, who tried to persuade him against pleading not guilty, since he didn't think the jury would go for self-defence. This public defender wasn't a very bright guy, but he was right about that jury. While half-a-dozen witnesses said it certainly looked like self-defence to them, there having been a reasonable appearance of the necessity for deadly force on George's part to prevent his own immediate death or serious injury, not a one of these witnesses was white. The jury didn't even stay away long enough to order dinner. This was 1976, and, at the time, like I said, I thought capital punishment was out of fashion for good, except in places like Iran and South Africa. But after three appeals and seven years on Death Row, George Hall was about to become Mitchell Bazemore's next victory on his way to the national record. Friday morning I told George's brother I never thought it could go this way, and George's brother told me to go fuck myself. Friday evening I went to a dance.

*

8

For ninety-six years running, on the Saturday before Christmas, the Hillston Club had held its annual Confederacy Ball. Every year the town's inner circle, which liked to refer to itself as 'our number' or just 'us,' let a committee at the Club tabulate this 'number' and send them creamy gilt-bordered invitations. The elected drove through North Hillston, where they all lived on windy roads, over to the Club, and there they two-stepped around a mildewed ballroom for a couple of hours, pretending it was 1861 and still possible they were going to win the War. The men grew moustaches and strapped on swords they claimed were inherited. The women ballooned out of BMWs in hoop skirts, with gardenias pinned to their hair. My information comes from Justin, who loved any excuse to dress up in a costume, and had a handmade grey brassy outfit looped with gold tassels that he frisked about in there every year.

Except this year. This year the Entertainment Committee had not only dropped the word *Confederacy* from their invitations, they'd changed the date from Saturday to Friday. A black man was scheduled to be executed at Dollard Prison on Saturday, and there'd been considerable publicity regarding the case, because in the years George had waited on Death Row, his younger brother, Cooper Hall, had become a pretty well-known political activist, with an instinct for what his enemies (and that was most of Hillston) called media manipulation. I'm not saying the Hillside Club acted out of worry over what Coop Hall could do with their planning to dance the Virginia reel while his brother was being gassed to death. The number'd been raised on good manners, and they were feeling genuinely queasy. Peggy Savile, Justin's mother, and my source, made a motion to cancel the ball entirely, but after some 'frosty' discussion, the motion was defeated five to four in secret ballots that fooled no one. Still, even Judge Henry Tiggs, Retired, who'd once called an attorney with a sardonic black colleague up to his bench and drawled at him, 'Get that nigrah out of my courtroom,' even Judge Tiggs probably wasn't comfortable with the thought of stumbling through a waltz under the mistletoe at the exact same moment somebody he'd sentenced to death was paying his debt to society by inhaling for three or four minutes (up to six, if, like Caryl Chessman, he was determined not to breathe too deeply) the vapours from a sack of sodium cyanide eggs dropped into a little sulphuric acid.

So it was decided to move the dance to Friday, and unanimous to substitute black tie and formal gowns for the antebellum

9

costumes, which undeniably had the smack of nostalgia for the Age of Slavery, or at least might give that tacky impression to people not of the number. That last included me, but the doorman didn't notice when I tugged Justin's invitation out of my rented tuxedo, laid it out on his open white glove, and strolled into the foyer, ducking a chandelier that burned real white candles.

Earlier, back at my bureau mirror in River Rise, I'd tried putting different hands in different pockets, looking for the nonchalant effect. Martha Mitchell was disgusted; Martha's this little more-or-less poodle I found dumped out, just a puppy, on Airport Road the day I got home from Vietnam; she had Mrs Mitchell's nose and bangs, and she appeared to have been treated about the same by her relations. Since I knew the feeling, what with the Nixon gang dicking us both around in the worse way, I gave her a ride to Hillston, and we've been splitting Big Macs for nine years. So Martha, lying on my king-sized water bed, lets go with this sigh while I'm practising nonchalance at the bureau. She's a proud lady. Well, hey, here I am, youngest chief of a city its size in the whole South, modernized my department with some drastic innovations like computers, women, and blacks; dropped the crime rate 11.75 per cent my first year, not to mention the crime rate *inside* the force – bribery, bigotry, and occasional mild brutality being the oldest favourites; with a half-column and my picture in *Newsweek* magazine stuck to my refrigerator door by a magnetized tiny pineapple. 'SCHOLAR COP' is the headline on this piece: I'm going for a history PhD. At a slow pace.

So Martha squirmed on the water bed, embarrassed for me, while I tried out one hand versus two in the slippery pockets of those rented trousers. I told her, 'Honey, don't give me that Marxist wheeze. There's things about my life story you don't even know, so get your toenails out of my water bed before I find you floating around in the closet.' Martha's listened to my conversation a lot longer than my ex-wife Cheryl did; she's not much on repartee, but she hangs in there.

I decided on one-hand, so that's how I walked into the Hillston Club ballroom, heading for the waltzy music and hum of voices, past a ceiling-high Christmas tree burning some more real white candles, past a blond beautiful drunk girl in a strapless red satin gown, lying on a couch against the wall, her arm over her eyes, past Mr Dyer Fanshaw trying to unhook his wife's stole from the catch on her necklace.

'Well, why, Chief Mangum, surprised to see you here.' A. R. Randolph, short, stout, shrewd, and ignorant as a hog, was shoving towards me, one hand in his back vent, tugging his pants loose from the crease of his buttocks. These folks were so used to their Rhett & Scarlett rentals, they were having trouble with their own clothes. 'Dammit.' He jerked his head at the girl in red satin. 'That's my damn granddaughter passed out on the damn couch, and it's not even ten o'clock.'

'Looks like she might be a real pretty girl when she's feeling better.' We shook hands when he'd finished playing with his underwear. 'Surprised to see me? Why's that, Atwater?' I let Randolph's Lions Club set up their October carnival in my Municipal Building parking lot, so I called him Atwater and joked some circles around him. He got a kick out of it. He was more than twice my age, and a thousand times my income, inherited the construction company that had built Haver University and just about everything else in Hillston, including the River Rise complex and the state-funded four-lane bridge over the Shocco River that you could play a full game of softball on without worrying about interference from traffic.

He stepped closer for confidentiality. 'Figured they'd need you over at the state prison. What I hear is, the Klan's going there tonight and bust up that vigil. All those "Save George Hall" nuts. That's what I hear.'

'Well, now, rumours. A rumour's kind of like the flu bug. You don't know where it came from, and you don't want to spread it around.' I gave him my country grin. 'Those Klan boys aren't as young as they used to be. They'll all be home watching HBO. It's too cold and messy out there for politics.'

'I heard you had a tip they were going to hassle those Pro-Lifers tonight.'

Luckily I was already grinning, so my laugh sounded friendly. 'You got to keep up with the lingo, Atwater. Pro-Lifers are the ones that are against killing fetuses, and *for* killing grown-ups. Whereas Coop Hall's group is anti-pro-capital punishment, and most of them anti-Pro-Lifers too. You with me?'

'Well, they're wasting their time, whatever they call themselves.'

'Probably.'

'Cuddy, the historical fact is, mankind has a right to protect ourselves against scum. And that's always the type that gets themselves executed.'

11

'Um hum. Historical-wise, three popped right into my head. Socrates, Joan of Arc, and Jesus Christ. Talk about scumbags, whoowee!'

His plump face wrinkled. 'Now hold up, Chief, if Christ hadn't been killed, we'd none of us be redeemed today.'

'Well, you got me there, Atwater.'

Neither one of us was looking at the other one during this chitchat. He was watching his friend Dyer Fanshaw still trying to detach his wife from her stole while she ignored him and hugged everyone who walked close enough. I was looking over Randolph's head into the ballroom to try to spot either the man I'd told myself I was coming to see, or the lady I'd told myself I didn't care if I saw or not. The man was Julian Lewis, once attorney general, now lieutenant governor, hoping to move up another step. The lady was Mrs Andrew Brookside, wife of the man Lewis was running against. Except when I knew her best she wasn't married; she was sixteen and her name was Lee Haver.

One wall of this ballroom was glass doors; each one had its own wreath. In front of them, tables floating with white linen stretched along, crowded with crystal punch bowls, beds of oysters in their shells, and platters of tiny ham biscuits. Every four feet, a waiter stood waiting to tilt a glass ladle of champagne punch into any receptacle held up in his vicinity. (Some members had obviously lost patience with their little crystal cups, and had moved on to water glasses.) The waiters were the only black people I saw in the room, except for the mayor, the mayor's wife, the president of Southeast Life Insurance Company, and half the band, which sat on a little dais, behind shiny red shields draped with holly garlands and labelled THE JIMMY DOUGLAS ORCHESTRA. The band was pumping through 'The Anniversary Waltz' (maybe celebrating a near-century of these affairs), but only about fifty couples were dancing (or forty-nine; I don't know what old Judge Tiggs and his wife were doing, maybe the tango, or maybe one of them was trying to leave the floor and the other one didn't want to). The rest of the guests looked like they were scared to lose their places in the punch line.

'You know Dyer Fanshaw?' Randolph tugged me towards the couple.

'Let me take a wild guess. Does he own Fanshaw Paper Company?'

'Chief, you kill me. Dyer, will you leave that woman alone

and say hello to our chief of police? You see him in *Newsweek* last month?'

'Cuddy Mangum,' I said, just as Mrs Fanshaw broke loose, tossed me a fast hello, and rushed into the party.

'Everything under control?' Fanshaw asked while we shook hands.

'Personally, or criminally?'

'Mangum kills me,' Randolph explained. 'He means the George Hall business, Chief. Don't you, Dyer?'

Dyer did, so we talked a while about whether the governor would stay Hall's death sentence (they didn't think he would), and whether there'd be a riot at Dollard Prison between the vigilante protesting execution and the enthusiasts demanding it. I explained why I had my doubts. 'First of all, it's freezing rain out there, which discourages philosophical debate, and second' – I shared a little of the inside track – 'I talked to Warden Carpenter an hour ago, and the place is quiet as an opium den. I talked to the FBI, which pays about two-thirds of the dues at our local Knights of the KKK, and they don't have a plan rattling around in their heads. And I talked to somebody working with the George Hall vigil, and she says they can't get Action News to come, which they surely could if there was a hundred-to-one shot of even a poke in the eye, much less blood in the dirt.'

My business leaders were relieved and disappointed, and tickled to be in the know. Then they talked for a while about how Governor Wollston could follow his heart since he wasn't up for reelection, and about whether Andy Brookside had made a mistake resigning the presidency of Haver University to run on the Democratic ticket, since – even if he was a war hero married to a millionairess – having an assistant campaign manager like that Jack Molina mouthing off against capital punishment was going to kill him in the polls; not that they cared – they were Republicans, and loved to see Democrats beat in their own heads with their own baseball bats. I asked if Brookside was here tonight, and they said, sure, he went every place there were more than a dozen voters penned up in a room with only one exit.

Then some more stocky financial spokes of the inner circle herded around us. A lot of this group I knew by name, but we weren't exactly what you'd want to call golf partners. I recognized a bank, a towel company, a 'Hot Hat' barbecue franchise (all the roofs had red neon pigs tipping top hats), and a lot of real estate. Most of these men looked like their bow ties were choking

13

them. The bank (still growing the moustache he'd started for the reclassified Confederacy Ball) jumped right into the George Hall business with the interesting theory that the problem with capital punishment these days was that it wasn't cruel enough. 'Listen here, it's painless! They put you the hell to sleep, come on! In the old days, they'd flay you alive, burn you – you'd think twice.'

'Dead is dead,' said the towel company, shifting his cummerbund to the right.

'You wouldn't say that, Terry, if it were your feet in the fire.'

I had to agree with the bank; between gas and disembowelment, or getting stuffed with gunpowder and blown all over China, or having my head crushed by an Indian elephant, I'll take American technology any day. I told them, 'Folks don't have any imagination anymore. You know what happened if you killed your daddy in ancient Rome? They sewed you in a cloth with a monkey, a poisonous snake, a fighting rooster, and a wild dog, and they tossed you in the Tiber.'

The notion stopped them cold for a minute, then the bank nodded. 'That's what I'm talking about. Punishment. And I'll tell you something else, it ought to be in public, like they used to. Put them on TV. It's supposed to be deterrence, right? Make people watch.'

I said, 'Speaking as a keeper of the peace, gentlemen, crowds make me nervous. Last time we hanged somebody in public was in the 'thirties, over in Owensboro, Kentucky. What I read is, twenty thousand folks piled in for the show, and a third of them set up refreshment stands. "Make them watch" isn't exactly the problem. It's the fights over good seats.'

My figures led the real estate man to mention how he'd managed to buy six seats for the Super Bowl, which led to complaints about Cadmean Stadium at the university, which led to speculation about the illness of 'poor old Briggs,' meaning old Briggs Cadmean (of Cadmean & Whetstone Textiles Industries), a big bald sly SOB of about eighty-five, and, to hear him tell it, the private owner of Hillston. I had to walk by Cadmean's picture on the way to my office every day; he'd paid for the Municipal Building and wanted everybody to know it. In this eight-foot oil painting in the lobby, he's got the rolled-up blueprints in one hand; the other hand's pointing down the hall towards the men's room. Once the old bastard had claimed to my face that he was personally responsible for my promotion to chief. I was dating his youngest daughter at the time. The rest of his offspring were male, long dead, or looked it, and this girl (he'd named her Briggs after himself and called her 'Baby') was his favourite. She hated the sight of him, and turns out he thought I'd bring them together as a thank-you note for my new job. I had to disappoint him. Deep down, Briggs Junior wasn't any fonder of me than she was of her dad, though she just about convinced me otherwise. She was an astronomy professor, and I think what she really loved the most was stars. Justin always said she was about that cold, too. Last I heard, she'd taken a position out West, where there wouldn't be so much population between her and the sky. She sent me back my ring before I finished the Visa payments, and about a month after she left, Cadmean flagged me over to his limousine on Main Street, and accused me of reneging on a deal he'd never bothered to call to my attention. He had the morals of a grizzly bear. Justin liked him.

'Poor old Briggs,' Fanshaw was saying as he looked over at the passed-out girl on the couch, who was about to deep-breathe herself out of the top of that red satin strapless. 'Well, God knows, Cadmean had a good long life, and he's dying the way he wants to.'

'How's that?' I said. 'Just temporarily?'

'See what I mean?' Pointing at me, Randolph nudged Fanshaw. Then the quartet of business leaders said they were headed to the bathroom before their wives cornered them, and did we want anything. I was the only one who appeared to find this question peculiar.

Randolph told them he'd be down later, and turned back to me. 'Nahw, Dyer means Briggs won't go to the hospital. What I heard was, he said, "I paid for the damn hospital, but that doesn't oblige me to let those suckbutts get their hands on me, so I go meet my Maker with my fanny in a pan and a tube up my dick.'"

Fanshaw tightened his nostrils. I gave him a wink. 'A sweet-talking man. He's got a lot more to explain to his Maker than a bare backside.'

They both chuckled their agreement. And that's when I saw Lee Haver Brookside. Actually it was Justin I saw first, as they swung past the crowd on to the dance floor. Justin stood out, due to being the only man at the party in white tie and tails. He was the kind who'd wear an English hunting outfit to a barbecue picnic. Now he and Mrs Brookside were waltzing in big slow loops, so I saw her back where his hand rested just above the black folded silk, then the white of her neck and shoulders as her head turned. A diamond flared like a match in the braided coil of dark gold hair.

I said I thought I'd go get some punch. 'Nice to meet you, Mr Fanshaw.'

'Same here.' He nodded at Randolph, like I'd passed a test, and told me, 'Call me Dyer. The real bar's downstairs in the men's lounge. That punch won't do a thing for you.'

'Mr Fanshaw, what I paid for this outfit, I don't want to waste it on a john. I see enough line-ups of men during the day.'

Fanshaw chuckled, and Randolph said, 'Hunh?,' and I gave one shoe a quick rub on the back of my trousers, put my left hand in my left pocket, and walked into the party.

For the most part, the Club style seemed to be to mix the sexes for dancing, and split them up for conversation. Seated at little tables, women, their long dresses glittering, smoked themselves almost invisible while telling each other what must have been mighty funny stories. Men stood in black glossy huddles, nodding at everything everybody else said. The Reverend Thomas Campbell (an old tall Presbyterian, in a tuxedo) and Father Paul Madison (a young short Episcopalian, in a collar) had crossed the line and were chatting with our new black mayor's wife, whose fixed smile must have been hurting her jaws.

'Chief Mangum,' called the rector, grinning dimples in his cheeks. He didn't look any older than he had in college, and in college he'd looked about seven. 'Come buy a ticket to Trinity's Christmas lottery. And talk Mrs Yarborough here into it too.'

'Well, Paul,' I said, squeezing in, 'maybe I should remind you, soliciting in public's against the law. Plus, our first lady's a Baptist, right, Dina? How you doing?'

In her fifties, pleasant-looking but not pretty, Dina Yarborough was a thin light-skinned black woman with stiffly waved hair and a careful voice. 'Fine, thank you. Nice to see you, Cuddy. Isn't this a lovely party?' I'm sure she'd almost rather have gone to the dentist for a root canal, but you couldn't tell it from her eyes.

'It's my first time,' I said.

'Mine too,' she nodded. 'It's an annual affair?' I didn't hear any sarcasm, so maybe she didn't even know about those ninety-six years of hoop skirts and yellow sashes under the Stars 'n' Bars.

Both ministers leapt in fast, Campbell by nodding in a cough-

16

ing fit, and Madison by waving a thick card in my face. 'Worthy cause,' he wheedled. 'Add sleeping quarters to our soup kitchen.'

I said, okay, I'd take five. He said I could send a cheque; I said I had money in my wallet, and he said, 'Five hundred dollars?'

Old Campbell (his was the richest church in town) laughed while I was gasping, 'A hundred dollars each?! What are y'all raffling?!'

'A Porsche. Only two thousand tickets to be sold.' Paul Madison put his hand over his heart. 'You've got a great chance, Cuddy.'

'You're raffling a Porsche for a soup kitchen?'

Madison grinned like a pink conscienceless baby. 'Jim Scott donated it. Here's the thing, you raffle small-change stuff like, oh, a cord of wood, nobody wants it. A Porsche, that's a big temptation.'

I winked at Dina Yarborough. 'Paul, I thought you guys were in the business of fighting temptation.'

'Frankly,' coughed Campbell, a sad craggy man, 'we at First Presbyterian have stayed away from this sort of thing.'

Madison already had his pen out and was writing my name on the damn ticket. 'If Trinity had y'all's endowment, we'd stay away from it too. How many did you say you wanted, Cuddy?' My glare hit his dimples and bounced off.

'One,' I whispered.

'One?'

I snatched the ticket away from him. 'Thank you, Father Madison . . . Mrs Mayor, would you care to dance?'

'Hey, There' thumped to a close about thirty seconds after we got going, so we stood waiting while I asked her, 'Where's Carl? Off hiding one of those vile cigars of his from the public? I keep telling your husband, tobacco *made* Hillston. A smoking mayor'd be patriotic here.'

'Not if they're Cuban cigars.' Her face loosened into what so suspiciously looked like wryness that I decided her question about this ball's being an annual affair was about as innocent as the Trojan horse.

I laughed. 'Lord, Dina, tell the mayor to give me a raise, or I'm going to leak it to the *Star* how he's trading with Fidel. Come on, let's go get a drink.' But before we could squeeze out of the crunch of dancers, Dina's brother, the president of Southeast Life Insurance, tapped her for the next number. Tapped me, that is;

his fingers boring into my shoulder like he was looking for a major nerve to paralyse. He said, 'My sister promised me this next dance,' in a tone that suggested I'd dragged her on to the floor at gunpoint. And I dropped her hand as if I'd got caught doing it. Lord, the South. None of us can shake off all the old sad foolishness.

On my way to the food alone, I smiled at anyone who smiled at me. Then out of nowhere, a wide elderly lady in a lacy bed jacket stopped me with two steel forefingers on my lapels, and dared me to contradict her. 'You were in that magazine. *People*.'

'Excuse me?'

'I saw you. I forget what it said.'

I told her, 'Ma'am, I missed that one. *Newsweek* said I was tall, gangly, innovative and indefatigable.'

'That's the one I saw.' She eyed me suspiciously. 'What did it say your name was?'

'*Newsweek*? Seems like it said my name was "Chief Mangum."'

'That's right.' Reassured, she patted my elbow. Thousands of dollars of diamonds were slipping dangerously around on her fingers. 'I'm Mrs Marion Sunderland.'

'Not *the* Mrs Marion Sunderland that owns the *Hillston Star* and Channel Seven? Listen, what happened to those reruns of *Ironsides*? You know where Raymond Burr's in a wheelchair and has to catch the crooks secondhand? I wish you'd put those back on the air.'

Mrs Sunderland took a beat before she surprised me. 'I believe that article also described you as "whimsical." They misused the word. You're a little odd, but you don't strike me as capricious.'

'Well, I think *debonair*'s really the word they were after.' I leaned over and patted her arm in return. 'Mrs Sunderland, I want you to take some professional advice. Next time you go honky-tonking, you ought to leave those rings home in a vault.'

'Mr . . Mangum, I only go out in public among friends.'

'I bet that's what Julius Caesar said.' She surprised me again with a laugh that would have been loud on a woman twice her size. Then she invited me to 'call on' her, then she introduced me to two friends hovering nearby, a fresh-scrubbed octogenarian widow of a department store, who said she couldn't hear and just ignore her, and a Sunderland grandnephew who appeared to ski for a living. I spotted Paul Madison hunting through the dancers like Cupid through a cloud bank, so I slipped away without a word of warning to his next victims. No one else stopped me before I reached the buffet, where Judge Tiggs was trying to load his plate with devilled eggs, and his wife was trying to block his hand.

'Hey.' Somebody pulled me down by the elbow and kissed my cheek. 'I'm surprised you came.' It was Alice, Justin's wife. She's a small beautiful copper-haired lady from the North Carolina mountains. Justin met her three years ago while we were investigating some folks that worked on her floor at Cadmean Mills, and the best move he ever made was to marry her as soon as he could talk her into it. Bluest eyes you ever saw, clean as the sky, and clear as we all used to figure truth was. Alice believes in truth, and loves politics, and claims she can keep the two in shouting distance. We argue a lot. Justin says that's why he invites me to dinner twice a week, so he won't have to 'box around about ideas' with her himself. 'Can you believe this man?' Alice would say. 'Smart, educated, and he sits here and says he's not interested in ideas, whatever that means.'

Justin would check his wine sauce. 'It means, for Christ's sake, I don't care why Prohibition got voted in when it did. I thought we were trying to figure out if Billy Gilchrist's too bad a drunk to be a reliable stool pigeon.' Justin would talk your head off about the people in the case at hand, but analysing history bored him.

I put down my buffet plate and kissed Alice back. 'Well, look at you.' I turned her around. 'An old commie union organizer like you, used to go out to dinner in a sweatshirt with Emma Goldman on it, used to love a good brainy fight and a Hostess cupcake and don't try to deny it 'cause I've seen the wrappers.' The waiter offered me a cup of punch, which was hard to drink because of the baby strawberries floating in it. 'Now, Lord, Lord, Alice. Justin the Five's got you all pregnant and dolled up in this swanky thing, looks like you borrowed it from Jackie Onassis last time y'all got together.'

'How do I look?'

'Like Christmas.' Her gown was a dark green velvet and her red curls were like ribbons. 'You look like the prettiest Christmas present anybody ever got, by which I'm sorry to say I don't mean me.' I kissed her. 'Congratulations, Red. But please don't name that child Cudberth, 'specially if it's a girl. Is that Scotch? Where'd you get it, the men's room?'

'Ladies' lounge. You know, I don't like the way liquor tastes anymore. I guess that's lucky.' She gave me the drink. 'I'm going to kill Justin.'

'You're talking to the police chief. But I didn't catch what you said.'

'I told him, *I* wanted to tell you I was pregnant.'

'You know he can't keep a secret. Good detective though, I'll give you that. He tells folks his secrets, then folks tell him theirs, then we put the cuffs on them and haul them off.' I reached for a ham biscuit, but the waiter waved me away and tweezered one on to a plate stamped 'Hillston Club.' I held up four fingers; he held up one eyebrow, then humoured me and piled them on. 'Alice, tell me about Mrs Sunderland. How much say does she have at the paper?'

'Does have? Probably none. Could have? Probably lots.'

'You know her? Didn't the *Hillston Star* endorse you?'

'She's one of Justin's godmothers.'

'Can't hurt.'

She laughed with her chin raised. 'Cuddy, I never denied it.' Alice is in the state legislature now, which she wouldn't be if it hadn't been for Justin's name, and for old Briggs Cadmean's tossing a big chunk of money into her little campaign – out of some peculiar impulse that had nothing to do with late-blooming feminism. Now I'd heard she was also working to get Andy Brookside into the governor's mansion, but I'd avoided discussing it with her.

We watched Justin waltz Mrs Brookside in and out of duller dancers. The Jimmy Douglas string section was giving 'Lara's Theme' all they had, fighting back against the buzz of talk. 'Isn't my husband beautiful?' Alice smiled, happy as a cat.

'Motherhood hormones are eating up your brain, Red.'

'Well, he is. He looks like Paul Newman used to.'

'When was that?' We watched some more – his black coattails, Lee's black gown lifting as they turned; her shoulders, his shirt front a bright white blur. 'Married him for his looks, hunh? I always thought it was his cooking.'

'Go break in on them, so I can dance with him. You know Andy's wife?'

'I did a long time ago.' Alice gave me too straight a look, so I turned towards the buffet to scoop up some cashews, and I had a handful near my mouth when Lee saw me staring at her, and smiled. It was just a polite smile, then it went away as she recognized me; her body tightened, pulling Justin out of step for an instant.

Alice was talking. 'Well, I feel like I ought to be at the vigil anyhow, but Jack Molina agreed if I could put some pressure on Andy's position, or get to Lewis tonight, that might do more than holding up another placard at the prison. And now he's not even here.'

'Who's not here? Brookside?'

Alice was either looking at me funny or I was getting too sensitive. She said, 'No, Julian Lewis, Julian D.-for-Dollard Lewis, Justin's whatever he is, cousin, the lieutenant governor.'

'He's not here? Damnit.' I had promised George Hall's new lawyer, an old friend, that I'd come to this dance, corner Julian Lewis, and give him some reasons why he should persuade the governor to stay tomorrow's execution. Not that a lot of people hadn't been giving the governor a lot of reasons for a lot of years, but last-minute reprieves appeal to some politicians. They're catchy; the press likes them too. But as for Lewis caring what Alice thought, I didn't see why she thought the lieutenant governor would listen to anybody who was trying to stop him from taking over his boss's office, even if Alice's mother-in-law was Lewis's aunt. Plus, Lewis wasn't going to think a damn thing the governor didn't tell him to think. As for her influencing Brookside – in public, he too had stayed away from the Hall case, soothing his liberal constituency by keeping Professor Jack Molina (one of the Hall Committee coordinators) on his campaign staff. I looked around the ballroom. 'Where is Brookside?'

'Go ask his wife.' Alice took my plate away from me.

'I don't dance.'

'Oh bullshit, you're a great dancer.'

'Honey, now that you're a mama, you got to watch your language.'

She mouthed something that was pretty easy to lip-read, as I let her nudge me on to the floor. I eased my way through a cluster of younger dancers calling coded jokes from couple to couple while they circled. One pair just stood with their eyes closed, rocking softly back and forth.

Justin stopped the instant I touched his shoulder, and smiled like I'd brought him a million dollars, his long-lost dog, and news that the lab was wrong about his having cancer. I tell him, with that smile I don't know why *he* isn't in politics, except a year in the loony bin makes nervous voters nervous. I said, 'Excuse me, may I?' And he said, 'Hey, Cuddy, wonderful, you came!'

'Why is everybody so surprised?'

'Have you two met? Lee Brookside. Cuddy Mangum, my commanding officer.' Justin did a little bow – I suppose straight from childhood dance class – said, 'Thank you,' to her, 'Pardon me,' to us, and walked backwards smooth as a skater through the crowd. When I turned around to Lee, she had her hand up ready to rest on my shoulder. 'Hi,' I said. Her hair was pulled back in its loose knot, away from her face, a smoky ash-blond, and her eyes, which I'd remembered as blue, were actually grey, like an owl's feather, flecked and warm. I hadn't looked this close in her eyes in a long long time; the last time I'd looked, on a Saturday morning in June, we'd both been crying. It's easier to cry at seventeen. We were standing on a little wooden Japanese bridge in her backyard – except with that much land and trees and gardens, you don't call it a yard – and she was telling me her mother wouldn't let her see me again, not through the summer, not after she returned to private school in the fall, not, in fact, ever. I kept saying, 'Why?,' but we both knew why, and I don't blame her now for not letting me force her to say it. After that, I'd next seen her a year or so later, when she came to my house in East Hillston, called me a coward, and slapped me across the face. After that, only in passing.

I took my hand from my pocket now. 'You still mad?'

She said, 'My God, how long has it been?'

'Don't start counting. How'd you like that French college?'

And she laughed years away for a minute. 'Oh my, was I ever young enough to go to college?'

'Hey! I'm still going.'

'You are? You're the police chief.'

'That's true, too.'

She still had her hand held near my shoulder, but lifted it back, so I moved forward, and circled her waist, and we started dancing. I couldn't really remember what it had felt like all that while ago, pressed together in the gym under the sagging streamers and balloons, or in some school friend's hot dim living room, not moving when the records changed. Now she felt cool and sure, accustomed to dance with strangers. There was something sad about her eyes, but it was hard to imagine her crying easily anymore. We danced at first without speaking, at one point

22

passing close to Justin and Alice; Justin was humming, Alice smiled at me, and wiggled the fingers woven with his.

Finally Lee moved her head and asked me, 'So you stayed in Hillston. You always wanted to travel.'

'I've travelled some.' I summed up two years in Southeast Asia, then six months in Europe (on the GI savings I'd planned to use to buy Cheryl and me a house), seventeen months teaching school in Costa Rica, a summer in New York City, when I decided I wanted to be a police detective. I said I still like travelling; I take a special package charter some place new every vacation I get. Last year it was Nova Scotia; the year before, Haiti. I said, 'But mostly Hillston, since I've been with the police department here.'

'Why the police? . . . I mean I guess I always expected to read how you'd . . . I don't know, written the history of the United States.' She was squeezed against me by a wild-spinning couple.

I backstepped us away. 'Well, probably the more history I read, the more I figured, crooked as the law is, it's straighter than lynch mobs and posses on the loose, right? I'm a great believer in capital-L Law. And Hillston's home. So here I am, enforcing the law in Hillston.'

'. . . Hillston's got so big.' Her hand lifted out of mine to gesture at the room. 'I used to think I'd find myself seated beside you at a dinner, but I never did.'

'I used to think that too.' I didn't tell her that when I'd first gone to Paris, I'd get the dumb notion to rush off to a certain park or museum because I was sure that's where I was going to see her stroll by.

She'd stayed abroad after college. Her first husband was a French mountain climber; I'd read in a paper that he'd died in a hotel fire, only twenty-seven years old. I remember thinking: the French mess up in Vietnam, the US sends me over there, I'm lucky and escape, Lee's husband makes it up Mount Everest but can't get out of a suite on the Riviera. Six years after his death, she'd married Brookside. She had no children.

'Andy was there the same time you were,' she said, her neck arching back to look up at me. 'In Vietnam. Have you two met?'

'Over there? Nope, we never did run into each other.' It was interesting – 'Andy' – the matter-of-fact assumption that everyone knew who her second husband was, which of course everyone did. The 'Have you met?' probably meant local politics, since I doubt she figured young Major Brookside had ever swooped down in his jet to shoot the breeze with the boys in the mangrove swamp. Well, maybe she'd lived so long in a world where everybody knew each other, that's all the world she thought there was. I mean world, too. Randolphs and Fanshaws, now, they counted in Hillston, and Cadmeans and Dollards might own the Piedmont, and have a long lease on the state, but Havers had been so rich for so long, they were on the big map. When Chinese and Kenyans and Danes smoke your cigarettes, you can build universities with your loose change, and you can expect even your collateral daughters to marry heroes; you don't need them to marry money. That message her family had sent to the little Japanese bridge – well, you could see their point. I've got my All-State Guard plaque, and my dinky combat medals in my bureau, I've got my three-inch *Newsweek* clipping on the refrigerator door. Andy Brookside's got a cabinet full of football trophies, and a Congressional Medal of Honor, and a presidential committee appointment to study that sad war, a Pulitzer Prize for the book he wrote after he studied it, a *Time* magazine cover, and Lee Haver. There's no catching heroes. They've got the gods running interference for them, you know what I mean? The gods keep them wrapped in a glow, you can see the shimmer when they come in a room.

I said, 'Well now, this is a pretty place. Never been in here before, myself. You come to these Christmas parties with your family back then?'

She didn't answer. A tiny blue vein in her neck tensed against the diamond necklace around it. Then, after a silence, she said, not smiling, 'You know, I hated you for a long time.'

The rush of old intimacy shocked me. I tilted my head to look at her; it felt like that sudden fall that jerks you awake when you nod off in a chair.

Her eyes searched in mine until finally she said, 'You remember that day I came to your house with the box of letters? Right before I left for France? You wouldn't even talk to me. You wouldn't *look* at me. Your mother left us standing there in your living room, and shut the door to the kitchen. I think she was crying too. She asked me if I wanted a glass of tea, and you snapped at her, "No, she doesn't."'

I said, 'I remember it very well. You threw the letters at me, and slapped me in the face.'

Her palm moved inside mine as she pulled her hand away. We stopped there in the middle of the dance floor.

'You're the only man I ever hit,' she said.

She put her hand back in mine. Other couples seemed to be moving around us, but far away, small and shadowy, as if the room had suddenly doubled in size. We moved together. Then I heard, coming from a distance, the rustle of applause, and I realized the music had already stopped.

I was going to ask her if she'd like that glass of tea now, when through the knots of applauding couples I saw Andy Brookside walking towards us, tall, bright-haired, full of energy, his handsome head nodding right and left; maybe he thought folks were clapping for him instead of the band. He touched Lee's arm, and claimed her. 'I'm sorry, darling, I got caught up in a conversation.' (It was the first I'd seen him all night, and I wondered if he'd been down in the men's lounge where the 'real drinks' were.)

She said quietly, 'There you are.'

He put his arm through hers, saying, 'Shall we?,' before turning to me with a friendly, expectant face; I didn't see a twitch of phoniness in it, and I was looking hard.

Lee stepped away from him to introduce us. 'Have you met my husband, Andy? Cuddy—' And then the beeper in my breast pocket went off, which meant that Sergeant Davies at headquarters had decided I needed to make a decision, which to him could mean anything from Mrs Thompson had called again because Clark Gable was back in her attic crawlspace, to Officer Purley Newsome had put another dead cat in Officer Nancy White's locker, to a gang of terrorists with Uzi machine guns were holding the entire downtown population of Hillston hostage.

I turned the beeper off. 'Excuse me, I better go phone in.'

'You're a doctor?' Brookside smiled, then showed me how he'd won the nomination. 'No, wait ... Cuddy, Cuddy ... Of course, Mangum! Our police chief. Last spring at the Jaycee's breakfast panel, "Improving Town and Gown Relations." Right?' His handshake was professional but not stingy. 'Good to see you. Tell me, what's your sense of the George Hall situation?'

'Lousy for George Hall,' I said.

'Naturally, yes. Of course, I meant the governor. Clemency.'

I said, 'I don't think so. But then I'm not in tight with the powers that be.'

Lee had been standing there, her fingers touching a jewel on the necklace. Into our silence, she suddenly said, 'Andy phoned

25

the governor yesterday, asking him to extend mercy,' then she looked up at Brookside as if to make sure it was all right to have told me. There was something uncomfortable between them, which was odd in such a poised couple. I mean, I knew why I felt uneasy – I was half back to eighteen years old – but I certainly didn't suppose I was what was troubling the Brooksides.

'Um hum . . .' I looked from her to him. 'Well, there's mercy, and then there's justice.'

'True.' There was nothing in his eyes but earnestness.

'Hall's supporters wanted not just clemency, but a pardon. At this point, they're just trying to get the stay of execution. And if you're planning on making any statement about "mercy" of a little more of a *public* nature, seems like waiting much longer might make it pretty moot.'

He gave me a stare. 'I know.'

Mr and Mrs Dyer Fanshaw shuffled in a bored fox-trot near us. Mrs Fanshaw smiled brilliantly at Lee, then patted the clumps of diamonds strung on her own neck. Every city employee in Hillston (including teachers, including tax clerks and garbage collectors, including me) who filled out a form or washed his hands or signed a cheque, did it on Fanshaw Paper. It adds up to diamonds fast. She cooed as they swerved close, 'That is just a beautiful beautiful dress, Lee.'

Lee smiled brilliantly back. 'Oh thank you, Betty. Yours too. Merry Christmas.'

I excused myself again to go telephone, but Lee touched my arm. 'Cuddy, before you go? Is it true there've been threats against the group George Hall's brother organized? Jack Molina, on Andy's staff, says so. He's been working with – is it "Cooper" Hall?'

I nodded. 'There're threats against just about anybody who steps in front of the public and moves enough to catch their eye.'

She stared at her husband. 'But you're protecting them?'

'Coop Hall? I can't. Not unless I locked him up, and maybe not then. Oh, I could catch whoever did it, but if they don't mind going to the trouble, and they don't care about getting caught, anybody in this country can kill anybody they want to.'

'Lee?' Brookside reached for her arm again.

I backed away. 'Thanks for the dance, Mrs Brookside.' She offered her hand again, so I took it. Her fingers were cold, colder than they'd been when I'd held them before.

Out in the lobby, I saw Father Paul Madison, small and eager, selling Mrs Sunderland's grandnephew a chance to own a Porsche. I waved good-bye, but he held up a palm to stop me, so I waited.

'Cuddy,' he said, brushing blond hair out of his eyes, 'don't take this wrong, please, but would you know anybody I could lean on to make a contribution to the George Hall Fund? We're seven thousand in the hole.'

'You mean, like me? And why should I take it wrong?'

He blushed. 'Well, you're the one who arrested George in the first place, but then I know you're a friend of Isaac Rosethorn's . . .'

'Isaac's charging you guys seven thousand to represent Hall?'

'Oh, no, nothing like that much. It's the *paperwork*, and phone calls, and now we need to hire an investigator to go back over—'

My back was still tightened with memories of Lee. Paul stopped in midsentence, peered at my face, then he lowered his head. 'You don't think we'll get the stay?'

I said, 'No. Do you?'

'I'm praying we will.'

'You are? Looks to me like you're selling Porsches.'

His blush spread over his ears and neck. 'Cuddy, I'm sorry I upset you,' he said. When I didn't answer, he gave my arm a rub. 'You still mad about what happened at Trinity?'

I said, 'Only when I think about it.' He was referring to a protest rally that the Save George Hall Committee had staged in October on the steps of his church, Trinity Episcopal, to which they'd invited a very left-wing movie star who happened to be on location in North Carolina; they'd sent a lot of news people advance word, but neglected to do the same for the police – meaning me. I also suspected they'd taunted the Klan into coming; at any rate, ten showed up in robes, with a few Aryans in combat fatigues, plus a hundred hoods with nothing else to do. I didn't have enough men there to handle it. Mud clots got thrown; we made four arrests, and the evening news shot a lot of footage. I was so angry at Paul and Cooper Hall, I came close to arresting them too. It was right after that that Isaac Rosethorn offered to take on the Hall case. It was also right after that that *Newsweek* called me up.

Paul was saying, 'And look, drop by the soup kitchen someday. We've got a new stove. Eight burners and a built-in grill. Mr Carippini bought a range for his restaurant, so he gave us his old one.'

'Isn't he Catholic?'

'Sure. Listen, this stove's been blessed by a bishop.'

'Father Madison,' I grinned back at him, 'please don't turn to crime; you'd run me ragged ... About your Hall Fund, why don't you ask Mrs Andrew Brookside?'

'You think?'

'I think she's sympathetic. But you may have to say you won't use her name.'

Madison looked puzzled, then nodded. 'Oh, right, Andy Brookside. Politics.' He acknowledged that little world with upraised palms, then with a soft whistle blew it away.

As I waited for the cloakroom attendant – an old black man with a completely specious grin, and 'Hillston Club' embroidered on his jacket – I glanced at the couch by the tree, but the girl in red satin was gone. Inside the ballroom, Justin and Alice were talking to Mayor and Mrs Yarborough. They all turned when the Jimmy Douglas Orchestra struck up 'God Rest Ye Merry Gentlemen,' while behind them brass-buttoned waiters trooped out of an open door, carrying gleaming platters of shiny roasted turkeys, with red ribbons on their legs, and circled by white candles burning in bright little apples. Everybody clapped.

Chapter 2

On a sticky hot summer night seven years ago, George Hall sat drinking in an East Hillston bar called Smoke's; it was a loud rough old place in an all-black neighbourhood known as Canaan because of a gigantic AME Church of that name, now demolished, that had once dominated all the cheap-shod houses around it. George often spent his evenings at Smoke's; his mother didn't allow alcohol in her home. He was a very dark, stocky young man, thick-cheated, with a broad flat face and a long moustache; a Vietnam veteran, with a small government cheque as payment for two lost toes on his left foot. That summer night, he was twenty-eight, unmarried, unemployed. The prosecutor Mitchell Bazemore was to remind everybody at his trial that George hadn't kept a job for as long as a year since he'd been twenty, his age when he'd come back from Saigon. He'd had a lot of chances – loader at the tobacco warehouses, roof tarrer, jackhammer operator, driver for a doughnut supplier, driver for Fanshaw Paper Company. But as the court's psychiatrist explained to the jury, despite these opportunities, time after time George had 'gotten himself fired,' or he had simply quit. He had a 'problem with authority,' had lost his stripes in Vietnam for insubordination, and returned home to lose his jobs in Hillston from the same 'antisocial disorder.' Moreover, as Captain Fulcher testified (without objection from the public defender), George had a police record – three arrests since his return home, one for a fight at the ballpark, one for interfering with a police officer who was trying to cuff a burglary suspect, and one for running a red light. The second arrest was made by Bobby Pymc, the man

Hall subsequently shot outside Smoke's on that hot August Saturday.

Smoke's offered more than liquor; it had the ball games on TV, a coin-operated pool table, and, reputedly, cards in a back room, plus three girls upstairs, plus a bookie bartender who'd take your money for anything from a numbers game to a spitting contest. On weekends it had a blues band and dancing, and from time to time it had fights. Occasionally, an ambulance had to be called, which, occasionally, brought the police. So George had been in trouble before, and Smoke's had been in trouble before, and the only thing that was unusual about this trouble was what a white, *off-duty* policeman like Bobby Pym might be doing in all-black Canaan in all-black Smoke's, when he lived way across town in West Hillston, and when his wife thought he was at a bowling alley south of I-28. The question was asked, but not pressed, and nobody ever knew the answer. All the customers at Smoke's that night said they'd never seen Officer Pym before, hadn't even noticed him in there until the fight – which was pretty hard to believe, no matter how crowded the place, or how bad the light was. Captain Fulcher might have claimed that Pym was there working undercover, if he hadn't blurted out to me, as soon as he saw the bloody body, 'What the g.d. hell was Bobby doing *here*!?' That question came up again at the trial, but was overruled by Judge Henry Tiggs. According to the judge's instructions as to the law, a man had a right to go to a public bar of his choice, even if others might find his choice 'peculiar and frankly unsavoury'; he had a right to turn on a jukebox even if somebody else was playing a guitar and singing (this somebody was the blues performer); he had a right to carry a licensed weapon (this was in reference to the .38 pistol stuffed in Pym's belt under his bowling shirt); being told by George Hall, in abusive language, to get out of a public bar, Pym had a right to 'object' (presumably the judge referred here to Pym's inserting the barrel of this gun into George's nostril). And, as Mitchell Bazemore heatedly summarized for the jury, most assuredly, a man, a *policeman*, a man with a wife and a baby, a man whose dying groans (tape-recorded in the ambulance) the jury had heard for themselves, a policeman had the right to leave a public establishment without being chased outside and shot down in cold blood by a state-supported black troublemaker with three arrests, a bad army record, and an abandoned and malignant heart.

George's refusal to plea-bargain annoyed the Court; his taciturnity on the witness stand annoyed the jury. All he would say was that after his interference with Pym's arresting the burglary suspect, Pym had harassed him; and that, in fact, he assumed that Pym might even have come to Smoke's that night in order to harass him further. (The DA objected to these conclusions and conjectures, and was sustained.) Two, George claimed he was convinced by Pym's assaulting him with the gun that his life was in danger. (The DA demonstrated that even if Pym had responded to Hall's obscenities by 'provoking' him – which of course the DA didn't believe – such provocation was certainly resistible by 'any reasonable man similarly provoked.') Three – while admitting he had chased Pym outside in the heat of passion – George claimed that he'd seen the cop run to a blue Ford down the street, reach inside it, then turn back towards him; that he'd believed Pym had taken a second gun from the car, and so had fired in self-defence. Well, the DA was very sure the jury wasn't going to fall for a story that didn't even make sense. Heat of passion! There was 'appreciable time' between the moment George wrenched the .38 out of Pym's hand, and the moment he shot him on the sidewalk – time for cooling reflection, or for premeditated, intentional malice aforethought, and which did George choose? And as for his thinking Officer Pym had gone for a second gun! There wasn't even a blue Ford around, much less a gun in it! Pym drove a Dodge, and it was parked *across* the street from Smoke's, not down the street. Pym was not running for a gun, he was running for his life! The DA knew the jury would agree.

And so they did. They found George guilty of first-degree murder. Told to go back and determine whether he deserved the death penalty, they returned to say, yes, they thought he did. Judge Tiggs thanked them for doing their duty, and sent them home.

The assistant public defender had taken exception to at least a few of Judge Tiggs's overrulings of his objections, and on that basis he filed an appeal for George; it was denied, and the defender, having discharged his obligations, quit, after telling George not to worry, because while lots of people got the death penalty, nobody had actually been executed in the state for ages. George filed his own appeal, claiming an incompetent defence; it was denied. More petitions were written, filed, and denied. Years passed. Despite the defender's sanguinity, three men and one woman were executed at Dollard Prison. George's mother hired another lawyer. George's younger brother organized the Save George Hall Committee, using contributions to buy public attention about the case. On Death Row, George did three hundred push-ups a day, and grew African violets from seedlings in paper cartons. Years passed, almost seven since the bullet had entered Bobby Pym's skull. From that moment, most people in Hillston had been sure that George Hall was going to the gas chamber. And a lot of them were angry that it was taking the state so long to get him there.

Unless you found yourself behind a farmer too bitter to let you pass his tractor, or a teenager itchy to ram you into a tree, Old Airport Road was the shortest route from Hillston to Dollard Prison, twenty minutes away, just beyond the city limits of the state capital, and in my county. This late on Friday night, I had nothing to dodge but ice. Needles of sleet were crackling on my windshield hard enough for me to hear them, and the wipers made weak swipes that just smeared the slush around. I listened to a tape with Loretta Lynn on one side, and Patsy Cline on the other. That's a lot of love gone wrong.

Out in front of the Hillston Club, I'd used my car radio to call downtown. The night desk sergeant, Hiram Davies, is a Baptist deacon starched clean as his undershirts, who almost never goes home because he's past retirement age, and he's scared we won't let him back in if he leaves. After he'd stopped apologizing, he'd given me a message. It was from a man I've known for a lot of years, and it upset me enough to make me risk my Oldsmobile to Airport Road in a sleet storm. 'Maybe I should have just sent a car, Chief, and I hate to disturb you during your social occasion—'

'Dance, Hiram. I got to this place, and I want you to know these folks are dancing! Drinking, probably even cussing and card-playing in the back rooms. It makes a man want to fall to his knees and pray.'

'I hope so, Chief.' (Jokes slide off Davies like chestnuts off a steep tin roof.) 'But since Mr Rosethorn did say to tell you personally, that's why I decided—'

'Tell me what?'

I could hear Hiram shuffling his notes. 'A pickup truck, licence AX four one five seven nine, passed Dollard Prison gate twice, slowing near the vigil group; male Caucasians, obscenities and verbal threats shouted.'

'Who told Isaac Rosethorn this? Who, and when?'

'He's over there at the prison.'

'Isaac?'

'Isn't he, he's Hall's lawyer now, isn't he? At least that's—'

'Jesus Christ, what's a man his age doing marching around with a sign in the middle of the night in this weather?!'

Davies pinched off his words, one at a time. 'I couldn't say, sir. That truck is registered to a Willis Tate, Jr, lives in Raleigh, one previous arrest, vandalism.'

I started my motor. 'You're a hot dog, Hiram, no getting around it. Call Raleigh, ask them to go after that yahoo. I'm heading out there.'

He said he'd send a car for me, and I said never mind it, and he said it wasn't his place to argue, which had never stopped him before, and didn't this time. Finally he got around to sharing a second part to the message from Isaac. 'He said to tell you Lieutenant Governor Lewis had just driven up with another man in a limousine, and gone inside the prison. He said you would want—'

'I'll be goddamned!' I slapped my hand on my thigh so hard I hurt both of them. 'Fuck the ducks, they stopped it.'

'I couldn't say, sir.' There was a faint snort at my profanity. 'And Chief Mangum, what would you like me to do? The holding cell's full, and I've got a drunk-and-disorderly keeping everybody awake. Four joyriders, two breaking-and-entering. And Norm Brown on wife assault again.' Davies loved a full report, though he usually phrased it in terms of questions he didn't need the answer to, so I listened while I drove. 'Attempted burglary, Maplewood Pawnshop, apprehended on the scene. Three purses snatched in River Rise Mall. Purley Newsome caught one of them.'

'He didn't kill him, did he?' (Officer Purley Newsome was a leftover from the old regime, with a brother on the City Council.)

'—And considerable shoplifting. It's busy tonight.'

'Well, it's only four more shopping days to Christmas. Folks get tense.' I turned the heater higher and turned on to Airport Road.

'—And we had a jumper on the roof at Showtime Cinema; Officer White talked him down, and then Officer White had him

33

admitted to UH for observation.' (Davies' refusal to acknowledge, by name or pronoun, that we had women – like Nancy White – on the force, drove him into a lot of syntactical byroads. He was like an old monk, stunned to find nuns sleeping in his monastery.) 'Officer reports his condition satisfactory.'

'Tell Nancy she's a good lady. Aww, humankind, Hiram. Makes you wonder where God went, and forgot to turn on His answering machine. Who's the loud drunk?'

Davies squeezed his voice so tight it turned falsetto. 'The Lord answers all who call on Him . . . The drunk's Billy Gilchrist.'

'Lock him in the interrogation room, he can sleep on the table.'

'I already did.'

Sergeant Davies signed off in a huff. I put on Patsy Cline. I still hate to think of that woman's plane crashing. 'Why can't I forget the past, and love somebody new . . .' Her voice was so sweet with sadness, I slid down into a memory of Lee Haver as if other heartbreaks – as if my wife, as if Briggs – hadn't worn the first loss away years and years ago.

Twenty minutes later, the black brick turrets of the old penitentiary rose up at me, caught by big searchlights. The place sat there in miles of flat meadow and rows of broken tobacco stalks, like a backwater castle built by some paranoid, third-rate baron that the king never came to visit. In summer you could watch convicts slouch through the yellow grass swinging their thick wooden scythes. Families picnicking in the public park across the highway would point at them, maybe hoping they'd be lucky enough to see one of the blue-shirted reapers slice a guard in half, then race off without much hope towards wherever he figured freedom was. Or maybe the picnickers pointed to show their children what could happen to them if they didn't stop talking back. In summer, the convicts played baseball in the meadow and grew tomatoes against the fence. In winter, unless herded off to fill some highway potholes, they stayed indoors like everybody else in the South. The sixty-three men on Death Row never went outside at all.

Now the prison looked wide-awake, so many lights on, you could tell that the coils of barbed wire on top of the turrets were shiny with ice. Out front, I saw some huddled cars, and a dozen or so figures, most in plastic ponchos, crowded together under the gate house ledge. Inside his steamy cubicle a guard was eating doughnuts and reading a magazine. Four more people hunched beneath umbrellas around a forty-gallon drum where

34

burning sticks hissed at the sleet. Nothing was going on, and nobody looked injured, just miserable. Obviously the pickup truck hadn't come back. There was a stretch limo, a black Lincoln, parked near the gate.

As I slowed, a Mustang behind me passed in a hurry, then cut left into the prison drive, skidding sideways next to the high iron gates. I pulled in fast, and jumped out the same time the driver did. We had both run, spraying slush, halfway across the wide lot towards the vigil group before I recognized Bubba Percy, reporter for the *Hillston Star* – star reporter according to him – a handsome good-ole-boy gone to pudge in his late thirties, with a nose for news like a jackal's after maggoty meat. Clamping me on the shoulder, he yelled, 'Mangum! That pickup come back? I miss anything?'

I snapped open the umbrella I keep in my raincoat pocket. 'I bet you heard that on the scanner, didn't you, Bubba? Breaks my heart you got nothing else to do on Friday nights. And lashes pretty as a girl's, except if this ice hardens on them, it's gonna freeze your weasel eyes shut.' I kept walking towards the four-some at the fire watching us.

'Oh shut up, Mangum.' He ran, zigzagging puddles. 'You know in 'eighty-two, there was a W. Y. *Tate* arrested in Raleigh for tossing a stink bomb in that synagogue window on Yancy Street? You know that? Do you?' His hair snagged on one of my umbrella spokes, and I hauled him under it with me.

'Bubba, you just hang on, one of these days the *New York Times* is bound to call.'

I didn't recognize anybody in the crowd scrunched under the gate ledge – most were black, some were female, all were bedraggled as cats. Slush had blanked out half the letters on the big signs propped up beside them: FREE GEORGE HALL. STOP THE KILLING. JUSTICE FOR *ALL*. I did know the four people under umbrellas around the fire drum. The tallest, slender and long-muscled, wearing an old army jacket that had probably belonged to George, was Cooper Hall, the condemned man's younger brother, who'd just started college when George went to prison, and now worked for a civil rights organization that ran a legal-aid society, engineered legislative lobbies, and published a journal called *With Liberty and Justice* which Coop pretty much ran. He was better looking than George, with a fine-boned arrogant face.

The woman in a yellow slicker beside him was his fiancée,

Jordan West, a caseworker at the Department of Human Services; time to time I'd see her in the Municipal Building when she'd come to testify about a welfare violation or child custody trouble. In her early twenties, she had the kind of looks that will turn your head on the sidewalk, women and children's too. Bubba Percy put it differently, stopping to whisper, 'Shit, now that's fucking brown sugar! That's the best excuse for miscegenation I *ever* saw. Hey! Cut it out!' I gave his wrist another sharp twist before I dropped it. 'That was a *compliment*, Mangum!'

'Yeah. Here's another one. Your mama must be the first woman in history to give birth after getting fucked up the ass by a hyena.'

'Something bugging you? Something happen out here tonight? Come on, what's the story!'

'Jesus!' I kept walking.

The thin white man by the fire was Brookside's assistant campaign manager, Jack Molina, a communications professor at Haver University and a founding editor of *With Liberty and Justice*. The considerably older and broader white man next to him, smoking in the rain, his nubbly Russian hat on sideways, his dirty camel's-hair overcoat gaping at the buttons, was the one who had sent me the message: Isaac Rosethorn – for just a month now, George Hall's lawyer; for a whole lot of years, a friend of mine. He was maybe Hillston's only native-born Jew, probably its only native-born legal genius, and undoubtedly one of its most perverse citizens. He said, 'Thirty-five minutes?'

I said, 'Road's icy. Hi, Isaac. Evening, folks, how y'all doing? Coop, Dr Molina. Jordan, nice to see you.' Jordan made a place for me.

Rosethorn gave up on his wet cigarette, and asked, 'Could you trace that truck? There was a second one. Both pickups, big Confederate flags flapping out the windows. We only got the plates on the last one.'

I said, 'Raleigh's already traced it. A Willis Tate.'

'Ahhh? Tate? . . . The synagogue?'

Bubba Percy grabbed me. 'Didn't I tell you!'

'Bubba, damnit, will you stop stomping on my toes? Y'all know Bubba Percy of the *Star*, clubfooted hound of the free press?' While I talked, Coop Hall and I kept our eyes on each other; if looks could freeze, you could have snapped my arms off like icicles on a drain sprout. Behind us, the dozen young vigilants pressed nervously in a semicircle near him. I nodded at them. 'Any word from Warden Carpenter?'

A few of them shook their heads and a young man said, 'No. Nothing.'

I said, 'I'm sorry . . .'

Coop Hall stepped around Percy; his face was a lot younger than his eyes. Hatless, he seemed indifferent to the weather; his close-cropped beard and hair glistened with rain. He shook his head at me slowly, scanned his eyes down the ruffled tuxedo shirt. 'You don't belong here.'

Jordan said, 'Coop, please . . .'

He pulled away from her with a twitch of his arm. 'What are you supposed to be, Mangum, fuckin' police protection? We don't need it. Why don't you go do something for my brother? Why don't you go figure out how—'

Rosethorn said, 'Cooper!'

I said, 'Isaac called me, okay? Listen, I know how you feel—'

Coop said, 'Ha.' It wasn't a laugh.

I nodded at him. 'I meant, how you feel about me. Okay? . . . I'm just trying to do my job . . . About these pickup trucks, didn't the county sheriff send somebody over here with y'all?'

Isaac dismissed the sheriff with a swipe at the air. 'He had two bozos drive by every now and again, but naturally they haven't been back since before our visitors showed up.'

'Did these guys stop? Anybody see any weapons?'

Jack Molina wanted to take charge, but Coop cut him off, his breath steaming out in the cold. 'Okay. They came twice, they didn't stop, they threw a glass bottle—'

'Did you recognize anybody, anybody from that bunch that tangled with you back at the Trinity Church meeting?'

Molina pushed forward. 'They were going too fast. They yelled out stuff like "Gas the nigger"—'

'And "Fuck the nigger lovers,"' Jordan added, her eyes bright and hard.

Coop winced with impatience. 'So what? You think my mind's on filing some more complaints about what a few more chicken-shit rednecks spew out of a truck window?!' He pointed at the prison looming over us. 'Julian Lewis is in there with the warden right now! And I can't find out if it's even about my brother or not. So, do *you* know, Mr "Police Chief"?'

'No. I don't know any more about it than you do.' I looked at

37

Isaac Rosethorn. Hall walked away from us back towards the gate. The other vigilants followed him immediately, and Bubba Percy grabbed Molina, tugging him aside.

Isaac finally budged; he'd just been watching me and Coop. 'Here's the bottle they threw. That makes it assault. Ron Rico rum, a pint. Disgusting.' He pulled a bent McDonald's milkshake cup out of his fat coat pocket, and handed it to me; it was full of chunks of glass.

'I tell you what's disgusting, Isaac. The thought of you out in this weather, drinking a milkshake.' I walked him back to my car and he pulled himself in, lifting his bad right leg with his hand.

Isaac Rosethorn's a fat old bachelor who's never done a thing to deserve still being alive at sixty-four. Living in the South, his family had totally tossed away all the healthy habits of their race. When Isaac wasn't eating spareribs or fried chicken wings, he was drinking bourbon; when he wasn't napping on his worn-out couch, he was sucking on unfiltered Chesterfields, holding the smoke down until it puffed out of his wide mouth like steam from a train. I never could decide if his eccentricities were natural, or if he'd put them together out of all the books he must have read to get away from being a poor, fat, brainy Jewish boy in the South, in the Depression. But he'd eat lasagna for breakfast and cereal for supper; he'd wear a ratty wool tweed suit in July, and sleep with his windows open in February. His career was built on his brilliance and ostentatious peculiarity, not to mention a spectacular head of white wavy hair, a voice dark as molasses, and eyes like a cocker spaniel's – all very effective in the court-room. When I was younger, I'd tell him, 'Get off your fat butt. You could be rich and famous!' He'd say, 'Probably,' and go back to identifying weeds or birdcalls, or reading Rumanian poetry, or whatever weird fancy he'd dodged off into at the time.

'Ahhh, God.' A sigh rumbled down Rosethorn like an old elevator as he settled into the seat. 'Poor Cooper hates you, still hates you.'

'No kidding. It's not exactly the way to get folks behind you.'

'So who are you, Dale Carnegie? ... What's this "Auto-Reverse" mean?' he said, then he sneezed on my dashboard.

'Tapes, they play one side, then they play the other. Isaac, you're too old not to mention fat to try dodging shotguns in the slush. Why are you out here?'

'Who said shotguns?' He checked his watch, then started

through his soggy pockets, dropping crumpled papers and file cards on the seat, looking for his cigarettes. 'Our lieutenant governor's now been in there forty-two minutes. That's his chauffeur over there in the stretch limo.'

'I figured. You know why?'

His round shoulders shrugged inside his overcoat. Then straightening a cigarette, he pointed it at the prison gate. 'You know who carved those letters over the gate?' I glanced across at the deep Gothic incisions in the stone ledge: EUSTACE P. DOLLARD STATE PRISON. He smiled, 'W. O. Wolfe, Thomas Wolfe's father, that's who. Interesting, hunh.'

'Yes, interesting.' Back by the fire, I saw Bubba was still cornering Jack Molina, or vice versa. I said, 'Okay, Isaac, besides nobility and architectural tidbits, what are you up to? Yesterday you said you had to rewrite a petition for some District Court judge.'

'Mrs Hall just drove it to Greensboro.'

'In this weather? She's too old to go to Greensboro in an ice storm. Why couldn't Coop go himself? What's the matter with him, sending his mother!'

'God almighty, Cuddy, what's the matter with *you*? The main business here is not you and Cooper. The main business here is George.' He yanked off his hat and jerked his hands through the shaggy white hair. 'Anyhow, that priest at St Stephen's took her ... I thought if maybe she drove all that way herself, personally, *especially* on a night like this ... Judge Roscoe's an ignorant dotard, but he's sentimental.' Now he was looking for his box of kitchen matches. 'Slim, I've got some bad news.'

'The governor already said no. Why didn't you say so!'

But he shook his head. 'No, nothing to do with that ... Old Briggs Cadmean died a few hours ago.'

'Cadmean *died*?' I guess it surprised me, not just because I'd enjoyed tangling with the old bastard about his daughter, but because Cadmean *was* Hillston. Growing up in the east part of town, his smokestacks and sawtoothed mills were my skyline. The mills were where grown-ups' paycheques came from, and Cadmean was the man who owned the mills. I wondered how Cadmean's daughter had felt when they called her, high on some western starry mountain, to tell her the news; or maybe all the while she'd been by his bed right here in Hillston, the past forgiven.

Isaac patted my knee absentmindedly. 'Well, well, well well. But he died in his sleep, and since he was so convinced he wasn't mortal, it's nice he never found out he was wrong.'

'Whooo . . .' I rubbed my eyes fast. 'Almost hard to believe he couldn't work a deal on this one too . . . How'd you hear?'

'Professional courtesy. He kept a drawerful of lawyers by the bed. Could there be an ashtray hidden in all this machinery?'

I said, 'It's a virgin. Those vile cigars are probably what killed Cadmean.'

'He was ninety-one. Why blame cigars?' Rosethorn fluttered his thick fingers down the ruffle on my rented shirt. 'Slim, hope he rests in peace, swine that he undeniably was . . . So, how was the Confederacy Ball? You leave a glass slipper, I hope?'

'If I did, it's still sitting on the steps, unless it got tromped under somebody's galoshes . . . Lord, Cadmean dead . . .' I looked towards all the squares of light in the black brick wall of Dollard Prison. The sleet had lightened to a drizzle of rain now. Jordan offered Coop a Thermos cup of coffee that he didn't want. I said, 'Julian Lewis never showed at the dance, but I guess you already figured that. What else could he be here for, but the Hall case?'

'Maybe.' He threw his cigarette out the window. 'We'll have to wait and see.'

'Maybe, wait and see? Jesus! And you jump all over me about forgetting the "main business." Seven years, I can't get you interested that a racist judge and jury railroaded George Hall into—'

'It's not necessarily racist, Slim, to take exception to a white policeman's getting shot through the eye by a black assailant. Not *necessarily* racist. People have strong feelings about eyes.'

'I bet you could have pulled off the self-defence.'

'With that jury? I don't think so.'

'At least murder two, Isaac, manslaughter; not first degree. But, okay, you're not interested. Then five weeks before the man's scheduled for execution, you suddenly volunteer to represent him—'

'The Hall Committee offered me a moderately substantial fee to represent him—'

'Don't tell me about money, Isaac. Money's not worth dick to you. And don't tell me about the Halls, and don't even tell me about capital-J Justice. Tell me the *idea* you decided might be interesting.'

He smiled with a sweet bogus incomprehension. Over the

40

decades, Isaac Rosethorn had been preserved not just by some alchemic mix of tobacco, alcohol, and animal fat, but by an avoidance of all major human emotions, except a cupidinous curiosity. Whenever I thought I'd detected in those deep round eyes some mild stirring of anger or envy or hurt, it always slid behind the cloud of abstracted serenity now floating over his face. He took law cases because they 'interested' him, variously outraging acquaintances both on the left and the right, who had decided he was one of them. A full pardon for George Hall wouldn't have satisfied Isaac; what he wanted was a new trial. Stopping the execution was a necessary first step. I said, ' "Maybe" what? Tell me.'

The spaniel pouches under his sad beautiful eyes crinkled. 'Tell me, tell me, tell me, ever since you were a skinny kid with ears out to here. What kind of food did they have at this fancy dance?'

'Aww, shit . . .'

'Did you meet anybody you liked?'

'Isaac, you've been trying to find me the right girl since the day I met you.'

'Don't exaggerate. You were five years old then.'

'Don't you. I was nine.'

I'd met Isaac the day he'd tapped me on the shoulder in the drugstore and hired me to run to the library for some book nobody'd checked out since 1948, that I had to beat the dust out of like an eraser. For the next five years I ran to the courthouse for his messages and to the corner for his newspapers. Isaac Rosethorn never ran anywhere, or did much walking either. His right leg dragged a little – from polio, he said. Sometimes it seemed to work almost fine, sometimes it limped along downright pitifully – depending on the jury. He'd lived then where he lived now, in the Piedmont Hotel, and if he ever went any farther, he drove a Studebaker that I know an antique auto show would love to get its hands on. He went to visit his sister-in-law every Saturday, and every Sunday he went to the cemetery to visit somebody called 'Edith Keene, 1920–1947, Gone to a Better Place,' which first I thought maybe meant that she'd had the sense to get out of Hillston – since a better place was where my daddy had always wished he could go, out of Hillston, 'this armpit.'

Isaac said, 'I hope you aren't going to argue with me that your own efforts to find the right girl have been terribly successful.'

I said no, I wasn't going to argue with him.

Outside the car, the drizzle had slowed, almost stopped. Behind us, Jordan West, checking the rain's pause with an upturned palm, pulled thick white candles from her canvas purse, lit them in the fire, and passed them around to all the vigilants, who moved out in a line from under the gate ledge to take one each. Then they began singing, clapping the beat. 'Ain't gonna let nobody turn me around, turn me around, turn me around . . .' The guard in the cubicle, licking glaze from his fingers, clearing a circle of steam from the windowpane with his forearm, stood up to watch them. '. . . Walking down that freedom road.' Their voices sounded eerie, disembodied, in the outdoor night.

Bubba Percy broke away from Molina and trotted up to my car, looking excited, his new Burberry trenchcoat flapping. When I rolled down the window, he stuck his head all the way inside. 'That guy says Briggs Cadmean died! Tonight!' We nodded back at him. 'And here I am all the fuck out here like an asshole!'

'That's strong, but factual,' I said. 'Just stop eavesdropping on police business, and you won't get led so far astray.' Behind the waves of Percy's auburn pompadour, I saw a second prison guard opening the long gate. A man walked out with an umbrella, raised it, then lowered it, then Julian Lewis stepped out behind him, tucking his scarf inside the velvet collar of his coat. As soon as they saw him, Coop's little group grabbed up their signs and ran over, chanting, '*Free George Hall! Free George Hall!*'

'Bubba,' I said, 'on the other hand, eavesdropping just made your day. The lieutenant governor's about to give you an exclusive.' I turned his soft pink cheek with my forefinger. Percy spun around and took off, probably before he even believed Lewis was there. 'Come on,' I told Isaac; but instead, settling his wide buttocks down in my upholstery, the old man pulled a bag of pistachio nuts out of his pocket. I walked off after Percy, who'd already wedged himself between Lewis and his assistant.

Like most Dollards, Julian D. Lewis was good-looking, personable, and not too bright – not dumb, just not bright; he was also as tan in December as he was in August, because he represented the state at a lot of winter conferences in warm golf resorts. He was also polite, not to mention wanting to be governor himself if he could beat Andy Brookside, so when a newsman with a circulation of 110,000 asked him what he was doing at Dollard Prison at midnight, he stopped to answer, though I could tell the circling crowd made him nervous: he kept his back to the limo and his eye on the guards by the gate.

'*Free George Hall!*' yelled the vigilante again.

Looking solemn, Lewis held his bronzed hand up, then combed it briskly through his hair, like he was revving a motor, and said, 'I'm here on behalf of the governor. To inform Warden Carpenter. That the governor has decided to grant. A stay of execution to the prisoner George Hall.'

There was a second of pure quiet, then Jordan screamed, leaping up and down against Coop, who stood still as a rock, like he couldn't feel her. The candle slid out of his fist into the mud.

Behind them, Molina raised both arms and silently shook them. Jordan ran to the young protectors, who threw away their signs, cheered, and pounded each other on the arms and backs. Lewis forced a smile, but at least he didn't wave. I pushed through so I could hear.

Bubba Percy, topping from foot to foot, jerked out a little spiral pad. 'You mean, the governor pardoned Hall?'

Lewis shook his head. 'No. Governor Wollston has granted a stay of four weeks in response to petitions regarding the case.'

'Is there new evidence?'

Lewis's assistant, wearing an exact replica of his boss's clothes, leaned over to whisper at him. Lewis nodded at the chauffeur, who opened the back door of the Lincoln. Then he replied, 'I'm simply here to convey the governor's decision; that's all.' Coop Hall jammed his hands in his jacket, and pushed through the cheering group to Jordan; I was standing next to her, and held out my hand, but he never looked.

His voice was hoarse. 'Get to a phone and call Mama.' Jordan hugged his arm as he spoke to the group behind him; he had to yell over their whoops of pleasure. 'Okay, everybody. Hey! Come on! Pack up and go get some sleep. Okay? And, listen! Be in Raleigh tomorrow, just as planned.'

They broke off, and dutifully collected their placards. Hall moved Jordan towards the cluster of cars. 'Go on. If Mama doesn't answer, you drive on home and wait for her to get back from Greensboro. I'll be there soon as I talk to Rosethorn.' He turned away, acknowledging her rub on his back only by a nod.

Bubba was still talking and writing at the same time. 'Mr Lewis, you were state's attorney general when Hall shot Bobby Pym, and that was *seven* years ago. Wasn't that a fair trial? I mean, how much more "study" of the case do you think—'

'Mr Percy.' Lewis looked at him, hurt. 'I did and do believe the first trial was a fair one. But when a man's life is at stake, naturally the state must take every—'

I didn't wait around for the speech, but ran back to the Oldsmobile, where Isaac was pouring pistachio shells into my ashtray. As soon as I opened the door, yelling 'Hot damn!,' he said, 'The stay, how long?'

'Four weeks. . . . Hold it, how could you hear him say "stay"?!'

He sucked on his lip, looking morose. 'Too bad. Twelve, eight, I was hoping. Just as easy to say eight as four, the tightwad.' Stuffing all his notes in his pockets, he said, 'I remember back, Governor Pat Brown in California, the State Department asked him to give Caryl Chessman a reprieve. Ike was starting that goodwill tour of South America, and there was a lot of sympathy for Chessman down there. Sixty days, Pat Brown gave him. Not that it did any good. Later on, I remember, Brown said he was sorry he hadn't pardoned Chessman. Ahh, I'm tired, I'm going home.'

I caught hold of his coat. 'Okay, Isaac, who's going to South America? I get the funny feeling you *knew* there'd be a stay. Hummm? Is that why you hotfooted it over, and had me yanked from wassailing with the upper crust, when I paid forty-five bucks to rent this suit? So, okay, were you tipped off?'

Rapping his knuckles softly on my head the way he'd done when I was a child, he rumbled his sigh of a laugh. 'I use my noggin.'

Bubba was bamming on my window again; the Lincoln limo had left, and the vigilante were crowding into their cars. 'Mangum,' he wheezed, thrilled out of breath, 'give me a statement and I'll print it. Wollston granted a stay!'

I said, 'There was a report of a threat to disrupt a peaceful assembly. I came to check it out. That's a statement. Now will you stop trying to crawl into my car? It's crowded enough with Rosethorn spread all over the seat.'

Bubba leaned past me. 'Mr Rosethorn, your client's got a reprieve. How do you feel?'

Isaac said, 'Better.'

'That's it?'

Rosethorn sighed. 'I'll feel even better when the State Supreme Court grants my client a new trial.'

Bubba switched back to me. 'Look, Mangum, you've been

involved in this Hall business from the beginning. You were just a patrolman when it started.'

'Sergeant.' I tapped on his spiral pad. 'I apprehended the suspect, but I was not assigned to the investigation, nor in any other way "involved" in the case.'

But Bubba had his story line already set. 'Here you are trying to put criminals away, and the courts drag it out for seven years. Is that frustrating for the police?'

'The police keep the peace and enforce the law against people who break it; they don't try people, and they don't sentence them. Leave me alone.'

'But isn't it frustrating, when the law said to execute George Hall seven years ago?'

'Nope, Bubba, that's what the jury and the judge said.'

'Okay, okay. You're close friends with Savile's wife, Alice, what's her name, MacLeod, the one that keeps trying to bring up that bill in the legislature to outlaw capital punishment. She says capital punishment's imposed unfairly against minorities. What do *you* think about that, or, say, about the death penalty in general?'

It was the question I'd worried about getting asked for a long time, worried about asking it of myself. I just shook my head.

No denying Bubba's shrewdness. He grinned at me. 'Come on, Cuddy. Should a moral man accept a job to enforce the state's laws if he doesn't believe those laws are morally right? That's my question.' He kept grinning. 'No comment?'

'Bubba, please go on home and write your story before you miss a chance for a headline.'

Rubbing his cheeks with his sheepskin gloves, Percy grimaced. 'Shit, y'all know what the boonie *Star* headline's gonna say, gonna say that old fart Cadmean finally croaked. Black border and big photo. Lewis back there tells me the governor's declared tomorrow a fucking official day of mourning. Half-mast, factory whistles, the whole boo-hoo. Okay. See you assholes back in Deadtown. Basketball tomorrow.' He dodged off on tiptoe, to keep his Italian boots out of the puddles.

Isaac Rosethorn and I looked at each other for a while before I said, 'Be a little tacky to have executions and racial demonstrations on an official day of mourning, wouldn't it?' He just fished around in his mouth with his baby finger for nut husks. 'My my,' I shook my head. 'You must of zipped out of Hillston the minute they smoothed the covers over Cadmean's eyes, and his soul soared off to South America. You didn't by some chance kill Old Fart yourself, did you, Isaac? Pull the plug, trip over the oxygen line, anything of that nature?'

'I don't believe in killing, you know that.'

'Well, you must have planted the "day of mourning" notion mighty fast, that's all I can figure. Who with?'

Like in the old days, he waggled his fat finger at me, smug as Churchill. 'To predict is not to plant. To conclude is not to cause . . . And four weeks is only twenty-eight days.' He pulled his gloves back on; one was black, and the other one brown. 'I need to ride back with Cooper. Come have Chinese with me Sunday, unless, I hope, you did meet a girl at this dance and are otherwise occupied.'

I sighed. 'Make it Buddha's Garden at seven-thirty.'

'Interesting question, Mr Percy's. The one about moral lawmen and moral laws.' He patted my knee as he pulled himself out of the car, and walked – his right foot dragging a line through the slush – across the empty lot towards his old Studebaker, where Coop Hall stood waiting for him, staring up at the high brick turrets.

The old prison was settling to sleep. Lights like stars in the chinks of blackened bricks had blinked out, one by one, except for a row on the second floor. Death Row is never dark; in darkness a prisoner might contrive to cheat the state, might braid a noose out of his clothes, or, while a guard yawned, fashion a razor from a bit of blade secretly broken off from the supervised shaving tools. It happened. Or almost happened. Men had been led to the chair with bandaged wrists or throat. But not often, not anymore; there were no sheets, no belts, no shoes, no metal utensils, there were head counts every few hours, there were naked body inspections whenever a guard decided to do one, there were trusties to watch the prisoners eat to make sure they didn't choke, there was no privacy in the solitary cells, and no darkness, not even on this winter solstice, the longest night of the year.

I thought everybody had left until I saw Jack Molina still standing by the drum can, watching smoke push through the dirt he'd thrown in to smother the fire. I stopped my car beside him. 'Come by yourself, Professor?'

'What?' He looked at me as if he were trying to remember my name; then he walked over. Molina had a lean, narrow head, all angles, except for round John Lennon glasses and huge dark eyes like a Byzantine saint. He kept his hair short now, and wore a tie. In the sixties, he'd looked a lot like Jesus on a diet. He'd been a sixties star at the university. Shoved through crowds by a phalanx of students, he'd jump up on cafeteria tables or the library steps, and give speeches that drove folks crazy – one way or another. After the sixties died, he'd settled for classroom forums and ghost politics; taught courses on 'The Rhetoric of Mass Communication,' and wrote speeches for Andy Brookside.

Turns out he'd come over to ask me about the Hillston Club ball, and whether I'd noticed the Brooksides there. I told him I had.

'Did you happen to see my wife, Debbie?' He was glancing around inside my car as if he thought I might have brought her along.

'At the dance? I don't think I've ever met her, so I can't say. Was she there?' He didn't bother to answer me, so I asked him a different question. 'You knew that Briggs Cadmean died?'

'Rosethorn mentioned it when he drove out to bring us some coffee.' His eyes weren't paying any attention to what he was saying. 'Rosethorn's quite a character.'

'No argument.'

Molina poured more dirt into the smoking can, and stuck his bare hand in to spread it around; I don't know why it didn't burn a hole in his palm. 'Yeah,' he nodded, 'Rosethorn defended Piedmont Chemicals in that big negligence suit in 'seventy-three. I was in the line picketing his clients at the trial. He got them off. You know the one thing all Utopias share . . . No lawyers.'

'That and failure.' I asked him again, 'You come alone?'

'Yeah.' He pointed at a midsized motorcycle leaning under the shadow of the gate; it surprised me – he didn't seem the type; plus he was wearing chinos and loafers.

'Whooee, Professor, your balls must be charged with antifreeze.' I meant it friendly, but he took offence and walked away, stiff-backed, without a kiss-my for a tired police chief, on his night off, driving twenty miles through sleet to stop some rednecks from maybe chucking a brick at his head. I bet back in the sixties Hillston cops must have just loved Jack Molina.

Before I rolled my window up, I heard a strange sudden howl, so sharp in the dark quiet that Molina jumped back a step, his heel striking the drum can like a gunshot. It was a sound like a mountain lion might make that had somehow managed to walk out of the Smokies down to the Piedmont, and was claiming the territory. I called to Molina, 'Keep in touch if you see any more of those trucks.' He turned around, nodded, and raised his hand in good-bye.

It wasn't until I was halfway home that I wondered if the yell had been George Hall, finding out they weren't going to kill him in nine more hours. When they told him, twenty-eight days probably sounded like a long time.

Chapter 3

Clouds had quit and hurled themselves out of the way of the moon and a few stars; the slush had washed off, so the drive back to Hillston was fast. On both sides of the highway, winter trees twisted up like coral reefs, and the road was so lonesome I might just as well have been under the sea. Patsy Cline sang 'Crazy' and Loretta Lynn sang, 'You Ain't Woman Enough to Take My Man.' Some folks fight, some folks cry.

Airport Road comes into town from the north, so I figured I'd go by the Hillston Club to tell Justin and Alice what I'd heard at Dollard Prison. It was one A.M. when I drove down the poplar-lined entrance. The Mercedeses and Cadillacs had thinned out in the parking lot, but there were still plenty of Saabs and BMWs left, Justin's old Austin wasn't among them, but maybe they'd come with somebody else, or maybe Alice had left early with the car. Out on the pitch-black fairways, I could hear some golf carts tearing around, girls shrieking 'Faster!' and guys hollering 'Fore!' The whole white-columned wood front was still lit up with twinkling Christmas lights, and the Jimmy Douglas Orchestra appeared to have shucked off the past, at least as far as Early Motown, because even outside I could hear them chopping up the Supremes' 'Baby Love' in the worst way.

It was clear that the older half of 'the number' (as well as most of the staff) had abandoned the ball, or been locked in the basement by the younger set. On the couch where I'd seen A. R. Randolph's granddaughter passed out in her red satin gown, I now saw a young dishevelled couple kissing like they never expected to get another chance; they'd pull apart, gasp for air, and plunge back in like they were trying to save somebody from drowning. Two young men in their ruffled shirts were fencing with brass pokers beside the giant Christmas tree. Somebody smart had blown out all its little candles just when there'd been nothing left but wax nubs between that tree and a flaming inferno; Hillston's whole high society could've burnt up like Confederate Atlanta. On the parquet floor, two young barefoot women sat, their dresses spread like bright parachutes, each chugging a bottle of champagne while watching the fencers. 'Aren't they silly?' said one. 'I think men are the silliest things I ever saw in my whole life, I really do, I mean, you know, don't you? Don't you think, Steffie, men are just, well, I don't know, silly? Or something.'

Steffie opened her mouth, but then slowly shook her head as if her thoughts on the subject were too complex.

In the ballroom, the guests still on their feet (there were some stretched out on chairs and tables) were gyrating like they'd stuck their hands into a fuse box. I gave a half-hearted look for Justin, but knew I wouldn't find him; he's not a modernist and was probably already home one-fingering Cole Porter tunes on his upright. And I didn't see the mayor and Mrs Yarborough, or Paul Madison, or the Brooksides, or anybody I much knew. Maybe the older crowd had got word of Cadmean's death, and all gone home to mourn the passing of an era. If this group here had heard, they hadn't let it get them down. Three very good-looking drunk girls (one, I realized, was Randolph's granddaughter) stood on the band dais, imitating the Supremes. They'd giggle when they'd turn wrong and crash into each other.

I stood by the door in my wet raincoat a few more minutes. At a table beside me, a young freckled woman in a blue strapless evening gown sat alone, picking without much interest slivers of meat from a turkey carcass. She had a drunk tragic look to her, but it may have just been the smeared mascara. She said, 'Know who you look like?'

'Me?' I shook my head. 'No. Who?'

'You know who, he goes to the train station and it's raining and she doesn't show up, and then she walks into his nightclub, you know the one.'

'*Casablanca?*'

'My mom rented the video. You look like that.'

'He was shorter.' I sat down at the table, and ate some of the turkey. I said, 'George Hall just got a stay of execution.'

'Execution?'

'George Hall. The governor granted a stay. He was going to be executed tomorrow.'

She nodded. 'Oh. The black man?'

'Yeah.' We watched Randolph's granddaughter pretend to be Diana Ross. Then she said, 'Hey, wait, I've seen you before. Like on TV? Were you on TV?'

'Sometimes I'm on the news.'

'No! It was a magazine, or something.'

I said, 'Right. I'm the Hillston police chief.'

She slapped my hand, presumably for lying. 'Come on! Give me a break.'

'Okay. I'm an investment banker. My name's Cuddy Mangum.'

She nodded, but didn't offer her own name, and as if by way of explaining her disinterest, she lifted the tablecloth so that I could see a ruddy young man sprawled in a dead drunk sleep on the floor, his head in her lap. 'I don't want to wake him up.'

I said, 'Honey, you could leave his head on that chair, drive to Charlotte, and it'd still be there when you got back.'

She wanted to know why she should want to go to Charlotte, and I admitted I couldn't think of a reason.

In the lobby, the fencers' dates were taking their pokers away from them because tempers had apparently run high; one guy had blood running from his nose into his shirt front; I now recognized him as Mrs Sunderland's grandnephew, the professional skier. The girl who thought men were silly was crying.

Downtown Hillston had made it through another day, and turned off its Christmas trees and its store lights and its six blocks of neon sleighs flying without any reindeer across Main Street with Santa holding tight to his toys. Somebody was still awake at the *Hillston Star* (probably Bubba Percy), a half-dozen lonesome people still sat waiting in the coffee shop at the bus station, the Tucson Lounge was filling its dumpster with the night's rubbish, but the rest of Hillston had gone to bed when I drove up to the wide stone steps of the Municipal Building, flanked by two Confederate cannon that Cadmean had arranged to have hauled over from the old county courthouse. As far as I know they'd never been fired. Sherman bypassed Hillston to the west, missing the surrender party waiting for him on the banks of the Shocco.

According to a plaque, some of his stragglers did stable their horses overnight in a farmhouse near Pine Hills Lake; it's now the fanciest restaurant in town, and a favourite with the inner circle.

Above the courtroom doors in the dark marble lobby, old Cadmean shook his painted blueprints down at me. Upstairs, the holding cell was asleep and peaceful. From the poster on my office wall, Elvis looked like he was having too much fun ever to get fat and sick and die. While I was checking in with Sergeant Davies, we heard loud shouts and sobs coming from the interrogation room. Hiram said, 'Billy Gilchrist, on a crying jag. Seems to think they executed George Hall tonight, and he's praying for him.'

Gilchrist, a local low-life alcoholic, had got religion about a year ago; it hadn't stopped his binges, but it often gave them a remorseful flavour. I said, 'Come on, Hiram, drunk prayers are still prayers, aren't they? Seems like Christ hung out with lots of boozers himself.' Turning his back on me, Davies snapped paper into his old Royal and typed away.

Unlocking the interrogation room, I spotted Gilchrist literally on his knees, banging his head on the carpet, still shouting and still blotto. He took a tone with the Lord that explained why Davies hadn't been sympathetic. 'God, help me, goddamnit! Where are you, you fucker!' He was about sixty, wino-skinny, bleary blue eyes, yellowish-white hair combed forward over the baldness. He stank to high heaven – wherever his prayers were going. When he saw me, he sobbed, nose, mouth, and eyes all running. 'He put me by myself! Get me outta here! Not my fault. Can't stand be all lone. Ostrichized. Need a drink.'

I pulled him to his feet; he was so light he flew up like a paper puppet. 'Billy, you need to get yourself calmed down. Stop that bawling.' I walked him to the corner where he'd dragged the pallet Davies had made, laid him down on it, and covered him up with a blanket. 'The sergeant says you think they killed George Hall tonight? Well, they didn't. Fact is, Hall got a reprieve from the governor. A *reprieve*.'

He snorted back tears in jerks. 'Reprieve? Not dead?'

'No. Now, Billy, you lie back. We can't have you keeping all our other guests awake. You can leave in the morning. George Hall, is that what's got you all upset? You used to be a pal of his or something?'

But Gilchrist had abruptly passed out, snoring. Safe and sound in the sleep of the dead drunk.

Home in River Rise, a grin of a moon was laughing at A. R. Randolph's bridge over the Shocco. My apartment was freezing cold, one of the strings of coloured lights had burned out on the little spruce I had in a bucket with its bad side to the picture window. Martha Mitchell had pooped in the kitchen for spite, right next to the magnetized swinging door I'd had specially built so she could lead an independent life. She was upstairs in my bed, burrowed under the quilt Alice MacLeod made for me. 'I got your message, Martha,' I said. 'Bitch.' She gave me a nasty look, which I returned.

Yawning, I piled suit, cummerbund, tie, and shirt back in the rental box; even the cuff links came with the outfit. In the mirror I saw a tall skinny man with thick hair the colour of tobacco, a bony face, and blue eyes. One day a long time ago Lee Haver came to school with a robin's egg. She held it up near me and said, 'Cuddy Mangum, this is how blue your eyes are.' From then on, I liked my eyes best of my features, though my ex-wife, Cheryl, didn't appear to single them out as anything special. Cheryl and I had some great times in bed, but the memory must have faded fast while I was sleeping solo in the soggy Mekong; it's clear that a sense of history wasn't Cheryl's strong suit.

History's what I study. Time's witness, Ben Jonson called it, advertising Sir Walter Raleigh's *History of the World*. History of the world. Imagine thinking you could think that big. 'Course, Raleigh never finished the story. Twelve years on Death Row before they cut off his head. He ran his finger along the axe blade and joked, 'A sharp remedy, but a sure one for all ills.' I've been told I've got a sense of humour, but I've got nothing to match that sailor.

Me, I study history in small sections. Even so, it makes me think, if God's doing the best job He can, He picked the wrong profession.

Mrs Mitchell growled in her sleep when I pulled back the covers. I told her, 'George Hall got reprieved because old Cadmean died. Now, you suppose God thinks that's pretty funny, Martha?' She didn't answer, and I slid the top book off the stack by the bed.

Chapter 4

When I wake up, it's usually with relief to find out my dream's not true. In this one, they'd accidentally locked me inside the gas chamber while I was trying to apologize to George Hall. I heard the hiss of that cyanide sack hitting the acid, and then two rows of witnesses just watched while I ran around, beating on the glass windows and the green metal walls. Most of these witnesses were people I knew. Nothing moved but their eyes. Tugging against the straps of his chair, George was missing his own death, he was so upset about me.

Saturday morning the phone rang too early; by the time it was clear to me I wasn't getting gassed, and neither – today – was George Hall, I'd said yes to everything Sergeant Caleb wanted to know without hearing what it was.

'"Yes," you'll come on downtown, or "yes" you'll call her back? . . . Chief?'

'Yeah, sure. What time is it, Zeke? Call who back?'

'She said, Lee Haver Brookside. It's ten o'clock. I didn't wake you up, did I?' Caleb, farm-raised, sounded appalled.

' 'Course not. I was out sanding my walkway.'

'You still got ice out there, Chief? Golly, it's about sixty degrees downtown.'

'Zeke, start over. Mrs Brookside called.'

What she'd wanted was to speak with me 'officially' about an 'important' matter. Told this was my day off, she'd asked if she could call my home to 'arrange' for me to 'meet her' anyhow. I was curious, eager, and oddly annoyed. 'Call Mrs Brookside, tell her the earliest I can "arrange" to come to my office is three, if she wants to meet me then.'

My phone's not listed. You put some folks in jail, they'll hold a grudge till they get out. Once one of them rang my doorbell and threw a Carolina pancake in my face. I got my hand up in time, which was good for my future love life, because a Carolina pancake is lye and Crisco mixed in a batter and set on fire with a dab of kerosene. It burned right through my bathrobe sleeve and left an ugly scar on my forearm.

'And, Chief Mangum, we got a college kid in here Purley Newsome brought in for going seventy in a twenty zone, driving without registration, and resisting arrest. This boy says he told Newsome he wasn't doing more than thirty, says Newsome took his registration away from him and ate it right in front of his eyes.' Zeke Caleb, day desk sergeant, was young, rawboned, probably never been west of the Appalachians or north of the Mason-Dixon line; he had Indian blood, Indian pride, and he wouldn't lie if you held a branding iron to his neck.

'You believe this kid, Zeke?'

'He . . . well . . . Yes, sir.'

I rolled out of bed, shuffled through the carpet to wake up my feet, and drew the drapes back on my balcony slider. Winter sun almost blinded me. 'Let him go. Is he out of state?'

'No, sir. Black boy from Kingston.'

'Okay, tell him to go to Motor Vehicles Monday, and they'll give him a new registration. You call Darlene about it.'

'What about this speeding ticket?'

'Purley's going to eat it. I want him in the squad room at two-thirty, and I want an audience there too. Whoever you can round up.'

Zeke rasped out a laugh. 'Ohhh, he's 'bout bound to get hinky over this. Can I call Nancy? She's off-duty, but I sure hate her to miss it.'

'Let's don't get vengeful on a maiden's behalf, Cherokee.' I suspected Zeke of being in love with Officer Nancy White, but neither one of them seemed to know it yet. I'd had to pull Zeke off Purley Newsome, after Newsome had hung a dead cat, with sexist remarks attached, in Nancy's locker. A week later, someone put deer rut spray in the heater duct of Zeke's Chevy Blazer, and Purley's denials didn't much convince me. (The only redeeming feature to Purley Newsome's entire character's a relative one – by which I mean his brother Otis, who's the city comptroller.)

First thing I do every morning is race fat Martha down to the river, and carry her back. She hates moving, and I hate moving in the cold; maybe because my folks were always running out of furnace oil about halfway through the month, I've got a strong dislike to blue lips and numb toes. But we do it, then Martha goes back to bed, and I turn on the radio.

While I ate breakfast (bananas and mayonnaise, toasted), did some wash, some windows, and some bills, WNNC played me 'White Christmas,' which was just wishful thinking, then took me on a quick tour 'around the world,' where folks were up to their usual tricks, crawling out from under earthquakes, crashing aeroplanes, swapping gunshots, and pilgrimaging to Jerusalem for holy week. 'Around the nation,' a cold snap was wiping out Florida oranges, the country's infrastructure didn't look good, and on his ranch in California the president had chopped down in person a Christmas tree his wife had personally picked out. 'Around the state,' today, flags would be lowered on public buildings to mourn the death of a great Tarheel, Briggs Monmouth Cadmean; Monday, Andy Brookside was going to address a convention of black business leaders in Winston-Salem; and Governor Wollston had given George Hall a last-minute reprieve. Discussing this bit of news on 'In My Opinion,' local evangelist Reverend Brodie Cheek announced that Governor Wollston was a spineless worm bought off by a Jewish-financed conspiracy of black agitators, liberal sob-sisters, and secular humanists in high places – like Andrew Brookside, president of that Communist-atheist breeding farm, Haver University. WNNC said that wasn't necessarily their opinion, and Elvis sang 'Santa, Bring My Baby Back to Me.'

Justin showed up while I was tucking a sheet around the bucket I had my Christmas tree in, draping the folds to look like a snowfield, and setting up Mama's old plaster creche scene on it. A sheet doesn't look a damn thing like a snowfield, the creche was tacky to start with and now had only one wise man, plus Joseph's head was broken off, but family habits die hard.

Soon as the bell rang, Martha tore out of the bedroom like the Charge of the Light Brigade, but Justin told her, 'Who are you kidding?' and she took offence and went back to sleep.

Justin asked if I'd heard about Hall's reprieve – he'd kept calling here until two A.M. with no answer – so I explained where I'd gone last night, and why. 'Alice is delirious!' he said, taking off some outer layers of L. L. Bean paraphernalia. 'She ran off to Raleigh with Jordan West, and that group. Distributing those handouts because somebody from the Supreme Court's visiting at the governor's mansion. That's a nice tree.' He perched on one of my denim couch sections with his Thermos jug of French coffee and his bag of croissants on his lap; he's convinced there's nothing in my refrigerator but Pop-Tarts and discount beer. I gave him a 'Go Tarheels' mug, but he set it down on the glass table, and walked over to fiddle with my tree lights. 'Cuddy, you know Cadmean died last night?'

'Isaac Rosethorn told me. Frankly, Old Briggs never seemed the type.'

He nodded, not turning around. The top string of coloured lights came back on. '. . . Want to hear something weird? He left me that black Thoroughbred of his. Manassas? Boy, that surprised me.'

I said, 'My my, touchy as you are about your little knickknacks in that old Victorian icebox of yours—'

'It's Queen Anne—'

'Somehow I can't see you moving a giant-sized not to mention vicious stallion with no potty training into your guest room. Still, it was a sweet thought. You want me to nuke those rolls of yours?' (I already know he won't eat anything heated in a microwave.)

He said, 'They're hot enough just sitting in this room. Christ, it must be ninety degrees.'

I said, 'Go look. I'm smack in the middle of the "comfort zone." . . . Mr C. didn't happen to leave me his mills, did he? I could stand to retire.'

'Sorry.' Justin pulled off his Argyle sweater. 'You're not going to believe this.'

'Try me.' I lay down on the rug with my can of Pepsi and a cold pizza slice.

'Well, my cousin Buchanan drew up the will, so he called Mother this morning, and that miserable shit—'

'You're not talking about my Peggy Savile, are you?'

'—Cadmean cut out his sons, and left everything to *Briggs*! But, *but*, Cuddy, with this codicil – that she has to quit teaching astronomy, and move back to Hillston. Or else the sons divide it all. Well, a few million to Haver University for a textiles technology lab.'

'My my my.' I hugged my knees hard. 'Oh Lord, I hope there's an afterlife, so Mr C. can watch when Briggs Junior tells your cousin Buck where he can stick her father's will. The old bastard.'

Justin had a cloth napkin on his knees while he ate his croissant. 'Are you kidding? You think Briggs is going to turn down ten and a half million dollars?! Why, she could get that codicil thrown out.'

'Don't drop those crumbs on my wall-to-wall. Listen here, Justin, I stood in the draught when Daddy Warbucks tried to give Briggs Junior a *Buick* if she'd just come pour coffee at a board dinner. I'd rather gone to the Pole with Admiral Byrd. She's going to turn it down flat, plus now she probably won't even come to the funeral.' I went to the closet for my parka. 'Hell, she turned me down flat and this is nothing but ten million dollars. Put that bag in the trash compactor and let's go tear up some courts. Maybe if I hoisted you up on my shoulders, you could get the ball in the basket once in a while.'

Whenever we can, a group of us in the department play basketball against other nostalgic types sponsored by local merchants. We call ourselves Fuzz Five, and the only teams we ever beat are The Rib-House Rousers and the Stags of Stagg Hardware Store. If I could just persuade our lab man, Lieutenant Etham Foster ('Dr Dunk-it' to every NCAA fan with any memory at all), to play with us, we'd sweep the series, but he says he never even liked the game, just wanted the education. So we mostly lose; well, hey, Justin only *claims* to be 5'9", and Nancy White can walk under my arm without its tickling. But this morning we were going against the Cosmics of Carippini's Italian Restaurant, so we had a chance, since their captain's Father Paul Madison, who's shorter than Justin, and their forward's Bubba Percy, who's scared to mess up his hair.

Driving to the Y, I pushed in a tape cassette. Loretta Lynn came on loud and feisty. 'Lay off of my man if you don't wanna go to Fist City.'

'Fist City?' groaned Justin, sticking his fingers in his ears. He took them out in a minute to ask me a favour: his amateur theatrics group, the Hillston Players – they put on 'classics' in an old bankrupted downtown movie theatre, and pestered their friends to come watch them – needed someone to play Malvolio in their holiday production of *Twelfth Night*. Justin said, 'We lost a male member to a broken leg.'

58

I said, 'That's a tough way to lose one. What'd he do, land on it funny?'

He turned down my tape. 'Is that supposed to be vulgar?'

'Mildly. Listen, I'm a man of the *vulgo*, *vulgaris*, that's the people, yes!, to you.'

'That's *vulgus*, *vulgi*, to you,' said Justin, naturally enough a classics major way back when. 'Come on, this is a great part. And we need somebody quick, I mean a quick study.'

'Forget it, I never acted in my life.'

'Are you kidding? With all your affectations? And you look right too, tall and thin. See, Malvolio's this Puritan steward to a countess, but he thinks he's better than everybody, and keeps telling them to stop having fun, so they trick him into thinking the countess is in love with him, and she has him locked up as a madman.'

I gave Justin the long raised eyebrow I'd seen on the waiter at the Hillston Club. 'You're telling me I'm *right* for this part?'

'You've got the best lines. "Some are born great, some achieve greatness, and some have greatness thrust upon them."'

'Doesn't sound like greatness you're fixing to thrust upon me; sounds like public humiliation.'

'See!' He socked my arm. 'Just what Malvolio would say. Blue Randolph's playing the countess, and I'm playing her drunk uncle.'

'Well, that fits. Who's Blue Randolph?'

'Oh, you know. Atwater's granddaughter. At the dance? Wearing bright red?' He pantomimed an hourglass.

'I seem to recall her.' We turned in at the YMCA, where the state flag was lowered to half-mast. A squad of women jogged past us, looking like they wished they hadn't signed up. 'Why don't you ask Paul Madison to do this part?'

'He's playing the Duke . . . Well, just promise me you'll think about it.'

'I'll think about it.'

Justin tells me Paul's in a great mood today, because he's already called him to leak the news that Briggs Cadmean had left his big ugly Gothic mausoleum of a house to Trinity Episcopal Church for a "rest home." This was going to surprise people, since the old robber baron had attended First Presbyterian; not that he paid much heed to any moral reminders he might have heard there. Well, the Reverend Thomas Campbell might gnash his teeth on his pulpit over this raiding of wealthy parishioners, but I've about decided there's no con Father Paul Madison's not capable of pulling on unsuspecting sinners while they're smiling indulgently at his unworldly face.

I said to Justin, 'God, what a blabbermouth you are. What'd your cousin Buck do, come over at five A.M. with a copy of the will?'

'Oh, you know how families talk. It's going to be a convalescent home, and the stipulation is, anybody that worked more than thirty years at Cadmean mills can stay there free till they die.'

I said, 'Too bad my daddy couldn't wait.'

In the locker room, Justin says, 'You know, Alice told me you probably could have sued the mills over your father's death. Brown lung disease.'

'Yeah, and bought him a bigger tombstone. Or maybe I could have sued Haver Tobacco Company for those four unfiltered packs a day Daddy smoked. Or maybe just sue Adam for loving his wife.'

'Boy, you're in a rotten mood.'

'Am I?'

'You know what? Sometimes I think you do it just on principle.'

'Well, hey, Justin, somebody's got to.'

Paul Madison was in a good mood. While jabbering about his new convalescent home, he kept passing the ball to Bubba Percy, who appeared to be catching up on lost sleep under the basket, so my Fuzz Five moved out of last place. Nancy White (a tough East Hillston kid who used to lead a girls' gang that would tear your face off, and your hubcaps too) ran about forty miles during the game, scored eight points, and yelled, '*Punk power!!*' after every one.

Back in the locker room, I told Father Paul he ought to put in a good word with his Boss Upstairs for old Cadmean (now undoubtedly in hell, and as hot as one of his factory smokestacks), since the industrialist's opportune croaking had not only given Trinity Church more beds than that Porsche was going to buy them, it had temporarily saved George Hall's life. And Paul told me that at tomorrow's mass, he was reading Cadmean into the General Prayer, plus dedicating the altar flowers to the repose of his soul.

I said, 'You figure that'll get the SOB moved some place cooler?'

The rector blithely tossed his towel in the bin. 'Any hell that poor old man was in, he left when he died. And God bless him for dying when he did.' Snapping on a white collar over the black shirt, he laughed as he left the locker room. 'Oh, wondrous are the ways of the Lord!'

'How 'bout "ruthless"?' I yelled after him, and he stuck his head back through the door, grinning. 'You betcha,' he said.

Justin and I left Bubba in front of the mirror admiring his nakedness while he combed his hair for half an hour. He said, 'Check the front page. I gave you a quote, Mangum. You owe me.'

I said, 'I hope it was the one about your mama and the hyena.'

'Man, you're so touchy. Lighten up.' He swirled the comb through a complicated auburn wave. 'Life's too short to get too heavily invested in it. Trivial pleasure, that's the way to go.'

'Bubba, life's too short to spend half of it combing your goddamn hair.'

'You keep missing the point, Mangum. Shallowness is the secret of happiness. That's the point.'

Justin said, 'You must be the happiest man alive.'

'Believe it, friend,' called Percy over his bare furry pink shoulder.

At the Municipal Building a basket of lilies had already been placed beneath Cadmean's portrait. Justin dropped me off there on his way to East Hillston to chat with Preston Pope, a local thief on whom my predecessor Fulcher had once tried to unload a homicide rap. I had Justin working on what looked like a case of rivalry among some upwardly mobile gun smugglers: two months ago we'd found a Peugeot driven into deep woods off the 28 bypass; the trunk was full of guns; the front seat was full of the driver, who'd been dead so long he had to be shovelled into a plastic bag, but whose loafers Justin was still able to identify as Ballys of Switzerland. If Preston Pope knew anything about the smuggling (anything that didn't involve his family), Justin would be the one he'd tell.

Down in the holding cell, the drunks had sobered up and gone. Billy Gilchrist had left Zeke with an IOU for five dollars. Upstairs, there was a sullen tension around the place because of George Hall's reprieve; a couple of the older patrolmen sat by the coffee table telling anybody who came over how the lousy system was rigged to let killers walk: to them, George Hall was a cop-killer, pure and simple, and they wanted him dead. A young recruit, John Emory, who was black, started arguing with them that Hall hadn't had a fair trial; voices got loud, then they got ugly. Finally Zeke sent all three men down to wash the squad cars.

There was too much paperwork on my desk; moving it from the In side to the Out is the bulk of my job. For the rest, I spend a lot more time with feuding families and worn-down social workers than I do with big guns and fast cars. The duller my job, the better a job I figure I'm doing. Like I say, I'm a peacekeeper. After Vietnam, peace is my idea of a party. I gave up even carrying a gun a long time ago; because if you've got it on you, chances are you'll get scared enough or mad enough to use it. Nothing's simpler than squeezing a trigger. It's quicker than reasoning, and a lot less tiring than giving chase. I came so close one time to killing a guy who jumped me with a screwdriver in his living room, it still gives me bad dreams. Since 1925, Hillston police have records of fourteen suspects killed while 'escaping' or 'resisting arrest.' Twelve were black, and those are just the figures *on* the record books. No suspect's escaped and no suspect's been injured, much less died, since I've been chief, and I'm proud of that. I don't want any more macho jocks and hot-rod cowboys on my force looking for a legal chance to speed around and shoot their rods; aside from Purley Newsome, I don't have too many of them left either. The best way is to convince them to resign. One gave up after three months on traffic duty at Polk Elementary School. One developed a perforated ulcer from refilling out departmental forms till he spelled words like 'apprehended' right.

The worst one (a close pal of the guy George Hall shot) left before my promotion. His name was Winston Russell. I kicked him in the nuts once, after a prostitute told me in the hospital what he'd done to her with his nightstick. He called me a 'fucking sick idealist,' but he misunderstood me. By the time I finished coaching that woman, they should have put him away for life. But he was out on parole after eighteen months, and came ringing my doorbell with that Carolina pancake. If I'd been an idealist, I

62

would have been more surprised when I'd opened my door. This time Russell got five years, and served two. He was supposed to have got out again a few months back. I kind of doubt he'll drop by and ask for his old job. Winston Russell was a sadist; I didn't know his pal Bobby Pym all that well, but I bet the two had a lot in common. They made the Black Panthers' views on their profession sound understated. A clue to Purley Newsome's character was that when he first came on the force, he'd admired those two goons, and was always sucking up to them, offering guffawing anecdotes of his own puny tyrannies for their approval.

At 2:30, I met the shift in the squad room where Zeke had sat Newsome down in a front seat. I went over some routine business, then said I wanted everybody to listen hard for any rumours about Klan rumblings, any talk connected to the Hall reprieve. 'We don't want another Trinity Church incident, okay? It makes Hillston look bad, it makes you and me look bad . . . Now, one last thing before I turn you loose to fight off crime and Christmas shoppers.'

Then thirty police officers, eight of them women, sat sober-faced at their plastic desks while I wrote 'A, B, C' on the blackboard. 'This, girls and boys, is a pop quiz. "Question: Harassing folks because they're different coloured and better educated than you is something (A) the police do? (B) assholes do? (C) nobody in this room had better ever do again?" I'd like Officer Newsome to step up here and check off the right answer. Purley, I'm gonna give you a hint: don't pick "A."'

Purley Newsome – good-looking if you like big, dumb blonds – slumped surly and thick-faced down in his chair.

I said, 'Purley, we have just talked a Haver student, whose car registration you apparently mistook for your chewing tobacco, and whose papa happens to be a *judge*, out of filing a million-dollar suit against you for false arrest. We finally beat him down to one condition that seems downright mild mannered considering early on he was asking for one of your *ears*. One condition. You're going to eat that speeding ticket for dessert. Zeke, give him the ticket.'

Newsome laughed, but stopped when nobody joined in. 'You're crazy out of your skull, you think that,' he spluttered and pushed back hard in his chair.

'Well, your other option is to resign. I'll certainly understand, and be willing to accept your resignation.'

He just stared at me, shaking his head like a truculent bull. I gave him a silent count of ten before I yelled, '*Then get the fuck up here, you prickhead!*'

That brought him to his feet; bullies are suckers for bullying. But he stalled and took a high tone. 'I'm not sinking down to your level.'

'You want to clarify that, Purley?'

'Regarding your verbalization.'

I smiled. 'How 'bout this: I'd appreciate your coming up here, Officer Prickhead – before I rip that badge off your fat shirt, and shove your fat ass through the goddamn window!'

'You're gonna be sorry' was the best he could do, when he slouched past me over to Zeke.

'That's harsh,' I said. 'I'm glad you warned me.'

Not a soul cracked a grin while Purley balled up the speeding ticket, crammed it into his mouth, and stomped back to his seat, his cheek bulged out like a blowfish. I saw him spit it out in a trashcan when he left, but I didn't push the point; at least he used the can.

After I dismissed the squad, Zeke shook his head. 'That black boy from Kingston, his daddy didn't say a word to me about suing us for a million dollars if Purley didn't eat the ticket. He was pretty mad though.'

'Right. And when the city comptroller, Otis Newsome, comes down here in a hissie about me harassing his baby brother, you tell him we're just lucky Hillston didn't get slapped with another mess like the one he hushed up when Baby Purley told that seventeen-year-old girl he'd tear up her traffic violation if she'd do him a "personal favour." Okay? Remind Otis of that.'

'Yes, sir.' Zeke frowned uneasily. 'You mean you made that bit up about the judge's suing us to scare Purley?'

'Truth is a mountain, Sergeant. Sometimes you got to drive up on a windin' road.'

'I guess.' He didn't believe it for a minute, which is why when Nancy White asked him if he thought she was a little overweight, he said, ''Bout eleven pounds.'

A few minutes later, Zeke knocked at my office and stooped under the doorsill. 'Mrs Brookside here for you, Chief.' He stepped back as she came in, looking at her like she was a kind of flower he'd never seen. Lee was wearing a lilac wool suit, with a blue and gold necklace. Light Carolina blue, about the colour of my shirt and new tie.

I said, 'Hi, Lee—'

She said, 'Hi, oh, don't get up,' and hurried to a chair before I could get out of mine. 'You see,' she nodded, 'you were wrong. Governor Wollston did reprieve George Hall.'

'Well, every decade or so, I'm wrong about something.'

We stared at each other, both of us, I think, trying to look past a stranger to find the person we'd seen there years ago. Then she tilted sideways to glance at the poster behind me, and laughed. 'Elvis! I remember you loved Elvis. And, oh who was that woman singer . . .'

'Patsy Cline.'

'Right. Patsy Cline. Country.'

'Like they say . . . when country wasn't cool . . . You liked Johnny Mathis.'

'Did I?'

'Um hum. I told you it wouldn't last.'

I studied her studying my office, and wished I'd put away the sweaters and cleared off the Styrofoam coffee cups and all the crumbled candy bar wrappers that had missed the basket. When I get nervous, I talk. While she wandered around the room, I heard myself sounding like a tour guide in a hurry for lunch. 'And that chess set's from Costa Rica; see, the pawns are peasants. When I left there, I gave a guy my car for it. 'Course, you never saw my car. And that plaster bust up here's supposed to be genuine Rodin, according to this street vendor in Paris who sold it to me for ten dollars.'

'Oh, Cuddy.' Lee's laugh didn't sound familiar, and I wasn't sure if I'd forgotten, or she'd changed it. 'I tried to imagine . . .' She put down one of the bright-painted pawns. '. . . what your police captain's office would look like . . . It looks like you. Books, and a blackboard . . .'

'No folks chained to the wall and a bowl full of blackjacks?'

'You obviously haven't given up those awful candy bars.'

'I tend not to give up on things.'

The room felt too quiet after we stopped smiling. She stepped back to her chair. Nothing came to mind, so I said, 'Could I get you some coffee? . . . That glass of tea maybe?'

She didn't seem to catch the allusion, but kept tilting her head to feel an earring as if she was afraid she was going to lose it. 'No, no thanks. There's a real reason I came.'

'Well, now, I sort of figured that, Mrs Brookside. You haven't exactly got in touch to shoot the breeze over the decades.'

'Neither have you . . .' Her lips pressed together in a way I could still recognize as anger, and pink streaked across her cheekbones.

'True.' I started drawing triangles on a notepad. 'My sergeant said something about "official problem." You haven't been stealing loose grapes from the A and P again, have you?'

She looked up, smiled; then frowned the joke off. 'Last night . . .' I nodded when she paused, wondering what in the world she was going to say. I sure didn't expect what she did say. 'At the Club last night, you seemed aware of how much pressure there's been on Andy to take a public stand against the Hall execution.'

'I've heard a little about it.'

'Not just the Hall case, but against the death penalty itself. Jack Molina, for example . . .' She stopped; I watched her right hand twisting her wedding ring.

'Jack Molina . . .' I prodded her. 'I know him.'

'Well, you can imagine Jack's position. There's also tremendous pressure, both on and off Andy's staff, *not* to take any such stand: that the polls say, in this state, it will cost him the election. This isn't New York.'

'That's true . . . But listen here, New York would have its old electric chair back popping sparks like Frankenstein in a thunderstorm, if it wasn't for their governor's veto. Amazing, how people with principle can make a difference every now and then.' She didn't answer. I felt uncomfortable behind my desk, so I walked over to lean by the window. Pigeons waddled a few steps away, but didn't bother leaving. Finally I asked her, 'So, which side of that pressure are you on?'

Her chair swivelled to face me. 'Neither. I'm a politician's wife . . . as it turns out.'

I said, 'I'm not real sure I know what you mean by that.'

'It means, doesn't it, I'm on my husband's side.' Window light struck her face and she frowned trying to see me. 'On it. At it.'

Last night came back. The little signal of Brookside's 'Shall we?' with a tiny touch on her arm. The years of reception lines and meals with strangers that had fine-honed the shorthand. 'Okay,' I said. 'So which side of the pressure is your husband on?'

'Personally, he's convinced by studies that prove the death penalty is not a deterrent. And that it's discriminatory.' The way she said it didn't make it sound too personal.

66

'Um hum. And is he going to say so?'

Her answer was a preview of a speech. Monday in Winston-Salem, Brookside would talk to a banquet of black businessmen. He would remark on the rights of all Americans to adequate legal counsel for as long as necessary, regardless of ability to pay – now the state's obliged to pick up the bill only through a first round of appeals, after which court-appointed defenders usually skip away fast, since there's neither loot nor laurel to be gained by sticking it out with indigent convicts. At this point in his speech, Brookside would mention George Hall as a case in point: that having lost his first appeal, he had lost his public defender, and had lost years before obtaining new counsel. Brookside would then say that he applauded Governor Wollston's decision to stay George Hall's execution, and would urge the governor now to offer clemency.

It made me wonder what Brookside had planned *yesterday* on saying at this banquet, since until last midnight nobody had any reason to think George Hall wouldn't be dead and buried by Monday morning, and way beyond the clemency of Wollston or anybody else. I almost said so, but stopped myself.

Plus, it sounded to me like Brookside was still fox-trotting on the fence rail, but of course that's the trick of political balance: his comments on capital punishment would be limited (apparently against Molina's urging) to Hall's case alone.

'The staff's been arguing all morning,' Lee said, 'how even saying this much is going to cost Andy votes.'

Not a one, I thought, that Brookside had a blind pole-vaulter's chance of winning anyhow, but I didn't say that either. All the while Lee spoke, light in a dance on her hair, her eyes lowered against the sun, I hadn't a clue if she felt this upcoming speech of her husband's was the best thing she'd heard since Kennedy's inaugural, or political suicide, or a mediocre mishmash, which made me realize how dumb it was to think I knew who this woman was, just because a long time ago we'd talked on the phone for hours every night, till my bones would ache from lying on the cold kitchen floor. A long time ago, I knew the quickest detail of her feelings: fret over a grade, tears over a lost ring her grandmother left her, pleasure at a stepfather's rare compliment. Now, here was this woman, with sad eyes and elegant clothes, a photogenic politician's photogenic and very rich wife, and a stranger. I didn't know what she thought, or wanted, or didn't want, or even what she'd done with her life except marry a mountain climber who'd died, and a college president who wanted to be governor.

Coming around to sit on a corner of my desk, I rearranged a set of little fold-out photos – Mama and Daddy on their wedding day, my sister Vivian's yearbook portrait; a snapshot of some kids I'd taught in Costa Rica, in front of our school's new shade tree; a photo I took of Justin and Alice in the stocks at Williamsburg.

Out of the blue, Lee said, 'He'll be a good governor. If you think Andy is only president of Haver University because of my name, you're wrong. He had offers from *Washington* he turned down.'

'I don't doubt it. And if you think your name didn't help a *heap*, here *and* in Washington, you'd be wrong too, because let me tell you—'

'That's not the—'

'It is too the point, and—'

We both stopped, and laughed at the same time. 'God, Cuddy, can you believe we're already arguing again just like we used to?'

'Hey, what else are old friends for?'

She moved to the front of the desk, and looked at the photograph of my parents. 'For good advice . . . like always? That's what I hope.'

'Okay. Did you want to ask my advice about this speech, or what?'

And she surprised me by saying, 'Somebody's threatened to kill Andy.' She held up a hand to stop my response, then reached into a small leather purse and took out an envelope. 'I know, I know. Public figures are always vulnerable, but . . .'

'Who threatened him?'

'It's a letter. And I feel a little, well, guilty, coming to you without his knowledge. Because he thinks it's silly to take this seriously.' She handed me the crumpled dime-store white envelope, penciled 'BROOKSIDE.' 'It was stuck under the windshield wiper of his car, on campus. Andy started to tear it up, but I asked to see it. It gave me the creeps.'

I tapped the letter out, and shook it open by a corner. Also in pencil, printed in block letters on paper torn from a spiral notebook, was an unsigned message, which I read aloud. It was succinct.

BROOKSIDE.
WE DON'T WANT ATHIEST YANKEE COON-LOVERS
RUNNING OUR STATE. WE KNOW HOW TO TAKE CARE OF
YOUR KIND. REMEMBER DALLAS. 11/22/63. THIS IS A
WARNING.

I said, 'That last bit sounds a little redundant, doesn't it?'

Lee leaned over the desk towards me. 'This is a direct threat, doesn't it sound like that to you? The Kennedy thing? I told him to call the police, the FBI, but he just kept saying, it's a typical nut, it's a scare tactic.' She crossed her arms tightly, her fingers rubbing the lilac wool. 'He said he'd been finding them like that since he announced, telling him to get out of the governor's race. I was so upset I called Jack, but he . . . I guess what I'm asking is, would you come see Andy? Tell him, he can't make light of this.' She lifted a hand towards me, then let it fall to her side. 'It's like the sky-diving, and the rest of it.'

'Excuse me? What?'

'That speedboat he races.'

'What are you talking about, Lee?'

'About risks, needing danger, liking it.' She sank into her chair. 'He misses the war, isn't that strange?'

I pulled back on my hair. 'Well, honey, it's strange to me. But if there weren't the kind of guys who're going to miss wars when they're over, starting wars probably wouldn't be so popular.'

I was thinking about her first husband, the young French mountain climber who'd died in the hotel fire. She must have come to believe that, like Love and Glory, Death is after heroes too, tries to steal them away as young as it can. Funny, I felt a low kind of sadness about how much she must love Brookside.

I pulled out a plastic folder to slip the letter in. 'You called Jack Molina? What was his attitude?'

'Like Andy's; he brushed it off. I think he was mostly angry I was going to try to use it to get Andy to pull back from some of the positions Jack wants him to take. Because I did say it made me worry more about this speech in Winston-Salem Monday . . . Jack and I aren't . . . close.'

'Okay.' I pulled a pencil out of the Cherokee bowl I keep them in. 'Give me a number where I can call your husband.' I wrote down the three different phone numbers she recited. 'Lee, probably it *is* just some vile-spewer with nothing on his mind but shooting off his mouth. But anybody running for office in this country ought to recall enough history to know that sometimes nuts do exactly what they warned you they were going to do. I'll check it out.'

'Thank you, Cuddy.' She rested her hand on mine for a second; the rush of my response scared me.

My phone buzzed; Zeke said he was sorry, but a car had swerved across the 28 divider, got sideswiped by a semi; there was a fatality, and Wes Pendergraph had called in to say he thought there was something I needed to look at.

Lee stood up quickly. 'I'm sorry to take up your free time.'

'Don't be stupid.' While I walked her to the door, I asked, 'Is there anything on your husband's car to identify it as his?'

'Oh. You mean, the letter's being on the windshield? The parking space. There's a sign. "Reserved. President Brookside." The car's just a grey Porsche.'

I grinned at her. 'He didn't happen to win it in a church lottery, did he?'

She smiled back, puzzled. 'I don't think so.' Then she looked up at me. 'But there're a lot of things in Andy's life I don't appear to know.' She touched my arm while she said, 'Cuddy, it's good to see you again.' And her smile came back.

Outside in the corridor sat a young black man in a navy-blue suit; on the chair beside him was an immense glistening fur coat. He was on his feet, holding the coat out as soon as he saw her. 'I'm sorry, Mrs Brookside. They made me move the car. I brought your coat.' She smiled at him too, like he'd done her a kindness, but she didn't introduce us.

The accident was on I-28, south of Hillston, a little west of the Shocco River. I took Cadmean Street, named for old Briggs's grandfather, who'd built it right after the Civil War to get from the river up to the railroad tracks that he'd also built so he wouldn't have to pay a Virginia line to haul his wares. Every block or so, I'd see a lowered flag mourning the mill owner. From the sidewalks Christmas shoppers gawked, hearing my siren.

I sped the last half mile along the break-down lane; traffic on the Interstate was still backed up. When I reached the wreck, I saw 'Action News' already videoing a stretcher being shoved into one of the ambulances parked on the shoulder. An attendant with 'Haver University Hospital' sewn over his pocket kept his face to the camera. Under the low, grey-clouded sun, flashes of red and blue lights gave the scene that ghoulish look passing sightseers can't resist slowing down for. Highway patrolmen near the smashed-in truck were flagging a single line of traffic along without bothering to answer all the 'What happened?'s shouted from car windows.

Officer Wes Pendergraph leaned against the side of an over-turned, crumpled Subaru, his head in his arms. His uniform was wet with the blood and urine of the young man who'd been flung through the window down into the culvert. Wes had sat there holding him till he died. Wes is twenty-three. He keeps asking me if he should quit the force: 'The other guys say I take things too hard.' I tell him that's why I need him to stay. Now I just looped my arm over his shoulder and walked him, not talking, beside the highway until he was ready to show me the body. At the bottom of the incline, in scrub brush and hard red clay, the driver lay still covered by a hospital blanket. Another ambulance attendant stood beside it, yawning, his fingers laced over his upstretched arms.

Wes said, 'I didn't want them to move him, till you got here. It's hard to tell, all the blood, and everything's so mangled up. But was I right, Chief? Look over here.'

The dark face was crushed in, covered with blood and clay, but I knew who it was. It took me a while to get my throat to work so I could say. 'No, you're right. It's Cooper Hall.'

But that's not what Wes meant. He'd never seen Coop Hall before, except on television news, and hadn't recognized him. Wes knelt and turned the head to show me why he'd wanted me to come here. It was a small round cavity just under the ear. He said, 'I didn't notice it at first. But, Chief Mangum, I swear that looks a lot like a bullet hole to me.'

Chapter 5

The factory whistles kept crying over Hillston, grieving for the old industrialist who'd built them. Decade after decade they'd summoned the town each morning to come weave for him, told it at noon to eat lunch, sent it home each evening to rest; now they wailed that Cadmean was dead, wailed loudest here in East Hillston where the factories loomed. Messengers of death, like me. From the porch of Nomi Hall's house on Mill Street, past the patrol car that would wait and watch all night, I could see lights glitter the sooty brick smokestacks, the stained pastel water towers, the lowered flags, and the rusty teeth of the skylighted roof with its neon greeting, 'HAPPY HOLIDAYS!' Mrs Hall lived a few blocks from the C & W gates; a few blocks from the stucco duplex I'd grown up in. The Hall house was a one-storey box, with an asphalt walkway, and an old scarred sugar maple in the dirt yard. Years ago, somebody had added a porch, but hadn't got around to painting it the yellow with blue trim that was fading from the rest of the wood.

I told Cooper's mother myself. Jordan West was still somewhere in Raleigh with the vigil group, and I couldn't find Isaac. Mrs Hall and I stood together just inside her front door, because she stepped back when I tried to lead her to the couch behind us. She was a small woman, her hair still a crisp black, her features – like her son George's – almost oriental, flattened across the dark plane of her face. She'd come from the kitchen, flour on her hands and apron. Seeing me there meant something bad, why else would I come? And naturally she thought only of George. Living all these years under his sentence, four different specific days and times pronounced for the death of her child, how could she think it would be anything but George? Before I spoke, she said, 'The governor stopped it. He stopped at ten-thirty last night. What's the matter?'

At first she couldn't hear 'highway accident' and kept asking, 'Has something happened to George?' The word *Cooper* struck her like a fist, so hard her breath rushed out with the sound of wind.

She repeated the name. '. . . Cooper? . . . Cooper?'

'Yes, I'm sorry.'

'But he's not gone? He's alive?' Carefully, she took off her glasses, and her eyes in a strong unblinking pull drew the truth out of mine.

I said, 'I'm so sorry, Mrs Hall. No.'

'No?' She was staring hard in my eyes for some chance of a different meaning. Then her pupils shrank away from mine, and she cried out, 'My Saviour, no! Lord Jesus, no, not my boy.' I reached for her hands, but she lifted the apron to cover her face.

Finally when she took it away, wet white flour splotched her cheeks. Her head still shook that 'no' while she said, 'I want to see him. Where is he?'

I said, 'He's at the hospital. Mrs Hall, we're going to have to do an autopsy . . . I'm afraid, there's evidence that Coop went off the road because he was shot—'

She stepped back. '. . . Shot? I can't understand you. You said nobody was in the car with Cooper.'

'We think he was fired at from a passing car.'

She swayed suddenly forward, and I reached out for her. 'Ma'am, please, come take a seat here, please.'

But her fingers rested on my arm only an instant, then she straightened, and wiped the backs of her hands across her face. '. . . Let me be alone by myself for a few minutes now.'

'Are you—'

Her arm pointed past me. 'If you would just step two doors down and get me my sister Verna.' Shoulders hunched tight, she turned without waiting for my response. On top of the television stood framed colour photographs – studio portraits of George in his army uniform, Cooper in his graduate gown, a daughter with two small girls in Easter dresses – and she paused there, then took the picture of Cooper with her towards the dark back of the house.

For the next half hour, I sat outside on their porch in an

73

aluminium beach chair, my neck tucked down into my overcoat, while behind me the house groaned with the grief and prayers of her gathering family and neighbours and minister. They'd stop in their hurry up the walkway, nod at me nervously, then quickly step inside. I didn't want to go back in the house, which Mrs Hall had asked me to leave, but I couldn't make myself walk away, sick with a feeling that something else horrible would happen if I left her there. I'd sent Wes Pendergraph to Jordan's apartment. Three of the young vigilants came back with her in his patrol car, and helped her up the steps. She moved like a blind woman. Wes said she hadn't spoken after he told her. I didn't try to talk to her now either. The other three couldn't tell me much; they kept insisting that somebody must have followed Coop when he left Raleigh – though they'd seen nobody suspicious hanging around. All they'd done was stand on the sidewalk in front of the governor's mansion and hand out copies of *With Liberty and Justice*. They'd waved signs at the Supreme Court judge when his car sped through the gates. After Coop had left them, they'd driven to a restaurant, then returned to Hillston. They said Alice was probably still in Raleigh; she'd gone to the library. I didn't try to question them further, just offered my sympathy. None of them acknowledged it.

Ten minutes later, Isaac Rosethorn's Studebaker bucked to a smoky stop across the street. He stumbled out, tugging impatiently at his bad leg. I met him at the curb, where Wes sat in his squad car waiting for further radio reports from downtown.

Isaac said, 'I just heard at the courthouse. A fellow who'd been over at University Hospital when they brought Coop in.' He gave a yank to straighten his frayed black tie. 'Poor woman. Poor woman.' His eyes burned in their deep shadowed sockets. 'Is it definite? He was shot?'

'Yes. It's like a goddamn nightmare. You better go in and see about getting word to George at the prison before somebody like Bubba Percy does.'

'I already called Warden Carpenter; he'll let me spend "a few minutes" with George tonight.'

'You want a ride out there?'

'No.' He yanked off his gloves, linted with loose tobacco, and pushed them at his baggy coat pockets. 'Slim, what I want from you is try not to feel responsible for this.'

'I *am* responsible.' Angry, I scooped one of his gloves up from the sidewalk where it had dropped, and slapped it into his hand. 'I'm the chief of police in this city, and when one of its citizens gets shot to death driving his fuckin' car home, I am responsible.'

'. . . Well, we'll argue that another time.' He used the glove in a halfhearted attempt to buff the tops of his oxfords. 'Nomi. Does she know how Cooper was killed?'

'I told her, yes.'

'God help us all.' The old man lifted his head to the starless early winter night. 'Stupid, endless stupid evil . . .' He twisted to look at the house. 'What are you still doing here?'

'I don't know . . . I think maybe I was waiting for you.'

His arm hugged through mine. 'Here I am. Now, how did it happen?'

We walked together towards the porch while I summed up what little I knew. 'Looks like Coop left the demonstration in Raleigh early. Mentioned having to meet somebody in Hillston. None of these kids seem to know who. He was hit just before coming over that rise on I-Twenty-eight, you know, about a mile west of the Shocco Bridge. Jumped the divider and went head-on into a semi. The driver's still unconscious, and the hospital's not hopeful.'

Isaac watched the silhouettes moving slowly behind the Halls' front windows. 'Witnesses?'

I said that we had two drivers who'd stopped, plus the one who'd called in the accident on his CB. But all any of them had seen was Coop's Subaru smashed into the oncoming truck, just after it happened. This stretch of 28 was heavily wooded, uninhabited, and a search through the area hadn't turned up a thing. According to Dick Cohn, our medical examiner, the shell was fired at too short a range to have come from the woods, or probably even from across the median strip; his guess was that someone had fired from the passenger side of a vehicle travelling in the same direction down the Interstate. The bullet had entered under Coop's left ear, passed through his brain, and out the right temple. No slug had been found, and given the extent of the wreckage, we couldn't even tell if the bullet was still in the Subaru.

Isaac poked at my arm. 'Listen. One of those witnesses *saw* the car that fired at him. Had to. Cars can't evaporate. Maybe didn't see it *when*, but right before, or after, they shot him. That car had to have been following Cooper, and it had to pass Cooper. And it had to keep going.' Isaac shook his yellow-stained finger in my face. 'You stay on the witnesses, Cuddy, stay on them.'

I said the possibility of some psycho firing at random from his car window couldn't be ruled out yet.

'Oh, don't feed me your municipal pabulum!' Isaac jerked off his fur hat in disgust. 'It's because of George's reprieve. A black man named Hall was supposed to die today, and somebody felt cheated! Why, I heard ignoramuses this morning that thought George had been pardoned outright, and they were *mad* about it. It's the Klan, the Invisible Empire. Arrest the vermin!'

'We're already going down our list, checking alibis, but, Isaac, a lot, a whole lot of people in this town, in this state, hated Cooper Hall's guts. I can't go arrest them just for being racist.' I pulled my coat collar higher around my neck. 'So you listen, I want Mrs Hall out of here, okay? Her, and Jordan, too. I don't have the resources to protect them.'

He stopped me with a wide paw across my breastbone. 'You're expecting more?'

'Goddammit, I didn't expect this! Plus, the press is going to surround the place any minute now. If you already heard about it at the courthouse—' I saw Wes Pendergraph waving me over to the patrol car. '—Go on in, will you, Isaac, I'll be there in a second.'

Wes had changed out of his bloody uniform, but Cooper Hall's death was still in his eyes. He hung up the radio mike, and leaned from the open car door. 'Chief, it's bad. About five minutes ago. The truck driver died in OR. You know, he's just coming over the hill, and then – he's dead. Lived in Athens, Georgia. Had a wife and three kids. She's already on a plane, flying up to the hospital, and doesn't even know it's too late.'

I kicked at the tyre. '. . . Okay, Wes, get Nancy White, tell her to go to the airport, meet this woman's plane.'

'Do you want Nancy to tell her, or let the doctors?'

'Oh, Jesus wept . . . Maybe we should *all* quit the force . . . Look, tell Nancy it's up to her. Either way.' I started to walk off, but Wes called me back.

'Chief, McInnis called from Raleigh. He saw this Willis Tate. Says the guy's out for us; they brought him and his three friends in about noon on that harassing incident at the prison last night, and they still haven't posted bail.' Wes checked his opened notebook. 'The names you wanted checked, from the Trinity

Church arrests, one's in Fort Bragg and the other two got airtights from employers, all day long.'

'Well, that's seven maniacs down, and a couple hundred buddies of theirs to go. Any word from Dick Cohn on the autopsy?'

'Yes, sir, he's not finished, but Hall was definitely shot through the head, one wound.'

'Rifle or pistol, can he tell?'

'He didn't say. Lieutenant Foster is still working on the Subaru. He *thinks* there was a second bullet fired that missed the victim, exited through the windshield. The search squad left the site, but he went back.'

'Etham's still out there in the woods? It's pitch-dark.'

'I guess so.'

I tried to reach Etham Foster by radio, but he didn't answer. He often wouldn't answer in his lab either; you had to go downstairs to root him out, and even then he'd take his time swivelling around from his microscope, his six-and-a-half-foot frame S-curved over a high stool; his black elongated fingers, that had once made a basketball look like an orange, tweezing with patient precision a fluff of fabric from a shoe sole, a fleck of blood from a coat sleeve. I told Wes to keep calling him, to tell him to come back to headquarters. 'And look here, soon as you can, you go get something to eat.' But he said he wasn't hungry, and I knew how he felt.

At seven Isaac was still inside with Mrs Hall and the others, and by now the news-seekers, professional and amateur, were inching past the edges of the Hall yard, blustering their way to the porch, where two big deputies the county sheriff had sent over, uninvited, blocked the steps. The 'Evening Edition' and 'Action News' vans arrived almost simultaneously, perhaps drawn by the secret synchronicity that puts the same covers on *Time* and *Newsweek*. Right after them, a crew from Raleigh's CBS affiliate and an Associated Press stringer drove up in a cab. Carol Cathy Cane spotted me and shoved her bearded cameraman past Bubba Percy. Thrusting her mike at my chin, Carol, a tall young woman who thought she resembled Jane Fonda, looked about as revved as a college cheerleader at the homecoming game. She never took a breath. 'This is Carol Cathy Cane for "Action News." We're here with Police Chief C. R. Mangum at the home of the slain civil rights activist, Cooper Hall, brother of condemned murderer George Hall whose execution—'

'Evening Edition' and CBS smashed their mikes against hers, while Bubba yelled, 'Cuddy, is that confirmed? It wasn't just a crack-up, he was shot?!'

I said, 'Mr Hall was involved in a head-on collision on I-twenty-eight. He died at the scene. The driver of the truck struck by Hall's vehicle has now been pronounced dead by Haver University Hospital. There is evidence of—'

Shifting from cheerleading to offensive line tactics, Carol Cane jostled around 'Evening Edition.' 'Our sources at University Hospital say Hall *was definitely shot!*'

'There is evidence of a bullet wound. We're waiting for the autopsy report before making any official statement.'

The stringer shoved back at Cane. 'Was the killing racially motivated? Do you see a connection between this shooting and the governor's surprise stay of George Hall's execution yesterday?'

More questions piled on before I could answer his. 'Wasn't there a Klan-instigated assault on Hall last night at Dollard State Prison?' 'Is the Hall family inside?' 'Coop Hall told Channel Seven two months ago that racist threats had been made on his life. Did the police make any attempt at all to investigate those charges?'

'Carol, every effort will be made – and has been made – to pursue all leads regarding racist threats against Mr Hall, or anybody else in Hillston.' I heard a motorcycle approach. One of the mikes hit the side of my mouth when I pulled my head up to see over the cameras. While I was talking, I watched Jack Molina park the cycle, then get stopped at the curb by Wes Pendergraph. 'And I urge anyone with *any* information about this tragedy – now, however insignificant it may seem to you – especially anybody who was travelling from the direction of Raleigh into Hillston on I-Twenty-eight this afternoon, to *please* come forward.

'This is a sad, horrible loss of two lives here today. You can believe that whoever is responsible is going to be caught. That's all I have to say now. Except I want to ask you media folks to let Mrs Hall alone; she's with her family and her minister. I know you can imagine how she's feeling.'

Bubba Percy had slid around behind me, and was running towards the back of the house, when Eli Johnson, a 280-pound sheriff's deputy, leaned over the porch rail and grabbed him by the back of his Burberry. I motioned to Wes to let Molina through, then helped shoulder a way for him up the steps. It was thirty degrees, Molina's breath fogged his round wireless spectacles, but he wasn't wearing a coat over his sports jacket, so at first I thought he was trembling from cold; one look at his eyes showed me it was rage. It burned like sparks out of his face, even his hair looked electric. He said, 'I just heard. The goddamn Nazis.'

Carol Cane swung her cameraman to face us. 'You're Jack Molina, aren't you?' When he nodded, she twirled her finger to signal the video to start taping. 'This is Professor Jack Molina, Andrew Brookside's campaign manager—'

'I'm not his campaign manager—' Molina began.

'—And, am I right, Dr Molina, you're a member of the Save George Hall Committee started by his brother Cooper? What's your response to today's tragedy?'

I'd thought Molina would brush by her, but instead, his glittering huge eyes stared straight into the lens atop the young cameraman's shoulder. 'Yes, this is a tragedy . . .' His voice was sharp and slow, not at all like his conversational voice, so reverberant that everyone turned to look. 'A tragedy for the Halls, and a tragedy for Hillston. A tragedy that's happened too many times for too many years in this country, and made too many martyrs. Martyrs to the white hate of groups like the Klan and Brodie Cheek's Constitution Club. Martyrs to the white indifference of powerful political interests that allow that hate to go unpunished!'

CBS started taping too, and Molina turned his face to the new camera. 'Cooper Hall was killed today because he stood up against prejudice and against injustice, because he fought for his brother George, and for all black victims of our racist society. *George Hall was sentenced to die because he was black. And Coop Hall is dead because he was black!'*

A murmur swelled from the small neighbourhood crowd stirring on the sidewalk.

He had everybody's attention. Like I said, I'd heard Jack Molina give speeches back in the sixties. He was good. He was also dangerous – maybe mostly to himself. Linking the rightwing radio preacher Brodie Cheek with the Constitution Club, a conservative fund-raising league to which some of the most important political figures in the state belonged, and equating either one with the Klan, was about as far left of the most radical remark Andy Brookside had ever made as Che Guevara was to JFK. And trust Bubba Percy to dive right for the bottom line. He asked Molina, 'Are you speaking for Andy Brookside?'

Molina answered the cameras. 'I've come here to offer Mrs Hall the personal condolences of President Brookside, who shares the horror and outrage we all feel tonight. Shares it more fully because the same ugly elements responsible for the Halls' tragedy are the ones who have from the beginning of his campaign opposed, slandered, and threatened Andy Brookside.'

Bubba looked puzzled, an unfamiliar expression on his satisfied face. 'Wait a minute, are you implying that your candidate's political opponents are in any way connected with what's happened to Coop Hall?'

Molina shook his head, but the pause he took first was long enough for anybody who wanted to, to think that's exactly what he meant. Then he raised his arm, and spoke over the tops of the cameras to the growing cluster of blacks in the yard and street. 'I'm saying racist fear and hate don't want Andy Brookside to be governor! *I'm saying racist fear and hate killed Coop Hall!*'

'That's right!!' yelled a man's voice from the crowd, and another shouted, 'Yeah!'

The Associated Press stringer muttered to Bubba Percy, 'What's this guy doing, a campaign kickoff or what?'

'The fuck I know,' admitted Bubba. 'Looks like he picked up about ten votes out there in the yard.'

Behind us a shadow moved from the front door, and the news crews leapt forward to see who it was. Isaac Rosethorn squeezed towards the steps, motioning for me. Carol Cane got her mike as close as she could. 'Sir! Is Mrs Hall in there? Can you give us a statement? Could we speak with her?'

Isaac's fat fingers closed around the microphone, lifting it right out of Carol's hand, as if he thought it were connected to a PA system. His rumbling baritone made the 'Action News' cameraman jerk his headphones away from his ears. 'Folks! My name is Isaac Rosethorn, and I'm the Halls' attorney.' He rubbed his fleece of white hair for a while. 'Mrs Hall thanks you for your sympathy and your concern for her family's grief. She's in bed now, under her physician's care. Nobody will be making any other statements tonight. Except this. Nothing is going to deter our struggle to win a new trial for George Hall, the new trial his slain brother was fighting for.'

The stringer asked, 'What did George Hall say when he was told about his brother's murder?'

Isaac sighed. 'If you want to ask him that, well, you'll have to go to Dollard Prison and do it.'

With a terrible shriek, Cadmean's factory whistles pierced the air again. I gestured at the two deputies as I pushed to the top step to shout over the noise. 'Okay, everybody, that's all! Any further reports, you'll get them as soon as we have them. No more questions.' Eli Johnson and his partner began moving the news people back through the yard, and five minutes later, they were all gone, either because they had all they wanted, or didn't figure they could get more, or just couldn't hear over the C & W whistles. The crowd faded back into the shadows of Mill Street.

Isaac Rosethorn, swaying bearlike on the top step of the Hall's porch, reached for Molina on the step below him, pulling him back by a wad of his jacket. 'What did you think you were doing just now, Jack?' The mildness of his tone was incongruous with his tight grip on the much smaller man. 'This isn't a political platform, this is a woman's home. She just lost her son.'

Twisting around, Molina jerked free. 'I was saying exactly what her son would have wanted me to say.'

Rosethorn dropped his hands to his sides, then put them in his pockets. 'Possibly. But I'm not so sure Coop would have wanted you to say it for Andy Brookside.'

Molina stepped around the old lawyer without replying.

'Just a second,' I said to him. 'Couple of questions, Professor.' His pale long face twitched impatiently as he listened. 'First off, did you know who it was Coop Hall planned to meet this afternoon in Hillston?'

'No idea. Ask Jordan.'

I said she'd told us she didn't know, and he said if Jordan didn't know, then nobody knew. He kept trying to move into the house. He was so keyed up, I felt like I was speaking across static wires. I asked if he had any knowledge of any written threats against Coop Hall.

He said no. 'But I've got plenty of firsthand knowledge of, okay, mud clumps and bottles, okay, thrown in our faces, and fires set in our office, and hecklers at our vigils, okay?! Curses, taunts, spit – do they count? I've got a lot of knowledge of *threats*! Shit, man, Cooper's been *threatened* on the lousy radio!'

I leaned against the front door, which he was trying to open. 'But not written threats? I'm asking because, see, I understand you do have some knowledge of written threats against Andy Brookside, and so I'm wondering if there's a connection.'

My question surprised him; his eyes widened as he ran his

fingers over the stems of his round, wired glasses, pressing the loops behind his ears. 'Andy told you that?'

I said, 'No. He should have. You should have too. His wife told me. Have you seen any of these letters? Do you or Brookside *have* any of them?'

'Yeah, Andy showed me a few. I don't know if he kept them or not.'

'*Death* threats?'

'Yeah. Typical redneck ravings.'

I tilted my head to look at him. 'Well now, how 'bout clarifying that a little bit? I'm a redneck myself.'

Molina balled his fists under his arms. 'Lay off me, all right? I'm talking about run-of-the-mill Klan-type garbage. Rabid right-wing racist stuff. Look, politicians attract psychos. You can't freak every time you get a poison-pen letter. Anyhow, Andy's got good security.'

'Right. Cooper Hall was just killed driving down an interstate highway at four in the afternoon. *Nobody's* got good security. I want to see you and Mr Brookside about this. Try to find some of those letters. I'll be in touch.' I stepped away from the door. 'One last question. Do you know of anyone with any *personal* reason to want to kill Coop Hall – grudge, rivalry, anything like that? Somebody that hated him, that he hated?'

'You mean, besides you?' Molina's thin lips spread open over his long narrow teeth. It may have been a smile.

'I said, a *personal* reason.' I kept my eyes looking at his, and he didn't blink either, so finally we called it a draw. 'I have to discount a personal motive – jealousy, love affair. Most people do hate each other for personal reasons, you know.'

'Coop wasn't most people. He "hated" *the system*. He was fighting a system, fighting two hundred years of history. He didn't give a rat's ass about "personal."' Molina pushed past me, opening the door without knocking, then looked back over his shoulder at me. 'Just ask Jordan West.'

Chapter 6

Justin Savile had loved old styles and stuffy traditions long before they got to be the fashion with yuppies who'd had flower children for parents, and seen a better life-style by watching Edwardian miniseries on 'Masterpiece Theatre.' But Justin'd been wearing a pocket watch, bow ties and braces, trotting around on horses, and slapping Stilton on water crackers since he was a toddler. When he'd first bought his brick Victorian – excuse me, Queen Anne – row house south of Main Street, across from Frances Bush College for Women, all the society folk had long ago moved off to the woods and meadows of North Hillston, abandoning the town like gold rushers who'd run out of ore. Soon as they left, country people and blacks, who'd been stuck out in the woods and meadows, crowded into the old neighbour-hoods, until inside the city limits got to be beyond the pale. Justin's relatives thought his buying a tacky shell of abandoned 'old Hillston' was another instance of his 'problem' – by which bland term they always referred to his past drinking and/or nervous breakdown. 'Course now that some of the old tobacco warehouses are shopping boutiques, and the old mills are apart-ment complexes, and a couple from Massachusetts tried to buy his house for twenty times what he paid for it, and the state folk art museum offered him five thousand dollars for a pine cupboard he kept his shoes in, everybody congratulates him for being a pioneer of gentrification and a shrewd investor in tra-dition. Fact is, Justin never cared a damn for real estate, and couldn't use gentrifying – he was gentry by nature.

Me, I like modern. I like wall-to-wall, I like trash compactors, swivelling recliners, compact discs, automatic redial, frozen gourmet I can nuke in sixty seconds. I've got a gadget that will start my coffee before it wakes me up, I've got a car that will talk to me about changing the oil. Modern's pretty damn nice. I bet Tom Jefferson would have just loved to get his hands on my computer software. Listen, I grew up with a tin kitchen sink, pull-chain toilet, rag rugs, scratchy records, and laundry on the line. Believe me, my Hoover Deluxe's got a lot more going for it than a broom. I like progress, and I like heat, only two reasons why, as far as I'm concerned, Alice MacLeod was the best thing that ever happened to Justin Bartholomew Savile. When she moved into that draughty gargoyle of his, she stuck her colour TV in his sideboard, her popcorn popper on his hutch, her Jesse Jackson campaign poster on the wall, and she turned up the thermostat high enough to wear a T-shirt in January.

But now – five hours after I'd left the Halls – Alice came to the door with a quilt wrapped around a bulky sweater. It wasn't from cold but for comfort. There was no need to ask if she'd heard about Coop Hall. When I stepped inside, she walked into my arms without speaking. I pressed my hand against the bright copper curls, and we stood there in the quiet hallway until with a long breath she pulled away.

'Oh, Cuddy. Dammit, dammit. Not again.'

I said, 'How'd you hear?'

'Justin called me.'

'Red, you told me on your wedding day, you were gonna get to be governor of this state, and straighten all the bad old shit out. You better make your move. I can't take much more.'

'I was supposed to ride back with Coop, Cuddy. Leave Jordan my car. Then I said no, I wanted to drop by the library, catch up on some things over the recess. I keep thinking, if I'd only just gone on with Coop, it wouldn't have happened.'

'Aw, shit. Thank God. Those motherfuckers could have killed you too.' My hand on her shoulder, I walked behind her along the high narrow hall into the front parlour, where Justin had his piano, and where Alice kept a loom she'd carted down with her from the mountains, but never much used anymore.

She wiped her eyes. 'You want a beer?'

While she was gone, I stretched out on a puffy couch with wood paws, with my feet hung over. Channel 7's 'Action News' was on TV without the sound, showing Manhattanites fighting to Christmas shop in a blizzard. Alice shuffled back in the quilt from the kitchen with a six-pack and a bag of Nacho chips. I said, 'Where *is* Justin? I've been up at headquarters for the last four hours, and over in the mayor's office trying to keep Carl Yarborough from telling me, "Do something," long enough to do something. Your spouse didn't bother to call in. Etham Foster's disappeared from his lab. I've got about five hundred suspects, I've got no witnesses, I've got nothing for ballistics, I've—'

'Here, drink this. Justin said if you got in touch, he's with Preston Pope. And Preston's in-law or some such who's something like a local "commando captain" in the something like "White Southern Patriot Party." Move over.' She popped open her beer can. 'He called from the Tucson Lounge 'bout an hour ago.'

'Hillbilly music and piss in a pitcher.' I raised my can to her. 'Poor ole General Lee, you know how he hates that Tucson Lounge.'

You can tease about J.B.S. the Five only so far with Alice, then she jumps on you, even knowing nothing's talking but love. 'Well, you'll recall Justin did almost get killed right outside that dive. For *you*.'

'Darlin',' I quoted at her, 'I never denied it.'

From her next news, I realized she'd reacted to what she figured was going to bother me, because it was already bothering her. 'Well, he says he's got about four of these Patriots in a booth, they're all getting ready to go to a meeting tonight, and he's going too, to keep fishing for any word out on . . .' She rolled the beer can slowly against her forehead. '. . . who shot Coop.'

'How many times do I have to tell that man not to set up these capers without checking with me? What's he supposed to be, Imperial Wizard from some preppy Klavern club? I swear I'm gonna fire him. Meeting where? Right, he didn't say.' I went over to what was probably one of the last black rotary dial phones in Hillston, and finally got through to Dave Schulmann in Raleigh, a regional FBI agent with Klan contacts, whom I'd already talked to once tonight about Cooper Hall's death. He'd said then he'd heard nothing about plans to stir up things in response to George's stay of execution, much less any talk about shooting George's brother. He said now that the local White Patriot Party was pretty moribund, but he'd heard rumours about a splinter group with paramilitary fantasies that had broken off from them and the Klan. He said he was already checking into it. When I hung up, Alice tore nervously with her teeth to open the bag of chips.

I said, 'Look, don't worry. If these yahoos are letting a total stranger tag along, this ain't, in the parlance, no heavy-duty meeting they're going to. Probably just sitting around somebody's tacky living room, smoking pot, watching videos of *Deep Throat* and *Birth of a Nation*.' She laughed. 'Right,' I grinned. 'Justin's gonna delight in telling us every tasteless detail.'

All of a sudden, I saw myself on the TV screen, speaking to the crowd at the Hall house. I felt around fast for the remote control, but naturally they didn't have one. By the time I got the sound up, the camera was on Jack Molina. Carol Cathy Cane, in voice-over, was saying, 'While police so far deny any connection between the savage gunning down of Cooper Hall, and the governor's last-minute stay of his brother George Hall's execution on Friday night, others, including gubernatorial candidate Andrew Brookside, feel strongly that today's shooting was racially motivated. Speaking for Brookside – his campaign manager, Dr Jack Molina.'

The lens zoomed on to Molina's thin passionate face. 'Cooper Hall was killed today because he stood up against prejudice and against injustice, because he fought . . .' As he went on, with the off-camera crowd sounding much louder and larger than they'd actually been, Alice leapt up to stand inches from the screen, her mouth open at Molina's speech. '. . . *Coop Hall is dead because he was black!* . . . I'm saying racist fear and hate don't want Andy Brookside to be governor! *I'm saying racist fear and hate killed Coop Hall!*'

Alice wheeled towards me. 'Andy let him do *that*?!'

'Got me. But I betcha – if "Andy's" watching, you could pitch a horseshoe in his mouth without touching the sides.'

'God, I heard *I* was outspoken!'

I said, 'Least ole C. C. Cane left out the part where Molina claimed Brodie Cheek was running the Constitution Club, and the United Klan made it a threesome . . . Oh, fuck it!—'

Cane was now back in the 'Action Newsroom,' where she only got to be 'Anchorwoman' on weekends, and had to make the best of her chances. With her were three 'guests,' all black. One was Mayor Carl Yarborough, one was Dr Judy Templeton, a psychologist, and one was Franklin Smith of the 'Afro Revolutionists,' who'd once told Officer John Emory that if he – Emory – had any balls, he'd be busy stockpiling guns out of our weapons room, preparatory to exterminating honkies, instead of fucking with a brother like him – Smith – just for threatening to blow the head off a gas man who came to read his meter. 'Why's she giving that lunatic a public forum? Jesus! Poor Carl, getting this sprung on him. He hates Franklin Smith.'

Mayor Yarborough didn't look pleased. He said Hall's death was a shocking loss, that it was painful to think it might have been racially motivated, when Hillston (though still with a long way to go) had grown in recent years into such a heartening symbol throughout the state of reform and progress. That it was premature for him, or anybody else, to speculate on what we could be sure would be a swift and thorough investigation by Chief Mangum of our nationally praised police department.

I raised my beer to him. 'Thank you, Carl. You're the best mayor this town ever had, and when I say that, hey, I'm not just whistling "Dixie."'

Dr Judy Templeton talked briefly (since Cane cut her off) about the psychological factors underlying bigotry, and the current socio-economic conditions that might explain a resurgence of Klan violence.

Cane cut off fast-talking Franklin Smith even sooner, but not before – having dismissed Carl and Dr Templeton to their startled icy faces as 'honkie stooges,' 'establishment dupes,' and 'Oreo cookies' – he called on blacks everywhere to embrace the fire of revolution, to burn white America to the ground and sweep its – beepbeepbeep – ashes into the sea. A commercial whipped on quickly; by freak mischance (or tasteless programme director), it was for an insurance company and showed your typical middle-class white family standing in their yard in bathrobes watching their house go up in flames. When 'Action News' finally returned, six commercials later, Carol Cathy Cane and her guests had been replaced by a string of basketball scores. Fifteen minutes later the programme ended with an old clip of Cooper Hall at the Trinity Church demonstration, followed by a shot of his body, not even fully covered by the bloodstained blanket, being carried up from the highway gully into the ambulance.

'Oh Lord,' I groaned, and punched off the television.

Alice said, 'Freedom of the press.'

'Right. And to think I used to be a great believer in it. Why'd they have to show that last shot?'

'I just hope nobody that cared saw it.'

'This is making me real nervous. Do me a favour? Call up, see if you can find out if Isaac talked Mrs Hall and Jordan into leaving.'

Alice went upstairs to phone; she was gone a long time. When she came down, she said she'd talked to a friend in the vigil group, who told her Jordan West was in Richmond with her parents.

'Good. I'm glad.'

'And Sandy said somebody drove Mrs Hall and her sister out to their brother's house in the country.'

'Good.'

'Sandy said Coop's funeral's Tuesday.'

We sat there a while, not talking. Then I lay down on a thin little oriental rug next to the couch. 'Why don't y'all get some decent carpeting?'

She didn't answer.

The porcelain clock on the mantel ticked like a faucet leaking.

Finally I said, 'That's Christmas Eve ... On Tuesday. Coop's funeral. It's the twenty-fourth ... I heard they're burying Cadmean on the twenty-fourth, too.'

The clock kept on.

'Alice?'

'Want another beer?'

'Nope. Tell me about Andy Brookside. You like him?'

'Yes, I do. It's kind of hard not to like him. He's bright, good politics, interesting, incredibly good-looking, sexy, he listens, amazing energy—'

'Okay, okay. You plugging for a spot on his ticket or what?' I pulled a pillow off the couch and bunched it under my head.

She pointed a finger at me. 'I've been wondering how long it was going to take you to admit you don't like him. The first time I mentioned the campaign to you, you started talking about the goddamn weather. Okay, tell me why. You think he's too slick? Fake liberal? Shallow?'

I rolled my head to look over at her. 'Your words, honey. I didn't put them in your mouth.'

'I've heard other people say them.' She shook the finger again. 'I've also heard all the womanizing rumours, so don't bother filling me in, because, frankly, you could say the same about FDR and JFK, and I'd still rather have them than Nixon and Reagan any day.'

'Hey, slow down, Red. I didn't say a thing. This is the first I heard of "womanizing rumours." But I'm not gonna say I'm surprised.'

Alice threw off her quilt and stood up in a flush. 'People'll say anything! Christ, a guy in the legislature told me just last fall – and I never even mentioned it to you – told me he'd heard that the Hillston police chief – that's you, buddy – was taking kick-backs from a ring of suburban prostitutes in Catawba Hills, and that you were sleeping with the woman who'd organized it.'

'Is that *true*?!'

'Yes! He said he knew it for a fact.'

I started laughing. 'Lord God Almighty. And I thought all those ladies and I had been so discreet.' My laughter wouldn't stop, until finally Alice got the giggles with me. 'He said, sub-urban prostitutes in *Catawha Hills*?'

'Yes! Can you believe that?! Like maybe Mrs Marion Sunder-land! Mrs Dyer Fanshaw!' Laughing, she flopped back down on the couch, beer splashing over her wrist. 'His face was so solemn when he told me. Ed Blackman from Sanderton.'

I wiped my eyes. 'Well, hell, maybe I ought to investigate.'

'God, Cuddy, how can we be laughing now?'

'I guess it's a different way of crying.' I reached over and gave her foot a tug. 'Tension. Hysterics. Life force.'

'Oh shut up . . .' She wiped her eyes. ' 'Course, Ed was right. It would be the one who'd *organized* the ring that you'd sleep with. That much was right on the button.'

I propped up on an elbow. 'How do you know who I'd sleep with?'

'I don't.' She stood and started out the room. 'But I do have my theories. Want some more Nacho chips?'

I stood up too. 'You got anything real to eat? When I'm tense, I need to eat.'

'You eat all the time.'

'I've got to. What theories?'

'Come on in the kitchen. God, what's your secret, why don't you gain weight?'

I followed her back through high-ceilinged rooms. 'I think it's sorrow over the fall of man.'

Alice and I were cooking a pan of fried potatoes and onions when my beeper went off at midnight. At the desk, Sergeant Hiram Davies had just got a call from squad car 32, which was patrolling the Canaan section of East Hillston. The two officers in it were screaming for backups, fast, and for fire trucks, fast. There were twenty to thirty young blacks rioting in the streets. Some of them were throwing bricks at store windows, upending automobiles, starting fires in trash dumpsters. Some of them were chanting, *'Coop Hall! Coop Hall!'*

Alice ran back with my overcoat while I was telling Hiram, 'Instruct car thirty-two to get on their horn: order everybody in the area *inside*, away from the windows. I want a square cordoned off quick, East Main along Pitt to Maplewood, *nobody in but us.* No press! Call Ray at the State Patrol for a couple of mounties, and get me as many more of our guys out there as fast as you can, okay? And listen to me, Hiram, make sure some of them are black. Fisher. Emory. Mike Jones. Pull in Summers.'

'Chief, you want the canine team?'

'Jesus, no. No dogs, and no tear gas, you hear! That and the fuckin' news is all the fuck we need now!'

He hung up.

As I raced out of the house, yelling back to Alice to phone Carl Yarborough, I bet myself that if Bubba Percy had his scanner on, he'd beat the 'Action News' van out to Canaan, where I hoped they'd both run right into my roadblocks. I made some more wagers too, with my siren speeding east towards the sound of other sirens, past the old brick dilapidating sprawl of C & W Textile Mills: First off, if Governor Wollston had any feel for irony, which I doubted, he'd be struck with admiration for this latest twist of the Lord's whimsicality. Here Wollston had let his lieutenant governor, Julian Lewis, put some hometown pressure on him to postpone an execution, lest a racial disturbance mar the dignity of Briggs Cadmean's death, and here he was going to open his Sunday paper and see on page 1 a photo of a racial disturbance, instead of a photo of his press conference declaring a day of mourning for that great fallen captain of southern industry. Plus, George Hall was still alive; plus, his brother was now a martyr; plus, Wollston still had the decision about clemency or pardon to make, only with the stakes considerably raised, not to mention that in four weeks both State and Haver University would be back in session, and if only one out of ten students gave a damn about George Hall, that still meant 4,200 more possible protesters loose in the area than there would have been if he'd kept to his original execution date.

So I also bet myself: That Lieutenant Governor Lewis would lose some points with his boss for ever having come up with that last-minute 'stay' idea – maybe he'd even get dropped from a holiday dinner-party list. That Mitchell Bazemore, the DA (who, I'd heard, had had a temper tantrum about Hall's reprieve), would jump right on this mess like a whole family of acrobats on a circus springboard. *And*, that off in his yellow stone chateau-style estate on Catawha Drive, A. R. Randolph was sparking at his wife that if she hadn't changed her damn vote, the Club could have gone right ahead with the damn Confederacy Ball on the damn day and in the damn way they'd had it for the past ninety-six damn years.

The 'Race Riot in Canaan,' as the *Hillston Star* dubbed it, was not really much of a riot, and it was all over by two A.M. Still, my cops were so terrified – with the strangeness, and flames and smoke and gushing fire hoses, and curses screamed out of the dark on poorly lit, rumble-strewn streets – that it was a near miracle they didn't hurt somebody. The calmest creatures involved were the horses the three state patrolmen rode. I climbed up on a fire truck hood, to see over the chaos, and used a megaphone to send two squads circling out a few blocks to flank the rioters (luckily, ganged pretty close together in the bitter cold wind). 'Doesn't look like they've got any serious weapons,' Sergeant Ralph Fisher shouted up at me.

I yelled against the noise, 'Okay. Listen hard, everybody. We're as good as they come. Prove it! Keep your guns holstered, keep your shields up, and don't swing those sticks 'less you can convince me afterwards you *had to*!'

We did better than good; it didn't take too long to funnel most of the rioters back towards Smoke's Bar, into a dead-end alley. Only one of what the *Star* called 'the inflamed mob' (about two dozen black males, aged fourteen to twenty-two) sustained any injury needing treatment – a sprained ankle from a fall – and on our side, only Officer Titus Baker, who'd taken off his helmet, had to go to Emergency – nine stitches over his eyebrow where he was hit by a chunk of stone hurled from the crumbling steps that were all that was left of Canaan AME Church. Oh, and a photographer pal of Bubba Percy's got knocked down by firehose spray, and broke his wrist. Most of the property damage was minor – graffiti, broken car and store windows. But a new Thunderbird with Alabama plates had been rolled on its side, and wind had blown a fire in an open dumpster across into a lot selling Christmas trees, sending stacks of pines flaming up in pitch-crackling explosions. The heat scorched the near wall of the Greek grocery next door; inside, produce was smoke and water damaged. But the fire team had saved the store, had saved the *block*, and their chief and I (I didn't like him and he didn't like me) exchanged congratulations. The trucks were rewinding their hoses by the time 'Action News' sneaked around my roadblocks. And by three A.M., our wagon was heading downtown with the last of the arrests.

The outbreak had started when four of the older boys, drinking at Smoke's, heard about Cooper Hall's death on the bar's television. One had flown into a rage, and kicked his foot through some wood panelling. The bartender had promptly tossed them all out on the sidewalk. (He later denied he'd ever served them alcohol.) On the street, they'd run into other small groups, all of them 'just hanging around,' telling each other rumours about the highway killing, and rumours that the Klan was behind it, a few sharing a bottle, a few sharing some coke, until finally somebody spiralled up enough frustration and rage to heave a stray grocery cart through the plate-glass front of Acme Loan Company (whose absentee owners, the Wister brothers, were well hated in the neighbourhood – due to being a couple of shoddy white-trash gougers). Then somebody else threw a brick, and somebody else smashed in the Thunderbird's windshield, and from there, the hot pleasures of destroying things took all of them off on a group high. Herd adrenaline, anger, and young testosterone pumping together – it's a hit that crack can't touch. I saw it at work in Vietnam, doing stuff the Mother of God wouldn't forgive.

By five in the morning the parents of most of the juveniles had come to post their bail and take them home. Hiram Davies was good with parents, consoled the distraught ones, and preached forgiveness to the furious: one father was promising us that as soon as he got his son home, he'd beat him as close to death as he could manage.

The vandals we were left with in the interrogation room ranged in personality as widely as most groups do. Some were surly, some flip, one in tears, most scared. A seventeen-year-old (grabbed as he was enlarging the hole in the Thunderbird's window with a two-by-four) had a garrulous bravado way up there in Mercutio's league. Sergeant Fisher took away this boy's sunglasses and, having examined his pupils, nodded at me with a tap on his nose. 'Flying high.'

'No way,' announced the youngster with a solemnity that was

an uncanny replica of the expression on Hiram Davies's face. 'Let me tell you, okay,' he said, then bounced around the room, squeezing at the crotch of his pleated pants, while he confided in me that he was a victim of mistaken identity.

'Meaning you weren't there?'

'Meaning I wasn't there to be there, right? Check this out now, man, listen to what happens to me, I'm going down Maplewood, you know, doing my thing, you know. *Wham*, I'm in Rambo Land! I mean *lumber's* flying around my head, man, so listen, I'm lookin', curious, you know what I mean, got my human curiosity same as you, all right, I'm *lookin'* at the T-Bird, maybe some dude's inside, needs some help maybe, all right?' He paused, looked at Hiram Davies, who appeared sceptical, then turned his attention fully on me.

'I'm all ears,' I assured him.

'*Wham*, cop looks like a space monster comes arresting my ass! Listen to what he says, tells me this ain't no way to "*protest*." Don't dis me, I don't run with these turkeys here, don't lay that shit on me, protest is capital N-O-T my bag.'

'What's your name?'

'Walker. G. G. Walker. Check your books. You won't see it. Go ahead.'

'Okay, G.G. Get back over there with the turkeys, my man, and check *this* out: misguided protest is gonna go down better with me than private enterprise, like looting a T-Bird. Think about it.'

'See any merchandise? Hey, no way.' He opened his oversized tweed coat like a fashion model on a runway, presumably to invite us to search him for stolen property as he backed up, adding, 'I'd like a receipt for those shades.'

The young man who'd originally kicked in the panelling at Smoke's Bar, slender, coal-black, with sullen handsome eyes, stared at the wall as I questioned him. His jeans were ripped down one side. Cuts on his knuckles were bleeding. 'They tell me you started all this. That true?'

He shrugged, coiled at the end of the long bench, away from the others.

I nudged his foot with the toe of my shoe. 'Make you feel any better? . . . Listen, who do you think owned that car, who do you think was selling those Christmas trees? You think it was the people that shot Coop Hall? You think it was even *white* people?'

He shrugged.

93

'You punk assholes know somebody could've got *killed*?'

His eyes burned up at mine, then away.

'What's your name?' I pulled a chair over. 'Come on, I asked you your name.'

He spat the word at the floor. '. . . Martin.'

'Martin. Martin what?'

His eyes glared back at me, not blinking, and I was already seeing the resemblance when he snarled, '. . . Martin Hall.'

Almost seven A.M., false dawn, a hard empty blue, I'm on Cadmean Street driving home. The fact that the city didn't burn down feels like a minor accomplishment that nobody much appreciates. In the last few hours, I've been accused of brutality and a bleeding heart both. Carl Yarborough has burst into my office with a suit on over his pyjamas, and reminded me that he's the first black mayor Hillston ever had, that he intends to keep on being mayor, and that if I intend to keep on being police chief, I'd better get on top of the Hall case fast. I find a message in my box from President Andrew Brookside's administrative assistant, telling me Tuesday's the earliest her boss has a moment free to chat about threats on his life. I find a message that Mrs Etham Foster wants to know where her husband is. The Channel 7 station manager's called me a fascist obstructing the First Amendment. Alice has phoned me because Justin hasn't come home yet. Cooper Hall's teenaged cousin has stared at me with the dead man's eyes while I mumble platitudes like 'What you did tonight's not the answer.' Stared at me, and said back, 'It's *a* answer. Just not the one you motherfuckers wanna hear.'

I'm driving, I can't think of anything good, except that off in a ten-by-five solitary cell in Dollard Prison, George Hall is still alive.

It's almost seven A.M., my face feels like I've been lying in sand, my eyes feel like the sand got rubbed under their lids, a rightful of rank coffee and gooey rolls aren't getting along in my stomach, and I'm heading home, two days before Christmas, to the longest relationship I've managed to hang on to for the past nine years – an old foul-tempered poodle. I reach for a tape, not looking. It's Linda Ronstadt. She's singing, '. . . Some say the heart is just like a wheel; when you bend it, you can't mend it.'

I tell her that's too sad a point of view.

I drive on past my turn-off, on over the Shocco Bridge, on

down I-28, like I'm gonna just keep on driving west till the gas runs out. Then I see, sulphurous in the rising dew, the yellow flashers on the police trestles that mark where the Subaru and truck collided. They're gone now, but near the skid marks and debris and gouged clots of red clay, there are two other cars parked on the shoulder. I know both of them. They belong to two detective lieutenants of mine. On a tarp near the rear of the station wagon lie neat rows of tools. I pump brakes, make a U-turn.

Etham Foster's shoving a flagged stick into the clay; tall, lean-fleshed, in jeans and sheepskin jacket, he looks like a black cowboy up at dawn, staking fence on the range. Thirty feet off, holding the other end of a tape measure, crouches Justin Savile in a cheap hick get-up he must have bought at a thrift store to wear bigot-slumming tonight. He waves at me like we'd run into each other at a cocktail party. As usual, Foster doesn't bother looking up.

I pull over between them, get out and lean on my door. 'Y'all's wives are thinking of divorcing you. Me, now, I was thinking of firing your butts, but I see y'all already quit and took state jobs surveying the roads anyhow. I like your new outfit, Justin; it suits you. Dr D., you been out here all night?'

Foster says, 'Some,' then writes in his notebook, slowly sticks the pencil down its spiral loops, slowly winds the tape measure like reeling in a fish he knows is too little.

I lean one foot over the other, scratch at my chin stubble. 'I thought I sent Wes Pendergraph out here to tell you to return to headquarters. Etham?'

'He told me.'

'Well, that's good.'

Foster licks his bristly moustache with the underside of his purplish lower lip, and yields enough to add, 'Was out at the garage with the Subaru some.'

'Umm. I was out at a little riot in East Hillston. Even mounted patrols, Justin. I know you always wanted to be one. So, y'all didn't happen to hear about a riot, did you? Guess not. Both been pretty busy, I guess.' I find some loose M&Ms in my pocket, and eat them. 'You run into Savile here at his White Patriots' hooten-anny?' Foster doesn't answer. I watch Justin brush clay off the knees of these orange-checkered polyester pants that are too tight. I lick my fingers with a sigh. 'Lieutenants, I'm in a real bad mood. I'm in the kind of mood where I lose track of old times and camaraderie. Y'all got five minutes to tell me something good.'

Justin took longer. But it was good. This meeting he'd gone to with Preston Pope's contact wasn't a very interesting meeting: this group called itself the 'Carolina Patriots.' They'd read an article from *The Fiery Cross*. They'd served ribs from Hot Hat Barbecue. They'd listened to an ex-Green Beret sergeant lecture on survivalist tactics – what roots to eat, how to booby-trap your lean-to, where to cache your ammo – tactics for when white folks have to take to the woods to keep themselves pure from the Tainted Races. During the refreshments, Coop Hall's death had come up – they gave the news a cheer, but nobody tried to take the credit of knowing any insider gossip about who might have shot him. What had interested Justin was the fellow the rest seemed to think had the most right to an opinion: not because he said a word about it, but because he had a personal stake in anybody named Hall. Because his name was Willie Slidell, and as somebody happened to mention, his sister was the widow of Bobby Pym, and Bobby Pym was the cop George Hall had killed. So after these freedom fighters ran out of beer and adjourned, Justin decided he might as well follow Willie Slidell home, instead of checking in with me, or bothering to phone Alice. And this trip was interesting, too. Turns out, Slidell's home was a farmhouse just off Exit 9 on the Interstate, and Exit 9 is less than half a mile from where we were standing right now.

So that's what Justin had to say. Etham didn't talk. He opened the beautiful initialled briefcase I knew his wife had given him for his last birthday, because I went to the party, and he showed up a half hour late. With a carefulness slow enough to make you hyperventilate, he took out a plastic bag. Inside it was a tiny crushed brassy cylinder, a fired bullet shell. He stretched up, tall as the sun lifting above the bare tobacco field behind him. 'Thirty-eight,' he said. 'Like I figured.'

Chapter 7

Sunday morning I slept, drapes drawn, pillows over my head, Martha exiled. Early afternoon, I sat in a groggy stupor on the stool at my breakfast counter, staring at the smooth white lacquer surface, staring out my balcony sliders to the feathery horizon of dark winter trees behind the Shocco. Coffee eventually brought me back my brain, and with it yesterday's events. On a legal pad I drew a map of the section of I-28 along which Cooper Hall had been shot, sketched in Exit 9's turn-off, with Willie Slidell's farmhouse, and a question mark that stood for Justin's theory: Since how could a car follow Coop all the way from Raleigh to Hillston without his spotting it, what if, Justin says, what if Slidell, or somebody, had waited at Exit 9 for the Subaru to pass, pulled out then, and fired the shot? His theory didn't answer the 'how' and 'why.' This somebody still needed to want Coop dead. Why? That seven years ago Coop's brother had shot Slidell's sister's husband might, I suppose, be a reason – especially if Slidell was attending white supremacy shindigs – but that didn't answer the how. This somebody still needed to know that Coop would be coming down that highway at that time. I made phone calls to set up a serious search of Coop's apartment and the office of *With Liberty and Justice* on the floor below it. The person I wanted to find was the one Coop had been on his way to meet, because that's the person who *had* to know when and why he was driving into Hillston.

Meanwhile, the nervous green light on my answering machine kept trying to catch my eye, and deliver its messages – several from newspapers, one apparently from Isaac Rosethorn – he'd started talking before the beep, but appeared to be cancelling our dinner tonight at Buddha's Garden – one from Officer Nancy White, who sounded upset, two from Father Paul Madison, and three from our Haver County district attorney:

'Mangum, this is Mitchell Bazemore. Call me. It's nine-o-six.'

'Bazemore, Mangum. It's ten-thirty-eight. I'm leaving for church. I'll be in my office at one.'

'Mangum, call me immediately.'

'Chief? This is Zeke Caleb here. The DA is on my back about where are you. You coming in?'

Two other messages I didn't expect, and not only because I wondered who'd given the callers my unlisted number:

'Mr Mangum, my name is Edwina Sunderland, Mrs Marion Sunderland. I had the pleasure of meeting you Friday at the Hillston Club, and I trust you'll pardon my presuming on the briefness of our acquaintance, and the shortness of this notice, but I'd like to invite you—' Mrs Sunderland's stately pace had made no allowances for modern impatience, and the machine cut her dead here. She didn't appear even to realize she was speaking with a machine, for she phoned back, saying, 'Mr Mangum, I believe we were disconnected. Would you be free to accept an invitation for dinner at my home on Boxing Day? The twenty-sixth? At eight o'clock. I look forward to hearing from you, good-bye.' She ignored instructions to leave me her number.

The next and last call was the first one I returned.

'This is Lee, Cuddy. I just heard the radio. Are you all right? When you get a chance, phone me? I'm here till seven.'

The maid said she'd be willing to see if Mrs Brookside were at home. It was more than the maid had been willing to do back when Lee's mother had first forbidden me to see her daughter. Different maid, same house. 'Briarhills.' Up in North Hillston near Haver University. The kind of house you give a name to. Lee's parents were dead and the Brooksides were living there now, instead of on campus. Maybe the university president's house, which came with the job, hadn't had a sky-diving landing field. The maid said Mrs Brookside would be with me in a moment.

Lee and I talked for half an hour. I think it surprised us both. Talked about Cooper Hall and the Canaan disturbance. She didn't know how Brookside had responded to Jack Molina's televised outburst, or even if he'd heard about it: he'd flown to Asheville yesterday and she hadn't seen him since his return. Saturday she'd mentioned to me that she and Molina weren't 'close.' I was getting the feeling that the same might be said about her and Andy. Or maybe cosy conjugality was just another one of those rise-of-the-middle-class notions that never rose as far as the upper crust.

That was all we said about Andy. We talked about Cadmean's funeral, and about Justin Savile: what did I think of his wife Alice? I said, the world. We talked about Mrs Sunderland, since Lee was the one who'd given her my telephone number, which she'd got out of Sergeant Zeke Caleb.

I heard myself laughing. 'So you got around Zeke. Well, that Cherokee can't resist a woman in distress.'

'A woman in distress . . .' Her laugh was throatier than the young Lee's. 'My God, is that what I sound like?'

'You sound—' But I stopped, scared, because I was going to say, '—lonely.' And what was that supposed to mean? Instead I said, 'You sound a little naturally worried, that's all.' She was quiet, so I added, 'It's going to be all right. Nothing's going to happen to your husband . . . Lee?'

'Did Edwina invite you to dinner?' She asked as if it weren't a peculiar change of subject.

'Pardon me?'

'She told me she wanted to ask you to her Boxing Day dinner. She said, "I like a man whose eyes don't fidget. Made me laugh. Found him charming." Naturally, I agreed.'

'Charming? I don't think anybody ever called me "charming." You say she's a widow? Would it be tacky to ask her to marry me at my first Boxing Day dinner, and what is Boxing Day? Sounds too violent for a woman of her years.'

'Oh, you know, it's British. Edwina's president of the state's English Speaking Union. Besotted Anglophiles all claiming to be descended from some Plantagenet crusader or Stuart jailbird. My stepfather was in it. But then he really *was* the grandson of a viscount . . . As well as a son-of-a-bitch . . .'

'God, I'm glad you finally admit it.'

'So did you tell her yes?'

'Mrs Sunderland? Why? You fixing to warn me she lures charming bachelors with steady eyes to these parties and drives them wild with London gin and Portsmouth oysters?'

'No,' she said, 'I wanted to say I hope you'll come. Because I am.'

I telephoned Mrs Sunderland, and told her I'd be happy to accept her invitation.

Driving downtown I thought about, well, about whether Lee meant she was coming alone. Then I told myself to stop it. Then I thought about it some more. Then I regretted making that dumb lewd remark about oysters. Then I thought about her laugh. Then I wondered if she'd mentioned going to Cadmean's funeral because she was maybe hoping to see me there. Skirting around the plastic Christmas tree in the Municipal Building's marble lobby, I felt old Briggs Monmouth C's bearish eyes glower down at me from his oil painting, like he wasn't surprised to hear me planning to use *his* funeral to spend time with a married woman.

When I walked by Zeke Caleb at the desk, his wide red-knuckled fist waved the phone at me, as he yelled, 'Chief! Father Paul Madison. *Chief!*'

I told him, 'Sergeant, don't bellow. I've got ears.'

'Well, use 'em.' Zeke's never acquired the hang of deferential subordination. It's not an Indian notion. That's why there're a lot more family dogs in white America today than there are American Indians. 'You look like shit,' he casually added, and handed me the phone.

Paul Madison was distressed about Cooper's death, distressed about the Canaan riot, wanted me to know that he was helping Elmore Greenwood, pastor of Hillston's largest black Baptist church, to raise bail money for the five young men we were still holding, and wanted to ask me if we'd arrested Billy Gilchrist again.

I said, 'Again? We just released him Saturday morning. Hold on a second.' I put the receiver to my chest. 'Zeke, is Gilchrist in again?' Zeke shook his head and swung back to his typewriter. 'Sorry, Paul, no. What's the problem?'

'He didn't show up last night. Wasn't here this morning, didn't do any of his chores, and he knew there was a processional at eleven o'clock mass. Billy never misses a processional when he can carry the St Michael banner, *never* after he's just come off a binge.'

Billy Gilchrist used to be a fairly successful local con man, till booze ruined his coordination, his concentration, and his looks. About two years ago, I'd sent him to an AA group that met at

Trinity's parish house. He didn't take to AA, but he did take to Paul Madison, and claimed to have taken to religion as well – maybe he just admired it as a more lucrative, bigger-time con than any he'd ever pulled. At any rate, he'd convinced Paul, who gave him room and board at the soup kitchen in exchange for his doing odd jobs around the church, including setting up all the gold platters and silver chalices for mass. About once a month, he jumped off the wagon, tore up a bar or two, and stayed with us a while for old time's sake.

Paul said, 'Nobody's seen him. He's just gone. Nothing's missing from his room—'

'How 'bout the vestry? Anything missing from there? Collection plate maybe?'

'Cuddy, I'm serious! Billy hasn't missed a procession in a year, unless he was in jail. He *loves* to carry that banner.'

'Could be he had a crisis of faith . . . Okay, okay, I'll put out a bulletin for your lost sheep . . . And listen, if you're in touch with Reverend Greenwood, tell him I'd like the details on Cooper Hall's funeral as soon as possible. By the way, Coop wasn't planning to meet you or anybody else on the Hall Committee in Hillston yesterday, was he? He had to leave Raleigh to meet somebody here, but apparently he didn't say who.'

'Jordan and Isaac don't know?'

'No. Why would Isaac know anyhow?'

Paul said, 'Well, I know Cooper was up at Isaac's hotel almost every night last week, because Jordan kind of, you know, made a joke about never seeing him . . . I spoke with her this morning. She's in a very bad way. Christ help her.'

I said, 'Right. Wondrous are the ways of the Lord, Father Madison. I betcha another of your damn raffle tickets that the slimeball who shot Coop calls himself a Christian.'

'You keep blaming Christ for Christianity, Cuddy. Talk to you later. Find Billy for me, will you? Bye.'

The DA was in my office ten minutes after I sat down. Probably kept a spy in the halls. It's no news on the upper floors of the Municipal Building that Mitchell Bazemore and I aren't exactly pals. He's got a voice like a machine gun, I'm pretty quick-tongued myself, and we've bounced some fast exchanges off the corridor walls over the years. Our views on crime and punishment take different etymological routes: he believes in prisons, I believe in penitentiaries. What he lives for is capital crime convictions, big ones, and lots of them. Like I say, what I'm after is as much peace, with as little injustice, as this sad greedy race of creatures can be cajoled, trained, or bullied into tolerating.

Bazemore's about my age, local-bred, chisel-chinned with a dimple in the middle, like somebody stuck a pencil in it hard, which wouldn't surprise me. His contact lenses are too green. His hair's so black there's speculation that he dyes it, but no proof. Some women say he's handsome; he's one of those naturally skinny, Nautilus-fanatic, artificial mesomorphs whose muscles are too big for his head and hands. Like his hair, his chest looks faked. He gives off a straining-at-the-seams energy, a kind of virile moralism, like a top recruiter for a fundamentalist college with a big athletic programme. 'Go For it' is the printed motto cased in plastic on his desk top – as if getting folks sent to the gas chamber was the same as aiming for a gold medal in the Olympics.

'I left you half a dozen messages,' he said by way of hello.

Well, he'd only left three, but I had to let that go, because I said, 'Gee, I'm sorry, Mitch, damn machine's on the blink again. What's your problem?'

'What's my problem?'

'Grab a chair.' I even picked one up for him, and shook the books off it. 'No? Well, grab a door and do some chin-ups while we chat. Little on edge today, Mitch?' (That was a joke; Bazemore's so hyperkinetic, you'd figure him for a speed freak if he weren't always campaigning for a drug-free society – he doesn't drink or smoke either, though of course, as an elected official in North Carolina, he never makes public statements about his aversion to tobacco.)

'No, I'm not on edge. I'm just a little darn annoyed.'

'Oh? Why's that?'

'Why's that? Why am I annoyed?' Like a lot of people whose mouths run faster than their brains, he repeats things. 'I leave town, I take twenty teenagers to Boone on a church retreat—'

'That *does* sound annoying—'

I watched him pace along my desk like it was a jury box. Mitch wears his white shirt sleeves rolled up tight around his biceps, his collar open as if his neck were too pumped full of maleness to allow him to button it, his sombre trousers just a little too tight across the buttocks, and his vest straining at his chest. He wears a wedding ring and a college ring, a tiny American flag as a tiepin, a gold belt buckle with his initials on it, and tasselled wing tips he can see his face in. Marching, he flicked his Phi Beta Kappa key. 'I leave, I come back, and Wollston's screwed up the George Hall execution. As a direct, I mean a *direct* result of which, we have a homicide. We have a homicide, and we have a race riot. A race riot!'

'As a direct result of your going on this teenage church retreat? Don't be so hard on yourself. Cheese cracker?' I held one out as he strode past.

'I don't snack,' he informed me.

'Ah, right. Empty mind in an empty body.'

'I don't joke.'

'Mitch, you sell yourself short. I think you're real funny.'

'You think I'm real funny. Well, I don't find you at all amusing.'

What I didn't find at all amusing was the list of indictments he was planning to ask the grand jury to bring in against the young blacks we'd arrested last night in Canaan. I tried reason: setting fires in dumpsters was illegal and dangerous (especially in windy weather around a pile of cut trees), but it wasn't intentional arson; throwing chunks of cement randomly into a crowd was illegal and dangerous, but it wasn't attempted murder. I tried politics: most of those involved were juveniles, and we were unlikely to get convictions on charges that stiff; all of those involved were blacks, responding to what might very well be the racist killing of a highly visible civil rights activist whose brother—

'Whose brother should have gone to the gas chamber years ago! Mangum, please. Don't talk to me about the Hall brothers.'

I said, 'I don't have to. You can read about them in any paper you pick up. And if you go bulldozing into this Canaan thing, before we make an arrest in the Coop Hall case, I'm telling you, Mitch, you're going to read about that in the papers too. And so are the voters. Not everybody in this county's white, and not everybody who *is* white's a bigot. Follow me?'

He pressed his knuckles on to my desk top and twitched his biceps at me for a while. 'You follow *me*, Mangum. You get me a suspect on this highway shooting, and you get me one quick, and I don't care if he's white, black, purple, or green. Am I coming through?'

I said, 'Like a rainbow.' I stood up to pat his shoulder; it was hot and quivery. 'Mitch, you've just proved my point. Those civil libertarians always on your back, trying to get your convictions overturned, I tell them they got you all wrong. I tell them, colour's not an issue with our DA.'

He eyed me suspiciously. 'I don't care about colour. I care about crime.'

'Right. That's what I tell 'em.'

Officer John Emory was waiting outside the door when the DA strode past him with what looked like a Black Power salute, but was probably just that Mitch was too hurried to unclench his fist. Emory set a huge cardboard box down on a side table, carefully lining it up with the edge. A small, well-made young black man, he had perfect posture, a pristine haircut, and his shirt and trousers were as sharply creased as if he'd just taken them from a dry cleaner's bag; John had been an army MP, and I couldn't get him out of the habit.

'Sir, here's the personal property from the Subaru.'

'At ease, John. Anything interesting?'

Emory didn't like to commit himself to value judgements, so he'd brought, and itemized, the entire portable contents of Coop Hall's car, including flares, rope, manual, a gym bag with dirty shorts and towels, a baseball cap, two dozen back issues of *With Liberty and Justice*, one tennis shoe, a raincoat – balled up and still wet – an unpaid parking ticket, three library books on criminal law, a paperback by Toni Morrison, and an unravelling briefcase with the handle held on by a twisted paper clip. Among the papers in the briefcase were printer's galleys; a report compiled by the NAACP Legal Fund on race and capital punishment; a copy of Isaac Rosethorn's petition to Judge Roscoe, citing a dozen questionable rulings by Judge Henry Tiggs at George Hall's original trial; an old newspaper clipping from that trial with the headline, 'COP KILLER TAKES STAND'; and a scuffed bulging address book, crammed with loose slips of paper. I thumbed through its pages: neat entries in ink – 'Jordan' the first name under 'J,' Isaac Rosethorn the last name under 'R' – scribbled entries in pencil; names crossed out and dozens of numbers jotted in margins. Cooper must have used it sporadically as an appointments book as well, because on blank pages in back there were notes like 'Tues, 5:30, Silver Comet' (a bar), and 'Brookside, W-S, Marriott, 23rd' (the date and place of Andy Brookside's Winston-Salem speech to black business leaders). As I leafed through the thick book, I said to Emory – still in his military at-ease position, hands behind his back, 'Okay, John. All these names in here? I want to know how Hall knew them, and I want to know where they were yesterday afternoon.'

He said, 'Sir.'

'Hang on.' I'd already seen some names that interested me. One was 'Gilchrist,' in a corner of the 'G' page, with a number under it. I dialled it. After a long wait, a young girl's out-of-breath voice said, 'Trinity Church soup kitchen, sorry to keep you waiting.'

'Pretty busy today? This is C. R. Mangum, chief of police. I'm looking for Billy Gilchrist.'

'Oh! Hello. Father Madison's been looking for him all day.'

'He hasn't come back then?'

'No, and he didn't even clean out the coffee machines. But I found, can you believe this, an IOU in the refrigerator for two pounds of cheese.'

'Doesn't sound like mice, does it?'

She giggled. 'Hey, did you say you were the *police* chief? You don't sound like one.'

'Darlin', it's a brave new world. Keep the faith.'

Also in Cooper's book was an old business card belonging to one 'Clark Koontz, Senior Sales Representative, Fanshaw Paper Company.' It wasn't odd that Cooper should know a paper salesman, since he edited a magazine; it was odd that on the back of the card, in faint handwriting, was written, 'Newsome, Sat., 3.' This Saturday? Purley Newsome? But he couldn't be a suspect; late Saturday afternoon, Purley was right here in the squad room, swallowing the last bits of a speeding ticket. Purley's brother, Otis Newsome, our city comptroller?

I called Otis Newsome at home. His wife said he was over at a neighbour's watching TV. 'It's a bunch of men that like to watch games together,' she explained sort of wearily.

'Lionel Tiger will tell you why,' I said.

'I don't know him.' She sounded as if she didn't want to either. I called the neighbour's. Otis clearly resented the interruption. Yes, he'd known Koontz, so what? He'd bought city paper supplies through him. No, he hadn't known Cooper Hall, nor could he be bothered to try to imagine why Hall would have a card of Koontz's with 'Newsome' on it. I asked how I might reach Koontz.

'You can't,' Otis told me. 'He's dead.'

I looked up after the call to find Emory still fixed in place. 'Go on, John. You can take the rest of that stuff back.'

But he didn't move. 'Sir?'

'Yep?'

Staring straight over my head, Emory tucked in his chin as he spoke. 'This is out of line, sir, but, but, the thing of it is, we just got our new rotation with the new partners listed . . .' He paused so long I lifted my eyes from the notepad I was writing on. Suddenly his face opened in shocked grief. '. . . And I've been assigned to Nancy White!'

I leaned back in my swivel chair. '. . . So?'

'I know I'm out of line . . .' Earnestness tightened his whole body. 'But well, but but . . .'

'But could I switch you? . . . Nope.' I let my chair fall forward. Now I knew why there was a message from Nancy on my machine at home. 'Exactly what are your objections to Officer White? Maybe her name?'

Emory shook his head vigorously.

'Her sex?'

He shook his head again, but much more slowly, and without a lot of conviction. 'I'll tell you the truth—'

'Please do, John.'

'I don't feel good about that.' Indeed, he looked miserable, sweat starting to bead on his handsome forehead.

'Will you sit down?' I walked around my desk and shoved him into the vinyl armchair. He froze in it like a pharaoh guarding a pyramid. 'Now you listen, Nancy's a good cop. But she's a little, well, individualistic.' He nodded quickly. 'You're a good cop. But you're a little . . . what'll we say? . . .' I tilted my head at him, grinning. 'Let's say . . . fussy.'

His face went rigid. 'Sir?'

'Gung ho. By which I mean, John, you arrest people for spitting.'

'It's against the law!'

'But you bring them downtown, and we just don't have the space. You arrest married couples for shouting at each other on the sidewalk.'

He was out of his chair. 'That was an oral altercation, Chief Mangum. It says in the manual—'

'I know, I know. The point is, I think if you and Nancy meet somewhere in the middle, you'll make a fine team.'

'I don't feel, sir, that—'

My phone rang. 'Okay, John. We'll discuss this after you try it, two weeks. Start on that address book.' I gave him a salute.

It was Zeke Caleb with a message from Wes Pendergraph, reporting from the *With Liberty and Justice* office. There'd been a break-in there, probably late last night. The place was trashed, and a file cabinet had been stolen.

'What the hell does Wes mean, a file cabinet? The cabinet or the files?'

'Says, a file cabinet, Chief. Says, that fat old lawyer fellow came on the premises, claiming this cabinet's got taken.'

'By "fat old lawyer fellow" do you mean my friend Isaac Rosethorn?'

'Don't ice up on me, Chief. I *like* that old lawyer. Also, Savile's down in the lab if you got a second.'

I tossed my crackers wrapper at my Hong Kong Rodin; it bounced off Balzac's head down into the trash can below.

Out in the main room, Officer Brenda Moore was twisting loops of red and green streamers around the doors and guardrail. Zeke was standing on his desk, attaching mistletoe to a ceiling wire. I said, 'Cherokee, you sure about that mistletoe? You want a string of holiday drunks smacking their lips at you all day?' His sharp-winged cheeks blushed bright.

'Wasn't any idea of mine,' he mumbled, jumping off the desk like he was figuring to fly across the room.

'Zeke, what did Purley Newsome do after the briefing broke up yesterday? When was it, quarter to three?'

''Bout. Purley? Hung around the locker room, runs his mouth like a dirty river to any what would listen. Mostly laying shit on you.'

'Till when?'

'Still here when I signed out at four. Playing pinochle with McInnis, seems like.'

'McInnis his new partner?'

'Yeah, and he don't deserve it.'

I said first thing tomorrow morning I wanted to see McInnis.

'You got a meeting with the Board of Finances first thing tomorrow.'

'Right. I was gonna ask if I can get us some band uniforms in the budget, maybe a couple of majorettes. Didn't you used to love majorettes? Whooo, I did.'

'Band uniforms? We don't even have a band.'

'Well, hey, New York's Finest's got one, why shouldn't we?'

'A band?'

'Cherokee, when are you gonna get used to me?' I turned to

Brenda Moore, a young black officer, plump and happy-tempered. 'Hey, Brenda, ask me over for supper again?'

She came back quick, like always, hands on her big-hipped trousers. 'Soon as you give me a raise. Last Easter you came, I had a whole basket of painted eggs, and you ate 'em all. Ate the rabbit too.'

Zeke said, 'Be kind of nice to have a band. You know Nancy can play the trombone?'

I winked at Brenda. 'I'm not real surprised.'

Actually, Justin wasn't in the lab, but in the hall outside it, because Etham Foster doesn't allow smoke anywhere near his equipment. Nose in a paperback Cajun cookbook, Justin stood puffing away on his Dunhill, in his Harvard sweats – with the 'Veritas' shield across his chest – his fine Arrow Shirt features contorted in a coughing fit. 'Don't say a word,' he told me as soon as he could manage to.

'If you won't listen to the surgeon general, why should you listen to the chief of police? Don't put that butt out on my floor.'

'This isn't your floor, Cudberth, it belongs to the city of Hillston. "*Salus populi suprema lex est.*" Or: "The people's good is the highest law." Marcus Tullius Cicero.'

I took his cigarette and crunched it in the sand bucket across the hall. 'It ain't necessarily so. George and Ira Gershwin.'

While I waited for him to finish hacking, I pulled down some out-of-date notices off the bulletin board beside him, including one in crayon from Brenda Moore. I sighed. 'Brenda's married now. So she's *probably* not still looking to share an apartment with "one or more females." Doesn't anybody ever read these boards? . . . Alice let you back in this morning, or could I maybe replace you in her affections? Tell me, J.B.S, what have you got that I don't have anyhow?'

'Her,' he said, stuffing his book into his sweatshirt pouch. 'Plus looks, savoir faire, family connections—'

'I notice you don't mention brains.'

'You and Alice would bore each other to death. You're too much alike. Besides you'd both be dead in a year from grease, sugar, preservatives, and salt. Y'all ruined one of my frying pans last night burning those oily potatoes. Let me show you something.' He opened the door to the lab.

'You had the frying pan analysed?'

The lab was empty and immaculate: microscopes covered, sinks scrubbed, photo blow-ups of tyre tracks and skid marks, of bullet shells, of shattered windshields, thumbtacked neatly to a corkboard. Immaculate, except that one long counter was strewn with garbage. Real garbage – sparerib bones, coffee grinds, broken light bulbs, salad goop on crumpled newspapers, cigarette butts, all kinds of disgusting stuff poured out of a smelly brown plastic trashbag. Justin leapt up, perched on the edge of the counter, and smiled. 'First,' he said, 'let me fill you in.'

'I hope this wasn't your lunch.'

'Listen. I sent Parker out to talk to Willie Slidell this afternoon, you know – "We're investigating this shooting on the Interstate. Did you happen to see anything, and by the way where were *you* yesterday from etc., etc." So Slidell says he was at his sister's all afternoon. So Parker asks him if anybody else lives there at the farm with-him, and he says he lives alone. And he's acting hyper. Meanwhile—'

'Justin, what's this junk doing all over Etham's lab?'

'*Meanwhile*, I'm waiting down the road at this filling station. Right after Parker leaves, Slidell leaves.'

'Let me guess. You follow Slidell?'

'No, Parker tailed him. He went straight to West Hillston to see his sister, Lana. Bobby Pym's *widow*? I find that interesting.'

'Jesus, Justin, I've known folks to visit their sisters that weren't murderers.' I took a pencil and poked through some greasy napkins. '"Meanwhile," back at the farm, I hope you're not fixing to tell me you entered Mr Slidell's house without a warrant.'

'Who me?' He gave me his old Boy Scout pledge, three fingers and a grin. 'No, I just looked in the windows. Somebody was asleep in a bedroom, but I couldn't really see very well.'

'Male or female?'

'I don't know. Big though. The point is, he'd said he lives alone.'

'Maybe he has a big girlfriend. This by any chance Slidell's garbage?'

He looked at it affectionately. 'Yeah. I took it out of his dumpster by the side of the road on my way out. You can tell a lot about people from their garbage.'

'Um hum.' I gave my hair a tug. 'You did say you were *released* from that loony bin up in Asheville, didn't you? I mean, you didn't escape out a window maybe?'

'Very funny. That was ten years ago. And I wasn't crazy. I was a drunk. You could hurt somebody's feelings one of these days.' But he brushed this possibility aside by jumping off the counter and slapping me on the arm. 'Let me show you something you can learn from garbage.' He reached around me to pick up a small flattened paper box. It had once held, according to its cover, two dozen .38 calibre bullets.

'Okay?' he asked.

'Okay,' I nodded.

Justin was rubbing his hands together in a way I'd seen before, on homicide cases, or when he was about to slap down a Scrabble word on a triple point square. 'We can pull Willie Slidell anyhow. He's stealing from his job! I didn't go in the house, but I did go in the barn. And, guess what, there's about eight giant cylinders of paper in there behind an old car.'

I startled him, snapping the pencil in two. 'Slidell works at Fanshaw Paper Company.'

'Christ, how'd you know? He's a shipping clerk there. And he's stealing paper. I just can't figure out why. I mean, it's just paper. It couldn't be counterfeiting or something, could it? Printing?'

I gave Justin the business card from Fanshaw Paper Company, and told him to check out the dead salesman, Koontz. Also to pull the personnel file on Otis Newsome.

My mind was running all over the place, a fact nagging for me to remember it. Justin sent Parker back to Slidell's, to say we were doing a general search for hideouts the killers might have driven to after the shooting. He could insist on looking in the barn, and then question Slidell about the paper containers. I agreed to let Justin keep on undercover. 'But you go talk to Dave Schulmann first; the FBI's got much better files on these Patriot yahoos than we do. And you stay away from that farmhouse, unless this Willie Slidell of yours *invites* you over, understood?'

Justin solemnly promised. 'I was thinking,' he added, 'well, these Carolina Patriots were listening to that ex-Green Beret sergeant, you know, tell them to start stockpiling weapons and ammo, for Armageddon. So I was thinking of saying I know where we can get a bunch of guns.'

'Where? Sears and Roebuck's?'

'No. Rob the Crawford Sons warehouse over in Bennville. You know, that mail-order firearms place? Get some M-sixteens, twenty-two-calibre machine guns, stuff like that. I'll say, I've figured out a no-risk way to break in there.'

His eyes danced like some artist had painted the twinkles in with a tiny glitter brush. I sighed loudly. 'Justin, these jerks are never gonna suspect you're not one of them.'

'I'll take that as a compliment, despite your intentions.' He pulled on a wide-collared, wide-shouldered, magazine ad-looking jacket. 'Now, what about Malvolio?'

'Say who?'

'*Twelfth Night.* We had to postpone. We lost Blue.'

'Y'all are getting careless. First, a male member. Now, Miss Randolph, who, as I recall, was quite a lot of flesh to mislay.'

'All of a sudden, she flew to Vail with this moron Chip Sunderland.'

I said, 'My my,' wondering if that's whose chair at Mrs Marion Sunderland's table I'd been invited to fill. I started out the lab door. 'Look here, Justin, I don't have time to play. I don't have time to *work*.'

'You need a *personal* life, Cuddy. Like Alice says, you've just cut yourself off, like a kind of misanthrope. Hey, maybe we ought to do Molière.'

'Play-acting is not a personal life.'

'Sure it is. It's personal. It's *people*. Playing together.' He jogged backwards in my path as I headed down the hall. 'You want to know my theory? Bring back all the old feast days, harvest festivals, jousts, guild pageants. Make ritual, not war. Societies that *play* together stay together.'

'That's not a theory; that's an ad campaign. And I don't think I'd look so hot with yellow ribbons crisscrossed up my legs. Get somebody else to do this social-climbing steward of yours.'

He caught my arm. 'Ah ha, you've read *Twelfth Night*! You read it last night!'

I removed his hand with two fingers. 'I read it in high school. Last night I put a stop to a race riot. See the difference? And don't tell me if those kids got more chances to do Shakespeare's plays, they wouldn't have torn up Canaan.'

'Exactly right!' Well, one thing about old Justin, you can't repress him with rationality. '*Coriolanus, Henry the Fourth*, I bet they'd be great!'

I told him there was a fast-talking young man in the holding cell right now, wearing sunglasses and an overcoat down to his high-top Reeboks, a natural actor, trying to raise bail. ' "Politics is N-O-T his bag." Why don't you go audition him, leave me alone.'

'What's his name?' asked Justin.

On my way out, I passed Sergeant Fisher with a chest-high stack of arrest files. 'Any luck, Sergeant?'

He scratched at grey stubble on his black cheek. 'Nothing but alibis tighter'n a bank on a dollar. Looks like most of these Klanners work Saturday jobs.'

'Well, just keep on rounding up the usual suspects. Like the movie says. You know, I met this girl, thought I looked like Humphrey Bogart.'

He kept going. 'Can't help you. White people all look alike to me.'

It was when I saw George Hall's picture on the poster that the fact nagging at me pushed through. All those lost jobs of George's that Bazemore had run past the jury to show how the defendant was a troublemaker – hadn't one of them been a job driving for Fanshaw Paper Company? I didn't know what to fit this fact *to*, but I was getting the angry feeling that maybe in all these nightly meetings Paul Madison had said Isaac and Cooper were having, they were fiddling with the same facts, and hadn't bothered to share the news with me.

The poster that said 'SAVE GEORGE HALL' was on the door of the *With Liberty and Justice* magazine office. This magazine was staffed by volunteers – mostly students – and financed by the civil rights organization that paid Coop Hall's salary. Its office was squeezed between two boarded-up clothing stores on a dark side street off Jupiter, near the old train station, now a shopping gallery called Southern Depot, modelled, according to its developers, on the Bourse in Milan. But *With Liberty and Justice* hadn't developed into anything as affluent as the Depot, and, when I'd sent Wes Pendergraph to run a search on the office this afternoon, it had still looked, apart from some computers, pretty much as it had fifteen years ago, with one room of secondhand desks, mismatched chairs, crowded metal bookshelves. Except that Wes had found a back window open, had found 'NIGGERS OUT' and 'KKK' dripped in black painted letters down a wall, and books and papers littered across the floor.

Three college kids I'd seen at Dollard Prison Friday night, and again at Nomi Hall's house, stood close together in a corner, watching the kneeling Etham Foster peer in disgust with a penlight at the windowsill. Wes told me that Isaac Rosethorn had come by shortly after he'd arrived; that he hadn't explained how

112

he'd known files were missing; and that he'd left immediately. The three college vigilants told me they weren't leaving until we did. They looked stunned, and hostile. Friday, they'd got their stay of execution; Saturday, the world – whose amenability they were affluent enough to assume – had revealed a malevolence so indifferent, it must have felt like a betrayal.

There were little posters of quotations on the wall. Splattered black paint dots speckled them now. Someone had painted 'NIGGERS OUT' over the one that said:

> YOU'RE EITHER A PART OF THE SOLUTION OR PART OF
> THE PROBLEM.
>
> ELRIDGE CLEAVER

And 'ATHEISTS' over this one:

> EVERY HUMAN BEING THAT BELIEVES IN CAPITAL
> PUNISHMENT LOVES KILLING AND THE ONLY REASON
> THEY BELIEVE IN CAPITAL PUNISHMENT IS BECAUSE
> THEY GET A KICK OUT OF IT.
>
> CLARENCE DARROW

I said, 'Dr D.?' When Foster stood up, I asked, 'How about Hall's apartment upstairs?'

'Not touched since our folks were there yesterday.' He wrote in his notebook, slid it in the sheepskin pocket. 'These three here say they can't really tell if anything but those files're missing. Hall pretty much ran the place singlehanded.' He pointed at the paint on the wall. 'Could be, robbery was just a side show anyhow. Came and left by the window, paint smear on it.'

'Carrying a file cabinet?'

Wes stepped forward. 'Mr Rosethorn said a "cabinet," but it sounds like all it was, was a locked metal box Hall kept in his desk.'

'Isaac tends to exaggerate,' I said. 'Wes, how 'bout giving him a call, at the Piedmont. Tell him I said, stay put till I get there. And see if you can get a phone number for a Jack or John Molina.'

The students – two male, one female, one of the males black, all wearing bulky jackets with a strip of black cloth tied around their upper arms – waited silently, their faces a battlefield of numb grief and anger. They seemed to think we didn't believe them when they said that the last time they'd seen Coop Hall was at noon when he'd left the governor's mansion. They said he'd seemed happy, even exhilarated. When I asked if they were sure he'd left as early as noon, they looked at me as if I'd accused them of killing him.

Noon? You could make that drive in twenty-five minutes. Hall had been shot entering Hillston at 2:45. Where'd he gone for over two hours? I asked them if they thought he might have come back here to the office. They didn't know. Pressed, they sullenly said they knew nothing about the contents of the file box, though the black male added that he thought Coop kept personal papers in it. The last time any of them had been in here themselves was early Saturday morning. Coop had been typing at his desk then, the girl said, and had told them he was waiting for a call, so for them to go ahead and pick up Jordan for the Raleigh trip. I said, 'Typing what?' The girl said she had no idea, probably a piece for *WL&J*. He wrote a lot of the copy himself. I asked about the most recent subjects he'd been working on.

'The House of Lords series, I guess,' she admitted begrudgingly.

'You mean the British Parliament?'

She looked disgusted by my lack of familiarity with their journal, and gave me a copy of the last issue. I glanced at its headline. 'FROM CAMPUS TO CAPITOL: NETWORKING, SOUTHERN STYLE. PART I. By Cooper Hall.' A quick skim of the lead paragraph told me that the House of Lords was a secret society founded in the 1920s for select male undergraduates at Haver University, and that membership in that club was the only open sesame to any future success in state politics or industry. I had no reason to doubt it, which made my modest advancement to police chief even more astonishing, I suppose, since I'd never even heard of the House of Lords. The names listed ended in the 1940s, but later details promised in Part II. I flipped through the thin newsprint, then stuck it in my coat pocket.

As I sat down at Coop's desk, the girl bristled. His typewriter was empty. Neat piles of paper revealed nothing startling. There were no photographs, no ashtrays, no paperweights, no knick-knacks. Just a wind-up clock that was still ticking, a calendar, a phone, and framed in plastic, another handwritten quotation.

IF A MAN HASN'T DISCOVERED SOMETHING HE WILL DIE FOR, HE ISN'T FIT TO LIVE.

MARTIN LUTHER KING, JR.

Holding the frame, I looked over at the college vigilants. Tears started down the girl's face, and the young black man, putting his arm around her, bit his mouth to keep from crying too. Well, they'd worked so hard to stop a death – succeeded, too, for years – focused so long on ending the death penalty, it was like they'd come to believe they were ending the very notion of death. So Cooper's annihilation must have been like a trapdoor, a side-swipe, the sudden crashing of a monster through barricades built to defend against more predictable enemies.

Foster's neck swivelled as he studied the room. 'Didn't happen till after five A.M., 'cause it rained 'bout an hour then, hard. No moisture under the window. Maybe tied to that blow-out in Canaan?'

The girl slipped from under her comforter's arm. Anger swelled her face. 'This is the Klan!' She pointed at the graffiti. 'Who else! They . . .' Her voice stumbled. '. . . murdered him, and then—' The two males closed around her, drew her away. She said to the black one, 'They aren't going to do *anything*! Look at them!'

Foster went on as if she hadn't interrupted him. 'Happened early. Everything in here's ice cold even with the heater pumping hard.'

Wes Pendergraph said Rosethorn wasn't answering his phone – which didn't mean he wasn't there. A baby-sitter at the Molinas told Wes she thought Dr Molina was in Winston-Salem, and that Mrs Molina was 'out.' In fact, Dr Molina had just called home, thinking his wife would be there. Like the Brooksides, the Molinas didn't appear to sit by the fire together much. It's clear my notion of marriage is way out-of-date.

Augustine Summers, Etham's handpicked assistant, showed up with a folder Etham had called him to bring. In it were enlarged copies of the anonymous letter Lee'd given me – which I'd handed over to the lab. Together they studied the copies, then the wall. Then Summers started photographing the graffiti. 'See it?' Foster said to me, holding an enlargement from the letter to Brookside ('ATHIEST COON-LOVERS') against the painted word 'ATHEISTS' on the wall. 'Bars on the Ts, the H?'

'Yeah, I see it,' I told him. 'I already thought it, too. Looks like his spelling's improved, doesn't it?'

Wind from the open window ruffled the months on Coop Hall's desk calendar. The black student struggled with himself, I watched it in his face; then he volunteered: 'I don't think Coop came back here yesterday, before, before it happened ... I got back to Hillston I guess around two, called here a couple of times, and just got the machine. The tape ran out on me the last time, so I don't figure he'd dropped by for messages. Anyhow ...' He gestured at the trashed room. 'This stuff, it's nothing new. October, they threw a rock through that window there.'

I nodded at him. 'No, nothing new. 'Bout four thousand years older than you and me. But you're still trying to stop it. So am I. You believe that?'

The girl said, 'Eric, that's bullshit.'

I said, 'Cooper Hall died yesterday. Today is Sunday. My detectives have already interrogated over thirty people with Klan connections or records of civil rights violations, including those we charged in the Trinity Church demonstration. Police officers who were up all night trying to stop a riot are out today trying to find out who killed Cooper. And that includes me. So you want to watch your mouth, young lady.' She turned her back on me.

Eric kept staring at me. 'What's going to happen to those Canaan kids you arrested last night? One of them's related to the Halls ... I don't know if you know that.'

'I know it. He's been released on bail.'

'Martin's never been in any kind of trouble before.'

I nodded again. 'I know that too. All I can tell you is what I want to happen. Suspended sentences, and time on Canaan Street repairing the damage they did. What I don't want is for them to do it again.'

The white male snapped, 'Sure! I bet the Klan's going to repair the damage they did here, too. What about the "damage" to Coop Hall?!' He poked his upper arm at me, jabbing his finger at the black strip tied there. 'What about Coop Hall?'

I looked a while at the anger in his reddened eyes. 'Oh, I want whoever did that to go to jail a long long time.'

His lip curled. 'One thing's for sure; he won't get the death penalty, not if he's white! You can bet the fuck that's for sure.'

'You're not telling me that's what you want, are you?' I buttoned my overcoat and felt for my gloves. 'The death penalty for whoever killed Coop Hall?' With my glove I tapped Foster, bent over the open windowsill with his penlight and magnifier.

'Going to find Rosethorn.' The back of his head lifted an inch in acknowledgement.

A siren shrieked, short, loud, and right beside me, scaring a bunch of us on the sidewalk into banging up against each other. In a patrol car, Officer Nancy White was trolling along Jupiter, waving her arm to catch my eye. She was alone in the front; in back behind the screen squirmed a big, unshaven, wild-eyed, ugly mental case, handcuffed to the steel mesh. Pedestrians pushed for a look, as I climbed in the front. 'Friend of yours back there, Nancy?' The man growled and kicked at the seat. 'Drive me to the Piedmont Hotel, we're collecting a crowd. Where's your partner DiMallo?'

'Already took him home.' She drove with the forefinger of her left hand. 'Then I see this squirrel here, listen, he's *peeing in* a Salvation Army Christmas pot right in front of Belk's. Folks screaming their heads off. I'm unloading him at UH.'

'Jesus, yes. Don't bring him to our place!'

I estimated the man's weight at 190. Nancy's is probably 130. She's five-seven, wears her hair in a sort of floppy flat-top, her skin's too pale and you can see some acne scars, but her eyes are a fine thick-lashed hazel, and she's got a great smile. Nothing scares Nancy, at least not since her dad died when she was twelve. He used to beat the shit out of her, but nobody's done it since. First week she was on the force, she broke up a fight outside the Tucson Lounge between two hicks I wouldn't have got near without a sledgehammer. One of them tried to stuff her in a trash can. McInnis was with her, but he said all he did was help her pick the two guys up off the floor and put the cuffs on them. I told her then, she ought to be careful who she took on, because I didn't want her hurt. She said, 'Chief Mangum, if I'm messed with, if somebody gets in my face, they're the one you better tell be careful, 'cause, listen here, no man alive's gonna shove me in no trash can.' Like I say, she'd run a girls' gang. Natural leader. I asked her now, 'You subdue this charming character on your own?' He was shaking the screen hard behind my head.

'Couldn't dance around.' She popped her gum. 'These type squirrels, you know how they get all muscled up? They can *hurt* you. Had to use my stick on him.'

'Doesn't seem to have bothered him much.' Muttering a mantra of 'Fucking yeah I know I know fuck yeah I know,' the man punctuated each word with kicks and rattles. 'Fact, Nancy, I don't believe you even got his attention yet.'

She pulled up in front of the shabby genteel Piedmont Hotel, and wiggled sideways to face me. Her collar was open showing a gaudy gold heart on a gold chain – the kind of gold that's likely to go green on you. She said, 'Listen here, Chief—'

'Officer White, where's your tie?'

'Oh, come on, I'm in the *car*. My shift's over. Why do I have to wear the tie in the car!'

''Cause you keep hopping *out* of the car to make the streets safe for democracy. Put the tie on.'

She said, 'Crap,' snatched the already looped tie from behind the sun visor, and pulled it over her head. Behind the screen, the 'squirrel' appeared to have lulled himself into a stupor with his chant. 'Chief,' she began again, talking fast. 'I know you're dealing with heavy shit now, but you said how if something bugged us, come and tell you.' Her voice sped up. 'They just put me partners with that hemorrhoid Emory. I can't hack that type detail. I mean, it's not gonna go down. That man gets his rocks off shining his *badge*. I'll pull night shift, holidays, but *please*—'

I picked up her hat off the floor by my feet. 'Nancy, no. Nope. I already had this same talk with Emory—'

'What'd he say!'

'Well, he didn't accuse you of polishing your badge. Look, we rotate so everybody gets to know everybody, gets to learn from everybody, gets to feel like a family—'

'Crap, forget that!'

'—After two weeks, you come and tell me five things you *like* about John Emory, then we'll talk.'

'What am I gonna *like* about that turkey?'

'I don't know. Find out. And put your hat on.' I handed it to her. 'That true, you play the trombone?'

She was still shaking her head. 'Yeah, I played it in stupid high-school band so I could get away from home, that's all.'

'Well, Emory plays the piano.'

'With his gloves on? . . . Okay, can't blame me for trying. Sorry I bugged you at home. I mean, bugged your machine.'

'That's o——' I slapped my leg. 'Make a U, and take me back down Crowell. Then you get this guy to UH. Go on, go on.'

'What's the matter?' She swung the car into its turn.

I shook a finger at her. 'I wasn't listening. Cops shouldn't talk, Nancy. Cops should listen.'

Machine. The student Eric had told me he'd called the *With Liberty and Justice* office, but got 'Coop's machine.' And if the tape had run out before Eric could say anything, it must be full of messages, the last ones Coop Hall had heard, or maybe had never heard. At any rate, the callers were potentially very interesting.

Somebody else had obviously thought so too, because when I opened the top to the small machine on his desk, the cassette for incoming messages had been removed.

I let myself into Isaac Rosethorn's smoke-rank, crammed and jumbled two-room suite on the top floor of the musty Piedmont Hotel, and found something else missing from its regular place. The little aluminium suitcase that Isaac kept under shoe boxes of bird nests on the shelf of his closet was gone. So was his electric shaver, his bathrobe, and the old photograph of Edith Keene that always sat on his bedside table. Ashtrays were stuffed with cigarette butts, Chinese food cartons on the big desk were pretty putrid, I couldn't see the floor for the law books and newspapers on it, I couldn't see the view for the grime on the windows, and I couldn't see the ugly flowered bedspread for the clothes, legal pads, and record albums tossed around there. In fact, everything looked fairly normal, except that Isaac wasn't lying on the sagging, cracked leather couch, or slumped in the swivel chair behind the eight-foot worktable, or seated on the toilet in the tiny bathroom, through whose open door he would continue to carry on conversations with me (an informal style of receiving visitors that he claimed to share with Louis XIV and L.B.J.). Isaac doesn't like to travel – except mentally. But his home was small, he was large, and it was clear in seconds that he wasn't anywhere around.

I called down to the desk clerk, who said he hadn't noticed Rosethorn leave, but added he'd been 'pretty busy' all afternoon – though certainly not in welcoming new guests or vacuuming the Piedmont lobby, which was consistently both filthy and deserted. I told him to go find out if Isaac's Studebaker was parked in its spot in the hotel garage behind the building. He said he was still pretty busy, I said I was the chief of police, and he said he'd be right back with the information. While waiting, I shamelessly picked the lock of the desk drawer where Isaac kept a cigar box of 'emergency cash,' usually about a thousand dollars in twenties. The box was empty. Last time I'd seen him empty that box – a dozen years ago – he'd been gone for two months. He'd come back with a woman whom a client of his had been accused of murdering.

The desk clerk must have run the whole way; he panted that the Studebaker was right there. 'What did Rosethorn do? Something serious?' he asked hopefully.

'Library fines,' I said and hung up.

I phoned the department (that's what I call our floors of the Municipal Building; Justin calls them 'headquarters'). It took Brenda Moore a few hours to learn that Isaac had not taken a plane or rental car out of the area, at least not charged to his own name, nor taken a cab or bus with anyone who'd recognized his picture (and believe me, around here, his face stood out in a crowd). Before I left his room, I read through the top pile of papers on the desk. Among them was a recent State Supreme Court decision rejecting an appeal claiming disproportionate use of the law against blacks. Isaac's fat inked comments on their ruling were mostly obscene. I knew he'd been hoping for (without expecting) a favourable decision on this case so he could use it for George Hall. Except that he'd always known, as he'd once said, 'Listen to me, Slim, you don't get your appeals by great legal leaps in enlightenment. You get them by little procedural screw-ups. The law's an anal-compulsive. That's its virtue and vice both. Law is like that British clerk at the labour camp in *Heart of Darkness*. He keeps off the jungle by wearing a pressed suit and tie. Meanwhile, his company's working poor Africans to death. You read *The Heart of Darkness*? Extraordinary tale.'

I told him, 'I did better than read it. I went to Vietnam.'

I was remembering this conversation about procedural screw-ups now because I'd noticed a clipping from a recent *Hillston Star*, stapled to a folder labelled 'Hall appeal' on his desk. It was a small article: a local man had won a malpractice suit against a doctor who eight years ago had performed an operation that had so permanently impaired this man's hearing that two years later he'd been fired from his job, and the following summer been struck by a motorcycle he hadn't heard approaching. The man's name, Darwin Wheelwright, was circled with Isaac's thick black pen. It sounded vaguely familiar. But I couldn't place it. That's one of the differences between my brain and Isaac Rosethorn's. He must have recognized it immediately. Because when I turned on some lights, after the sun gave up trying to slip through the grime on the windows, the long blackboard against the far wall finally caught my eye. The 'thinking board,' he called it. Ever since I'd known him, it had been covered with squiggly diagrams and cryptic outlines. Now I realized my name was scrawled in block letters in a free space near the top margin.

CUDDY. I'll be back. And by the way, Juror #9 at George's first trial was deaf as a post.

Chapter 8

On Christmas Eve morning, Mayor Carl Yarborough told me, 'Give me a present, Cuddy. A suspect on Cooper Hall, okay?' I had to give him a bottle of Scotch instead. Our highway witnesses had proved pretty useless. One teenaged girl said 'an old white car' had sped past her 'real fast' seconds before she drove over the crest and saw the wreck, but she could give no other details. Nobody else had come forward with information of any sort, and the fact is (*pace* the little-grey-cells techniques of brainy-type detectives like you meet on the Orient Express), most of our cases get solved on the phone-in-tip method. Somebody squeals on X, and *then* we apply detection to figure out how X did it. I didn't have any X yet. Justin was assuming it was Willie Slidell, especially after Bruce Parker went back out to the farm and found it shut up, with the barn emptied – no giant cylinders of Fanshaw paper, no white Ford on blocks. And no Willie Slidell, when Slidell's supervisor thought Willie was home on sick leave. Slidell's sister said that he'd driven his station wagon to Kentucky Sunday night to try to patch things up with his estranged wife. Justin had located the estranged Kentucky wife by phone; she said she had neither seen Slidell, nor expected him. Trying to patch things up with her would have been futile anyhow as she'd 'been with somebody a lot better for three years,' which was when she'd lost patience with 'Willie the Wimp.'

According to Willie's sister, Willie had never had a white Ford, had never had anybody staying at the farm with him, had never stolen from his job, never attended any white-supremacy meetings, and in general never done a single thing to warrant Justin's asking her these questions. And yes, Willie'd been right there at her house Saturday from noon till nine, so he couldn't have killed Cooper. Justin had a feeling she was lying.

So we had a bulletin out for Slidell. And a bulletin out for Billy Gilchrist; not just because Paul Madison was pestering me twice a day, but because I wanted to know what Billy's name was doing in Coop's address book. Meanwhile, when I cornered Otis Newsome and his brother Purley in the Municipal Building lobby, Otis told me he still had no idea why Coop Hall should have Clark Koontz's card with the name Newsome written on it. Purley Newsome sneered, 'Me neither,' and walked off. Dead of cancer, Koontz was in no position to contradict either of them.

Otis was a short fat blond man, like the result if somebody had put his baby brother Purley in a trash compactor. His devotion to Purley was as strong (and misguided) as his opinion that I ought to be fired, Carl Yarborough (against whom he'd run for mayor) ought to be impeached, and 'left-wingers' like Alice MacLeod ought to be burned. Otis was a devout Julian Lewis man, and a suckbutt to the North Hillston crowd. He was in charge of the town's purchases, and the town purchased tons of paper supplies, all of them from Fanshaw Paper Company. I asked him if he knew a Fanshaw clerk named Willie Slidell. He said no, why should he?

'Who do you deal with at Fanshaw?'

He said, 'I deal with Dyer Fanshaw direct.'

'You two were in college together, at Haver, weren't you?'

'So what?'

I said, 'Well, Otis, I'd hate to think you weren't taking time to entertain some competitive bids on those paper contracts.'

His fists twisted inside his Madras pants pockets like he was struggling to get them out, and couldn't. He said, 'I'm not going to waste any time talking to you, that's for sure. And I heard how you made Purley eat that ticket in front of his friends.' I said, 'What friends?,' but he talked right over me. 'Don't you think it's going to be forgotten. There're a lot of us who never wanted you appointed chief.'

I said, 'But not enough of you.'

Otis had dry blinky eyes, but his smile was greasy, like his hair, and he always flashed his teeth when he jabbed me with his favourite needle: 'There were a *lot* of us. But you had old Cadmean behind you.'

123

I wanted to tell him to go to hell, but instead I smiled back. 'Right. So I heard.'

'Well, you don't have him anymore. Things are going to change in this state, soon as Lewis gets in. We're going to get rid of your kind.'

'Meaning what, Otis? No more intelligent tall people?'

With a scowl, he trotted away across the lobby's loud marble floor.

According to the paper, there were five funerals in Hillston on Christmas Eve. I went to two of them. The first, Briggs Cadmean's at Presbyterian, drew the larger crowd. The pews were so packed, the furs so thick, the floral displays stacked so high, that by the time Mrs Atwater Randolph warbled 'Abide With Me,' the whole place, despite the frigid weather, felt like a steamy greenhouse. 'Our number' from North Hillston attended en masse – as if everybody I'd seen Friday at the Club dance had changed out of their evening clothes and hurried off to church together. Sprinkled among them were distinguished out-of-owners: men whose hired drivers waited outside, stamping their feet like carriage horses; men who would fly back home to Atlanta or Richmond or Birmingham in time to sing carols with the family tonight. It crossed my mind as I studied this crowd that an anarchist could lob a single bomb through First Presbyterian's plate glass right now and take a big chunk out of the top junta of southeastern industry, politics, and social life.

Accompanied by their wives, both gubernatorial candidates – Julian Lewis on the right aisle between the governor and the Dyer Fanshaws, Andy Brookside on the left between Mayor and Mrs Yarborough and a US senator – prominently displayed bowed heads during the prayers. Lee didn't close her eyes, but did look solemn. She wore a black wool suit with a small grey cap that had a black feather across it. At two points, Brookside leaned over to whisper something to her, and the feather brushed across his face. At one point Carl Yarborough whispered something to him that made him smile. Just the mayor's sitting there beside Brookside was in itself talking loud and clear to Hillston, as had a standing ovation from those black business leaders in Winston-Salem on Monday. It looked like Jack Molina's impromptu speech about Coop Hall to the TV cameras up on that porch stoop had swept his candidate right into the arms of the black vote, or maybe Brookside had finally got out his calculator and realized that 100 per cent of 20 per cent of the voters meant he only needed 31 per cent of all the rest.

High above us in his white wood pulpit, Thomas Campbell swallowed his chagrin at losing old Cadmean's cavernous estate to Trinity Episcopal, and preached a sad pious eulogy about the good servant who had made his talents multiply, grown prosperous by Divine Election, died a symbol of his nation's great blessings (blessings he had returned sevenfold to his city, state, fellowman, beloved family). And now he was welcomed to his heavenly home by the Christ Child Himself, here on the very eve of that Child's wondrous birthday. Home for Christmas, home for all eternity. Old Briggs would have guffawed through the first ten minutes, and slept through the next twenty. As for his beloved family, the few ambulatory sons he had left sat with a mingle of grandchildren, great-grandchildren, in-laws, distant relatives, and a sobbing elderly woman with a black veil, who turned out to have been his fifth ex-wife (whom he'd left thirty-five years ago for Briggs Junior's mother) and who'd come all the way from Sarasota to make a play for a cut of the old man's estate. Her noisy presence and the even noisier absence of Briggs Junior (the presumed heiress) were the two human-interest highlights of the service. From the hiss of indignation I overheard on the steps (as old Cadmean's silver-handled casket was carried past the news cameras by a palsied son of his, the bank, the towel company, A. R. Randolph, Senator Kip Dollard, and Justin Savile), it was clear that Hillston was outraged by Briggs Junior's failure to attend her own father's funeral after he'd left her ten million dollars that all she had to do for was give up her career and come back home. I took considerable satisfaction in having predicted her response to Papa's codicil; as at least Alice admitted while we were waiting near the hearse for Justin to get their car. 'Okay, Cuddy, you were right.'

'My favourite words in the language, honey.'

'Thank God you didn't marry that bitch.'

I was shocked and said so. 'Alice MacLeod, a feminist like yourself, and you can't see why she was insulted by that SOB's will!'

Alice shivered as the freezing wind flattened our coats against our legs. 'Of course I can see why Briggs was insulted. I'm not saying she shouldn't have told him to fuck off. I'm saying she should have come to the bastard's funeral.' Alice turned to shake

125

hands sweetly with Judge and Mrs Tiggs, who were quarrelling about whether it was too cold to go to the cemetery, or too rude not to. Then Justin pulled up, and as I helped Alice into the Austin, she asked, 'Any word from Isaac?'

'Zip-a-dee-doo-dah for two days. Vanished. You don't suppose that after sixty years a man would suddenly decide to take a Christmas vacation and fly off to Bermuda or Squaw Valley?'

Justin said, 'He's working on the Hall case, betcha five bucks.'

'Let's hope. We could use some help. Drive careful, J.B.S., this lady's bearing my godchild. See y'all at the grave, which is bound to be a big one. I'm imagining something about on the scale of Rameses the Second.'

Out on the church steps, I stopped Dyer Fanshaw, and asked him to tell me about his salesman Clark Koontz. 'What about him? He died,' said Fanshaw, annoyed at being separated from the governor and lieutenant governor, who were getting photographed by a Raleigh reporter. 'You better talk to my sales manager,' he added, admitting, 'I don't really know all that much about lower-level employees. Excuse me.'

I held him by the cuff of his herringbone tweed. 'Well, Dyer, that may be a mistake. We have reason to believe that one of them – fellow named Willie Slidell – may be stealing your paper, great big old rolls full.'

Fanshaw changed colours fast, his ears turned as red as his cheeks, his lips as white as his hair. 'What are you talking about?' he asked, then apparently decided he didn't want an answer, because he pointed at the hearse, waiting behind two of my motorcycle cops, looked at me with extreme annoyance, maybe because discussing robberies was bad manners at a funeral, maybe because I'd made him miss his photo opportunity with the governor, and he walked away.

I noticed that Andy Brookside, bright hair ruffled in the wind, had paused at the top of the church steps, chatting with the Yarboroughs, until Governor Wollston and Lewis had reached their limousine. Then he touched Lee's arm and started down, brisk but saddened. He looked as good outdoors as he had at the Club dance. I also noticed that the reporters took more pictures of him than they had of anyone else. What struck me, seeing him, was the literalness of the metaphor 'magnetic.' People lining the steps actually leaned towards him, as if pulled there.

'Hello, Cuddy, how are you?' Lee paused beside me, and already halfway past, Brookside turned back.

'Hi, Lee. Not the merriest of Christmas Eves, is it?'

She and I talked about the funeral while Brookside shook several hands thrust at him; after which he grinned at me cheerfully. 'Hello again. My apologies. I hadn't realized Friday that you and Lee were such old friends. She says you knew each other when you were kids.' He took her gloved hand in his. 'That's what's so wonderful about these small Southern towns. The past keeps coming back.'

'Wonderful or horrible,' Lee said, and smiled.

'Isn't that true in New England too?' I asked him.

He laughed. 'I have no idea. Because *I* don't keep coming back. I'm a Tarheel now, an adopted son of the South.' A grey Jaguar sedan stopped near us, and the young driver I'd seen holding Lee's fur coat outside my office scooted around to open the door for her. She nodded good-bye, as she slid inside the leathery interior.

Brookside gestured at the open door. 'A lift to the cemetery?'

'No thanks. My car's right up there.'

He looked at her, then me, then suddenly took me by the arm, and stepped me away from the kerb. His eyes were as aquamarine as a travel poster for the Virgin Islands. 'Jack Molina said you wanted to talk to me about those, what'll we call them, anonymous threats?'

'I did. I phoned your office twice.'

'Sorry I didn't get back to you, Captain. Things have been crazy.'

'Yes.'

He shook his head. 'God, for *you*. The Canaan fallout from the murder! You must be half nuts.'

'Does it show?'

His smile, I admit, was a beauty. 'So it seems hardly worth even—' He waved good-bye to three men that people claimed owned a county apiece in the western part of the state. 'Sorry. Anyhow, cleaning out the last little bits in my Haver offices, I did find an earlier one of those "your-days-are-numbered" notes. How about this, we go right past Haver on the way to North Hills Cemetery. You give me a ride. We'll whip in and I'll get the letter for you.'

'. . . Well, actually I've got my dog in my—'

'Just a second. Let me tell Lee.'

He was so quick, I'd been so unprepared for his suggestion, I hadn't realized fast enough how little I wanted to have him in my car. Plus I hated to think why. Hated to think I was embarrassed by an Oldsmobile that my daddy would have sold his soul for. Hated to think that I couldn't stand to be around Andy Brookside because I was jealous of him.

I didn't hear what he was saying to Lee, but she nodded and looked at me gratefully. Well, after all, I *had* promised to help.

Like everybody else in his life, Martha Mitchell fell for Brookside as soon as she laid eyes on him. She squirmed right into his lap and he patted her as he admitted he'd thrown two or three earlier anonymous letters away, 'afraid I just balled them up and tossed them like the rest of the garbage. You can't fret over flak. You have to gun the throttle and fly through it.'

'Well, maybe you can, but *I* can't afford to dismiss anonymous threats on your life, Mr Brookside. Guns are cheap, and brains are rare.' In my rearview mirror I watched the funeral cortege pull out behind the motorcycle escort, then I cut off down a side street. 'And by the by, you keep on letting your speechwriter accuse Reverend Brodie Cheek of being in the Klan, if not in on a murder, you're gonna piss off a lot more anonymous people than the one already writing to you. There're two hundred fifty thousand right-wing born-againers on Cheek's mailing list. Lot of votes.'

He cocked his head at me. 'Yeah, I heard Jack's rhetoric got a little fervent at the Hall house.' It didn't seem to bother him. Apparently, he saw Molina as a stalking horse to herd in any stray believers still waiting around left field for the old dream to show up. He said, 'It's all true, though.'

'Well, it's true Brodie Cheek's a foaming reactionary. But I'm not sure he's in kahoots with the Klan, much less the Constitution Club, and I *am* sure the members of that club, including Senator Kip Dollard and Julian Lewis and probably a fifth of the guests at that funeral we just left, aren't going to appreciate hearing Molina lump them in with the lumper. Not to mention hearing on TV how Cooper Hall's a "martyr to their racist fear and hate."'

Brookside glanced out the window at two young women at the stoplight who laughed as a gust of wind lifted their shopping bags almost sideways. 'Jack had that SDS gleam in his eye, hunh? ... That's a beatiful girl there, the one in the blue coat.' He rubbed at his neck where a thin scar ran from his hairline down into his collar. 'Well, he keeps a small altar fire burning to the flame of the sixties.'

I nodded. 'I heard Molina at a few rallies, back when he was in college. He was wild in those days. Campus cops bashed him on the head once; he soaked his shirt in the gash, climbed up on the shoulders of the Charles R. Haver statue, started waving that bloody shirt and yelling, "Not 'my country, right or wrong!' My country, *right* the wrong!"'

Brookside's laugh was affectionate. 'Sounds like him.' One of the women's scarf blew off, and they chased it down the sidewalk. 'Jack thought very highly of Cooper Hall.'

'And you? Ever meet Coop?'

He reached down to straighten a black silk sock. 'His loss strikes me as a far greater waste than his brother's would have been. From what I've heard, at least. Not that I don't commend the efforts to stop the brother's execution. But I haven't shared Jack's passion about it.'

A considerable understatement; and his tolerant tone provoked me into saying, 'From what I hear, Molina's trying to haul you off the fence on the capital punishment issue, but you got both legs locked tight around the rail.'

He looked bemused. 'Who told you that – Alice? You're friendly with her, right?'

'Right.' His dropping in Alice's name so casually set my teeth on edge. Or maybe I was just mad at Martha Mitchell for her downright sickening eagerness to get her head under Brookside's hand. I said, 'No, it was Lee who told me.'

The bemused look stretched into surprise. 'Lee? Really? That's interesting.' Then the pleasant smile returned. He crossed his long, elegant legs and gave one a pat. 'Yes, you could put it that way, I suppose.' The smile was replaced by earnestness. 'But I do agree, in principle, that the death penalty's barbaric.' He ticked off his points on his fingers. 'It's also discriminatory, it's not a deterrent, and I'm sure innocent people do get executed, et cetera, et cetera.' He let the other hand stand in for the rest of the arguments. 'But frankly where do we set our priorities? How many convicts are even on Death Row in this country now?'

'About nineteen hundred.'

'Not even two thousand.' He held out a palm in a 'Okay, case proved?' gesture. 'In the general scheme of things we're talking *very* small numbers, and let's admit it, most of them *are* criminals of one sort or another.'

I was in more of a position to admit it than he was, and did so. 'Yep, most of the folks we kill have killed somebody, or at

129

least been in the vicinity emptying a cash register while a friend killed somebody.'

He hadn't quite decided about my tone yet, but it only showed in a slight squeezing of his eyebrows. 'Most murders occur during robberies?'

'No, most murders occur during jealous fits or marital spats. A passion crime, and a one-per-customer crime. But the state picks and chooses the little per cent it's going to *execute* for murder, and the state's partial to robbery murder, because the state's partial to protecting property – especially white property.' I mentioned that nothing made our DA, Mitchell Bazemore, happier than a felony homicide; he'd get himself twelve males, wave the capitalist flag in their noses, and turn them into a hanging jury faster than you could say Dirty Harry. Brookside was with me now; his eyebrows had relaxed. He had a fine listening style, so intense I could feel it without looking at him. I said, 'So folks get the notion that the death penalty's going to hold down stickups and muggings. It won't.'

'You don't like Mitchell Bazemore.'

'No.'

'He has an impressive record of convictions as prosecutor.'

'So did the Inquisition.' It occurred to me that I was maybe talking to the next governor, a guy who'd have jobs and judge-ships jingling in his pockets like loose change. Could be he was interviewing *me* right now; he was for sure checking out Baze-more, whose possible rising future I did my best to sink fast, when Brookside asked me to 'describe the man.' I told him, 'Mitch is honest, dedicated, hardworking, mean-spirited, small-minded, moralistic, bigoted, and rigid as Rasputin.'

He smiled. 'His reputation—'

'His reputation is for capital convictions – what he calls his "winning streak" – and the more he's got, the more he gets. Juries are just as much suckers for reputation as the rest of us. He's sent nine men to Death Row from Haver County since I've been chief.'

'And one's George Hall.'

'No, Hall's been there a lot longer than that . . . I watched one of those men get executed myself, which believe me, judges and juries should be obliged to do.' (His neck stiffened on that bit of info.) 'Three got out on appeals. And of the five that are still waiting, four are black, none had private lawyers, or educations, or money, or connections – or any of the goodies that if you do have them, nine hundred and ninety-nine times out of a thousand, you don't end up on Death Row.'

Brookside nodded carefully. 'I grant everything that implies. It still seems to me there're more productive battlefields to fight on than capital punishment. Welfare's a racist tool too, and a far more pervasive one. Poverty itself – 'He stopped himself – and rumpled his hair. 'But, well, Jack doesn't agree, of course.'

That was so transparent, it made you wonder why in the world he'd ever wanted Molina to help with his campaign.

He appeared to be fine at reading faces as well as listening, because he said, 'Why did I hire Jack? Because he's a very, very good speechwriter. The real question is, why'd he take the job?' Martha had flopped right over on her back, and he was rubbing her stomach as he smiled at me. 'Jack finds me hopelessly pragmatic, a cool impurist of the most unpalatable sort. In fact, he doesn't really even like me. But he's killing himself to get me elected, because he'd rather have Impure Brookside than the alternative, which is just more of the same dumb smug thieves.'

I turned off Main Street under the canopy of flying Santas, and passed the post office where the flag was still lowered for Cadmean. I said, with a grin, 'And are you?'

He grinned back. 'A dumb smug thief? No.'

'How 'bout a cool impurist?'

I watched from the corner of my eye as he folded his arms on his overcoat and appeared to give the question some thought; he had a way of making everything he said (for all I knew, stock phrases from standard speeches) sound spontaneous. 'Purity in politics fails. So it's useless. So, yes, I have no use for it. Too many things need to be done to waste time failing.'

Stopping for the light, I turned to him. 'Well, there's pure, and then there's Pure. I don't like the one kind much myself.'

'Which is?'

'The kind that leads to the stake. Usually the type Purist who ends up in the fire himself has felt just fine about sending other guys there ahead of him. Savanarola. Thomas More. That type Purist. But then, you're not that type, are you?'

Brookside swivelled around, throwing his arm along the seat back, giving me a slow look, as if he'd decided I was a lot more interesting than he'd thought. I've got that look from other folks of his background over the years. He asked, '. . . So, why'd you join the police? Aren't they our Inquisitors?'

'Because chaos always made me nervous. After Vietnam, it made me *real* nervous. So I build my little roads of law and order, and folks can walk around then, and don't have to worry much about getting their feet blown off every time they take a step.'

From the way he nodded, I figured he'd followed me back to the Mekong, where guys like me – sweat-slick, bug-stung, and scared shitless to move on or stay where we were – would look up when we heard those bright cool planes diving into clouds miles above us.

The light changed, and we were both quiet for a couple of blocks. Then he picked up the two political biographies lying on my seat (just purchased – in fact, just published), and asked if I didn't think one was 'excellent' and the other a 'disappointment' after a previous work by the same author. I mentioned his own book on Vietnam, and he brushed it aside ('It's okay, but I've read better'), dismissing his Pulitzer as 'a fluke,' just the result of all the press hoopla he'd got for 'this and that' (the Medal of Honor? the White House job?). Then he solicited my views on the state's law enforcement and prison systems; he asked good questions and listened to the answers.

All right. As Alice had said, he was bright, knowledgeable, charming, interested, and interesting. I was ready to vote for him myself by the time we'd passed through the gates of the high stone wall that protects Haver University from Hillston. And I didn't even like him.

Inside the walls, perfectly placed trees lined perfectly paved drives through acres of Gothic architecture perfectly replicated in Appalachian stone. Even in winter the grass inside the walls seemed richer than the grass outside. Brookside pointed out various new dormitories he'd had built and the sites for additions to come, including the future Cadmean Textiles Laboratory. Without any students on campus, the place looked strangely private; without all the cars, it looked timeless. It was as if some affable medieval lord were taking me on a solitary tour of his ancestral duchy.

I asked him if he were going to miss being president of Haver.

He looked out over the cloistered buildings. 'Not really. I got some cobwebs cleared out, and blew away some dust, but academia, well, you know what it's like. It's, oh, the sonorous drone of long-winded big frogs croaking at each other across a little pond. It's cream soup with dowagers who may leave you Eliot's money if they don't leave it to Vassar instead.' He stretched, as if three years in the Groves had cramped all his muscles. 'Nope, I find it just a little slow.' He gave a bored glance at the Eustace Dollard Memorial Library, where I'd sat up a lot of nights reading history to pass my MA orals.

I said, 'Even with ten thousand twenty-year-olds running around loose? My. What do you think you'd find fast enough?'

He smiled. It was hard to believe he hadn't paid a fortune for those teeth. 'Captain – I'm sorry, that's your rank, isn't it, as chief, Captain?'

I shrugged with a nod. 'Captain's as high as it goes downtown, Major.'

It wasn't that he was missing my irony; it appeared to appeal to him. I didn't much like the idea of his liking me, but he gave me the feeling he did. 'Course, that's his profession, giving folks that feeling. He said, 'What's fast enough? Well, your job. When you're really *there, in* it, that's what I mean by fast enough.' He swivelled around on the seat again; his face had the star glow to it. 'Imagine what we could do if we used *everything* in ourselves? All of it, full out! But whoever does? That's what I want. To *move* with everything in me. Like the first hundred days of Roosevelt's presidency. Bonaparte's consulship—'

'Hitler's blitzkrieg?'

He looked at me, more disappointed than annoyed. 'No. Mozart. Keats's odes. Einstein.'

'Well, now, I believe Einstein lived on a college campus, didn't he?'

Brookside tapped his head hard. 'He lived *in here*. He used what he had. We should all do that. People are sloths.'

I said, 'Yeah, thank God. We all ain't got that much up here.' I tapped my own head, 'I've met a lot of folks in my line of work, I don't *want* to see them using every messy thing they got mucking around in their noggins. Trust me, let 'em stay slothful.'

He shook back a lock of hair impatiently. 'Come on, I'm not talking about ordinary people. I'm talking about people like *us*.'

'Oh.' I cracked open a window; the VIP view of life always made me feel stuffy fast. I asked, 'What kind is that?'

'You'd like to change things in this state, if you had the power? You already know what at least some of those things are? You'd like to *have* the power?' He shook one of the biographies at me. 'Exactly. So would I. Well, most people would rather have a bigger television set. They haven't the imagination, the energy, the soul, the whatever it is, to demand beyond the personal. Not on their own. Of course, they *want* to want more. That's why the single Kennedy line everybody remembers is the "Ask not" line. Right? ". . . ask what *you can do* for your country."'

'Tell you the truth, I could use a bigger TV set myself.'

'I'm quite serious,' he told me sternly.

'I know. This where I turn?'

Frowning, he pointed to an entrance. It was clear I'd let my maybe future governor down. No doubt, I could kiss state commissioner of police adios. But at least I was sure now that it wasn't just because of Lee that I *wanted* to rub him the wrong way. 'Look,' he told me. 'I'm as much a little-d democrat as the next man. Absolutely – "As I would not be a slave, so I would not be a master." But it's sentimental horseshit to deny *vast* differences in capacity.'

I said, 'Um hum. But let me paraphrase your little-d democrat, old too-honest Abe. As I would not be a star, so I would not be a star-fucker.'

I got the eyebrow squeeze, but he rallied fast and said, 'Depends on the star, doesn't it? Aren't some fucks more desirable than others?' He lifted Martha into the back seat, and that ended our two-man symposium.

Parking behind Rowell Hall, where the president's offices were, I saw a grey Porsche at the end of the lot, and asked if it was his. He flicked at his handsome forehead. 'I forgot! Right, the driver picked me up here for the funeral.' He jumped out of my car, then leaned back in. 'How'd you know it was mine?'

'Lee told me you'd found the note on the windshield. Parked here?'

'Right. Hold on, I'll be back in a second.'

He didn't invite me to come along, so I looked around the area near his Porsche. As Lee had said, there was a little sign on a post: RESERVED: PRESIDENT BROOKSIDE. But still, sticking a death threat under a car windshield seemed an odd choice. Why not mail it, or shove it under a door? I glanced up at the ivy-latticed grey stones of Rowell Hall. Just as I did, on the second floor, at a set of arched windows, someone pulled back a drape, and looked down. She was a young woman, slender, black-haired, and she seemed to be staring in my direction. She pressed one hand flat against the glass, and held to the drape with the other. When she saw me, she stepped back from the window. I walked to my car, and got in. Five minutes later, Brookside strode across the parking lot towards me. He came around to my door, and handed me two manila folders.

'Here you go, Captain Mangum. You appear to have trouble seeing why Jack Molina chose to – shall we say? – hitch his wagon to my particular star. Read this.' He looked down at me, his head tilted the way he held it when he listened, or had his picture taken. 'The other folder's the crank letter. If I get any more, I promise I'll let you know. This one was under the windshield about a month ago.'

I opened the folder with the letter; it looked to be along the same general drift as the one Lee'd given me. Also the same strong upward slash on the *Ts* in 'QUIT BEFORE IT'S TOO LATE.'

The larger folder held a typed report. Its first page made clear that it was the source of Jack Molina's remark about 'Brodie Cheek's Constitution Club.' A neat diagram graphed lines of connection among (A) public officials belonging to that club – including Senator Kip Dollard and his baby cousin, Lieutenant Governor Lewis – (B) private money men belonging to that club – including Dyer Fanshaw and the now departed Briggs Cadmean – and (C) leading corporations, trusts, organizations, alliances, and/or drives around the state on which these officials and moneymen had sat as boards, directors, trustees, consultants, and/or honorary members. Arrows pointed down to (D): smaller businesses, etc. owned by the businesses, etc. listed in (C). From (C) neat arrows shot at a list of contributors to 'Christian Family, Inc.' (of which the Reverend Brodie Cheek was president). So, if you skipped from the top of this page to the bottom, it did give the impression that fancy folks (who'd sure never invite trash like Cheek to their dances) just might be contributing money to radio shows of his that told the Common Christian White People that they might be down-and-out, but in God's book they were better than blacks, homos, Jews, Commies, and Secular Humanists like Andy Brookside. There were no lines leading from Christian Family, Inc down to any little box labelled 'KKK,' but that was going to be a hard line to draw. If Christian Family was donating to the Klan, they probably didn't bother filing deductions with the IRS.

I told Brookside, 'Somebody's been working hard. Who dug it up for you?'

He gestured around him, as if at the university itself. 'I have a very bright, and dedicated, and passionate staff.'

'Like Jack Molina?'

'Among many others.' He pointed at the folder. 'Actually, there's nothing here that wasn't available. It's just that nobody connected the dots before.'

'Nothing here necessarily illegal either ... but I'll give you interesting. And I doubt Lewis would like seeing it analysed in public.' I put the folders down on the seat. 'Okay. You ready to go?'

But he suddenly reached in his overcoat, pulling out keys. 'Look, you know, since my car's already here, why don't I just drive myself, then Lee won't have to run me out to the airport after the burial. I take off at two-thirty. Thanks a lot.' He shut my door with a brisk click, and stood there slapping his keys against his palm.

Once again, I felt a little caught short by his abrupt shifts in travel plans, and by his decisiveness in altering mine. But then, I guess when you're 'moving everything in you, full out, energy and soul,' you do move fast. Fast and forgetful, if I was really supposed to believe he'd forgotten where he'd left his Porsche, or that he was supposed to catch a plane in an hour.

As I drove out of the parking lot, I looked back at Rowell Hall. The dark-haired woman still stood in the window. Even from this distance, I could tell that she was, in Brookside's phrase, 'a beautiful girl.'

North Hills Cemetery looked down over Hillston, which is why, I suppose, the first Cadmeans and Havers with money had themselves buried there. So they could keep an eye through the ages on their property. Right beside 'ENOS CADMEAN, AVE ATQUE VALE' – entombed in a small-scale replica of the Pantheon (modified by a grief-stricken lady angel flinging up both arms as if she'd just crossed the finish line after a torturous quarter-mile dash) – Old Briggs, son of Enos, was electronically laid to rest. He descended under a huge blanket of nearly black roses that everybody was whispering had been sent by Briggs Junior. 'Everybody' was only about a tenth of the capacity crowd who'd come to the church, which admittedly had been a good sixty degrees warmer and minus the wind chill factor. The tears rushing down the faces of the mourners around the grave were probably as much from cold as sorrow. In fact, Reverend Campbell was praying so fast, the ceremony was over five minutes after I arrived, and Andy Brookside didn't make it at all.

As soon as the coffin was lowered, the whole group hurried off to the warmth of their waiting cars. I told Justin and Alice I'd meet them later, then I walked over to speak with Lee, who stood saying good-bye to the Fanshaws, her dark fur pulled around her ears. On the cypress-dotted knoll behind her rose a thirty-foot marble obelisk with HAVER carved down its front in letters you could read a block away. Surrounding it were dozens of tombstones, temples, and crypts, all memorializing the death of some Haver or other. I wondered under which of them her parents were buried: Her father, Gordon Haver, who'd been shot down over Korea, and her stepfather, Dr Blount, who'd asked me on each of the three occasions that I'd eaten dinner at Briarhills if I wasn't a caddy at the Hillston Club (I wasn't), lying on either side of her mother, who'd apologized a number of times (with a distinctly unapologetic significance) for her inability to remember my name.

Lee didn't seem surprised that I'd misplaced her husband during a fifteen-minute drive. I mumbled something about Brookside's bringing his own car so he could go to the airport; she mumbled something about, well, she wouldn't wait then. Her driver stood leaning against the Jaguar, smoking a cigarette – probably one from a Haver factory. She said, 'Walk me to my car?' I took her arm and we walked slowly back together over the hard earth, over the still sleeping past, the 'Beloved' wives, 'Blessed' infants, over generations of forgotten decent, and indecent, men.

I said, 'Do you mind, just a second?' and led her carefully through a crowded plot of Randolphs, over to a bare dogwood tree beneath which sat the small stone inscribed 'EDITH KEENE 1920–1947, GONE TO A BETTER PLACE.' Over the years I'd accompanied Isaac Rosethorn dozens of times on his Sunday visits here, though he'd never answer my questions about who Edith Keene was, or why he brought her a yellow rose every week of his life. Naturally I'd imagined a tale of tragic young love from which the old bachelor had never recovered. After I joined the force, I'd even gone to Town Records and looked up her death certificate. I still remember how cold the room got when I read that Edith Keene, unmarried female, had died 'by misadventure' while a patient in the state hospital for the insane. I never told him I'd found that out. Today, the rose in the bud vase was withered, petals already fallen on to the dry winter grass. Isaac had missed this Sunday's visit.

Lee said, 'I remember your telling me about Edith Keene. That strange lawyer, Isaac, the one you were always going to see?'

'Isaac Rosethorn. He's still pretty strange.'

'It sounded so romantic, bringing roses to her grave, and, look, he must still be doing it!' She rested her hand on the curve of the stone.

I said, 'After we broke up, I remember planning on doing the same for you, in case you died. I'd have these fantasies about standing there by your tombstone, an old white-haired bachelor, holding my rose, and young folks would wander by, whispering, "Now, that's love."' I'd intended a joke here, but instead a hot embarrassment rushed over me. I couldn't even make my mouth smile – not with her eyes looking straight up into mine.

Finally Lee saved us both, by laughing. 'You were so angry, it was probably the idea of my being *dead* that you liked the most.' Then I could smile, and she reached for my arm again and we walked on.

At the Jaguar, the young chauffeur held open the door for her. She said, 'Thank you, Arnold,' and he got back in behind the wheel. Standing by the door, Lee took my hand. 'See you Thursday at Edwina's?' I nodded. She said, 'Andy has to be in New York.'

'Oh. Is that where he's flying today? On Christmas Eve?'

'Today? Oh, "airport." No, he meant flying himself. He has a little Cessna. You know, at that private field on the way to Raleigh.'

'Ah. Well, I'm glad to hear it. I hated to think you were going to be by yourself Christmas Eve.' I was still holding her gloved hand, but made myself let go of it.

She looked up, into my eyes so long I could hear my own heart, and was worried she probably could too. I said, 'Merry Christmas, Lee.'

She said, 'Where are your gloves? Your hands are blue.'

I pulled my gloves out of the pocket of the new overcoat I was wearing for the first time. I said, 'So are your ears.'

'Are they?' She put her hands over them. A flurry of wind swung the car door towards her, and jumping forward to catch it, I jostled against her. She reached out, holding on to my arms.

138

I could see the flush heat her face, and a sudden sure sense of its meaning shot through me, almost buckling my knees.

Then she was in her car, and the driver had started the motor. As I was closing the door, she said, 'Merry Christmas, Cuddy.' Then she was gone.

The cemetery where Cooper Hall was buried, only an hour after Briggs Monmouth Cadmean, was not on a hill, but in a stubby pine grove behind Holy Sion Baptist Church. Besides me, I saw only six people who went to both funerals: the Yarboroughs, Justin and Alice, Bubba Percy, and Father Paul Madison. And Bubba and I stood outside in the yard during the Hall service. Sion Baptist was on the outskirts of Canaan, that easternmost section of East Hillston that the rest of Hillston had finally – about a hundred and ten years after the Civil War – got out of the habit of calling 'Darktown.'

Coop's political colleagues were planning a memorial service for early January. Today was private – for his family, and the friends they wanted with them. I had five policemen near the doors of the small stucco church to keep it private. Still, a lot of people came that afternoon to sit with Nomi Hall, and with Jordan West. I watched them all go past me, and inside, Officer John Emory watched too, asking the deacon who stood in a back corner with him to put names to faces. It's a sad fact of nature that killers sometimes show up at funerals they're responsible for. Sion was nearly filled when the two cars from Dollard Prison drove into the lot – two cars, four guards and rifles to bring George Hall to his brother's burial. And days of red tape, political favours, political pressures to grant him the privilege.

When George stepped out of the cruiser, his eyes squeezed shut behind his glasses, and he turned his head away from the hard winter light. His hair had greyed. They'd given him a tie and a blue suit to wear (too tight for his stocky, overmuscled body), but they had his hands cuffed together. He walked between his guards with an odd tentativeness, faltering as gravel changed to grass, testing his footing on the church steps, as if he'd lost in those seven closed years his sense of space and distance.

Standing by the door with Paul and Bubba (who had a wool scarf up over his nose like he was planning to rob the congregation), I nudged them both back to clear the entrance for Hall. I felt Bubba's resistance, so I squeezed my hand down on his shoulder, but he shook it off and growled at me, 'Oh get fucked, Mangum, what kind of a creep do you think I am!' I didn't bother to answer this question. Meanwhile, Paul slipped around me, grabbed the prisoner's hands, and murmured, 'Oh God, George, all my sympathy, Christ be with you.' One of the guards, about twice Paul's size, stepped between them with a polite mumble, 'Excuse us here, sir.'

'There's no reason in the world,' snapped Paul, 'to have this man *chained*.'

They ignored this exaggeration.

George kept moistening his lips and clearing his throat while he spoke, as if he'd lost that habit too. 'It's okay,' he said to Paul. 'You know Isaac Rosethorn? He around?'

When Paul looked at me, I shook my head, and answered. 'No. We don't know where he's gone, but he's been gone since Saturday. Fact, I'm getting real worried.'

George pushed at his glasses with his wrist, he nodded when he recognized me. 'I need to see him. You tell him that. Okay?'

'Okay.'

George turned to Paul. 'Mama said you came by a lot. Thank you.'

The first guard muttered, 'Okay. Excuse me,' pulled open the doors, and they led Hall past us inside. A soprano voice flew out of the church into the bright air like a sparrow. 'Deep river, Lord . . . I want to cross over into camp ground.'

It was not until after the service, when I saw her at the grave, singing with the others, 'Precious Lord, take my hand,' that I realized the voice I'd heard was Officer Brenda Moore's.

I realized something else that surprised me. As the small crowd was assembling around the opened grave, behind Nomi Hall and her minister, I saw a couple who must have already been inside the church when I arrived, because I know I would have noticed them go in. First, because there weren't that many whites in attendance. Second, because I could have picked out Jack Molina's Byzantine eyes on Coney Island on the Fourth of July. And third, because the person whose arm he kept linked through his was the slender blackhaired woman I'd seen two hours earlier looking down with such intensity at Brookside and me from the window of Rowell Hall. I moved next to Paul and whispered, 'Who's that with Molina?'

Paul twisted his neck around. '. . . His wife. Debbie.'

'Does she work at the university too?'

He shook his head no, then he bowed it, closing his eyes.

The rich bass of Reverend Greenwood, a big round-shouldered man of seventy, lifted over the field, and over the sounds of crying.

'Dear Lord, we send You a man we love. Cooper David Hall. His life was short in years, but it was long, long in the light of Your truth, in the strong armour of Your battle, in the bright hope of Your sweet promised land. Yes, he was young in years, but a leader for those without one and a warrior for those who need one. Young in years, but Cooper David Hall had put away childish things, and he spoke as a man . . .'

The shovel was passed from hand to hand as they covered Coop's coffin with cold red earth. When it reached Jordan West, she stepped back to where George, his face stung with tears, stood with his guards. Jordan embraced him, brought him forward to the edge of the grave, and placed his bound hands around the shovel's wood shaft. The guards kept their eyes lowered to the ground when George turned to hand the shovel to his cousin, the thin young man I'd last seen downtown in the interrogation room – Martin Hall. He wore the black armband of the vigil group, and stood with the college student Eric who had talked to me about him after the breakin at the *With Liberty and Justice* office. Martin jabbed the blade into the dirt hard and fast.

Reverend Greenwood said a prayer, and then he told us, 'Cooper's not here, my friends. He's not cold and he's not lonesome. God Almighty's got him safe and warm in His bosom. Let's us go on home.'

Then George walked around the red upturned clay over to the row of metal folding chairs, where his mother sat, motionless, her sister's arm around her. He dropped down on his knees, opened his hands at the manacled wrists, placed them on Nomi Hall's face, and pulled her towards him. She cried out then, as he rocked her back and forth, 'Oh son, son. Oh my Lord. Cooper, George, Cooper!'

Behind me I heard the click of Bubba Percy's camera. The picture later appeared in dozens of newspapers, even the *New York Times*.

Chapter 9

When WNNC rang in Christmas at midnight with Mario Lanza shouting 'Joy to the World,' I was seated on a stranger's rug surrounded by two hundred pieces of an unassembled ten-speed, pink-and-white bicycle. That hadn't been my plan. But neither had the stops along the way. For example, Paul Madison invited me out to dinner, then took me to the Trinity soup kitchen, where I ate spaghetti and sponge cake with his eighteen other guests – at least a third of whom I'd already met, for a variety of reasons ranging from prostitution and panhandling to grand larceny. The young fellow handing out coffee was one of the kids from 'the Canaan riot.' (They were all out on bail now, and a defence counsel from LDF was dickering with Mitch Bazemore about reducing the charges.)

After the meal, Paul lured me into the church vestry where a dozen folks, aged six to seventy, were rummaging through cabinets to find robes they wouldn't trip over. There he tried to bully me into carrying that damn banner in his processional at Christmas Eve mass; even claiming St Michael was a sort of celestial police chief.

I refused: 'I already turned down a lead in *Twelfth Night*, and all you're offering me's a walk-on.' Paul threw in the chance to 'read the Lesson instead then.' I said, 'Rector, I don't go to this church.'

'So? You don't go to any church.' He pulled this bright embroidered outfit down over his Buster Brown haircut.

'Doesn't that sort of give you a *hint* about my feelings on the subject? What is this, a membership drive?'

'Absolutely.' He winked at the other priest in the room, who was struggling to tuck up a choirboy's skirts, while the boy surreptitiously picked his nose and wiped it on his snowy lace sleeve.

I said, 'Well, Paul, not me. I already gave at the office.'

'Classic workaholic. You need a personal life, Cuddy.'

'Yeah, like you? You live here, work here, sleep here, and I'm sorry to say, you eat here. I'm getting tired of everybody I know telling me I need a personal life.'

'Doesn't that sort of give you a *hint*,' he grinned at me, 'of our feelings on the subject?' He handed a stout teenaged girl a cross on a silver pole that looked heavy enough to bash in your head if it fell on you; then looped a thin stole around his neck, and clapped his hands to his line-up of candles, flags, smoky pots, and threadbare cassocks. 'Bless this mass to the glory of God. Show time!'

So when the choir called, loud enough for me to hear them in the parish house, 'O come all ye faithful, joyful and triumphant,' I was back in Billy Gilchrist's closet of a bedroom off the hall of the soup kitchen. If Father Madison had been right in telling me nothing was missing from this room, Billy was not a man of property. There were a few cheap, pretty ripe clothes in a couple of drawers of a bureau, a few more hanging on hooks behind the door; a worn-out suitcase under the bed with an unopened fifth of Canadian rye in it; a tabletop with ten packs of gum, a Bible (guidance for the new life?), an Elmore Leonard paperback about gamblers and racketeers (nostalgia for the old life?), and a half-dealt hand of solitaire. In a jacket pocket I found a matchbook from the Silver Comet, which interested me because Coop Hall had written the name of that bar in his address book. Taped to a supporting slat inside a bureau drawer I found the numbered key to a public locker, which interested me because it was the only thing Gilchrist had bothered to hide.

The Silver Comet Diner was a railroad car from the old Raleigh-to-Atlanta line, up on blocks behind the once also old train station, now the brand-new mall, Southern Depot. Formerly offering cheap eats to drifters from the Piedmont Hotel ($1.99 specials of chicken steak, mush potatoes and collards, slapped on a grimy counter by a fat pasty waitress named LuBett), the Comet had got a liquor licence when the county finally broke the Baptists-and-bootleggers filibuster against going wet; service shifted, then, from watery coffee to watery booze. Its days as a dive were numbered. Upscale hadn't quite reached the Comet yet, but it was moving in that direction. Pete Zaslo, the owner – stringy and grey as a rag – told me, 'Some developer's nosing around. Price's right, you can forward this old man's mail straight to Florida. *If* the price's right, now.'

It took a little imagination to see Hockney prints replacing faded photos of fried eggs, ferns hanging where the Pabst clock was, bleached oak instead of Formica – but all that would come. Meanwhile, tinsel ropes and cardboard bells drooped from the ceiling, big coloured lights blinked on a baby-blue plastic tree in the corner, and Elvis sounded kind of scratchy on an old radio, doing 'I'll Be Home for Christmas.' Well, it's hard to think of something sadder than the type folks who sit around a cheap bar on Christmas Eve, listening to songs about counting on them to get home for the holidays when it's transparent they either lost track of home a long time back, or don't want in the worst way to go to the one they've got. It was this type I saw staring solitary into their filmy glasses when I walked into the Comet; they sure weren't chumming around the bar, perking each other up with a round of 'God rest ye merry gentlemen, let nothing you dismay.' Most of them looked beyond dismay, and on the way to catatonia; dismay takes a little effort. Still, a woman on the stool next to mine – she looked like she'd lived fifty years, two or three real hard times without a break – had enough heart left to tell me, 'I don't guess I'll ever stop missing Elvis.'

'If you can hang on, never do stop,' I told her. 'I miss him too. What's your drink?' She said, Tequila Sunrise – because she liked the sound of it – so I bought her two. Sunrise. Some hearts keep on hoping.

The Comet owner said, sure, he knew who Cooper Hall was, from TV, but couldn't say if he'd ever been in the place or not. On the other hand, Billy Gilchrist was a regular, 'except when you guys nab him, or that runt buttinski priest pal of his busts his balls, gets the poor fucker boo-hooing, and makes him swear off booze.' He glanced through the smoky dimness at his clientele. 'Haven't seen Billy for a while. But he'll be back. They're always back.'

'Well, it's a charming place, Pete, easy to see why.'

'Don't make me laugh, Mangum.'

'I keep trying. Looks like you could use a laugh . . . Anybody Billy hung around with special?'

144

Zaslo scratched his grey stubble. 'New, not really. Liked to gab, you know, so whoever was around. While back, he used to pal up with this coloured fellow, Butler ... Something weird Butler.'

'Moonfoot Butler?'

'Yeah. Haven't seen him either though, long time.'

I finished my beer. 'I'd say, be 'bout five more years 'fore you're likely to. Moonfoot Butler went North. Extradited to Delaware. Little matter of loading up a truckful of videotapes that didn't belong to him.'

'That so? ... Wanna 'nother beer? ... On the house.'

'Pete, it's against the law for me to accept presents from taxpayers.'

I'd been joking with Peter Zaslo for years; this was the first time he'd laughed. Not just laughed, but volunteered more conversation than answers to direct questions. 'Mangum, account of it's Christmas, I'm gonna pay you a compliment. How long you been chief now, three, four years? All the guys in Hillston, got joints like mine, we waited and waited for the squeeze – you know, what the fuckin' bill was gonna be, one thing or another ... You know what, we've 'bout decided it ain't never coming. We've 'bout decided there ain't gonna be a squeeze, not even a free lousy beer, 'cause you new guys are fuckin' *clean*. So that's the compliment.' He walked to the end of the bar, and eased the glass out of the hand of an old fellow who appeared to be napping, maybe soothed to sleep by Perry Como's crooning 'The First Noel.'

When Pete came back, he said, 'So with the lady's tequilas, that'll be eight seventy-five.'

I gave him a ten. 'Pete, I want to thank you for that compliment. Now, tell me, who were the old guys that weren't so squeaky clean as yours truly? I hate to think any of them are still on my payroll.'

'Naw, somebody killed 'em, didn't he? Pym and Russell? Coloured guy that got the chair. Yeah, what's his name – the governor just let him go.'

I skipped over Pete's shaky information about George Hall's crime, and just asked, 'Are you telling me Bobby Pym and Winston Russell were extorting money from you?'

First he looked hurt, like I was teasing him. Then he laughed for the second time tonight, even louder. 'Mangum, now *that's* funny. From me, and you name it. Them two fuckers extort the fillings out of their grandmama's mouth. They was like clockwork, them two.'

Now I'd heard rumours, of course, back when Van Fulcher ran HPD, of cops cadging freebies, cops taking little bribes to look the other way, but nothing specific, or systematic. And while I knew for a personal fact that Russell and Pym were a couple of legalized thugs, nobody'd ever said they were on the *take*. I lifted my elbows so Pete could give the bar a swipe with a cloth I think he'd used since he bought the place. 'So, tell me. They'd just breeze in and say, "Hey, Pop, I'm here for my week's allowance"?'

'Oh come on, Mangum, you know. It was more like we had to buy – their price – what it was, whatever, they was pushing at the time.'

'Meaning what?'

'Whatever. Booze, tapes, mostly a shitload more cigarettes than you could move. I tell you this, I'm a white man, but me and a lot more, we raised a fuckin' glass when that black boy shot them two cops.'

I reminded Zaslo that George had only shot one cop – Bobby Pym; that Winston Russell had gone to jail soon afterwards, for assaulting a prostitute, and then gone back to jail for assaulting me. But, far as I knew, he wasn't dead.

'Too bad.' Pete admitted his memory was doubtless clouded by wishful thinking. 'Well, you know, it was always the two of them together, Pym and Russell, so they stick in my mind that way, I guess.'

When I left the Comet, half an hour later, with the names of a few of Pym & Russell's other former customers, Bing Crosby was waltzing out of the radio into a winter wonderland. As my Tequila Sunrise neighbour thanked me for her drinks, she sighed, 'I miss Bing too. All the great ones – they're going fast.'

I said, 'That's true. But look here. Peggy Lee, Ella, Loretta, we got a lot of great ones left.'

She wiped the corner of her mouth with a surprising daintiness. She said, 'All women. Women last longer.' The thought appeared to cheer her up a bit.

Downtown, not a proverbial creature was stirring. Stores were closed, their shelves stripped bare. Everybody'd gone home with however much they could haul, or charge. Even in my business, business is slow the night before Christmas. Hiram Davies, at the night desk browsing through his Bible under the mistletoe, attributed the half-empty holding cells to the spirit of God.

'Right, Hiram. But like the song says, why can't we have Christmas every day of the year? Don't you think it's kind of laissez-faire of the Lord to slough off the way He does, the other three hundred and sixty-four? He worked for me, I'd fire His butt.'

Davies' thin neck moved inside the starched collar as he carefully placed the attached string of ribbon in his Bible to save his place. Then he closed the book, and looked at me, his eyes big and earnest behind the old gold glasses. 'Cuddy Mangum . . .'

Well, that was a shock; he hadn't called me by name since I'd first outranked him when I made lieutenant. 'Um hum?'

He took a long breath. 'You're a smart man. Smarter than me, I know that . . .' He took another breath. 'But if you think making fun of God shows how smart you are, well I'm here to tell you, in my opinion, the one you're really making fun of is just yourself.' He pulled off his glasses defiantly, blinking hard. 'That's my opinion, and you can go ahead and fire me if you want to.'

His face was red, and the fact is, so was mine. We stared at each other, then I nodded at him, and reached over the desk. He flinched – I don't know what he thought I was going to do, maybe rip off his stripes – but I put my hand over his for a second (his was trembling). I said, 'Hiram, in my opinion, I suspect maybe you're right . . .' I stepped back, took a notepad, wrote on it. 'Now . . . You think you could locate some old shift logs for me? Bobby Pym, Winston Russell. Also a couple of arrest records. Billy Gilchrist's, and you remember a guy we shipped to Delaware, called himself "Moonfoot" Butler?'

Still stirred up by his unprecedented challenge, Davies looped his glasses back over his long-lobed ears, and patted down the careful strands of white hair. He smoothed the piece of paper gently. 'Butler.'

'Right. Moonfoot. Long-legged guy, they called him that 'cause he had these high bouncy steps like he was walking on the moon?'

The old Hiram was back, shoulders stiff, chin tight. 'Arthur Butler. Two convictions for grand larceny, 'seventy-four, 'seventy-seven, or maybe it was 'seventy-eight.'

'Hiram, I love you.'

He ignored my grin. 'And something funny. What was it now? . . .' Davies pushed slowly at the nose bar of his glasses. Finally he nodded. 'Yes, Haver Tobacco Company; a warehouse robbery, that's what it was . . . We pulled him in on it. But they dropped the case. Officer on the scene said he'd seen a suspect run off, but couldn't make the ID. Said it wasn't Butler.'

I slapped a drumroll on the desk top. 'Sergeant Davies, not only would I *never* fire you, not only would I never *allow* you to retire, I'd like to kiss you under the mistletoe! And you can tell me who that officer was, I swear I'm *gonna* kiss you.'

His lips pinched tight as if trying to escape the thought. 'Don't remember.'

'You sure you're not lying to keep me from kissing you?'

'Captain Mangum, I have as many faults as the next man, but *I'm not a liar, I never—*'

'Oh, Hiram, calm down. Go pull that Haver robbery file. I'm gonna bet you ten dollars that officer's Bobby Pym or Winston Russell. Okay, okay, you're not a better either. How 'bout this? If I'm right, you'll call Officer White "Nancy" to her face. If I'm wrong, well, I'll tell you what, I'll go to church next Sunday. How's that? Deal?'

It took him a while to weigh the sin of gambling against a chance to save a soul, and I was proud of him. He said okay.

So, I guess I'm going to church next Sunday. Because the officer's name was Purley Newsome, Russell & Pym's little tagalong.

Martha was glad to be home; I mean she's got the run of the department, and her own private suite in the back seat of the Oldsmobile, bed and all, but home's where the munchies are. Listening to a new compact disc of Vivaldi (country's not the only sound I like), I changed into jeans, and the sweatshirt Justin gave me last Christmas. Here's what's printed down its front:

> **Policeman**, constable, peace officer,
> detective, arm of the law, inspector,
> *flic, gendarme, carabiniere,*
> bailiff, catchpole, beagle, beadle,
> reeve, tipstaff, bobbie,
> peeler, cop, copper, narc,

trooper, John Law, bull, flatfoot,
gumshoe, shamus, dick, fuzz, pig,
the Law.

Then Mrs Mitchell had some fried chicken, and I nuked some frozen enchiladas, and then we lay on the carpet looking at my Christmas tree lights, and at the old crèche with its headless Joseph, and its one wise man staring behind him for those two missing kings of Orient-are, like maybe they'd fallen off their camels back in some quicksand, or maybe they'd lost heart in their pal's plan to chase a star across the Sahara, and turned around.

Now, the truth is, what I really felt like doing was reading the files Hiram Davies had found, and the folder Andy Brookside had slipped me before shutting my car door in my face. But I made myself put them down on the glass coffee table, under a lead minié ball I'd dug up at the Bentonville battlefield. What with its being Christmas Eve, and everybody accusing me of an addiction to work, I figured I'd go cold turkey – at least for the night. So I looked up 'Holiday Drinks' in my Bartender's Guide, made myself a pitcher of eggnog, and turned on my downstairs TV, which is in a wall shelf with my CD, FM tuner, VCR, beer bottle collection dating back to college, and 2,765 alphabetized books that I counted one night when I was real depressed. I'd hate for Andy Brookside to know it, but I've got another TV up in my bedroom, in another wall shelf, with more books, plus my, what I call, rocks collection – these are stones, gravel, bricks, little broken bits of the past, I've picked up loose in my travels, from rubble heaps of historical significance, like the ground around the Acropolis and Cheops's tomb.

For an hour, I lay on my wall-to-wall by the tree, and clicked at the channels with my remote control. The Pope was in St Peter's, Billy Graham was in Berlin, Johnny Carson had a rerun. And no *Chainsaw Massacres* tonight. Movie stations had gone spiritual (*Song of Bernadette*, *The Robe*), or classical (*How to Marry a Millionaire*, *The Great Caruso*), or seasonal. I sipped eggnog, which I don't much like, and flipped from old Scrooge getting terrorized by a peek at his own tombstone, to little Natalie Wood shaking down Kris Kringle for a house in the suburbs, to Gary Cooper just about jumping off the top of a building so he won't let down the John Doe clubs who'd had faith in his suicide vow. By the time I caught up with *It's a Wonderful Life*, Jimmy Stewart had pretty near got the picture from his angel that – however puny, broke, and wasted he might be feeling – without him, his sweet small town would have turned into Boston's Combat Zone. I confess it was a personal fantasy of mine that the same might be true of Hillston without me.

Now here's something else I don't think I ever told a soul: I'm a sucker for angel movies. *Angels in the Outfield, I Married an Angel, The Bishop's Wife, Heaven Can Wait* – I've seen them all. I love it when Claude Rains and Cary Grant and James Mason pop down from Above to fix things. I love *It's a Wonderful Life.* I even get the sniffles when all Jimmy Stewart's neighbours show up with cash on Christmas Eve so he won't lose the bank and go to jail. So when my doorbell rang, I was blowing my nose. I clicked off the set, scuffed over in my socks, wondering who'd come calling at two A.M. I admit I had a rush of hot irrational hope that Andy Brookside had disappeared in his Cessna, and Lee had driven to River Rise to tell me about it. When you watch a lot of movies, things like that seem possible.

But life's not a movie, and it wasn't Lee. Squinting through the chained gap, I saw a stranger – a pretty woman about my age, also in jeans and sweatshirt (except hers didn't have thirty synonyms for 'cop' on it), and also sniffling; at least, her eyelashes looked wet. She had the greenest eyes I ever saw; they sort of tipped up at the ends. And very black hair in a loose ponytail. She had a screwdriver in each hand – not the kind you drink. I said, 'You want to put those away? Somebody tried to kill me with a screwdriver once.'

'Really?' She looked at the tools, then squeezed them down in her jeans' pocket. She glanced at my door plate. 'Are you C. R. Mangum?'

'Yep.'

'I'm Nora Howard. I'm sorry to bother you this late, but I'm next door, Two-B—'

'TV too loud?'

'Oh no. The thing is, I just moved in a few weeks ago, and I looked out on my patio and saw your lights were on. What I need is a smaller Phillips screwdriver. Do you happen to have one? I think I'm just going to drink down a can of Dran-o if you don't.'

Despite her violent turn of phrase, I decided she probably wasn't fixing to stab me, so I flipped the chain and invited her in.

I peered across the foyer; she'd left her door open, and a

bright-coloured Indian teepee looked to be taking up most of her living room. 'What happened to Henry and Dennis? Two-B? The landscape architects?'

'I'm subletting. They broke up. You didn't know they left?'

'I guess I've been pretty busy.' Well, I'd miss the smell of their nouvelle cuisine, but not their affection for heavy metal rock groups.

Nora Howard explained that she'd been trying to assemble her daughter's bicycle for the last three hours. 'This is my first Christmas as a single Santa, and let me tell you, a sixty-eight-page instructions manual is a humbling experience.' Then she frowned at me. 'Say, are you okay? I probably busted in on something. I'm really sorry.'

'*It's a Wonderful Life.*' I pointed at the TV.

'Oh.' She grinned, and gestured at her wet lashes. 'Me too!'

In the kitchen I found her a small Phillips screwdriver. 'Bless you, C. R. Mangum.'

'Most people call me Cuddy.'

'Do you like it?'

'Not much, but it's better than Cudberth.'

She nodded. 'That's true. My family used to call me Angie; I never liked it. That was my middle name, Angela. Nora Angela Carippini.'

'Aha. The restaurant?'

'It's my older brother's.' Then she frowned again. 'Do you all wear those shirts?'

'Pardon?'

'Hillston policemen? Mrs Falliwell – Three-A? – she was telling me about you. You're the chief of police. I thought you'd be about sixty.'

'Sometimes I think I am.'

She laughed. 'Oh boy! I know that feeling.'

I opened my refrigerator. 'Do you like eggnog?'

She squinched up her face. '. . . Actually, I hate it . . .'

I nodded. 'It's *horrible*, isn't it?'

She was looking over my shoulder into the refrigerator. 'Look, I know Laura – my daughter – would say, "Mom, you're embarrassing me, *jeez*!," but is that a tub of Kentucky Fried Chicken in there? I'll trade you a glass of white Chianti for a wing, and *one* question about "Figure thirty-b" in this assembly manual.' She studied my face for a moment. 'You're sorry you answered your door.'

151

Well, in a way, I was. I'd been looking forward to a bath and a book. But conceit's always been my stumbling block. One look at those two hundred loose bike parts, I figured she'd be up all night, whereas I never met instructions I couldn't translate into objects as fast as I could read, and I'm a fast reader.

So that's how I ended up on a strange floor bolting a reflector to a pink fender when Mario Lanza sang in Christmas with 'Joy to the World.' Nora's daughter Laura was ten. The teepee was for her son Brian, who was five. They were upstairs sleeping, unless they were faking it, waiting for dawn. Nora had lived with her husband, Warren, in Texas, where he'd worked for NASA. He'd died of meningitis almost a year ago. She'd come to Hillston because her brother and sister-in-law, who'd moved here a long while ago to open the restaurant, thought it was a great place to raise children. And she did like Hillston. The only problem was she wasn't licensed to practise in North Carolina.

I said, 'Practise what?'

She said, 'The Law. Just like it says on your shirt.'

Justin and Alice always invite me for Christmas breakfast. Well, we start at breakfast, and by the time Alice finishes opening all the presents Justin's bought her, it's time for lunch. She keeps begging him not to buy her so many, and he keeps hinting that she ought to buy him more, if she's so embarrassed by us just watching her make her way around the tree where he's stacked up the boxes. Myself, I gave him a record, and her a book. I'm not all that imaginative when it comes to presents. Alice gave me a sweater. Justin gave me a piece of the stone-carved pediment from the old statehouse, a pair of pink Argyle socks, a videotape of *The Maltese Falcon*, and an honest-to-God signed studio photograph of Patsy Cline, that who knows where he got it, or how much it cost.

We were drinking our bloody Marys, admiring the Scotch pine (no tacky lights and tinsel, just genuine little Victorian knick-knacks scattered here and there); listening to the Preservation Hall Jazz Band record I'd got him; Alice was saying, 'Oh, sweetheart, *another* dress!,' when we heard the beeper go off in my jacket.

Justin said, 'When constabulatory duty's to be done, to be done, / A policeman's lot is not a happy one, happy one.'

Alice said, 'Shit.'

Zeke Caleb said Merry Christmas, he was sorry, but call Etham Foster right away at the following number. Etham didn't say he was sorry, he said he was at a filling station near where they were pulling a body out of the Shocco River.

I said, 'Dr D., I hate to sound unfeeling, but I've seen bodies, I've even seen bodies pulled out of the Shocco, and so have you. And you're supposed to be *off* today with your family; Ruthie's starting to hate me as it is.'

He said, 'Just come on, Cuddy. I-Twenty-eight, left on Exit Nine, past that farmhouse, one-point-six miles in, path to the river, you'll see us. Body's in a car.'

'Slidell's farmhouse?'

'Right.'

'Somebody drove off the bank?'

'Didn't. Pushed.'

Justin said, 'Okay, this makes two episodes, same place! I told you!'

'Whatcha want, J.B.S., a raise? Looks like about double last year's salary's lying around the room here anyhow.'

Alice walked us to the door. 'Don't mind me, boys, I've got at least two hours of packages left to go.'

'Don't open anything till I get back,' Justin told her; he loves to watch folks tear into presents. 'Just be an hour.'

But it was more like three before I sent Jay the Bountiful home.

Where Cooper's Subaru and the truck had collided, the skid marks looked fresh, the shoulder torn open. We bounced along a packed-clay road, through fields that had probably once been ploughed for brightleaf tobacco, corn, and soybeans, but now were back to grass and young pines; if you don't fight her hard, Nature's fast to reclaim her own. The tractor in the yard at Slidell's farm hadn't been driven in years, and the rusted pickup near it didn't even have its tyres anymore. Since we were there, we stopped for a second. The doors were still locked; nobody was home. Justin showed me the barn; as Parker had reported, there were now no huge rolls of paper squeezed in with the other junk.

'There was an old white Ford right here.' Justin pointed. 'See the oil drip?'

'Maybe Slidell drove it off for the holidays.'

That proved not to be the case. About a mile farther in from the highway, three of our cruisers had their lights flashing. We walked the clearing towards the river; it was drivable, more or less, but not by me in my new Oldsmobile. Obviously the car in the river had made it through the dead kudzu, sumac, and maple saplings to the edge of the steep eroded bank. And obviously my men had got a tow truck down in there, because they'd winched the car half out of the thick brown water. It was gunked with slimy weeds and mud, but it was still unmistakably the white Ford Justin had seen in Slidell's barn. We leaned over the crumbling ledge; you could see the car's path down to the Shocco gouged in red clay and broken roots.

' 'Sixty-eight Fairlane,' said Etham Foster, looming up behind me. Under his sheepskin, he had on a new red sweater; no doubt a Christmas present. 'Been in there a few days.'

'Merry Christmas, Dr D. Get the body out?'

He pointed at a plastic bag near the bank. Dick Cohn (our medical examiner, fellow about my age) sat on a stump, sadly puffing a pipe.

Justin asked, 'Etham, the car was pushed?'

'Drove it in Low to the ledge, jumped, it went over. You'll see,' was all we got for an answer as he headed back for the tow truck. I asked him if he'd identified the body, but he didn't hear me. It didn't matter, because as soon as Justin pulled the tarp down, he said, 'It's Willie Slidell. I knew it.'

I sighed. 'If you were figuring to pin the Hall shooting on this guy, you need a backup man, 'cause I don't believe Willie here would go to the trouble to plug himself in the chest this many times before driving off a twenty-foot ledge into a river – no matter how remorseful he'd got to feeling.' Because we didn't need Dr Cohn to tell us Slidell hadn't died from a bump on the head, or water in the lungs either.

'Three shots, probably dead when they put him in the car,' Cohn said. 'Where's my ambulance? I gotta get out of here, I'm blue.' Dick Cohn had emigrated from Brooklyn for 'the weather,' and now did nothing but complain about it. Like a lot of New Yorkers, he had a shaky sense of geography beyond the Hudson, and had apparently figured the 'South,' *anywhere* in the South, meant warm as Miami. He pulled his ski cap farther down his narrow bald head. 'Cheesh, my kid wanted a car for Christmas. Oughta bring him out here, show him what can happen.'

I said, 'For Christmas? Y'all were just celebrating Hanakkah last week.'

He laughed. 'Yeah, if my kids heard they handed out gifts on Buddha's birthday, we'd be celebrating that too.'

Justin was going through Slidell's pockets like a derelict in an alley. I left him at it. There were about half a dozen cops on the scene now, including a diver and photographer. John Emory, soaked up to the knot of his neat tie, was shivering inside a thick blanket. He and Nancy White had taken the call, and found the body – a rough way to start their partnership. I saw Nancy a few yards off, also wrapped in a blanket, leaning against a big oak. She had her arm around a skinny boy of eleven or twelve, in a cheap cut-down coat, sneakers, and a just about shaved blond head (quick cure for lice, probably). Nancy was nodding as she listened to him. 'Hey, Chief, c'mere,' she yelled at me. 'Talk to Wally.'

Wally lived about two miles up the road in a rental farm – modern lingo for a tenant shack with a couple of worked-out acres and a few dozen scruffy chickens. He'd found the car because he'd got a Daisy air rifle for Christmas. Forbidden to leave the yard with it, naturally he'd rushed off into the woods to shoot anything that happened to be there. Not much was, so he'd kept walking until he'd come upon the clearing of smashed undergrowth, which he'd followed to the ledge above the Shocco. There he'd hidden, pretending to be somebody like Rambo, firing down on 'stuff' in the river. It wasn't that he'd deduced the car from the rutted bank, or even seen the car, which had been completely submerged. He'd just leaned out too far from his ambush spot, the ledge had given way, and he'd tumbled down the bank, losing his brand-new rifle to the muddy water. So he'd dived in, coat and all. And that's when he'd bumped up against the Ford. If he'd hit it diving, it might have killed him.

The dive had been instinct; the decision to tell his parents about it was courage, because as Nancy told me later, 'his fuckin' daddy whipped him good' – I suspect because the boy'd lost a BB gun that they'd doubtless had on lay-away since summer. But after Wally's folks had taken a look at the ruts, and weighed the pros and cons of isolationism vs. citizenship, in the end they'd decided to call the police. Nancy had already talked to them, then brought Wally back with her to the scene.

I leaned down, shook the boy's cold skinny hand. He wore a cheap digital watch that looked big as a clock on his wrist. 'Thank you,' I said. 'You did the right thing. I'm Cuddy Mangum. Merry Christmas.'

He was clearly scared speechless, but he nodded up at me, then looked back at Nancy.

She said, 'Chief, I told Wally we'd get him a new rifle, okay?'

'That seems pretty reasonable, Officer White.' (She not only didn't have her tie on; she was wearing a bulky purple-striped turtleneck over her khaki shirt. Looks like everybody got sweaters for Christmas.)

I sat down on the cold grass beside them. 'You lived around here long, Wally?' He nodded. 'Your folks know Willie Slidell pretty well?'

His small Adam's apple gulped. 'Some. Not too good, I guess . . .' He looked across the clearing at the plastic mound where Justin knelt. 'Is it him? Mr Slidell?'

'Yes.' I gave him a little while to adjust to this. '. . . Wally? Is that Mr Slidell's car? You recognize it when we pulled it out?'

'No sir. He's got a tan station wagon.'

'What about this white Ford?'

His pale blue eyes stayed bravely on mine. 'He didn't drive it that I know of. But I think I maybe saw it once or twice.'

'In the barn?' No answer. I took out two packages of cheese crackers, threw one of them in his lap, and opened the other one. 'Wally, what grade you in, eighth?'

'No sir, sixth.'

'Really? You sure look older.'

'I'm eleven and a half.' He opened the crackers carefully and slid one out.

'The school bus take you all the way home, or let you off out on the exit road?'

'By the road.'

'Didn't you ever sort of check out Slidell's place when you were passing by? Look around, you know? Like lately, I'm wondering if he had somebody visiting him for a while?' Wally studied the ground and I chewed up a cracker. 'You know what? My teachers used to say to me, "Cuddy, curiosity killed the cat." But those teachers were wrong as they could be.' I popped another cracker in my mouth, and finally he started to nibble on his. 'Curiosity made me the youngest chief of police Hillston ever had.'

He looked up suspiciously. Well, I did have on jeans, sneakers, and a down jacket. I said, 'Nancy, you wanna tell this man I'm the chief of police.'

Nancy vouched for me.

Wally thought it over, finished his cracker, and slid out another. 'I think he lived all by himself.'

156

'Um hum. Ever get a good look in his barn?'

'. . . I guess I saw the Ford there.'

'Good. See any big rolls of paper in there?'

'It could have been paper. Tall round things in cardboard?'

'Right. That's good. Slidell ever run you off his place? That used to happen to me a lot, I'd be snooping around.'

Wally slowly nodded yes, without looking up. 'But I never took anything, or even touched it,' he mumbled. He took his time over a few more nibbles. '. . . I think somebody was staying there last week maybe. I think a couple of times I saw him out in the yard.'

'You think you could describe him?'

Wally described a large muscular man, neither young nor old, dark nor fair, 'just regular.' One time Wally saw him through the window without his shirt on; he had a red scar sideways on his back. One time he watched him out in the yard firing at coffee cans with a big pistol.

I asked him, 'Good shot, this man?'

'Yessir.' He nodded seriously.

'Did you happen to check around for bullets? I would, if I'd been you.' Blinking slowly, he nodded again, and admitted he'd picked up some of the slugs after the man had gone back in the house. I told him Nancy was going to take him home, and borrow those bullets, tomorrow we wanted him to come down to my office and look at some pictures with us, and then we'd give him a new BB gun. I threw in a promised tour of the jail, and he ate a half cracker in one gulp. 'One more thing, Wally, you remember Saturday, when there was the big accident right up here on I-Twenty-eight. When the two men got killed?'

He looked sorry to let me down. 'I just saw it on TV.'

'Too bad. I was hoping you maybe noticed something. Because you're a good noticer, real good.'

Wally was disappointed to have to say that he hadn't been anywhere near the car crash. He'd ridden his bike five miles west, over to Lake Road Airport, the small private landing field where they gave flying lessons, plus Piper Cub rides for twenty-five dollars, which if he ever had twenty-five dollars he was going to take. 'Saturdays I go to watch them sometimes. They don't see me. I sort of hide,' he admitted, though with some trouble breathing – apparently he'd been forbidden to go to the airport, or warned off by the people who ran it. When I said he ought to be careful riding a bike along a highway, he gave me a look that was pride pure and simple. 'I'm careful. I noticed something at the airport,' he added.

'What was that, Wally?'

'Saturday, the one you mean? That man was there riding in a plane with this other man that comes a lot.'

'What man?' I thought he meant the man at Slidell's.

But he didn't. 'I 'membered him when they showed his picture on the TV. That black man, that the news says they shot him.'

'Cooper Hall?'

'My daddy don't believe the news though. He says y'all just want people thinking somebody shot him 'cause it's like Martin Luther King.'

Nancy and I looked at each other. I said, 'Are you sure about this, Wally? You saw Cooper Hall at the airport. Are you *real* sure?'

He thought about it. 'Yessir.'

Wally didn't know who the other man was, but thought probably somebody at Lake Road Airport could tell us his name, because he had his own plane. 'They all treat him like a kind of a big shot, I guess. Just the one that got shot was black. The other one looked kind of rich.'

He'd even noticed the time when Coop Hall and the other man had gone up for their plane ride on Saturday, and when they'd come down. While he was watching, he kept track of flights on his watch, which he told us he'd bought with his egg money and it was 'a good one.' They'd stayed up an hour, and landed at 'two-thirty-something.'

'Did they leave together?'

'No, just the black man. He drove off in his car, sort of a beat-up car.' Wally folded the plastic around the rest of his crackers, and put them in his coat pocket. He looked at us both. 'Does that help?'

I said, 'Wally, that helps. That helps so much, in a couple of days, Officer White's gonna come back out here and take you up for a twenty-five-dollar plane ride. That's a Christmas present.'

Nancy said, 'Forget it. I've never been in a plane in my life.'

Wally gave her a solemn stare. 'Me neither. So it'll be okay.'

Chapter 10

Christmas night I spent downtown in my office, reading articles and reports, drawing circles around names on my blackboard; 'thinking with chalk,' as the man called it who'd given me the habit, whose name, in fact, was on my board now. 'Isaac' with a question mark. Where was he, and what did he know was missing from Cooper Hall's file box?

From my window, high up in the Municipal Building, I could see the flying Santas frozen in midair above Main Street, the choir of cutout angels lit up on the roof of the new Macy's Department Store, the sparkle on the tree atop the Hillston Star building; on almost every shop, office, and restaurant, I could see some wreath or words sprayed in snow or garlanded lights, some *something* that people had gone to the trouble, Christmas after Christmas, to fix up in public celebration. Tonight Hillston was peaceful, quiet, and satisfied it had made that communal effort. Tonight in the dark it was looking its best. Of course, it wasn't as long-lived, or as good-looking, as, say, just about any homely, unimportant little town you zip past on a train in italy. It wasn't as civilized, or as wise in the sly campaigns of the world either. Just an unimportant, decent, homely American town that had built back against entropy and chaos for 205 years.

Still, Hillston had got civilized enough even now in its adolescence to have kissed good-bye those naive vows of its national youth – for example, the ones about no entangling alliances, no House of Lords. It didn't take me much reading in Coop Hall's article on the Haver secret society with that undemocratic title, or much checking of Brookside's data on the

Constitution Club, to predict that there was going to be a lot of entangling overlap in the names of the membership of both. Like peers and party leaders of all times, all places, the nobles of Hillston were thick as thieves, and always had been. And like peers and party leaders of all times, all places, they were such hogs at the board of plenty that the poor folks waiting below for the trickle-down of the lords' crumbs stayed mighty skinny.

But revolution's not my business. I'm not paid to stop systematic corruption on a cultural scale. I'm paid, by the system, to stop the petty thieves from fouling the machinery. I work at the bottom, keeping the lower decks of the ship of state clean. It's when the nobles visit the hull to get things done that they don't feel like doing themselves, that's when they step into my territory, and that's when I make them my business. And that's what I spent Christmas night thinking with chalk about, writing circles of names on that blackboard.

Finally, I must have fallen asleep on my (or rather the city's) imitation leather couch, Martha Mitchell at my feet like on a duke's tomb. I dropped off, going over – for maybe the thousandth time – the few minutes, as it turned out, crucial minutes, I'd been on the scene the night George Hall had shot Bobby Pym, sending himself to Death Row, and his younger brother Coop into a political activism that had ended with another bullet to the head.

In memory I think I might have heard George fire the gun, from blocks away, but I'm not sure. That hot summer Saturday night, there was a lot of loud music from open windows, and car noise and crowd noise along that section of East Main. I'd just finished my shift, and was driving over to Mill Street to check on my father. (He'd lived alone since Mama's death, and he was starting to die, too, but we didn't know it yet.) When I turned on to Pitt Street, the people bunched by the door of Smoke's Bar spotted my squad car, and most of them slipped back inside, or off into the shadows. My next memory is George sitting on the sidewalk, and then another clump of people farther down the street, squatted around a twisting body that lay near the kerb; I remember I noticed how the leg spasmed. And I remember being aware of all the dark, silent faces staring out from doorways, and down from windowsills. I radioed for help, but the next squad car got there so fast (three minutes, with the ambulance only a few minutes later), that I knew somebody had already phoned before I did. I found out later, in fact, that an anonymous call had come while Pym and Hall were still fighting over the gun inside the bar. As it happened, Captain Van Fulcher himself was in that squad car, along with two officers, cruising nearby on Maplewood, set to pay one of his periodic calls on the Popes (a huge extended family of fairly incompetent thieves, generations in the trade) to see what he might parenthetically find on their premises while harassing them. Fulcher had a thing about arresting the Popes – they were his token whites, to keep his arrest record from charges of racism.

George sat alone on the kerb, in T-shirt and jeans; arms hanging down between his legs. Soon as I saw the pistol lying beside him on the sidewalk, I pulled my gun. That's when he raised his arms and said, 'I'm not running. Just don't shoot.' His nose was bleeding, and he kept wiping at the blood that dripped into his moustache. He asked about Pym, but didn't say much else, just stared out at the street. He didn't say much more at his trial, except that he'd thought Pym was running towards a blue Ford to get another gun, and so had shot in self-defence. Of course, by the trial, who knew what cars might have been parked on that dark crowded street.

I didn't recognize Bobby Pym at first; he was out of uniform, and besides, his whole face was oozy with blood. A red hole gaped right through his eye, but incredibly enough he was still alive. There was a swarm of people (almost all black) hovering about, everybody pushing at each other, shouting; it was all pretty confused. I was yelling, 'What happened?!' over the sound of sirens coming. But all I got was head shakes, shrugs, the mumbled 'Didn't see it,' or 'Look like a fight,' and the blur of people's backs retreating fast into doorways. It's hard now to sort out what I *saw*, from what I heard at the trial, not that I even heard much of the trial; I wasn't on the record as the arresting officer. Like I said, I was only on the scene about five minutes before Captain Fulcher careened around the corner, and took over. I was told to follow the ambulance to University Hospital Emergency Room. An hour later Fulcher showed up there with Bobby's wife and father, and half a dozen police officers (including, I recall, his partner, Winston Russell). Word came soon after they arrived that Officer Pym had already died in OR. When I left, Mrs Pym (who looked about eighteen) was hysterically insisting that Bobby's killer had robbed him first, because Bobby's wallet wasn't in the plastic bag of personal effects the nurse gave her. No one ever found the wallet. George certainly didn't have it.

That was the end of my official involvement. The arresting officer of record was Van Dorn Fulcher, publicized as the captain who still works the toughest beat in town. Of course, I had no claim to the case, other than my having accidentally driven past the scene. I wasn't even in Homicide yet – not till I made lieutenant. And as I already had more than enough of my own cases, and my own troubles, George Hall gradually faded for me to just 'the Hall case,' department gossip, maybe a little chagrin at a missed chance for 'the big collar' that can speed promotion. It was only after George did the unexpected, when everybody had figured he'd go for guilty to second-degree, and pleaded innocent; and only after Mitchell Bazemore asked the jury for the death penalty, and they gave it to him, only then did my mind start going back to the image I'd first seen of George Hall, sitting slumped on the kerb of that Canaan sidewalk, arms between his knees. From then on that image would push its way into my thoughts at odd times, and on bad nights George began to show up in my dreams.

Lying on my couch now, I dreamed he was with me on a search-and-destroy near my last fire base in Vietnam. Pitch-black steamy night, we were huddled together in the weeds of a hollowed riverbank; incoming whistling down on us, throwing up chunks of mud, the sky bright with red and green tracers. I yelled at George, 'Where's it coming from? Theirs or ours!' His mouth was next to my ear, kind of chuckling. He said, 'If you *knew*, man, you think there'd be any difference?' Then blood suddenly spat out of his mouth, hot and sticky across my face. It woke me up, sweating.

Later, Hiram Davies must have sneaked into my office, turned off my light, and draped my overcoat across me. At dawn the pigeons, gossiping on the window ledge, woke me again. I listened to Brodie Cheek selling tapes of his salvation seminars on the radio while I did a few knee bends to get the kinks out. On my desk was a neatly typed report from Hiram, who preferred the slow formality of his old Royal to the faster pace of the computer, or just telling me whatever it was he had to say.

TO: C. R. Mangum, Capt., HPD
FROM: Sgt. H. Davies
RE: Suspects' Access to HPD Impoundment Facility.

The 'Hillston Police Department Impoundment Facility' was a little concrete building next to a chain-fenced lot on the west end of town. In the lot we kept unclaimed/abandoned, and recovered/stolen cars, motorcycles, and bikes, along with broken-down police vehicles. In the building we stored confiscated illegalities – by which I mean shelves of guns, rifles, and knives of considerable variety; shelves of pills, powders, and weeds of considerable variety; shelves of lewd and lascivious entertainments of the same considerable variety; and shelves of other people's property, even more various. The 'suspects' I had in mind here were Offficers Robert Earl Pym and Winston M. Russell, Jr. Their 'access' to this 'facility' in the period immediately preceding Pym's death had been, according to Hiram's research, 'definitive and unobstructed.' In other words, flat-out easy, since (a) inventory procedures at the time had been lousy, and the records were a mess, (b) the night watchman at the time was an old retired cop on a pension who could have slept through the bombing of Dresden, and (c) Winston M. Russell, Jr had once been assigned to duty there – long enough to get to know the place very well.

Now as soon as Pete Zaslo at the Silver Comet had let me in on news about the bad old days before the reign of Mangum the Incorruptible, my theory was that Russell & Pym had been selling off impounded HPD goodies to customers who were in no position to argue about prices, since they were themselves violating some stuffy old statute or other – like the ones against prostitution and gambling, both of which were rumoured to have flourished, for example, upstairs at Smoke's. The first call I made after the pigeons woke me up was to Justin, so he could get an early start working on my theory. He responded with a string of preppy profanities and silly demands that I tell him the time.

I said, 'It's six-o-nine, A.M., Lieutenant. Turn on your radio; Brodie Cheek's already on the air telling us Jesus hates abortions and our pinko Mayor Carl Yarborough condones riots. I'm already at my desk. That's how I've risen to the top of the heap while you wallow in the shrubs below, clipping those coupons; how I climbed the ladder of success, beating the Peter Principle, while you were lying around just beating your peter; how I maximized—'

'Oh God, I can't stand it,' he whined. 'I'm up, I'm up, goodbye.'

The next call I made was to Warden Carpenter at Dollard

163

Prison. He hoped I was phoning with news of Isaac Rosethorn, since George Hall continued to be overwrought in his demands to speak with Rosethorn immediately. I said there'd been no word from the old lawyer, but I'd let him know; meantime, I said, ask George if there was anyone else to whom he'd like to talk. Carpenter said George had made it clear he wanted Rosethorn, and nobody but Rosethorn.

Warden Carpenter was a big, rawboned, rural man, a former police chief himself, a WW II vet with a burn scar down the left half of his face. He was slow spoken; I got my desk straightened up while I listened to him. 'He's real different, George, these last few days. All along, and even, you know, the day before we were scheduled to carry out the sentence, well, George was . . . resigned, I guess. Kind of just pulled back real far inside himself, not fighting a thing, not interested, like he'd already died or something. Then the governor's stay—'

'You know I was out there the night Lewis dropped by?'

Along pause. Then, 'No . . . Well, maybe the shock of the reprieve, what happened to his brother, but George is real different now. Real agitated. Yelling at the guards, not eating, getting out of control. It's rattling the other men. Hate to think George could lose it, after holding on all these years.'

I said, 'Well, sir, you know if Hall does go crazy, the state can't execute. Not till we cure him of the insanity enough so he can pay attention when we kill him. Now, how's that for proof that capital punishment's there to deter killers, not for vengeance?'

Carpenter sighed into the phone. 'The ones that *don't* go crazy over here are the ones I wonder about, young fellow. We're up to eight years wait time on Death Row. Kind of like getting forced to play Russian roulette eight years solid. The only ones don't go crazy are the psychopaths, and the retards and the suicidals begging for it. Oh, hell, I ought not to talk, you know, in general. You got to look at the individual situation. Every last one of them's a different case when you get down to it.'

Ten years ago, he'd walked into Dollard Prison a hidebound authoritarian, an unthinking racist, a guard of the guilty. But somehow, ten prison years had taught him the opposite of what you might predict – not more bigotry but a struggling tolerance. Now he was about as fair-minded as a warden in a crowded, antiquated, badly staffed, barbarically designed prison system could be. Fair-mindedness had given him a great reputation and bad stomach ulcers.

He said, 'So what can I do for you, Cuddy? Not sending me anybody today, are you? We're full, no vacancies.'

I said, 'Just information. You remember a cop you had there, Winston Russell? Aggravated assault.'

There was another pause. Then, 'Oh, yeah. Now there was a real SOB. I thought about arguing with the board to nix his parole, but hell, who wanted him around?'

'He's out, isn't he?'

'Think he went down to his folks' home in north Georgia, had a security job lined up. What's the problem?'

'This goes way back. Looks like he and Bobby Pym were in tight on an extortion scam, including maybe shakedowns at that bar in Canaan, Smoke's, where George Hall hung out, where he shot Pym. We're just starting to dig into it—'

'What are you saying: George knew Pym and Russell were on the pad?'

'I'm not saying George knew it.'

'Well, still, I'd just leave that sucker down in Georgia. Somebody on the street'll kill him down there sooner or later. Somebody in here just about did already. Otherwise Winston would have been out couple of months back. We had him in the infirmary seven weeks.'

'Wait a minute. When was he released? I thought it was a couple of months ago.'

'Well, would have been. Let's see. Been about a week, I guess.'

'A week! Like last Thursday? Russell got out last Thursday?'

'Let's see ... Yeah, that's right. Thing was, prisoner in the kitchen pulled a knife on him.'

Zeke Caleb had just opened my door with a bag of doughnuts, a quart of coffee, and Martha, whom he'd taken for a stroll to the ladies' room (the parking lot). Zeke looked at me funny, I guess because I was slapping the wall, in fact smacking Elvis on the face. I said into the phone, 'Zackery, you say a *knife* fight? Was Russell scarred? Across the back?'

'That's right. You hear about it? Back and side. Fifty-eight stitches.'

Carpenter said he'd have somebody call back with the north Georgia address. The rest of the information I wanted – including a record of Winston Russell's visitors during his time at Dollard

– he said he'd 'see' about. I said, 'Let me ask you this, Zackery – just off the record, okay? Why'd Governor Wollston stop the Hall execution? Folks were saying all along, no chance in hell he was going to. You think he really had second thoughts, or, one theory is, it was out of respect for Cadmean's dying. Scared there'd be an incident.'

Carpenter said, 'I heard there was an incident anyhow. Because of the brother's murder . . . Got a line on that one yet? Hell of a thing. Racial?'

'Maybe. So what about Governor Wollston? What did Lewis tell you?'

'Just that the governor was granting a stay. Next morning the official call came, and confirmed. Off the record, Cuddy . . . I was glad to get it.'

'Why send Lewis out here in the rain when Wollston could just call?'

'. . . I don't guess that's my business.'

'What was he doing in there for almost an hour?' I didn't get an answer to this. 'Or you don't guess that's *my* business?'

'I guess it's not.'

We talked a little more, not to leave it at that, then I wished him a Happy New Year, and hung up.

Zeke shovelled a mound of my gum wrappers into the trash, as he gave me a hard look. 'Chief, you oughta take a shower. I mean . . .' He blushed. 'You don't look too good.'

Jam squirted out of my doughnut and ran down my unshaven chin. 'Looks aren't everything, Sergeant. You get in touch with Purley?'

'Not yet. Otis Newsome, he's in Fayetteville with his wife's family, but Purley's not with them.'

'Find him. And call Nancy, tell her to get that kid Wally back over here.' Zeke, who made rooms look small and furniture flimsy, sprang across the carpet in a couple of steps. 'Zeke, hold up . . . You never mentioned – have a good Christmas?' He blushed again. 'You do like I told you, and ask Nancy to dinner?'

'Sort of . . .' He wrung the door handle a while. 'We ate there at the bowling alley.'

'Took her to the bowling alley, hunh? Well, that's pretty romantic. You give her a present?'

He brightened. 'I got her one of those Water-Pik kits for her teeth. She don't take real good care of her teeth.'

I said, 'I bet you told her that, too. Cherokee, you gotta learn a little more of the white man's forked-tongue approach.'

He looked puzzled. 'Well, she oughta take care of 'em . . .' He tapped his own perfect teeth. 'She's something. She bowled two sixty-four. Just clean wiped me up and down like a old floor mop.'

'Not exactly going the Annie Oakley route, is she?'

'Nancy? Naw, she's a terrible shot.'

'That's not what I meant. Annie Oakley deliberately blew her match with her boyfriend 'cause you can't get a man with a gun.'

Now Zeke really blushed. 'Nancy's not trying to get a man; you oughtna to say that, Chief.'

'It was an *Indian* gave Annie Oakley that advice. In the movie anyhow.'

He frowned, confused, made a part with his hand in his stiff black hair, shook his head, and left to call the unsuspecting love of his life. I took a shower.

Most of the morning on Boxing Day, as Mrs Marion Sunderland liked to refer to December 26, I listened to reports from the team I'd assigned to what I was now thinking of as the Cooper & George Hall case. First, John Emory had checked out the names in Coop's address book. Coop knew a lot of people, but most of them were the people you'd expect him to know – relatives, school friends, and the Piedmont area's young left-leaning social conscience – what there was of it: other civil rights activists, social workers, teachers, union types, pro bono lawyers, ex-SDSers like Molina, liberal Democrats like Alice. 'Three of these people,' said Emory tersely, close-shaved black chin tucked into immaculate khaki collar above painfully tight black tie, 'at least three are known Communists. These three.' He pointed at his list. 'The woman, sir, has an arrest record. She spoke to me with some violence.'

I looked at the names. 'Yep, they're Commies. Fact, Janet Malley here's been the Communist candidate for City Council the last four elections. Placed tenth out of ten every time. I tell you this, maybe she's a little, well, strong tongued, but we could use ole Janet on that council.'

Emory's nostrils reacted like I'd uncorked some ammonia under his nose. 'Yes, sir . . . All three had alibis for the time Hall was shot.'

'Well, John, I hadn't really been figuring them for prime suspects.'

'I considered the possibility that they might want to create a martyr situation.'

'It's an interesting notion, but a little harsh for Janet's style . . . Look here, John, when are you ever going to take that sergeant's exam, so I can promote you into using that brain more than those feet?'

'I'm studying. I don't feel I'm prepared yet.'

'Um hum. I wish you'd study with your partner. Nancy's already flunked once, due to not cracking a book, be my guess. How y'all getting along?'

He took a deep breath, and confessed, 'She's . . . reliable, and very committed to the job, and I think she's . . . smart.'

'But how're y'all getting *along*? . . . Mmm . . . That bad, hunh?' His handsome face was contorted in a struggle to find something polite to say. I let him off. 'Well, you'll get used to each other. Now, let's forget Janet Malley's fondness for Fidel. What about these names here?'

The predictability of Cooper's address book made a few entries in it stand out like Shriners at an anti-nuke rally. Two I'd noticed before: Billy Gilchrist, drunk con man and missing Episcopal convert. And the deceased paper salesman Clark Koontz, whose card with 'Newsome' on the back seemed a funny thing for Coop to hang on to, especially when *With Liberty and Justice* had never, as we now knew, done business with Fanshaw Paper Company. But there were other odd names there, like Hamilton Walker. Him, I knew personally. He'd been the king of East Hillston pimps for a decade, having inherited the title from his mentor, the late great Woodrow Clenny, who was stabbed to death by a jealous prostitute, after a long flamboyant reign. His successor, Ham Walker, ran the business *as* a business. It was impossible to imagine Cooper Hall as one of his customers.

Another name, Bunny Randolph, I knew only by reputation. He was Atwater's son, and presumably the busty Blue Randolph's father. According to Justin (who could appreciate it), Bunny was the black sheep of his family, apparently because of his drinking escapades. Seemed like Justin had once mentioned that Atwater had fired Bunny, his only son, from his only job, but still paid his alimony for him and kept him at a distance on an allowance.

I looked up at Emory, who was studying my blackboard. 'You asked those two how and why Coop Hall might have had their phone numbers?'

'Yes, sir. Hamilton Walker said—' Emory took out his notepad. 'I'm quoting Walker now. "How the blank would I know? Half the blank-blank males in this blank-blank town know my blank phone number." He persisted in that.'

'I bet.'

'Yes, sir. Bunny Randolph is really Atwater Randolph the third. Lives in Southern Pines. He said he had contributed to the George Hall Defence Fund, and Cooper Hall had telephoned to thank him.'

'Um hum. Hard to believe.' I rattled the list of names at Emory. 'Now, John, what's the *most* interesting name you came across in that address book?'

His chin worked back and forth. '. . . Cadmean?'

'Right. Ole Mister BM himself, hanging down there in the lobby right this minute. Why interesting?'

Emory just about smiled. '. . . Because that's his home number. And it's unlisted.'

'Right.'

'You knew that, sir?' He tried hard not to look surprised.

'I was a friend of the family. For a while.' The desk phone rang; it was Etham down in the lab, and I said I'd call him back in a second. 'Okay, John. What I want you to do – You have people in East Hillston, don't you?'

His eyebrow flickered. 'I suppose it's easy to assume, sir.'

'. . . Hey, come on. Not everybody in East Hillston's black. Everybody's just poor. I grew up there, on Mill Street. Nancy grew up on Maplewood.'

He said the first person-to-person thing to me since he'd come to HPD. '*Almost* everybody in East Hillston's black. It tends to go along with being poor.'

I tossed my pencil down, and leaned my chair back. 'You're right. It sure does.'

He blew out an audible breath. '. . . I have family in Canaan, yes.'

'Any teenagers that might know Martin Hall? The kid we had in here on—'

'I know who he is.'

'Talk to him. Get out of the uniform. Forget the manual. I want to know everything Martin, or anybody Martin can get you to, can think of about Cooper that can help us. Including anything about Hamilton Walker. Anything about Smoke's Bar.'

Emory nodded, fingering his belt of bright polished equipment as if it'd be hard to do without it. 'As per who might have shot him?'

'And behind that. "As per" what happened the night his brother shot Bobby Pym. For now, let's say the Cooper Hall case is also the George Hall case.'

Then I returned Etham Foster's call from the lab. And that's when the Cooper & George Hall case became the Hall & Slidell case, because that's when Etham reported that the bullets removed from Willie Slidell's chest had been fired from the same .38 pistol as the bullet that had killed Cooper Hall. And a bullet the boy Wally had taken from the target-practice coffee can outside the farm had come from that gun too. I made it clear to everybody that this news was not to become news, if we could possibly keep it that way. We hadn't even released a statement that the body we'd recovered from the river yesterday was full of slugs, much less those particular ones.

Next Dick Cohn, sniffling with a cold, came in to report that Slidell had been dead at least three days before Wally had found him. Saturday or Sunday was his best guess. If Wally hadn't been so desperate to save his BB gun, chances were, in so inaccessible a part of the river, the body could have sat in that car underwater until time and fish had stripped it of anything personally recognizable. Whoever put the body there must have counted on that likelihood, since Slidell's pockets had been carefully emptied. Darlene at DMV reported that it might not be possible to trace the ownership of the white Ford, from which someone had not only removed the licence plates, but chiselled off the metal ID number.

'Slidell? Not shot at close range,' Cohn added, zipping up a padded coat he could have crossed the North Pole in. 'Fantastic placement, though, Bam, team, team, tight as a bull's-eye.'

'Before or after Cooper Hall was shot?'

He shrugged. 'I'm a doctor, not a Ouija board.'

'Come on, Dick, help out here! What's your best bet?'

'Within the same thirty-six hours.'

'Thanks a lot.'

'Anytime.' He checked the sky out my window. 'You think they could use a good medical examiner in Miami? It's in the eighties there today.'

'It's warm a lot of spots they could use a good ME. How 'bout El Salvador, Honduras, around there? They get heaps and heaps of bodies need examining.'

'Don't speak Spanish . . . By the way, Slidell was on coke.'

'Down in these parts, that usually means Coca-Cola, but I bet you're talking about the other kind.'

'Sure am.' He pulled on some fat ski gloves, and waved good-bye like he was leaving to walk to Canada instead of the parking lot.

After Cohn left, Nancy White came in with the young boy, Wally. She took him into the squad room to look through a stack of photographs I had ready for her. The stack included every picture Dave Schulmann at the FBI could give us of known or suspected KKK'ers, or any other fraternal order of white supremacists, including two yahoos Justin had identified from the Carolina Patriots gathering where he'd met Willie Slidell. It also included the photo I'd removed from Winston Russell's HPD file. An hour later, Nancy reported that Wally (whom Zeke was now taking on a tour of the department) had considered all the photos carefully, and finally admitted that he'd really been too far away to be sure he could recognize the man he'd seen target-practising unless maybe he saw him in person.

I asked Nancy, 'He pay any special attention to the shot of Russell?'

She pulled her gold neck chain up over her chin, and bit on it. 'That kid paid 'bout five minutes special attention to every one of them! When he got done, I pointed to Russell and asked him directly, but he wouldn't make the ID. Then he goes through the whole stack again! That kid's beginning to remind me of Hemorrhoid Emory.'

'Caution's a virtue.' It would have been nice if Wally'd pulled Russell's ten-year-old photo right out of the bunch, but I didn't really need Wally to convince me it was Winston Russell who'd been staying out at Slidell's. I'd been feeling my way to Russell all night, even before Zackery Carpenter'd confirmed it with the news about the knife scar.

But Wally did make one positive ID while taking his tour. He identified the 'kind of big shot' who'd taken Cooper Hall for a plane ride just an hour before he was killed. Wally saw the man on the campaign poster Brenda Moore had put up on a bulletin board outside the squad room. In this poster, Andrew Brookside looked like St George with a high IQ and a great tailor.

Now, I'd already had a report that the red mud embedded in the tyre treads of Coop's Subaru was compatible with the mud at Lake Road Airport, though no one at the airfield appeared to have noticed Coop Hall out there boarding a plane. And I'd had a report that of nine private planes that had logged flights that Saturday, one of them, a Cessna, belonged to Andy Brookside. So I was prepared. But still surprised.

According to a switchboard operator (presumably all alone on campus), Haver University was 'closed for the holidays.' I called Brookside at home. 'Briarhills?' said the maid who answered. Only Lee was there; the fast-travelling Andy was up in New York, being the main speaker at a national teachers' conference. But Lee was expecting a call from him, and would give him the message to phone me. 'You sound funny. Is something wrong? Is this about the letter I gave you?'

I said, 'No, it's about Cooper Hall. Your husband have much contact with him? Were they friendly?'

'Cooper Hall? I don't think so ... No, I never saw them together. Andy never mentioned knowing him. Why?'

'Just a detail I need to clear up, that's all.'

'Detail? ... Could Jack Molina help? He knew Cooper Hall well.'

I said, 'According to the grandma that the Molinas left home with their kids, the Molinas are up in New York too.'

'Oh . . .'

'These college types all tend to run off at Christmas, don't they?' It'd be a lie to say I was suspicious of my motive in mentioning where the Molinas were; I *knew* what my motive was, and didn't much admire it. It seemed more than likely, even from the little I'd observed at Rowell Hall the day of the funerals, that Brookside was, as they say, involved with Debbie Molina. I wasn't sure if Jack suspected – though he did appear to be pretty nervous about his wife's whereabouts. I wasn't sure if Lee suspected, and I wanted to be sure. I wondered if I didn't even want to make sure.

But all she said was, 'I expect Jack's helping with the speech. He's very committed to Andy's campaign.'

I said, 'How about you? How'd you feel about your husband's resigning from Haver, and going for this long shot at governor? Well, they say it's a long shot.'

'Andy thrives on long shots. He expects to win.'

'I asked you about *you*. You want to be First Lady?'

She said, 'As opposed to what?'

'Well, Lord, I don't know. Brain surgeon. Chanteuse in a

nightclub. Last I heard you wanted to be a newspaper reporter. 'Course, that was back in high school.'

She laughed. 'Oh God, that's true, isn't it? Maybe I ought to ask Edwina Sunderland to hire me. I'll see you there tonight, at Edwina's?'

'Yep. Our hostess said "seven-thirty," like we better not mistake it for seven-thirty-five.' My hand was sweaty on the receiver. 'Look, Lee, would you like a ride, show me exactly where in those windy woods fifteen sixteen Catawba Drive is? Close to your place, isn't it? I could drop by and give you a ride.'

She said, 'Well, I've already agreed to drive over with the Fanshaws.'

'Oh, sure, okay. That's okay.'

'. . . But they always like to leave so early. Edwina loves people to just sit and talk . . .'

I kept staring at Elvis on the wall. What I was seeing instead of him had taken place about as long ago as that picture on the poster. Lee and I making out for the first time – neither of us knowing what we were doing, neither of us believing there was a world beyond the glassed walls of her family's greenhouse where we'd hidden ourselves; neither of us imagining a future outside that April night. It had taken me years of that future to get over her.

Now she said, 'So . . . maybe you could give me a ride home, Cuddy.'

And I said, 'Fine.'

After we hung up, I pushed the phone away from me, turned around, and told Elvis that after the way he'd messed up his own life, he had no call to sneer at my apparently dumbheaded willingness to do the same to mine.

At two-thirty, I officially announced to Mrs Sunderland's newspaper, the *Hillston Star*, that Justin Savile, detective lieutenant of Homicide, was officially in charge of the Hall murder, reporting directly to me. Bubba Percy, the *Star*'s representative, who'd made himself at home on my couch, yawned and said, 'That must gripe Savile's ass, working for you, when his people've been running this boonie state since they killed off the fuckin' Indians; when they've been buying and selling your kind wholesale.'

I said, 'Bubba, now that's impressive; in one fairly short sentence you've managed to insult me, Lieutenant Savile, the upper class, the common folk, the native American Indian, and the proud state of North Carolina. Get out of here. I'm busy.' I was wondering if he'd nosed out some rumour about Willie Slidell's death already, and was waiting to spring it at me.

Bubba flapped his Burberry trenchcoat; maybe to show me the label, maybe to fan himself. Then he pulled out a clipper, and began snipping his fingernails. 'What'd you think of today's editorial?' He always assumed I spent every spare minute poring over his newspaper. 'We're endorsing Julian Lewis for governor. Snore, snooze.'

'Little soon, isn't it?'

'Oh, everybody knows he and Brookside'll take their primaries. But it's starting to look like a crapshoot about the real election. Brookside's coming on.' Bubba patted his crotch. 'Course ole Andy'll have to keep his dick zipped. The Brodie Cheek moral Babbitts get hold of that little black book of his, they'll nail our war hero to the cross by his hyperactive balls. Shit, I could die happy on a tenth of the pussy that man puts away.'

I didn't look up, but kept signing the forms Zeke had left on my desk. 'What sewer's the source of your information, Bubba?'

'Well,' he grinned, 'one source said she was speaking from, let's call it, firsthand knowledge.' He leaned across the couch to brush nail clippings on my carpet. 'Hey, big deal, right? I don't care who Brookside fucks, as long as he fucks that asshole Julian Lewis. And if he'll keep his yap shut on this death penalty junk, he may just go all the way. Probably got the Lewis money men nervous already.'

'Probably.'

'I was just talking to Mitch Bazemore; he's hinting around that Lewis is going to tap him for attorney general. True?'

'Probably.'

'Vomit ... And Bazemore says y'all are close to making an arrest on the Hall case. True?'

'No comment.' I found a tie in my 'In' basket, and put it on. 'I'm overdue at the mayor's. You planning to take a nap on that couch, you'll have to sleep with Martha.'

He laughed so affably, and his pretty, pudgy face turned so earnest, I knew he wanted a favour before he said, 'I'll go, but, look, I need a favour.'

I said, 'I need a lot.'

'Tell me what you've got on the Hall shooting. I heard Raleigh police pulled in those goons joy-riding at the prison with Willis

174

Tate, but it's near one hundred per cent they had zilch to do with the shooting.'

'Tell me something I don't know, Bubba.'

'You tell me. *Are* you close? Slip me something, will yah? This could be big for me. I think I could go national with a real piece on Cooper Hall. I'm serious.'

'Go national?' I walked over and moved his Italian boot off my couch arm. 'I thought shallow triviality was the secret of happiness. Sounds like you're coming down with that "last infirmity of a noble mind." If you read anything besides newsprint, you'd know what that was.'

Bubba rolled off the couch, tucking his cashmere turtleneck into his pleated trousers. 'It's ambition – according to an old blind man named Milton.' He grinned. 'You're always underestimating me, Cuddy. Just 'cause I'm gorgeous, doesn't mean I'm dumb. Sometimes shallow waters run deep. Okay, okay, I'm going. Keep the peace, Captain Pig.'

I caught the newspaper he tossed at me from the doorway. 'Hold up, Bubba.' I tossed him back a copy of *With Liberty and Justice*, with Cooper's 'House of Lords' article in it. 'Read this. And do *me* a favour. Find out for me why Cooper had Bunny Randolph's phone number in his address book.'

Percy winked a long-lashed eye, made some disgusting smacky kissing noises, and left me alone. The *Star* still had the Hall shooting on the front page. There was also a little piece captioned 'BRODIE CHEEK TURNS TO TELEVISION.' In the popular evangelical tradition, Cheek was leaving syndicated radio behind for cable TV, where the real money was. Unless Brookside's information was right, and Cheek's real money was falling from the heaven of corporate industry, courtesy of the Constitution Club. While I was thinking about his motive in giving me a copy of that report, Brookside himself telephoned.

I'm not sure why, but I got out of my chair and stood beside my desk to take the call when Zeke put it through. While I waited for Brookside to come on the line, I kept moving the wood chess pieces that Lee had admired, arranging them randomly around on the board. The bright-painted pawns were Costa Rican peasants, the castles plantations, the knights Quixotic warriors on horseback, and by a touch I'd admired so much that I'd traded my admittedly defunct car for the set, the kings and queens looked suspiciously like modern wealthy Americans.

'Hello, Andy Brookside speaking. Captain Mangum?' Brookside was pleasant, but wasted no time. 'I'm in New York. I just spoke with Lee, who seemed to feel this was urgent. I have a moment now.'

I took a breath. 'This will only take a moment. In our little car ride recently, you told me you didn't know Cooper Hall.'

He was so quick I figured Lee must have mentioned something to him about my questions. 'No, I recall you asked me that, and I recall I did not reply.'

'You implied—'

A warm chuckle. 'As I believe your purist, Thomas More, reminded his interrogators, silence implies consent, not denial.' His voice had none of the tight tone that defensiveness usually produces. 'In fact, I met Hall . . . on a few occasions. Jack Molina introduced us. Why?'

I decided not to waste any time either. 'Did one of those occasions take place in the air in your Cessna, about an hour before he was killed, and in the same vicinity where he was killed?'

Well, I'd stopped him for about four seconds, but no more than that, and when he answered, he was succinct. He said, '. . . Yes.'

'You admit that you were with—'

'Why should I deny it? You obviously know it to be true, someway or another. Who told you?'

I thought about telling him he was in no position to ask, but it wasn't worth shutting down the conversation. I said, 'It came up accidentally during questions in a different investigation. A boy watching the planes happened to see the two of you together and recognized Hall from the news.'

'Jesus Christ.' He sounded disgusted.

'Right. A fluke. Now you tell me why he was in your plane.'

'To talk to me, of course. Perfectly legitimate.'

I was jumping a knight in and out of a cluster of pawns, and Brookside's cool formal easiness so irritated me, I broke the tip off the knight's lance. But I kept my voice down, and my diction up there with his. 'Then why, Mr Brookside, didn't you inform me as soon as you learned of the shooting? There's nothing "legitimate" about withholding material evidence in a murder. Spending an hour with the victim immediately before his death is, as you perfectly well know, material evidence. At the *least*, material evidence. I could have you arrested.'

He wasn't fazed. 'Why? Do you suspect me of shooting this man?'

'Did you?'

'No.'

I believed him. Not on faith. I'd already established his alibi. I asked, 'Do you know anything about who did?'

'No. Look, Hall wanted a meeting. In private. I was planning to leave for Asheville. We arranged for him to come to Lake Road Airport. He was interested in going up in my plane, so we did. For approximately half an hour. Then I set him down, and immediately took off again. At two-twenty-three. It's logged. He had his own car, and, I assume, left in it. I was flying over Raleigh fifteen minutes later, *before* – I gather – the time he was shot. I radioed their tower, checked the weather, and they cleared me through to Asheville. You can verify my Asheville arrival time.'

'I already have. Also your conversation with Air Traffic Control in Raleigh.'

'Jesus Christ.' He forced himself into patience. 'Understand my position.'

'Try me.'

I pretty much knew what he was going to say, and he said it: 'I hope to be governor of this state. A great many people share that hope, and have worked damn hard for it. This Hall meeting was the kind of awful coincidence that can do terrible damage.'

'Withholding evidence can do terrible damage.'

'Look. I was in Asheville. I didn't know until Sunday morning that Hall had been killed, and I didn't know until much later how and *when* he'd been killed. I did know that while our meeting had absolutely nothing to do with his death, the fact that I might have been the last person to see him alive, my being in *any* way involved in testimony in a homicide—' Brookside sighed, briskly. 'I was wrong. I made a mistake.'

'Because we happened to find out?'

'No, I've been distressed about the whole thing. I planned to speak with you as soon as I got back from New York.'

I didn't know whether I believed this or not. At any rate, I assured him he *was* going to speak with me as soon as he got back. Meantime, despite the 'quite a few people waiting in the next room' for his attention, I insisted that he talk to me before joining them. He did so as if he were taking questions at a hurried press conference.

Did Hall come to, and leave from, the airport alone? Yes – as far as he knew. Was there anyone in the vicinity who might have been watching Hall? Not that he'd noticed; the access road was empty. Did Hall say where he was going afterwardss? No. Did anyone else know about this meeting? On his end, no. Not Jack Molina? Hadn't Molina set up the meeting on Saturday? No, Hall himself had. How far in advance? Not at all in advance, early that morning. How? By phone.

I said, 'Friday evening at the Hillston Club you didn't seem to me all that interested in Cooper Hall. His brother gets reprieved later that night. Saturday morning Coop calls you up, and you agree to meet him?'

'You misinterpreted me if you thought I was uninterested. He struck me as a savvy young man of tremendous political potential. Anything else?'

We went on, while I made up scenarios with the chessboard: Coop the black knight alone in the centre face to face with Brookside the smiling white king. And me? I couldn't see myself in any of the pieces.

He said he'd naturally encountered Cooper Hall through the latter's political activities, but only in public settings. More recently, at Jack Molina's request, he'd agreed to see Hall, who'd asked him to take a position on George Hall's death sentence. Had that been what the two had talked about on their Saturday flight – George's stay of execution? In part. What about the other part? The gubernatorial campaign. Would he be more specific? No. Why? Their discussion was irrelevant to the issue at hand.

'I'm not sure I can go with that, Mr Brookside. Was the talk personal or political?'

'It was not personal.'

'Then why did this meeting need to be private?'

He said I should be able to figure that out myself: many of his supporters, and even staff, strongly opposed his taking a stand on the George Hall execution; moreover, they felt that in general he should move his position further centre, away from the left, and certainly away from such highly publicized representatives of the left as Cooper Hall was becoming.

I said, 'Seems like you claimed it was *Coop* who wanted the meeting private.'

Now he chuckled. 'I'm sure people on his side had similar feelings about his associating with a reactionary like me. Our talk was preliminary, speculative. A formal meeting would have been premature.'

'Are you saying you were discussing Coop Hall's joining your campaign?'

'It's immaterial now, isn't it? Captain, I have fifty visitors waiting. I'll be back in Hillston the thirtieth. Should I bring a lawyer?' He asked in the friendliest style, like we were in this together, and just had to say these formulas for the record.

I said, 'That's up to you. We'd just like a formal statement.'

'Ah. Iron fist in the velvet glove. All right . . . Now, let me ask you something. Did you read the Constitution Club folder?'

'Yes. What was your motive in giving it to me?'

'Why, to win you over to my side.' I could hear the smile in his voice, just as I could see him up at the phone in that New York conference suite, perfect features, perfect clothes, perfect tan; while behind a door the fan club of teachers milled about, clutching wine and crackers.

I said, 'Not because your data's sort of "speculative," and it'd be "premature" to go public until somebody did all the footwork to check it out for you at taxpayer's expense?'

'Of course.' Brookside's voice was warm as a soft scarf. 'If I didn't think you'd be interested in that kind of misuse of money and influence to manipulate people's worst prejudices; if I didn't think you'd be interested in that old atrophied network's clutching power by keeping poor whites hating blacks and abortions more than they hate their own poverty – well, I wouldn't want you on my side, Cuddy . . . I'll see you then, soon as I get back. And by the way, I hear you're going to Edwina's tonight. Tell her, will you, I'm disappointed that the *Star*'s endorsed Julian Lewis. She won't know anything about it. She owns that paper, but she never reads it. Bye.'

The moon was already hanging dully around outside my window, though the sky was still grey enough for me to see the tops of the Haver Tobacco Company buildings off to my west, and the Cadmean Mills off to my east. I didn't hear Zeke knock, or maybe he didn't knock.

'Chief? Chief? Why don't you turn a light on? I'm leaving now. You want that phone call typed up in the morning?'

I said no, but to save the tape.

He clicked on my desk lamp. 'How come you got your blackboard turned around?'

I said, because I hadn't wanted Bubba Percy to read what was on it. Zeke laughed, and flipped the board back to the front. He shook his head at all the names, arrows, question marks in chalk. 'Chief, looks like you're fixing to arrest everybody in Hillston . . .' Moving quietly around the room, straightening things, he kept shaking his head. 'Know what, I wouldn't want your job. It's too worrisome. I bet you got this whole blackboard jammed up in your brain all the time. You spending the night here again?'

'No, I'm going out to a dinner party later on.'

'That what that tuxedo in the bag there's for? I rented myself one of those suits too, once, back in high school. It was a really pretty blue.'

'This one's black.'

'Then I chickened out, didn't even go to that dance anyhow. I never heard how people wore 'em to eat dinner in, though. Y'all gonna dance after you eat or something?'

I said, 'I'll let you know tomorrow, Zeke.'

Zeke went to work on my desk. 'Don't leave these french fries sitting here for the ants. Shit, you got gum stuck right to the wood.' He picked up a chess piece beside the phone. 'This lady part of that chess set? Where's it go?'

I said, 'The queen goes next to the king.'

'Chief, sometime, you wanna teach me how to play this chess game? Sort of like checkers? It's a pretty old game, ain't it?'

'Pretty old. It was a royal game. I think it came from India.'

He grinned. 'Like me, hunh? . . . Well, is it the kind where it's hard to learn the rules, 'cause if there's too many rules, forget it, far as I go.'

I looked back out across the Hillston skyline, fading into night. 'Yeah, I guess I'd say it's the kind where it's hard to learn the rules.'

Leaving work, my tuxedo on under my coat so nobody would see it, I forgot a much simpler rule – one I ought to have known by heart. Never assume that any dark empty basement parking garage – not even the police department parking garage – is safe enough to bend over and tie your shoe in, without checking around first to make sure it *is* empty. I keep my Oldsmobile on the opposite end from the elevator, back in a far corner spot, because I'm nervous about protecting its flanks. I should have felt the same about my own flanks. I didn't hear, see, or sense a thing. It did flick through my mind that an awful lot of the lights were out, but I figured the circuit breaker was acting up again, and we were really going to have to give in and replace the whole box. Otherwise I just strolled towards my car, thinking I hoped Justin was right that a Sunderland Boxing Day dinner party was 'definitely black tie.' Then I tripped on a shoelace, then I knelt down to tie it, then I felt a sort of whoosh of air, after which my head exploded like an ammo dump hit by NVA rockets.

The next thing I was looking at after my shoe was Etham Foster's face, actually two or three of his faces. There were also bright haloed lights glaring down at me. I was lying on the concrete floor on Etham's huge sheepskin jacket, and he was squatted beside me. He held my head in one hand; the other one was poking through my hair. I said – well, I think it was me, but it sounded more like Marlon Brando in *The Godfather* – I said, 'Doctor D, you haven't been dribbling around the floor with my head, have you? Maybe a few dunk shots?'

'Lie back down.' The hand he pushed on my chest was the size of a catcher's mitt. 'You got sapped.'

'I had a feeling that's what happened.' I tried a grin. It was a mistake. I rubbed the back of my head. It was a worse mistake.

'Didn't break the skin,' he said encouragingly.

'How about the skull?'

'Too hard. What happened? Saw you lying here. Whoever it was, was gone. Drove out or ran out. You see who did it?'

I groaned. 'Well, I doubt you did, Lieutenant, but that's about all I can tell you. This is what I get for leaving Martha with Hiram. She could have at least bitten somebody's ankle. Okay, okay, I can get up. I'm fine.' Etham didn't bother to debate this shameless lie, but slowly pulled me to my feet. The best I can say for the experience is that I felt worse in a village outside Da Nang when the medics dropped my stretcher on the way to the helicopter.

Wes Pendergraph and a couple of other guys were down here too now, checking out the garage. Nothing and nobody. They'd found a circuit breaker off, but maybe it had just blown. None of the cars looked vandalized or broken into, including mine. Mine had a real high-strung alarm system anyhow; it would have a fit if you leaned on it funny, much less jimmied a door lock. My wallet was still in my jacket. Had I somehow just thought I'd bent down, but instead had tripped over the shoelace, lost my footing, and knocked myself out?

181

'No way,' grunted Etham. 'Got sapped.'

'Stop rubbing it in.' My head was shrinking a little, about down to the size of a medicine ball now, and my vision had cleared enough for me to see my watch. 7:22.48. I'd been out cold for fifteen minutes. 'Shit, I've gotta go. I've gotta be at a party.' I started towards my Olds. 'Tell Wes to follow this up, okay? Probably juveniles. Shit, look at these pants!' I swiped dirt off my trousers (or rather Saddlefield's Formal Fashions' trousers). 'I'm okay, Dr D, I'm okay.'

'Go get your head looked at.'

I turned back to him; his dark, long-jawed face was furrowed in a frown. All of a sudden I realized he had as much grey in his hair as black. 'Etham,' I said, 'we're getting old, you and me. You realize that? Just the other day we were playing varsity—'

'I was playing varsity. You were mostly on the bench.'

'—Now we're getting old. It's too late for me to get my head looked at. I've gotta go to this party.' While I babbled at him, I was feeling in my overcoat for my car keys. They weren't in the right pocket. I mean the right-hand pocket. I also mean the correct pocket. Now, I'm a creature of strong habits – maybe bad habits some of them (dietary), and maybe messy habits some of them (sartorial) – but strong habits. My books are alphabetized, my bills are filed by date, my toothbrush is on the right-hand side of the sink, my shampoo on the right-hand side of the tub, my radio's on the right-hand side of the bed, and my car keys are *never* in the left-hand pocket of my coat, which is where I found them. I said, 'That's funny, I put my keys in the wrong pocket.'

Etham grabbed the key chain out of my hand by its wornout rabbit's foot, just as I was about to unlock the door. 'Get away from there!' he snapped. 'Pendergraph! Go see if Augustine's still in the lab. Get him down here.' He had his flashlight pressed against the Olds' window; then he crawled under the hood and flashed it around.

'Etham, come on! Who's going to put a bomb in my car?! I don't have time to sit around here while you get paranoid. Give me those keys.'

I heard his voice from under the Olds. 'Use a squad car. This one's not leaving here. I smell something weird. It's gonna take a while.'

I nudged his tennis shoe, which looked like a size fifteen. 'That smell was probably Martha. She farts a lot. Get out from under there. Hey, I'm a captain, you're a lieutenant. Ever heard of the chain of command?' I didn't get any answer. 'You're saying somebody unset and reset my alarm? Knew the Olds was mine, knew it had an alarm system, knew where the fuse box was, plus wired a bomb in ten minutes?'

'Yeah. Kind of narrows it down, doesn't it? But didn't say bomb. Could be a bomb. Maybe not.'

I didn't believe Etham enough to stick around, but I believed him enough to tell him I'd check back later, and to drive to North Hillston in a HPD squad car. I even almost made it on time, because I used the siren. Well, there ought to be some perks to the job, to make up for the long hours, and the sore knob swelling out of the back of my head.

When I pulled in among the parked Mercedeses, I wondered if Mrs Sunderland's neighbours were peeking out the windows, figuring her place had finally got itself raided by the police for throwing parties they weren't asked to. Then I remembered that up here on Catawha Drive, nobody had to put up with neighbours, except the few and far between kind.

I bet my apology to my hostess, regal in a floor-length beaded number that matched her blue hair, was the first one of its kind she'd ever been handed in her double-storeyed, marbled-floored, holly-garlanded hallway. 'Mrs Sunderland, you're gonna have to forgive me for being eight minutes and thirty-three seconds late. I was sapped with a blackjack in my parking lot, knocked out cold, and my lab people are defusing a bomb in my car.'

My hostess said, 'You lucky man. Nothing's worse than a boring life, as I can testify from seventy-two years of nothing but, and you do not appear to be leading a boring life. Call me Edwina. The others are in the sitting room swilling cocktails. I was just on the phone to Atwater Randolph. His moron of a granddaughter, Blue, ran off to Aspen with my moron of a nephew. You remember Chip, my nephew, grandnephew? Well, Blue just called to inform Atwater that she and Chip had got married today.'

'Is that good or bad?' I handed my overcoat to a maid who'd popped up beside me and appeared to want it.

Mrs Sunderland walked me down the hall at her stately pace. 'I imagine they'll find out in a few months. Maybe they'll be perfectly happy. Ignorance is supposed to be bliss. Of course, Atwater's gone berserk. Threatening to disinherit her. He's going to run out of heirs. He already cut Blue's daddy off.'

'You mean Bunny Randolph? Why'd he do that?'

'I could give you two dozen reasons, none or all of which might be true, so I won't give you any. I always liked Bunny, though he had a spine like a wet mop. You know Atwater? He's an admirer of yours.'

'That's good to hear. I'm hoping he'll leave me his bridge over the Shocco. I look out on it from my kitchen balcony, and since nobody ever uses that bridge much, I thought maybe I'd build some shops on it and lease them out. You know, like the Rialto, Ponte Vecchio.'

She gave my arm a squeeze that shot right up to the knot on my head. 'Cuthbert, I'm sorry I didn't meet you fifty years ago. No, let's say thirty. Then I'd already have poor Marion's money.' She had a carnal laugh with a growl in it. 'And we could have built our own bridge.' She jabbed open some double doors into a room full of people. I was glad to see the men wearing tuxedos. I was gladder to see the woman introduced to me by Mrs Sunderland as Lee Haver Brookside.

'Cuddy and I are old friends,' Lee said.

'Maybe so.' Edwina handed me a Scotch and water that was more like a Scotch and a few drops of dew. She grinned, her sharp old incisors cutting into her full lower lip. 'Maybe so, but then you're already married, Lee darling. And I'm available.'

I had the feeling Mrs Marion Sunderland might be more dangerous than a clonk on the head. And not much more subtle.

Chapter 11

'Nobody will discuss current politics this evening,' commanded Mrs Sunderland, as we all rose after our cocktails in the 'sitting room,' which could have sat a few dozen more than had gathered around the hefty marble fireplace for Boxing Day. 'Nobody will discuss anything that appeared this morning in the *Hillston Star*,' she added, leading me to suspect that, despite Brookside's assumption, she was aware of that paper's contents. 'The "news,"' she informed us with a contemptuous drag to her full and brightened lips, 'the "*news*" is the preoccupation only of those who have no culture. No knowledge. And no memory.' She paused to extend an arm from which round rich flesh swagged, and to drop her empty Scotch glass on a tray that a maid whisked under it. 'And *that*, God love us, describes to a tee the *vast* majority in this nation of ours.' Her pouchy eyes gave us all the once-over. 'No sports scores, no weather reports, and no politics.'

Arrested on our way out the double-sized doors, to cross the parqueted hall into a dining room that disdained electricity, all the guests froze in a cluster, nodding at these instructions from our hostess as solemnly as recruits getting the battle drill from General Patton. I moved over to Lee, who still stood by a grand piano covered with lace, loose sheet music and framed photographs, including one of Mrs Sunderland in a long line of red-eyed people bowing and curtsying to Queen Elizabeth II.

Lee smiled at me, whispering, 'The no-politics orders are for Kip Dollard. Sometimes he forgets where he is, and starts filibustering the dinner table. It drives Edwina nuts. She believes in "conversation."'

I whispered, 'Why does she invite him?'

'Oh I think they had an affair about a hundred years ago, and she's sentimental.'

'Um hum, like the Borgia popes.'

'What happened to your head?'

'I'm okay. Somebody knocked me out.'

'Are you *serious*?'

'Sometimes I'm real serious.' I smiled at her. 'Listen, tell me, why does Edwina—'

She put her finger to her lips. 'Shhhhh.' Lee's neck and shoulders were bare. Her long dress was a sheath of white glimmering fabric that rustled when she moved.

I whispered, 'She keeps calling me Cuthbert. Did you tell her to?'

'No, she had a great-uncle whose name was Cuthbert, and he was called Cuddy. She thinks maybe you're related.'

Hands clapped once. They were those of our hostess, who had caught us whispering while the other guests marched obediently to dinner. Chastened, we joined the end of the line.

Turning to me between the salmon and game hens, as I sat enthroned on her left in a high-backed stiff velvet chair with knobbed arms, Mrs Marion Sunderland explained that her Catawba Hills house (which had always been her house, and not *Mr* Marion Sunderland's, because it had always been a Nowell-Randolph house, and that was exactly what Edwina Sunderland had always been, even after her marriage – as was testified by the worn N-R on my thin silver napkin ring), Mrs Sunderland's 1857 white-brick, porticoed and columned house had always been called Palliser Farm. Though, until, as she bluntly put it, she'd 'gotten her hands on Marion's money,' and fixed it up again, Palliser Farm had been a ghost house, having lost over the generations all of its livestock, and much of its furniture.

Presumably the other guests, spaced like a conference of cardinals in their own narrow thrones, already knew the name of their hostess's home; they were at any rate not listening to Mrs Sunderland give me her genealogy, but were all busy between courses, turning from their seating partners on the right to those on their left: Lee from Dyer Fanshaw to Judge Tiggs, Mrs Fanshaw from me to the bank, Mrs bank from Father Paul Madison to Senator Kip Dollard, and so on, along the dark oval expanse of a dining table the ten of us could have probably slow-danced on, if the party had got wild enough – which it wasn't likely to do, despite Judge Tiggs's two-handed pumping of a crystal wine carafe whenever his wife wasn't looking. The very old and very shrunken widow of the department store, who'd told me at the Club dance to ignore her because she was hard of hearing, must have told her dinner partners the same; at any rate she was talking quite happily to the oblivious Fanshaw, while he was picking at his pearl onions as if he was afraid somebody's eyeball had got mixed in with them. He'd avoided me during cocktails, but then so had Kip Dollard – though maybe only because Dollard had always found his sister's son, Justin, an embarrassment, and I reminded him of Justin. Tiggs, on the other hand, had been friendly all evening (apparently having never noticed in our forensic dealings – before his retirement after the George Hall trial – that I thought him a disgrace to his profession who'd filled Dollard Prison with the victims of his bias or boredom or sore fanny).

'Why's your place called Palliser Farm?' I asked Edwina (as she'd insisted I call her). 'Is it because you were a Trollope as well as a Nowell-Randolph?'

Her raucous laugh bounced the loops of garnets and yellow diamonds on her ample, wrinkled bosom, and startled Mrs Fanshaw, beside me, into spooning too much salt on her yam. 'Cuthbert, you and I shall be friends,' Edwina announced, with a squeeze of my hand that left the impression of those loose diamonds of hers dinted into a few of my fingers. 'Mangum . . . Mangum. What was your mother's maiden name?'

'Cobb.'

'. . . No, it's not familiar. But good English names. Well, a Hillston policeman who reads Trollope. I want you to call me Eddie.'

I gave her the country smile. 'Lord, what do folks read who get to call you "Ed"?' This set her off again, but I snatched my hand away in time by grabbing one of my sharp-stemmed wineglasses – these with a fat 'S' cut into them, so post 'N-R,' maybe part of Mr Sunderland's dowry. I said, 'But I've got to disabuse you, Eddie, I saw my Trollope on TV, and it wasn't even your channel. It was the good channel, you know, the intellectual one. The one you own goes more in for blood, sweat, tears, and smut. Terrible shows about tacky rich families deceiving one another, and shows with these old has-been comedians sitting up in little Tic-Tac-Toe boxes—'

'Oh, yes, yes, I know.' She picked up a tiny game hen wing

with her fingers and took a sturdy bite out of it, so I dropped my useless knife and fork, and did the same. 'Channel Seven is unwatchable, except by the mentally and morally retarded.'

I said, 'Lucky for you, there's so many of both crowded around the Piedmont tuning in.'

'Lucky for me? Explain yourself.'

'Well, their tacky taste supports your good taste.' I gave a nod at the furnishings.

Mrs Sunderland took a hefty sip of wine. 'Cuthbert . . .' She swilled the wine around like a mouthwash for a minute. 'Cuthbert, capitalism is not a benevolent system. It is, in fact, the pure opposite. And I have always believed it's damn silly to pretend otherwise, though I have many mealy-mouthed acquaintances who do exactly that.' Paul Madison opened his mouth, but she reached across and stopped him with one of those bone-crunchers to the wrist. 'Girls I went to college with back in the impressionable thirties. They'll sell off their chemical stocks one year, and their South African stocks the next year, whatever horror gets to be the style, and then they'll buy themselves something "nicer," that's just as profitable.'

I buttered a roll and held it up. 'Have their cake and *caritas* too.'

'Yes, sir!' Another laugh that set her ear bobs swinging, though I don't think a hurricane could have budged those laminated blue waves of hair. 'Well, it's damn silly. I say, in or out. By the luck of birth, I'm in. I enjoy the fruits of other people's labour. And my charities I take off my taxes.'

Senator Kip Dollard, white haired and red nosed – sort of what a Dorian Gray portrait of Justin might have got to look like – heard the word taxes, and launched a multi-metaphoric salvo across the candles that flickered their flames. 'If handed the reins of this good state of ours, the Democrats will gallop their Taxation Chariot over the backs of business, sowing the seeds of inflation and misery like dragon's teeth—'

'Kip, confound it!' Mrs Sunderland gave her crystal goblet such a crack with her spoon, I was surprised it didn't shatter. The sound did, however, shatter the old senator, who sputtered out one more classical allusion, to the many-headed Hydra, then continued his speech privately to Mrs bank in a hushed murmur.

Somebody from behind my shoulder slipped my plate away while I was saying, 'Oh come on, Eddie, what about good capitalists, laissez-faire philanthropy, what about everybody rising to the top by the action of the cream? Wasn't that the American Revolution's plan?'

She said, 'Horse shit.' Mrs Fanshaw looked up, scared into trembles, and her peas slid right off her silver fork into her lap; she sneakily shook them on to the floor as her hostess boomed on. 'The American Revolution was to protect middle-class capitalism from aristocratic exploitation. The Civil War was to protect Southern capitalism from Northern capitalism, and vicey versy. Slaves picked the cotton in Georgia; immigrants made the shirts in Massachusetts. And both sides paid sweet boys like Paul here to preach to them about camels and needle eyes.'

I leaned over to whisper in her powdered ear. 'You know what I think you really are deep down, Eddie? A Marxist.'

She grinned, swiping her napkin across her lips and leaving it with a bloody look. 'No sir, I'm a Nowell-Randolph. A Sunderland by acquisition.'

'Well, I wish your Channel Seven Newshound acquisition wouldn't root around quite so much in all the *carnage*. Stirs the viewers up; it's like flashing full moons at werewolves. Then they rampage, and I have to deal with the messy results.'

'Cuddy has a very cynical opinion of human nature, Mrs Sunderland.' Paul Madison grinned at us from behind a fat candelabrum. 'He's a Puritan at heart. Calvinist. Original sin.'

Edwina shook her leg, or rather the little hen's leg, at Paul. 'Paulie, you don't believe in sin at all, which is mighty peculiar in a man of the cloth, and probably grounds for dismissal.' They both laughed at this risqué flirtation with orthodoxy.

I said, 'Yep, Paul's unfallen. That's why he looks thirty years younger than he is.'

Paul blushed in a peculiar hurt kind of way. Then he smiled. 'Maybe that's my sin.' He turned to Mrs Tiggs, leaving me feeling like I'd said something wrong. I looked down to the other end of the table where Lee, dark gold in the candlelight, raised her wineglass to her lips as she nodded at something Judge Tiggs was saying. She turned her head towards me as if she could feel me looking at her. And she smiled. The frail judge babbled on, abruptly laughing, jerking his bald skinny head back like a chicken somebody was choking. I'd seen him laugh that way at his own witless jokes in the courtroom a lot. His jokes were the laughingstock of the Municipal Building, but not the way he imagined. His wife made a flanking grab for the carafe, around the flower bowl; she and Tiggs did a silent little tug-of-war, which she won.

Lee put down her wineglass slowly, still looking at me. All the other guests seemed to go static and silent, like painted figures in an old mural. But they didn't know it, and kept on chattering.

Back in the sitting room for cordials, Lee played the piano for Paul, who sang a few comic songs from *The Mikado*, dedicating 'Let the Punishment Fit the Crime,' with a wink at me, to Judge Tiggs. The judge merrily choked out that high spastic laugh of his; it's clear there were no bad ghosts in his memory. The widow of the department store started clapping a few notes before 'Tit Willow' was over. The bank had set her down like a slumped baby in a deep flowered armchair, and she finally gave up trying to pull herself out of it and get to the dish of chocolates. She cooed, 'Just so pretty. I love hymns. I thought the hymns at Briggs Cadmean's funeral were as moving as they could be. Didn't y'all? I did.'

Senator Dollard raised his snifter. 'A great man, a great North Carolinean, a great—'

'Lovely, lovely hymns. And you couldn't see the coffin for the flowers. That was so nice. Eddie, it's downright tragic your arthritis wouldn't allow you to attend.'

Eddie brought over the silver candy dish, setting it down in her friend's lap, where it stayed until there wasn't a Godiva left for the rest of us. She said, 'Sue Ann, I despised Briggs Cadmean. And it wasn't my arthritis that wouldn't allow me to attend. It was my stomach. I wasn't about to sit listening to Hillston fawn over that pile of bull manure the way it did his whole life.' No one defended the dead man.

Dyer Fanshaw, having kept carefully out of my vicinity all night, suddenly stopped poking at the fire with a brass tong, crossed the room, and led me into a corner. 'Look here,' he said, then scratched at his upper lip where he'd shaved off that moustache he'd grown for the Confederacy Ball. 'Sorry I cut you off, back at the funeral, but you know, upsetting circumstances, so on. You said one of my shipping clerks might be stealing paper from me? I've looked into it. There're no indications of any such thing. What made you say it?' He had us squeezed between a highboy and the Christmas tree, and kept nervously glancing out at the room, like he was going to whip some dirty pictures out of his dinner jacket. At the piano Lee and Paul were taking requests now; they appeared to have the entire Gilbert and Sullivan corpus at their fingertips – maybe a prerequisite for these Anglophiliac affairs.

I said, 'Mr Fanshaw—'

'Dyer, Cuddy.'

'What made me say it, Dyer? About a ton's worth of paper rolls my detective saw in Willie Slidell's barn. Or was that a holiday bonus?'

He shook his head impatiently. 'Our inventory's intact. And I did check into this man. He has a good record. Why was a detective even out at his house? I was told he's on sick leave now. The flu.'

'Worse than that.' But I wasn't going to mention how much worse just yet. Instead I told him, 'This detective of mine, well, he thinks this Slidell of yours might have killed somebody. Cooper Hall.'

Fanshaw's eyes bulged, he was staring so hard. 'My God, why?' He was shocked. Maybe he was a little too shocked. 'You're arresting Slidell?'

I said, 'Nope. He disappeared from his farm. Seems like working for you can be pretty high risk. Slidell gone. And here's George Hall, drove one of your trucks, didn't he, and he's on Death Row.'

It took Fanshaw a while to focus; when he did, his mood had changed. 'Look here, what are you getting at, Mr Mangum?' We seemed to be back to last names fast.

As I answered, I turned to join the polite clapping for Paul and Lee, who'd finished up with a fast-talking tune from *Pinafore*. 'Well, I'm still wondering about that Mr Koontz, that died? Why his card, with "Newsome" written on it, showed up in Cooper Hall's address book.'

We stared at each other a little bit. Then he muttered, 'I have no idea. I would assume Clark tried to sell the man some paper supplies, and gave him the card.'

'Since Hall didn't buy paper – from you folks or anybody else – odd he would have kept the card so long.' Fanshaw shrugged. I said, 'Otis claims he never met Cooper Hall. Should I believe him? Y'all pretty close?'

As he made a show of not knowing what I meant, I prodded him. 'Otis Newsome? City comptroller? You know, the guy who gets you the contracts to supply Hillston with all its paper needs? Otis Newsome whose little brother Purley that works for me used to pal around with a cop named Bobby Pym, that had a brother-in-law named Willie Slidell that works for you? You follow me? That Otis Newsome. Are you and Otis close friends?'

Fanshaw went the colour of his cummerbund, which was red in honour of the season. 'I don't know what you're trying to suggest by these remarks.' As he left me standing there, and stomped over to the couch where Mrs Fanshaw was yawning behind her hand, I guess he didn't want to know either. He whispered something to her. She nodded pretty eagerly, leapt off the couch, sneaked around Judge Tiggs (who was telling a very long joke, the plot of which his wife kept correcting), and took Lee aside to whisper to her. Lee looked over at me, questioning. I nodded, and Lee shook her head no at Mrs Fanshaw.

Mrs Sunderland told me where I could find a phone, and I excused myself to call the department. I asked Hiram to send somebody over to bring me my Olds and take back the squad car, so I wouldn't have to drive Lee in the latter. Hiram said I couldn't have my car. I asked if I could at least have the fingerprint report I'd asked for. 'Five minutes,' he said, then connected me to the HPD garage, where Etham Foster was still at work. Etham wanted me to know that he was right and I was wrong. It was something he pretty regularly wanted me to know. I said, 'I didn't think it was a bomb, and it wasn't.'

'You'd have been just as dead if enough of that cyanide had seeped through the vents in your firewall. And probably would have, high up as you turn your heater. At the least you'd have passed out, crashed that new car, maybe killed somebody.'

'Okay, Doctor D, you were right. That old rabbit foot on my key chain saved my butt in Vietnam, and looks like it's still got some hoodoo left. Enough to bring you on the scene. I know you don't want me to thank you. Thank you.'

Whoever had lifted my keys had opened the hood and poured a solution of acid and cyanide under the cowl of the circulating system. With the heater fan on, the fumes would have been blown right in at me. This whoever obviously knew a lot about the parking garage, my car, and me, just not enough about me to know I was such a strong creature of habit regarding things like key chains. Etham said, 'Couple of months back, didn't somebody get blasted with some deer rut from the heater ducts in a squad car?'

'Zeke. Purley Newsome probably did it.'

'Think he did this?'

'On his own? I don't think he's got the guts. But I've about decided he's not on his own.'

I had Etham connect me back with Hiram Davies at the desk, where I got the information I'd expected. Winston Russell's fingerprints were all over the Slidell farmhouse. He might have had relatives in north Georgia, but he sure hadn't gone down there to take an honest job when he'd left Dollard Prison. 'Okay, Hiram, call Savile, tell him to get folks on this fast. That fuck Russell was right here in Hillston, but if he hasn't gone by now he's going quick. So get it on the wire. And I want Purley Newsome picked up too. Check his brother's house. Then put out a bulletin – oh, and have the prints at Slidell's checked against Purley's file.'

'You want a bulletin out on Purley Newsome? Don't want to wait, see if he shows up here for duty? – Due in a few hours anyhow.'

'I got a feeling Purley took early retirement this evening, and didn't bother to do it in writing. He's wherever his pal Winston is.'

'You think *they* tried to kill you? But good gravy, Chief!'

'Hiram, I want you to watch that strong language. Kiss Martha good-night. Call you later.'

When I returned to the sitting room, the Fanshaws had left, pleading her headache (though I seriously doubt her head hurt anywhere near as much as mine did, despite all the alcohol I'd sent up to help it out). The eight of us guests remaining were then commanded by Edwina to play bridge. She picked me for her partner, and after I overrode some of her greedier swoops on the bid, we came out the winners, with $38.55. Well, I'm a good bridge player, despite a lack of practice opportunities other than the games in the newspaper. At any rate, Edwina was impressed, and between that and the Trollope and my violent job, she got carried away enough to propose that we have Judge Tiggs marry us then and there. I had to disappoint her on the claim that I was too old to keep up with her, but I grabbed the opportunity to recommend a more hedonistic bachelor – Bubba Percy. She'd never heard of Bubba Percy. I told her that despite, or because of, fatal character flaws, Bubba was the best journalist on the *Hillston Star*, much better than the man who ran that rotten rag. She said, 'Send him to me.' Rather, I imagine, as old Queen Elizabeth One would have said it when she was in the mood for a set of well-shaped gartered legs with a Renaissance brain on top. I promised to send Bubba around, if she promised not to throw me over for his pompadour and curly eyelashes.

This chatty flirting wiled away the time while Lee was saying good-bye to Senator Dollard and the Tiggses. They all kissed her cheek affectionately. Well, she was one of them, even if she'd married a Yankee-born liberal who was trying to steal the governorship from their native son, Julian D.-for-Dollard Lewis. In Edwina's terms – terms of pure, unadulterated capitalism – Lee was not just one of them, but *the* one. She was the international royal princess to their regional lords and ladies. And they'd have loved her no matter whom she'd married, as long as he was white and well-bred, because they'd known her not only all her life, but known her for generations before she was born, because she was born a Haver. There was *no one* that Andy Brookside could have married (including the Virgin Mary, because there're not that many Catholic voters around here), who could have helped him more powerfully to pull that gubernatorial chair out from under the junta who'd shoved Wollston into it, the man before Wollston into it, and – if they had their way – the man after Wollston into it too.

Lee was the perfect choice for a candidate's wife. Not just because campaigns cost money, and she had money; not just because politics is photo opportunities, and she was photogenic. Not just because she had relatives and friends in the state. Lee Haver was the state. She summed the state up in her family's history of private success and public service, of scandals, philanthropies, and heroics – her great-great-grandfather's university, her wastrel grandfather's celebrity, her noble father's death fighting Communists. And most of all, that history of money, money, money. She summed up, in her name, the state's century-long climb out of rural poverty and illiteracy; she industrialized the state, modernized it, capitalized it; she brought the Yankees to their knees, and then moved them in and built them shopping malls. She was the dream of *winning*. Was that why Andy had married her? Why she had married him? Was his victory to be Lee Haver's service to her state?

Standing in the hallway, I watched her, wrapped in her black fur, bend to hug the little widow of the department store, whom Paul Madison was driving home. I saw Paul take Lee's hands, thanking her. Heard him say, 'Your cheque will mean a lot to the

Hall Fund; we're just very grateful for your, your, your incredible generosity.'

She said, 'I was glad to be able to help. I share Andy's deep concern about this case ... And Paul, please, let me know more about this new convalescent home you were talking about? Will you?'

'Oh absolutely!' Paul nodded, still holding her hands as if he was going to kiss them.

Yep, even if Brookside didn't love her (and I had no reason but envy to think he didn't), he couldn't have made a better choice. And if he was jeopardizing it for a few more trophies on his cocksmanship, he did indeed, as Lee had said, need to take deadly risks.

Edwina had sneaked up behind me in the hall, while I was watching Lee. 'Is that cracked skull bothering you, Cuthbert, or are you just sad to leave me and get back to your much more fascinating criminals?'

I sighed, turning to her. 'Most of my "criminals" are boring, Eddie. Dumber than they think they are, poorer than they wanna be, and resentful as shit of folks like you.' I buttoned my overcoat. 'Your TV shows that keep most of the underclass comatose; well, those shows make "my criminals" all mean and itchy, know what I mean?'

She flashed those long yellow incisors at me in a grin. 'That's what my TV shows are there for. To keep the vast majority comatose. Lucky for you. Otherwise, the streets would be full of guns, wouldn't they? And that's mighty bad for business.' She got in one last hand squeeze. 'Now. kiss me good-night.' I did so, and smelled talcum powder sweet alcohol, and a flowery odour like old sachets in musty linen. 'Look at that.' She pointed me at the window. 'A nice seasonal touch for my party. I wanted it to snow. And it's snowing.'

A few flakes were floating slowly down and settling on the long stone front steps. I said, 'You see some causal connection between your desire and the weather, Eddie?'

Patting her yellow diamonds, she frowned at me. 'No, I've never thought for a minute I could get snow if I wanted it, or anything else of that *nature*. I sensibly limited my desires to things I could buy ... Good-night, now, thank you for coming, and go give Lee Brookside that ride home – since that's what she informs me you've offered her. I suppose she dislikes imposing on her driver.'

Edwina's old pale eyes were hard as her diamonds, but I wasn't about to let her stare me down. I said, 'Thank you for having me. I enjoyed it. You're a brainy woman. It's a crime you were too lazy to run that newspaper yourself. Maybe you'd have got a real kick out of the power of the press. Since you claim the power of money's done nothing but bore the pants off you for seventy-two years.'

I suspect I'd nicked her a little, but she came right back. 'Power of money *is* the power of the press – without getting your fingers inky.'

I gave her the look she was giving me. 'Well, inky fingers might have been better than wasting away your whole life bullying your friends over a deck of cards.'

She backed off a step and rubbed the corners of her mouth with her two middle fingers. 'Ah . . . I don't think I'm going to worry anymore about your safety among our little group, Captain Mangum. Because you've got a nice mean streak in you. So go on now and take her home.'

Maybe Mrs Sunderland didn't need to worry about me, but I did. I mean, I thought I *ought* to worry, ought to worry about consequences, and responsibilities – all those things I've got a long habit of worrying about. But I'd put off thinking until it was too late. It took only ten minutes to drive to Briarhills, which wasn't long enough. Neither Lee nor I spoke. All I could do was feel her beside me in the enclosed still space of the dark car. I felt enveloped by intimacy, familiar, strong as a pulse. And at the same time an almost panicking sense of freedom and strangeness surged in my chest. The fact that I wore formal, uncustomary clothes, the fact that the car was an anonymous, unmarked patrol car, with its Spartan interior and all its metallic equipment, the fact that snow, unusual in Hillston, was swirling like moths into the car lights – all of it made more intense both the intimacy and the strangeness. As long as we kept in motion, neither in her world, nor in mine, but just winding along the dark wooded roads, we were free. We could drift, suspended in the night, circling our lives like a sky of stars.

But we weren't circling. We were moving across North Hillston towards Briarhills, and in the ordinary sublunary amount of time, we reached the brick columns of the gates, and turned in. The driveway was as straight and as long and as bordered by lights as an airline runway. High-branched rows of sycamore trees on either side of the drive blocked my view of the grounds, but I could remember where the wooden Japanese bridge had crossed the creek, and where the gazebo had looked through lattice over the pool, and where the greenhouse was hidden by the grove of cherry and willow trees. I could remember the house, the tall, impregnable expanse of brick façade, with its sixteen shuttered windows across the front. (I'd stood on the steps and counted them one afternoon after Lee's mother had gently lied that Lee wasn't home, and then softly closed the door on me.)

There were lights burning in carriage lamps on either side of the wide varnished door, and lights on in most of the windows. And ground lights where the driveway ended in a paved oval with a fountain in its centre. From the pool rose a statue of a young woman in a tunic with her arm around an antlered deer. The pool was circled by flower beds – except now in December, there were no flowers; I just remember them having been there, the extravagant patterns of unfamiliar colours.

Onto the trees and brick and statuary, snow now fell, and vanished. I stopped the car, and turned to Lee. 'Who's having the party? All your lights are on.'

She looked at me, then vaguely at the house as if she didn't recognize it. 'Oh. The lights? Nobody. No one's home.'

'Oh . . .' Around us, night was lightened by the falling white snow, and softened. Everything was losing its shape, the outline of the shrubbery, the sharp corners of the house.

She said, '. . . Well, the Reeds, but they're probably all asleep by now.'

'. . . Bessie Reed still works here?'

'Yes . . . and her son and his wife. You remember her?'

'Yes.' I turned off the motor, and listened to the fullness of the silence.

She said, 'Bessie gave me a note from you once. Brought it up to my room while my mother was having a lunch party. A note that you were—'

'—That I was waiting by the little Japanese bridge.'

'Yes . . .'

I stared at my hands moving up and down on the steering wheel. Finally I asked her, 'Why did you tell Brookside I'd be at this party tonight?'

She looked at my hands as she answered, 'So if anyone

197

mentioned it to him later, he would have already heard it casually from me.'

I thought of ten or fifteen things I could ask or say next, then felt each one get caught in my throat and slide burning back down inside me. We sat watching the silent snow curtain the car windows, enclosing us. I could see her without looking at her, the line of her cheek and mouth, the dark gold hair brushing the curve of her ear, the pale blue vein in her neck. I could hear her breath, and the slippery sound of her nylons as she crossed her legs. I could smell the cold air caught in the black fur of her coat.

Then I looked at her. 'I'm not casual.'

She said, 'I know that.'

I kept holding to the steering wheel, hearing each small movement of the seat cover as she turned towards me and placed her hand over my hand. Her fingers laced through mine; they stroked my wrist under the cuff of my coat, and their heat ran up my arm into my chest, poured in everywhere, melting the tightness.

I heard her breath catch before she whispered, 'You have beautiful hands. Like they could build or heal or mend anything they wanted to. Like they could set everything right, make everything all right.'

Her fingers tightened over mine, then she loosened my hand on the wheel, and with a small moan, she pulled me against her, drawing me to her side of the car. My arms closed around her, and my mouth grazed her hair, the clean cold sweet smell tingling into me. She tilted her head back, opening her neck into a white curve, her lips parting just before my mouth touched hers.

When we pulled away, I cupped her face in my hands, and we looked at each other, long, close, deeper than in the past, looked right through those years apart as if we were living each one in an instant, living them all together in an instant, coming through them, bright and fast as lightning, to this moment. Then my hands moved down the lines of her neck, across her shoulders, gathering her to me, and we fell together, easily as the snow, down against the seat.

I opened her coat, slid it down off her arms, and kissed the scented hollow of her breastbone, dizzy with the keen spiced fragrance of her skin, the soft swell of flesh between her breast and arm. Her hands kept stroking up my neck into my hair, clasping my back under my coat, drawing me closer. Her skin

198

was warm as my lips, smoother than the white satin that slipped rustling under me as I pressed myself to her. I could feel her words prickling my neck, but I couldn't tell whose breath I was hearing, mine or hers.

Her eyes were all I could see: the full dark irises ringed by the smoky, gold-flecked grey. There were faint lines at their corners now that hadn't been there the last time I had looked this close. Those clear, young eyes had always fluttered closed when we kissed. Now they were wide open, dark with desire, staring into my own. My voice was a strange low whisper coming from somewhere beyond her eyes. I said, 'This is as far as we ever got before.'

Her eyes smiled back into mine. 'I know. Weren't we silly?'

Our legs coiled, squeezing together in the close space.

She whispered, deep in her throat, 'I used to wonder what it would have felt like.'

'Like this.'

She pulled my hand to her mouth and slowly kissed the inside of the palm. '. . . Would you like to come in the house with me?'

'No.'

Our hands couldn't stop moving. She slid hers between the studs of my laced shirt and on to my chest. I pulled the thin strap of her gown down from her shoulder and circled the curve of her breast. Her fingers were tight and quick in my hair. 'Then here,' she said. 'Let's just stay here. Hidden in the snow. In the back seat. Like we were young again.'

I whispered against her breast. 'We didn't have a car then . . . especially not a police car.'

She laughed out loud, and my lips felt her low, soft laughter lifting her breast.

I said, 'I don't feel like being young again. I feel like finally being young the first time.' At least I think I said it, maybe I just thought it, because her hand moved up my thigh, like a flame racing over the black wool.

Chapter 12

My mother's son, I never leave any lights burning in my apartment while I'm away. In my childhood, whenever we went out of our house, even for an hour, Mama would fretfully rush back from the car to check again that the lamps were turned off, and the stove, that the faucets weren't leaking, that the iron was unplugged, that all the doors were locked. Often, to my father's patient sighs, to my sister Vivian's and my own impatient disgust, she'd be overcome a second or a third time – even after we were blocks away – by fear of profligate waste of light and water, of catastrophic loss by fire or flood, and we'd have to return home 'just to be sure.'

My mother was never sure. She was never not afraid that debts and sickness and accidents would drag us under, like sharks in the ocean, and chew us to bits. On the few vacations when we'd had money to rent a cottage at Wrightsville Beach, she would never enter the surf with us, but would stand frowning at the tide's edge, scurrying backwards if the foam rushed at her feet. Helpless, she'd watch the waves rise behind our bobbing heads, and would stretch out both arms, frantic to haul us back. 'You're out too far!' she'd scream uselessly into the vast roar. 'Malcolm, don't take them out so far! Viv! Cuddy! Come back!' Beyond her reach, we'd cling to my dad's arms, thrilled by her anxiety.

My mother's son, I had an instinct for danger; since childhood, I'd studied the waters of my life carefully; brooded on those waters, planned for emotional riptides, for sudden drop-offs into bad luck, for hidden moral shoals. Well, if ever I'd gone out too far, it was now, with Lee Brookside. I was swimming against the tide towards open ocean. But for tonight, at least, there was no reason not to figure I could float all the way to Spain on my back, happily gazing at the sky.

In this buoyant suspension, I parked the patrol car and ran to my building's entrance, zigzagging a design in the fresh thin coat of snow. At two in the morning, there were few lights on anywhere in River Rise (a less prodigal place than Briarhills), and in the dark breezeway shared by four apartments, I banged my shin on a bicycle. Outside my door, which was at the far end of the corridor (the river-view side, which I'd picked over the parking-lot-view side for an extra eight thousand dollars), I had to fumble for a while with my key. Instinct is stronger than euphoria: the instant the key turned, I knew the door had already been unlocked, and a rush of adrenaline tightened my muscles; the instant the door opened, I knew the white swag light over my dining room table, the lamp by my denim couch, and the track lighting in my kitchen were all burning, and that somebody besides me had turned them on. I still had my hand around the knob, pulling the door closed, cursing the fact that I wasn't carrying my beeper, much less a gun, or anything heavier than a rented black patent leather shoe, when I heard someone in the hall behind me. Let me tell you, the beat of a lover's heart is nothing compared to the pounding mine now set up, trying to get out of my chest. I whirled around, dropping to a crouch, arms up, already thinking about Winston Russell's Carolina pancake, that gob of ignited lye and kerosene flying into my face again.

'Cuddy?'

'What!'

'It's me.'

It took a second before I recognized Nora Howard, from the apartment across the hall, standing there in her doorway with a wineglass in one hand, a yellow legal pad in the other. She'd had her hair in a ponytail the night I'd helped her assemble the bike – probably the one I'd just tripped over – and now it was in loose black waves to her shoulders, which gave her a very different look. 'Goddamn, you scared me!' This time I was whispering. 'Get out of the light!' I scuttled over to her, and yanked on her jeans' leg. Shocked into obedience, she crouched next to me. I gestured at my door, whispered again.

'Somebody's in my apartment.'

She shook her head at me, bewildered; then she said in a normal tone, 'Oh, no, it's okay. It's a friend of—'

But before she could finish, a big shadow, already talking, filled her doorway. 'Nora? Cuddy back?' I knew the voice and the shadow both, but I was so surprised, I just stared at him as he said, 'Why are you two squatting in the corridor, or whatever these modern condominiums like to call what looks like a hotel hall to an old man like me?' In his socks, with his frayed plaid flannel bathrobe on over his shirt and pants, Isaac Rosethorn rumbled towards us.

Nora stood up, wiping the sloshed wine from her hand, but I couldn't move, even with Isaac swaying over me. He clucked. 'Slim, you appear to have gone on a café society binge over the holidays. At least it looks as if you've been sleeping in that tuxedo for a week. Where have you been? Sergeant Davies had no response from your pocket gizmo, or the car either.'

He gazed down at me mournfully with those deep sad eyes, and I actually ran a guilty hand through my dishevelled hair, before the outrageousness of his remark struck me and brought me to my feet. 'Where've *I* been?' Between terror and relief, I got so angry I actually grabbed his lapels and gave them a quick shake. 'Where've *you* been, for a goddamn *week*? Don't tell me you've been holed up in this lady's apartment while I've had half of HPD out rooting through the entire countryside for you. Jesus! Where *were* you!'

'Delaware. And don't exaggerate, Slim.' Isaac gave Nora a consoling smile, as if to comfort her for being neighbours with a lunatic. He smoothed down his robe. 'Nora and I only met, oh, six hours ago. But we are already consociates of the most amiable sort, aren't we, my dear? *Amicita curiae*, one might say. You weren't home, and she was kind enough to invite me—'

I strode back to my door, and flung it open. 'You broke into my apartment?!'

'Ah, no, I haven't the knack. Your superintendent let me in. I told him I was your father. Nora kindly corroborated this mild prevarication. And, of course, being a man of sentiment, I always keep your photo in my wallet, and showed it to Mr Morrison, who was quite touched by my paternal devotion.' He gave a pat to his breast, where his jacket pocket would have been, had he not for some peculiar reason been lounging around a strange woman's home in a bathrobe which was not only pocked with cigarette burns but stained with God knows how many years of dribbled barbecue sauce.

I said, '*Delaware?*'

Isaac's hostess (also in her socks, but otherwise fully dressed in jeans and a green sweater) suddenly gasped, 'Our potato skins!' and ran back into her apartment, calling over her shoulder, 'Don't stand there in the cold, Isaac. Cuddy, you're welcome to come on over.'

But I blocked the eager Isaac from trotting after his new buddy. Prodding him to my door, I nudged him inside. A ratty suitcase – his, no doubt; obviously, my place was just a changing room for visits across the hall – lay open in the middle of my carpet. I pointed at it. 'You came over here with your bag in the middle of the night, after disappearing for a week, to tell me you went to Delaware?'

He took his long-winded time explaining: He'd just driven straight back from Delaware (in 'a friend's car') to Dollard Prison, where he'd met with George Hall this afternoon (or rather yesterday afternoon, since it was now two A.M.). He'd called HPD about 8:30, and talked to Hiram Davies, who'd told him about my getting sapped down in the garage. After Hiram couldn't reach me (I'd left my beeper on my bureau, and turned off the car radio), and had telephoned everybody he could reach, like Justin and Etham (though not, I fervently hoped, Mrs Marion Sunderland), he and Isaac had convinced each other that I was in 'trouble,' that whoever had rigged my car had come back to finish me off, and that I was probably lying in a puddle of blood on my wall-to-wall, or had suffered a delayed concussion and drowned while taking a bath (leaving poor Hiram stuck with Martha Mitchell for the rest of his – or her – life). 'So,' said Isaac, scrounging in his robe. 'I was seized by an intuition of disaster, luckily quite off the mark. But we drove over here to check things out.' He pulled out his bifocals, shook lint and nut husks off their case, and put them on. 'Besides, I felt we should stay hidden, and here's as safe as a jail, which of course was another possibility.'

'You and Hiram Davies wanted to hide here?'

'*Billy*. Billy and I.' He picked up the phone by my couch, and started dialling, his nose an inch from the numbers. 'Gilchrist. What's the matter with you, Cuddy?'

As he said it, I heard a sudden wheezing snuffly sound coming from upstairs. I pointed towards the noise. 'Billy Gilchrist is *here*, in my bedroom? Isaac, what the fuck is going on?'

'Shhh.' The old lawyer waved a fat paw at me as he said into the phone, 'Sergeant Davies? ... Yes, speaking ... Yes, yes, we found him ... No, quite unharmed. Appears to have stayed late, at some, ah, party, and not been, ah, in a position to respond to his beeper ... Yes, you're welcome. Good-bye then.' He turned to me, peering over his glasses. 'Concerned about you. Davies.'

'I wasn't lost, Isaac. I didn't need to be found!'

'Shh shh shh! Billy's not well. He can't sleep.'

'Maybe not, but he can *snore*. You know Paul Madison's gone nuts worrying about Gilchrist?'

'So we'll call him. What's his number?' He picked up the phone again.

'Jesus, it's two in the morning. Hang up. I'll call him tomorrow.'

'Well, you said he'd gone nuts. Cuddy, didn't you get my postcard? I wrote you from Delaware; I explained where we were.'

'No! I certainly didn't get your "postcard." So I'm *real* curious.'

'Keep your voice down. Well, I mailed it. Billy knew an individual who could give us some information, a man Billy saw with George at Smoke's the night of the shooting.'

This stopped me on my way up the stairs to evict my uninvited guest, or at least turn him over on his side. '*Gilchrist* was in Smoke's that night?'

'Only by happenstance. This other fellow, who's now in prison in Delaware, is a friend of Billy's, so we went up and talked him into giving us a deposition.'

Thoughts jumped like a horse locked in the starting gate. 'A guy called Moonfoot Butler?'

'Ah, you *did* get my postcard.'

But no, I hadn't got it (and never did; he'd probably neglected to put a stamp on the thing). Instead I had, in his phrase, 'used my noggin,' and, in fact (as he nobly allowed later), he was 'impressed' that I had independently begun to formulate a theory about the Pym shooting so close to the one he had worked on with Coop Hall for months. Of course, we'd each got a break – mine had come from the Willie Slidell connection. Isaac's had come after Coop's death, by means of Billy Gilchrist.

When I arrived, Nora and Isaac had already been talking through the case together for hours, and it was a little unsettling to hear her sound so familiar with names I'd been fretting over for a long time, names she'd probably never heard before tonight.

But Isaac had a way of forming these strong initial impressions, and acting on them instantly. Turns out that when he'd banged on Nora Howard's door to see if she knew me (she told him she didn't think I'd been home since Christmas morning – which was maybe a little too nosily observant of her), she'd offered to help him get into my apartment by tricking Mr Morrison – with whom I was going to have to have a serious talk. Then she'd invited Isaac over so Billy could 'sleep,' and twenty minutes later, Isaac had hired her to clerk for him on the Hall case while she was studying for the state bar exams. She'd told him she'd read some of his briefs, and that she figured that working for Isaac Rosethorn would be the best cram course for passing the bar she could take. Her admiration undoubtedly flattered any reservations out of the old egomaniac, so Nora and he were now fast pals. Maybe she was even planning to put him up in her extra bedroom (mine had no bed, just books). Her little boy and girl were off in their Christmas teepee with her brother's kids, all of them camping out on the floor of Carippini's Restaurant for the adventure of it. This family news was given me by Isaac himself, who appeared to have made himself at home with the Howards mighty quickly, what with his wandering around in his stocking feet on his first visit, and to have taken an unprecedented domestic turn – cooking those nocturnal potato skins she referred to as 'ours.'

'That woman's got a very fine brain,' he told me. 'Wasted, wasted on tax law in Houston of all places.'

'Her husband worked for NASA.'

'I know, I know, poor dear, a tragedy to be widowed at her age, and with young children. But time and faith, time and faith. And extremely fortuitous that she moved to Hillston. Very good ideas. We've come up with *twenty-eight* points for our appeal to Judge Roscoe, only twenty-four of which I'd already thought of myself.' (He delivered this compliment with his typical complaisance.) 'Let's get back over there. But first . . .'

But first, Isaac thought I should, as he tactfully put it, 'go freshen up.' Taking me by the arm, he rubbed his wide thumb across the side of my mouth. His soulful eyebrows lifted slowly as he then examined his thumb. 'Slim, you look a little . . . obvious.'

Off in the bathroom mirror, I saw what he meant, and why Nora Howard had been giving me such peculiar glances – though frankly she had no right to make judgements about the personal business of a complete stranger, and I was annoyed that I felt, well, embarrassed, even guilty, when I saw myself. It wasn't just the lipstick smears; my mouth was swollen, there was a blood-bruise on my neck, a stud was missing from my ruffled shirt, and my bow tie hung loose around my neck. I looked (even to Isaac Rosethorn, who might still be a virgin, for all I know) like I'd been doing exactly what I'd been doing.

Walking across the hall to Nora's, I asked Isaac what Coop Hall thought of Andy Brookside. He said he didn't know, that Coop and he had never discussed politics – for which Rosethorn had a Swiftian contempt – though he knew that Coop himself was interested in someday running for public office, and that Jack Molina had encouraged him about it.

In Nora's living room, over potato skins and beer, I was initially a little irritable with Isaac and his new law partner. It didn't seem fair that after all this time when I'd led my work-aholic monk's existence, that the first chance I got at the private life which everybody had pestered me to find, I should end up the object of a search party. Why couldn't I have spent a few hours alone with a woman, without half a dozen people trying to track me down? Why couldn't I make love to a woman without, two hours later, having to listen to two lawyers analyse the political bearing of a murder case on that woman's husband's career? Why couldn't I have come home to dream that Lee and I were more than just one night's fulfilment of an old interrupted infatuation, without finding a wheezy wino convict hiding in my bed? Why couldn't I say, no, I don't want to argue evidence at three in the morning, when I could be floating to sleep in a reverie about a woman whom I'd wanted half my life, and who'd just told me that tonight had been the most intense sexual communion she'd ever felt.

Well, but I didn't say, No, I'd rather sleep. So maybe that's why I don't have much of a personal life. Because as soon as Isaac Rosethorn said that the person Billy Gilchrist was hiding from was Winston Russell, I was wide awake, and on the phone to Hiram Davies to send over copies of the files I'd already collected about the case. That's when Isaac allowed that I'd 'impressed' him. That's when I told him that if he'd come to me as soon as Gilchrist had come to him, maybe we could have saved somebody's life.

*

I didn't mean Cooper Hall's life. I meant Willie Slidell's. Because Billy Gilchrist hadn't shown up at Isaac's hotel until late on the night of Coon's death – at about the time of the 'Canaan Riot.' The story Billy'd told Isaac then was this; in fact, exactly this, because I woke Billy up and made him tell it again.

Gilchrist looked horrible and sounded worse; apparently he'd slipped away from Isaac a few times on their trip North and skidded into the nearest bar; apparently he hadn't brought along a change of clothes either. Scrawny and shaking, grey faced, he sat swallowed by Nora's wing-backed chair, with an electric blanket wrapped around him, and gave me a weak hopeful smile. 'Chief, this don't come easy. It hadn't been for Father Paul showing me the light, no way I'd be blabbing my fucking guts out to the law – excuse me, Mrs Howard. But all those years I kept mum, well, I'm sorry for them.'

I sipped what I'll admit was a lot better coffee than my freeze-dried. 'Mum about what, Billy?'

'Lifting that cop's wallet. 'Course, I didn't figure him for no cop at that particular time. Just some boozed-up redneck busting into Smoke's, picking on a spade happens to be sitting there with my acquaintance, goes by the tag Moonfoot.'

I checked out my translation. 'That night in Smoke's, you stole Bobby Pym's wallet while he was preoccupied with harassing George Hall?'

Gilchrist nodded.

'Deliberately and specifically George Hall?' prodded Isaac from the blue couch where he and Nora sat together, sharing notes on their legal pads.

'Hunh?'

I repeated it. 'Pym picked on George in particular?'

'Yeah, he went straight up his ass – I'm sorry. I mean, he was ugly to the whole joint, and feeding the jukebox while they had this spade guitar player doing his number, junk like that, but he was riding Hall the most. Yeah, deliberate.'

'You had the impression Pym *knew* Hall?'

'I didn't have no impressions, Captain. I'm a bystander. They're shoving each other around, and Pym takes a fall. I sort of help him up, and I cop his wallet, pants pocket, you know. Then the cop leaps up – I mean, later on I hear how he's a cop – and Christ Almighty the fucker pulls a gun, sticks it up Hall's nose. Think about it, here I am with the man's wallet and he's waving a gun at the joint. So I think, "What's going on?" Plus I knew Moonfoot was in the business—'

'Like breaking into cigarette warehouses and selling the merchandise out of state, that type business?'

'Yeah, well, you hear these rumours, you know.'

'And you thought maybe George and maybe Pym were in this business too? Well, Billy, I sure wish you'd done your civic duty and mentioned it back then to somebody like me.'

He snorted at the stupidity of this suggestion. 'Sure, I got a dead cop's wallet, I got a record, and I'm gonna volunteer my "impressions." Sure.'

'At any point did Bobby Pym say anything to Butler?'

'Moonfoot was out of there the second that gun showed up.'

Nora asked a question now. 'There was trial testimony that as Pym pushed the muzzle into George's nostril, he said, "Your ass is grass, buddy." Did you hear anything like that?'

Gilchrist whined, tugging the blanket around his skinny shoulders. 'I can't remember all these details! Rosethorn's already put me through this with a fucking lice comb. Awh, shit – excuse me – all I'm giving you's the picture, okay? Pym was in the black guy's face.'

Nora leaned forward. 'But the "picture" you had was that Pym was threatening George's life? That was your sense of it?'

'He wasn't asking him to dance. Listen, y'all spring for a drink maybe? Look at my hands.' It was hard to get a clear look at them, they were shaking so much. Finally Isaac let him have a bottle of Guinness Stout, which Gilchrist said tasted like motor oil – a pickier palate than you'd expect in a wino. He drank it though. His description of the fight itself tallied pretty closely with the trial record. After the shot, Billy said he followed the crowd outside and saw Pym lying on the sidewalk. When I showed up in the patrol car, he slipped back into Smoke's and hid upstairs, where he also kindly warned the private party shooting craps to clear the cash off the floor, in case the cops came up. Not that Captain Fulcher ever went to the trouble. But Billy had kept a lookout from the upstairs window. And he was still looking out, after the ambulance had left, and Fulcher's team was inside the bar questioning whoever hadn't managed to leave in time.

It was then that Billy noticed a large white man running out of the cheap hotel across the street, and driving off in a Ford parked down the block; Billy noticed him because he was white, and because he had *run* to the car, and because he assumed the man had got into some kind of trouble with a black hooker or her boyfriend, since the 'hotel,' locally known as 'Clenny's Cathouse,' was 10 per cent flop joint and 90 per cent brothel.

Nora flipped through pages of her legal pad. Isaac leaned over, circling a note on a page. She said, 'And you later decided this man was Winston Russell?'

'Yeah, like I said, I hear rumours this cop named Russell is nosing around Smoke's, putting the word out he wants to know who maybe lifted this wallet of his pal's, okay, and somebody by way of a friend points Russell out to me, okay, and it's the same redheaded guy I saw beating it out of Clenny's.'

Nora said, 'You're sure of that, Billy? When you saw him, it was dark and he was running.'

'I saw him pretty good, standing in Clenny's doorway.'

I said, 'Meanwhile, you had Pym's wallet, with, I believe Isaac mentioned, eight hundred dollars in it. Which you spent.'

His rheumy eyes looked sadly at his hands. 'I didn't have no self-esteem at that particular time in my life, Captain Mangum. I was lost. I'll tell you the truth, I hit the bottle, flew to Vegas and blew every cent. If it wasn't for Jesus leading me to sal—'

'Um hum.' I forestalled his born-again testimony, which I (and everybody else in HPD) had already heard a number of times. 'Now, you also found in Pym's wallet, according to Isaac, a public locker key. Is that right?'

'That's right. When I get back from Vegas, I scout around with this key, and finally I hit it at the bus station in Raleigh.'

'And what did you find in this locker?'

'Suitcase.'

'And in the suitcase?'

'Forty-seven thousand, seven hundred and sixty-nine dollars in cash.'

I stared at Nora and Isaac, both of whom nodded at me. I said, 'That's a lot of loose cash.'

Isaac said, 'When Cooper told me the rumours that Robert Pym was not the sterling police officer Mitch Bazemore had conjured so successfully for that jury, but a thief and an extortionist, my first impulse was to find a record of irregular income –

had he bought his wife a new freezer, put in a pool, made odd bank deposits, that sort of thing. But we came up empty. We came up empty because the money was still in that locker.'

Billy said, 'I open the suitcase, and I see forty-seven thousand, seven hundred and sixty-nine dollars.'

I asked him, 'You counted it?'

'I hid it, then I counted it. I relocked the locker, and I hid the key too. I still got it. It's taped under a drawer in my bureau.'

I said no, actually, the key was at this moment in an envelope labelled 'B. Gilchrist,' in the In basket at my office. 'I hope you had a warrant,' Isaac said.

'Nah, it's all right,' Billy shrugged. 'Captain Mangum's done me favours too.' The con man sank deeper into the heat of the electric blanket, and sucked on his beer bottle. 'So, anyhow, I gotta figure the way Russell's been pushing for info, he's after the dead guy's wallet because of that key. Wasn't no sentimental journey, like maybe he was gonna bronze that wallet for a souvenir of his buddy, you know? I do some asking around too. Word's out 'bout two cops doing a hustle, and I peg Pym and Russell for it. Moonfoot Butler, he fills me in, how these two put the squeeze on him after they pulled him on a B and E rap. So how he was getting merchandise for them – heavy quantity stuff now, too, cigarettes, even guns and ammo, is what he said. So I know all this cash ain't 'cause these cops won big at bingo over at the station, you know? Then, next thing I hear, Moonfoot skips, like he dropped through a hole. Not a trace. Tell you the truth, at that particular time, I figured the cop had pumped one in him.'

I asked Isaac, 'Moonfoot Butler confirms this in his deposition?' Nodding yes, Isaac pulled a folder from the pile on the floor, and shook it at me. I said, 'Okay, Billy, so you find the money. Hall goes on trial for first-degree murder. Then what?'

'Well, for a while I lay off, real quiet. Then I hear on the news how Russell's got *himself* busted, A and B on some hooker, I hear, and he's pulled six to nine at Dollard. So I say to myself, "You're home free, Billy," and that's when I start unloading the other stuff. What I did was wrong, but I know my Lord forgives me, and I want to thank God for punishing me in His fire, and then washing me in the waters of—'

'Yes, that's fine, that's good,' I said. 'This is "other stuff" you found in the suitcase in addition to the money?'

Gilchrist yawned. 'Yeah. Plastic bags with police tags on them;

mostly pot, some coke, two or three were pills.' He yawned again, his eyes flickering. 'Couple of guns. I dumped the guns. I never messed with guns. That was always a strict rule with me.' His eyes closed, and his head fell to his shoulder.

Nora said, 'Maybe we should let him go back to sleep now.'

I could sympathize with Billy's desire. Not Isaac; unless forced up early by a trial, he'd always flipped night and day, claiming to reach the 'peak of his powers' between three and five in the morning. It looked like Nora Howard was going to fit right in; she was rummaging around in all those notes of hers, bright-eyed as a nocturnal raccoon in a trash can.

Yawning, I walked over and shook Gilchrist's bird-boned arm. 'Wake up, Billy ... Okay, you sold the drugs – let's not discuss whether or not you suspected from those HPD tags that you were selling confiscated evidence that was the property of the police department—'

Isaac sighed, and blew a puff of smoke at the ceiling. 'Yes, let's don't discuss it. Billy repents his former life.'

Gilchrist was swaying back and forth, either from exhaustion or the beer or religious ecstasy. 'Repented and found salvation in the redemption of my Lord Jesus Christ—'

I said, 'Right. Let's *not* discuss it. Sorry I brought it up. You sold the drugs. What did you do with the forty-seven thousand dollars?'

He answered with his eyes closed. 'I spent some. And I lost some down in Florida.'

'I assume you don't mean you mislaid it, but lost it gambling?'

'Yeah, mostly dogs and horses, craps, some cards, little jai alai, you know. I guess it was about twenty thousand dollars I lost. I mean . . .' He opened his eyes to explain. 'Not all at once. Different trips.'

I said, 'Well, that's reassuring. I'd hate to think you were reckless enough to lose twenty thousand dollars on one visit to Florida.'

'I had a kind of a serious drinking problem.'

'I know.'

'Yeah well, I kept waking up and finding myself on an aeroplane headed some place like Vegas or Miami.'

'My my. Must have been pretty nerve-racking.' I watched Nora trying not to smile. She hopped off the couch and went to the kitchen.

Billy popped the lip of the beer bottle out of his mouth. 'Blackouts. It's one of the symptoms of alcoholism, Father Paul says.'

'Sounds like an expensive one. Okay, you lost twenty thousand dollars under the influence. Where's the other twenty-seven?'

He pulled himself up with what I guess you might have called a radiant smile if his teeth had been in better shape. 'I gave it to God. You know, after I got saved. Like a kind of thank-you, see, for redeeming me.'

Isaac had been waiting for this. He pointed at the look on my face, and started chuckling. 'That's right, Slim, all that sinful money has been laundered in the blood of the Lamb.'

I ignored him. 'All right, Billy. But I'm assuming you didn't give it to God *directly*, right? Who was the go-between?'

Billy said, 'Hunh?'

Isaac said, 'Trinity Church. He put it in the collection plate.'

'Not in a lump,' explained Billy quickly. 'Twenties at daily mass, fifties on Sundays. Father Paul says, you don't want to be like the Pharisee praying in the marketplace, you know, for the reward of it, sort of. It's gotta be just between you and God, so I kind of tried to spread it out.'

Nora stood by the kitchen counter holding up the offer of a beer in one hand, a Pepsi in the other. I pointed to the Pepsi, as I said to Gilchrist, 'Let me just be sure I've got this. While sleeping at their soup kitchen, you made daily contributions to Trinity Episcopal Church, adding up in the past few years to twenty-seven thousand dollars?'

He wriggled sheepishly. 'Not exactly daily. Maybe I'd miss a week here and a few weeks there.' He lifted his chin. 'But I'd always try and make it up soon as I got back out of the slammer. Except the thing is, like I been telling Mr Rosethorn and this lady, giving the money was kind of a way of making up for things, but it didn't do me no good in my ... my ... mind.' In his struggle for the right words, he sat up, throwing off the blanket. 'After a while, I couldn't feel easy, okay, about that guy George Hall. The way his trial had gone down so bad, and him never saying nothing bad about those two cops, even when the judge hands him the Big One. 'Cause the way I figured it, Hall knew what they were up to, and they came gunning for him, and it got fucked up. But I say, "Billy, stay out of it, you don't know what was going down, and you don't stick your neck out 'cause some spade's getting gassed." But then Father Paul, you know, he's always talking to me about how Jesus figured things, how He didn't go for that eye-for-an-eye stuff, how He said we *gotta* stick our necks out for our neighbours, same as if they was us. And I see how Father Paul's always meeting with this bunch of people trying to do something for George Hall, and a lot of them never even laid eyes on him. And I see Hall's kid brother all over the place, asking questions over at Smoke's, doing these marches, all that. But it's coming down to where it's just a matter of days before Hall's gonna get gassed, and I'm in a sweat 'cause I can't stop thinking about it, but I'm chicken to go to the cops or even Father Paul. I'm chicken.' Gilchrist gave a deep sigh. 'So I take a dive. I get myself good and plastered, and figure time I come to, it'll be all over. But I wake up . . .' He looked at me. 'With you guys downtown.'

I said, 'And that was Friday before Christmas, right? I came in late that night and told you Hall had got a four-week stay from the governor, you remember?'

He stared at me, his eyes shiny. 'That stay wasn't from no governor, Captain Mangum. Jesus did it. I know that as sure as anything, and I'll tell you this too. Jesus talked to me, right then and there in that room.' Gilchrist looked at each of us in turn, waiting for a response. We all gave him a nod, and, satisfied, he went on. 'Jesus told me, straight-out, "Billy . . ." Jesus stood right by the window and He said, "Billy, I appreciate that money. But that money don't mean a fucking thing to me compared to George Hall. Don't mean diddlyshit to me compared to *you*. And Billy, the best thing you can do for you, is do something for George Hall, okay. So you know what I'd do if I was you, Billy, I'd go cold turkey on the booze, and I'd get out of here and try and help save that spade from the gas chamber. 'Cause I already took that Last Walk, and I know what it feels like." That's what Jesus said to me.'

Isaac and Nora nodded as solemnly as if Gilchrist had just quoted them a little Thomas à Kempis. Isaac even came over, slouched on his chair arm, and patted his knee, as he told me, 'So that's exactly what Billy did. Early Saturday morning he went to Cooper Hall at the *With Liberty and Justice* office, talked to him and gave him Pym's wallet. Then he drove with Cooper to Raleigh to the bus station and showed him the locker; the empty suitcase was still in it, which Cooper took. Afterwards Cooper drove on to the governor's mansion and his picket line, and Billy took the bus back to Hillston.'

The old lawyer pushed himself to his feet, and began pacing around the living room, in the style I'd watched a lot of times from the balcony of the Municipal Building courtroom, when his voice could make you cry. 'Saturday afternoon, poor Cooper is killed ... Saturday evening, Billy goes back to the *With Liberty and Justice* office. A kid there gives him my address at the Piedmont, because Cooper's told Billy my name. But when he comes out of the office, he sees somebody parked in front, sort of casing the place. It's Winston Russell. And Billy recognizes him, and he panics. He hides all night. Sunday dawn he hitchhikes about ninety miles north of Hillston. Then he gets a call through to me. I borrow a car, and drive up to meet him.'

I said, 'And you and Billy keep right on going, hunh, Isaac? Straight to Delaware, instead of telephoning the police?'

The great lawyer was not to be sidetracked by petty accusations. He dragged his bad leg as he swung into a turn. 'Now, what if Winston Russell, released from Dollard only a few days prior to this, had been in the Raleigh bus station when Billy took Cooper there to show him the locker? Had followed them there, or simply gone there at the first opportunity to check the locker? At any rate, saw them there together? And where is Russell? Since he's apparently slipped right through your fingers.'

I said, 'Maybe he wouldn't have, if you hadn't been such a goddamn grandstanding, secret-hogging Lone Ranger you had to do it all yourself.'

Nora looked startled, but my anger shot right by Isaac without ruffling a hair. He said, 'Shhh. Poor Billy.'

I glanced over at the armchair. Poor Billy was sound asleep.

On a charitable impulse (or maybe because I'd already caught a whiff of my usurped sheets), I let Gilchrist finish out the night in my bed. Isaac and I took him there. Downstairs in my living room, I stopped Rosethorn from rushing back to Nora's apartment. 'Hold up a second. What's bugging me, what's *been* bugging me, is *did* George know what Pym and Russell were up to? Is Billy right, and George was involved? And if he was involved, or at least knew something – why didn't George say so at the trial, or even after the trial, to a lawyer, to *Cooper*?'

Isaac frowned. 'George said nothing to Cooper beyond his testimony.'

'Because that's all he knew?'

No answer.

'Why was George so desperate to talk to you?'

No answer. The old lawyer pulled open the door to the hall, but I shoved it closed. 'Isaac, you're pissing me off. Whose side do you think I'm on anyhow?'

The old bathrobe spread open as his chest swelled. 'You're out of line, Slim. I work for a client. I'm bound by a pledge to defend him against the state. You work for the state, directly under a district attorney I don't respect or trust. I'm not going to provide the prosecution with information it failed to obtain itself, and may even use against my client. I have to decide when I have more to gain by hogging my secrets, and when it's useful to share them.'

I reached around him and flung the door open. 'Well, let me know when I'm useful!'

'I will,' he said, and shuffled across to Nora's.

I stretched out on my couch, too sleepy to stay angry long. The next thing I was vaguely aware of was somebody tucking a blanket around me.

And the next thing after that, I opened my eyes and saw two small faces about an inch from my own. A little boy and girl, both with black curly hair, both wearing blue NASA sweatshirts, both fairly rigorously chewing gum, were kneeling beside the couch, solemnly watching me for signs of life. The girl said, 'Are you really a policeman?'

I managed to make a fairly human noise. 'Yep. Did you get a bicycle for Christmas?' She nodded. 'Then I bet you're Laura Howard.' She thought it over, and nodded again. 'Is this your brother Brian?'

'My *little* brother,' she clarified.

Brian scooted forward. 'It's time to wake up.' I got both eyes open, and checked out his statement. He was right. It was full sunlight. I'd pretty undeniably fallen asleep in my rented tuxedo, after – as I recall – telling myself I was just resting my eyes. I hadn't even dreamed about Lee, as I'd intended to. I'd dreamed about George Hall.

Brian propped his elbows on the couch arm. He had the same tilted-up green eyes as his mother. 'We slept in a teepee,' he announced, and curled his gum-covered tongue out towards his nose.

'Um hum. I heard. You like it?'

But that was all he had to say, and he ran off, making motor noises, back out the opened door, and across the hall. His sister was more conversational, if a little facetious. She asked, 'Do you always sleep in a tuxedo?'

'Who him? Captain Mangum? Absolutely.' Another face suddenly leaned into my view. It was Justin Savile's, disgustingly bright. The head of my Homicide Division was grinning. 'Always in a tuxedo, partying day and night. Dapper Dan Mangum we call him at the police station.' (Justin himself looked unusually casual this morning in a three-piece Harris tweed suit from some episode of *Brideshead Revisited*.) He whispered at Laura, 'Let's be nice to him. He's my boss.'

'He is?' Laura looked dubious. I don't know why children have such trouble believing in my rank. In any case, she changed the subject. 'My mom said come have some coffee. Bye.' She whisked away as quickly as her little brother.

Justin grinned as I pulled myself into a seated position. 'Cuddy, I always told you Billy Gilchrist was a staggering mine of information.' I glanced up at my stairs. Justin nodded. 'Still snoozing. Quite some story Isaac just gave me. Told you Willie Slidell would be the link.'

Now the fact is, I'm used to waking up alone, not to mention in bed in my pyjamas. I grumbled, 'Just a second, okay? Just hold down the gloating till I can cope with it. And make some coffee.'

'Let's go to Mrs Howard's.'

' "Mrs Howard's?" '

'What a smart woman. Beautiful too.'

'I'm not going anywhere till I take a shower and drink some caffeine.'

When I returned from my shower (I could hear Gilchrist's snores even with the water running), Justin cheerfully handed me a mug of coffee, and picked up where he'd left off. I sat on a stool, staring out at the Shocco, while I listened to him.

'So it's got to be this way. Pym and Russell branch out, start smuggling their merchandise out of state. Inventory gets a little low at the police warehouse, you just get thieves like Moonfoot Butler to steal more for you, and shipping clerks like Willie Slidell to provide transportation in Fanshaw trucks. I knew Slidell was the key.'

'I'll make sure you get your name in the paper, okay?' I poured more coffee. 'Just what are you doing over here, Justin?'

'Reassuring myself. Listen, Alice thought you were *dead*. But then she always takes a radical position. You know we got a call from Hiram around midnight that you were "missing"? He said you carelessly let someone bash in your skull, and had probably wandered off in a coma. You ever get to that dinner party of yours?'

'Yes. Did you talk to Pym's widow?'

Flipping the omelette he'd insisted on making, Justin reported that Lana Slidell Pym was prostrate with shock after seeing her brother Willie's body in the morgue. She had trouble believing we'd found him in a car in the Shocco River. She clung to her version of a Willie Slidell who knew nothing of guns or enemies. Her late brother and her late husband Bobby Pym were innocent victims of their violent fates, and no facts could make them otherwise. Justin said he had also phoned Slidell's Kentucky wife again; she said she was sorry to hear that 'poor dumb Willie had got the shitty end of the stick again, like always.'

I asked, 'Meaning what?'

'Meaning, and I quote the lady, "doing the shit work for that jerk-off brother-in-law of his, Bobby Pym, and his jerk-off buddy Winston Russell."'

'This omelette's really good,' I admitted. 'Could you get anything specific out of her?'

Justin grimaced at the contents of my refrigerator. 'No. The former Mrs Slidell felt strongly that having climbed out of "that shit pile," she had no desire to climb back in. But don't worry. She and I are going to be having some more talks.' Justin made a face at the messy remains of some Hot Hat brunswick stew. 'My God, what is that?'

I ignored his question. 'What time is it?'

Nora Howard had stuck her head in my front door, and answered me. 'Ten o'clock. Coffee?'

Justin said, 'I'd love some.'

Back in her living room, Isaac Rosethorn, his white hair sticking out like a cap of spiky feathers, sat smoking away at the dining room table, his nose in a scroll of computer printouts. Mrs Howard (as Justin kept calling her, though she was younger than he was) certainly was hospitable; she appeared to be happy to throw open her apartment to anyone who happened to pass through the hall; maybe it was her Italian background.

While I drank my third cup of coffee by the balcony window, I watched her children play outside, trying to scrape together enough of the inch-deep snow to make a small snowman. Isaac hadn't moved, and Justin was on the Howards' phone. Then he came to the kitchen, shaking his head. 'Mitchell Bazemore wasn't exactly charmed with our request for a warrant against Purley. He says Otis Newsome is a good friend, a good man, and a high-ranking city official, and that it wasn't easy to tell Otis that we were accusing his brother Purley of half a dozen serious felonies. In fact, Bazemore wants us to know that he never had to do anything sadder in his life. He says Otis was shell-shocked, outraged, and doesn't believe a word of it ... Wonderful coffee, Mrs Howard.'

'Call me Nora.'

He gave her a short bow.

I said, 'Bazemore's our DA.'

Nora said, 'I know.'

Justin said, 'But he backed off a tad on the indignation, when I told him Etham had found Purley's prints, as well as Winston Russell's, out at Slidell's farm.'

I said, 'You tell our friendly DA about Arthur "Moonfoot" Butler's deposition?'

'Yep. He said he'd prefer us to find somebody besides convicted criminals to, quote, "substantiate these allegations." ' Justin stood with his cup and saucer, like he'd come for a tea party. 'Meanwhile, the best evidence we've got against Purley is that he's gone. He's definitely skipped town. No leads on him or Russell either. Could be in Bangkok or Sweden by now.'

Nora turned to him. 'From what I've heard, Winston Russell doesn't sound like the Sweden or Bangkok type.'

I said, 'Justin's parochial. He figures everybody for a cosmopolitan.'

'He's been telling me,' she said, 'you're the one who takes vacations all over the world.'

Justin smiled at her. 'Oh, and I talked to Dave Schulmann; he said FBI could justify some help on the Cooper Hall homicide, if we demonstrate conspiracy to deprive him of his civil rights.'

Isaac shouted from the dining room table. 'If *murdering* a man doesn't deprive him of his civil rights, I'd be intrigued to know what would qualify!'

I said, 'It's the conspiracy we have to prove. We haven't tied Purley to the Hall or Slidell shooting, except that at some point he was in Slidell's house. In fact, he was in the squad room when Coop was shot.'

I accepted more coffee from Nora, who was wearing a dress for the first time, I mean it was the first time I'd seen her not in

218

jeans. She said, 'He doesn't need to have been there at the actual shooting in order to prove conspiracy.' She paused, and looked at me. 'Would you like an outsider's opinion?'

I said, 'Outsider? Last night, I thought you and Isaac announced you were now co-counsel for the defence.'

She smiled. 'I am. To the police, that's usually an outsider's opinion.'

Justin said, 'We're not usual police.'

I said, 'Speak for yourself.'

He said, 'Look, I'm not the one who sleeps in a tuxedo.' He turned to Nora. 'Have you known many police chiefs who sleep in tuxedoes?'

'Not lately,' she told him.

'What's your opinion?' I asked her.

'That Willie Slidell was driving the car Saturday when Russell shot Cooper Hall. *Somebody* had to be driving. But that Slidell hadn't realized what he'd got himself into, and either broke down, or at least Russell believed he *would* break down. I think by Sunday Russell and Newsome decided they had to get rid of Slidell, and get rid of the car. As soon as you found Slidell's body, they both took off. So Newsome had to be involved. Because nothing had been publicly released yet about Slidell. Only the police knew.'

Justin said, 'Makes real sense. Cuddy, you awake? What do you think?'

I said, 'I'm awake. Don't I look alert and alive?'

Nora smiled. 'You look better than you did last night.' The weird thing was, when she put her hand on mine to take the coffee cup, I felt, well, I felt aware of the flesh of her fingers, as if her touch was familiar to me. And that recognition must have been in my eyes, because I think she saw it there; I think I saw it in her eyes too. At any rate, we both looked away fast. It was the last thing I would have expected, and I thought, Jesus, what's the matter with me? Is this just a residue of arousal from last night with Lee, or just overstimulation from no sleep, or just that once I cracked the ice of my accidental celibacy (meaning I've been too busy to look for somebody), I was thawing in a hurry?

Justin looked up from his appreciative inspection of Nora's copperware. 'Captain, any plans on coming to headquarters today? Etham and I have a few more little tidbits for you. For one, we found both Purley's and Winston's prints on your ostentatious Oldsmobile, so that little stink bomb was definitely their good-bye present to you. Two, their prints are *not* at the *With Liberty and Justice* office, and the graffiti on the wall does not match either of their handwritings.'

Isaac roared from the dining area. 'Find out who broke in there and took Cooper's file box. I want Pym's wallet. I'm sure that's where Cooper put it, in his file box.'

I walked to him and tapped my finger on the table top. 'How 'bout letting us find Winston Russell first. If we *can*.'

His jowls twitching, Isaac peered at me over his bifocals. 'You *better* find Russell. I need him for my retrial.'

'I want him too, and for more than "your" retrial. Besides, you don't even know if you'll get a retrial.'

He stuck his nose back in his papers. 'I'll get it,' he grumbled.

Justin was pulling on his Chesterfield overcoat. 'And here's another present from Etham and me,' he said. 'That white Fairlane we found in the Shocco with Willie in it? Well, guess what? Seven years ago, it was one of the many unclaimed vehicles in the HPD impoundment lot. Seven years ago, somebody with access to that lot borrowed it and didn't bother to bring it back, and nobody even reported it missing. And guess what else? Etham and I did a little chipping away at the paint on that Fairlane. It didn't used to be a white Ford. It used to be a *blue* Ford. I bet it used to be *the* blue Ford that Mitch Bazemore said didn't exist, at George Hall's trial.'

Well, this news perked Isaac Rosethorn up enough to think about sending out for brunch spareribs from Hot Hat Barbecue. Justin and I left then, first going across the hall to get my coat. Billy Gilchrist was still sleeping.

If Justin hadn't stopped to give me a lecture about spraying my corn plant for mealy worms, we would have been on our way downtown before the phone rang. As it was, I was prepared for the scene I was to encounter fifteen minutes later at the Municipal Building. It was Zeke Caleb calling. He sounded like he was out of breath.

'Chief, shit, Chief, get down here. Whole place is gone haywire. Second floor. Got a fatality.'

'What's wrong? Is it Mayor Yarborough?' The second floor was where the mayor and the city council had their offices, and my first thought was that Carl might have had a heart attack.

'No, it's the comptroller. Otis Newsome. He's dead. His secretary couldn't get into his office. They had to break in the door. Everybody's running around downstairs going batshit.'

'Otis Newsome's dead?! How? A stroke?'

'I'm sorry to tell you, Chief. I don't know if y'all were friendly, but it's bad. Mr Newsome killed himself.'

'What? Jesus! Are they sure it was suicide?'

'Real sure. He hanged himself from a ceiling pipe. They got Dick Cohn in there as soon as they found him, but it wasn't any use.'

'Did Otis leave a note? Get down there and ask about a note.'

'DA said there wasn't any note. DA and another fellow were already on their way to see Newsome, so they're the ones got in there first. DA ran for Dick Cohn. After Dick gave up working on Mr Newsome, this other fellow fainted flat on the floor so Dick had to revive him. Name of Fanshaw, something Fanshaw. DA said he was a friend of Mr Newsome's.'

Getting out of the car at the Municipal Building, I saw Mitchell Bazemore at the top of the steps, leaning on one of the Confederate cannons, staring hard off into space. When we came back out, half an hour later, he was still there, staring. Everybody else standing around was staring hard at what was going on down on the sidewalk. It was a small group of young picketers slowly moving in a loose circle at the foot of the block-long steps. They were all carrying signs, and what they were picketing was the Hillston Police Department. I knew some of these people – I recognized the three Haver students from the vigil group, and the two teenaged Canaan blacks from the riot, Martin Hall and G. G. Walker (who – despite his somewhat inappropriately jaunty grin and bebop walk – had clearly changed his mind since his vaunt to me that 'protest was N-O-T his bag'). Most of the signs the group carried said the same thing. They said, 'JUSTICE FOR THE HALL BROTHERS.'

I nodded to the group as I hurried by, but Justin stopped beside the long-legged, young Mr Walker and told him, 'Rehearsal tonight at eight, G.G. See you.'

'I'm easy, my man,' said Walker and kept moving with the circle of picketers.

I asked, 'What was that all about?'

'G.G.'s playing your part in *Twelfth Night*,' Justin wheezed at

221

me as we hurried to the car. 'Malvolio. Thanks for suggesting him. Of course, he's *charging* me to be in it. By the line. But wait'll you see him. He's really great.'

I turned and looked back at Walker, bouncing along with his solemn sign. 'Well, he's a braver man than I am. Some are born great,' I said. 'And some achieve greatness, against mighty considerable odds.'

I noticed that many of the young protesters wore campaign buttons. They were light Carolina blue. They had Andy Brookside's face on them.

Part Two

A Kind of Puritan

Chapter 13

It was three months after the city comptroller took his own life – the official word on the suicide was that grief at a bad brother's misdoings had temporarily overwhelmed a good man – before Isaac Rosethorn slapped down his bulging briefcase on the defence table, and began 'his' new trial. That's how he put it. Sometimes he said 'our' new trial, referring, I assume, to himself and Nora Howard, and possibly George Hall. Of course, all George had to do was wait. Isaac had to work, an activity about which he professed some ambivalence, as it took time from his hobbies – like teaching himself Russian so he could read Dostoevsky, who he believed shared his philosophical point of view; that's the way he phrased it, not 'I share Dostoevsky's view,' but 'he shares mine.'

At any rate, two weeks after Nora and he submitted their written briefs, one week after they presented their oral arguments, and seventy-two hours before the governor's stay of execution expired, the justices of the State Supreme Court did in a few minutes what Cooper Hall had worked for seven years to bring about: they remanded the case of *S. vs. Hall 2179 N.C.* to the District Court to be retried, with a new defence, a new jury and a new judge. During this time, Isaac had practically moved in across the hall from me, since for some bizarre reason, he'd decided it would be 'improper' for Nora to work in his room at the Piedmont Hotel, but fine for him to soak his big carcass in her tub for hours (he claimed to think better in the tub), smoking cigarettes and getting volumes of the *General Statutes* so soggy the pages stuck together.

Nora didn't seem to mind his being in her house, and her children treated Isaac like an unusual old toy they'd found up in the attic – sometimes they played with him, sometimes they threw him over for the modern gadgets they'd collected at Christmas. I was often invited there for dinner, but most evenings I wasn't free to go, either because I was downtown working, or because I was with Lee, or home waiting for her to call me. Besides, that 'general conversation' which Edwina Sunderland had insisted on at her parties was by no means forthcoming around the bleached oak table at 2-B River Rise. Instead, what you got was in this vein:

Nora: 'Isaac, look back at page three fifty-six. Following the verdict, Judge Tiggs failed to instruct jury that death penalty was *not* mandatory sentence. We can use General Statute fifteen-A-two thousand. Brian, please, *please*, eat one little piece of broccoli, just one.'

Isaac: 'Absolutely the best lasagna I ever tasted. Quoting that racist yahoo Henry Tiggs now, in his charge prior to sentencing: "As for these people who have testified that they saw the victim Robert Pym grossly and recklessly provoke the defendant, consider that the witnesses may have come to that conclusion out of feelings of" – listen to this, Nora – "*allegiance* with the defendant. If you so decide, you will disregard their testimony as in any way mitigating the defendant's crime." Well, God Above! If that's not a clear violation of fifteen A-twelve thirty-one, I don't know what is. Believed him because they were black! Put it down. Comment to jury as to the weight of the evidence or credibility of the witnesses, et cetera, ET CETERA . . .. Really, delicious lasagna! . . . On the other hand we can't slash so heavily at Henry Tiggs that we suffer a backlash. Extraordinarily enough, he still has a few friends in Raleigh.'

Laura: 'Mom, would you just *listen*? If I don't have four big green sheets of poster board by tomorrow, I can't do my science project, and I'll flunk *out*.'

Nora: 'They're in a bag in the hall closet, sweetheart. Maybe Cuddy could help you with your project this evening. I bet he was very good at science. Cuddy, would you? Oh, Isaac, I'm not sure about making too big a deal of defence's failure to object to state's introduction of prior criminal record. What do you think? I think we should drop it. Too many precedents for exceptions. Look here, for example, *N.C. vs. McClain* two forty (nineteen fifty-four).'

Brian: 'No books at the table, Mommy. You *said*! Cuddy, she says we can never ever bring *our* books to the table.'

Isaac: 'Nora, where's that transcript of the voir dire?'

Yep, general conversation didn't have a chance. My hostess and host talked shop, read shop, wrote shop, and pretty much ate shop. The budding firm of Rosethorn and Howard must have had to ship its appeal briefs to Raleigh in a tractor trailer. Those briefs were longer than the United States Constitution on which their favourite points were based. But in the end, as Isaac had predicted, when the court finally set aside the first verdict against George Hall, and granted a new trial, it was not because his Fourteenth Amendment rights to equal protection under the law had been violated by a biased judge and an all-white jury, nor because his Eighth Amendment rights against cruel and unusual punishment had been violated by his receiving a death penalty conviction for a homicide that was not of an 'unusually heinous nature,' that was devoid of 'malice aforethought' or 'cool deliberation,' and that resulted from 'a situation of mutual combat' (regarding which, Isaac and Nora listed four precedents of similar cases in which the charge was not first-, but second-degree murder; fifteen precedents in which the charge was not even homicide, but manslaughter – most involving black victims of black assailants; six precedents in which the defendant was found not guilty by reason of self-defence – white assailants, white victims, and two in which the charges were simply dropped – white assailants, black victims). All these heavy-duty arguments failed to elicit much comment from the justices one way or another.

No, George appears to have got a new trial because NC General Statute 9:6–1 had been violated in his old trial: that's the law that says everybody has a right to a jury who can hear what's going on. And Isaac was able to demonstrate that juror number nine, one Darwin Wheelwright (perhaps out of the same pride that had kept him from admitting he was deaf until after he lost his job, got hit by a motorcycle and sued his ENT surgeon), juror number nine had answered falsely when he replied no to the question of whether or not he had any physical impairment that might handicap him from well and truly trying the case. In Mr Wheelwright's defence, maybe he hadn't meant to perjure himself, but had just misheard the question.

So Isaac got his new trial. And his new judge. He got Judge Shirley Hilliardson (it's a male name in these parts, and Shirley

Hilliardson was definitely male, though less definitely human, for his cold-eyed face resembled a falcon's, and his thin elongated frame, a crane's). Most lawyers I knew hated Hilliardson, but Isaac claimed to be pleased, and would rub his hands together so fast and long you'd start waiting for spontaneous combustion to incinerate them as he crowed, 'If I have to have a judge with a missing organ, I prefer it to be the heart, not the brain. Shirley Hilliardson has a brain. He knows his law. Ah, Slim, I can smell it! The heat and dust of battle is in my nostrils!'

Despite this eager snuffling of war, as soon as a date was set for the opening of the trial, Rosethorn launched another marathon paper drive to have it postponed. He won that skirmish too. In his request for a continuance, I was one of the culprits. The state of Delaware was another one, for taking so long to decide if they'd lend him Arthur 'Moonfoot' Butler for the day, so he could put him on the witness stand. I was presumably among the law enforcement officials who had failed so far to locate one Winston Russell, in order to serve him with Isaac's subpoena. I was more concerned that I hadn't been able to serve Russell with warrants for his arrest on two counts of first-degree murder. I wanted Russell more than Isaac did, and Isaac was the least of all the reasons why I wanted him. I wanted him for the Halls, for Jordan West, for Carl Yarborough, I wanted him for me, and maybe most of all, I wanted him for, well, I guess you could call it the reputation of the Hillston Police Department.

In January, in conjunction with the FBI, HPD went public with part of our case: we charged Russell and Purley Newsome both with extortion, robbery, the sale of stolen goods, felonious use of the interstate highway system, with the murder of William Slidell, and with conspiracy to deprive Cooper Hall of his civil rights by bringing about his death. We also charged them both with attempting to murder me.

By now, we'd made a fairly good reconstruction of the two men's last day in Hillston. On the morning of December 26, Officer DiMallo had mentioned to Purley that Homicide had pulled a murder victim out of the Shocco River. On the evening of the twenty-sixth, Purley had been visiting his brother Otis's office on the second floor of the Municipal Building; he then had waltzed into HPD, cleared out his locker (Officer Titus Baker: 'I didn't think much about it, figured he was cleaning it up'), then had stolen Titus's patrolman hat. He must have left by way of the parking garage. Probably Winston was with him. Nobody noticed them hanging around, but cops don't look at cops, and it turns out they were both wearing uniforms. They must have thrown the circuit breaker, then waited down there in the garage to see if they'd be lucky and I'd be dumb enough to walk alone in the dark to the far end where I kept my car. They were lucky.

They dropped by the Trinity Episcopal soup kitchen (where Purley asked three of the regulars if they knew where Billy Gilchrist was, and where Winston shoved aside a black panhandler who was leaning against the side door of his car – or rather, Purley's car, a new red Fiero). By this time the bulletin had gone out to all squad cars to bring Russell and Newsome in. Nobody did.

Near midnight on December 26, the new red Fiero – with two big light-haired men in it, not in uniform now – stopped for gas at a Texaco station on the 28 bypass, then headed east. The car was not seen again until it was found abandoned in a shopping mall parking lot near Spartanburg, SC, on February 8. By then, of course, we'd offered a reward for information, and people were seeing the wanted killers everywhere: Two men fitting our suspects' descriptions held up an armoured car outside a Winn-Dixie in Atlanta. The same day two men fitting their description held up a 7-Eleven in Danbury, Virginia, and molested the female clerk before robbing her. Neither lead worked out, and when the Danbury pair were apprehended, and I saw their pictures, they looked as much like my two guys as Justin and Zeke do. They were next 'seen' simultaneously in Houston, Texas and Baltimore, Maryland.

But finally the calls slowed down. Then silence. Purley didn't show at his brother's funeral, didn't get in touch with his relatives or friends, didn't use his credit cards, didn't go to a hospital. He just disappeared. Sometimes, I decided Winston had long since killed Purley the same way he (or they) had killed Willie Slidell. I even sent a search party back out to the Shocco. After three weeks, we dredged up one giant, largely disintegrated roll of Fanshaw paper, ten feet downstream from where Wally had found the Ford Fairlane. Well, I could explain that paper now: Slidell had hidden the paper in his barn, and filled the empty containers with whatever stolen goodies his partners had come up with for him to ship to their buyers. I could explain a lot of things, but I couldn't find two men, themselves trained in surveillance, who didn't want to be found. Just as anybody can kill a stranger without getting caught, anybody can hide among strangers without being seen. And the world is full of strangers.

Finally, even Mayor Yarborough grew hoarse with explaining that I was doing my best, that *I* hadn't hired either of the suspects (one of whom had been thrown off the force five years ago anyhow), and that two rotten apples didn't mean we should throw out the whole barrel. Finally, even the *Hillston Star* got tired of screaming 'KILLER COPS STILL AT LARGE,' and finally Carol Cathy Cane at 'Action News' lost interest in leaping out at me with her microphone and demanding that I 'produce the criminals who've shown the Hillston Police Department to be rife with corruption, racism, and brutality.'

Sad but true, Winston Russell and Purley Newsome were former Hillston police officers. Sad but true, I had not produced them. By late March, when Isaac's continuance expired and Hall's retrial finally began, I was under pressure from not only the DA, but from his boss, the attorney general, and from *his* boss, the governor, to shut down the case until somebody somewhere else (a highway patrolman, an FBI field agent, an airline security guard, a good citizen) called up and said, 'Hey, I just saw those two guys you're after.' It wasn't going to be somebody in Hillston, because I'd torn Hillston apart looking. I'd also torn apart Willie Slidell's farm and its five square miles of surrounding woods. I wasn't the first one to do it either. When Etham had gone back to check fingerprints, he'd found the place in shambles. Obviously, Russell and Newsome had slipped back in, and gone through the house in a hurry, trying to find something. I didn't know if they'd found it or not. Things you might have thought they'd be interested in, they'd uncovered, but left. For example, loose floorboards had been pulled up in the back of the barn, and still lying exposed under them were twelve single-gauge shotguns, six .45 automatics, and two 9mm machine guns. We found traces of cocaine in a can of talcum powder in the open medicine cabinet, and a whole packet of it taped inside the toilet tank.

In the process of searching Slidell's house, we'd also come across a library of Ku Klux Klan literature, several newspaper clippings about George and Cooper Hall, quite a collection of smutty magazines, a lot of video camera equipment along with some smutty videotapes (one homemade, with two hookers whom I recognized). We'd found a sock with the Dollard Prison laundry marker on it, and in an old telephone directory, the underlined home number of the dead Fanshaw salesman Clark Koontz. In the fireplace, we'd found minute fragments of burnt cloth that had blood on them; we'd found a bloodstain in the crack of the woodwork on the kitchen wall, probably where Willie had slid down to the floor after he was shot. And in the drawer of a bureau, we'd found Polaroid photographs of the former Mrs Slidell, taken in the nude in the days before she'd given up on Willie the Wimp. (They were in a cardboard box with the marriage licence, the divorce papers, and three postcards she'd sent him from Myrtle Beach.) We staked out the farm in case Winston and Purley came back to look some more for whatever they were after. They didn't.

I'd kept Russell's and Newsome's faces on the local news so much, they were as familiar as Johnny Carson to anybody in the area who owned a TV set. Both were big men, tall and bulky, but Winston's bulk was harder and tighter. Both were fair; Purley wore his yellowish blond hair long, and invariably hid his soft stupid blue eyes behind aviator sunglasses. Winston kept his reddish hair cropped short. He had almost no eyebrows, and the dead evil unblinking eyes of a shark. I dreamed about them both.

Slidell's sister, Lana, the former Mrs Bobby Pym, had been brought in for questioning so often, her lawyer got a court order to enjoin HPD from 'undue harassment.' She also wanted us to give her back Willie's tan station wagon, which we'd impounded when we found it abandoned near Pine Hills Lake. In the car was a packed suitcase, and in that, two wrapped Christmas presents, which made us think maybe Slidell really had planned to go try to patch things up with his ex-wife -- one gift was a red lace nightgown and robe, the other was a 'Jane Fonda Workout' videotape.

Justin had spent so many hours consoling the bewildered widow Mrs Otis Newsome about her husband's suicide while trying to pry information from her about Purley's whereabouts that he'd gained three pounds from the carrot cake she always served him as she asked over and over, 'Why didn't Otis leave me a note, something to explain why? I can't understand why he would do it, even if Purley is guilty of the things you're saying. Why didn't Otis talk to somebody, to *me*?' Justin decided that Mrs Newsome was telling the truth. He still thought the widow Pym was lying about not knowing what her husband and brother had been up to with Russell.

We planted an article in the papers that a Mr Billy Gilchrist was wanted for questioning about a suitcase said to have been stolen from a Raleigh bus station locker; then we sent Billy out on the street as bait, just in case Russell was still lurking around. Nothing happened except two former drinking buddies of Billy's tried to turn him in for a reward. I had the Georgia police doing surveillance in Russell's hometown, to the indignation of his relatives, who protested that they'd struck his name from the family Bible twenty years ago, hadn't heard from him since, when a teenager, he'd left for Vietnam, and hoped they never did hear from him. I had inquiries out along selected Fanshaw truck routes for possible buyers on the receiving end of those stolen shipments. Ten HPD officers had logged 1,205 hours of interviews with anybody they could find who'd ever met either of the suspects. We turned up nothing.

Well, that's not true. We found out more about Winston Russell and Purley Newsome than people generally get to know about each other; enough to discourage those with any faith in human nature from ever wanting to pry into their neighbours' secrets. We heard from people they'd bullied for sex and kickbacks, or just for the fun of it. We heard that they'd been known to socialize with members of the KKK We learned that when Purley had closed out his bank account on the twenty-sixth, he'd had a little too much in it for a man living on a cop's salary. We learned there was riverbank mud still caught in the ridged soles of the shoes he'd washed, then tossed damp to the rear of his closet. We knew that when Winston was in Dollard Prison, he'd had fifteen visits from Purley, and that he'd bragged there that he had 'a shitload of money' stashed waiting for him when he got out. (He also boasted that as soon as he was released, he was going to kill me, for sending him up.) All we didn't unearth, poking at the worms turned up under the rocks of Russell and Newsome's pasts, was their whereabouts. That, and their place in the puzzle.

Because I didn't think we had the puzzle in place yet. My new computer (its relational data base manager is a much more patient fellow than I am) fed itself years of daily patrol logs for Russell, Pym, and Newsome, cross-referenced them with unsolved robberies, coordinated that with Fanshaw Paper Company truck shipments signed out by William Slidell, and so substantiated for me the dates, figures, and routes of their racket. Etham Foster (just as patient as my computer) matched two single strands of hair from inside Slidell's tan station wagon with hair taken out of Purley's bathroom brush. But I already knew these particular men were stealing, and they were smuggling, and that at least one of them had killed. I just wasn't sure I knew for whom they were doing it.

'For money. For themselves. That's why. For themselves, for money,' said Mitchell Bazemore, who by February had briskly flip-flopped under the weight of the evidence, from his first position – that Billy Gilchrist and Moonfoot Butler were lying scum; Pym and Newsome, paragons of law and order – to his present position – that Pym and Newsome (along with Russell and Slidell) had been a gang of crooks, working with Moonfoot Butler and George Hall. Together, they were responsible for every item missing from HPD, and every warehouse burglary in Hillston, during the past ten years. In the DA's new theory, Willie Slidell had got himself killed in 'one of those typical falling-outs of thieves over the money.' We went around about this again and again under the colour photo of Ronald Reagan on Bazemore's office wall.

'What money, Mitch? Billy Gilchrist got the locker money. And now you're saying Russell and Newsome shot Slidell because he wouldn't tell them where he'd hidden some more money? My mama would call that cutting off your nose to spite your face. Because they sure were looking for something at Slidell's they were having trouble finding.'

'They found the money, and took it.'

'And why'd they shoot Cooper Hall?' I'd ask this because, much as he wanted to, Mitch couldn't get around the fact that the same gun had killed both Cooper and Slidell.

He twisted his knuckles into his biceps as he fought the facts. 'You can have it one of two ways, Mangum. Russell was driving along, alone—'

'I've told you. No. He couldn't have fired across the width of his car *and* through a window, not with that kind of accuracy. I don't care how many firing range awards the bastard won.'

'Then he was with Purley Newsome, then. No, okay, that's out. Newsome was here at Municipal at the time, correct? . . .'

I'd already pointed this fact out on a dozen occasions, but Bazemore's the tenacious kind of guy who won't let go of even useless ideas until he mulches them to pulp. I just stood there, looking at Ronnie.

Bazemore poked his thumb in his chin dimple. 'Slidell has an alibi for Saturday afternoon. He was with his sister.'

I fiddled with the fringe on the flag by the window. 'Lana Pym is lying.'

'You haven't proved it. And you aren't catching the point. I'm proposing that Russell drove along, saw Hall as he passed him, in other words saw a black man with all sorts of leftwing slogans stuck to his car, maybe recognized him for the radical on the media all the time. We know Russell has a violent, a very violent record. It's possible he simply impulsively shot out his window at Hall, simply out of impulse. Spur-of-the-moment type thing.'

'Oh, Jesus!'

Rubbing his Phi Beta Kappa key, Bazemore paced around his desk as if he were measuring it, taking the corners square. 'Well, your only other choice is to assume there is a connection. That's your second choice. There's a connection between the Hall brothers and Russell that—'

'If you'll recall, I picked number two a long time ago.'

'—a connection that goes back to the original murder of Pym. If in fact there's any truth in that bus station locker story, it may have been that Russell thought Cooper Hall had taken his money out of that locker.'

'Then why kill him in such a way that he couldn't check that possibility out? Sorry, Mitch, doesn't work.'

'Then, it may have been that Russell and Slidell were just revenging the killing of Bobby Pym. After all, Pym was their partner and relative. That may have been it. Newsome had nothing to do with it. The state fails to execute George. So in revenge Russell and Pym execute George's brother. That really may have been it.' Bazemore's pacing was stopped short by a jolt of pleasure with this notion.

I said, 'Then too bad they missed the lesson when you were teaching your teenyboppers up at Bible camp that vengeance is mine, sayeth the Lord. You do hit them with that lesson, don't you, Mitch?'

'I don't enjoy your sarcasm.'

'No? Well, it's an acquired taste.'

He pointed his finger at me like an Uncle Sam poster. 'Listen, I know what's behind all this. Your bleeding-heart obsession with George Hall. That's what's behind this. The man's a murderer, a *convicted* murderer, and nothing anyone did or didn't do to his brother will change that fact.'

I moved his finger away, and he jerked his arm back. 'We're discussing *why* something was done to his brother, Mitch, okay?'

The DA then told me the State Supreme Court had been nothing but *tricked* by 'that conceited Jew,' Isaac Rosethorn, into wasting a lot of useless time and money on a new trial for George Hall. But winning the death penalty against Hall this time was going to be even easier than it had been on the first go-round. It was going to be, Mitch announced, lacing his fingers backwards so the knuckles cracked, 'not only a piece of cake, but a down-right pleasure.' If the original jury had bought first-degree when they didn't think George even *knew* Bobby Pym, they were going to hand it over to Mitch on a platter this time, if they heard George had been 'in the racket with Pym up to his nose.' Poor Pym – mused Mitch aloud, rehearsing his opening statement no doubt – poor Bobby Pym, desperate for money for his new baby, had probably been led into crime under the influence of black low-lifes like Hall and Moonfoot Butler in the first place. Of course, the DA realized he couldn't throw the jury his favourite, sure-fire pitch – that a black man who shoots a white cop is threatening the whole American way of life – since he was going to have to paint this particular white cop pretty (morally) black himself. But on the other hand, the prosecution had a curve ball that would win the game anyhow – a black crook who turns on and shoots the white crook who hired him, and paid him, is threatening the whole American way of life.

'Yes, yes, yes.' He did a few neck exercises, and studied the ceiling a while. 'Slidell and Russell shot Cooper Hall to avenge Pym. That's not going to hurt me in the retrial one little bit. Not one little bit.'

I picked up a photo on his desk; in it the DA stood proudly between Governor Wollston and Lieutenant Governor Lewis in some overstuffed hotel banquet room. I said, 'So why do Russell and Newsome turn around and kill Slidell a few days later?'

Then we were back to the 'thieves falling out over money' line. I put the banquet photo down beside the one of the DA's perky wife and their six starched children, all lined up by height and all looking at the camera with the same tense smiles and tight muscles, like they were in the last round of a do-or-die spelling bee where the losers were going to be flogged.

In all our discussions, there were two things Bazemore was sure of: First, the whole case – thefts, smuggling, murder – did not go beyond the two black men (Hall and Butler), the two missing men (Russell and Newsome), and the two dead men (Pym and Slidell). 'The buck stops here,' he informed me forcefully. 'Let's get that straight. Dyer Fanshaw has explained to me, voluntarily came in here and explained to me, that he was utterly and entirely ignorant of the misuse to which Fanshaw trucks were allegedly subjected.' Bazemore assumed a tragic stare, focused out the window. 'And Otis Newsome has already suffered enough. I don't want him going through anything else.' (An odd way to put it, since Otis had been dead for months.) 'He loved Purley like a father. Otis did *not*, did *not*, know what his brother was up to, and when he found out, it crushed the life out of him. Crushed it out.' Bazemore acted this out by pressing his palm down hard on a stack of folders. 'We are not dragging Otis Newsome's memory into the gutter where his brother may have chosen to lie down.'

'Nice, Mitch. Save it for the trial.'

But Mitch couldn't stop, and used his empty sofa for a jury box. 'Otis Newsome was not his brother's keeper, but we could say that he died for his brother's shame. Now, let him find what peace he can, Above.'

Now I *did* believe that Mitch believed what he said. He was a bigot and a bounty hunter, but he had to justify his opinions to that Bible-camp moral thermometer he was always taking everybody's temperature with, including his own. In the years I'd known him, Mitch had never asked me, or – as far as I knew – anyone else in HPD, to plant evidence or perjure testimony or cover up problematic facts. What he did with those facts in a courtroom might be slimy as raw sewage, but he did it while thumping a pure breast. So I didn't suspect Dyer Fanshaw had confided to Mitch that he was heavily into graft and smuggling, and then slipped him a few thousand to keep it a secret. I didn't suspect that Otis Newsome had left him a note confessing crimes, and that he'd destroyed the piece of paper. Well, in the end, I guess both of us were going to be surprised by how much the Pure can justify to an Upright Heart.

When Bazemore finished trying out a few more pieties on his imaginary jury, I said, 'I'm telling you again, you're wrong. We're dealing here with more than a couple of greedy cops.'

He flexed his pectorals, straining the buttons on his wool vest. 'No, Mangum. We're *not* dealing with more than that. And really! Isn't that bad enough for you – Hillston police officers stealing and murdering?! Maybe you're the one who's greedy.' He sat down, pompous in his chair, leaning back against the eagle embroidered on its cushion, nodding with the smug derisive smirk that drove me wild. 'You've already bitten off more than you can chew, wouldn't you say? You can't find a murder weapon. Can't find an eyewitness. You can't even find the two suspects you've already got.'

Heat was rising fast through my body. 'You want to suggest some approach I've overlooked?'

'Right! You've thrown so much personnel at this thing that our overall arrest and conviction statistics are down, way down.'

'Wait a minute, okay, wait a minute! You're telling me, do more, find them. *And* telling me, don't do so much, don't—'

'I'm telling you we're losing our standing state-wise. We're falling behind. That makes *me* look bad.' He leapt up and slammed his fist on his desk. 'I'm taking the flack because *you're fumbling the ball! That's what I'm telling you, and you better understand it fast!*'

I came around the desk at him, steaming. '*Go fuck yourself, Mitch! I'm not working my ass off to beef up your goddamn fucking body count!*'

His head went scarlet, and his neck bulged so much his collar spread. '*Get your dirty mouth out of my office before I put my fist through it!*'

We went eyeball-to-eyeball for a while, breathing hard. But he wasn't about to hit me, and I wasn't about to hit him, and we both knew it. We'd done this more than once over the years. The problem was to get out of it. He was never much help. This time I was too mad to think for us both, so we just stood there, counting each other's blinks, until luckily his secretary scurried in – maybe she was alarmed by our shouts, or maybe I'd underestimated Mitch and he'd called her with a foot button under his desk. At any rate, she said, 'Sir, you're due in court in five minutes.'

I let out my breath, and said, 'Well, I hate to leave, Mitch, but I guess you better get downstairs and gain some yardage on those statistics alone. Least, a field goal or two. Basketball's my game.' This was a deescalation move, but he was too much of a clod to take it gracefully.

Hurriedly squeezing his shirt sleeves down over his biceps so he could get his jacket on, he muttered, 'Alone is right. I'm certainly not getting much help from your end of the line. That's one thing I'm certainly sure of. And I mean what I said. I'm going to put George Hall away, and I better get your full cooperation in doing it. Follow me?'

237

I didn't bother answering, and he didn't wait to see if I would.

Like Rosethorn, Bazemore was war hungry. Like all glory-hound blood-lusters, both of them could already taste not only the dirt of the battlefield, but the wine of the victory cup. But that game, in which the field was the courtroom, the jury was the scoreboard, and I guess George Hall was the ball, that game was between Mitch and Isaac. My game was to find out where the buck really stopped. Because I didn't believe it stopped with two dumb thugs like Russell and Newsome. Over the long winter, while George Hall waited for his trial, I waited for a break. Finally, slowly, new puzzle pieces were handed to me; they were the kind that keep people addicted to jigsaw puzzles, the linking kind that makes sudden sense of whole sections of loose fragments.

I said I turned down invitations to eat dinner with Nora and Isaac because I was either working, or waiting for Lee to call. Through those months of long winter nights, usually I was working. Half the nights I slept on my office couch, and therefore half the nights Martha Mitchell slept at the Howards'. Something about that family obviously brought out the grandparent instinct in old cranky spinsters and bachelors like Martha and Rosethorn. Neither one of them liked noise, mornings, or children, and they couldn't stand each other, but both appeared to be irresistibly drawn to 2-B River Rise, where noisy children got up at seven A.M. Martha set down some quick rules with Brian and Laura – don't pick me up, leave the ears and tail alone, don't chase me or expect me to chase you, avoid high-pitched squeals, and so on – but, that settled, she took a benign, even protective, attitude towards the Howards, occasionally leaving my bed to sneak out the back, and whine at their patio doors. (I strongly suspected them of slipping her chocolate candy, for which she had an unhealthy weakness that her doctor had already warned me about.)

With me, Martha took the injured icy tone of a neglected wife. And she was right that I didn't pay much attention to her these days. Paul Madison was right that I never laughed much these days. Lee was right that I was losing weight. Justin was right that I was 'obsessed' with the Hall case; out of guilt over Cooper's murder, he said. I don't know if he was right about that or not. I do know that the only time I could stop thinking about the Hall brothers was when Lee Brookside was in my arms. And the only way I could stop thinking about what I was going to do about my feelings for Lee was to work on the Hall case.

Not that Lee was in my arms that often, or even that she would have been there if I'd had all that world enough and time to give her. I was available but preoccupied, trying to keep a hundred thousand people from robbing, raping, beating, and generally bothering each other, or at least trying to remove from circulation the ones who went ahead and did such things. Lee was *un*available, and preoccupied, trying to get her husband elected governor, or at least win over to his side as many as she could of the Inner Circle, at whose hub she sat in a series of gowns, supporting the arts, dispensing charity, and oiling the social axle with endless luncheons, dinners, dances, parties, hunts, receptions, and other such fund-raisers. Between us, we didn't have time for an affair.

We also didn't want to think that's what we were doing, having an affair. But we didn't want to think about the two alternatives either; at least we didn't want to talk about them. The first alternative was for her to leave her husband, either in the middle of a political campaign, or after he won it, or after he lost it. The other alternative was for us to stop falling in love again. We tried the second plan a few times, but then she'd telephone me late at night, or we'd brush against each other in the crush of a cocktail party, and that would be the end of our ending it. We never discussed the first alternative. So months went by, with us meeting at my apartment at very rare intervals; I didn't feel real easy about it, not with the zoo across the hall, not with Laura and Brian likely to bang on my door to watch my eighty-eight cable channels while enjoying some microwave popcorn, not with Isaac likely to want to borrow a book at one A.M., not with Nora giving me looks that irrationally made me feel even more guilty than I already did.

Often Lee and I would go driving somewhere we hoped was out of the way; we'd take walks or sit in the car. It was cold weather for love. Sometimes, not often, we'd meet out of town. Once we spent a weekend in a hotel in Bermuda, when Brookside had gone to Boston; we flew there on separate planes, because I figured it would be just my luck to have Carol Cathy Cane lunge out at us with her 'Action News' cameraman at the airport, or for Mrs Marion Sunderland to show up, or a Democratic party official, or any of a thousand other possibilities. And in fact, that particular night while I was waiting for my flight to board, I was greeted within half an hour by a police chief from a coastal town, by Mrs Atwater Randolph (on her way to Colorado to annul her granddaughter's marriage), and by two strangers who said they'd seen me on the news. The fact was, too many people in the Piedmont knew not only Lee Haver Brookside, but me. Adultery made me aware for the first time that I was, well, I guess you'd say, a public figure; I'd never thought of myself in that way before, nor as a 'public servant' as Justin was wont to define his job, nor as a 'public official,' though that came a little closer. If I had to describe my position, I suppose I thought of myself as the executive head of a law enforcement bureau. But of course, it was a public bureau, dealing with the lust, greed, and violence that draws media the way carrion lures hyenas, so I was in, and on, the local news pretty regularly, and that makes you locally pretty public. As it turned out, Lee was worrying that *I'd* be recognized, while I was worrying that the regional paparazzi would pop out of a closet to snap a shot of *her*. The result was, between our lack of privacy and our lack of time (throwing aside, now, morals and reputation), our affair mostly took place by telephone (which ironically was exactly how it had been when we were in high school; I hadn't been welcome at Briarhills then, I wasn't welcome at Briarhills now).

I did go to her house twice, once alone, once to a campaign fund-raiser; it was a mistake, and both times I left early. But Lee's life was rigorously social. Brookside had turned over his university duties to his successor, and was now deep into the gubernatorial campaign, so public events were really the only way for us to see each other anywhere near as often as we wanted to. It wasn't the *way* I wanted to see her, but desire takes what it can get. She arranged for me to be invited to the most populous of these winter galas (the Haver Foundation Valentine's Ball, the Children's Museum benefit, the buffet for the Cancer Society, the string quartet for the Historic Hillston Restoration Drive), and I went every time I was invited, and I usually ended up feeling miserable. It wasn't as easy as meeting her in the old days at somebody's rec-room sock hop, and those days had been hard enough. Now Lee was on a public stage, co-starring with Brookside in a show that had already been written, and in which it was hard to find a part for myself other than the one that Ralph Bellamy types got stuck with in the movies – faithful old Dobbin who hangs around in the wings to remind the woman he loves that she's lovable, even if her husband appears to have forgotten it. I didn't like the role.

On the other hand, I couldn't really imagine myself swinging down from a chandelier, grabbing Lee out of a reception line, waving a carving knife at the crowd, shouting 'Back off, she's mine!' and leaping out a window with her into a future of – what? Somehow, I couldn't see her in jeans, nuking frozen enchiladas and watching *Coal Miner's Daughter* on video out in River Rise. Somehow, I couldn't see me in a tuxedo for the rest of my life, wineglass in hand, turning slowly from left to right in that endless circle of smiling small talk. But we didn't talk about the future on the phone, which was the only time we talked. If we were alone together, we made love. If we were in public, we looked at each other. We wouldn't even have needed to speak the same language. And sometimes I wondered if in fact we did.

I told no one about Lee, and was careful (after Edwina Sunderland's innuendos) to make certain nobody was ever in a position even to speculate about us. It therefore worried me that Justin and Alice attended every one of the Brookside galas. But neither ever said a word to me, and as I'd never known Alice to hold back if something worried her (and I knew she loved me enough for this to worry her), finally I decided I was too discreet for them, or they were too absorbed in their own lives to notice. Justin was working as hard as I was on the Hall case; Alice was taking a very active role in the legislative session, giving a lot of speeches here and there, and people were talking about her. There were, for example, rumours that Brookside was thinking of Alice as his nominee for lieutenant governor; she did nothing to discourage these rumours, and neither did Brookside. In fact she made jokes about arranging to have her baby patriotically on the Fourth of July because the publicity would be good for the campaign. I'd given up hoping she was faking her friendliness to Brookside to further her own career; she really thought he was the most exciting possibility to hit North Carolina since the Wright brothers blew in from Ohio and put a flying machine in the air for twelve seconds before it crashed into a sand dune.

Justin too was a fervent Andrew Brookside supporter by now, mostly because of Alice, but also because Brookside and he had struck up an acquaintanceship, about which I had to hear a lot more than I wanted to. Justin felt he and 'Andy' had a great deal in common; I assume he meant their preppy pasts, because their personalities certainly weren't similar. Brookside didn't have the

241

innocent kindheartedness that drew folks to Justin. And Justin was no visionary for a better tomorrow. Nor was he a war hero, having been locked up in an alcoholics sanatorium during his draftable years. His missing that macho rite of passage may have had something to do with their new friendship, because 'Andy' was teaching Justin how to fly his Cessna. Now, I'd long suspected that Justin Bartholomew Savile V had considerably more money – what he called 'old money' – than he ever let on when he pestered me for raises, but he didn't have the kind of money it takes to buy your own aeroplane. So I admit it was probably nice to have a friend who did happen to have one, if you were after what Justin called, in his Byronic way, 'Experiences.' (An instance of Justin's innocence is that when I called him Byronic to his face, he assumed I meant it as a compliment.)

Meanwhile, Andy Brookside (Boston bred) was learning how to ride from Justin (treasurer of the Hillston Hunt Club). And Justin did own his own horse now: Manassas, the black stallion old Cadmean had left him. The fact that Justin could generally stay semivertical on top of that vicious brute is, I suppose, a testament to his prowess, or at least his passion for the sport. He even belonged to a polo club, though they could rarely get up enough players for a game. I'd never envied him his equestrian skills until I found out Lee loved to ride, which may have been why Brookside wanted to pick up some tips from Justin, who, by Lee's report, had 'the best seat in Hillston.' Not that there were many in town vying for that distinction. I heard that Justin rode Manassas at the Briarhills Hunt, where he won himself a foxtail by outriding everybody who'd had more brains than to take a shortcut by jumping a five-foot brick fence. It was the same approach to life that had led his ancestor, old Eustace Dollard's papa, into the Wilderness a little too far ahead of his troops, so that the Yankees sensibly seized the opportunity to blow his head off. All Justin did was break his arm. I wasn't too sympathetic, for more reasons than he knew, which maybe wasn't fair.

The same sense of my own unfairness had kept me, so far, from mentioning to the DA, or to Isaac, that Andy Brookside had spent the last hour of Cooper's life with him flying around in a plane, discussing politics – assuming that's what they were doing up in the clouds that Saturday. Bazemore, a fervid Julian Lewis man if for no other reason than a shot at the attorney generalship, would have liked nothing better than to haul Lewis's opponent into court on a charge of withholding evidence in a felony. Isaac would have liked nothing better than to haul a celebrity like Brookside on to the witness stand, if only for the dramatic effect. But I'd had two hard talks with Brookside about that Saturday ride, and although I wasn't satisfied that he was telling me the whole truth (I didn't believe Cooper would care much for a *theoretical* conversation about the future of the state), I was satisfied that Brookside knew nothing about what had happened to Cooper twenty minutes after they parted. I don't know, maybe the honest truth is, if the man *hadn't* been Lee's husband, I would have been even harder on him. He was, in a way, sheltered under my guilt.

Guilt (which may have had at its roots some rotten wishful thinking) kept me very anxious, as the campaign developed, about those threats on Brookside's life. My worst nightmare was that somebody would kill him *in Hillston*, and it would be my fault. He'd received two more anonymous letters. The handwriting was bothering Etham Foster, who'd taken the material to an FBI calligraphy expert. This woman made two 'qualified' observations: She didn't think the earlier letters Lee and Brookside had given me were in the same handwriting as the subsequent letters and the photostats of the *With Liberty and Justice* graffiti. The similarities were close, but 'possibly' not identical. Second, there was some 'suggestion' of a 'tentativeness' about the latter, as if they were imitations. This worried Etham. Myself, I was more worried that whoever had written any or all of those notes was planning to take a potshot at Brookside's bright shining head one of these days, and that I wasn't going to be able to stop it. I couldn't force him to agree to police protection, but I did insist that HPD be kept informed in advance of his schedule. This, of course, felt pretty morally awkward for me, and I dealt with it by a private vow not to take advantage of my knowledge of his whereabouts, unless Lee told me independently that he would be away. I admit it's a Jesuitical distinction. I also admit I broke it twice, when I couldn't stop myself from telephoning her.

I think I would have preferred it if Brookside knew about Lee and me, but she said he didn't know, hadn't asked, and (this to me was the saddest part) 'possibly wouldn't care. Oh Cuddy, I mean, of course, Andy would *care*, he would care terribly, but his reasons would be . . . not completely personal. That doesn't mean the reasons wouldn't be . . . valid. Valid to us both. Do you see?'

'Yes.' That was as close as we came to discussing the political nature of their union. Once I asked, 'Are you going to tell him?'

She said, 'Don't ask me to. Not now.'

Whether Lee was aware of the rumours about her husband's extramarital activities, I never knew for certain. It seemed wrong that I should point the rumours out, and I never did. But I think she suspected his promiscuity, and that the way she imagined Brookside would feel about us was a description of how she felt about him. She would care, but the reasons for her concern would be 'not completely personal.' If in the beginning they had been in love, if they'd ever cared enough for real jealousy, ten years of public life had worn away all the sharp edges from their private feelings. Lee talked about her pain at not being able to have a child; she didn't talk about how her husband's affairs might once have hurt her. In the beginning, one night at my paranoid worst, I'd wondered if she was sleeping with me to get even with him. But that was never true. She talked about him with admiration, but impersonally, as if they were not so much a marriage of convenience as an alliance of state. It didn't make me any less jealous, or guilty, or sad. Maybe because Mr and Mrs Brookside looked like such a successful alliance, such a permanent one.

It ought to be no surprise that I avoided Andy Brookside as much as I could. So it wasn't easy when finally it seemed necessary for me to call him at his campaign headquarters to insist that he stop Jack Molina from broadcasting the news about these threatening letters whenever he had the opportunity.

By now Molina had resigned from the Communications Department at Haver, and was working full-time on the Brookside campaign. He was more at the centre of things than the official campaign manager, a moderate, and very influential, Piedmont Democrat with three decades of party contacts behind him. Jack was the unofficial coordinator of the left branch, the black branch, the female branch, and the college branch of Brookside's supporters. Together, they made up a sizable chunk of the voting tree, and it was beginning to look as if they were solid as oak for Molina's man. Obviously he thought he could help keep them that way by telling them how much their enemies were Andy's enemies too: He'd even given a copy of one of the letters to the *Hillston Star* to print.

I'd talked to Molina about his inflammatory tactics, but had got nowhere. Just as I'd got nowhere asking him again about what papers might have been in Cooper's file box when it was stolen, or whether Cooper had done any further research beyond his first short article on the Haver House of Lords. Molina appeared to hold me if not responsible for Cooper's death, then probably part of a cover-up. At any rate, his black blazing eyes did not look on me with any kindly flame the day I had him brought to my office, and asked him if we couldn't cooperate.

'I can think of no case,' he told me, glaring at the shoulder holster that hung from the back of my door, 'where the revolution and the police stood on the same side of the barricades.'

'Well, how about the *Industrial* Revolution?'

He didn't think this was funny. 'Yes, that proves my point.'

I said, 'I don't believe I ever heard Andy Brookside describe himself as a "revolutionary."'

Molina's short hair and tidy suit hadn't affected his rhetoric from the old denim days. I got a pretty high-flown answer about practical instruments of the Cause, and reinterpretations of dialectical imperatives. I said, 'I'm also not so sure Mr Brookside would care to hear himself described as an instrument of the underclass, Hegelian or not. He seems to have a sort of Take Charge, Hands On, notion of history.'

Molina turned back from an examination of my bookshelf. 'Yes. If Andy Brookside didn't believe he was a hero, he wouldn't be such an effective instrument, now would he?' There's a chance the man smiled here. I'm not sure. Leaning against the wall of books, he told me, 'The march of history is not brought about, or even led, by heroic drum majors wearing plumes. But they *think* it is, and that can often be very useful.'

I said, 'Well, y'all are welcome to overthrow the government at the *polls* as much as you like. But you wanna march, you need a permit. And you keep on sending out open invites to the lunatic fringe by yelling about assassinations, you could lose your drum major before you get much use out of that plume. It doesn't help to polarize and agitate nuts like the Klan.'

'The Klan is actively trying to stop Andy. That isn't something I've made up.'

'We're keeping a close watch on the Klan. So is the FBI. Why don't you leave that to us.'

He couldn't stand his tie another second, and jerked it loose. 'A few years ago, Mr Mangum, the Greensboro police said they were keeping a close watch on the Klan. They stood there and *closely watched* the Klan shoot and kill half a dozen people. People who *had* gone to the police for a permit to march. That was their mistake. Cooper Hall is dead. George Hall is behind bars on Death Row. And you're behind this big desk, stamping pieces of paper to keep everything legal. The world is polarized. Half the people on Death Row in this country are in six Southern states; more than half of them are black; and the blacks are the ones you people are going to kill. Look at the records. From nineteen thirty to nineteen sixty-two, Mississippi had a hundred and fifty-one executions, one hundred twenty-two of them were of blacks. Georgia had—'

'I'm not arguing with your statistics, or your interpretation. It's simplistic of you to assume I would.'

'It's you who sends them to Death Row. It is that simple.'

'I don't send anyone to Death Row.' I said, 'Professor Molina' – which he winced at – 'I use what I've got to work with. You use what you've got to work with. You've got Andy Brookside. I've got this notion called "law." Maybe neither's exactly perfect, but like you say, an instrument of a cause.'

He walked to the door, setting the holster to swinging as he flung it open. 'I doubt our causes have much in common.'

'Oh, I bet they do. Ask around, you'll find out I'm one of those old of-all-the-people, by-all-the-people, for-all-the-people type guys.'

'If that were true, you'd resign. Your laws were written by a few of the people, *for* a few of the people.'

'Why should I resign? I don't see you trying to run Hillston's local commie comrade Janet Malley for governor, I don't see you polishing *her* unpopular baton for the big parade.'

He started to say something, changed his mind, gave me a mock salute, and set the holstered gun swinging when he shut the door. A week later, I heard him on public radio, reading one of the threatening letters to a fascinated talk-show hostess. So I went over his head and called his boss.

I told Brookside that there might be some trigger-happy imbeciles out there who hadn't even thought of assassinating him until they heard on the news what a popular notion it was getting to be.

Brookside didn't seem to think this was likely, adding, 'Jack just wants people to know what we're fighting against. But I'll talk to him, tell him to ease up.' He laughed happily. 'Hell, I don't want to alienate the right-wing trigger-happy bigot vote, if I can possibly swing it my way.'

'I'm not sure swings come that big.'

'Well, why not? After Bobby was shot' – I assumed this meant Robert Kennedy – 'a chunk of his supporters threw their votes to

George Wallace. People vote for the *man*. The far right's still looking for John Wayne. Well?' His words sparkled with humour. 'Here I am. Escape from a POW camp, Rambo trek through the jungle, barefoot, bamboo spear, eating wild dogs, hand-to-hand combat, Medal of Honor, all that good stuff. Pretty damn macho, right? What do you think? Can I turn the Brodie Cheek? Pull the far right out from under Lewis?'

'Well, watch out for the spikes in his golf shoes.'

I don't think I'd ever heard Brookside in such a festive mood before. He was ebullient as he chatted on. 'Wouldn't that be something? Get the rednecks to help vote out the old Magnolias and Money Club that's been siccing them, poor dumb sons-of-bitches, on the blacks instead of on the rich for centuries. Now, *that'd* be a rainbow coalition! Blacks, white yuppies, rednecks, and women of all colours. I tell you, Captain, I'm beginning to make Julian Lewis's masters *extremely* nervous. And that's *great*!'

I actually smiled. 'I'm glad things are going well.' And, hell, the truth was – Alice was right: He would be a better governor than Julian Lewis. I admit it.

'Just tell your friend Isaac Rosethorn not to lose Hall's retrial. Let's get that capital-punishment mine field safely behind us.'

Us? Apparently nothing could persuade the man that I wasn't a member of his team. Of course, I suppose on the birds-of-a-feather principle, he had every right to his assumption. I'm talking about his knowing he had my closest friends, Justin and Alice, already waving from his parade float. I'm not talking about his knowing about my closeness to his wife. I said, 'Isaac will do his best for Hall, and it doesn't come any better than his best. But that's not going to solve the death-penalty issue for you. Lewis will make his strong capital punishment stand a big part of the campaign. He's going to tackle you directly.'

'If you'll pardon my immodesty, Cuddy, I scored four touchdowns for Harvard against Yale my senior year. At the time quite a few men were making a concerted effort to tackle me directly.' The way he said it, it didn't even sound like boasting.

'Let me ask you something. If you get to be governor, are you going to use executive clemency across the board to suspend executions? Alice MacLeod assumes you are.'

'After I get into office, I'll answer that. Let me ask you something. When you joined the police, the death penalty was unconstitutional, right? What if it hadn't been?'

I said, 'I'd have to think about that. Tell you what, if you win, I'll give you an answer, after I find out what your answer to my question is.'

Laughter came as easily to him as everything else. 'Fair enough. Now. You know Ken Moize, fairly young man, used to be your county solicitor? The guy Bazemore defeated.'

'I know Ken. I was real sorry to lose him. He's good.'

'What do you think? Attorney general material?'

'Sure. Ken'd be my choice.'

Jesus, he hadn't even won the primary, and he was picking out his cabinet. Well, later I found out he'd just got the results of a *Time* magazine poll on upcoming primaries. He was the featured 'Spotlight' in the article, which not only projected that he'd wipe up the floor with his Democratic opponent, Harold De Witt (an old party machine fart from the western end of the state), the *Time* poll showed that he was pulling votes from independents, and even some Republicans. A covey of journalists had joined the noisy flock of staff already flying by his coattails as he zipped around the state, dropping in on factories, schools, churches, and shopping malls. I told him now that I was planning to put an unmarked squad car escort in his caravan when he was in the Hillston area. And that's when one of those small unexpected puzzle pieces fell into my hand.

He laughed. 'What do you mean, *planning* to? You've had somebody following me since November. I admit it took me until I saw them trolling behind me in a *patrol* car, to figure it out. I was going to tell you to back off, but after Christmas I lost track of them, and decided you'd either quit, or got better . . .. Mangum? Mangum? You there?'

I said, 'I never had anybody following you.'

'Come on! You fed me a line about some kid noticing Hall and me at the airport. You had me tailed there, didn't you? It was a late model Pontiac or small Buick, that time. Red. I thought I shook him.'

I repeated it. 'I haven't had anybody following you.'

'I'm telling you, there were two or three different cars – one a tan station wagon, one a *patrol* car. I got a glimpse of the driver, in *uniform*. Big guy wearing sunglasses. In December!'

I looked at the photo of Purley on my bulletin board. '. . . Right. His name's Purley Newsome.'

Now Brookside's end of the line went quiet.

I said, 'Don't you watch the news?'

'Newsome and Russell? Right, Winston Russell. Police all over the South are looking for them.'

'All over the country. Right.'

'He's related to the city comptroller, guy who hanged himself.'

'Right. I'm sending a detective over right now. I want every detail you can give him.'

'I can't give you much more than I just have.' He took a breath. 'What the fuck's going on? Why should they be following me?'

I said, 'My guess is, like you pointed out, you were making some people "extremely nervous."'

Nobody could have persuaded me that I could be any more desperate to find Winston Russell and Purley Newsome than I already was. But now I was a lot more desperate. Because now I wanted them not just for what they'd done, but for what I was scared they were going to try to do. If I let something happen to Andrew Brookside, when I was in love with his wife, well . . . if I didn't know how she would feel about me, I did know, real well, how I'd feel about me. And I didn't ever want to have to feel that way.

Chapter 14

Justin wasn't about to let a broken arm interfere with his heading the homicide investigation; he kept busy at 'the Patriots angle,' or at least he told me that's what he was doing. I never saw him anywhere around the department, but then he'd always described himself as a 'field man,' not a 'desk man.' Reports from the field weren't frequent, but again Justin wasn't an 'organization man,' preferring to surprise you by showing up with the solutions to cases you'd almost forgotten about. Not that there was any chance I was going to forget this case. Through the winter, Justin was working closely with Dave Sichulmann, because the FBI had more extensive intelligence on Klan activities than we did; he was also in touch with Klanwatch at the Southern Poverty Law Centre, which had even better intelligence. (They needed it the most, too, since the Klan had already firebombed their headquarters, and tried to assassinate their chief trial counsel.) In Klanwatch's photo files, Justin found a fuzzy shot of fifteen men on the steps of a cabin, somewhere in the deep woods of north Haver County. You might have thought they were buddies posing for a memento of a weekend hunting trip, except that they wore combat fatigues, and instead of showing off pheasants, they proudly held out automatic rifles, shotguns, and pistols. The photo was dated eight years ago, and more recently labelled 'FUTURE CAROLINA PATRIOTS?' The Carolina Patriots called themselves that because, as one member had told Justin when (thanks to Preston Pope's cousin) he'd got himself invited to that December meeting, 'it's what every last one of us is, a patriot for the free white Christian state of North Carolina.'

Justin brought me to the lab to study the huge blow-up of the photograph; he had a magnifying glass ready, and six faces circled in red, with numbers above them. 'Recognize anybody?' I studied the blurred images.

He couldn't wait. 'Numbers two and seven, I saw that night at the Patriot's slide show, when I met Willie Slidell; number two is Sergeant Charlie Mennehy, who was giving the lecture on survival tactics in the wilderness – Dave Schulmann's had his eye on him for, get this, supplying the Klan with explosives stolen from a US Army arsenal. When this picture was taken Mennehy was still active-duty, drawing taxpayers' dollars. Tsk tsk tsk.' Justin pinned up on the board enlargements of two of the other faces. 'Now, look. Number eight, number nine.' While I was examining them, he pulled out two studio photographs, placing them beside the enlargements. Both were Hillston Police Department photo IDs – one of Officer Robert Pym, one of Officer Winston Russell, Jr. They were the same faces as in the cabin photo.

Justin said, 'Okay? Now! The man in the doorway. Number six. Number six happens to be Clark Koontz, and—' He clipped two more blow-ups to the board. The first, taken at night, showed a huddle of men talking beside a car in a crowded parking lot. Justin pointed at a thin, stooped fellow. '—Here's our Mr Koontz, late of the Fanshaw Paper Company, again. This was taken four years ago. State fairgrounds in Raleigh, October fourteenth. You know these other gentlemen. There's number two, Sergeant Charlie Menneby again. There's poor Willie the Wimp Slidell. And there's Winston Russell – in between prison terms.'

Justin tapped a second blow-up, cropped from the same scene, that focused on the car around which the men stood. I held the magnifying glass to a blurred figure in the driver's seat. I said, 'It looks a little like Otis Newsome to me.'

'Doesn't it though? October fourteenth. Now, maybe you remember what happened two days later, on October sixteenth, in the Williamsville auditorium?'

I remembered very vividly. At a concert rally for the benefit of the man running against Governor Wollston, then up for reelection, a huge amount of tear gas had been suddenly shot off throughout the hall. In the pandemonium, a lot of people got hurt, and one person was trampled to death. He happened to be a black judge, among the few in the state, and a judge with a very liberal record. Those responsible for the tear gas had never been identified; some blacks accused the Williamsville police of

251

doing it themselves. There was a violent protest on the campus of a local black college. Governor Wollston sent in the state troops. The press commended his action. Three weeks later, Governor Wollston was reelected.

Justin now projected a slide on to the lab's wall: an enlargement of a single frame from a videotape taken at that concert, a quick pan shot of the audience. 'There's the judge who got killed. Now look at the guy, one row back, over to the left. I think it's Winston Russell. And I don't think the tear gas was the main event. I think the judge was the main event.'

It was hard to be certain with that smudged image. Of course, it was also possible that Russell was a big fan of the folk singer performing that night, and it was possible that that group gathered at the fairgrounds were discussing a blue-ribbon zucchini they'd just seen, and it was possible that it wasn't Otis Newsome in the car anyhow. But I bet it was.

Justin said, 'I want to go back to another Carolina Patriots get-together. With a wire on. I want Preston to tell his cousin that good ole Jefferson Roy Calhoun is really gung ho to join the battle for white survival, really serious.'

'You told those assholes your name was Jefferson Roy Calhoun? Jesus, don't you think that was a little much?'

'Nah. I told them I was from Charleston, and how a black mugger had stabbed my younger brother to death, and how the courts had let him off. They ate it up.'

I said, 'Forget it. There're too many ways your cover could have got blown.'

'You saw what I looked like. Even if anybody had been there that *knew* me, they wouldn't have recognized me. How do you think I got to be president of the Hillston Players? Talent, that's how! I imitated you doing your hillbilly number.'

I shook my head. 'Wait'll your arm heals.'

'I was going to tell them a homosexual hippie broke it.'

'Hippies are a thing of the past, Justin.'

'That's what you used to say about the Klan.'

Justin's love of acting was too exuberant for him to let his injury deter him from performing at the Hillston Playhouse in *Twelfth Night*. As the character he played, Sir Toby Belch, was a lewd, belligerent drunk, Justin thought it quite likely that somebody *would* have broken the man's arm in a brawl, and so with his modern plaster cast hidden by a doublet, he made much of his red silk sling on stage.

It was at the final intermission of this *Twelfth Night* performance that I was given, from an unsuspected source, another piece of my puzzle, one I hadn't been looking for. G. G. Walker's uncle, Hamilton, was the source. The information had to do with Andy Brookside and Cooper Hall, and what they might have talked about in that private plane.

Alice had cajoled me into escorting Justin's mother and her to the play's opening night, which due to 'casting problems' did not take place until late February, considerably after its original date on the twelfth day of Christmas. So on a rainy Saturday I sat through three hours and twenty-two minutes of revels by amateur thespians, who loved Shakespeare not wisely but too well. They hadn't cut a word of his play, thereby blithely mystifying their audience with long swatches of totally incomprehensible Elizabethan jokes. Despite their slavish integrity, the Hillston Players always sold out the house. In the first place, there were so many of them, their families alone filled half the seats. In the second place, they were one of the town's Grand Old Traditions (Justin was a fourth-generation member), and so the Players were an Annual Event in the social calendar of Hillston. The Mayor and Mrs Yarborough came. Lee was there, with a party that included Edwina Sunderland, as well as the department store widow, who clapped at odd moments.

The *Twelfth Night* cast was not, as Eddie Sunderland put it, uniformly gifted. Blue Randolph (forcibly retrieved from her combination elopement and ski trip, and to judge by her sullen expression still angry about it) looked a lot like Cheryl Tiegs and sounded a lot like Shirley Temple, neither of which struck me as exactly what the Bard had had in mind for the Countess Olivia. On the other hand, I was perfectly convinced that this particular Olivia was too dumb to tell the difference between Viola and Sebastian, the twins that she'd fallen in love with, even though there was about a foot's difference in their heights, thirty pounds in their weights, a couple of octaves in their voices, and profound anatomical discrepancies in their physiques. Playing the Duke, Father Paul Madison kept forgetting to come on stage when called for, so that the others had to mill around throwing out lame improvisations like, 'Methinks the Duke is somewhat TARDY!' This added considerably to the length of a show that didn't need any help.

Some people said Justin's cavortings stole the evening. But the actor who interested me the most, and unsettled the audience the most, was young Mr G. G. Walker, who played the part I'd turned down – Malvolio, the puritanical steward tricked by Justin's Sir Toby Belch and his bunch of cronies into believing the Countess wants to marry him. This in-crowd doesn't like Malvolio much, because he objects to their boozing themselves blotto and bellowing dirty songs all night. But it's when he gets uppity that they really turn on him. That a house servant can so forget his place as to imagine Olivia loves him just drives them wild. And he's easy prey to their practical hijinks – like shutting him up in a dark cage and pretending they think he's gone crazy. Malvolio's jolly superiors find this all hilarious. Usually so does the audience.

Well now, when my man, the young high-stepping G. G. Walker, came on stage for the first time in his life, all in black, and I mean *all* in black, he took that audience by surprise. Then he took them with him places they weren't sure they wanted to go. G.G. got them to laugh, and he got them to *stop* laughing. He may have blown a few lines, and put his own inimitable twist on a few of the others. (Instead of 'Go hang yourselves all! You are idle shallow things. I am not of your element,' we got, 'Y'all can go hang yourselves! Bunch of idle shallow things. Hey, I'm not in your element.') But he was so *real* on that stage that he threw the whole comedy out of kilter. When Malvolio crouched in the dark cage, while the clown kept claiming the place was all sunshine and light, I could hear the giggles die out, and the seats start to creak from the squirms in that Hillston audience. Then, when the clown told him, 'Madman, thou errest. I say, there is no darkness but ignorance,' G.G. stood up, shook the bars of that cage, and he didn't just shout, he wailed. 'I say, this house is as dark as ignorance, though ignorance was as dark as Hell. And *I* say there wasn't ever any man abused like me. *I am no more mad than you are.*'

Nobody laughed.

Peggy Savile, Justin's mother, leaned over to me and whispered. 'This isn't funny at all. Are we supposed to think it's *comic* that they're treating him like this?'

I whispered back, 'Peggy, I'll say this for your boy Justin. As a casting director, he's got a lot of guts.'

Some members of the audience were offended by what they not so obliquely called 'a break in traditions.' Judge Tiggs was overheard (by Alice) to ask his wife, 'What's a darkie doing in this stupid play?' But most people were too polite to notice anything different, though at intermission quite a number made a special point of rushing over to Carl and Dina Yarborough in the lobby, and telling them they thought the whole show was just simply wonderful, as if the mayor and his wife were somehow responsible for it.

Nobody (including the Yarboroughs) ran over to say anything to the only other blacks in the lobby. There were a dozen of them, standing for protection in a huddle by a watercooler, a few feet from where I was waiting for Alice and Peggy Savile to come back from the laciest room. The middle-aged couple with three teenaged daughters, I assumed to be G.G.'s parents and sisters. The rest of the group I already knew. Officer John Emory was there; I'd never seen him before when he wasn't in uniform, and I was surprised that he was such a stylish dresser, in a modern-looking baggy suit with pleated trousers, and a dark checkered shirt. He held back shyly from the others; I assumed he hadn't come in their party, but on his own. And he kept trying to look at Jordan West without her noticing, which wasn't all that hard since she was deep in conversation with a young psychiatrist – I recognized him because he did some pro bono work at Human Services, downstairs from me in the Municipal Building. Beside them, Martin Hall and Eric from the vigil group were talking to the oldest of the teenaged girls, while her sisters nudged her in the ribs and giggled. And bringing over two handfuls of little plastic glasses of wine was G.G.'s uncle Hamilton Walker, resplendent in a maroon leather suit with boots and hat to match.

Now Ham Walker and I had met a number of times, in connection with his work. Ham's predecessor, the late Woodrow Clenny, had called himself, with perfect justice, Hillston's 'El Primo Pimp.' Ham, however, preferred the term 'business manager of a hostess service.' I was idly wondering how many of the men in this lobby had had occasion to meet if not Mr Walker in person, then one of his hostesses. I was imagining him strolling about, shaking hands with his clients, making remarks like, 'How's it going, John? The girls in Canaan say hello.' But of course he didn't do it; his interests were, as he often told me, 'strictly business,' and publicly discomforting hypocrites was never good for business. I was also wondering what he made of his nephew's abandoning that very American interest in business, in order to join picket lines and amateur theatrical companies.

At this point, G.G. himself, in tights and yellow ribbons, bounded into the lobby. The cast did not usually join its audience until after the play was over, and this additional break in tradition caused a ripple of whispers that followed behind the Players' first black member like the trail of a loud taffeta cloak.

'Hey hey, the man's fan club!' G.G. pushed himself into the middle of his family group, slapping hands, hugging shoulders, kissing faces. They all offered as many congratulations as they could shout into his whirl of talk and embraces. 'Don't be shy, y'all. Listen, be more than happy to give you my autograph. Step up, wheeew, watch it, now. Don't y'all crowd the *star*. Y'all like it? Listen, this is some weird show, I mean can you *believe* it? Awh, come on, Daddy, loosen up. Think Sidney Poitier, man. Richard Pryor, Eddie Murphy. Those dudes are actors. *Rich* actors. Y'all hear me okay? Great. That's 'cause I'm *projecting*. Y'all got good seats? They said they were gonna give me some prime seats. Mama, these *are* my pants. Right! That was the *style*. What's happening, Uncle Ham? Lookin' good. Okay, I gotta split. I don't do much in the last act. Watch for me. Martin, my man! Hang in there. Can't every night be Tina Turner.'

He spun away through a crowd parting like the Red Sea in a silent movie. Alice came up behind me and pointed after him. 'The Hillston Players,' she said with a grin, 'will never be the same.' Then she pinched me hard on the shoulder. 'And that, Mr Mangum, is one reason why I love Justin Savile.'

'Who's arguing?'

'Oh, come on.' She patted her stomach through the blue silk dress. 'I'm an old pregnant lady. Let me go on believing you're secretly pining away for me, scheming how to send my handsome lieutenant out to be slaughtered in battle, like King David sent . . . who did he send? I want to say Uriah, but that's Heep, isn't it?'

(Were these adulterous references really about Lee, who had just joined the Yarboroughs at the far end of the lobby?) I said, 'It's both. Uriah Heep, and Uriah, Bathsheba's husband.'

She gave me a stare. 'For such a nonbeliever, you certainly know your Bible.'

I gave her a fatherly pat. 'I know my *Das Kapital* too, honey, but that don't make me no commie pinko like you used to be before you bought into the capitalist system.'

I got another hard pinch on the arm, as she said, ' "Honey," you're the *right arm* of the capitalist system.'

'You know' – I rubbed where she'd pinched me – 'pregnancy is turning you violent, Alice.'

'*No alcohol, no coffee, no Cokes, and a terminal case of gas*, that's what's turning me violent. See you.' She went off, smiling, to hustle up some votes in the crowd.

I was watching her some, and watching Lee some, when I heard a polite cough beside me. It was John Emory. He restrained himself from saluting when I turned, but I did see his hand spasm at his wrist. 'Sir, I have something for you.'

I said, 'If it's hard liquor, opium, or filthy pictures, let's step outside.'

He realized he was supposed to laugh, and made a dutiful but unconvincing effort. 'No, sir, it's concerning Cooper Hall.'

'Ah, John, I thought you were just here enjoying the show.'

His handsome jaw twitched. 'Oh. I guess I don't like his comedies as much as, well, *Hamlet* and *Lear* and the others.'

'I don't think the Hillston Players can risk doing the tragedies.'

Now he did smile, and became so interested in what he might have been saving up to say to Jordan West (I'd seen him lean towards her, then step back a half-dozen times), that his entire stance, gestures, even his vocal tone changed. 'You know, if it was me, well, I'd do *Merchant of Venice*, or maybe *Measure for Measure*, you know, where you've got the comic relief, but there's a, there's a *theme*, something with meat to it, anti-Semitism, sexual repression, that the modern audience can relate to. You know, more than all those cuckold puns, and this cross-dressed stuff.'

'Good Lord, John! You're over my head, man. Why don't you talk to Savile about joining up?'

He backed off, embarrassed. 'No. Well, I just . . .' And he stiffened into Officer Emory again. Turns out, he'd taken a 'Classics of the Theatre' extension course while in the Marines, and had 'brushed up' on Shakespearean comedy prior to attending this performance. Before John Emory would change a light bulb, he would read everything the Hillston Library had on the history of electricity. He could pass the sergeant's exam hungover in his sleep, but all I ever get from him is, 'I don't feel totally prepared yet.'

From across the room, Lee smiled straight at me a long, long second, then turned back to her conversation with Dina Yarborough. My pulse raced. She was better at this sort of thing than I was.

'Concerning Cooper Hall, sir,' said Officer Emory. 'I've had a couple more talks with Martin Hall, and he put me on to G. G. Walker. Well, yesterday, G.G. introduces me to his uncle, Hamilton Walker – that I talked to about Cooper Hall's address book? He's here to—'

'I know Ham Walker.' I glanced over at that gentleman, six feet of sinewy self-assurance, who despite his greying sideburns and broken nose was one of the best-looking men in the lobby. A Junior League type behind the Subscription Drive table fought unsuccessfully to stop staring at him, which he was perfectly aware of, and appeared to find mildly amusing.

'Yes, sir. What I found out was: when Cooper Hall was asking around about that night at Smoke's, somebody put him in touch with Walker. And Walker did some checking.' John looked behind him, as if to be sure his source hadn't disappeared. 'Walker can place Winston Russell in the vicinity for us at the time of the Pym shooting.'

Now *I* looked to be sure Mr Walker didn't go anywhere. I noticed he had his eye on me, too; just a glance now and then while he was talking to G.G.'s parents. An interested, sardonic glance. I said, 'Where in the vicinity?'

As Isaac was going to be happy to hear, Walker's information confirmed the story Billy Gilchrist had told. John said, 'That night, Russell took a girl upstairs in the Montgomery Hotel.' (The Montgomery or 'Clenny's Cathouse' – across the street from Smoke's – was where Billy had seen Russell lurking in the lobby.)

'Did they drive there together?'

'No. Apparently, he saw her outside on the street, and allegedly—'

'Prostitute?'

'Yes, sir. And allegedly threatened her with arrest if she refused to perform oral sex—'

'Without charge, I bet.'

'The girl said he was only up there fifteen minutes at the most.'

'Um hum.'

'She told Walker they both heard the gunshot. That Russell looked out the window, and then he, well, dressed himself, and ran out of the room.'

And then Russell ran right into the sight of me jumping out of my squad car, at which point he obviously decided his buddy Pym was beyond help, and that discretion, as the Bard would say, was a hell of a lot safer for a fellow's police pension than

258

valour would be. So he hid in the Montgomery Hotel doorway until his fellow cops had left, and standing there was spotted by Billy Gilchrist. I said, 'The girl worked for Walker?'

'I assumed that.'

'Black or white?'

'Black.'

'You got her name from Walker?'

'He wouldn't give it to me. He said the girl no longer lives in Hillston.'

'I don't care if she lives in Kathmandu. I want a statement from her.' The warning lights for the last act were already blinking as I started towards Hamilton Walker, but John caught me by the sleeve.

He shook his head. 'Captain. No. He doesn't want you talking to him in public.'

'Oh, really?' I looked across at Walker, and saw him look back at me over the heads of his cluster of relatives, one corner of his mouth slightly smiling. I turned away, and saw Lee Haver Brookside accept a kiss from an elderly couple. She was someone else I couldn't talk to in public.

John said, 'Yes, sir. He wanted you to know that what I just told you was a "present." That he has some "other information" he *may* be willing to give us. But this time it won't be "free." And he'll only give it to you directly. I'm to tell you, he's inviting you for a drink after the show tonight—'

'Well, that's sweet. I thought he didn't want to be seen with me.' Walker and I were still watching each other across the lobby. 'Is this more information about Winston Russell?'

John frowned. 'All he said to me was that it involved Cooper Hall, and, I'm quoting him, "heavy honkie shit" about the governor's race.'

I said, 'Okay, where? He inviting me to his home?'

If I hadn't known better, I'd have said John was trying not to smile when he said, 'Smoke's Bar.'

The crowd was hurrying back to their seats, Lee nodding patiently at the department store widow's chittering monologue. I caught Walker's eye, and raised my hand as if I were toasting him. He nodded, then leisurely strolled into the theatre to watch his nephew tell all the happy Illyrian wedding folk that he didn't want to accept their easy apology, didn't want to come to their party, and hoped in fact to get revenge on the whole careless pack of them. I knew how he felt, which I suppose was why

259

Justin had offered me the part. After G.G. stomped off, the clown ended the show by singing, 'The rain it raineth every day,' which went over well, because it was pouring outside, and you could hear the storm showering down on the theatre roof like it did have plans to keep at it every day from now on.

Like the Players, and the Confederacy Ball, Smoke's was a Hillston tradition. While it didn't have a plaque announcing its date, of the sort bolted on the side of the Pine Hills Inn, Smoke's was, in fact, the oldest continuously operating bar in town, apparently opening its doors in 1927, and never closing them since, unless forewarned of an approaching raid. It had been a beer bar during the brown-bagging forties and fifties, when the Pine Hills Inn was still an abandoned livery stable. While calling itself 'Smoke's Coloured Restaurant,' it had even been a bar during Prohibition, thanks to a mutual arrangement with the then chief of police, John Wesley Doad, 'Pork Doad,' to his friends. For a long time, Smoke's had been the only bar for blacks in Hillston, as the Montgomery had been their only hotel.

Legend was, Smoke, a mysteriously wealthy black man from Chicago, had come South on the lam from the Mob, built the place, and given it the name bestowed on him either because of his complexion or his prowess with a gun. Two Haver graduate students, researching the town's history, repeated this legend in the monograph they wrote for the Bicentennial; excerpted from there, it now appeared in the Historical Society's 'Official Guide to Old Hillston,' and there was even a movement afoot in the Society to have Smoke's listed with the National Historical Preservation Trust, so that its owners would be prohibited from renovating it. In fact, no one really knew whether the original 'Smoke' was a person, or a style of cooking, or an acknowledgement that the whole town smelled like tobacco because of the Haver factories. Still, in the tradition of Caesarian emperors, successive owners of the bar adopted its presumed founder's name, and many were known to their customers simply as 'Smoke.'

The Society had little to fear in the way of modernization. Like the Hillston Players and the Confederacy Ball, Smoke's kept a pit-bull hold on its traditions, kept its legends of the past alive with faded memorabilia on the walls. Most proudly, Smoke's had a signed photograph of Bessie Smith, who (again according to legend) had driven through town one night, stopped in, drunk down a eight-ounce glass of gin without batting an eye, and then – accompanied by a local youngster who happened to have his guitar with him – had sung blues until word got out and the place got jammed with so many people, a man took her away out the back door, and they drove off together in a dusty car. On a shelf above Smoke's nickel-plated cash register was the glass out of which Bessie Smith was said to have drunk. It looked original. The walls, too, looked original, and maybe the paint; certainly no one had altered the little round iron tables, the curved wood booths, the black ceiling fans, the cloudy panelled mirrors, the wrought-iron bar rail like an old Singer sewing machine pedal, twenty feet long. Smoke's had gone, indifferently or obliviously, in and out of fashion, as fashions came and went, dozens of times over the decades. The saying around Canaan was, you could grow old and die in Smoke's, and your bones fall in a pile on the floor, and nobody'd move them till Judgment Day. According to legend, a few people *had* died in Smoke's, some of them not all that old, and most of them not expecting to. I was there tonight because someone had died like that, though Pym had actually made it as far as the sidewalk outside.

The only thing that had changed at Smoke's since 1927 was the customers. And only their faces changed, not their colour. Maybe today was the eighties, and maybe it was the New South, and maybe Carl Yarborough was mayor of Hillston, but there sure weren't many white people living in Canaan, and none of them were drinking at Smoke's. The Historical Society might be trying to preserve the building, but it didn't appear to be because they liked to visit it. As I walked the long length of that room, which had sounded mighty noisy when I shook out my umbrella and opened the doors, and sounded considerably quieter by the time I made it to a back booth, it occurred to me again that there was no way that Bobby Pym had gone entirely unnoticed in Smoke's before he called attention to himself by waving a gun at George Hall.

Another thing crossed my mind, as backs turned on me when I passed by: Justin may have had some chutzpah to add G. G. Walker to the roster of the Hillston Players, but the worst that was going to happen to Justin was that people in his set would whisper that he'd always been a little peculiar for a Dollard. On the other hand, to bound on to that stage, to bounce into that lobby, G. G. Walker himself, at the age of only seventeen, had to be in possession of a pair of balls that if Ernest Hemingway had had them, he'd be alive today. Hell, I had the *Law* to keep me company, and I felt lonesome as General Custer, on the few occasions I'd come into Smoke's.

G.G.'s uncle Hamilton was in a booth watching me approach, while he twirled a swizzle stick around his long fingers like a tiny baton. At some (at least to me) invisible signal, the woman seated beside him scooted off the bench, and left. She had both a very short skirt and very long legs, and shoes with such high stiletto heels that I'd hate to think she had to walk in them in this cold rain any farther than across the street to the Montgomery Hotel (where it was pretty safe odds to bet she was headed).

Before I reached Walker, the owner – or current 'Smoke,' also known for evident reasons as 'Fattie' – squeezed his way through the tables towards me with the speed of a maitre d' at a nice restaurant trying to stop a drunk from tossing his dishes in the air. He even held up both round hands as if to catch the falling plates as he said, 'Good evening?'

I said, 'Good evening, Fattie.'

'Raining hard?'

'Letting up.'

'Some problem?'

'No problem.'

A bubbly sigh of relief was replaced by a blank smile, behind which he kept asking questions with his round close-set eyes, placed like buttons side by side over his nose. If there was no problem, no *serious* problem, what was the police chief doing here at midnight on a rainy Saturday? Fattie and I had met personally only a couple of times over the past three years, for talks about little irregularities of his, like serving to minors, and running a numbers game for his customers. It was enough times for him not to like me much. He said, 'Something particular?'

I said, 'Um hum. A Budweiser.'

He checked my eyes for the trick. 'A Budweiser?'

'Um hum. Or, Miller's, be okay.'

He stopped a cocktail waitress, maybe hired for her corpulent resemblance to her employer, and told her to bring me the beer. Then as if he'd forgotten having just asked, he said, 'Look, I got a problem?'

I said, 'I don't know. Do you?'

His eyes were vanishing. 'You tell me, okay.'

I nodded. 'Well, I guess I'd say you look like you might be carrying a little extra weight for good health. That might be a problem.'

He decided not to play anymore, just wait until I hit him with whatever the charge was going to be. The waitress was back so fast with a bottle of Bud on a tray, you might have thought I'd called ahead. I stepped around Fattie, and sat down across from Ham Walker, who'd watched this exchange with his ironic half-smile shaded by the maroon leather hat. Maybe he had hats to match all his suits – I don't think I'd ever seen him without one – or maybe he kept them on because he was losing his hair.

When I slid into the booth, Fattie's whole body, of which there was an unbridled glut, relaxed with a shiver: the world made sense, there was a serious problem, but it wasn't his, it was Ham Walker's. Happy, he set the beer and glass in front of me, said, 'Budweiser,' and disappeared.

Walker spun the swizzle stick off his fingers, raised his high-ball glass, and gave me a nod. '*À votre santé*,' is what he said.

I poured some beer, and lifted it. '*Salud*. Sorry to keep you waiting. I had to drive somebody's mother home.'

'I'm not waiting. I'm here.' ('Here' had an existential flavour to it.) 'Emory gave you my message?'

'Right. It's too bad you couldn't have persuaded that girl to come forward at the time, about her little rendezvous across the street with Winston Russell. It might have made a difference to George Hall.'

'That so?' The sardonic smile spread across his mouth.

'Well, it might make a difference this time. Hall's getting a new trial.'

'I heard.' He scratched a sideburn, then picked up a small card on the table and tapped it against his glass. 'I heard this time he got a real lawyer.'

'True. So where is this woman? Emory said she'd left Hillston.'

He flicked the little card so it landed on my side of the table. On it was written a woman's name and a phone number; the area code was Washington, DC.

I said, 'Thank you. Did, in fact,' – I looked at the card – '. . . "Denise" tell you about this episode with Russell at the time it happened?'

'In fact?' Walker took a slow swallow of his drink. 'In fact, no. I got that story a long way down the road. After a sweet young lady, friend of Denise's, woke up in the hospital following a "little rendezvous" with that same' – he set the glass down and smiled – 'motherfucking pig.'

I smiled the same way. 'I put Russell away for what he did to her.'

'I heard.'

Twisting out of my jacket, I rolled up my right shirt sleeve. Years later, the burn scars were still fish-white and bald. I said, 'When Russell got out, he came to see me.'

'I heard that too.'

'You hear everything that goes down in this city, Mr Walker?'

He took off the hat, and stroked its lines; his hairline was, I noticed, slightly receding. He said, 'Everything? Oh no, sir, Captain, sir. I only hears the kinds of things a nigger pimp need to hear.' The man had a truly nasty curl to his lip. 'I don't hear a lot of honkie things, like what's happening over at the Hunt Club. I just hear honkie things in the way of business. Like which of you fuzz I can buy, which I can fuck, which are gonna fuck me, and which I can invite over for a drink.'

I poured some more beer. 'Your busy grapevine mention how bad I want Russell? Well, I want him *real* bad. He shot Cooper Hall.'

Sipping at his drink, Walker shrugged. 'That's what they say on the news.'

'You don't believe it?'

'Oh I believe it. Russell, or somebody else. The man's dead, I believe that ... Excuse me one second.' Suddenly sliding out of the booth, Walker took a leisurely tour of the crowded bar, pausing to slap a hand or rub a back. The noise had gone up as the night went on and the alcohol went down. People were laughing like they weren't convinced tomorrow was a sure thing. On a raised platform against the wall, three young men were untangling the electric cables to large, *large* amplifiers. Walker ended up as if by accident near the entrance beside a plump black woman with extremely red hair, a short fur jacket to match, a tangle of bright necklaces, and, again, dangerous-looking shoes. He leaned down with a smile, said something to her, hugged her by the waist, put a spin on the hug, and sent her back out the doors.

While he was gone, Fattie-Smoke brought over more drinks. 'One vodka tonic. One Budweiser.' He tried to hang around the booth, but on his return, Walker told him bluntly to 'beat it,' then announced to me with a drumroll of his fingers on the table that we needed to talk some business because in a few minutes he needed to leave to do some business.

I said, 'Hamilton, that escort business of yours keeps real late hours, doesn't it? Customized service must be your middle name.'

'Haver's my middle name.' His smile on the word *Haver* startled me. 'But, yeah, we rocks around the clock, Captain. Demand and supply.'

'Right. Well, *skoal!*' I clinked my beer mug against his glass.

He toasted me back silently; I'd half-expected him to say something like '*L'chaim!*,' but he didn't. He was 'strictly business.' He said, 'I've got something to offer you—'

I said, 'We don't take bribes. And we don't pay them.'

He said, 'That so?'

I let the sarcasm float off before I said, 'We expect citizens to be proud and eager to come to the aid of their police department. And when they do, and when what they tell us is helpful, well then, we're proud and eager to thank them. What helpful thing do you have to offer?'

Leaning back in the booth, he pulled one leathered knee up, and looped an arm around it. A gold-linked watchband hung from his wrist. He shook his head. 'Politics is not my bag.' (So that's where his nephew G.G. had got the philosophy from which he'd now apparently converted.) 'Democrats, Republicans, right, left, black, white, yellow, straight, homo, they're all horny, and you strip 'em, they all look about the same.'

I said, 'Well, you got the jump on politicians. You're in the oldest profession. They're just the second oldest.'

This made him laugh; there was a gap in the strong upper teeth, which may have been why he usually only smiled with one corner of his mouth. Then he settled back against the bench, and slowly spun the new swizzle stick through his fingers. 'I'm a businessman, Captain. But like you, I have a human weakness. We're all born of women, and those cords are hard to cut. You had a mama?'

'I assume that's a rhetorical question, but the answer's yes.'

'Nomi Hall was good to my mama. During a time of troubles. Later on, I got to know her son Cooper when he was hanging around here, asking stuff about his brother smoking the cop. Sometimes, he'd show with this white buddy he had, named Jack ... Medina, Molina, some wop name. Man always talking political shit, 'bout Andy Brookside doing good stuff for the brothers. Man's a maniac.'

'A believer.'

'That so? . . . At the time, I didn't know where this girl Denise was at. But I told Cooper I'd check it out. I checked it out. Then I talk to Cooper. Then I turn on the tube one night, and I see the man's been wasted.' He tossed the plastic stick on to the table. 'That's the thing about "believers." I was in insurance, I wouldn't want to sell one any big policy. Not a black one anyhow. Too many folks wanna figure the nigger that's gonna make some noise, and take him out so he stops making that noise. I see a believer, I see women crying by a pine box. But this kid Martin – he hangs round close with G.G. – he took it hard about Cooper.' Walker shook his head irritably, as if disappointed in his human weakness. 'And, well, I like G.G., he's a crazy motherfucker, but I like him—'

'So do I.'

He nodded. 'I'd just as soon no bad shit went down on G.G.'s record. His mama wants him to go on to college. G.G.'s book smart, always was.'

I nodded back. 'I'm a great believer in a college education. So, let's talk about politics. I believe Offficer Emory said you had information involving the governor's race.'

'That depends, Captain. Here's a taste of what I've got. A while ago, I met this class-act number calls herself Jamaica Touraine—'

'Are you talking about some hooker?'

He smiled. 'Let me put it like this. You know that joke? Dude asks the lady, "You sleep with me for two million dollars?" She's kinda shocked, but, you know, she thinks it over, finally says, "Okay." Dude says, "I ain't got two million dollars. You fuck me for twenty bucks?" well, now she smacks his face, screams and hollers, "What you think I am, a whore?" Dude says, "We already 'stablished what you are, lady. We just haggling about the price."' Walker's eyes glittered hard as coal. 'That's what you and I are gonna do, Captain. Haggle some about the price.'

I wiped my mouth with a cocktail napkin. 'That charge about the Canaan riot that's troubling G.G.? Judge Roche is on the bench. Dolores Roche.' He nodded. I said, 'Well, Judge Roche shares my high opinion of a college education.'

Reaching for his hat, he adjusted the brim with care. 'You know Judge Roche personally?'

'I know her professionally. We both have a real lofty notion of our duties. We think we need to punish the wrong and save the wrongdoers if we possibly can. Especially young wrongdoers . . . Okay?'

He talked to the hat. 'Okay, I'll buy that. Sounds like a nice easygoing attitude. I'd like to think you had that attitude about other things too, about, oh, a little love and companionship between consenting adults. I'd like to think you were passing on your easygoing attitude to your boys on the beat around here.'

I said, 'Lovers don't usually expect cash payments for their companionship.'

The look Walker gave me was oddly expectant. 'There's all different kinds of costs to love. Money's one of the cheapest. You'd agree with that, wouldn't you? All kinds of costs.' His smile flashed like a snake suddenly slithering past you in a lake. Then he tapped my fingers with the end of his swizzle stick. 'Now, I'm reasonable. I don't mind your boys taking my ladies on a little drive downtown every once and a while. Keep your books straight.' He shook the stick in front of my face. 'But not twice a month, and sure not twice a week. That's harassment. Some of your boys have picked up the pace to where it's fucking with *my* books. I don't know if these boys are bored, or born-again, or bucking for a bonus. But I do know, I don't like what it's doing to my overhead.'

I said,'I can understand that. I'm sure so much transporting your ladies downtown adds to my overhead too. My budget's not big. I'm sympathetic.'

'I was hoping you would be. I'm counting on it . . . Now, I believe we were talking about a "hooker" named Jamaica Touraine.'

I nodded. 'Um hum. I don't believe my boys ever introduced us.'

He laughed at this notion. 'They never will. It's hard to tell a real rich whore from a real rich . . . lady. Mostly, folks don't even try.'

'This Jamaica's in your two-million-dollar category?'

'Class act. One of the finest-looking women *I* ever saw, and I've seen a lot of women.'

'She works for you?'

This time the laugh was rueful. 'Nooooo. Jamaica mostly does sort of semipermanent arrangements, high-rollers, gentlemen only, with a little short-term freelance in between. But Jamaica and I have some—' He rubbed the glass rim over his upper lip. '—Some mutual interests. I had an occasion to invite her for a drink one evening over at the Hilton—'

I said, 'You invite Jamaica to the Hilton, and invite me *here*?'

His eyes widened. 'Man, I'd invite that woman to the moon, I thought she'd go. Fact I did invite her to Bermuda once, told her how I loved Bermuda, had a boat down there. But she turned me down. Like to kill me.' At all this talk about Bermuda, my head flinched. What's more, Walker seemed to notice it, and seemed to understand it. This suspicion stabbed further into me when he added, 'You know how it is, Captain. Some women a man would crawl over briers on his belly to get to.'

All expression faded from his eyes as I stared at them, and finally I decided I was being paranoid. Why shouldn't he like Bermuda? Lot of people do. I gestured for him to go on.

He said, 'All right, that evening at the Hilton, these hightone honkies come in the lounge. First, one of them looks like he maybe knows Jamaica, then he gives her the freeze. She laughs, says, look at that motherfucker frost her, after he paid her five thousand dollars to do a number.' Walker sighed, I guess at the difference between what he could command for the services of his hostesses, and the fees of the mythical Jamaica. 'That's heavy bread.'

I said, 'Certainly more than I make in a night. Do a number on *him*?'

'No, do a number on another dude. Find him, fuck him. This guy just wants her to let his man set up a video in her suite so she can turn it on when the time comes, and make herself a home movie of her and the other dude. The buyer wanted the movie. So she gets to the dude, she fucks him. But 'fore she called the hired hand to come pick up this tape, she has me make her a little copy for a souvenir. She didn't mention that little copy when she handed over the original.'

I said, 'Why did you think I'd be so particularly interested in this?'

'Just pay attention. She and I, we have our drink, talk about families and troubles, and so on, then she says, so long, she's off with a gentleman friend, he's taking her all the way to Buenos Aires ... don't some folks live the life? So she thinks she'll give her copy of the tape to me, 'case I can put it to some good use. She said, "Contribution to the cause." Could be, Jamaica's interested in politics. I'm not.'

I drank the last of my beer. 'But I bet you could tell me if you wanted to, who these high-tone political honkies in the Hilton were.'

'I could tell you who the one humping Jamaica was. You could tell it to yourself, you took a look at this videotape. I think he's the one going to interest you most, but I guess Jamaica could tell you about the one doing the hiring, if I could reach her long-distance. I don't know if I can.'

'Could you describe the buyer and his friend?'

'White.'

'That's it?'

'Money.'

'I'm talking short, tall, thin, fat, hair, glasses. Would you recognize them? Say, if I showed you some photos?'

'Would you thank me for doing that?' His eyes watched me thoughtfully behind their long, stiff lashes. 'See, I've still got this problem, Mr Mangum. Nothing worse for business regularity than have your staff keep calling up, telling you they're unavoidably detained down at the Municipal Building. Imagine it.'

I gave what I was going to say a minute's thought. 'Um hum. I've got a problem too. I want you to imagine mine.'

'Help me a little.' He smiled.

'Too many crimes with *victims*. The sad fact is, I've got so many crimes with victims to worry about, I'm forced to make it a strict priority not to tie up my facilities with crimes that *don't* have any victims. You know what I mean, crimes that don't hurt anybody but the people committing them, things like smoking pot, household sodomy, escort services, private gambling, that type thing. Every now and then I *should* remind my cops that we have to live in a world of priorities. I'll do that.'

He thought about my remark, then he made up his mind, looked at his Rolex watch, and said, 'Ask questions.'

'Where's the tape?'

'I gave it to Cooper Hall. Sitting, right here. Friday night, round midnight, December twenty-third.'

'Wait a minute. That was the night of the governor's stay of execution.'

'That's right. Cooper came in here, 'bout midnight, flying high 'cause he'd got word his brother had his reprieve. He said, "Now I got some time to *move* in." I give him the tape, and he said, "Ham, I'm goin' into politics tomorrow morning!" Said, "I'm

269

gonna change things around, do some good shit for our people. I'm gonna buy us some *good* shit!" '

'Because of the tape?'

A shrug. 'He spins that videotape like a Ferris wheel, and he takes off with it. Saturday, I turn on the tube, he's lying in his own blood. My girls went all to pieces, carrying on, said how it was like King and Malcolm X. Shit. "Change things around." Right, man.' Standing up slowly, Walker pulled the leather hat on, checking the angle in the cloudy mirror above the booth.

I said, 'I'm not through asking questions. Did you tell Cooper the story, that there was another tape, and who had it?'

'I told him somebody had it. At the time, I didn't know who.'

'What do you mean, at the time? Do you know now?'

'I might do. Wouldn't testify to it. Hard to tell from the TV. But the man in the Hilton looked like the city hall man on the news.' Walker made a bizarrely vivid pantomime of a man hanging himself with a rope.

I tried to keep my voice level. 'The man Jamaica pointed out as the one who'd hired her looked like the city comptroller, Otis Newsome, who committed suicide.'

Smiling, Walker shrugged. 'Looked like to me.'

I caught his hand as he scooped up the soggy change Fattie had left. 'Who was the man in the tape?'

'Oh, that man?' The grin pulling at his mouth's corner had that same expectant feel to it that made me tighten up inside. 'I figured you weren't asking about that man, Captain, 'cause you already knew about him. Figured y'all must . . . share things. The one humping Jamaica?' He shot his forefinger at the fat waitress who was cleaning dirty glasses off the table beside us. Pinned to her shiny blouse was one of the light Carolina blue buttons that I'd been seeing more and more people in Hillston wearing lately. The buttons with Andrew Brookside's picture on them.

I said to Walker, 'You're sure?'

He smiled at me. 'Yeah, I'm sure. They may all look alike in the dark, but with Jamaica you don't wanna be in the dark.'

I sat there, waiting for him to leave. Then when he kept looking at me, I said, 'Thanks for the beer.'

He tipped the hat. 'My pleasure. Stay cool.'

Walker had gone, the blues band had begun to play, its amplifiers thumping like the heart of Leviathan must have sounded to Jonah. Nobody bothered me in my back booth at Smoke's, where I sat not even dealing yet with the significance of what I'd learned, because I was trying to accept the fact that somehow Hamilton Walker knew about my involvement with Lee, at least suspected it. The irony in the curve of his lip when he said the word *Bermuda* kept coming back to me. His grin reminded me, though they were, at least on the surface, an unlikely pair, of Mrs Marion Sunderland's nasty smirk. Their smiles had said the same thing to me: 'It doesn't much matter how I know. I just want you to realize *that* I know. I'm not even going to do anything with the knowledge, except share with you the fact that I find it mildly amusing.'

Chapter 15

In the time between the *Twelfth Night* performance and George Hall's new trial, the following things happened:

I kept seeing Lee.

Billy Gilchrist fell off the wagon again, and disappeared.

I kept trying to find Russell and Newsome.

I kept hard at work policing Hillston, logging arrests for arson, rape, homicide, child-molestation, larceny, manslaughter, embezzlement, robbery, fraud, indecent exposure, assault, shoplifting, kidnapping, drunk-driving, and all the other sad ways folks vent rage and satisfy craving.

Arrests of prostitutes near the Montgomery Hotel were, on the other hand, kept to an all-time low.

Andy Brookside told me indignantly that he most certainly had not discussed with Cooper Hall, during their aeroplane ride together, a videotape of himself and anyone named Jamaica Touraine. That he could not have possibly done so since he had never known anyone with that name. And who in hell had told me otherwise? And why in hell was I even coming to him with such filth?

My reply would have been a little more forceful if I'd had a copy of that tape, but I didn't. Coop had either given his copy to Brookside, or to someone else (nobody we'd talked to, unless they were lying), or it had been stolen out of the *With Liberty and Justice* office. It seemed likely that Otis's cameraman had been Willie Slidell, given all the video equipment and porno tapes we'd found at his farm. Slidell had either given the original to Otis Newsome (as they were both dead now, this possibility couldn't be checked), or to someone else, or left it at the farm where it had, or had not, been found by Russell and Newsome. All I could say to Brookside was that my information had come from an unimpeachable source, and that he, Brookside, had better hope *I* found his X-rated romp before it showed up on the Brodie Cheek show.

Mr Hamilton Walker, my unimpeachable source, regretted that he was unable to locate Ms Touraine (or maybe that wasn't her real name) on her round-the-world cruise with the Argentine (or maybe he wasn't Argentine) businessman. We did, however, find Ham's former employee 'Denise' plying her trade in the nation's capital, and Wes Pendergraph flew up there to take a statement from her. She told him she'd be happy to come testify that Winston Russell was on the scene when Pym was shot. She said she hated Winston Russell so much, she'd be happy to testify that he had shot Pym himself if we wanted her to. Wes, who kept wondering if he was 'tough enough,' came home 'shocked.'

I had my own shock when Professor Briggs Mary Cadmean suddenly returned to Hillston, having resigned from her western university, to collect the millions her chauvinist pig of a papa had left her on the condition that she do just that. Alice was also shocked. Justin was not. 'You simply don't renounce that kind of inheritance,' he informed us, somewhat smugly it seemed to Alice and me, as if how could we be expected to know such things, having grown up so poor and trashy. Alice and Justin had a fight about Briggs Junior's 'character,' he spent the night on my couch, she came over at two in the morning, and from up in my bedroom, I had to listen to them, from 2:15 to 3:30 A.M., decide that they were (a) totally incompatible, (b) having a problem communicating, (c) madly in love.

Sergeant Zeke Caleb informed me that he and Officer Nancy White were madly in love. I wasn't surprised. That he and Nancy White were having a baby. I was very surprised. That they were going to get married. I thought this was a good idea.

A munitions salesman tried to get me to buy a dozen electric stun guns to have on hand for any future race riots. 'A weapon

273

of compassion,' he called it, but turned me down flat when I said I'd buy as many as he'd let me shoot at him pointblank range, right here in my office.

Judge Dolores Roche sentenced each of the 'Canaan Riot' teenagers to two hundred hours of community service. If they stuck with it, their records would then be cleared. The older of the Wister brothers (whose loan shop's window had been broken) called out from the rear of the courtroom, 'You mean they're not going to jail?!' The judge replied that as a cure for social problems, jail was incredibly expensive, largely ineffective, and usually inhumane. Mr Wister stood on his seat and cursed her, and was sentenced to either one hundred hours of community service, working with the teenagers, or a fine of $500. Having to choose between losing money and having to sweep sidewalks with blacks proved too much for Mr Wister, whose face went purple and whose open mouth appeared to be paralysed. His brother paid the fine.

I assigned John Emory and Nancy White to supervise the teenagers as they were cleaning, repairing, and repainting the block of East Hillston where they'd 'rioted.' One of them did not 'stick with it.' A few weeks later while stealing a neighbour's TV set, he hit the neighbour with a lead pipe. Judge Roche sent him to the state reformatory. She sadly said to me afterwardss, 'One more failure, Cuddy; yours, mine, and the whole messed-up system's.'

Old Dolores had never been a happy judge, and she was getting gloomier by the year. I told her she was losing her capacity to look on the bright side; after all the other eleven young men *had* stuck it out: That section of Canaan looked cleaner than it'd been for years. They'd cleared away the informal junkyard that had grown on the site of the demolished AME church, and then they had painted a big, bright mural of local black history on the church's single still-standing wall-section; you could see it for blocks away, because Canaan AME (to which the wide stone steps remained) had stood atop a small hill. In this mural, Bessie Smith was depicted singing in Smoke's; two black children were depicted being escorted by state troopers into Polk Elementary School through a gauntlet of ugly-faced white parents; five young civil rights demonstrators were depicted seated cross-legged in a row across Main Street, and the Hillston police were depicted hauling them off, while one of my prede-cessors as chief stood watching, left hand on a megaphone, right hand on a gun. A pro-basketball superstar who'd grown up in East Hillston was depicted in flight across the top of the mural. Coretta Scott King was depicted shaking hands with Mayor Carl Yarborough, and Cooper Hall was depicted dead-centre, his head about as large as Lenin's in Red Square, his hand raised beneath the sun, as if he'd just tossed it into air. With John and Nancy's help, the teenagers also built two wood benches, laid a path with the old church bricks, chained a trash can to a post, and called the place 'Cooper Hall Park.'

Justin discovered through his informant, Preston Pope, that last fall the Carolina Patriots had been expecting a shipment of arms for their much-discussed Armageddon against the Tainted Races, but that the (prepaid) guns had never shown up. The missing supplier turned out to have been the fellow (or what was left of him) we'd found dead in the abandoned Peugeot off in the woods last November. Turns out he'd done time in Dollard Prison during the same period, and in the same cell block, as Winston Russell.

Mayor Carl Yarborough appointed a black to replace Otis Newsome as city comptroller, and was accused of 'nepotism' by Brodie Cheek on his new cable television show, 'Call to Christ.'

Andy Brookside was the main speaker at Cooper Hall's memorial service, organized by the 'Hall Committee.' That night Haver Auditorium was so jammed with students that Nomi Hall's sister couldn't make her way through to the family seats, and had to stand in the back to listen to the eulogies. A black rock star sang a song he'd written about Cooper called 'My Brother's Keeper.' Jack Molina read telegrams from national civil rights figures. Jordan West introduced Alice MacLeod, who introduced 'our next governor Andrew Theodore Brookside.' (Maybe he was laying the groundwork for folks to call him ATB – as in FDR and JFK)

In his speech, Brookside never mentioned the death penalty

against which Hall had fought, but I'll give him this: he brought that crowd to its feet with his final words: 'Whenever a young man like Cooper Hall dies by violence, then a little of all that is best in this country dies with him. Whenever his voice is silenced by hate, then the voice of America is silenced too. Let us pledge tonight to join our voices to those who have had the courage to sing alone. Until together, our song is a shout of liberty and justice! Tonight is not our memorial to Cooper Hall. *The future is our memorial to Cooper Hall!*'

Jack Molina, who had presumably written this speech, was the first to leap cheering out of his seat.

Martin Hall was expelled from Hillston High for insubordination to a history teacher. Officer John Emory offered to talk to the school; Martin told him to 'get fucked.'

G. G. Walker was admitted to Haver University for the fall term; he was also offered, and accepted, the Dollard Scholarship, a full free ride granted each year since 1928 to six native male North Carolinians considered by the judges to be 'mentally, morally, and athletically outstanding.' Justin's mother, Mrs J. B. Savile IV (nee Peggy Dollard) was one of the judges.

I found out I had aced the last extension course I'd needed before my PhD orals; I decided to put off those orals for a year, when presumably my 'personal life' would have resolved itself one way or another.

I saw Debbie Molina (Jack's wife) outside civil court in the Municipal Building; she was deep in conversation with a lawyer I knew, who handled a lot of divorce work. I had an irrational spasm of certainty that she was leaving Jack in order to marry Andy. The lawyer told me she was there to testify for a friend in a hospital negligence suit.

Justin had a small beach cottage on Okracoke Island in the Outer Banks, left to him by a man named Walter Stanhope, a friend of his father's, and a former Hillston police chief. I asked him if I could use it to get away by myself for a weekend. Lee and I spent

Valentine's Day there, walking along the grey beach huddled together under a blanket.

Bubba Percy told me he was 'still working' on the Buddy Randolph-Cooper Hall connection. Maybe he was working on it when I saw him in the Municipal Building following Jordan West down the hall, grinning and jabbering at her. She sidestepped him into the ladies' room, where I was amazed he wasn't gross enough to follow her.

Mrs Marion ('Call me Eddie') Sunderland invited me to two dinner-and-bridge parties; she invited Lee to neither one. Bubba showed up at the second of these in a tuxedo with a bow tie the colour of his auburn hair. Eddie laughed her head off at his impersonations (mostly stolen from 'Saturday Night Live' reruns) of Nixon and Reagan. He also did Senator Kip Dollard after that gentleman left the party.

A week later I saw Bubba and Eddie both laughing their heads off over a luncheon of stuffed crab at the Pine Hills Inn, where I'd taken Alice for her birthday. It was a shame that when Bubba had finally found a rich, available woman as smart and jaded as he was, she turned out to be seventy-two years old.

A week later, Bubba ran an article implying that in the late 1950s and early '60s, Haver students in a secret club called the House of Lords had engaged in the 'intimidation and harassment' of local blacks and of fellow students sympathetic to the civil rights movement. This article (which gave no credit to the previous article by Cooper Hall in the largely unread *With Liberty and Justice*), claimed that, according to an unnamed source, members of that secret club at that time included former Hillston official Otis Newsome, and Lieutenant Governor Julian D. Lewis.

Julian Lewis issued a denial.

Bubba was fired by the managing editor of the *Hillston Star*.

The managing editor of the *Hillston Star* was fired by the editor-in-chief after a private meeting with Mrs Marion Sunderland.

The new managing editor was listed on the masthead as 'Randolph P. Percy, Jr,' which was the first anybody had ever heard of Bubba's real name, if in fact it was his real name, and not something he'd quickly put together as soon as he'd listened to Edwina Sunderland's spiel on the Nowell-Randolphs of Palliser Farm. I told Eddie it looked like she'd thrown me over for Bubba's eyelashes after all. She told me her impression was that I was 'already taken.'

I said, 'Meaning what?'

She said, 'Meaning, Cuthbert, I just hope you aren't going to waste your life – as you so bluntly implied I had wasted mine.'

I said, 'I just hope you aren't ever going to bid four no-trump with a singleton again.'

On his new cable television show, Reverend Brodie Cheek endorsed Julian Lewis for governor. So did everybody in the Constitution Club, which meant nearly every business leader in the state did.

Mayor Carl Yarborough endorsed Andy Brookside. So did a whole covey of national figures, both white and black, including members of Congress, sports stars, rock stars, and movie stars.

Under its new management, the *Hillston Star* reversed itself and endorsed Andy Brookside.

Julian Lewis won his primary with 47 per cent of the votes.

Andy Brookside won his primary with 89 per cent of the votes, the largest plurality on the polling records.

Fuzz Five ended our basketball season with three wins and five losses.

Isaac tried to get me to 'date' Nora Howard.

I kept seeing Lee.

Chapter 16

Miss Bee Turner, the clerk, sang each word like a loud bell. 'Hear ye, hear ye, hear ye, the Superior Court of Haver County in the State of North Carolina is now in session. The Honourable Shirley Hilliardson presiding. All please rise!'

The State versus George Hall, Part II (as Bubba Percy called the trial) was taking place daily. According to the Hillston Historical Society, which had avidly involved itself in the restoration, our new Superior Court (1947) was 'an enhanced replica' of our old Superior Court (burnt 1912), which, parenthetically, had never been called Superior Court, but simply Court, just as the wood building that had housed it had been called simply Courthouse. A second wood courthouse had caught fire, and a third was bulldozed by Progress when the civic-spirited Mr Briggs Cadmean built Hillston its stone Municipal Building, which by now had expanded to a block-long complex of annexed structures that included the police department. From the rolled-up blueprints that Cadmean shook down at folks from his lobby portrait had come the enhanced design of our new courtroom. Opening by massive double doors off our new marble rotunda, it was his philanthropic showplace, a huge handsome room with a forty-foot ceiling, tiered seats, a viewers gallery, sixteen brass chandeliers, and sixteen ten-foot-high windows. The walls, the seats, the bar, and oak wainscoting were painted authentic Federalist colours, and the seats were comfortably cushioned; the jury box, witness stand, and judge's bench were gleaming cherry-wood, handmade by Carolina craftsmen. The State and the defence both had rich leather chairs. The judge's chamber had on

279

its wall an authentic oil painting of Robert E. Lee, said by Judge Tiggs (who hung it there) to have been drawn from the life by his great-aunt, Miss Charlotte Victoria Tiggs. Above the bench, the Seal of the State of North Carolina was painted in gold leaf. The gavel had a silver handle. The big eagle-topped clock on the wall had been given personally to old Cadmean's father, Enos, by President McKinley, and had been presented to Enos right here in Hillston by Mark 'Boss' Hanna himself, the man who had personally given McKinley to the country, and vice versa. The clock was still ticking.

Naturally, time had dulled the courtroom wood, tarnished the brass and faded the paint; now the grand windows looked out at ten feet of air before running smack up against the concrete walls of later buildings; the visitors gallery (from which I had long ago listened to Isaac Rosethorn dazzle a jury) was now closed off as a safety hazard. Still, Superior Court looked, as the Historical Society's brochure told its readers, like a loving restoration of an architectural gem. The proportions were so fine, the space so rational, the props so solid in their symbolism, it was easy to sit in that room believing Justice was on her throne and blind as a bat to everything but the bright light of Truth.

Easy, but a big mistake. I'd seen enough examples in that room to know that Justice has got a real eye for colour (she prefers white), and for class (she likes upper and middle); that, in fact, she always was, and still is, a bitch on the poor, and a pushover for power. If you're connected to power, it's rare that Justice is going to tangle with you; it's rare you're even going to show up in a superior court, and if you do, rarer still that you're going to walk out of it into a jail; because by tradition in the game of law, the lower class gets to be the criminals, the middle class gets to be the jury, and the upper class gets to be the judge.

By tradition, crime is when you shoot up, take a knife to a spouse, write a bad cheque, bop someone on the head and snatch a purse, or steal $162.54 from a gas station. Crime is when you're on the streets where we can catch you. *Unorganized* crime, that's what Justice is used to. She doesn't mess as much with big-time corporate shenanigans and government slip-ups. CRIME DOES NOT PAY claims the sign over the Oklahoma electric chair, but of course that's usually depended on the size of the profits.

Well, of course, times have changed a little in Haver County since Judge Tiggs sentenced an East Hillston maid to ten years in women's prison for allegedly stealing a few dollars off her employer's bureau (on the grounds that if the money was missing, she must have taken it), the same month that he sentenced a North Hillston lady to a fine and five years probation for slipping her husband a sleeping pill, lugging him to the garage, and leaving him there with his Buick's motor running until he died (on the grounds that she'd succumbed to 'mental anguish' after hearing his plans to divorce her in order to marry his receptionist).

But by and large, Justice remains faithful to her old favourites. As the late great Woodrow Clenny told Judge Tiggs to his face, 'Money talks. And Money walks. Rich folks never do no time.'

At his first trial, George Hall wasn't rich. This time around, he still wasn't rich, but he knew some people who were; or rather, they knew him, or rather, they knew *about* him, and that's enough to make a difference. And when I say 'rich,' I don't mean ready cash; I mean what they used to call Society, Government, Church, and the Fourth Estate. I mean power. At his first trial, George was 100 per cent lacking in that desirable commodity. So before that first trial began, while still unconvicted and (presumably) innocent until proven otherwise, he'd sat for fourteen months in Haver County Jail in a cell he sometimes had to share with as many as five other men. The jail, unequipped for 'long-term prisoners' – fourteen months was (presumably) not in that category – had no facilities for counselling, medical treatment, or even exercise, other than the endless scrubbing of its floors and walls.

At his first trial, George never laid eyes on his lawyer, an assistant public defender, until he stepped into the courtroom. George's lawyer never saw George's file until it was handed to him that morning by another public defender, who'd interviewed George months earlier, and who'd lost patience with the defendant after he'd turned down the great deal this PD had worked out with Mitchell Bazemore in one of their games of flesh-peddle swap: Mitch would let Hall go for ten-to-twenty on guilty to second-degree murder, if the PD would give him a guilty plea on all three counts of rape by another client – a young thug I was pretty sure *had* committed at least two of the rapes. George's stubborn refusal to accept this deal loused up the court's busy schedule, and exasperated those who'd 'only wanted to help' him. He couldn't have annoyed them more unless he'd had the arrogance to act as his own lawyer and presume to tell them their own business in their own courtroom.

So George's first visit to Superior Court had been a brief one;

there were no pretrial motions, there were no challenges, there was no striking of jurors, there were no requests for directed verdicts against the state for not proving its case, no exceptions to overrulings, there was no wasting time on behalf of a stubborn man without friends or money. The whole trial took two days; the jury took fifteen minutes, and as we now knew, one of the jurors couldn't hear anyhow, and another had passed the time addressing Christmas cards.

But, *now*, on George's second visit to court, we were nine days into the trial, and hadn't even got to the opening arguments. Defence was still fighting over every single seat in that cherry-wood jury box. Isaac Rosethorn was dragging out the voir dire (questioning the panel of possible jurors) so long, I asked him if he wasn't stalling for time – maybe until Billy Gilchrist came back, or we found Winston Russell.

'Absolutely not. Verdicts,' said Isaac, with his wagging finger, 'are close to decided as soon as you pick those twelve jurors. Decided before that, the minute all the possible names are drawn. You've chosen your best juror bets before you ever get into that courtroom, because you've hired investigators to snoop out everything they can dig up about every damn one of them. If *I'd* been defending George's first trial, I'd have challenged the whole damn panel. Claimed box stuffing. Claimed intentional *and* systematic exclusion of blacks. That's the first thing I would have done.' But, of course, if Isaac had been an overworked, underpaid public defender, he wouldn't have had the funds to hire his private investigators, or the leisure to analyse their investigations, or Nora Howard to help him do it. He wouldn't have had time to care. Or to get anybody else to care.

So George Hall's second trial was a different affair altogether. After passing through metal detectors, spectators rushed to grab every handsome cushioned seat in Superior Court. Now George was the brother of a famous martyr (who even had a song about him on the rock charts). He had the undivided services of a famous lawyer. He had the attention of Society, Government, Church, the Fourth Estate, and the People. *Hall vs N.C., II*, was a standing room only show. Or it would have been if Judge Shirley Hilliardson – his long thin black-robed arm rising steady as a wing to strike the gavel – hadn't announced right off that the unseated would not be allowed, nor would television cameras, nor snacking, nor whispering, nor the unmannerly, the unruly, or the unkempt.

'We are here,' Hilliardson announced with a contemptuous glare, 'to serve justice to the best of our puny abilities. We are *not* here to serve the prurient curiosity of the idle, or the circulation goals of the so-called media. I will not hesitate to clear this courtroom whenever I see fit.' Nobody doubted it. Those precisely clipped words were sharp as the long beaked nose, and cold as the hawkish eyes.

Late on the ninth day, I slipped into Superior Court through the big glossy doors at the back, with a surprise present for Isaac Rosethorn that HPD had just received anonymously in the mail. When I arrived there, the first thing I saw was George Hall's back, straight and still, in the ill-fitting suit he'd worn to Cooper's funeral. The Haver County sheriff, accompanied by two armed deputies, was personally escorting George into the courtroom from Haver County Jail, where he'd been delivered last week by Dollard Prison guards and where he was (again) being kept for the duration of the trial. The first day, Sheriff Reese had led George into court with a chain running from his handcuffs to a leg shackle. People were shocked.

Sheriff Reese had spluttered, But, but, but George Hall was now, after all, a convicted murderer under sentence of death. The sheriff's splutter was in response to Judge Hilliardson's calling a conference in his chambers (Isaac told me about it), and demanding that 'all that medieval paraphernalia be removed from the defendant at once.'

Reese had whined, 'Okay, Your Honour, and what are we supposed to do if he tries to make a break for it?'

The judge had replied, 'You are supposed to stop him. I assume that is why you have added to my congestion by posting four fully armed men in my courtroom?'

Isaac hadn't protested the chains himself, because they were sympathy-getters, and for the same reason Mitch Bazemore didn't protest their removal. So after the first day, George was uncuffed as he sat down beside Isaac, and recuffed as he was taken away.

At the other end of the defence table sat Nora Howard, her black curls up in a sedate twist, her dress a muted grey. In the first row behind the bar, next to Jordan West, sat George's mother, Nomi Hall, in a black dress and hat; she kept her gloved hands folded over her purse in her lap, and kept her shoulders as straight and motionless as her son's.

When I walked in, Isaac Rosethorn was standing (deliberately, no doubt) between the prosecutor's table and the jury. He had another prospective juror squirming on the stand. I'd heard he'd already gone through one entire panel, and forced Miss Bee Turner, as clerk, to summons a new set of veniremen. By the end Isaac was to use up all fourteen peremptory challenges, the ones where you don't have to give a reason for bumping jurors, and where he sometimes didn't appear to have one. 'A hunch,' he'd say. Or 'Phenology.' He'd take a woman because she had 'a generous face,' or he'd strike folks because they were ectomorphs, or their feet twitched, or their hair was too tightly pinned, or their eyes kept wandering towards the court clock. He said research had been done analysing psychological profiles of people strongly in favour of capital punishment, demonstrating that they are more likely to be authoritarian, intolerant, and violent themselves, than people who strongly oppose it. It was these types that Isaac claimed he went after. He struck down an innocuous-looking housewife ('Hard mouth'). He struck down the plastic surgeon whose earlier request to be excused had been denied by Judge Hilliardson ('Prig, and already hostile'). The surgeon had looked insulted when Isaac gave him his wish.

Not to be outdone, Prosecuting Attorney Mitchell Bazemore (muscles bulging through his three-piece pinstripe) was also striking jurors right and left, playing his peremptory challenges defensively, getting rid of as many blacks as he could, as well as people with advanced degrees, and anybody who struck him as a 'bleeding heart.' Miss Bee (a plump grey dove of a woman who'd run the court for so many years, she acted as if she owned it) was by this point giving both lawyers ostentatiously nasty sighs; our court clerk might have looked like a dove, but it was camouflage for a much meaner bird. As soon as one juror was dismissed, she'd rummage her hand down in the panel box for a new name as if she were furiously groping for a key stupidly dropped through a sewer grate.

As I sat down to listen that afternoon, Mitch had a black engineer 'struck,' leaving five women (two black), five men (three black). I watched as Isaac then had a bookkeeper excused as 'unqualified,' after the woman eagerly claimed (probably because she thought total ignorance was the 'right' answer) that not only had she no fixed opinion as to Hall's guilt or innocence, but also that (although living in Hillston, possessing a TV, a radio, and a subscription to the *Hillston Star*) she'd heard, seen, and read 'absolutely nothing at all' for the past seven years about anything to do with the George Hall case. 'Madam,' said Isaac with a bow, 'you appear to be astonishingly, though perhaps blessedly, free of the remotest interest in your fellow man.'

She risked a dubious smile, and said, 'Thank you.'

Isaac said, 'Thank *you*. Challenged for cause.'

'Excused,' said Judge Hilliardson with a withering look.

Then Mitch challenged a young Catholic mechanic who admitted he had such religious scruples against the death penalty, that he would never convict in a case where death could conceivably be the sentence. 'Look, I'm sorry,' he said, with a glance at Isaac Rosethorn after he was excused, 'But I felt like I had to tell the truth.'

Judge Hilliardson scowled at him. 'Surely, young man, you don't suspect the defence counsel would prefer your *dishonesty*?'

Isaac, the old hypocrite, shook his head, sad solemnity in his eyes.

Then Miss Bee called one Curtis McHugh, a middle-aged, middle-management man at C & W Textiles. He took the oath with loud earnestness, and settled himself quickly in the stand, like he was eager to try on some new shoes. The State (via Mitch Bazemore) quickly found McHugh quite acceptable, and retired to its table for a sip of water.

Seated next to Nora Howard behind the book-cluttered defence table, Isaac nodded as she handed him a small slip of paper. Then he limped over to the stand (a very slight limp, just enough to make the Korean War veteran already seated in the jury box subliminally wonder, 'War injury?').

The old lawyer was wearing his shoes polished, his shirt snowy white as his hair, his old tweed suit freshly cleaned and patched ('suggests I'm a neat person but not a wealthy one'), a wedding ring (in the totally preposterous and conceited fear that otherwise jurors might think he was up to some 'hanky-panky with Nora'), a borrowed Civitans' pin in his lapel (one of the selected jurors was in that organization), and a new tie with tiny blue French fleur-de-lis all over it (one of the jurors had spent years trying to trace his ancestry back to the Bourbon monarchs).

Curtis McHugh watched Rosethorn's approach with studied nonchalance.

'Mr McHugh,' the deep voice purred, 'you've just told Mr Bazemore that you feel "fully and completely confident" you can give a disinterested, fair-minded hearing of this case. No question in your mind?'

'No, sir,' said McHugh, straightening his rather loud tie.

'What do you know about the defendant here, George Hall?' Isaac pointed at the defence table.

'Just what I heard on the news. He murdered a policeman a few years back, got convicted, but now they're giving him a new trial because sombody messed up the first one.'

'Messed up?'

McHugh shrugged. 'You know, threw it out on technicality-type stuff.'

'Ah. . . . Anything else you've heard about Mr Hall?'

'No. Well, he's the brother of the one the police think maybe got shot.'

'The "one"? The one what?'

'The protester. Cooper Hall.'

'Do you have any views about Cooper Hall's past "protesting" that might prejudice you against his brother, the defendant?'

'None a'tall.' McHugh folded his arms firmly over his chest. 'Why should I?'

'You shouldn't.' Isaac took a stroll as he talked. 'Do you think killing is ever justified, Mr McHugh?'

'Sure, in wars and things like that. Or protect your home and family. Things like that.'

'In self-defence?'

'Sure. But if it's a matter of just plain shooting somebody down or something, then I think you've got to pay your debt to society. If a human being takes a life, then he owes a life.' McHugh nodded up at Judge Hilliardson as if he expected to be commended; Hilliardson stared straight through him. 'Like the Bible says.'

Isaac nodded. 'In Leviticus, where the Bible also says it's fine to own slaves, and not fine to eat pork chops ... Now, Mr McHugh, you told Mr Bazemore a minute ago, you are "totally sure" there's not a "single shred" of prejudice against black people in your "heart or mind."' Isaac smiled sweetly as he quoted these phrases.

'That's right.' Serious nods.

'Well, that's a wonderful thing to be totally sure of. Let me ask you something . . .' Isaac leaned against the stand, scratching an eyebrow. 'You have any friends who're black?'

Confusion. 'What do you mean?'

A dismissive wave of the hand. 'No? Well, how about casual acquaintances? Ever had a black person to your house for dinner?'

McHugh's face twitched. '. . . No. But there're a couple of black people at C and W in my division, and I don't have any problem with them a'tall.'

'Ever go to a show with one? Or maybe out for a cup of coffee, ever socialize with one?'

Suspicion tightened the man's face. '. . . No. But just because we don't have anything in common doesn't make me prejudiced if that's what you're getting at.' McHugh pulled at his ear, then grinned. 'I've never had any Brazilians over to dinner either, so does that mean I'm prejudiced against South America?'

Mitchell Bazemore did his obligatory laugh, and a few of his jury-picks smiled. Hilliardson glared at McHugh, whether disgusted by his taste in jokes, or ties, I couldn't tell. But Isaac smiled too, then he said, 'Well, sir, it might mean you were prejudiced if you lived in Brazil.' Another stroll, ending up near the two black men already seated in the jury box. 'Mr McHugh, what do you think of Martin Luther King's birthday becoming a national holiday?'

Mr McHugh looked at the judge. 'Do I have to answer this kind of question, Judge?'

I think McHugh knew what was coming, because he'd turned sulky. I'm sure Mitchell Bazemore had figured out where Isaac was headed, too, because he stood up and said, 'Your Honour! I fail to see where this entire line of questioning is headed.'

Hilliardson (deadpan) to Rosethorn: 'Counsellor, unless you plan to arrive at a relevant destination soon, I suggest you take a faster train.'

Rosethorn: 'Your Honour, the train I'm taking is the one they used to call Jim Crow. But I'll speed it along.'

Hilliardson looked up from the notes he was taking, or maybe the crossword puzzle, and said, 'Please do. I will allow the question.'

Isaac: 'Mr McHugh?'

'I don't think much about Martin Luther King one way or the other, except you could say, there's lots of good Americans I could name maybe deserve a holiday more.' Someone in the back of the courtroom clapped, and Hilliardson slammed down his silver-handled gavel.

Isaac: 'On January twenty-fourth of this year, Mr McHugh, did you happen to attend, along with *uniformed* members of the Ku Klux Klan, a rally in downtown Raleigh staged *against* Martin Luther King Day?'

McHugh: '. . . Maybe I was there, lot of people were there. Doesn't mean we're in the Klan, you know.'

Isaac kept going. 'And at this rally was not a racial slogan chanted at a group of young black people carrying posters with Cooper Hall's picture on them? And was this slogan not as follows?' He took out the slip of paper Nora had given him, and slowly pulling on his bifocals, read, '"King's down, and Cooper Hall. What happened to them could happen to y'all"?'

McHugh: 'Maybe. I don't really remember.'

Bazemore jumped up, then decided against protecting Mr McHugh, and sat down; for all he knew, if Rosethorn had dug up this much background, he might be getting ready to produce a photo of McHugh wearing a white robe and carrying a jug of kerosene.

Isaac returned to the defence table, sinking into his chair with a sigh. 'Challenged for cause, Your Honour. Bias.'

Hilliardson looked at Bazemore, who looked at the neat stack of papers on his table. Then he looked at McHugh (or his tie). 'You are excused. Thank you.'

McHugh's face crumpled. 'You mean I'm not a juror?'

'Yes. You're excused.'

'But I've got a *right* to be a juror. I took off from work and everything. Your Honour!'

It took several more minutes, and another rap of the gavel, to get Curtis McHugh off the stand. After that, Bazemore and Rosethorn (warned by the judge that he'd 'very much like to see a jury selected before his retirement from the bench') zipped through their questions to a sixty-three-year-old farmer's widow, whom they both found acceptable. Then Isaac struck an East Hillston grocer (who'd been twice robbed by blacks). Miss Bee fished angrily around in the panel box for another number twelve. 'Mrs Albert Boren!' she bellowed. I saw Isaac and Nora Howard flip through their legal pads, then start whispering energetically at each other as if they were arguing.

Mrs Boren, a little overweight, a little dowdy, looked to be in her late forties, and as if she'd once been a pretty blonde woman, but that it had got harder and harder for her to remember when. She also looked very unhappy that her name had popped out of that box.

'Mrs Boren,' smiled Mitch, after the preliminaries established that she was a housewife, and her husband owned an electrical supplies store. 'Tell me now. Do you have a fixed opinion about

288

the rightness or wrongness of the original verdict that found George Hall guilty of first-degree homicide?'

A deep breath, a headshake, and a faint voice, as she nervously fiddled with the collar of her sweater. 'No, sir, I have no opinion.'

Hilliardson peered down in her direction. 'Please speak up, Mrs Boren!'

She nodded, clearly scared to death.

'And.' Mitch smiled, so that his chin dimple winked. 'Do you feel fully confident you can listen to the evidence in this new trial without being biased by that original verdict?'

'. . . I think so.'

He beamed more of the long steady smile at her before he spoke. 'Your Honour, the State accepts Mrs Boren.' Another long silent smile, and he came close to patting her arm, as he backed away.

Isaac was still head-down in his buzz of whispers with Nora Howard, when the judge finally scowled, 'Any day now, Mr Rosethorn!'

Scrambling up, Isaac bowed. 'Your Honour, I'm sorry. I thought the district attorney was still giving Mrs Boren an opportunity to examine all his beautiful teeth.' He displayed his own in imitation and was rewarded by a chuckle from the audience.

The woman on the stand studied his approach as if she was afraid he was going to bite her. 'Mrs Boren, nice to meet you. Sorry to keep you waiting so long. Just a few questions. You have children?'

'. . . Four.'

'Four . . .' He looked worried. 'How will they manage, if you're shut up here with this trial?'

Her shoulders relaxed just a little. 'My oldest girl's sixteen, she's very responsible.'

'You must be proud of her. Your husband play a lot of golf, Mrs Boren?'

A puzzled jerk at this sudden shift. 'When he gets a chance. He works hard.'

'Ah, I know, I know. The cost of raising a big family these days.' Isaac sighed. 'Do you play with him?'

Her mouth twitched. 'No.'

'You work pretty hard yourself, I imagine.' His nods were full of sympathy. 'But when Mr Boren *does* get a moment for golf, where does he play? A public course or a private club?'

'We belong to Greenfield Club.'

'Well now, Mrs Boren, any black members of that club?'

'. . . I don't know, I'm not sure.'

Isaac was benevolent as a lamb. 'Well, would you be surprised to hear that there aren't any black members; never have been any, and according to the bylaws of the Greenfield Club, there never *will be* any black member?' He didn't wait for an answer, but stopped in midstride and asked, 'You own a house in Hillston?'

She tensed. 'In Fox Hills.'

'Any black families in Fox Hills?'

'. . . I don't know everybody in Fox Hills.'

'Do you know if there was ever a meeting of the "Fox Hills Association" to try to stop a black family from moving into your subdivision?'

'. . . Yes.'

'And did you say at that meeting that you were opposed to that family's coming into your neighbourhood?'

She shook her head. 'No, I didn't say anything. My husband—'

'Your husband organized that meeting, did he not?'

Mrs Boren frowned angrily at Isaac. 'Yes.'

'Your Honour!' Bazemore lifted his chair out from under him as if he planned to throw it. '*Mr* Boren's views are irrelevant.'

Hilliardson said he fully agreed, and Isaac apologized. Then he asked the woman whether they paid taxes on their house.

'We pay taxes. A *lot*.'

'What do you think of the public schools that you pay all those taxes to support? Think they do a pretty good job?' (One of the seated jurors was a junior high principal.) 'A rotten job?'

'They're okay, I guess . . .'

Isaac: 'Do your children attend the public schools?'

'My oldest boy's in college.'

'May he thrive there, God willing. How about the other three?'

'CFA.'

'Pardon?'

'They go to CFA.'

Isaac appeared suddenly to remember what that was. 'Ah. Right, that's Christian Family Academy, that's a *private* school, run by the Christian Family organization, yes, yes. Mr Brodie Cheek is chairman of your board there, I believe . . . Ah . . .' He scratched thoughtfully at his gorgeous white hair. 'Tuition there's, let's see, I believe it's thirty-eight hundred dollars a year, isn't it, around that? Times three, that's, gosh, that's eleven thousand, four hundred dollars a year! Every year! Plus a boy in college! Goodness, Mrs Boren, no wonder you and your husband have to work so hard! That's quite a financial burden.'

Her chin pulled into her neck and locked. 'It's important to my husband that our kids get a good education.'

'You think our Hillston public schools are that bad, hunh? Any black students at CFA?'

'. . . Not that I know of.'

'Not that Brodie Cheek knows of either, I'm sure. Mrs Boren, George Hall here is a black man, accused of killing a white man. *Deep down*, now, do you feel that fact will have a different effect on how you judge this case, than if, say, he were a white man accused of killing a black?'

She stared at him, then at her hands, then back at him. 'No, I don't, I don't think so, at least I'd try for it not to.'

He looked back at her just as seriously. 'There're statistics proving that in this country if a black's charged with killing a white, he's far more likely to get the death penalty than if he'd been charged with killing another black. In some states, he's *eighty-four times* as likely. That means, there's a whole lot of people in a whole lot of courtrooms not quite so disinterested and fair-minded as they think they are.'

Bazemore waved his pencil in air. 'Your Honour, really! I object to this. Let Mr Rosethorn save his speeches for his summation.'

Hilliardson turned his icy glare on Isaac. 'Counsellor, I assume you plan to challenge this juror?'

Isaac surprised the judge, the DA, me – and probably everybody else – by shaking his head. 'No, sir. No, I don't. The defence happily accepts Loreen Boren. Thank you, ma'am.' He gave her another of his serious nods. She looked very puzzled.

High behind his cherrywood bench, Judge Shirley Hilliardson glanced at his watch, then at Enos Cadmean's eagle clock on the wall. 'As the miracle has occurred, ladies and gentlemen, and we appear to have a jury, and as it is late in the day, we shall postpone selection of the two alternates until tomorrow morning at ten.' And after five minutes of instructions and acidic warnings to the chosen twelve, he adjourned court with a sharp rap of his gavel.

George turned around and spoke to his mother while the deputies were putting the handcuffs back on him. As they moved him towards the side door, two young black men stood up to call

291

out, 'George, hang in there! Take it easy, George!' With a flap of his black sleeves, Hilliardson squinted down at them balefully, then stalked out of the handsome room.

For some reason, Nora Howard frosted me when I perched on the edge of the defence table, waiting for Isaac to finish flirting with the equally frosty Miss Bee Turner, who kept squeezing her fist around the little sprig of silk violets pinned to her blue serge jacket; if they'd been real, they'd have been pulp. I said to Nora, 'Isaac surprised me with Mrs Boren; she sounded unsympathetic to me.'

Nora said, 'Isaac followed my advice in the matter. Excuse me.' And she scooped up her briefcase and left.

Isaac was cooing over the clerk. 'Now, Miss Bee, I know we're driving you stark raving mad, raking through your jury candidates this way, but as Supreme Court Justice Felix Frankfurter wisely reminded us, "The history of liberty has largely been the history of observance of procedural safeguards."'

The plump Miss Turner stabbed a pencil into her tightly wound white curls so sharply it was lucky she missed her skull. Her whole head shook when she spoke. 'Nobody has ever driven me "stark raving" anything, and I don't plan on anybody's ever doing it either, thank you very much, Isaac Rosethorn.' And off she strode – if you can imagine a partridge striding.

'Marvellous woman.' Isaac grinned at me.

'Umm. She appears to hate your guts. What's the matter with Nora?'

'Nora?' He looked around. 'Nothing, why?'

'She appears to hate my guts.'

He stuffed papers sloppily into folders, a few falling to the floor. 'Oh, I don't think so. You have to see a person to hate him, and who's seen you lately? . . . Well, we've got our jury, what do you think?' He waggled his hand. 'Mezzo mezzo?'

Setting aside his oblique remark about my absence – from his life? Nora's life? – I waggled my hand back and asked, 'Mrs Boren?'

'I know. But Nora's got a hunch Mrs Boren's a morally uneasy woman, maybe even repulsed by her husband's racism, if only because it probably goes along with other unharmonious "isms" of his. So we're hoping *Mr* Boren's nastiness may work in our favour.' He shrugged, gazing mournfully at the empty jury box. 'Well, well. Who can say. We did our best. Now, we'll see . . . God, that school principal, Gerd Lindquist? I'd *love* to see him elected foreman.'

I tossed a plastic bag on the table. In it was the wallet that had arrived through the mail this morning in a brown envelope addressed to MANGUM, HILLSTON POLICE DEPT – with no explanation, no return address, and no fingerprints. 'I've got something you might want to look at, Isaac.'

'What's that?'

'Bobby Pym's wallet.'

'AH!'

'Somebody mailed it to me, anonymously. Funny, hunh? Gilchrist steals it from Pym; years later, gives it to Coop Hall. Somebody steals it from Coop; months later, gives it to me. What I'd love to know is who, and why.'

'You're sure it's Pym's?'

'Yep. Driver's licence, Master Card. Interesting piece of paper in there, a list with columns of money pencilled in, and initials beside them.'

Rosethorn's fat paw snatched at the package. 'In here?'

'Don't touch it! The contents are upstairs anyhow. And I'm turning the whole thing over to Bazemore. It's State's evidence.'

'Bazemore! What if he withholds it from me!' The thought made him yank his hair straight up from his scalp.

'He won't. It's not his style. But here . . .' I took an envelope from my jacket. 'Here's a Xerox of the list for now. Never say the kindly, if thoroughly self-serving bread you cast upon the waters of a lonesome little boy has not returned to you many-fold.' He grabbed the thing out of my hand, and read as I talked. 'Appears to be sort of a casual statement about income and outgo – both of them pretty hefty for what looks like only one run of merchandise. I thought you'd be happy to know most of the initials are just the ones you'd expect to see. But I'm not so sure how happy you're going to be about the initials of somebody who maybe got paid for doing something. 'B' (for Bobby) and 'W' (for Winston) get thirty-two hundred and fifty dollars each, and looks like Willie and Purley got twenty-seven hundred dollars each. But look down here, at the bottom. 'Five hundred dollars. G.H.' Counsellor, I can't help but think that G.H. refers to your current client, George Hall.'

The old man's face squinched like a bulldog's, but his moral disdain was not directed at George Hall. 'Five hundred dollars. The lousy cheapskates!' he growled.

*

'No beer. Have a Guinness.' Isaac Rosethorn's voice boomed in at me from his kitchen alcove. 'Anyhow, this Robert Elliot had been a professional executioner for decades. Three hundred and seventy souls he sent out of this world by his own hand. Even became a kind of celebrity, because he got the famous ones – Ruth Snyder. The Lindbergh baby's kidnapper. Sacco and Vanzetti. Anyhow, in the end, he fell apart, riddled with remorse, and spent his last days going around the country preaching against capital punishment.'

I yelled back, 'Remorse about what? That he'd killed *innocent* people. Or that he'd killed people period?'

'Both.' Rosethorn waddled in with two brown bottles of Guinness Ale. 'I was reading through the transcripts of the Sacco–Vanzetti trial last night. Tell me who said this: "Prejudice is not a specific violation of the Constitution and does not warrant taking jurisdiction away from the state." '

'I have no idea.'

'Chief Justice Oliver Wendell Holmes, that's who. The great man Holmes! Denying that the judge's clear bias in the Sacco–Vanzetti trial was grounds for a reversal. It's enough to make you vomit, isn't it?'

'Not really. Not as much as this egg roll. How long has it been lying here in this ashtray? Jesus!' I was cleaning debris from the floor of his Piedmont Hotel suite, a place that certainly had nothing to offer architecturally except that it looked out over Hillston's skyline – or would have if Isaac had ever washed the smoke stains off the windows. I could see a few smudged stars, the hulking back of Haver Tobacco Company, and down below, the neon locomotive on the Silver Comet Bar.

The fat old lawyer flopped down on his bed in a rising mist of dust motes, and sipped at his ale. 'Because that's the problem, isn't it? Hell, I know perfectly well that a *homely* person doesn't have half the chance in court that a good-looking one has.'

I said, 'Why do you keep expecting life to be fair?'

'I don't. But I do have a perverse hope that *Law* could be fair.' His arm reached across the silver-framed photograph of Edith Keene, a dark-complexioned girl in her twenties, whose eyes looked smart and whose mouth looked scared. He pulled the chain on his bedside lamp. 'I'm with old Earl Warren, when he threw out "separate but equal," the question always has to be, is it – in the actual reality of its enforcement – *fair*?'

Isaac had apparently settled in for a 'talk,' of the sort we had been having together for a lot of years, the sort he much preferred to other social entertainment – he had no television, and I'd never heard him mention going to a concert, a ball game, or a movie. After court tonight, I'd given him a ride home, then come up 'just for a second,' because he'd wanted to talk. He'd already said, 'Let's order up some Chinese,' and I'd already said, 'Maybe another time.'

But listening to him now, I realized it had been a long while since I'd sat in his crammed, messy rooms, and 'talked.' I'd grown up and got too busy for long conversations with Isaac Rosethorn. And thinking about this, I realized that back when I was a boy (when this congestion of law briefs, bird's nests, stamps, pottery shards, dried leaves, and mounted insects had all glittered in my eyes like Aladdin's cave), that back then, this man had never once said he didn't have time for me. He was never too busy to say, 'Let's us order in some Chinese food' – when both the notion of 'ordering in' and the strange food itself were irresistibly exotic to me – 'and you and I'll sit and have us a discussion, Slim.'

I looked over at him lying on the bed now, fat, rumpled holes in his socks, his old plaid bathrobe bunched around his worn baggy trousers. His face was *old*. Not just the jowls, the pouches under the sad spaniel eyes, but really *old*. When had it got that way? Had he always had those discoloured spots on his cheeks and hands? Had his hair been that white when I met him? Hadn't it been grey? I couldn't even remember.

On the day I graduated from Hillston High School, three large crates arrived UPS at our duplex in East Hillston. They were from Isaac, and they were filled with books. Four hundred and thirty-eight books, on all kinds of subjects, that he'd picked out himself, and that I was sure he'd already read himself. The card that came with them was scrawled in his large, tilted upward script.

Cuddy. Congratulations. Being valedictorian, you already know, I bet, that the word *educate* means 'to lead out.' Here in these cartons are a few scouts for the trip. Let it be a long, happy one. Keep going, keep going, beyond the hills. There are no edges where the world ends. Keep going, and you'll come back home a man who can then lead others out, a few steps further from the night.

Your friend, Isaac Rosethorn.

I wonder if he believes I've become that man. I know he's proud of the work I've got so busy at that I never noticed when his hair turned white. I know that had he not been in my life, I might never have travelled into any hills at all, much less beyond them.

Sitting back down in the pockmarked armchair, I said, 'Hey, Isaac. I'm hungry. How about we call Buddha's Garden? Shrimp with lobster sauce? And some cashew chicken, a quart of won ton, and spareribs?'

'I thought you had to go.'

'I decided I didn't. What's the point of being chief, if you can't decide you don't have to show up?'

'And egg rolls,' he smiled. 'Call it in. Nine six five, two two one one.'

I called it in. Then I said, 'Well, Isaac, look at it the other way. We did get rid of "separate but equal." We do keep hedging the law in *towards* fairness, don't we?'

Isaac grinned happily. '*Ah!* Now he lectures *me* with wisdom I had to prise into his calcified skull with the wedge of bribery. An Almond Joy here. An illicit sip of beer there.' He began patting aimlessly around the pillows and on the bedside table. I tossed him the pack of Chesterfields I spotted under the long, littered desk. As he searched for an unbroken cigarette, he said, 'Yes. We hedge law in. But the hedges don't always last. Like the one stopping the death penalty. Because it's people that plant hedges, and people that rip them out.' He squirmed around, patting some more, and I found a matchbook and threw that at him too. Smoke blew to the ceiling, ashes floated on to his chest. 'I *know* Bazemore's going to wave that "malice aforethought, appreciable time" flag in the jury's face. If George had to do it, I just wish to hell he'd shot Pym the second he grabbed the gun out of his hand.' Isaac wiggled himself slowly off the bed, and shuffled towards his desk. 'Now where's that damn pad!' Watching him riffle through papers on his heaped desk, I noticed a little tremor in his hands I hadn't seen before. 'Shirley Hilliardson on the bench. Interesting. Ah! No, that's not it. All right, here we are.' Holding the legal pad, he started patting his pockets.

I picked up his bifocals beside the telephone, handed them to him, and he ran his plump finger down the page. 'Blah-blah-blah-blah-blah. Okay. This is Hilliardson: "From the use of a deadly weapon, the law presumes malice but *not premeditation*. Premeditation and deliberation are questions of fact, not law."

Okay. Blah-blah-blah-blah . . . "It is *the duty not of the judge, but of the jury alone to determine whether the homicide was of the first or second degree.*"' The old lawyer pushed his glasses down his nose, and frowned at me. 'Say, God help me, I don't get the acquittal, and we go to the sentencing phase. Well, I'm going to hand Shirley Hilliardson his own instructions, and he's going to tell my jury, they don't *have* to send George to the gas chamber.'

'They don't have to. But they can if they want to. Can you stop them from wanting to?'

Isaac looked at the blackboard on which he's already scrawled circles around the names of the twelve chosen jurors. 'I just have to make *one* of them not want to, not want to so absolutely that no amount of bullying or pleading by the others can change his mind . . . Or her mind. I think I can.'

I sat forward in the chair. 'Isaac, tell me. Was George involved in the smuggling?'

The old man stared at me thoughtfully. 'He knew about the smuggling, yes. He knew Pym and Russell, yes.'

'Why didn't he testify about it? Will you tell me?'

'. . . All right.' His wide spottled hand rubbed across his face. 'All right . . . George kept quiet because he believed he was protecting his family . . . Your former colleague Winston Russell had got to George pretty quickly after the shooting, and convinced him – I think we can imagine how convincing Mr Russell could be – that if George let any word get out about what they'd been up to, that it'd just make things worse for him at the trial.' Isaac limped over to his window, and looked down at Hillston. 'Maybe it would have. But more important – and, believe me, it was stressed again and again to George at the time of the trial, and by messages given him on Death Row, when Winston was in Dollard – more important was, if George didn't keep absolutely silent, Winston said he would kill someone in his family. His mother, his kid brother – Cooper . . . That's why.'

I stood up. 'Awh, Jesus Christ. And George went along with that?!'

Isaac's long sigh lifted his hands across the old bathrobe. 'As we discovered, George was quite right to believe it wasn't an idle threat . . . God help us.' He turned back to me. 'The point is that he believed the threat, and he faithfully, I'd say, frankly, he *nobly* kept his part of the bargain. And even after Cooper involved himself actively in the case, and brought me into it, George refused to talk to me, or to Cooper, about anything to do with the Pym shooting. The night before he was scheduled to die, he didn't talk! I didn't find this out until I got back from Delaware. When George was asking to see me. After Cooper was killed.'

'You believe all this?'

'Yes. I believe he was willing to die to protect his family. I believe he shot Pym to protect himself.' He looked at the names on the blackboard. 'All I need is for the jury to believe it too.'

It was midnight before I left the Piedmont Hotel. Isaac didn't spend the whole evening discussing the trial, just most of the evening. But he also talked about Captain John Smith's changing views on Indians, about the current situation in the Middle East, about the Dead Sea Scrolls, and the life span of the male silk moth (six days, all of which time it spends looking for mates – doesn't ever even stop to eat a single meal).

Maybe it was the *carpe diem* determination of the silk moth that led him suddenly to ask, as we poked with chopsticks for the last bits of shrimp and pea pods clinging to the sides of the white cartons, if he could 'ask a personal question.' I said, 'Sure.'

Leaning back in his old leather reading chair, he rubbed his paper napkin around his mouth. 'When are you going to get married, Cuddy?'

'When are *you*? I've already been married once. I've already tried to get married a second time; the engagement ring's still in the drawer with my socks. It's your turn.'

'I'm in the grave to my knees, whom should I marry? But you, you've got half your life left, God willing. You want to spend it with an empty bed, a lonely breakfast, and a wall of books? You want to end up like me?' He waved his arms around the musty room. It was a good argument.

I gave him a chance at the last sparerib, but he passed on it. 'Whom should *I* marry, Isaac? There's Miss Bee, but I know for a fact she's been in love with you for forty years. Got any other candidates?'

He brushed egg roll crumbs off his robe as he leaned over to me, his deep brown eyes warm and bright as dark candles. 'Yes. I do.'

'Who?'

'Nora Howard.'

'Aww, Lord.' I stood up, broad-stepped a stack of law journals

298

and headed for the kitchen. 'I had a feeling you were going to say that.'

'You had a feeling for a reason,' he shouted after me.

'Yeah? Listen, I don't even know Nora, and she doesn't know me.'

'After all these months how can you—'

'Furthermore, she doesn't even much *like* me.'

'Not true!'

I came back with a trash can and began dumping the food cartons in it. 'Oh really? She tell you otherwise? . . . Listen, just because I don't blab out my private life to you, doesn't mean I don't have one.'

'Wait! Don't throw away that egg roll.'

'Right, let's drop it here under the chair to rot.'

'What are you getting so angry about, Slim? . . . Tell me about this private life. Are you marrying somebody else?'

'Jesus, Isaac. No, I'm not marrying "somebody else."' I shoved the unused little packages of cookies and tea bags down on top of the cartons.

'Why not?'

I don't know what made me blurt out the truth, but I did. 'Because she's already married, okay? Okay?!'

'Ahh.' He relit a half-smoked cigarette, and stared at me a while. '. . . I'm sorry.'

'Right.' Grabbing the bottle of ale, I flung myself back in the old chair.

Isaac shifted his glance to the window behind me. '. . . And I imagine she feels it would not be . . . possible for her to leave her husband . . . under the circumstances.'

I glared at him. 'What do you mean by that?'

'I mean, I'm very sorry, Slim. I wish you were happy.'

Had he seen me with Lee? Yes, okay, a couple of times, but only at things like the reception after Coop's memorial service. Had somebody been talking about us? Maybe he knew Edwina Sunderland. Maybe Nora had seen Lee on one of the (very infrequent) occasions she'd come to my apartment. Or, maybe he hadn't meant anything at all by 'under the circumstances.' We both sat with our thoughts a while, but he could always outlast me. Finally I said, 'It's a very complicated – and delicate – situation. If someone's said something to you, I wish you'd let me know.'

His sigh sounded like an old lion's. 'I've known you since you were nine. It was this very room you sat in, eighteen years old, biting your mouth raw so you wouldn't cry, the first time you let your heart get broken. *Over the same damn thing.*'

'Okay, okay.'

'So don't you ask me "if someone's said something to you." Do I need to be *told* who you are, after all these years? Because, God help you, you apparently have *not altered one iota*. She won't leave Brookside, don't you know that?'

'It's none of your business!'

'Well, well, you're right. Ah, who knows . . . Certainly not an old shrivelled celibate like me. So I'll trust Juvenal: "Never does nature say one thing and wisdom another." If that's how you feel, Slim, that's how you feel.' He pulled himself out of his chair, limped over, and patted me on the knee. 'Now ask *me* a personal question. Come on . . .'

I smiled up at him. 'How old are you?'

'That's it? That's not an interesting question. I'm sixty-eight, or -six, or something. That's not personal.'

And it wasn't the question I'd planned to ask. I was finally going to ask Isaac what had ever happened between him and Edith Keene. But I decided I didn't have the heart to hear the answer.

Chapter 17

On my way out of the Municipal Building the next afternoon, I cracked open the court doors to check on the trial. Mitchell Bazemore was sermonizing his way through his opening statement. Stroking his Phi Beta Kappa talisman, he paced the jury box like a preacher too fervent to stand still behind his pulpit. 'The burden of proof is on the *State*, ladies and gentlemen, and in the name of our good state, I am *proud* to accept that burden. I honour that burden, because our Forefathers placed it upon me to *protect the innocent*. Unless the State establishes by an unbreakable chain of hard factual links, every charge we've brought against the defendant George Hall, we have not *proven* him guilty, and you are required to find him innocent. And that is one of the precious glories of the American system, and I cherish it as much as I'm sure you all do.

'But if we do establish the charges beyond a *reasonable* doubt – and, now, that doesn't mean beyond *any* doubt, or a *possible* doubt, but a *reasonable* doubt – then we have proved George Hall guilty. And *then* your duty – your duty to the victim, to the victim's family, your duty to the great society in which we all live; your duty to the *State* . . .' (Mitch pointed at the flag and the seal now, just like he always did.) 'Because, members of the jury, you *are* the State – your duty is to find George Hall guilty as charged, of murder in the first degree.'

He gave each row a stern gaze to be sure they'd got the message. 'Ladies and gentlemen. The State can and will prove during the course of this trial that on the night in question, George Hall did wilfully and with malice aforethought pursue

Police Officer Robert Pym, Jr with a deadly weapon – and a thirty-eight-calibre Smith and Wesson revolver is a very deadly weapon. That he did so with the deliberate intention of firing this revolver at Officer Pym. That he did in fact deliberately shoot and did in fact deliberately *kill* Officer Pym. That he killed him after a clear opportunity maturely and meaningfully to reflect on what he was doing. This was no accident. This was not negligence, or diminished capacity, or irresistible impulse. This was cool-headed, cold-hearted murder.'

Bazemore turned and shook a scornful finger at Isaac Rosethorn who was making a great show of scribbling away on a pad as if he were refuting every word out of the DA's mouth (he was probably writing a letter). 'The defence here,' sneered Bazemore, 'will try to persuade you that Officer Pym "provoked" George Hall. And no doubt Mr Rose . . . thorn here is also going to try to tell you that Officer Pym was no shining knight, but a corrupt man, a cruel man, even a criminal.'

Isaac stood up, leaned to the jury, and shook his head yes in a broad pantomime of eagerness. Several of them smiled. Bazemore whipped around at the defence table, where Isaac quickly dropped his pencil and pretended to be picking it up.

'Even so!' The DA did a snappy about-face, and stared down the jury. 'Even so! Even if Bobby Pym was an *awful* man, even if he flew into a heat of passion that night, and behaved in an inflammatory way towards the defendant, remember, ladies and gentlemen, Bobby Pym is not on trial here. Bobby Pym is dead. He's dead because George Hall murdered him. Because George Hall *chose* to follow him outside Smoke's Bar, and *chose* to shoot him down in cold blood. He made a *choice*.' Bazemore paused, contemplatively. He had the jury listening hard, and knew it. His voice hoarsened with honesty. 'We all get provoked sometimes.' He looked with sorrow at the older black man on the front row of the jury. 'We've all been treated badly, maybe been treated with the most painful unfairness, at some time or other in our lives . . . 'Head shaking, his voice lifted. 'But we *don't* all turn to *murder* as our answer. We don't all choose the ways of the *jungle*, the ways of an animal, the ways—'

I left Mitch in full stride, walked outside, and headed down Main Street. He had another good twenty minutes to go on his Murder One Speech. They wouldn't get to my testimony in the hour left before Hilliardson adjourned for the day. When the DA wound down, Isaac would ask to defer the defence's opening statement until after the State rested its case. He always asked to defer. Then Bazemore would begin calling his standard ground-work witnesses that always bored everybody: Coroner – yes, Pym died of a gunshot wound to the head, etc., etc.; UH surgeon – yes, I removed a bullet from Pym's skull etc. etc.; ballistics – yes, the bullet taken from Pym's skull was fired from the revolver registered to Pym. Is this the gun? Yes, it is. The State would like to place it in evidence as Exhibit A. And so on until the prosecution had made it inescapably clear that there was a body; the body had been shot; the body had been shot with Exhibit A. By whom, and whatever for, came later.

Outside, it was one of those clean, breezy, blue April days that gives spring its great reputation. The sky bright, the air sweet-smelling, the leaves a sharp new green, it was one of those days that made even Hillston look *planned*. Every little spot of civic earth left uncemented was wildly sending up flowers, gaudy red and orange tulips, whole pink hedges of azalea and rhododendron, buttery yellow walls of jessamine vines. I pulled off my tweed jacket, rolled up my shirt sleeves, took in a deep breath of North Carolina at its best, and started the first walk I'd taken downtown in a long time. I was back on the beat, you might say, checking out my city. It was something I'd done regularly in the first months after I'd been appointed chief of HPD, when I was restructuring the department.

Back then, I'd been just what *Newsweek* reported: 'Indefatigable.' I'd drive around in the middle of the night posting notices on different shop fronts and in isolated areas ('A robbery is now in progress at this store'; 'A rape is now in progress in this alley'). Officers were supposed to call in to headquarters as soon as they spotted one of these simulation notices. I got complaints about 'playing games,' but my game did put a stop to the old-style tour of duty favoured by cops like Winston Russell; the kind where you wile away the hours snoozing in the patrol car, or strolling the safer streets, cadging free drinks, meals, and sex from civilians. I'd also drive around in the middle of the day, spot-checking whether officers were where they were supposed to be; or I'd follow radio calls to see how quickly a squad car responded, or how quickly the backup arrived if an officer asked for one, particularly a female officer, because Nancy White had consistently complained about 'macho pigs' being slow to respond when she radioed for assistance. And she was right; they were stalling. I fired one of them, and scared another one (Purley

303

Newsome) into at least a façade of fair play. Yep, I was a holy terror in those early months. A lot of people didn't like me. A lot still don't. But not many of those still work at HPD.

On my walk, I saw Officer Brenda Moore at an intersection, kindly giving directions to a driver with Arizona plates. I saw Officer Titus Baker checking the lock on a ladies' dress shop that was closed for renovations while being transformed into 'Banana Republic, Arriving Here Soon.' Everybody on the streets today looked cheerful, friendly, and law-abiding, like they were extras in the opening scene of some 1950s movie, just before the innocent people of Happytown, USA, look up and see monster-sized cockroaches from outer space crawling over the tops of their nicest buildings.

At the corner of Main and Cadmean streets, next to an elegant wine store, Hillstonians sat on white slatted chairs under sidewalk umbrellas, enjoying capucchinos and italian ice creams. The new green-and-white awning said GIORGIO's. Three years ago, there'd been metal stools crammed along a plastic lunch counter, and outside a plywood sign saying GEORGIA'S PIZZAS. Upscale everywhere – the Song of the New South.

Somebody called to me as I walked past.

It was Father Paul Madison, who wore his black collar, seated next to Lee Haver Brookside, who wore a light rose silk dress, with a loose dark rose jacket. Seeing her when I was *expecting* to was jolt enough on the heart and knees; coming across her like this, before I could get my system prepared, was more like having a live power line drop out of the blue and land on your neck. Like old Patsy Cline said, 'You walk by, and I fall to pieces.' Of course, it didn't show; that's the amazing thing about the heart – it can carry on like a maniac, while the rest of you is politely shaking hands.

Lee's purse and shoes matched the rose jacket, and I'm sure none of them had been bought anywhere near Hillston, even at its boutique best. It wasn't that she looked like she didn't belong in Hillston, because she always looked like she belonged wherever she was. But she could have just as easily been sitting in a café in Milan, or Paris, or one of the other places where I'd imagined running into her in the past, when I'd walked by handsome restaurants, hearing foreign laughter inside.

'Hello there,' she said now, and let go of my hand.

I hadn't seen Lee for the past two weeks. For one of them, she'd gone to visit her stepsister in Palm Beach. Then four days ago, she hadn't shown up for what was supposed to have been our first night in 'our own place.' In March I'd read an ad in the paper for a 'waterfront retreat, a steal at $79,900. Privacy, and a great view.' It turned out to be on the unfashionable, northwest tip of Pine Hills Lake, where nobody much went, and where it wasn't easy to go, since the access road looked like no one had touched it since the Shocco Indians left town. The house was an old, brown-shingled cabin with a boarded-up stone fireplace, an ugly dropped ceiling, tacky pineboard walls, and a rickety open porch built out over the water's edge. No insulation, no electricity, no phone. I loved it. I bought it – for $71,500 – all my CDs down, and the rest on that thirty-year easy monthly payment plan. Lee loved the house too, and whenever we'd take a drive now, we'd bring it a present. Some Sundays I went there alone, and worked on ripping out the fake ceiling and panelling. But then the first time we'd arranged to stay the whole night there together, she hadn't come. There'd been a message on my machine back at River Rise when I gave up at five A.M. and drove home. 'Cuddy, I'm sorry. Andy didn't go! He's downstairs. They cancelled all flights to New York. A blizzard. I'm *sorry*. I love you. Bye. Dammit!'

'Join us, Cuddy,' said Paul Madison in high spirits. God knows what charitable scheme he'd been hitting Lee up for now. Equipment for the day-care centre? New cutlery for the soup kitchen? Maybe a dozen doctors for his Cadmean Convalescent Home? 'No, no, come on. Sit down. How *are* you? Have some coffee.' The two of them had sipped their way through their minuscule espressos, and were waiting for refills. I said I was in a rush. Lee smiled at me, and I sat down.

Giorgio's young waiter passed by looking like the Philip Morris bellhop. I told him, '*Scusi. Vorrei una tazza grande di caffè americano, prego.*' Scowling, he looked to the priest for help.

Paul said, 'The Rio Grande belongs to Americans?'

Lee smiled at me.

I said, 'Y'all carry American coffee in great big cups, then bring me one . . .' He slouched off. 'How have you been, Lee, nice to see you again. Looks like spring is definitely claiming the territory.'

She said, 'Nice to see *you*, Cuddy. It's been a while. Have you seen Edwina Sunderland lately? I've been so busy with the campaign and . . .'

We kept this gibberish up for five minutes, each trying not to

305

look at the other. Then Paul talked about Bubba Percy's expose of the 'House of Lords.' Lee said Andy was disgusted to think such a racist club could have existed into the '60s at Haver University. I said, what made them think it wasn't still holding secret meetings in some fret house right now in the '80s? The breeze fluttered the silk sleeves of her blouse, and the loosened gold hair at the nape of her neck. Her finger traced circles around the dark blue rim of the espresso cup.

'Cuddy, you're a damn recluse. I've missed you,' said Paul, completely unaware that in 'three's a crowd,' he was 'three.' 'You were even skipping basketball games, and that just isn't you. He's a wild man on the court, Lee.'

'Is he?' smiled Lee. 'He always looks so .. calm.' Her calf brushed slowly against my trouser leg.

'Cuddy calm?' Paul laughed. 'He's tense as a bridge cable, always has been.'

'Really?' smiled Lee.

I finished my coffee, and made myself stand up. 'Look, y'all, I'm already late. Nice to see you again, Lee. Paul, take it easy.' I turned back. 'Oh. Gilchrist come home?'

Paul shook his shock of pale bangs. 'No. I've been asking around. Pete Zaslo said he hadn't seen Billy since he called me to come get him the last time he passed out at the Comet.'

'Well, I told you and Isaac to let me lock him up until the trial.'

With a sad sigh, Paul tugged at his collar. 'Billy said he'd go crazy if you did. He promised me he'd stay sober. He was doing so *great*.'

'Ah well, promises.' I said good-bye again, put down a dollar fifty for my American coffee, and left.

I hadn't wanted to mention to Lee that my appointment was just around the corner, in the nice glass-fronted first floor of an office building on Haver Avenue. The glass front was covered with those Carolina blue posters with Lee's husband's picture on them, and all the way across the top of the glass ran a red-white-and-blue banner that said, 'DEMOCRATIC HEADQUARTERS. BROOKSIDE FOR GOVERNOR.' Inside, there were at least a dozen desks, with phones and computers. Young men and young women sat at the desks, staring at their screens, or talking on their phones, or stuffing envelopes. The whole back wall was covered with a multipanel photo-mural of Andy photographs. Andy amazingly poised in air, about to catch a football, with a hapless moil of pursuers in the mud below. Andy grinning from the cockpit of an F-4C Phantom fighter plane. Andy solemn in military dress at the White House receiving the Medal of Honor. Andy intense in Aran Island sweater, at a work session at Camp David with a lot of faces everybody would recognize. Andy energetic in hard-hat, shooting the breeze with construction workers while watching the new Haver University Medical Research Center go up. Andy aglow in shirt sleeves and tie, leaning down from an outdoors platform, shaking the eagerly upstretched hands of quite a press of admiring voters, two-thirds of them women. Andy noble in a suit, receiving a standing ovation from blacks of all ages after the Cooper Hall speech.

I said to the pretty girl at the first desk, 'Looks like you've got the whole spectrum covered – touchdown for the right, Coop Hall for the left.'

She looked up from a hardcover copy of *Lake Wobegon Days*, and smiled the way you would at someone speaking Swahili at you with a friendly expression. I didn't bother to translate for her. She put her finger in her book and said, 'Can I help you?'

I didn't bother to correct her grammar either. 'Jack Molina's expecting me. He here?'

She pointed at a hallway. 'Back there, out through the double doors, down the hall, then take a right. One-o-one. I think Andy's with him.'

She didn't even ask for my name. I could have had enough gelignite under my jacket to blow 101 back through the hall and into that photo-mural. Yeah, like Molina said, 'Good security.'

Andy wasn't, however, back there. From the other side of the closed door to 101 came two extremely angry voices. One I knew belonged to Jack Molina; the other one I deduced pretty quickly belonged to his wife, Debbie. She was saying, or trying to say between sobs, 'I don't care. At this point, I don't care!'

'I called *four times*.'

'I *was at the store!* Look! If you want a divorce, then go get a divorce! Just stop *threatening* me, Jack. Just stop it! *I can't stand it month after month!* It's over, but I can't change the past! And if you really want "the truth" so much, okay, I *wouldn't if I could!*'

I heard the sharp loud thunk of something hitting something.

I had my hand on the doorknob when she said, 'Oh for Christ's sake, stop it!' It must have been a wall he'd hit, and not her. If he'd hit her that hard, I would have heard it in her voice.

Jack's voice was like a whip. 'I can't even bear to look at your face. It makes me want to *eradicate* you!'

'*Then leave me! Or let me leave you!*'

'You're the mother of my *children*!'

I decided this wasn't the time to find out why Jack Molina had sent a message that he'd like to talk with me at my earliest convenience. I didn't know what about, but presumably it wasn't about his marital difficulties. I left fast, closing the hall doors behind me. Three things seemed obvious: Jack had known for some time about his wife's affair with Brookside; the affair had ended; that fact had not had much effect on Molina's feelings. I tried to imagine the Brooksides screaming at each other this way: her about Debbie Molina; him about me. I couldn't do it.

Back in the main office, I sat down, shaky, at one of the empty desks for a minute. Near me, some of the volunteers were discussing what sounded like a security nightmare – a huge outdoor rally in Cadmean Stadium. A young black man in jeans and a Haver sweatshirt walked by me on his way out, a package of leaflets under his arm. Then he recognized me, and stopped. 'Mr Mangum? I'm Eric Solomon. From the Hall vigil? I was at *With Liberty and Justice* when the police came about the break-in?' He waited for me to place him, then said, 'First, well, just – that was okay what you did for the Canaan Twelve. The community service sentences. Just wanted to tell you.'

The Canaan Twelve? I hadn't realized they'd named themselves in that leftist numerology style; it sounded like an idea of G. G. Walker's. I said, 'It was nothing I did. Dolores Roche is a good judge. There are a few. Tell the Canaan Twelve from me, will you, I like their Cooper Hall Park.'

He said he'd tell them, then added, 'I read you think an ex-cop killed Coop, but you haven't caught him.'

'Not yet.'

He shifted the leaflets to his other arm. 'Remember what I said about how Coop's answering machine ran out on me, the day he got killed? Did you ever listen to the tape? Because, I was thinking about it again, and—'

'Somebody had already removed that tape; we never found it.'

'Oh! Maybe that's why ... I mean, I was remembering how Coop had this trick he sometimes did. He'd wait till the machine

308

picked up, then he'd answer, and say through the recording, you know, "Hang on, I'm here." And doing that would make the machine tape the whole conversation, if it was something he wanted a record of. He played me a whole talk he had with a Raleigh reporter once. But, anyhow, I wondered if you'd listened to the tape. Just a thought.'

It was a good thought. I thanked him for it, and asked for one of his leaflets. It announced that the Hall Committee and the Progressive Coalition (a Haver student political organization) were co-sponsoring with Trinity Church a public discussion on 'The Klan in Carolina: Pawns of Power?' Speakers would discuss whether the KKK, neo-Nazis, and other packs of white-supremacy lunatics were just that (lunatics), or whether they were the 'manipulated puppets of powerful interests in the state.' (A little of both, had always been my assumption.) Guest speakers would range from Andrew Brookside to a former Grand Dragon who'd got born again and quit the Klan. The moderator would be Professor J. T. Molina himself. The cover of the leaflet was the newspaper photo taken at last October's confrontation at Trinity Church: in it, Coop Hall had his arms out to protect the people behind him (one of them Paul Madison) from the raised sticks of two young hoods in military fatigues.

Eric told me, 'We're expecting a big turnout. Dr Molina says this Grand Dragon guy's going to be on Channel Seven the day before, so that'll stir up more interest. The Carol Cathy Cane show.'

I said, 'I bet she asks him to wear his robe.' Ms Cane had her own programme now, a local talk show along the Oprah Winfrey model. According to Carol's ads, she wasn't afraid to 'ask her celebrities daring, confrontational questions' – like 'Mrs Wollston, are you and the governor *really* as happily married as you want us to think you are?' And, 'Mayor Yarborough, honestly now, haven't you sometimes wished you were born white?' I had no intention of ever appearing on the Carol Cathy Cane show.

Just after Eric left, Dr J. T. Molina himself slammed through the hall doors into the room, and stood there (in his uniform of old chinos and worn-out tweed jacket), deep-breathing, while his eyes, the round glasses glittering, shot from the photo-mural to the desks to me. His wife, Debbie, wasn't with him; either she'd left by another exit or was still in the back office crying. By the time he reached me, he'd got his breath under control, but the large, burning eyes didn't look at all calm. 'You didn't have to come here,' he told me brusquely. 'I was just on my way to you. I thought your sergeant said around five was good. It's ten till.' He looked at his watch. Two of his knuckles were cut open and bleeding.

I said, 'I was in the area, so I dropped by. What's the problem, Professor? Besides the ones I can already predict if you're really planning a rally in Cadmean Stadium.' I figured he was going to say that Brookside had got another threat, or suspected he was being followed again; they'd reported no one suspicious hanging around him since he'd told me about Newsome tailing him, months back. No more anonymous letters had been reported either.

By a painful effort, Molina tried to focus, but sounded rattled. 'Problems with the stadium? Oh, that's all tentative. Mind if we walk somewhere? I'll walk you back to Municipal, okay? Look, I'd like to get out of here.'

I could believe it. But before we reached the thick glass entrance doors, two young volunteers ran over with questions for him. I stepped aside, but I got the impression that they were trying to line up a very famous liberal movie star for this stadium rally. Jack said, 'Tell her people we'll schedule around her. Any date she wants.' The other volunteer wanted to know 'how far to go in Hickory tomorrow.' Jack said, 'If *they* start the razz, wait and see how Andy wants to play it. If nothing goes down from their side, and the crowd's limp, toss in a few, okay?'

Toss in a few what? Cheers? Jokes? Insults? I assumed they weren't talking about *bombs* in front of me. Probably hecklers: If there were no real ones, they'd supply their own, so their man would have something to spark off. Molina's ideological purity didn't seem to interfere with his nuts-and-bolts approach to the campaign, any more than his personal problems interfered with his ideology. He then swept a handful of Brookside brochures into a manila envelope, bit open a Magic Marker, scrawled in large letters across the front, 'First Methodist Church. 1500 Bush St., 9:30, ANTI-NUKES,' and handed it to the volunteer. 'Somebody should be there,' he told the student. 'Try Kim first . . .'

I said, 'Why don't you give that to me? I'm having dinner at Alice MacLeod's in a couple of hours. She said she was going to that meeting.' I took the envelope before they could answer, then said, 'Okay, let's go walk, Professor.'

Jack Molina walked fast. I've been called 'Lincolnesque' as much for my lanky legs as my lofty soul, but I had to damn near trot to keep pace with him. He wasn't in the mood to talk much either. That was okay, because I'd got some disturbing ideas about Molina in my head that needed mulling over. One of them had to do with his handwriting.

When we rushed past Giorgio's, I looked to see if Paul and Lee had left. They had. The waiter quickly turned away before I could hit him with any more of my Italian. (There wasn't much more, but he couldn't know that.) Persisting in sociability, I asked Molina if he'd seen Jordan West lately. He said, 'Not really.' I asked if Brookside had decided yet on a nominee for lieutenant governor. He said, 'I'm not in on that.' Since he'd resigned his teaching position at Haver, I asked what he would do should Brookside lose. He said, 'He won't lose.' Of course, what I was really wondering was why, if Molina both knew of, and was enraged by, his wife's fling with Brookside, he hadn't resigned from the campaign, in which, if anything, he seemed more fervently involved than ever. But I suppose his answer would have been that the dialectic imperative couldn't be bothered with a puny case of adultery, or that, as Bogie summed it up for Ingrid Bergman, the problems of three little people don't amount to a hill of beans in this crazy world. Still, it was clear that, inside, Molina was all twisted up about Andrew Theodore Brookside. Lord knows, I shared the feeling.

In no time, and with naturally none of this discussed, he and I were back at the foot of the Municipal Building. Or I was at the foot. He was halfway up the big stone steps. Suddenly he turned, and sat down, as if that step had been his destination all along. Below, on the sidewalk near the marker to Hillston's war dead, three college-aged picketers circled with 'FREE GEORGE HALL' signs. They shouted greetings at Molina, and he waved both arms at them in the old peace sign. Then – as people swept around us on their way out of the building – he abruptly started talking. 'Look . . . Okay, look, Mangum. The stakes are too high to dick around. I'm going to bare my fucking throat to your teeth here, and just hope I've read you right.' His glittering eyes blazed up at me.

This extraordinary image – from one who'd never struck me as the Jack London type – was unsettling; all I could manage was a shrug as I sat down beside him on the steps. He appeared to take it as confirmation that I didn't plan to sink my incisors in his jugular vein. He said, 'Lewis is very vulnerable on that secret racist college club shit.'

'True,' I agreed. '*Elitist* racism annoys just about everybody.'

'Andy wants to push on it. Drop the tone down a level. If he does, Lewis is going to get down and dirty too.'

I agreed with this also, but added, 'Lewis may not need a shove in order to squat down low.'

If Molina's eyes had actually been lasers, instead of just resembling them, there would have been nothing left of me but ozone. He nodded. 'Okay, that's what I want to talk about.' He moved his gaze to the picketers. 'Let's put it like this. Circumspection and prudence – in private matters, okay? – are not the virtues Andrew Brookside has always . . . valued in the past, as highly as other . . . perhaps more "heroic" virtues. There are possible dangers in such a position.'

Jesus! The man's detachment was downright freakish. Was I completely off the wall about the content of that screaming match I'd just overheard? Had the Molinas really been fighting about something else entirely – maybe her plans to dump family life for a singing career, something like that? No, I didn't believe it.

I smiled agreeably. 'Well, that's true. You don't read much about "prudent heroes" in plumed helmets. Most big heroes are more your hyperhormone type guys. They get a destination in their heads – like, say, Holy Grail, Golden Fleece, Moscow, Moon – and they just whoop and charge straight at it, hacking up the interference on the way. Nope, circumspection wouldn't do, would it?'

He could even smile too. He did so. But then his hand squeezed down on his knee hard, and the cut opened up on one knuckle. He sighed through tightened teeth. 'Okay . . . If Andy's put his ass in a sling, we need to know now. I'm told you asked him if Coop Hall had given him a copy of a videotape in which . . .' He flinched just a bit. 'In which Andy is having sex with a black woman, a call girl.'

Now if he'd just said 'having sex with a call girl,' I might have figured Brookside had told him I'd made this preposterous claim and that it wasn't true, but that, for obvious reasons, he (Molina) wasn't sure he believed Brookside, so he'd come to me. But Mofina had said 'a black woman.' That meant either Brookside had told him what was on the tape. Or, he'd seen the tape himself. Because I'd never mentioned to Brookside the colour of Ms Touraine's pigmentation. Of course, I'd already assumed Brookside was lying – he had a reason to lie, and Hamilton Walker didn't – but I'd only assumed. Molina was confirming it.

Why, was clear from his next questions. 'Do you have direct knowledge of such a tape? Do you know of the existence of any copies? Do you *have* a tape?'

I looked at his penny loafers. It was a little surprising he kept them so highly polished, given the mussed look of the rest of his clothes. I thought a while. I looked at my cordovans. They could use a good shine, not to mention new heels and soles. Finally I sighed. 'Jack, I hear a lot of questions from you. I don't see a lot of throat bared. If we're gonna dicker, let's do like Julian and Andy, let's get down and dirty, okay? So why don't you come on upstairs to my office. There's not enough flesh between me and this stone step.' I headed inside, and he followed me.

The marble lobby was crowded, because the Hall trial had just adjourned for the day. Bubba Percy stood scribbling notes in the open doors, wearing a new baggy linen suit, and a Panama hat. Inside the courtroom I saw Isaac and Nora piling paperwork on Miss Bee Turner. 'What a fucking asshole,' muttered Jack Molina, with a jab of his hand at Percy. 'All of a sudden, he's Zola. *"J'accuse!"'*

'Hey, be grateful. The *Star* flip-flopped and endorsed Brookside, right? You can thank Bubba for that.'

'Coop spent months trying to get Percy to do a piece on George. All he got was a run-around. Then *bam*, Coop's a big dead hero. People magazine runs a piece. The *Times* runs a piece. All of a sudden, Percy acts like he's Cooper Hall's official memorialist. Did you read his thing about Coop in *Harper's*?'

'Bubba had an article in *Harper's*?'

'Oh yeah. "The Day the Sixties Died."'

'You're kidding. Cooper was in elementary school in the sixties.'

'Read the article . . .' He looked at me carefully. 'How's Rosethorn feeling about George's chance this time?'

'Better than last time.' I gave up waiting for the elevator, and led Molina over to the stairwell.

'From everything I hear, Pym was a fucking criminal.'

'Right. But as the DA just told the jury, Pym's not on trial.'

'He will be. I've seen Rosethorn work.'

Up in my office, Molina slammed his back against the wall, and wasted no time returning to the main point. 'First, Coop did not give Andy a tape. That was true. But Coop did tell Andy, when they met that Saturday at the airport, that he had such a tape.'

I settled into my chair, balled up my lunch trash, and tossed it in the wastebasket. 'What you mean is, that's *why* Brookside agreed to meet him. Or let's put it this way: Your candidate had every reason to believe it was possible there might exist such a tape.'

'Yes.' He sucked at his bleeding knuckles. 'Apparently so.'

'So, Jack, how do you come into this . . . imprudence? You set up the meeting?'

He nodded. 'Coop called me after I got home from the prison that night, the night of the reprieve, really late, and he says he has to see Andy. I'd already arranged one meeting between them a few days earlier, about George. That's when Andy agreed to call Wollston with the request for clemency. So now Coop says he wants to warn Andy about something the Lewis campaign was up to.'

Swivelling my chair to the file cabinet, I took out a blank manila envelope, and placed it on my desk. 'When he called, did Coop mention the videotape to you?'

'No. Just that they—'

'Who's they?'

'He never mentioned names, not to me, or to Andy. Just that people working for Lewis were up to something slimy that could do us some heavy damage. I said I'd have Andy call him Saturday morning. I didn't find out they'd actually met that same day until, well, later. But Coop told Andy then that he'd got hold of this tape. He described enough to convince Andy the thing existed.'

'Did he say where this slimy tape was?'

'In a safe place.'

'You knew Cooper pretty well. You worked with him. Where would he put something to keep it safe?'

'I don't know.' He looked at the knuckles; they'd stopped bleeding. '. . . Listen, don't get the idea Andy sent me to talk to you. I'm on my own.'

'I figured as much. Excuse me a second.' I buzzed Zeke at the desk, and told him to ask Etham Foster to come up if convenient. Then I leaned back and said, 'So, Cooper just wanted to "warn" the good guys that the bad guys were playing dirty?'

Molina tightened his arms across his thin chest. 'He also wanted some guarantees from Andy – human services appointments, civil rights steps, that type thing. They talked about the upcoming Winston-Salem speech. I mean, it wasn't like, like Coop was blackmailing Andy. Andy was very impressed by him. I suspect he would have . . .'

'Put him on the team, as they say?'

'Yes. I just don't want you to get any stupid ideas about Coop, or any ideas that Andy had anything to do with his death.'

'You don't want me to get a lot of ideas I hadn't planned on acquiring.' I looked at the photos of Winston Russell and Purley Newsome on my corkboard. 'Brookside couldn't have killed Cooper. He has a very good alibi. But the people who probably did kill him knew where he was because they had followed Brookside to the airport. And possibly one of the reasons they killed Cooper was that he had been talking with Brookside.'

'Those cops you're looking for? Pym's cronies? Were they the people who made the videotape?'

'They were possibly involved.'

His eyes flamed. 'So they were working for Julian Lewis?'

'For him, I don't know. Possibly on his behalf.'

'What's the difference!'

'There's a considerable difference.' I found a black Magic Marker in my drawer. 'All right, just after they meet, Coop is killed, and Brookside never got to see the tape?'

'No.'

I looked up at him. 'How 'bout you, Jack? You see it?'

'Me?' With his back, Molina pushed off from the door, and headed around my desk towards the window. The skin had blanched around his mouth. Swivelling in my chair, I kept my eyes on him. He asked quietly, 'Why do you think that?'

'Well, one reason is because you knew the woman was black.'

He thought about this as he stared out over Hillston, where the late sun was turning the air to gold haze. He said, 'Andy admitted that he had . . . spent a few evenings with this Touraine woman . . . Look, will you tell me how you know about this tape?'

'Sure. The man who gave it to Cooper Hall told me he'd done so. He only gave it to him late that Friday night. Obviously just before Cooper called you.'

'Where did this man get it?'

'Miss Touraine made this gentleman a present of it before she left the country, apparently for an indefinite stay.'

I watched the movement of Molina's eyes as he sat down across from my desk. Then his long thin face so visibly relaxed that I was pretty sure of what I'd been suspecting. He relaxed because he thought I was telling him there was only one tape, and that it had never got to the 'Lewis men.' It had gone from Touraine to Coop. He relaxed because he already knew where Coop's tape was. Because he had it. I said, 'Your commitment to Andrew Brookside is very impressive.'

He took off his glasses, rubbing his nose; unfiltered by glass, the large dark eyes were even more piercing. 'I have no commitment to Andrew Brookside. I have an absolute commitment to social justice in this country.'

'It's Mr Brookside's ass you appear to be trying to extricate from the wringer.'

'Well, I believe you're the one who said, "We use what we have."' He fitted his glasses back on. 'Look, Mangum. It took me a long time to accept but . . . there's not going to be a revolution in America. The thirties proved that. The sixties proved it again. A country where laid-off factory workers are opposed to inheritance taxes, where bankrupt farmers vote for Reagan, isn't headed for a proletariat uprising. The great scam of capitalist democracy has been to trick the poor into believing they *could* be rich. So . . .' He shrugged.

I shrugged too. 'So, if they don't see the chains, they won't shake them off . . .'

'Yeah.' He looked sadly out my window. 'Well . . . we did register a lot of people to vote . . . We did stop a war.'

'Not in time to keep me from getting my boots soggy . . . You know, Andy Brookside said to me once that you didn't like him, Jack, just thought he was better than "more of the same dumb smug thieves."'

'He's right.' His long pale fingers spread out over the chair's arm. He wore a wedding ring. Leaning forward, he shook off whatever he was thinking. 'It's crucial to find these leaks, and try to contain them. Will you tell me the name of the man who gave Coop the tape?'

I shook my head. 'Nope. I will tell you he's a man of circumspection. And political indifference. But that's not going to help you, Jack. That was a copy Coop got. There's an original somewhere.'

His body twitched in the chair. 'How do you know?'

'We think Miss Touraine gave the original to a man named Willie Slidell, who'd set up the video camera in her apartment. Willie Slidell was murdered. We don't know if his killers have the original, or couldn't find it. We don't know if there's only the one copy now, or a dozen.' I opened a packet of cheese crackers. 'I mean, in addition to the copy you took out of Cooper's file box at *With Liberty and Justice*.'

He didn't move a muscle.

After I ate a cracker I added, 'The copy you took when you trashed the office. When you also took the incoming tape out of the answering machine, because you realized Coop had recorded Brookside's Saturday morning call on it, when they talked about that video.'

His hand shook but he pressed it under his arm. 'This is pretty far-out shit, Mangum.'

I cleared papers from the desk edge, and put the manila envelope and black marker in front of him. 'Prove me wrong. Address this thing with the marker. Just write "Mangum. Hillston Police Department."' I handed him the marker. 'Oh, and how about adding the word *atheist* down at the bottom.'

Molina and I looked at each other for a solid minute. Then he said softly, 'Why should I do that?'

'Why shouldn't you?'

He frowned, uncapped the marker, then slowly recapped it. '... Okay.'

I said, 'The thing is, Jack, I'm close to sure Bobby Pym's wallet had been kept in Coop's file box, along with the video. And somehow I figure if an ordinary thief had stolen it, or one of "Pym's cronies," or a goon from the Klan, I just don't think they would have felt so "absolutely committed to social justice" that they would have finally felt compelled to forward that wallet to a policeman who was a good friend of George Hall's lawyer.'

We sat a while in the quiet.

Etham Foster knocked on my door as he was opening it. He had to stoop to walk under the sill. He said, 'Yeah?' His typical greeting. I reached behind me into the jacket I'd hung over my chair back, and pulled out the big envelope I'd taken from the Brookside volunteer, the one on which Molina had scrawled the Methodist Church address. 'Etham, do me a favour.'

'Yeah?'

'Compare this handwriting with the address on the package that Pym's wallet came in? Also try it against the photos of the graffiti on the walls at *With Liberty and Justice*?' I tossed him the envelope, which he slapped down out of the air between his long black thumb and forefinger. 'There's a *TH* and an *IST*. Even a *K*. That enough?'

He said, 'Maybe.' And left. He never appeared to have looked at Jack Molina, but a week from now he could have described him well enough for a police artist to draw his portrait.

I said, 'So, Professor, did you write all those threatening notes to your candidate, or just the last few? Just to keep the interest up?'

Molina had an odd grin on his face. 'You arresting me right now?'

I said, 'Nope. I'm scaring you right now.'

'You pigs never change.' He stood up. 'Listen, Captain, I was at the Chicago convention in 'sixty-eight. I was in Greensboro in 'seventy-nine. Unless you grab that gun on your door hook, and start firing, you got a long way to go before you scare me.'

'Well, Professor. I was in the Tet Offensive in 'sixty-eight. You wanna take it down a tone from there?'

'Touché.' He laughed out loud. Fact is, I kind of admired old Jack. 'Okay,' he said. 'Maybe I ought to mention, for theoretical reasons now, that *I* still pay the rent on the *With Liberty and Justice* office out of my own salary. That file box was Coop's property; so at this point, it's Nomi's property. She's a "close friend" of mine. And, in fact, it was *my* answering machine. So what's it going to be?'

I smiled. 'Oh, we could start with those vague fascist catchalls. Obstructing justice. Withholding evidence. That time-consuming type of stuff. Or . . .' I ate another cracker. 'You could cooperate with the pigs.'

The side of his mouth twitched. 'How could I do that?'

'One, a signed statement telling me the whole story. Even the slimier details. Two, get Mr Brookside to do the same. I won't make them public unless I have to. Three, and I'll stop here for now, help me trap some ex-pigs by leaking a little fiction to the press.'

Molina stuffed his hands in his chinos, and thought it over. 'Trapping ex-pigs has a certain appeal.'

I wiped the cracker crumbs off my desk top. 'I had a feeling it might.'

Chapter 18

An hour later, Jack Molina and I spoke with Justin, who called in the *Star*, and planted the story. Bubba ran it the next day, and the wire picked it up for Sunday papers around the South. The gist was that HPD had picked Purley Newsome as the prime suspect in the murders of Cooper Hall and William Slidell. That we'd done so after one Dr J. T. Molina told us that he and Cooper Hall had been repeatedly threatened by a policeman, now identified as Purley, to stop their protests against the George Hall execution:

> ... According to Lt Justin Savile, head of the Hillston Homicide Division, Dr Molina also claims that only three days before Hall's murder, the suspect, Newsome, forced their car off the road, pointed a gun at Hall through the window, and made verbal threats on their lives ...

We said we could now place Newsome's car in the vicinity at the time and place Cooper Hall was killed. We said, thanks to information provided by an unnamed source, we now had evidence

> pointing to Newsome as the actual trigger-man in the shooting-death of William Slidell, whose body was discovered in the Shocco River last Christmas ...

In other words, we said we were firmly convinced that Police Officer Purley C. Newsome had masterminded both murders, personally carried out both murders, and had organized the smuggling ring that the murders were supposed to cover up. In his statement, Justin theorized that by now Newsome had probably killed his underling Winston Russell too. The Star went on to remind readers that the prime suspect's brother, Otis Newsome, former city comptroller, had hanged himself on December 27. It added that Mrs Claude Newsome, Purley's mother, was devastated by the charges against her only surviving son.

I called Bubba Sunday morning to say thanks. He said, 'I notice you don't ask me to *believe* that turkey-turd, just run it. What are you up to, Mangum? Purley Newsome couldn't mastermind a game of Slapjack. And it just slipped Molina's mind till now that a gun-waving cop had yelled "You're a dead nigger" at his friend a few days before that friend gets shot?! Come on, hey. What's the deal?'

'Ask Molina. He told your reporter the same thing he told us. Why should he lie?'

'Okay, stonewall me. Listen, pal, you could use a friend in the press, but have it your way. You owe me a big one.'

I said, 'I already introduced you to Edwina Sunderland's money. That's a big one. And I'll put in a good word if you ask her to marry you.'

He said, 'Don't think it hasn't crossed my mind.' I told him I was sure it *had*, and hung up.

I trained all day Sunday. I spent the morning out at the Pine Hills cabin, positioning pans under the larger holes in the roof. I spent the afternoon at my River Rise kitchen counter, reading reports, and watching the Shocco River rise closer to Atwater Randolph's untravelled bridge. Martha moped around, turning slow circles on her cushion. The phone kept ringing. Alice called to say Justin had flown to Kentucky to talk to Willie Slidell's wife. Two times, somebody hung up when I answered. Three times Lee called. She said, 'When all of a sudden you walked by Friday, I felt like my heart had stopped. I couldn't breathe.' I said, 'When I got halfway across that street and saw you sitting there with Paul, my legs buckled. I couldn't walk.' We said, in other words, the same ridiculous, true, tin-pan-alley things lovers have always said.

Later, there was a surprise call, from another woman: Professor Briggs Mary Cadmean, whom I had once briefly entertained the notion of marrying. Now I felt like I was talking to a casual acquaintance. Maybe it had always been that way for her. When she said she felt awkward about phoning me, I took some satisfaction in telling her there was absolutely no reason to.

She called to ask about Cooper Hall. And her purpose for doing so finally answered the question of how old Cadmean's home number had got into Cooper Hall's address book. It turned out that, upon Briggs Junior's acceptance of old Cadmean's chauvinist codicil to his will (which we didn't discuss), and her coming home to the inheritance (which we didn't discuss), the lawyers had given her a long letter of instructions dictated, days before his death, by her papa (who clearly intended to go on bossing her around from the grave). Along with, I bet, advice on how to live every minute of the rest of her life, these instructions told Briggs Junior what she ought to do with the Cadmean money. There was a list of proposed contributions that the industrialist hadn't put directly into his will.

She read me the proposal suggesting a bequest to Cooper David Hall of $25,000 'to continue his researching of racial harassment by a secret club at Haver University called the House of Lords.' In his instructions, Cadmean took his time expounding on (which in no way ever meant defending) his rationale: 'I never went to college, but I hold a man's education in high respect. And for young college men of privilege to betray the honour of their native state by acting like a pack of goddamn Gestapo goons, sneaking around to scare decent Negroes and smear their names, is a disgrace to the American way of life I love. Cooper Hall's father, Tim, worked for me at C & W, and he was a good man at his job till his death. I don't say I agree with most of Cooper's ideas, but I believe in a fair chance, and I have given him my help about this research of his, and a few donations to his magazine, because he looks to be a smart industrious boy, loyal to his family, and by his own lights trying to do what's best for the great state of North Carolina. $25,000.'

I said, 'I don't know whether to laugh or cry. It sure sounds like your daddy at the top of his form. Calling a twenty-eight-year-old man "a smart boy," and then leaving him a pile of money to fight racism.'

Briggs Junior said she was equally struck by the fact that her father's respect for the college-educated seemed to be confined entirely to males. Sounded to me like the two of them planned to keep on bickering across the Great Divide. She read a note old Cadmean had scribbled to her in the margin: 'Baby, this one will appeal to a goddamn left-winger like you.'

He'd also added a handwritten PS. 'If this secret club horseshit about Julian Lewis turns out to be true, take an ad and revoke my endorsement of the jerk. Also cancel my contribution (on p. 18, ¶ 2). Give the money to the man he's running against. Unless it's that two-bit Kennedy flyboy Andrew Brookside. I don't like him.'

Now, as Cooper Hall was deceased, Briggs Junior's question was, did I know anyone who was carrying on his work? From the series of House of Lords pieces in the *Star*, it appeared that one Randolph Percy was fighting the good fight, and she'd also read several articles of his on Cooper Hall himself, which led her to think they had been friends. Was this true? On the other hand, she felt reluctant to turn over the bequest to a professional journalist, if in fact there was someone closer to Cooper. She wanted to ask me whom she could talk to so she could discover what *Cooper* would have wanted done with the money.

Despite owing Bubba one, I said, 'Cooper wouldn't want you to give it to Randolph Percy.' I told her to get in touch with Jordan West at Human Services, and Eric Solomon at *With Liberty and Justice*, and with Cooper's mother, Nomi Hall. She said she would and thanked me. Before hanging up, I said I couldn't help but mention I was surprised to hear she'd left her job out West. She said Arizona wasn't the only place that had a sky with stars in it. I agreed she had a point. We both said we'd probably run into each other around Hillston one of these days; neither one of us suggested we pick a time to make it happen.

The rain slapped at my sliders, hard as gravel. I thought about Cooper Hall's showing up at Cadmean's house and asking for a donation to *With Liberty and Justice*. I thought about his playing upon that old ruthless capitalist's squire-of-the-manor paternalism towards his workers and their families. 'I'm Tim Hall's son. He worked for you.' (After all, because my father too had worked Cadmean's line, hadn't Mr C. actually come in person to my mother's funeral; a dazzling tribute, for which my father momentarily forgave him a quarter-century of low pay, long hours, and ruined lungs?) I thought of Cooper in the vaulted dark-panelled rooms of that brick mausoleum, listening to Cadmean's odes to textiles and North Carolina, his two passions – beyond himself and his daughter. Cooper had undoubtedly got into a fight with him about politics, and there was nothing Cadmean liked better than an antler-butting fight. You just never knew what side the old SOB was going to take, because the notion of *principle* never entered his head, unless 'I take care of my own' can be called a principle. With Cadmean, it was all personal. He'd liked Alice MacLeod, and he'd liked the fact that she was Justin's wife, so he'd put money into her state legislature campaign. He hadn't liked the pastor of his own church, so he'd left his house to Trinity Episcopal. And me? He'd liked me, so he'd bullied the City Council into making me chief of police because he'd wanted somebody in Hillston to marry his daughter and keep her from leaving town, and at the time I'd wanted the same thing.

Now apparently he hadn't liked what he'd heard about the Haver House of Lords. So his death had come just in time for Haver University – because he might have revoked that new Textiles Institute. And just in time for Julian Lewis and Andy Brookside both – because he didn't like either of them, and for half a century, it had been hard to carry the Piedmont unless Briggs Monmouth Cadmean was carrying you, and Mr C. only carried folks he liked.

I picked up the phone to see if Isaac was across the hall at Nora Howard's, so I could tell them about Cooper's inheritance. Nobody answered. I heated a can of chili, did my laundry, tried to get Martha to eat something, did my dishes, called again. Nobody answered. I called Bubba Percy back, and asked him to admit to me that Bunny Randolph (Atwater's middle-aged son) was the source behind his pieces on the House of Lords – in addition, of course, to what he'd ripped off from Cooper's article. I reminded him I was the one who'd given him Bunny's name in the first place, when he was supposed to find out for *me* some connection to Hall, and that he'd stalled me about it for months. I said I now figured it had been Cadmean who'd introduced Cooper to Bunny Randolph.

'Assume you're right,' said Bubba coyly.

And that Bunny had blabbed the old college dirt to Cooper (either because he hadn't liked Julian Lewis when they'd been in the House of Lords at Haver together; or because he hated his father, Atwater, a big Lewis supporter, for keeping him on the dole in Southern Pines).

Bubba said, 'Assume you're right.'

'So Bunny Randolph is feeding you information.'

Bubba said, 'I don't reveal my sources . . . Now stop bugging me, Mangum. I've got a girl here, halfway to the sack.'

I said, 'I'm tempted to send over a squad car to check her age. Or is it Edwina?'

'Nah, it's your mother. She's a wild woman. Catch you later, pig.' He made a rooting noise into the phone, and hung up. I wondered which was more likely – that he knew my mother was dead, or didn't.

Under a coverlet of loose newspapers, I fell asleep on my denim couch, listening to Dinah Washington, and when I woke up, the clouds were still black with rain. When I went out in the hall and knocked at Nora's door, a teenaged girl identified herself as the baby-sitter; to which phrase, the ten-year-old Laura strenuously objected. The sitter added that Nora was out. Laura, standing behind her, said, 'Out on a date.'

'It's not a date,' insisted her little brother Brian, darting forward and menacing her with a rubber tomahawk.

'You're a geek,' Laura informed him, and he ran away whooping down the hall, 'Geek, geek, geek.' The baby-sitter chased after him.

I said, 'Laura, tell your mom I dropped by, okay?'

'She'll be out really really late,' predicted Nora's daughter. 'Can we go get Martha Mitchell and play with her?'

'Oh, we ought to let her sleep, how 'bout? She's not feeling too well.'

The girl looked at me with a sharp suspicion. 'Is Martha Mitchell going to die?'

'Well, in time she will. It's natural. She's a pretty old dog.'

Laura frowned. 'My dad wasn't old, but he died.'

'I know . . . You must miss him a lot.'

'I do. But sometimes I can't remember.'

I leaned down to hug her, and her small thin arms brushed against my neck. She squeezed them around me hard for a second, then she quickly let go, and ran to help the sitter herd her brother home.

Downtown across the street from the Municipal Building was the sheriff's office and the county jail. Sheriff Reese and I were not friends, but he had finally stopped calling me 'kiddo,' stopped reminding me that *he'd* been elected to office for 'forty years running,' stopped treating the city police like a bench of second-string substitutes there to back up the county team. The sheriff still thought of Hillston as a little warehouse town in the middle of his big farming county. He hadn't figured out yet that everybody in the county had moved into the city, and so had a fast stream of white-collar Yankees. But over the years Reese and I had learned to save our guns for the big battles; day-to-day, we were perfectly cordial. And so his deputy went so far as to stand up and suck in his gut when I dropped by the jail Sunday night. There was no objection at all to my having a talk with the prisoner George Hall, even at this late hour. With a protective squeeze of the heavy .357 that dragged his belt down low on his hips, the deputy even invited me to walk back with him to get Hall. I followed him through the steel door, down the dark corridor and into the smell of urine and stale sweat. There were fourteen men in the eight cells, most of them were young and black, some of them were snoring, one had a harmonica, one sat hunched in a corner talking to himself. George Hall stood in a T-shirt and cotton pants, leaning his arms out through the bars, looking out at the window down at the end of the corridor.

The deputy shook the keys in his face and said, 'George, Captain Mangum from HPD's here to see you. You wanna step away, and I'll unlock you.'

George turned his eyes to me. I'd only been this close to him twice before – once at his brother's funeral, once that night on the sidewalk outside Smoke's Bar. In fact, other than those brief minutes, and from a distance at the trials, I had never been around George Hall. Now I noticed little traces of Cooper in his features. I said, 'You mind a few minutes' talk, George?'

Cooper would have probably said, 'About what?' or 'Do I have a choice?' or 'What's a few minutes to me?' All George said was, 'No, I don't mind.' And he pushed back from the cell door with arms so thickly muscled, they pressed the sides of the bars as they slid away. He took a pair of glasses from his shirt pocket, put them on, then waited quietly for the deputy to slide open the steel door.

As soon as we sat down in the cramped, dingy 'conference room,' George lit an unfiltered Camel cigarette; I suppose if the government keeps telling you they're going to gas you to death in two months, or two weeks, or two days, on this date, or that date, then the government's warnings about tobacco don't have much effect. Nor do you lose track of time – as he smoked, he sat watching the black arrow of the minute hand click up the face of the oak regulator clock that was on the wall beside the NO SMOKING, NO BEVERAGES sign. Opening the bag I'd brought, I set out two coffees and four glazed doughnuts.

George was thirty-five. His hair was grey. His brother had

325

been murdered; he'd been in Vietnam for two years, and on Death Row for seven; I'd say that was enough to do it. He sat there smoking while I offered my sympathy about Cooper, and asked if Reese was treating him all right, and told him Isaac had told me how Russell had threatened him after the Pym shooting. He kept his eyes on mine, he replied politely and succinctly, he drank the coffee, ate a doughnut, and showed not the slightest interest in whether I spoke or not. Finally I said, 'And Isaac says he's talked to you about our investigations. That thanks to all the work Cooper did, we were able to locate two witnesses who'll testify that Russell was at the scene that night at Smoke's?'

'He told me about all that, yes.'

Another silence, then I said, 'George, you've declined to talk to the police. I'm not saying that's not your privilege, but if you *were* making truck drops for those scum, and you told us where, it might help us track Russell to whoever's hiding him.' No answer.

'It would help us if you gave me the names of any Dollard inmates who passed on Russell's threats to you . . .' No answer. I shoved back my chair. 'Do you believe Winston Russell killed your brother?'

Carefully stubbing out his second cigarette in the tin-foil ashtray, he said in a voice lower and softer than Cooper's, 'Yes, I do. Believed it a long time before it happened.' Leaning over, he emptied the ashtray into the wastebasket.

'When Russell told you if you didn't keep his name out of your first trial, he'd – well, what *did* he say? Did he explicitly say he'd shoot someone in your family?'

George looked past me, out the small high window. 'He said I'd *wish* he'd shot them.' He was watching the rain. 'Winston's a killer. Just that way . . . Isaac says you went to 'Nam?' I nodded. 'Were a lot like Winston over there. Both sides.'

'Too many at least ended up killers. Sometimes I think Winston was *born* that way. With him at large, does it worry you for your mother? Because—'

'No. He's through with me and mine. He can't hide nothing now but himself. You already told it all to the papers. Seems like maybe you ought to worry about you.'

'Why do you think he shot Cooper when he did?'

He walked over to a yellowed philodendron plant in a plastic pot on top of a metal shelf. '. . . Because he figured I'd talked, and that's how I got my reprieve.'

'I don't think so. I think it had to do with what Cooper was finding out, and the importance of the people he was finding it out about. I think Winston was *told* to get rid of Cooper.'

Gently pulling off dead leaves one by one, he said, 'You're testifying for the prosecutor tomorrow.'

'Not for the prosecutor. As a policeman at the scene. Is that it? You won't help me, because I might pass on information to the DA that would affect your defence?'

'I got nothing that'll help you.'

'I think you have a lot.'

He slowly turned the pot, separating out a dried vine. 'Like what?'

I said, 'I want to know if Russell, Pym, and the rest were smuggling not just stuff like cigarettes, but guns. How a group like the Carolina Patriots was involved. If Otis Newsome, or anybody else in the Constitution Club, was involved, and how.'

'I don't know a Constitution Club . . . Look, I gave my promise to Isaac I wouldn't talk to people 'bout anything 'less he was here.'

One thing was certain; if George Hall said he wouldn't talk, then he wouldn't. He had already been within twenty-four hours of the gas chamber, already been given the new shirt and trousers to wear to his execution, already been moved to the special last-night cell with its bare mattress on the stone floor – and he hadn't talked.

The deputy opened the door, looked disapprovingly at the coffee cups, and asked if we were almost done. I told him I'd let him know when we were. Hall never looked in his direction. After he'd left, I said, 'I'm just sorry, George, you didn't feel like there was somebody you could trust to tell this whole thing to, way back then. Told *me* about Pym and Russell. There're laws to—'

His thick body hardened with anger so fast that I instinctively stood up. He said, '*They* was the law. So was you.'

'No, they weren't. Neither am I. The law isn't people . . .' I held my hands up. 'All right, people fuck with it so bad, I agree it's hard to hang on to the difference.'

With long deliberate breaths, he relaxed his body. Then he dropped one handful of dead leaves into the wastebasket by the long scarred table. He nodded. 'It's harder for some folks to hang on than others.'

'That's true.'

His other palm tilted, letting the leaves fall. His unhurried voice was quiet again, when he spoke. 'Isaac said your daddy worked the line at Cadmean Mills, right?'

'Right.'

'. . . So did mine. One time my daddy got taken on a joyride by some men that worked there. He said something they didn't like.' George walked without haste around the room. 'They took him on this ride, and when they brought him back, he couldn't get his eyes to open, or get his mouth to swallow food for 'bout a week. My mama got on him bad, said, "Go to the law, Tim, go *tell* 'em." So he went to the law, and he got beat some more. Lost a week off his job. Next time something bad happened, he said to Mama, "You asking too much. Let it alone, and just go along." He went on along, and along, and along, till he died.'

'My father did too. Just went along that way till he died.'

George nodded. 'I seen a lot of men die fast, didn't even know it. And I seen men die yelling, crawling in mud. Two years back, I watched them strap a man in a wheelbarrow and take him down the Row to the gas chamber, had to strap him, he was carrying on so, crying like a baby. But my daddy, he died the *slowest*, just going along.' He stopped at the window to watch the rain.

I said, 'Now I think my dad was trying hard to do the best he could. I'm sure yours did too.'

George was looking out the window into memory. 'Cooper was just a little boy, nine or ten, when Daddy died. The preacher says to him, "You grow up a good man like your papa." And Cooper says, "I don't want to. I don't want to grow up scared." He told the preacher that, right there at the grave, his face mad and crying both.'

'Yes,' I said. 'I never saw Cooper Hall scared of anything. Your brother had great courage. So do you.'

'Naw.' Hall's eyes blinked; taking off his glasses, he rubbed them. He came back to the table and quietly sat down. 'Cooper was a teenager, he called me just a worthless nigger headed for jail. Said, "You're too dumb to tell the difference in your kind of fightin' and my kind." Told me my bad-assin' was just another way of going along . . .'

I sat down across from him. 'You didn't go along with a guilty plea. To protect your folks, you were willing to take Russell's deal. Why didn't you take the DA's deal, at least protect yourself from the risk of a death penalty?'

Looking at his hands spread open on the table, he thought a while. Finally he replied, 'Some things you can make yourself say, and some things you can't. It's just that way.'

When I was growing up, in the small dark kitchen of that Mill Street duplex, my daddy said a lot of things, for which my mama never 'got on him bad' at all, though I knew she didn't agree with them. He was a scared, unhappy man, but he wasn't a cruel man – he was gentle to my mother, my sister, and, except when we fought, to me. And he didn't rant or yell; he just said ugly things that the world he lived in believed were true – mostly about black people. He just repeated things he'd been told – about jungle-bunnies, eggheads, longhairs, bra-burners, draft-dodgers, Pope-worshippers, queers, Northern agitators, and atheists. He talked a lot about liberal conspiracies, and Jewish conspiracies, and Communist conspiracies. He talked a lot about the conspiracies of Cadmean Textiles, landlords, stores, bills, and banks to work, freeze, starve, and cheat him to death. But mostly he talked about all the things that were wrong with black people.

When I was old enough to understand what he was saying, I talked back. I told my daddy he was a stupid bigot, I told him his facts were wrong and his theories were wrong. He whipped me. When I was fourteen, he said he'd take his belt to me if he ever caught me hanging around that coonloving kike Rosethorn again. I hit him in the face. Mama cried and begged us to stop.

The day I graduated from high school, Daddy and I had another fight because I wouldn't return those crates of books Isaac had sent me. I told him that Isaac Rosethorn was more of a man and more of a father to me than he would ever be. When he raised his hand, I grabbed his wrist and threw him against the kitchen table. I left before the fear in his eyes made me hit him again. This time Mama followed me back into my room, stood crying by the door, and asked if she could say something. I glared at her. She struggled with her breath, and then she told me, 'You got to forgive your daddy. You got to ask him for his forgiveness. Can't you tell the way it tears him up how we can't give you fancy books like Mr Rosethorn, 'cause we don't know enough and we ain't got enough?'

I was still shaking as I yanked my graduation robe off its hanger. I said, 'Just because you're poor doesn't mean you have to be an *ignorant racist redneck!*' I grabbed my valedictorian speech off my bureau top, and shook it at her. '*I'm* poor!'

'No, Cuddy. You ain't cold and you ain't hungry, and you've gone on through school, and nobody ever said to you, you got to stop going. You got so much more than he did. He's worked and worked so you and Vivian could do better than us.' She stood there a long time in tears, squeezing the cheap plastic belt buckle of her new dress. Finally she said, 'Cuddy, please. Please, don't take this day from Malcolm. He's so proud of you. Please, tell him you're sorry.' I didn't answer. Her birthmark flushed dark red; she hid it with her hand, and whispered, 'If you can't find it in you to do it for him, son, I'm asking you if you'll please do it for me. He's out to the garage.' Then she quietly closed the door behind her. It was one of the few hard things she ever asked of me. I walked out to the garage where he sat in his car rubbing at some dirt on the dashboard, and I apologized.

He and I never fought like that again. But from time to time I'd still get angry. Once I asked him if he'd ever been in the Klan. He denied it, and now I'm sure that when he'd spent evenings with the neighbour who worked the Cadmean line with him, he was doing just what he claimed: 'watching the ball game,' or 'going out for a beer,' and not plotting black genocide, not burning crosses, or taking Tim Hall on a midnight ride. But my father's unreasonable remarks, his unreasoning prejudices, went on alternately enraging and saddening me until I left home. After I came back from Vietnam, when I would go to visit him alone in that duplex, when he would wander from one small dark room to another as if he were looking in them for my dead mother and my dead sister, after that, he just made me sad.

Monday morning, I gave my testimony in the Hall trial to the seven women and five men who'd made it to the finals of the jury selection, and got themselves impanelled. They'd also got themselves quarantined at the Ramada Inn. Judge Hilliardson had sequestered the jury there, after he denied the defence's request for a change of venue, snarling, 'Mr Rosethorn, I am prepared to prohibit any local interference with the defendant's right to a fair trial, and I am perfectly competent to do just that, in this courthouse, or any other.' Isaac talked and thought about the jury constantly. He was happy that they had chosen the school principal, Mr Lindquist, as their foreman. On the other hand, he saw no thaw in Mrs Boren's glowering freeze, and he worried about the sour expressions on several of the other faces.

Mitch Bazemore didn't want me on the witness stand long, just long enough to confirm that when I'd arrived at what he continually referred to as 'the scene of the murder,' I'd observed Bobby Pym bleeding to death thirty feet from where I'd observed George Hall with what Mitch continually referred to as 'a smoking gun.' I think Mitch got a smug pleasure out of the fact that I was the first eyewitness for the prosecution. Meanwhile, Nora Howard glared at me from the defence table the whole time, George looked at the state seal above Judge Hilliardson's grey tufted hair, Isaac made a teepee out of three pencils and a rubber band.

After about ten minutes of establishing my credentials, and bringing me into the 'scene of the crime,' the DA (with the brisk, manly collegiality that marked his 'we're both professionals on the side of law-and-order' style) asked me: 'Captain Mangum, as you assessed the scene before you, what did you assume?'

Rosethorn (blandly): 'Objection.'

Hilliardson (uninterested): 'Rephrase.'

Bazemore, who now fell into a trap that I suspect Isaac had set up, said, 'Captain Mangum, you are a professional police officer. As it were, an expert on the assessment of crime?'

'I'm a professional police officer. From what I've been hearing on the news lately, some folks aren't so sure I'm an expert at it.'

Bazemore joined in the little laugh I got on this. Then forcefully he slapped his fist into his palm. 'Captain, on the basis of what you directly observed, what was your professional appraisal of the situation outside Smoke's Bar when you arrived?'

Mangum: 'A man had been shot. I ran over to him, and identified him as Robert Pym. He was alive, but unable to speak or move. The wound was critical. He'd been shot in the head.'

Bazemore: 'He'd been shot through the right eye, hadn't he?'

Mangum: 'Yes.'

Bazemore: 'Did you make an immediate assumption as to who had shot Officer Pym?'

Mangum: 'Well, I'm not sure about immediate, but . . . yes.'

Bazemore: 'Who?'

Mangum: 'George Hall.'

Bazemore: 'Is that man in this room? If so, please point him out.'

I pointed at George. Turning around, Bazemore pointed at

George. 'You are pointing at the defendant, George Hall?' I said yes, and he asked me what George was doing to make me think he'd been the assailant.

Mangum: 'He was sitting on the sidewalk beside a gun.'

Bazemore: 'A still-smoking gun ... Did you then speak to George Hall?'

'Yes.'

'Did you then *ask* George Hall if he had shot Officer Pym?' Isaac objected that the State was leading its witness, the Court sustained it, and the State rephrased: 'When you spoke to Hall, what did you say to him?'

Mangum: 'I went over and warned him fully of his rights under the Miranda ruling, then I asked, "Did you shoot him?"'

Bazemore: 'And how did the defendant answer, if possible, in his exact words?'

Mangum: 'He didn't say anything. He nodded.'

Bazemore: 'He nodded, signifying yes, he had shot Pym?'

'Yes.'

'Did his answer surprise you? Or did it conform to what you'd already assumed?'

'The latter. Then he asked me if Pym was alive, and I told him he was. He asked me if an ambulance had been called. At that moment, another patrol car arrived, and—'

'Thank you, Captain Mangum. That's all for now. We appreciate your help, and apologize for taking time from your pressing duties. Your witness, Mr Rosethorn.'

Isaac shambled towards me, fingering a collar point on his fresh white shirt. He looked as if he'd never seen me before in his life, and didn't much think I'd improve on acquaintance. Since he wasn't acknowledging me, I focused my eyes about an inch to the side of his head. 'Captain Mangum, the defence too apologizes for taking up your valuable time, particularly when I know from the newspapers that your department has been working very hard – though lamentably without success – to catch the two police officers with whom Bobby Pym had been stealing, smuggling, extorting—'

Bazemore, on his feet fast: 'OBJECTION!'

Rosethorn, fast: '—And who are also now wanted for the murder of the defendant's brother Cooper Hall and of—'

Bazemore: 'OBJECTION! OBJECTION! Irrelevant, immaterial, and—'

Hilliardson: 'Sustained.'

Rosethorn: '—William Slidell, their partner in crime.'

Judge Hilliardson, angry: '*Mr Rosethorn!* The prosecution's objection is sustained! Sustained! You are seriously out of order! *Had* you been asking a question, I might request that you rephrase it. As I heard, however, nothing at all interrogatory in your bizarre remarks, I order them struck from the record. The jury will disregard them.' The jury looked sheepish.

Miss Bee Turner watched with gusto as the court stenographer, old Mr Walkington, deleted the outburst.

Hilliardson, calmer: 'If defence counsel has questions for this witness, ask them. Otherwise, I will excuse the overworked Captain Mangum.'

Rosethorn, meekly: 'Yes, Your Honour . . .' Isaac gave me a polite, chilly nod, before limping over to the easel that displayed a large diagram of the street outside Smoke's, with my squad car, Pym's body, George's position, the Montgomery Hotel all indicated. His stubby finger inched along the map. 'Captain Mangum, from the time you heard the shot as you drove down Polk Street, to the time you leapt out of your patrol car in front of Smoke's Bar, how many minutes passed?'

'Two or three minutes at the most.'

'Three minutes. Pym lay on the sidewalk, a crowd all around, cars stopping, shouting, considerable confusion, right?' He swirled his hand around the area where Pym's body was outlined.

'Yes. More than a dozen people stood around on the sidewalk.'

Isaac slid his finger across the map. 'And you've told the district attorney that you found George Hall way over here, seated on the curb, his head lowered. So he had made no attempt in those long three minutes, in that crowded confusion, to fade into the crowd, to *flee* the scene?'

'None.'

'He was holding the gun?'

'No. A gun was lying on the sidewalk beside him. As shown there.'

'He made no attempt to hide it, *or* to use it to make good an escape?'

'None.'

'Did *he* say anything to *you* when you first approached him, Captain Mangum?'

333

'Yes. He said, "I'm not running. Just don't shoot." '

'Ah.' Isaac asked his next questions walking towards the jury, his back to me. 'At the time were you pointing your gun at him?'

'No.'

'No? Why should he think you might shoot him then? . . . What were you wearing at the time?'

'My police uniform.'

'Ah . . .' And the defendant, seated passively on the curb, looked up at a police officer and said, "Just don't shoot"? . . . Why?'

'I can't answer for him. I imagine he was scared I might shoot him.'

'Could that possibly be because over the years, a dozen blacks *had* been shot and killed by white Hillston policemen?'

Judge Hilliardson shook his head. 'Counsellor! As the witness has already, quite properly, told you, and as I feel sure you already know, it is not for him to speculate on the defendant's *thoughts*.'

'Yes, sir.' Slowly Isaac turned his sad eyes from the black woman on the front row of the jury, back towards the drawing. 'Yes . . . And then, Captain Mangum, you've testified that, picking up Pym's gun from the sidewalk, you walked through the crowd thirty feet away to check on the wounded man. Did Mr Hall take *this* opportunity to attempt to escape?'

'No, he hadn't moved at all when I returned. I asked him if he had fired the shot, and he nodded.'

'The district attorney failed to inquire, no doubt in his eagerness to let you return to your investigations, whether you asked Mr Hall any *other* questions. Did you?'

'Yes, I asked him what had happened to his face.'

Isaac frowned. 'Why should you ask that, Captain Mangum?'

'Because it was smeared with blood. His nose was bleeding heavily, and there was a cut at the base of the nostril. I repeated the question, but got no response from him.'

'Were you able to ascertain from others at the scene that Mr Hall was heavily bleeding because he had been assaulted by Robert Pym?'

I figured Bazemore would jump, but I went ahead. 'Yes. Several witnesses said that prior to the shooting, Pym had inserted the gun muzzle in Hall's nostril during a fight between—'

Bazemore jumped late. 'Objection.'

'—the two inside Smoke's.'

Hilliardson: 'Overruled.'

Rosethorn: 'At that time did you question witnesses as to the origins of this fight?'

Mangum: 'No. My superior, Captain Fulcher, arrived immediately, and instructed me to follow Pym's ambulance to University Hospital, which I did. I stayed there until after three A.M.'

'Did you *then* return, and question witnesses to Pym's violent and armed assault on the defendant?'

Mitch's arm went off like a rocket. 'Objection!'

'Sustained. Mr Rosethorn, please!'

Rosethorn: 'I'll rephrase. Did you at any time further question witnesses to events leading up to the shooting?'

'No, sir. I was not made a member of the investigation.'

'Ah . . .' Rosethorn looked out the tall handsome windows for a while. 'The first policeman on the scene, the one in the most immediate position to observe what had happened, and you were quickly removed from the case?'

Bazemore: 'Ob—'

Mangum: 'I was never assigned to the case.'

Rosethorn: 'Before you were never assigned to the case, did you bother to ask Mr Hall himself how and *why* this tragedy had happened?'

The question stopped me for a moment. '. . . I wasn't interrogating him. We're talking about a few chaotic minutes, about a wounded man.' I paused. All that was true, but it wasn't really why I hadn't asked George that question. I said, 'Well, in fact, it seemed obvious. I assumed—'

Now Isaac put his freckled hand on the rail of the witness stand, and tapped his fingers, springing the trap door. 'Ah, yes! Captain Mangum, among all these professional assumptions and impressions you were busy with that night, and on the basis of what you've already told us, what *did* you assume? What was your *appraisal* of the circumstances surrounding this shooting? Did you assume that George Hall had committed a premeditated homicide against Pym? OR, did you not rather assume that—'

'OBJECTION!' Mitch was in a high-step jig all the way around his table and halfway to the bench. 'The witness's conclusions, based on hearsay, are irrelevant, immaterial, and insubstantial.'

'Counsellor,' Isaac wheeled on him. 'When I objected to your soliciting "impressions" from Captain Mangum, you're the one who presented *your* witness as an "expert" entitled to a professional opinion. I'm simply following your line of questioning.'

Hilliardson looked wryly at them both, then stroked his beaked nose. Finally he said, 'Objection overruled. Witness may answer.' Mitch's neck swelled with protest but he swallowed it.

I said, 'It seemed likely that there had been mutual combat between Hall and Pym, that Pym had been armed, that in a struggle for the gun, Hall had got hold of it, pursued Pym, and shot him.'

I was thinking it was interesting Isaac had never discussed with me what he might ask me today, and what I might answer. Interesting too, Isaac didn't ask me now if I'd assumed a case of self-defence, because I'd once mentioned I could see a grey area there. Nor did he ask now if I'd made any investigations into Pym's death *subsequent* to the first trial. In the first place, Judge Hilliardson wouldn't have allowed him to use cross-examination to present new evidence. In the second place, no doubt Isaac was hoping Bazemore would cover up the whole Pym–Russell robbery/extortion/smuggling racket, that the State would then rest its case, after which Isaac, in his opening remarks, could accuse the State of a cover-up. At any rate, all he said now was, 'Was it your understanding that Pym had attempted to "arrest" Hall by this violent means, and that Hall was resisting arrest?'

'No, it was not. None of the witnesses described any attempt by him to arrest Hall.'

'Did you think that George Hall had previously planned, and took this opportunity to execute, a premeditated murder with malice aforethought?'

'No, I did not.'

Isaac walked away from me, back to stand near George Hall. 'Were you then *surprised* to hear that your "superiors" had charged the defendant with murder in the *first* degree? Just answer the question, yes or no. Were you surprised, Captain Mangum?'

Mitch Bazemore had his arms crossed over his biceps, squeezing them. He looked furious, but in a struggle to hide it, lest the jury think there was anything worth bothering about in what I was saying. I looked at George, just as his eyes moved towards mine. I said, 'Yes, I was surprised.'

Isaac nodded slowly. 'Yes. I would imagine you would be. And as a professional police officer, were you so *surprised* that this man had been sentenced to death, on the basis of the evidence as you knew it, that you wrote a letter to the state prison parole board saying so, and asking them to consider extending clemency to George Hall?'

Mitch stepped forward, staring at me. I could foresee a long unpleasant afternoon in his office; indeed, I could foresee that if Julian Lewis became governor and Bazemore became his A.G., I might get the chance I occasionally moped over when I was worn out – I could leave law enforcement and become a history teacher.

I said, 'Yes, I did write to the board.'

'You thought an injustice would be done if Hall were executed?'

'. . . Yes.'

Isaac didn't smile at me even now; the jury was never going to suspect he didn't dislike and distrust me immensely. 'I have no further questions for the witness at this time.'

On redirect, Bazemore did smile at me; it was reasonably scary. He asked me to confirm once more that Hall had brought the gun out of the bar, had shot Pym *outside* the bar, a hundred yards from where the fight had allegedly occurred, that Pym had been unarmed when he was shot, that he had been shot from a distance of approximately thirty feet, and so not in the midst of a struggle. He asked me to agree that it would be entirely legal for an off-duty policeman to arrest someone. He asked me to admit that at the time of my writing to the board, I had not known the full circumstances of the relations between Pym and Hall, as I now knew them (though he didn't ask me what those full circumstances were). He asked me, 'Captain Mangum, in your questioning of Hall, only minutes after the shot was fired, did he appear to be irrational, or out of control, or in any way of diminished capacity to reason? Any of those?'

'No. He seemed—'

'*Minutes* after he shot Pym, did he seem violently in the grip of an irresistible rage?'

'No. Numb.'

'He surrendered himself to the police because he knew he had shot a man, am I right? He was perfectly aware of what he had done?'

'If you mean, did he realize he had fired the shot, yes, I think so.'

'Did he say to you then, "I shot Pym in self-defence"?'

'No.'

'Or "I didn't mean to," or "I couldn't help myself"?'

'No.'

'Does a request for clemency necessarily mean a denial of the validity of a verdict?'

'Not necessarily.'

'Have you, as chief of the Hillston Police Department, made a *great many* requests for parole or clemency for criminals whom *you* have charged, and the courts have convicted of crimes?'

'Yes, I have.'

'Hundreds?'

'No. Perhaps two dozen.'

'Do those many requests mean that you repudiate the right of a jury to try, and to decide on the guilt or innocence of a man brought before it?'

'No.'

Bazemore came up on my side, and thrust his chin very near my face. 'Is it your duty to enforce the laws of the state under which you are empowered as chief of this city's police?'

'Yes, it is.'

'Is it the law of this state that a jury may sentence to death a man convicted of first-degree murder if they so determine?'

'Yes, it is.' Freezing sweat ran down the sides of my shirt as I watched his pale blue righteous eyes.

'Is it,' he said, 'your personal belief that if the death penalty—'

Isaac managed to move fast without sounding even much interested. 'Objection. The witness is not being challenged for jury duty. He is here as a professional police officer. His *personal* opinions, whatever they may be, and however interested we all might be to hear them, are irrelevant.'

The judge agreed, adding that Isaac should keep that in mind when tempted to share with us *his* personal opinions.

Still smiling, Bazemore backed off. 'If, Captain Mangum, your superior had not arrived on the scene that night at Smoke's Bar, where you found Robert Pym dying of a gunshot wound, and George Hall sitting there beside a smoking gun, would *you* have arrested George Hall?'

'Yes.'

'No further questions, at this time.' Bazemore thanked me as if I'd said everything he could have possibly hoped for.

Nobody at the defence table looked at me as I walked by them.

Chapter 19

Upstairs, Sergeant Ralph Fisher told me he'd heard that my testimony had been pretty good. I said, 'Good for whom? HPD?'

He smiled, his black cheeks pitted with old pockmarks. 'New, for George Hall. I heard you made HPD sound pitiful.'

'Yeah, well, Ralph, if Bazemore cans me, I hope you get stuck with my job.' I handed him a typed roster. 'Here, you can have five extra men Friday night. That do?'

'Have to, won't it?' Ralph was in charge of police protection at that Trinity Church public panel on 'The Klan in Carolina: Pawns of Power?,' which the Hall Committee was co-sponsoring, and which I hoped the Klan would not be attending in force.

Ralph said, 'This born-again Grand Dragon worries me more than the Communist. If the Klan hasn't killed that woman by now, after all the stuff she's laid on them, I figure they don't plan to.' (Like most of the force, he called Janet Malley – whom HPD had had occasion to arrest for numerous public disturbances – simply 'the Communist.')

I said, 'Well, put a vest on Janet, if she'll let you. And don't stand too close to that ex-Grand Dragon; I hate for something to happen to you if one of his old pals tries to stop his exposé with a Browning automatic. Put a vest on him too.'

Walking away, Ralph called, 'On top of his robe, or under it?'

I was standing in the squad room skimming the *Star*, when Justin sauntered in. I asked him how he'd got back from Kentucky so fast, and he said Andy had let him borrow his plane. I said Andy was some pal, and Justin handed me a big envelope.

Nancy White, at the desk by the door, two-fingering a report on her typewriter, called to Justin, 'Hey, love your jacket, man. Heavy metal.'

I said, 'What's this, Savile, a bill for the gas?'

'Signed statement from the former Mrs Willie Slidell, who said not to call her that. "Call me Karla," she said as we took a little sight-seeing flight together over bluegrass country.' He smiled, throwing off an old leather flight jacket he must have bought at Antique Apparel in the mall.

'So, what did Karla say?'

He perched on Nancy's desk. 'Said yes, they were smuggling stolen goodies in Fanshaw trucks. Yes, they were running guns. But, one, Willie the Wimp was a very reluctant partner in the whole deal, preferring making dirty movies to arming for a race war. He got suckered into it by his brotherin-law Pym. Once in, he was too scared of Winston Russell to pull out. He also had an expensive coke habit to support. Two, Willie called Karla in a panic two days before he was killed, and told her that Russell had got him into, quote, "really bad trouble," and that he, Willie, "was scared out of his mind," and "had to get away." He mentioned to her that he had something Russell wanted, and said holding it back was his only insurance.'

I said, 'Well done, Kemo Sabe. I bet the insurance was the porno Brookside video.'

'Willie didn't tell her what it was, and she didn't care to ask. She told him if he ended up dead, it was his own fault, and she hung up on him. Given what happened to her ex, she now says she's "sorry" she'd talked to him that way.'

'Okay. Go park your plane, Lindy. Where is it, on the roof?'

'No, on top of your Oldsmobile.' He lit a cigarette. 'Oh, Karla says it was Winston's friend Sergeant Mennehy who talked Bobby and Willie into joining the Carolina Patriots too. She described the Patriots as "just a bunch of jerk-off dickheads that like to hide in the woods and diddle with guns."'

'I bet I'd like Karla,' said Nancy. 'Hey, Juss, I just talked to the last one of those Patriots this morning. Same as the others. An alibi, and don't know nuttin' about nobody murdering nobody. Said, if Winston and Purley had been blowing people away, it sure wasn't for the Carolina Patriots, because "We're against killing." Gave me his best bad-ass grin, said, "You got that, lady?" Said he hadn't seen Winston in years.' She scrubbed a hole in the paper with her eraser. '"Uncooperative" got an *a* in it?'

Justin said 'Yep.' Then pouring himself some coffee, he asked Nancy if she'd made an appointment to see Alice's obstetrician yet. She hadn't. 'Come *on*, Champ! You need to start *planning*. The wedding, honeymoon, pregnancy leave—'

I said, 'If she doesn't get a move on, they're all three going to happen at the same time.'

They ignored me. He said, 'Are you and Zeke interested in Lamaze? Alice and I are in this class now—'

Nancy spit the heart on her gold chain out of her mouth. 'Listen, man, I've *delivered* eleven babies, including *twins*. I want the needle. I don't need classes.'

I looked over the top of Karla Slidell's statement. 'Nancy, what you *need*'s a preacher.'

Justin said, 'Why? She and Zeke have got *you* preaching at them all the time. You're always trying to get other people married, Cuddy, but I don't notice you in a rush yourself.'

'You don't notice me three months pregnant either.'

Nancy laughed. 'Yeah, if Zeke's Okie redskin relatives don't show up soon, I'll be waddling down the aisle with a papoose strapped to my back.' Standing up, she showed her unbuckled uniform trousers. 'What I *need*'s some bigger pants.' She laughed with her head thrown up, and I realized that while I'd seen Nancy grin a million times, I'd never heard her laugh before. A quick image flashed by of her and Zeke with two or three kids crawling all over them, and a little jab of jealousy flickered through me.

While I finished reading about Mrs Slidell's irritation with her ex, Nancy and Justin went over their report on Winston Russell's buddies in the Carolina Patriots. Justin had requested Nancy full-time, and I'd let him have her and John Emory, because Nancy had said she wanted to stay with 'Roid,' short for 'Hemorrhoid,' though I don't think she even remembered the origin of the nickname she'd first given John. Nancy had also come a long way since her first comments about Justin: 'Hey, Chief, what's the deal with that fag Lieutenant Supercop, got his fucking name hand-sewn into all his clothes, he on loan from Hollywood or what? All of a sudden he takes me out with a flying tackle, then he jumps out the damn window after the suspect!' No, It didn't take Nancy and Justin long to realize how much they had in common: they both were impulsive, insubordinate, and reckless, and as each took considerable pride in these flaws, they pretty soon developed a fondness for the same traits in the other. Both of them loved being cops, too. Myself, a lot of the time I don't even like it.

Back in Justin's office, I sat down on the press bench he keeps to exercise his right leg: He's had two bullets hit it – one when he jumped between me and a murder suspect. I said to him, 'J.B. the Five, I've got to make an arrest on the Hall thing. Carl Yarborough's stopped talking to me, and this morning the goddamn governor called me again.'

'Well, for what it's worth, Preston Pope's got a hunch the Patriots are hiding Russell and Pym right here in the Piedmont.'

'If I could still use thumbscrews, maybe I could get them to say where. Speaking of Preston the Stooge, when are we gonna hear some *squealing* instead of hunches?'

'He thinks the Patriots don't trust him anymore. You should have let me go to some more meetings before they got so suspicious.'

'If I'd let you clog-dance back to those rednecks with a wire on, I'd have probably found you hanging charred from a tree in a cloud of soot.'

'Oh bull.'

.'Yeah, oh bull.' I turned on to my stomach on the bench, hooked my ankles under the weights, and did a few lifts. I said, 'Besides, those meetings were dickshit. I don't want any more smudgy handouts comparing Negro and Caucasian brain sizes. I don't want any more reports about how this one says he hates Jews, and that one maybe made an obscene phone call. I want y'all to hand me those Carolina Patriots on a platter full of *felonies*, General Lee.'

'Barkis is willing. But Dave Schulmann thinks they've folded their tents – that this interrogation scared them into shutting down.' He handed me a folder labelled 'Carolina Patriots.' Then he shook his phone messages off their spike, where they looked to me like they'd been piling up for quite a while.

I let the leg weights clang, and flipped through his folder. The FBI had got its indictment against former Green Beret Sergeant Charles Mennehy, for robbing a federal armoury, but they still couldn't tie in our local yahoos. And Bazemore said we hadn't given him enough to do it either. The Patriots' lawyer claimed that the Carolina Patriots was *not* a white-supremacy, paramilitary organization at all, nor affiliated with the Klan, but was instead a 'social club for modern military history buffs': that the old group photo of them in fatigues, waving those M-16s in front of their camp cabin, commemorated a 'Vietnam War reenactment retreat,' rather like – explained the lawyer – the Colonial Club that restaged a Revolutionary War battle near Hillsborough once a year. All those firearms in that old picture were 'fake replicas, handmade solely for the purposes of the reenactments.' Forced to acknowledge that they'd met Pym, Russell, and Koontz (since they were in the photo with them), Mennehy and the other Patriots denied knowing anything about any crimes any of those fellows might have committed. They denied even knowing Otis Newsome (and the photo we had of him in the state fairgrounds parking lot wasn't good enough to prove them wrong). Justin was keeping a tail on them; they led very boring lives. I closed the folder and threw it back down on his desk. I said, 'They do seem to be, like Brer Fox, just laying low.'

Tilted back in his Harvard chair with *Veritas* stamped on it, he sighed at his messages as he rolled them into pink balls. Then he said, 'Preston says he's hearing rumours they're planning something. If we get wind of a big meeting, I say let's just swoop on them. If we could nail them with something, it'd be easier to pump them about Russell.'

I climbed off the bench. 'You want to do a Jeb Stuart, you get me a *date*, and a *place*, and a definite promise that I'm going to find a lot of guys doing *real* illegal things on the premises, and I don't mean pot and porno, I mean like drills with twenty-two-calibre machine guns, okay? I mean blueprints, showing where they're planning to put the bombs.'

He laced his hands behind his head, and thought a minute. 'What if we plant a rogue cop to sell them the weapons we found under the floorboards in Slidell's barn?'

'I don't think so, General.'

'Jesus, Cuddy, you just said we've got to do *something*. We nail them with Slidell's guns.' He tossed this idea around until his phone rang. After listening about five secounds, he began frantically gesturing for me to run to the next phone and pick up extension 15. Adrenaline went through me like ice on a bad tooth. Justin had mouthed the words 'Purley Newsome.'

The call hadn't come through the desk. I punched Zeke's button and told him to start a tape, and a trace, on 15. When I switched the line on, I heard the same slow, truculent, self-pitying voice I'd had to listen to for years. 'Listen, Say-ville, I know what y'all are up to. Every last word in those papers is a fuckin' lie. I don't know any Dr Molina and he's a fuckin' liar. I never pulled a gun on Cooper Hall, I never shot him, and y'all know it. And I never shot Slidell either. Y'all are trying to frame me, aren't you?' Newsome seemed to have trouble breathing.

Justin sounded calm and friendly. 'No, Purley, we're just going on the evidence we've been given. If we've got it wrong we'll be glad to listen to your version. Where are you?'

'Wouldn't you like to know?'

'I sure would. Is Winston with you?'

'You told the papers you bet I'd killed Winston. That was a fuckin' lie, Say-ville.'

'It's Sah-*ville*, Purley.'

'Fuck you.'

'You still hanging out with Winston? Listen, you two have really had all of us hopping these past months. Made us look pretty bad.'

'Damn straight. Made that shit *Mangum* look bad.'

'Yeah, the governor was on the phone to Mangum this morning, saying he wanted to call out the National Guard, bring you in dead or alive. Now, Mangum personally, he'd prefer you *dead*. I've never seen him like this before. The DA either. I'm going to tell you the truth, Purley – I mean, you and I never had any axe to grind, right – they're going to hang murder-one on you, both counts, plus about a thousand other little felonies that would put you away for life plus a hundred. Except of course you'll get the death penalty. Mangum says he's *living* for the day he looks through that gas chamber window and sees you strapped in there with pink foam spurting out of your mouth and ears.'

Not surprisingly, Purley had no answer to this. In the silence, I thought Justin might have blown it, and we'd lost him, but finally the sullen voice grumbled, 'I wasn't even around when either one of them got killed, and I can prove it. I can prove a lot of stuff.'

'What we hear is, you planned the whole thing. The smuggling, the cover-up, and now the shootings. Russell was your accomplice, but you ran the show. You and your brother Otis.'

'Jesus shit, you're trying to make me think you're talking to Russell, and I know you're not.'

'Because he's dead?'

'He's *crazy*, that's what he is. Winston's fuckin' crazy if he told you all that!'

'Well, Purley, you may be right. I hope he's not there in the room with you calling him crazy. As I recall, he's got a very nasty temper. On the other hand, if you've sneaked off to call me, he's too smart not to figure out what you're up to—'

'I'm not up to anything!' A horrible coughing spasm.

'Purley, are you okay? You sound sick.'

'I'm hanging up.'

Justin turned urgent and earnest fast. 'Purley, listen to me! Use your head. If Winston was the real trigger man, his best bet is to get you accidentally killed, and let us find your body. Otis is already dead. Mangum'll unload the Hall/Slidell murders on you and your brother, and close the case. I'm being straight with you now. If you didn't kill anybody, *your* best bet is come in. Come in, and tell us your side of it. I'll listen. I'll keep Mangum out of it. I'll talk to Bazemore.'

We all knew this is exactly what Purley had had in mind when he made the call, or he wouldn't have made it. But he said, ''I'm not talking anymore. You think I'm a moron? I don't know you're trying to trace this call? Listen, Sayville—'

At that instant, Zeke Caleb ran into the room, whispering, 'In state! Pay phone, Rocky Mount!' It was all I could do to keep from shouting into my extension to Purley that if he hadn't always been such a stupid, rotten cop, he would have known how fast computers can track down phone numbers these days. But, still, of course, by the time we got a Rocky Mount patrol car to the shopping mall he'd been calling from, Purley was gone. They threw everybody they had at a manhunt for him and Russell. It didn't much matter that they came up empty, because before he slammed down the phone, Purley told Justin he'd be calling him back tomorrow at six A.M. to find out what Bazemore had to say 'regarding his cooperation, and it better be good.'

I bashed down my phone, yelled at the top of my lungs, and leapt a good two feet off the ground, scaring Zeke Caleb into slightly lifting the edge of one eyelid.

Justin ran into the hall, slammed his bad knee against the door corner, and hobbled up to slap me on the shoulder. 'He's coming in! We hooked him, Cuddy! Four days. And who would have thought he could even *read* a newspaper.'

I said I hoped he and Winston had already split up, because Winston wasn't about to let Purley waltz home and turn State's evidence. 'That would mean Purley's got to be smart enough to get away, and Winston's got to be dumb enough to let him, and neither notion has the crystal ring of plausibility, Rocky Mount, shit! Okay, meet me here at five-thirty.'

Justin grinned. 'Jesus, I *hate* getting up that early in the morning.'

I turned back in the hall. 'In a couple more months, you'll be getting up that early every morning, humming lullabies with a burp rag over your silk robe. Hey, say it's a boy, you're not going to name it J. B. Savile the *Sixth*, are you?' Justin and Alice already knew the sex of their future baby, but she wouldn't let him tell anybody.

'Cuddy, stop trying to trick me. You'll just have to wait and see. Now, for a girl, I always wanted Katherine. And for a boy, well, I love Andy's middle name. Theodore. Theodore Savile. You like it?'

I said I thought it was fine. I stopped myself from adding, I thought it was particularly fine if Alice was still hoping Andy Theodore Brookside would pick her as his nominee for lieutenant governor.

As my mama often chastised me, you don't have to say ugly things, even if they're true.

That afternoon, when I slipped into the back of Superior Court, I saw Jack Molina hunched over taking notes in the last row, and I sat down beside him. Isaac was finishing up his cross-examination of one of Mitch's witnesses from Smoke's Bar, a middle-aged black postman, who'd said that (a) George had thrown the first punch in the fight with Pym, (b) he and two other men had tried unsuccessfully to hold George down as Pym ran towards the door after the fight. On cross, Isaac led the man to explore his motive in holding George down, and got him to say it was prompted not by fear for Pym, but fear for George. 'You tangle like that with white people, you gonna lose. They cops, you gonna lose bad.'

Isaac: 'At the time, sir, did you know Pym was a policeman?'

'No, I thought he was a drunkard.'

Bubba Percy, up front in the press section, laughed out loud.

Isaac smiled. 'Well, that wouldn't necessarily mean he wasn't a policeman. Why did you think Pym was drunk? Was he uncoordinated, weaving around, slurred speech?'

'He was in Smoke's by himself, that's mainly why.' (For some reason, this was the first thing that provoked anything resembling mirth from Judge Hilliardson – a silent snort.) 'And he was talking real loud, riling people, seem like on purpose, you know,

346

like when he started up the jukebox during the live music and all.'

Isaac asked him to think back. 'Think back to the fight, now. Was Pym just standing there, and George hit him?'

'No, Pym was pushing and shoving and talking ugly at him.'

'Ah ... And you've said that Pym pulled out his gun from under his shirt. At that point, did he speak to Hall?'

The postman looked embarrassed. 'You want me to say it right out?' Isaac nodded. 'Well, when he push the gun up his nose, he yell, "Buddy, your fuckin' ass is grass."'

'And what did George say or do in response?'

'Well, just stares at him; says, "Try it," ... well, his word was, you know ...' The postman looked at Hilliardson, who told him to repeat exactly what he remembered hearing. Nodding, the man turned to Isaac and said, ' "Try it, you motherfucker." '

Beside me, Jack Molina whispered, 'Jesus Christ! Pym's got a loaded gun up his nose, and George says *that*!' I agreed that the Hall brothers did not scare easily.

The postman went on. 'Well, like I said, it happen real sudden, you know. There was this crash. I believe somebody banged open the door and hit a chair, something like that. The white man wheels 'round to see, and George Hall, he knocked his arm away, then slams it down hard, three, four times, on the table, knocks the gun loose. So the white man runs off.'

On redirect, Bazemore brought the witness back to what he said were the 'significant factors.' That George had initiated the fight by shoving Pym aside, yanking the jukebox cord out of the wall, and telling Pym to leave the bar. That when Pym had followed George across the room 'to protest,' George had hit him with his fist. That three men had tried physically to restrain George from following Pym, and that he, the postman, had said to George, 'Forget it, forget it, let it go.'

'Did Hall,' asked Mitch, thumbs jammed in his vest pockets, 'appear to hear and understand your efforts to stop him from shooting Pym?'

A boom of objection from Isaac. 'This witness *never said* he assumed Hall was going to shoot anybody!' Hilliardson sustained, and asked the DA to rephrase, which he did by changing 'shooting Pym' to 'pursuing Pym with a gun in his hand.'

'Yes, sir,' replied the postman. 'Hall understood. He said, "Y'all get back. Stay back in here." '

On recross, Isaac asked if George had used the gun as a threat

347

to get free of his restrainers. No, he hadn't. By 'Get back, stay in here,' had the postman assumed George was threatening them?

'No, more like he didn't want anybody hurt.'

When they finally finished, I went up front, leaned over the dividing rail, and whispered to Mitch Bazemore that I needed to talk with him as soon as court adjourned; his look suggested he hoped I was planning to offer to resign. Then I had a deputy pass a note to Isaac; in it I said that Purley had called, and was going to surrender. Nora smiled at me when I waved, a nice change. And I would have kept on going, out of the courtroom, had I not heard Mitchell Bazemore call out the name of his next witness in that earnest camp-coach voice of his. 'The State calls Arthur Butler.'

I imagine my face looked about the way Isaac's did, and Isaac's face rushed from shock to anger fast. All spring, he'd tried without success to have the Delaware prison release Arthur 'Moonfoot' Butler to serve as a defence witness. Now here was the DA calling the suddenly available Mr Butler for the prosecution. Spinning around to glower at me, Isaac saw me staring dumbfounded at Bazemore. It wasn't so much that Mitch had *wanted* to keep his strategy secret from me that staggered me; it was that he had *succeeded*. Plus, he'd done the unexpected; his 'game plan' was obviously not at all what I'd figured, and Isaac had counted on. The *State* was going to risk opening the can of wormy cops itself, rather than wait for the defence to do it. There was no other reason for him to put Butler on the stand. I watched these calculations take place in accelerated form in a few blinks of Isaac's eyes. Then he leaned over to George, who was looking around the room as if trying to spot Butler. George listened, frowned, nodded. Standing with a sigh, Isaac said, 'Your Honour, there is no Arthur Butler on our list of the prosecution's witnesses.'

Bazemore stood across the room, pushing his knuckles into the table top. 'Your Honour, this witness's appearance was only insured yesterday. He is incarcerated in Delaware; we arranged for them to make him available to us, and today was the day they chose.'

Isaac then asked to approach the bench, where the DA followed with the bounce of a gleeful bushwhacker. I knew Isaac was asking for a recess. I knew from Mitch's hugging himself that Judge Hilliardson was saying no.

While the deputies were escorting in Mr Butler, Isaac whispered busily at Nora as he hurried her into her raincoat. She strode quickly by me out of the courtroom, passing Moonfoot, who walked towards the witness stand in pleated trousers. The cuffs flopped from the floaty, bent-leg walk for which he'd acquired his nickname. Arthur Butler was about George's age, but younger looking, a lighter brown, with a squashed chin not much helped by a wispy goatee, a small head with minuscule ears above a long thin neck, sloped shoulders, and a high, narrow, tightly belted waist. His jacket looked new. He listened to the oath as if it were fascinating, then perched on the edge of the witness chair, hands on his knees. It was that pose that the *Star's* trial artist sketched; the picture appeared on the front page of the paper the next day.

After establishing Moonfoot's identity, and without going into too many details about his past, or for that matter, his present, Bazemore asked the witness to tell us in his own words how he knew George Hall.

Moonfoot nodded his long neck eagerly to show his willingness to help out. He spoke without taking his eyes from Bazemore. 'I been knowing George ever since grade school. We grew up in the neighbourhood, and hung out some. He come on back from 'Nam, and good jobs is scarce. We both do roofing some, then he gets on at Fanshaw, truck driver – 'cause he got his licence. I tried for one myself but the man gave me the test . . .' Bazemore stopped this, and herded his witness to Fanshaw trucks. 'So well, all right, I know these three men working a little business where they could use a Fanshaw driver, so, well, I put them on to George, and that's how it all got started between him and—'

Bazemore interrupted what sounded to me like the start of a long rehearsed speech: 'What do you mean by a little business?'

Relaxing, Butler explained at some length that he meant these men had possession of certain goods in large quantities, including cigarettes and pornographic merchandise, which they were smuggling out of the state in Fanshaw Paper Company trucks, and then selling to prearranged buyers. The DA wondered if Mr Butler could tell us how these men obtained large quantities of such goods, and Mr Butler said he knew for a direct fact that they'd stolen some of them from the Hillston Police Impoundment Facility, and confiscated some of them from 'this dude and that one' (i.e., previous thieves and receivers of stolen or illicit goods).

'And who were these three men?' asked the DA sadly.

'Well, sir, who they were, was three policemen, here in Hillston. First ones I met was Newsome and Pym, then they introduce me to Russell. That was the one in charge, it looked like, and was.'

'You are referring to Hillston police officers, Purley Newsome, Winston Russell, and Robert Pym?'

'That's right. Purley Newsome, Winston—'

'And these *police officers* told you they were smuggling stolen property out of the state inside Fanshaw Paper Company trucks?' This revelation about the moral character of these policemen was, of course, news to no one who'd read a paper or watched a television in the last few months, but when Butler said, 'They told me, and they showed me,' Mitch bowed his head mournfully, as if the knowledge of such corruption had weighed him down. 'And why,' he asked when he recovered, 'why should they tell and show you, of all people, that they were committing these crimes?'

'Why indeed?' asked Judge Shirley Hilliardson, scowling down from his high bench.

Butler coiled his neck around towards the judge. 'Well, sir, supplies at the police got low, and they needed a good supplyman with the right contacts, and that was me, so I'm the one they picked.' A chuckle from the jury foreman at Moonfoot's self-appraisal.

Bazemore made himself smile. 'And why should you agree to be picked?' Butler allowed it might have had something to do with the circumstances under which he'd first met Officers Newsome and Pym. 'Where and when *did* you meet these men?'

'Seems like it was at a warehouse loading dock at Haver Tobacco. 'Round about three A.M., on a Sunday, back in seventy-nine. They come up on me out of the pitch-dark.'

'What were you doing there in the pitch-dark?'

'Well, I had about two hundred cartons right there on the dolly, and another three hundred in the van. I saw the two of them, I liked to had a stroke.' He grinned. The juror Mrs Boren looked disgusted.

Bazemore, who rarely tried for humour, in the wise knowledge that he was devoid of that quality himself, now managed a bit of irony. 'May we assume, Mr Butler, that you were not at the time *employed* by Haver Tobacco Company to engage in this nocturnal transfer of their property from the warehouse to the van?'

Most of the spectators laughed; the judge did not join them. Moonfoot acknowledged that he had not been on the Haver payroll at that particular time. Another half hour rambled by as Bazemore led his stubbornly garrulous witness through his testimony: how the cops had impounded all the cigarettes, then coerced him under threat of a maximum sentence into supplying them with forecasts of upcoming robberies in the area, and tips on the whereabouts of illegal commodities they might also wish to impound. During a direct examination rife with conjectures, hearsay, and irrelevancies, Judge Hilliardson kept glancing at Isaac Rosethorn with expectation, then impatience, but the defence attorney made not a single objection. Instead he wrote notes to George Hall. By now it was three-thirty in the afternoon, and I suspected Isaac was hoping that Bazemore wouldn't be able to move Moonfoot (who was in no hurry to return to Delaware) through to the end of his story before adjournment, which would give the defence all night to plan its cross-examination.

Even Mitch kept turning around as if to meet face-on inevitable objections from Rosethorn. In their absence, he tried his best to speed Butler along, flapping his arm at digressions as if they were flies. 'Never mind about the adult magazines now . . .' 'We don't need that conversation word-for-word, Mr Butler, just summarize for us . . .' Finally, he herded him back to George Hall. 'So it was *then* you introduced the defendant to Robert Pym?'

'Well, sir, that's right. Pym's kinfolk, this Willie Slidell that was working in the shipping department there at Fanshaw? Well, he say how they been just taking a truck when they want one, but they gotta stop that now 'cause the man's gonna get on to them. But then the problem is, Russell didn't trust any of the drivers Willie Slidell knew enough to cut 'em in, and I said how I could put them on to George, 'cause we go way back, and he's hurting for bread. And that's how it all got started. George was running the regular route down to Georgia, but they want him to make stops on the way where they tell him to. But Willie said to me, "I don't like this whole—"'

'Just a moment. To your direct knowledge, George Hall, at the instigation of Robert Pym and the others, transported stolen goods from Hillston, North Carolina, into the state of Georgia?'

Butler nodded. 'Yes, sir, that's my direct knowledge of the facts. He got five hundred a trip.'

351

The whole room stirred, like wind over wheat. This *was* news to most people at the court; it certainly appeared to be news to the judge, whose nose looked the way it might if he'd just stepped into an outhouse during an August heatwave. There was a surge of motion at the press table. Bubba Percy threw aside his doodle pad, and started writing as fast as he could. Back near me, Jack Molina looked stunned. So did Jordan West. Nomi Hall's head trembled, but her shoulders straightened even more stiffly against her seat. George didn't turn around. He kept his eyes on the state seal above the bench.

Throwing his arm out in George's direction, Bazemore said, 'Mr Butler, do you have any direct knowledge as to whether the defendant was *aware* that he was transporting stolen and/or illegal merchandise?'

'Well, sir.' Butler pinched his tiny ear. 'George told me one time he's near the Georgia line, and how he met four men come out of the woods behind this old shut-down motel off Ninety-five, 'round midnight, and they climb in the truck and haul away six of those big old cardboard tubs loaded back there. I don't guess George thought that motel was a regular Fanshaw depot.'

Hilliardson gavelled down the snickering. 'Mr Rosethorn? Mr Rosethorn, I realize this witness has come upon you unexpectedly. I feel compelled to inquire whether or not the State's line of questioning is acceptable to the defence?' The judge's thin lips twisted like he'd bitten on the bitter part of a pecan shell. The clear implication was that unless Isaac had slipped into a coma and couldn't hear what was going on, his prolonged passivity was, in Hilliardson's view, inexplicable, if not derelict.

Isaac stood up in slow motion, and spoke at the same pace. 'Your Honour, I'm very appreciative of your consideration. Thank you. Yes, the prosecutor did fail to inform me that he'd arranged to "borrow" this convicted felon from the good state of Delaware. But I hope I am correct in assuming that Mr Butler will not be whisked away from us, and returned to his cell up North, until the defence has an opportunity to cross-examine him. Assuming that is the case, I think we should hear Mr Butler's story of his partnership in crime with these three despicable disgraces to the distinguished name of the Hillston police.' Judge Hilliardson looked like he was sorry he'd given Rosethorn a chance to get his mouth working again, as the old man's gorgeous baritone kept languidly wafting across the room. 'Your Honour, I have been intrigued by Mr Butler's story, shared with us vividly in what the counsel for the prosecution keeps on so strangely insisting are the witness's "own words"—'

'Yes. Fine, then, Counsellor.' The judge used two fingers in a 'be seated' gesture, and Isaac very slowly sat. Hilliardson then turned his sneer on Mitch Bazemore. 'At this point, the *bench* will ask the State to satisfy this court that Mr Butler's evidence has some direct bearing on Robert Pym's *death*, as well as his allegedly nefarious life.'

Bazemore swayed in place. 'Absolutely, yes, it absolutely does, sir.' And his next questions to Butler were rushed, as if he hoped that would speed up the answers. 'Do you know if George Hall was still making these "runs" at the time Pym was shot?'

'No, sir, he quit on them. Had a bad argument right after—'

'When was this argument? What date?'

'I don't know a date. This was 'bout three, four weeks before the, you know, thing at Smoke's, you know, when George shot him. Could be it was more like six or seven—'

'And after this bad argument, would you say that George Hall felt extremely hostile to Pym?'

To everyone's surprise, Rosethorn suddenly hit the table with his fist. 'Objection. Leading the witness! Calls for opinion!'

'Hate'd be a mild—'

'Sustained!' With audible relief, Hilliardson sighed. 'Strike the answer. The jury will disregard it.'

Bazemore tried again. 'At any time between when George Hall severed his connection with Robert Pym, and Pym's death, did George Hall ever do or say anything to make you think he was hostile to Pym?'

Isaac: 'Objection! Calls for a conjecture on the part of the witness.'

Hilliardson. 'Sustained .'

Bazemore gave it another shot. 'In that time, did George Hall ever have a conversation with you regarding his feelings about Robert Pym?'

Moonfoot looked at his knees. 'Yes ... Said he wasn't fit to live.'

George Hall's head jerked up. Leaning over, Isaac wrapped his arm around George's shoulder, and said something to him.

Bazemore walked the length of the jury box. '"Not fit to live." Did he say anything else?'

'Told me if he thought he could get away with it, he'd kill him.'

Bazemore stood quietly, letting the words sink in across the courtroom. Isaac patted the table top in a furious impatience. I moved so I could see George's face. He was just looking at Moonfoot Butler, with a puzzled contempt. Then, to everyone's surprise, the DA after a glance at the clock, dropped that whole topic, and asked, 'Were you with George Hall at Smoke's Bar on the night when Robert Pym was shot?'

'Well, sir, him and me had a drink at Smoke's that night, but I didn't stay for the shooting.'

Mitch pounced. 'By that, do you mean you had reason to think there *would* be a shooting there that night?'

Isaac's hand shot up to object, but then he quickly lowered it and shook his head at the judge.

Moonfoot Butler was grinning. '*You* mighta thought there was gonna be a shooting *too*, you saw Bobby Pym near 'bout foaming at the mouth, shove that big old thirty-eight of his right up George's nose. Ever'body in that bar thought there's gonna be a shooting.'

A sharp hoot burst from a section of the courtroom, where I spotted Martin Hall with his fist raised. Hilliardson slammed his gavel a half-dozen times, and made some dire threats about further disruptions. Moonfoot kept talking, before Mitch Bazemore, beet red, could stop him. 'Yes, sir. 'Bout ten minutes after Pym walks in, those two go at it like cats in the air. But that's when I split, so I don't have no direct knowledge after that.'

I heard the courtroom doors open behind me. Nora Howard hurried back, a manila envelope under her arm.

Squeezing the rail of the witness stand, Mitch made a valiant effort to control his voice as he said, '*But before* this altercation began, when George Hall saw Robert Pym enter Smoke's Bar, did Hall make any comment to you about Pym?'

Isaac objected here, again on the grounds of leading the witness. Hilliardson overruled him on the grounds that direct remarks made by the defendant at this juncture might well have a vital bearing on our understanding of the subsequent events.

'A comment?' Moonfoot tugged at his little goatee, looked at the ceiling, then twisted sideways in the chair and lowered his head. 'Well, yes, he made a comment about him, yes, sir. Pym went over by the jukebox, and folks were arguing with him 'cause he'd punched some tunes, and there was a live entertainment going on, and so George said to me . . .' Moonfoot looked up at Bazemore, and swallowed carefully.

Mitch nodded. 'He said to you?'

'. . . Said, "If he mess with me, if he say one fuckin' word to me . . . I'm gonna kill that motherfucker dead. I don't get him now, then I get him later, but I get him."'

Hilliardson spoke into the thick silence that now filled the courtroom. 'I'm sorry, I couldn't hear your last sentence. Could you repeat it, and if possible speak more loudly?'

Moonfoot kept his eyes on the DA. 'George said, "If I don't get him now, then I get him later, but I get him."'

Bazemore: 'Those were George Hall's exact words, at least fifteen minutes before his shooting Pym?'

'. . . Those were his words.'

'And this was prior to the start of any fight between them? Before it started.'

'Prior to it, that's right.'

'At the time he said this, was Pym's gun in evidence? . . . Was it visible to you?'

'No, it wasn't visible till they got to shoving each other when Pym goes for it. Then it was visible.'

'When George said, "Sooner or later I'm going to shoot Pym," did—'

Isaac slapped the table. 'Objection.'

Hilliardson sustained it, adding, 'There has been no testimony that the defendant spoke the words you just used, Mr Bazemore.'

Apologizing, Mitch rephrased the question, through tightly locked lips: 'When George told you, "If he say one fuckin' word to me . . . I'm gonna kill that motherfucker dead," what was his tone of voice?'

'Beg pardon?'

The judge said, 'His tone of voice. Was he laughing, shouting in anger, et cetera?'

Moonfoot squeezed his eyes shut as if to recall. 'Well . . . Serious. Quiet. Kind of scary, I guess.'

Bazemore: 'And what did you say?'

'. . . I don't recall my exact words, but something about it didn't sound like a good idea.'

'What didn't?'

'Shooting Bobby Pym.'

Mitch walked to the jury box, then faced Isaac Rosethorn. 'Mr Butler, when did you learn that Bobby Pym had been shot to death and that George Hall had been charged with the crime?'

'Early morning, I heard it on the radio.'

'And were you, to borrow a word from the defence counsel, *surprised* to hear that George Hall had killed Robert Pym?'

Butler wiped his hand all the way down the front of his face. 'Well, no, I wasn't surprised.'

The DA looked at the clock, said, 'Thank you,' and sat down.

The judge looked at the clock, at Mitch, at Isaac, and at Moonfoot Butler. Then he said, 'It is nearly four. We could continue. But rather than begin cross-examination at this late hour, I am going to adjourn court until tomorrow at ten.'

Miss Bee Turner hopped up. Behind her, Mitch waved his arm like a first-grader desperate for permission to go to the bathroom. 'Your Honour, Your Honour! Delaware police expect to return Mr Butler to their jurisdiction tonight!'

'Well,' said Hilliardson, as he stood like a tall black heron on a high riverbank. 'Then I suggest, Counsel, that you offer them and their prisoner the hospitality for which the state of North Carolina is so justly renowned.'

Chapter 20

After court adjourned, I walked over to ask Isaac and Nora what they were going to do about Moonfoot Butler's testimony, and they said they were going to Pogo's, the closest bar. There they were going to study the deposition Moonfoot had given Isaac back in December when he and Billy Gilchrist had driven to Delaware (and which Nora had rushed out of the courtroom today to bring back). They planned to check it for discrepancies with the pretrial statement Mitch had tossed on their table as he finished his examination. But Isaac didn't want to talk about Butler now; he wanted instead to hear all about Purley Newsome, and told me he'd like a chance to interview Purley as soon as we had him in custody. I said, 'You'll have to wait in a long line.'

After Pogo's, Isaac and Nora were going to dinner at Carippini's; they asked me to drop in there if I was free. I said I had a hundred things to do. Nora said, Who doesn't? Isaac yanked me aside, whispered that it was a surprise party for Nora, and he wanted me to show up – even though I hadn't been invited – because Nora didn't actively dislike me as much as it seemed.

I said, 'On those grounds, I could drop in for supper parties at half the homes in Hillston: I wasn't invited, and the guest of honour doesn't actively dislike me. Good Lord, Isaac.'

'No no, I meant everybody's just been asking everybody and I was going to ask you, but it slipped my mind. So do your hundred things, and come on over.'

One of the things I did was see Moonfoot Butler safely escorted to our holding cell at HPD, where he should have felt quite at home, after thirty-four previous visits over a score of years.

Whether Moonfoot's memories of HPD were fond or not, he'd begged his Delaware escorts to let him stay with us for the night, rather than send him across the street to the county jail. Mitch showed up while I was in there, and told Butler he'd done very well, adding that tomorrow he should 'stick to his story' and not allow Rosethorn to 'bamboozle him,' and that, until tomorrow, he should 'keep his mouth shut' if anyone came to see him.

Moonfoot yanked on the bars as if to make sure the cell were locked. 'I don't wanna see anybody. Don't let anybody back here.'

'Frankly, I think Butler's afraid of Hall, that's my theory,' Mitch said as he jog-walked back to his office from the holding cell.

Furious, I walked even faster than he did. 'Frankly, Mitch, I think you've had a major insight here. Now, *I* also have a theory; it's about *why* Butler's afraid of Hall. If I'd just committed perjury in a capital case, I too would be afraid to be locked up in the same cell with the man I'd committed it against.'

His neck one scarlet bulge, he swung around on me fast, and started jabbing his forefinger into my sternum. '*Are you implying that I suborned a witness? Is that what you're implying, Mangum? Are you making that accusation?!*'

I slapped his hand away hard. 'Don't do that, okay? You touch me again, and I'm gonna hurt you, Mitch. I said, in my opinion, Butler committed perjury. I didn't say you told him to, or even that you believe he did it.'

Folding his arms tightly over his chest, Mitch stepped back, and locked eyes with me. 'Butler is telling the truth. He isn't lying. He told the court exactly what he told this office when he was subpoenaed. The truth. Is that clear? No one bribed him, and no one intimidated him. The truth is, George Hall planned to kill a man, planned to, and did it. He's a violent disruptive factor in our society, and these trials and everything surrounding these trials has been a violent disruptive factor in our society, and Hall should have been executed years ago. And Isaac Rosethorn's *deigning* to waltz in now and set up his fancy magic show for the jury can't make the truth vanish. Hall took a life, and he owes a life. End of discussion, Mangum.'

We were outside his office now, but I straight-armed my hand against the door to stop him from opening it. 'I know you believe that. But the real truth is – you want the real truth? – Hall and his brother and their supporters are a big ugly thorn in your side, and you're *mad*. You're mad, and you're scared of Rosethorn, because he already beat you on three other cases.'

'Just hold it right—'

'The real truth is, you've got your name in the papers for winning those big forty-four "Go for it" death penalty convictions of yours, and you can't stand it that you've only managed to get nine of those forty-four people actually gassed. And you've gone on record that you're going to make Hall number ten, and you *want* Hall.'

'*The state of North Carolina wants Hall!*'

'The state of North Carolina *should* want justice, not a victory! If you wanted the whole truth, you'd listen. I've *tried* to tell you that George Hall was repeatedly threatened by Russell, that if he didn't keep his mouth shut, his family would be hurt. He does keep his mouth shut. And Russell still shoots his brother. And we still don't know why.'

Mitch shook his head fast. 'I don't believe a word of George Hall's story. It's just something he came up with after the fact. Trying to make himself look heroic. Nobody goes to the gas chamber if he thinks he can get out of it, not just because of some vague threat against his brother. George Hall knew he *couldn't* get out of it. And he's not going to get out of it either. I'm going to nail him in this stupid retrial. You can tell your friend Rosethorn that Hall's going right back to Death Row where he belongs. That's something Rosethorn can set his clock by!' It was interesting that Bazemore accepted the idea that a man like Otis Newsome could get so upset by a brother's 'shame' that he'd kill himself, but wouldn't accept the idea that a man like George Hall could let himself be killed in order to save a brother's life.

He flung open the glass door with DISTRICT ATTORNEY, HAVER COUNTY painted across it. Caught reading a soap opera magazine, his secretary leapt to her feet, then snatched up a stack of message slips, which she offered him as a quick distraction. He didn't, however, even see her, much less her offering, but marched around her desk and slammed the door to his inner office. Immediately it was yanked back open and out came Bazemore's nasal command that I phone him tonight '*re* what to have Savile say to Newsome in the A.M.,' adding that he had to discuss things with the A.G. first. I suggested that if Purley was dumb enough to believe in deals made with murder suspects by lieutenants over the telephone, we should go ahead and promise him whatever it took to get him into custody.

'I don't make promises I don't intend to keep,' snapped Mitch, with his pious prosecutor expression.

'So, what'd you promise Moonfoot Butler that you intend to give *him*?' I snapped back. The DA said what he'd give me was five seconds to get out of his office.

I made it easy, and drove to Carippini's Restaurant.

That night Nora Howard's brother had closed Carippini's to the public. Gold and silver balloons bounced against the ceiling, twisted mylar streamers shimmered around the columns and swagged from the archways. Across the windows, above the bar, and along the back wall stretched some long multicoloured strings of big letters. They spelled out 'CONGRATULATIONS, NORA.' A huge white pastry concoction in the shape of a Greek temple (it turned out to be the Supreme Court Building) also said 'CONGRATULATIONS, NORA.' Tables had been pushed together into two long L's, and at them sat twenty noisy, cheerful people drinking wine and eating a meal cooked by Nora's brother, veal marsala with risotto and Roman artichokes. Her brother had invited everyone to his restaurant to celebrate the fact that on Friday, Nora Angelica Carippini Howard had learned that she'd passed the North Carolina law bar exams.

It was a good dinner party, with lots of songs and lots of wine, lots of children, and 'Golden Oldies' dancing; there were zippy accordion tunes by (I think) Nora's aunt's second husband, and tributes to the guest of honour: the presentation of a new brief-case by her kids, Laura and Brian, a comic skit by three friends from the Law Library, the recitation by Isaac Rosethorn in Italian of Dante's meeting Beatrice in the *Divine Comedy* (in honour, he said, of his meeting 'the more beautiful half of Rosethorn and Howard'). Later, there was a prize of little champagne bottles won by Nora and, in fact, me, for our energetic jitterbug to Jerry Lee Lewis's 'Breathless' – which was exactly how three minutes of that youthful pastime left me.

Among the people at the party was Jordan West, who sat with the young black psychiatrist from the Department of Human Services. He couldn't take his eyes off her; a feeling most people had about Jordan to some degree or other. Watching them together, a comment of Jack Molina's popped in my head, about how if I didn't believe him when he said Cooper had no interest in 'the personal,' I should just ask Jordan West. Well, this new man looked as interested in the personal as it was possible to be; every time she spoke to him it was like she'd tapped a tuning fork. They danced a slow dance in a way that made me think John Emory might as well quit struggling to overcome his shyness in order to ask her out. I sat with them a while, and we talked about the trial, about Moonfoot Butler's testimony (she assumed it was all a fabrication – including George's involvement in the smuggling), about Nomi Hall's faith that Isaac would win an acquittal for her son.

I said, 'I hope so too.'

Jordan looked at me. 'Nomi doesn't hope so; she *believes* so. To her, Cooper died for George. Saving George helps to redeem his death. Me, I don't think Coop . . .' Her voice faltered, and the young doctor put his hand quietly over hers. 'I don't think of it that way. Cooper *lived* for George and all the others, people he never saw. But he *died* for no reason, just . . . hate.' None of us spoke for a while. Finally, she slid her hand out from under her escort's. She stood up, which I took to be a signal for me to leave, so I stood up too, and she shook my hand quickly, then said, 'I hadn't known until your testimony that you had written to the parole board for George. Isaac always told Coop that he was wrong about you. And I think if Coop had heard your testimony today, he would have decided that Isaac was right.'

'Well, Coop wasn't wrong about some things. I wasn't good enough or fast enough to protect him.'

She didn't argue with me. I shook Dr Arnold's hand too. He turned back towards her and I left them alone.

Three more dances with Nora and I pleaded exhaustion. While I sat off at a far corner table recovering, replaced as her partner by (I think) her brother's wife's cousin, Isaac pulled up a chair beside me. 'So, Slim,' he said, licking white icing from his fingers. 'Nice people.' I agreed. We watched the party a while, then he gave me one of his tragic looks. 'Cuddy, tell me, do you think Billy's dead? Now we know how close Purley Newsome was to home, and maybe Russell, too, I'm sick with the thought that they grabbed Billy.'

I said I hoped not, but it was possible. ''Course, Paul Madison's convinced that Gilchrist held out on those contributions to the collection plate we heard so much about, and that he's off on another toot to Vegas or Miami.'

'Well, Paul's a man of faith. He's naturally optimistic.' Isaac's rounded shoulders shrugged up around his neck. 'Me, I imagine chain saws and pools of blood.'

'How badly do you need Gilchrist's testimony?'

Isaac's eyes turned even more mournful. 'Ah, Slim, Slim, are you really so pragmatic as that? I *liked* Billy.' We were both quiet a while, then he said, 'I've got the girl who was up in the Montgomery Hotel room with Russell.' Another silence. Then, 'You want to know the word you used on the stand that hurt most? "Pursued." "George got hold of the gun, and *pursued* Pym."'

'"Pursued" was the truth.'

'"Pursued" was hearsay. You weren't there, and I doubt whichever patron of Smoke's described the scene to you said, "And then he pursued him out the door." ... Interesting, how Judge Hilliardson will allow a bit of hearsay, a bit of conclusion. He gave us quite a speech in chambers before we opened. You know how he bites off his words like little pieces of rock candy?' Rosethorn was an excellent mimic (most good trial lawyers are good actors), and it was remarkable how he transformed his large bulk, Semitic features, and rolling baritone into the clipped nasal tenor, and the thin Wasp semblance of Shirley Hilliardson, as he gulped down a sip of watery whiskey and said, "Gentlemen, in my courtroom, the game of law must and will be subordinated to the quest for truth. In that – and I am unabashed in calling it, holy – quest, jurisprudence is the servant of justice, never the master. We are all three here to seek truth. Not a conviction, not an acquittal, but truth. Counsellors, are we in accord?' Well, naturally Bazemore and I bobbed our heads like fuzzy dogs on a dashboard, then ran out into the court shooting, dodging, blocking, and behaving like any sane lawyer would. Still, it was a lovely speech.'

I said, 'I'm with Hilliardson.'

'I'm with George Hall.' He smiled. 'But in general, your testimony was helpful.' A pat on the knee. 'The jury seemed to find you morally appealing.'

I wiped my forehead and neck with my handkerchief. 'Maybe because they figured I was telling the truth. Which I suspect is more than we can say for Moonfoot Butler.'

Isaac went on an unsuccessful pocket search for his cigarettes. 'Ah, Mr Moonfoot. What he said isn't as interesting as why he said anything at all. And even that's not nearly as interesting *really*, as I'm going to make it sound tomorrow morning. Poor Moonfoot Butler. It's never safe to sell your soul. The buyers can rarely be trusted to pay off ... So, Bazemore scared you on redirect, didn't he?'

'You noticed? Thanks for shutting him up before that catechism on the death penalty. I would have had to answer—'

'Why?' He had taken off his jacket, and unbuttoned his shirt cuffs, which flapped loose around his wide stubby hands as he nibbled at pieces of Nora's cake. 'Your beliefs aren't on trial; George Hall's actions are on trial. And I'd advise if you're ever in similar circumstances – deprive yourself of the self-satisfying pleasure of beating the breast of truth, *or* baring your social philosophy.' His finger ticked back and forth near my nose.

'I think Mitch Bazemore and the AG and the commissioner already have a pretty good idea of my social philosophy.'

He smiled. 'Well, pretty good ideas are very different from forced acknowledgement. Which is why I never allow my clients to tell me things I shouldn't know.'

'Things like the fact that they're guilty?'

'Oh, no. That they do need to tell me; it helps me plan their defence better ... I meant things like – they cajoled a friend into supporting a false alibi, or they've decided to bribe a juror, or skip bail.'

I grinned. 'My reservations about capital punishment are in the same category as skipping bail? Why, you have even stronger reservations than—'

'No, sir! I have none.' His deep black eyes blazed out at me. 'My position on that subject is utterly *without* reservation: Simply put, I deny the difference between a hanging and a lynching. Profoundly deny it.' He rubbed the napkin roughly across his face. '*And*, I might add, the statistics agree. The states that have *had* the most lynchings, also have had the most executions.'

'That doesn't make them the same, for Christ's sake.'

'Oh yes it does. The props and the sets are immaterial.' He reached out and grabbed a floating balloon whose string Brian Howard was leaping for, and handed it to the child. 'Who said this? "Murder and Capital Punishment are not opposites, but similars that breed their kind"?'

Neither Brian nor I knew the answer, and the lawyer told us it was George Bernard Shaw. 'What do you think of that, Brian?' he asked the five-year-old. ' "Murder and Capital Punishment are not opposites, but similars that breed their kind"?' Not surprisingly, Brian said he had no ideas on the subject. 'Well,' said Isaac, 'Say I kill somebody—'

'Who?'

'Somebody you don't know. A man. Say I get mad and shoot him. Let's say you're the police. What do *you* think my punishment should be?' He leaned down to Brian, awaiting his answer with real interest. 'Would you kill me back?'

Brian bounced his head against his balloon a few times. 'I'd make you go sit all by yourself till you said "I'm sorry." I'd put you on a boat and send you to the middle of the ocean all by yourself.'

Serious consideration from Isaac. 'All right. That's a good plan.'

'And then . . .' Another bounce. 'And then when you came back, you'd have to be nice to the man's family because they'd be sad.'

Tapping his own forehead, Isaac nodded thoughtfully. 'Brian, you have a very smart noggin. But suppose I didn't want to be nice? Suppose I kept being mean?'

Racing around in a circle, Brian squealed, 'Then you have to go back in the boat, and then you have to clean up the whole ocean by yourself, and then *you'll* be sad!' Suddenly, he scooted under the table, having spotted his mother's approach.

Nora was not at all out of breath, despite her nonstop exertions on the dance floor (she attributed her stamina to aerobics). Lifting the table cloth, she gave Brian a 'ten-minute warning' before time to leave. Then, leaning over Isaac's chair, Nora hugged the old man from behind. She looked happy. He patted her crossed arms, and told her she had a wonderful family.

She said, 'Aren't they? Look, I just thought of another discrepancy. In fact, in at *least* five places, Butler's testimony today contradicts *both* the deposition he gave you back in December, *and* his pretrial statement from Bazemore!'

I said, 'Good Lord, you mean you can do the Mashed Potatoes and think at the same time?'

She straightened, held up the black curls off the nape of her neck. 'Captain, I can think, do the Mashed Potatoes, chew gum, keep an eye on the kids, and smell if the coffee's done – at the same time. Multiple-focus skills, you get them when you've trained to outwit nuns at a convent school.'

'I've never seen you chewing gum.'

'I said, I *could* do it, not I did.'

Isaac laughed. 'Never argue with a lawyer.'

I told Nora, 'Seems to me you're wasting your talents on the courts, the way you can *dance*. Any old clodhopper like Isaac here can sway juries and confound judges. But how many folks still living can double-time Walk the Dog?'

She grinned. 'Well, you, for one.'

The deejay (I think, Nora's oldest nephew) had put on Glenn Miller's 'Moonlight Serenade.' I said, 'I always loved it when June Allyson got this thoughtful look and tugged at her earlobe every time Jimmy Stewart started working on "Moonlight Serenade." Remember that movie? And she hides all his pocket change till she's got enough to buy the band a car? What a woman. Care to dance again?'

Nora smiled at me, but she scooped her arm through Isaac's and pulled him out of his chair. 'Come on, partner.'

The man was actually embarrassed, which I don't believe I'd ever seen before. Shaking his head, he held back. 'Ah, Nora, alas, I don't do this. I can't dance.'

She tugged him away from the table. 'Everybody can dance. Just hold on.'

Watching them from under the table, Brian's comment, spit out in a giggling fit, was apt. 'Mommy looks like she's dancing with a big old white-haired bear.' Isaac, after a minute of riveting his eyes to Nora's feet, glanced up, smiled, and waved at us. I'd say he was probably the worst fox-trotter I ever saw in my life, but he was apparently enjoying himself.

Afterwards, he shambled over to say good-night. Since he'd asked me how to get from here to the By-Ways Budget Motel, and since that's where Mitch Bazemore (ignoring Judge Hilliardson's advice to make North Carolina look good) had boarded the Delaware state patrolmen who'd brought Moonfoot Butler down, I assumed that Isaac was on his way to the motel to try to pump the men for information. Then he'd probably go to the county jail to visit George Hall, then he'd probably see if he could get in to talk to Moonfoot Butler, then he'd go sit up all night with a pack of Chesterfields, a pint of bourbon, a bag of pistachios, and his yellow legal pad.

I left the party shortly after Isaac did, went home to River Rise, put on some Aretha Franklin, listened to my messages. One was from Warden Carpenter at Dollard Prison, asking me if I could spare the time to come talk with him tomorrow. He didn't explain why. I returned the call from Mitch Bazemore that said, 'Bazemore, Mangum. I said call me. Where are you?'

'I have a wife and children,' the DA informed me when he answered on the first ring. I told him I'd heard that rumour. 'I mean, we're in bed.'

'All of you? The six kids too? Kind of hard to picture.'

'Mangum, just stop right there. It's ten-thirty five! Do you realize that?'

'I didn't realize it, but I can assimilate it, Mitch.'

While I listened to him, I tricked Martha into taking her pill by shoving it into a cheese cracker. Mitch wanted me to know that the AG had told him to tell me to tell Savile to tell Newsome that if he surrendered by noon tomorrow, signed a full confession, and agreed to testify for the State, then the State would take all the above into account. I laughed and said Purley might find our part of the deal a little vague. 'He can read between the lines,' Mitch impatiently pointed out.

'Purley can't read *on* the lines, much less between them. Give me something concrete in big print, or he's not coming in, Mitch.'

'Savile can *imply* – imply, not state or delineate in any way that impacts on our deniability – *imply* that the indictment will exclude first degree on the Slidell murder.'

'And on Cooper Hall?'

'The AG is annoyed, very annoyed. The reputation of civic government, law enforcement, public trust itself is at stake. We indict Newsome and Russell. They're the only ones involved in these murders, and their motives were greed, greed and panic, *not* politics. The AG wants this whole mess settled quietly. Quietly, quickly, and simply. It's left a bad taste in people's mouths.'

'Yeah. Especially people like Willie Slidell and Cooper Hall. And Otis Newsome. They got mouths full of dirt.'

His voice tripled in volume, and I wondered if his wife resorted to ear plugs. 'For the last time, Otis is left out of this! And politics is left out of this. Do you understand me?'

My voice made no effort to meet his. 'Then tell me flat out, Mitch. You're asking me to suppress evidence?'

He spluttered into the phone. '*I absolutely am not.* I'm telling you *you don't have* any evidence.'

As patiently as I could bear to, I reminded the district attorney we had every reason to suspect that Otis Newsome, a town official, had (a) called in his chits on Dyer Fanshaw (to whom he'd handed over all the city's paper contracts at a fat profit), and (b) persuaded Fanshaw to overlook the illegal use of his trucks by Otis's little brother Purley. That (c), far from turning in Purley and his pals for smuggling, Otis had then (d) paid them to supply weapons to extremists, and (e) worked with extremists to stir up trouble against the political opponents of people he wanted in office. That (f) it was likely he'd been involved years back in the tear-gas stampede at Williamstown Auditorium. That (g) it was likely he'd been involved in an attempt to blackmail Andy Brookside into pulling out of the governor's race. That (h) we had every reason to suspect that if Otis hadn't known beforehand, he'd surely covered up afterwards, the murder of Cooper Hall. That (adding a through h) it was likely that Otis Newsome would have been indictable on a string of charges as long as my arm.

Bazemore responded as if he'd been in the kitchen snacking the whole time I was talking. 'You have no evidence against Otis.'

'For Christ's sake, Mitch, why do you think the man killed himself? A bad day at the office?' I was pacing fast around the kitchen counter, lifting the phone's spiraled cord to keep it from knocking things over.

'Mangum, no man who'd done the kinds of callous things you are alleging, no man like that *would* kill himself. A good man devastated by horrible revelations about a cherished brother, whom he'd raised himself, that kind of man is the kind of man who might get overcome by despair and take his own life.'

I made myself sit calmly on a stool, and keep my voice quiet. 'I respect your feelings for Otis, but he's not one of the good guys. I'm *telling* you, I can produce a witness who will testify that Otis Newsome hired her to blackmail Andrew Brookside.'

His reply was wide-awake. 'Blackmail how?'

'Someone hired by Newsome to seduce Brookside and video-tape their sexual activity. Willie Slidell was hired to set up the tape.'

He asked me if I had the tape. I said I didn't. How did I know such a tape had actually been made? I told him I hadn't con-firmed the tape's existence. He asked me if I had the *witness*. I told him she was out of the country. I'd been told about her by Hamilton Walker. Hamilton Walker? Was this witness then a black prostitute? A sigh like a death rattle. 'Mangum, you make me sick. On the secondhand word of a *pimp*, you accuse a dead man, a dead man unable to defend himself, of consorting and conspiring with whores and pornography scum to blackmail the president of Haver University, a gubernatorial candidate! You should be brought up on charges, *on charges*, and don't think I'm not prepared to do it! Don't ever come to me with that kind of sewage again!'

'And if I produce the tape?'

'Then Andrew Brookside is a man of loose morals, and I feel sorry for his wife. You aren't going to produce a tape showing Otis hiring this whore of yours, and that's what it would take to convince me he had. Period! Subject closed.'

I looked out my sliders at the moon rippling in the Shocco. I said, 'Tell me one thing. When you and Fanshaw found Otis, did you look for a note?'

Bazemore swallowed – I could hear it over the phone – and said I knew we hadn't ever found a note.

'We didn't, that's right. Maybe somebody beat us to it.'

He dropped the phone into the receiver from what sounded like a height of about ten feet.

When Purley called Justin at 6:43 A.M. (from a McDonald's across from the Raleigh bus station, as the trace quickly discovered), he was coughing and wheezing even harder than yesterday. Like me, Purley laughed at the AG's offer. He wanted 'limited immunity,' which he knew about from the Oliver North hearings. Justin said, 'That sounds fine.' He wanted reduced charges for pleading guilty to lesser offences, *and* a chance to prove he was innocent of all charges, by reason of 'brainwashing.' Justin said he totally believed Purley suffered from a washed brain, and thought he should stress that to the DA Purley wanted 'protective custody,' from Winston Russell, for which I certainly didn't blame him. In fact, he wanted a new house and name and job in another state, which he'd heard the FBI gave to people who testified against the Mafia. Justin told Purley that since Winston hadn't been in the Mafia, we'd have to get back to him on that one. He wanted Savile publicly to retract those statements to the papers about his being the trigger man and the mastermind, and to tell his mother they weren't true. Justin said he'd be glad to. Purley wanted a private meeting with the district attorney and the attorney general. He wanted a doctor. He wanted a lawyer. Justin said he'd see to it that he got them.

'Okay,' Purley wheezed. 'I'm turning myself in. I want it on the records, it's voluntary.'

'You got it,' Justin told him. 'Now, where's Winston?'

'He ain't with me. He's sick. We both got sick. I cut loose from him couple of weeks ago.'

'Where is he?'

'I'm hanging up now. You be standing at the fountain, first level, Catawha Mall, two P.M. Okay, Say-ville? Just you, and bring me a signed paper about how I'm cooperating.'

Justin looked up at what I'd just scrawled on the blackboard, which was what Brenda Moore had just told me on the intercom, after a call into a Raleigh police dispatcher. 'McDonald's. Raleigh bus station. Five minutes max.' Justin held up an okay sign, then spoke as gentle as a priest at a deathbed. 'Just stay right there, Purley. You sound like you feel rotten. You need medical attention. I don't want you taking the bus all the way from Raleigh.'

'Fuck you,' grunted Purley, and was gone before two RPD squad cars screeched right up on to the kerb in front of the golden arches. The girl behind the counter there said, yes, a tall blond man had run out the door just a few minutes earlier; she'd figured he was rushing to catch a bus. (It turned out he wasn't, because the Raleigh cops stopped two buses pulling out, and checked all the passengers.) Asked to describe him, the girl said he'd looked shaky, feverish, exhausted, dirty, and ragged; 'like a skinny beat-up bum that was sick as a dog,' was how she put it. The thought of Purley skinny was hard to imagine. She said he'd had to scrounge through his pockets for enough grimy change to pay for his Egg McMuffin. Back in December, Purley had withdrawn over nine thousand dollars from his bank account. Obviously, he hadn't budgetted well during his travels with Winston Russell.

With Bazemore on his feet the entire time, pouncing and snapping objections, Rosethorn kept Moonfoot Butler on the stand for three hours and forty minutes. I didn't hear all of it, and neither did the jury, because Judge Hilliardson sent the twelve out of the room four separate times while he heard heated arguments from the DA or the defence counsel on whether this or that precedent from these cited cases warranted a favourable ruling, or whether this or that comment by opposing counsel was inadmissible, inexcusable, and deserving of a horsewhip. The first time I wandered down to the courtroom, jammed with everyone who could squeeze in to watch the show, I heard Isaac lead Moonfoot backwards through a long and persistently unsuccessful career in crime. He asked him, to start with, if he hadn't come up for parole in Delaware last year, and been denied because he'd been caught stealing cigarettes and candy bars from the prison commissary.

On the stand in his same snappy jacket and pleated pants, Moonfoot looked hurt. 'They lied on me about that. The only real worst thing I did was drop a couple of racks of dishes, which got broke by accident, and they gave me five days in the hole.'

The old lawyer kept flipping through a packet of papers thick as the Hillston phone book (maybe it was the Hillston phone book, since not even the bank robber Willie Sutton had an arrest record that long), as he asked things like, 'For what offence *are* you in prison now, Mr Butler?' 'Two years ago, you were arrested here in Hillston for receiving stolen goods, is that correct?' 'And, again in nineteen eighty-one, were you not convicted of three more counts of breaking and entering, for which you served an additional eighteen months at Dollard?' 'Shall we call nineteen seventy-five the year of the bad cheques, then?' 'I'm looking at your juvenile arrest record here, Mr Butler, and I must say I'm overwhelmed. I see here *before the age of eighteen*, nine counts of petty larceny, four counts of unauthorized use of a vehicle – in other words, stealing cars – two counts of carrying a pistol without a licence, let's see, ah, purse-snatching, shoplifting, disorderly conduct, possession of narcotics. Maybe it would save us some time, sir, if you simply listed for us any crimes you *haven't* committed. Have you for example ever before been charged with perjury?'

Bazemore naturally objected to this. In fact, he stormed right over to the defence table, and yelled, 'All right, Mr Rosethorn, just stop it right there! Your Honour, I protest counsel's outrageous attempt to embarrass and discredit this witness under the guise of questioning him!'

Isaac, flapping the arrest document in the DA's face: 'I don't *need* to discredit him! His past discredits him! And there is no immunity to embarrassment guaranteed a witness. Under the Fifth Amendment, Mr Butler *was* protected against self-incrimination. *You*, Mr Bazemore, *you* ignored that right by bringing this man here (and we might well ask how you *persuaded* him to

370

come) to tell all these wild tales of robbing and smuggling and porno heists and warehouse—'

'Do you dare imply that—'

'Gentlemen! Gentlemen!' Judge Hilliardson whacked down the gavel hard enough to make Miss Bee turn around. 'Address yourselves to me, and not to each other. If you wish to make proper arguments, I will dismiss the jury again, and hear them. If you wish to bicker, do so elsewhere.'

Bazemore: 'Your Honour, I move that last question be taken out of the record. It was facetious and prejudicial and uncalled for.'

Hilliardson: 'What was the last question?'

Mr Walkington, the stenographer (who despite his advanced years could still do 195 words a minute): ' "Have you for example ever before been charged with perjury?" '

The judge had the question removed from the record, and suggested that if Isaac were simply attempting to establish this witness's character, perhaps we'd heard enough by now to catch the general drift. Isaac said that Moonfoot's character, his integrity, and his honesty were vitally at issue, but agreed that 'we have heard more than enough to draw our own conclusions about all of them.'

I'd already drawn my own conclusions about Arthur Butler, so I left Superior Court then for a conference upstairs with the new city comptroller about my budget, where I knew he would say my budget was too large, and he knew I would say it was too small. At the desk, Zeke was brooding over 'Houses for Rent' ads in the paper; he said there was still no word from Justin about Purley.

When I looked back in on the trial, Isaac (taking forever to blow on his glasses, then wipe them with a blue handkerchief) was saying, 'Mr Butler, it's now clear that you remember *nothing* from that night at Smoke's, do you? Not what you drank, or George drank, not what you wore, or he wore, not what else you talked about, not who else was there, not the time, not the weather, not the location of your table, and all the rest that you can't "recall," isn't that so? Yet you are asking us to believe you *can* recall, as you claim, *word for word* a few sentences George Hall said to you that night *seven long years ago?*'

Mr Butler said that was a different situation, because if a man says he's going to kill another man, then 'something important like that stands out in your mind.'

371

Isaac turned his back on the witness stand as he said, 'Would you say your testifying in this murder trial was "important"?' When Butler told him he certainly did think so, yes, Isaac (still with his back to him) said, 'You and I have been talking very earnestly now for two hours on this important subject, and I have been standing very close to you, Mr Butler. What colour is my tie?' Moonfoot said he thought it was blue. Isaac turned and showed him that it was red with yellow dots. Moonfoot said that seeing wasn't the same as hearing. Asked then to repeat the last question he'd heard the district attorney ask him yesterday afternoon, Moonfoot said he thought Bazemore had asked him if George had been laughing when he'd said he was going to kill Pym.

'No, sir, it was His Honour who inquired about Mr Hall's tone of voice.' And Isaac had the stenographer read out the DA's last question: 'And were you, to borrow a word from the defence counsel, *surprised* to hear that George Hall had killed Robert Pym?'

Folding his handkerchief, Isaac sighed sadly. 'I think we're all "surprised" at your peculiar style of memory, Mr Butler. It seems to work a whole lot better on things that happened seven years ago, than seven hours ago, or seven *minutes* ago!' Next the old lawyer brought Moonfoot to admit that he hadn't actually gone to Smoke's that night with George, but had simply run into him there, and sat down for a drink. Actually, he hadn't ever 'gone' to Smoke's at any time *with* George.

Isaac (his arms crossed over his tweed vest): 'Mr Butler, you said yesterday, "George and I were real close, we hung out together from childhood." Is that right? Good friends?'

'That's right.' Moonfoot was looking tired, but game.

Isaac smiled at him. 'What's George's sister's name?'

Butler couldn't 'call it to mind. Was it Dot?'

'No, sir, it's Natalie.' Isaac spun around to spot Mitch Bazemore, who was pacing the length not only of his own table, but the defence table as well. Through this whole cross-examination, the DA had been on his feet – and when not striding around the room, was rocking back and forth on the heels of his shiny wing tips. With a prayerful gesture, Isaac thundered, 'Mr Bazemore, would you *please* sit down? *And stop prowling!*'

The DA quivered. 'If you'd stop trying to block my view of the witness, I wouldn't need to keep moving!'

Isaac: 'Is it that you need to see the witness? Or that he needs to see *you*? Are you perhaps worried about signals not being caught?'

Mitch's fist hit his palm. 'Your Honour! These innuendos are outrageous! I move that remark be taken out of the record. *Out of the record!*'

The side of Judge Hilliardson's face twitched, and I thought both counsellors were headed back to chambers – like to the woodshed for a switching – but all he did was rub his cheek, and say with no expression that the remark would be removed from the record, that the defence would stand away from the witness, and stop making promiscuous accusations, and that the State would confide any further compulsory peregrinations to his own territorial domain. Bubba Percy laughed, and was told by the same frozen face that if the press wish to remain in court, the press would instantly stop these inappropriate noises. 'If you want comedy, young man, go to a movie, not a trial.' Bubba, Mitch, and Isaac all apologized.

Finally Isaac got back to questioning Moonfoot's familiarity with his 'close friend' George Hall by asking, 'What's George's mother's name?'

Butler couldn't 'recollect' Nomi Hall's first name. Nor could he recall George's father's name, or George's high-school girl-friend's name, or the name of the dog the Halls had owned for thirteen years, or the month of George's birthday, or the make and colour of the automobile George had driven for six years, or the location of his room in the Hall home, or the exact location of the house itself. He didn't know that George had had two toes blown off by a Claymore mine in Vietnam, that he'd had since childhood a burn scar down the back of his right thigh, or that his father was dead.

Slumped in the chair, Moonfoot tugged fretfully at his goatee. 'We hung out, is what I said; we was thick that way, but that's no reason he'd need to get into all this personal stuff.'

Isaac shook his head with a tragic slowness. 'Too personal to tell you his father had died, but not too personal to confide in you that he planned to kill a man?'

'Well, I happened to be the one there at the time.'

'Ahhh. And if any other passing stranger had happened to sit himself down at George's table that night, George would have "bummed a cigarette" from *him*, and said to *him*, "Oh by the way, see that drunk over there at the jukebox? I intend to kill him. If not tonight, then some other night." Is that it?' Turning to the jury, Isaac raised his arms in baffled sorrow. Then he pointed at Hall, who sat motionlessly straight, hands folded on the table top; his glasses had black plastic rims that he pushed at when Isaac said to Butler, 'That night in Smoke's, was George wearing his glasses?'

Bazemore was back on his feet, now jiggling coins in his pants' pockets. 'Your Honour, please ask Mr Rosethorn to stop interfering with my view of the witness!'

Isaac: 'Your Honour, let Mr Butler answer! It's a *simple* question.'

Mr Butler's simple answer was that he didn't remember whether George was wearing glasses or not. Asked if he remembered at what point in the argument between Pym and Hall he had decided to 'flee' rather than stay to 'protect, calm, or assist' his 'close friend' in the midst of an altercation with a white policeman whom he, Butler, knew to be a 'racist thug' – objection from Bazemore, sustained – Moonfoot said, 'towards the end.' Asked if he could pinpoint more specifically the moment when he had 'deserted' his 'childhood pal,' he said he thought it had probably been when Pym had pulled the gun, and shoved the muzzle in George's nostril.

Isaac's face sagged with contempt. 'Discretion was the better part of valour, that was your attitude, wasn't it, sir? Desertion, that was your style, wasn't it? A friend's life is in deadly danger, and what do you do? Try to disarm his assailant, try to telephone the police, try anything at all, besides slither away as fast as you could?' Without waiting for an answer, which, not surprisingly, didn't appear to be forthcoming anyhow, Isaac asked, 'You've told us yourself that you were "working" with Pym and his associates, as their "supplies man." Perhaps Pym had come to Smoke's to see *you*? Had you arranged to meet Pym there that night?'

Moonfoot emphatically denied it.

'What about Winston Russell? Maybe you were meeting him there?'

'I wasn't meeting anybody.'

Isaac looked dubious. 'Perhaps *you're* the one Pym had had this argument with? Is that possible?' Moonfoot said he'd never had any argument with Pym, or 'any of them.' 'Then why run off?' wondered Isaac, his hands opened out. 'In fact, if you were on such good terms with Robert Pym, and on such good terms with George, why didn't you interfere in their quarrel?' Moonfoot said it wasn't any of his business. 'Ah yes, your business of supplying merchandise and *names*, isn't it?' Isaac next wanted to know if during the course of their 'business dealings,' Butler had ever seen Winston Russell in a blue Ford. Yes, he had; he'd ridden in it. Had he seen it outside Smoke's that night? Objection, as irrelevant, from Bazemore, overruled by Hilliardson. Butler didn't remember whether he'd seen it or not. The old lawyer's questions now lashed out quickly one after another. 'Did you ever actually accompany George Hall on one of these alleged "smuggling" trips?'

'No sir, I never—'

'No, you did not. Did you ever actually *see* George Hall loading, or watching others load, illegal merchandise into a Fanshaw truck? See it go into the truck now?'

'Well, I wasn't there at the warehouse—'

'No, you did not. Did you ever actually *see* any money given to George Hall by Pym or Russell or anyone else, as payment for these so-called smuggling trips?'

'No, I never was—'

'No, you did not!' And Isaac, without pause, shifted to a whole different line of questioning, and abruptly asked, 'Mr Butler! Before you appeared in court yesterday, did you have occasion to speak with Mr Bazemore? That's the district attorney pacing up and down there? Have you ever at any time discussed your testimony in this trial with him?'

By the time Moonfoot revealed that over the past forty-eight hours he'd had 'two or three talks' with the DA regarding his testimony, and 'three or four talks' with our yuppie assistant DA, Neil Sadler (including the statement Sadler had taken from him up in Delaware), Mitch Bazemore's coins were jingling like a runaway herd of belled sheep. Wheelling sharply, he bellowed, 'Your Honour! For heaven's sake! Mr Rosethorn knows it is perfectly ordinary and perfectly legal for the State to interview a prospective witness prior to testimony. He is trying to sneak around and imply that the State has behaved improperly!'

Isaac lashed back: 'I intended no such implication! But, of course, if that's the way you choose to take it—'

Hilliardson sent the jury (who were getting more exercise than they'd anticipated) back out; they went with the look of children sure all the exciting stuff was going to happen as soon as they left the room. Then the judge called both counsels to the bench, lectured at them a while, and told them loud enough for everybody else to hear, if not follow, his remarks, 'Patience may be sitting on a monument, smiling at grief. But, gentlemen, Patience has advised me she will not be sitting on this bench with me much longer!' Mitch appeared to be upset about some papers which Isaac was showing both him and the judge, and which I gathered the judge was going to allow into evidence, as he had Miss Bee mark the packet for identification.

After the jury hurried back in, Isaac shambled over to the defence table, where Nora Howard handed him another sheaf of typed pages. Flipping this set to its last page, he brought it to the witness stand, where Moonfoot still sat sadly staring at his shoes. 'Mr Butler, this is a copy of the statement that you gave to the assistant DA, Mr Sadler, two weeks ago, is that right? Here's your signature, is that correct?'

After a thoughtful perusal, Moonfoot agreed that it was his signature, but added that he couldn't be sure about whether he'd signed it two weeks ago or not; if that's what the notarized date said, he guessed he'd go along with it. With a smile, Isaac stepped back. 'Unreliable as your memory is, sir, I hesitate to ask, but have you ever met *me*? Before this trial, that is?'

Happy to be of help after all this criticism, Moonfoot grinned. 'Um hum, met you up in Delaware Prison.'

A rustle through the courtroom, into which Isaac purred, 'It was in the visitors' room that we met, rather than in an adjoining cell, wasn't it?' Laughter from some spectators.

'That's right. Y'all brought me a carton of Kools.'

'It was on last December twenty-fourth, Christmas Eve, and I was in the company of a friend of yours named Billy Gilchrist, wasn't I?'

'That's right. Y'all brought a big bag of Milk Duds too.' Butler appeared proud of this recollection. He looked around the room which was now audibly stirring with interest at the news that he and Rosethorn had met months ago. Isaac handed him the second set of typed pages and asked if that too was his notarized signature. It was. Was this the statement that he'd given to Rosethorn on December 24? It was.

Isaac held a set of pages in each hand, sighed, then suddenly turned around as Mitch Bazemore (with a puffing noise) stomped past him in his fast circuit of the tables. 'Counsel, would you kindly return to your corner of the ring, as His Honour asked you to do?'

With a last loud steamy puff, Mitch snarled, 'All right, all right,' about-faced and sat down.

'I have a problem, Mr Butler,' smiled Isaac. 'Yesterday, you came in here and told us that George's exact words to you before the fight with Pym were – and Mr Walkington will please correct me if I misquote – "If he mess with me, if he say one fuckin' word to me . . . I'm gonna kill that motherfucker dead. I don't get him now, then I get him later, but I get him." Is that accurate?' (It was uncannily accurate, even to inflections, as everyone in the court seemed by their nods and murmurs to be acknowledging.) Butler agreed that it was. Now Isaac pushed his glasses slowly up on his nose, leafed through the State's pretrial statement a while, pursing his lips thoughtfully. 'All right. Now, let me read what you told Mr Neil Sadler two weeks ago. "Question: 'So George was already gunning for Pym, isn't that right? He hated him and was looking for his chance. What did he say to you about Pym before the fight?' Answer: 'Well, something about he was an asshole.' Question: 'Didn't he say he was going to get him good?' Answer: 'Yeah, something like that. Said, "If he hassles me, I'm gonna lay him out."' Question: 'You had the impression George was mad enough to kill Pym, didn't you?' Answer: 'Something like that." '. . . Now . . .' Isaac peered at Butler over his glasses. 'Is *that* correct? Is that what you told the assistant DA two weeks ago?'

'Well, yeah. If that's what it says.'

'That's what it says.' Isaac opened the second sheaf of papers. 'All right, in December, when I came all the way up to Delaware to talk to you, because I'd heard you'd been there at Smoke's that night – though never once in the first trial did you come forward with all these exact words and direct knowledge – when I asked you how that fight got started, what – in your exact words – did you tell *me*?' When Moonfoot protested he couldn't possibly remember, Isaac said, 'Ah, yes. I forgot. You can only remember things that happened seven years ago! Well, would you mind reading this paragraph, the one circled in red?' He handed Butler the paper, pointing at the top.

Butler moistened his lips, then silently mouthed some of the words. I began to worry that perhaps he couldn't read, but then he nodded and said, 'You want me to read this to y'all?' Isaac said he'd appreciate it. Clearing his throat, and pulling at his tiny ear, Moonfoot read in a slow singsong, with apologetic pauses at the profanity. 'It starts out, says, "Butler," then "Looked to me like Pym was raising a ruckus on purpose-like, had an attitude, you know. Nobody wanted to get into it with him. Most folks, they be out only for theirselves. But George, he say to me, 'That fucker can't come in here and do folks that way.' I told him, 'Pym's mean, drunk, and white. Leave it alone.' He say, 'The man start something with me, I'll wipe his butt on the floor.' And he jump up and go to the jukebox."' Moonfoot looked at Rosethorn. 'That's all you got circled.'

Taking back the paper, Isaac shook it, then he shook the first set of pages in his other hand. 'Mr Butler, the time has come for you to pick and choose! You've testified under oath that George said one thing. You've signed two separate statements that he said *two separate other* things. Now, is one of them is true and the two others are lies? Or are all three lies?! Which is it? Did George say, "I'll get him sooner or later, and kill him because he's not fit to live"? *Or*, did he say what you claimed, at the State's persistent leading and urging—'

Bazemore: 'Objection! Uncalled for!'

Hilliardson: 'Sustained.'

Isaac: '—Say to you, "I'll lay him out"?' *Or* did he say, as you told *me*, "I'm going to try to stop this man from disrupting a public place, and annoying other people. *If* he starts something with me, then I will fight back"? Which is very, very different from saying, 'I'm sitting here plotting and planning to murder this man at the first opportunity." Isn't it? *Isn't it, Mr Butler?!*'

'I guess.'

'Or did George say *none* of them to you?'

Fidgeting around in the chair, Moonfoot turned sullen. 'I guess maybe he said them all.'

Isaac threw the papers down on the defence table in disgust. 'You *guess maybe* he said them all! You guess! Well, guessing isn't enough. And maybe isn't enough.' Moving faster than he ever had before in this trial, Isaac charged at Butler, who literally shrank back in the chair, and boomed at him, 'I don't guess! I *know*! I know you are no friend of George Hall's. You *were* no friend of George Hall's. And I would be *ashamed* to call you a friend of mine.' The old man spun to face Mitch Bazemore. 'And I would be *ashamed* to bring you into a court of justice to *witness the sacred truth!*' After a long stare at Mitch, and then a long stare at Moonfoot, and then a long sigh, Isaac limped back to his chair, and sank into it. 'No more questions.'

I don't know what Mitch was able to do on redirect, because Wes Pendergraph tapped me on the shoulder and said they needed me upstairs. But the vote of the press and the lobby gossip was that the prosecution hadn't been able to do much, and that the Moonfoot Butler round went solidly to Rosethorn.

That afternoon, the State produced the former, now retired, HPD medical examiner, who testified that at his arrest George had had nitric stains on his hands, evidence that he'd fired a gun, and that he hadn't been drunk when he'd done it, evidence that he was in full possession of his faculties. Isaac asked the ME if he had checked George's eyesight. No, he hadn't, the old doctor replied querulously; no one had asked him to. The State then produced a man George had beaten up in a ballpark fight a year before the shooting; the man said George had a violent temper. Under cross-examination, the man admitted he'd dumped his beer on George's head. Two former employers of George's testified that they'd fired him for being abusive and intractable. Under Isaac's questioning, they sounded like they'd fired him for being an uppity black man. The State attempted to produce the audiotape of Pym's dying words made in the ambulance. Isaac objected to its presentation, as inflammatory, and was sustained. He tried to keep out the photographs of Pym's corpse for the same reason, but was overruled. He took exception to the ruling. And so it went, with Bazemore heaping wood on the pyre, Rosethorn pouring water on the flames, and the jury watching the show from the safety of their box.

Bubba Percy, who described the afternoon's events to me, said he scored the jurors at this stage as six convictions, two acquittals, and four undecideds. He didn't explain his betting system, and I didn't have time to ask him about it, because I was calling him from University Hospital. I called to pay off 'the big one' he'd said I owed him.

I told him we had Purley Newsome in custody, and that Justin was going to make a statement about that news tomorrow, which gave the *Star* a morning's advantage. Bubba demanded to know if we were holding our suspect at HPD. I said no, we were holding Purley in the intensive care unit at University Hospital, because he was suffering from acute bronchial pneumonia.

Chapter 21

Zackery Carpenter, warden of Dollard Prison, didn't have much time to give me. He supervised, after all, more boarders than there were in all of Haver University; kept more farmers out in his fields than were hanging on in some entire Piedmont counties; bossed more assembly-line workers in his factory (making all the linens, sewing all the uniforms, for every state institution in North Carolina – from the insane asylum to the school for the blind) than Cadmean Textiles had employed at the peak of its productivity. It was probable that George Hall was now sleeping in the county jail on a mattress and pillow made at Dollard; in pants and a shirt made at Dollard, and being guarded by a deputy wearing a Dollard-made hat.

Like that out-of-the-way baron's castle it reminded me of, Dollard Prison was medievally self-sufficient – grew its own crops, made its own clothes, mortared its own bricks, tended its own sick, buried its own dead. Or maybe it was really more like one of those nineteenth-century utopian farms; only Dollard had even less tolerance for criticism of its imperfections. Stepping out of line at Dollard led to solitary (sometimes naked) lock-up in the hole (without water, without a toilet); protest led to Thorazine. Dollard labourers were not exactly competing on the free market, and they weren't unionized, and their earning power ($25 a month) was less of an inducement than the two days taken off their sentences for each day on the line. They didn't have the option of declining the jobs either, and what they produced belonged to the state. The left hand of the state sold their products to the right hand of the state, and rumour was that along the

380

way, considerable change got left in some personal pockets. In fact, Warden Carpenter's predecessor at the prison was thought to have died a wealthy man, though not a popular one: inmates kept repeating the old prison joke that the man was mean enough to sprinkle thumbtacks on the electric chair.

An elderly hillbilly trusty who worked there was telling me about the difference between Carpenter and his predecessor as we waited in the warden's office for him to return from settling a shouting fracas on Death Row over which station to turn the communal radio to. The trusty said, 'Mr Carpenter now, he's a hard, honest man. You can take a hate to him, and some folk may have cause, but I've been doing life here, one day at a time, Captain, and the man, well, he won't cheat you, and he won't tell you a lie.'

It was an interesting preamble to what Carpenter had to tell me himself when he finally came back to his office – which, like him, was big and grey and homely – and sat down in his (prison-built) rocking chair. No small talk except, from him, 'Turning hot,' and from me, 'Yeah, I think God's dropped spring and fall from the line-up; going for a two-season year. You notice that lately?'

'No. I don't get outside enough to tell one month from the next.' Rocking forward, he used a kitchen match to light a large pipe with a charred black bowl, then frowned at me. 'Listen, you asked me something back a while, and I dodged it. It's been on my mind.'

'You dodged two questions, Zack.' I sat down in a plain wood chair across from him. 'One about Winston Russell. One about Julian Lewis.'

He nodded, sucking on the pipe. 'You wanted to know, when Winston was in here, about his visitors. Okay, I gave you a list, but not the full one.'

'Oh? Somebody didn't want his visit recorded?'

'Yeah.' Reaching into his grey bagged-out jacket, he handed me a sheet of paper; on it were typed dates and names. I saw the name Otis Newsome three times – the last time, the day before Russell had been released. The first time, very near the beginning of the list, back when Winston first went in, Otis had been accompanied on his visit by William Slidell. While I was thinking about this, Carpenter's desk intercom buzzed to say that a prisoner on East 7 had tried to cut his own throat in the showers, and was on his way to the hospital in Raleigh. Carpenter settled back in his rocking chair with a soft groan. 'Poor stupid dumb kid,' he sighed, and was quiet for a minute.

'One more question, Zack.' I held up the page from the visitors' log. 'Why're you giving me this now?'

He scratched his pipe stem against the burn scar that spread to the grey cheek stubble, and changed the subject. 'Other thing was, why'd Julian Lewis come over here personally that night to stop the Hall execution.'

'Because of Briggs Cadmean's death, right?'

'Well, they might've used that for a cover, I guess. But Lewis came because the governor *made* him come. Lewis was madder'n hell about that reprieve, and madder'n hell at Wollston for granting it. Seemed to me, he took it all a little too personal, whether George lived or died. Oughtn't to be personal, I don't figure.' Carpenter rocked quietly and talked, while around us buzzes and phones and machines and raised voices clattered. I watched him pausing to pick his words with a tight slowness, as if looking for the least distasteful ones to use to say things he didn't like saying. 'Oughtn't be political either. Now, the governor's always been real strong pro-death penalty. He feels that it's the will of the people of this state.'

'Well, executions do seem to be getting more and more fashionable these days, don't they? Especially here in the South. So why be unpopular and reprieve Hall?'

Carpenter looked out the window. 'The governor figured if something could make this fellow Andrew Brookside take a public stand *against* the death penalty, well, they could count him out of the election. George Hall's case was where most of the pressure was getting put on Mr Brookside to take that stand. But he hadn't done it. And George's time was getting close. So—' Carpenter tapped his pipe ash out in an ugly metal bowl. 'So, I guess the governor thought he'd slow things up a while. Give the Hall supporters time to push Brookside out on a limb . . . That's why the reprieve.'

'Jesus, Zack. Who told you this?'

He said, 'The governor told me.'

'Governor Wollston *himself* told you he stayed an execution for campaign reasons?' The sad fact is it wasn't the doing it that surprised me so much, as the talking about it.

'Bob Wollston and I go back a lot of years. Been friends for a lot of years.' Carpenter looked at me, his jaw stiff. 'That wasn't even the point of the story he was telling me. His point was, he'd wondered what the hell the matter with Lewis was, fighting him so hard on it, when getting Lewis elected was the whole purpose of the stay. Then, afterwards, he hears Lewis has got links to people who may be in some kind of trouble that's connected to George. But he says he doesn't know anything about it, and he told Lewis he damn well better never *tell* him anything about it.' A tiny sad crack of a smile opened Carpenter's thin lips. ' 'Course, it's all backfired now, with that Roseberg lawyer hopping on the bandwagon, getting George his retrial. I guess if you let things get political, they can jump both ways.'

A uniformed woman stuck her head in the door with messages: the fire in the kitchen was out, a prisoner had had a bad epileptic seizure in the visitors room, and the chaplain was waiting outside. Carpenter thanked her, then when she left, went on talking to me with his same slow carefulness. He said, 'I don't know exactly how to put this. But lately I've been asking myself, what are these ulcers for?' His thick hard fingers pushed in on his stomach. 'I've walked men to their deaths right here in this building, just the way I was set to walk George. Walked a woman too. Whole time all of us waiting for that phone to ring, and stop us. Some I took that walk with, they went singing hymns. Even whistling, one fellow, sure the governor's call was coming. Some we dragged sobbing through the door. Some said they were guilty as sin, some died swearing their innocence, and some, well, we'll never know.'

Carpenter shoved himself out of his rocker and walked over to the thick-glassed window. Down below, convicts were mowing grass, weeding flowers, raking gravel. He nodded his head to someone. Then he sighed. 'And you know what, Cuddy, it doesn't make a difference after that door clangs shut. They all shit their pants the same, all drool the same colour blood, fists grab at the chair just the same. And watching, there's always some witness who pukes and runs off. And I always feel like doing it too.' He turned back around towards me.'I got a black boy slated to die next month. There's no fancy committees fighting to free Joe Bonder. Won't be any either. He'll die right on schedule. Liquor store holdup; the other guy turned state's evidence, said Joe pulled the trigger. Maybe he did. I don't think so. But maybe he did. Other guy played the system. He'll be out in four years. Joe's got an IQ about sixty-five. He smiles at me when I tell him the date of his death; says, "Yes, sir. I under-stand." Next day he's asking me when he can go home and see his mama . . . Well, I guess I'm getting sick of it.'

I asked him if he meant he was quitting. He glanced around the large sombre room, then finally he shrugged. 'Maybe I won't have a choice.' The buzzer sounded again. So I stood up while I said, 'Are you saying you'll back me if I use what you've given me?'

He told the voice nagging him on the intercom to hold off the chaplain and send in the parole board member. Then he pointed at the photo of Governor Wollston on the wall. 'Bob Wollston gave me this job.' His lips thinned to a grey line. 'Yeah. I'll repeat what I told you if you need me to.'

'You know what I think now, Zack? I think Bobby Pym and Winston were *sent* to Smoke's that night to kill George.'

He rubbed the ugly face burn carried home from Korea. 'I never go into a man's personal case, unless he brings it to me, and George Hall never did. How much he was mixed in with, or knew about, what those rotten cops of yours were up to, or your city comptroller and his buddies were up to – well, I don't know the answer. My business was, the state convicted and sentenced George. My business was, carry out the sentence for the state.' The warden's pale blue eyes had a puzzled grief in them, as he turned to face me. 'But if there's no such thing as the "state" that's better than you and me and Bob Wollston, then . . . what in God's heaven am I killing this poor dumb boy Joe Bonder for?'

As planned, Justin had met Purley at Catawba Mall, where he'd found him huddled on a bench by the 'rainbow fountain,' looking as filthy, scrawny, and sick as the Raleigh waitress had portrayed him. He was almost dead from pneumonia. His skin was papery and bright hot, his breath ragged, and he was shaking so badly Justin had to get help walking him to the car. Purley passed out before he could be raced to University Hospital, but not before telling at least some of his 'side of the story,' in what Justin described as nonstop delirious self-pity, the theme of which was that Winston Russell was crazy. That he used to look up to Winston, but now he knew: Winston was crazy. That Winston had put him through hell, running and hiding, hiding and running. Thanks to the newspapers and TV, the police were looking for them even in Georgia and Alabama. Winston wouldn't let them stay in motels or buy groceries or even drive into towns. He stole them cars and food in out-of-the-way places. He made them hole up in three different abandoned cabins in wilderness areas, the last one in a national forest near Pisgah in the Appalachian Mountains. There, a hiker had stumbled on their camp, and Winston had *shot him and buried him*. He was crazy. Purley had tried to run away that night, but Winston had beaten him up. Winston was the meanest man that ever lived; he didn't care that Purley was hungry and sick and scared out of his mind. He took all Purley's money. He told Purley he'd blow him away if he tried to turn himself in, just like he'd blown away Willie Slidell. Winston didn't care about anything. He didn't care that Purley kept getting sicker and sicker. He didn't even care that Otis had killed himself; when they'd read the news, he'd called Otis a 'chickenshit.' Winston had abandoned Purley weak and helpless in the cabin one day, barring the door while he drove off to steal food. He never thought Purley would be strong enough, with his high fever, to break through a window, or tough enough to walk thirty miles out of the mountainous forest, or smart enough to find his way to a road. But Purley had showed him, hadn't he? And Purley was going to *talk*, because none of it was his fault, and nobody had told him it would be this bad, and all he'd done was go along, and he was just tired, too tired to run anymore, and Winston was crazy . . .'

Standing by the foot of the bed in the intensive care unit at University Hospital, I whispered to Justin, 'Okay, go on asking.' We'd agreed that I'd keep out of the interrogation, because of Purley's strong (and reciprocated) feelings about me. Except it was (almost) hard to despise the jerk as he lay there, flushed, pupils shrunk to scared dots, the once pink beefy limbs now lank and grey, tubes in his arms and his nose. Pulling a chair up close, Justin punched on his tape cassette as he crooned, 'Purley? You tell me if I've got it right.' There was a nod that didn't lift the head from the pillow. Justin gave him a friendly pat, as he said, 'Okay. Winston shot Cooper Hall. You weren't there. He told you he'd done it. Right?'

Purley tried to wet his lips so he could speak; his voice sounded like someone talking long distance. 'Willie Slidell told me. Willie was driving.'

Justin nodded. 'Now back up a second. You'd followed

Andrew Brookside to Lake Road Airport; you were keeping tabs on him for Otis. And when you saw Brookside meet up with Cooper Hall, you called Otis right away because you figured—'

With weary impatience, Purley interrupted in a low hurried voice. 'I didn't figure nothing. I told Otis I saw them, and he called up the farm, and talked to Winston. Winston comes and says Otis told him, "Take Hall out right now."'

Justin nodded. 'Now, you said in the car that Cooper Hall had phoned Otis early that morning and told him he'd found out about this videotape of Andrew Brookside. That he claimed he'd seen a copy. And that he also had information about Lewis's past affiliations that the press would be interested in. That he wanted Otis to set up a meeting with Lewis. Is that right?'

I looked over at Justin, surprised. So Cooper Hall had been going for a double squeeze, leaning on the left *and* the right, on the Brookside crew and the Lewis crew both, to grab as many guarantees for his people as he could. Christ, the man had the tactics of a ward boss, and the guts of a saint.

Justin went on. 'Otis was scared that Hall was really working for Brookside. Scared he'd got to somebody inside your group. Scared maybe somebody was leaking him stuff.'

'Winston *said* Otis was scared . . . Give me some water, Sayville. I'm burning up . . .'

When Justin took the paper cup away, Purley weakly spread the spilled water from his lips up over his flushed cheeks. 'Listen, Otis never gave any go-ahead to get rid of Hall. He never said it to *me*, and I was his *brother*. And Willie didn't know about it neither. Willie fucking freaked when Winston shot Hall. He thought they were just tailing Hall. He tells me Winston just yells, "PASS HIM!," then he plugs Hall right out the window. Winston is crazy, Say-ville.'

'That's right, you're right. Just lie back.' Justin got Purley's head back down on the pillow. 'But Winston hated Cooper Hall, didn't he, like you told me in the car? I mean, Cooper's brother had killed Bobby Pym, and Bobby was Winston's partner.'

Shaking his head, Purley mumbled, 'I guess. I don't know. Everything got messed up. It was the money. You know, in Raleigh? Somebody'd got it.'

Justin said, yes, we knew that. 'So when Winston got out of Dollard, he went to check the locker at the bus station. Bobby had had the key to the locker in his wallet and Winston had never been able to track it down.'

'Winston went straight to Lana—'

'Did he think Bobby's widow was holding out on him? Did he think she had the money?'

Purley's breath was getting shallow, broken by a hacking gasp. 'At first ... But he was paying a guy in baggage at the bus station. To, you know, watch the locker for him. And ... this baggage guy calls Winston at the farm ... says this little bum that's been around a lot – we find out it's a guy named Gilchrist – that he's just come back, opening up the locker for ... Hall. Winston *freaked*.'

'How did this baggage man know it was Cooper Hall?'

'Recognized him ... Seen him on TV ... So I bust into Hall's Subaru while he's up in the plane, and there's Bobby's suitcase in there okay, but it's empty.' Newsome was wheezing pretty badly.

'And before you left the airport you gave that suitcase to Winston, and he destroyed it, right? And you had also checked Hall's car for a copy of the videotape but didn't find it?' There was a weak nod from Newsome. 'Purley? Come on, Purley. Tell me about the Brookside videotape. After Winston killed Slidell, you two couldn't find the original of the tape either, is that right?'

'Couldn't find tape ... Willie hid it. Wouldn't tell. Wanted to turn us in. I said, "Don't kill him, Winston. Don't."'

'Did *Otis* have a copy of the video?'

'Don't know. Leave me 'lone.' Purley's big head turned fretfully side to side, as he gasped, 'Can't breathe ... can't breathe ...'

Justin turned off the tape and left to find a doctor.

'Newsome's not going to die, is he?' I asked this question half an hour later of a young doctor who gave me a sceptical look, as if she suspected a lack of sympathy in my interest. I returned the look. We stood out in the hall, leaning against the ICU desk. I said, 'If his condition is critical, we're going back in there right now with the tape recorder.'

'No, you're not.' This young woman came up to about my waist, the sleeves of her white jacket drooped over her knuckles, and she actually still wore braces on her teeth, but she had the self-assurance of Attila the Hun. 'No one's going in there. Mr Newsome's temperature's one hundred and three point two, he's on oxygen now, his condition's unstable and quite serious.'

Folding her arms around her clipboard, she added, 'He is not, however, going to die.'

I asked her if she were *sure*, and she said that all she was sure of was that no more policemen were going inside the ICU today.

I said, 'Tomorrow?'

She said, 'Tomorrow is conceivable.'

I gave her a sigh. 'Doc, all of civilization's been based on that very same assumption.'

'Then why shouldn't it satisfy you, Captain Mangum?'

'Why?' I tapped the tiny portable TV on the desk, where Channel 7 was hyping the news. 'Because history's just one big old messy junkyard of inconceivable civilizations.' Noticing she had an Andrew Brookside button on her jacket collar, I pointed at it, and added, 'And their conceivers.' Maybe we could have gone on shooting the philosophic breeze this way, but suddenly a male nurse burst through the unit's double doors behind us, and yelled at her, 'Doctor! Got a cardiac arrest!' Pushing past me, the tiny doctor took off like a sprinter. Seated by the doors, where he'd be keeping guard all night, Wes Pendergraph had to jerk his legs out of her path.

I said, 'Well, hell,' to Justin, who was squatting against the wall looking miserable. 'Okay, let's go on downtown. Try here again later. So where's that damn original videotape? . . .'

No response.

I tried again. 'You know, I think it's kind of sweet how old dickhead Purley doesn't believe Otis called the shot on getting rid of Cooper. But you can bet your Reeboks Otis *did* call it. Winston is crazy, but he's not dumb. He wouldn't have killed Coop to spite George unless he *knew* George had fingered him, and he wouldn't have blown away what might have been a lead to the money just for kicks. And most of all, he wouldn't have done it with Slidell sitting right next to him, not unless they were both already on the same payroll. Right, General Lee?'

Justin still didn't answer, and I nudged his leather sneaker. 'Come on, perk up! Purley's given us a direct link to Otis and his political pals. And Carpenter's visitors' log corroborates. Plus, we know Winston's vowed to kill me and Purley both, and me and Purley both are right here in Hillston. And I'll bet you my photo-mural of Cape Hatteras, Winston's pissed enough to come here gunning for us. That's when we'll get him.'

Justin nodded without much interest; he didn't even bother reminding me how much he hated my photo-mural, or predicting that Russell would gun me down before we got him. As we left the hospital (walking under a painting of Justin's dad in the entrance lounge), I tried talking about the Hall trial. Did Isaac Rosethorn really have the chutzpah to make a case that George had never run stolen goods for the Pym/Russell crew at all? And if so, was he going to keep George off the stand, so Mitch wouldn't get a shot at him?

Justin just mumbled a few 'I don't know's, and got in my car. Driving downtown, I pointed cheerfully at the stone side wall of the Hillston Playhouse, now lavender with wisteria vines. 'Yeah, it's pretty,' he said without looking.

'My my, your sprezzatura's got a sag in it, son. Why, things are finally looking good for our side. Now I want you to get in touch with Boone, help them find that cabin, and dig up that poor camper's body.'

'All right.'

'What's the matter with you?'

He shrugged, shaking his head. I gave up. I figured he'd been upset by memories of University Hospital, which Justin's father had not only run, but died in. Not to mention the man had had a heart attack while in a car accident with Justin drunk at the wheel. Then, a few years back, Justin himself had lain for months in the same hospital, getting over that bullet that took off a bit of his skull. All in all, just being there was probably enough to cause the sunk look on his face.

But, as he finally decided to tell me, turns out that UH wasn't the problem, neither was Purley, and neither were the two other homicides he was investigating now. He was 'upset about what happened to Alice.'

My whole body went cold as sleet, and staring at him, I missed the turn off Haver on to Main. 'Oh God, no,' Justin explained fast. 'She's fine, the baby's fine – we just had sonar. No, no, it's nothing *that* bad. It's Brookside. She met with him late yesterday.' Justin's jaw set tight. 'He's decided to go with Harold DeWitt for lieutenant governor instead of her.'

'Aw, shit! That's all?'

'That's all?! Can you believe it? After all the merciless stuff Brookside said about DeWitt in the primary!'

Well, in fact I could easily believe it. DeWitt was a mainstream party-machine man, with lots of pull in the western half of the state, with contacts, money, and twenty more years' worth of favours owed than Alice MacLeod had collected. Enough favours to make Andy apologize for any earlier 'merciless stuff.' Enough of a chance at the lieutenant governorship to make DeWitt accept the apology.

Pulling into the parking garage under the Municipal Building, I said, 'Politicians. Fuck 'em. How's she taking it?'

'Better than me. I'm furious at Brookside. I really thought we had a personal relationship.'

I said, 'Well, hey, so what? This isn't personal.'

His thick lashes opened wide. 'Are you kidding? Of course it's personal! Everything's personal. You think if Isaac Rosethorn wins, and those twelve people decide not to send George to the gas chamber, that won't be personal? Brookside was her *friend*, and he just drops this on her, *after* he's already made the decision. I mean, he just didn't do it right.'

'If it had been personal, he *would* have picked Alice; I'm sure he's a lot fonder of her than he is of Harold DeWitt.' Jesus, what was I doing defending Andrew Brookside?

'I worked hard for him, Cuddy; I mean I had some resistance to overcome, in, you know, my family's circle. Some people really didn't much approve of Lee's marrying a—'

'Yankee? . . . Liberal? . . . War ace? . . . Man who wears garters on his socks?'

'Oh, cram it.' Justin was feeling better.

As I drove down into the parking garage, I asked him, 'Hey, why don't y'all come over and eat supper with me tonight? Tell Alice, fried eggs, fried potatoes, fried ham, and we'll toss in some alfalfa sprouts for you. We'll watch my videotape of *Mr Smith Goes to Washington*, and she'll see what a cesspool she just sidestepped.'

Justin finally smiled. '*I'll* cook. But Alice is fine. I'm the one who's mad. She never expected it anyhow. You know Alice: She didn't have the power base. Too young. It was going to be hard to campaign in the fall with a month-old baby anyhow. Plenty of time later. Et cetera, et cetera. All the reasons why Brookside *was right* to make the decision the way he did.' (No more 'Andy' for Justin, I noticed; we were back to 'Brookside.') 'He did offer her the post of executive secretary.'

'That mean she gets to make his coffee? Hop out. I'm setting the alarm.' Since I'd got sapped, I parked right beside the elevators, but I also gave a careful look around before stepping out of my Olds. Right now I could almost feel Winston Russell pressed into the black shadows of the concrete walls, or crouched against the fender of a car, taking aim. I hurried to the elevator, and leaned on the button till it opened. 'So, what'd she tell Brookside?'

'I *told* her to tell him to stuff it.'

'Yeah, but she told him she'd think about it.'

'Right. That she'd have to believe that her views – you know, like on the death penalty – would get a real hearing from him. But listen,' said Justin as we slowly clanked upward in the elevator. 'Executive secretary's actually in lots of ways more powerful than lieutenant governor. You know when Reagan was governor of California, Meese was his secretary?'

'That's a recommendation?'

'I mean Meese had a lot of power.'

'I know, J.B. I was there when Alice told us that "personal" story about how Meese spent a lot of time lobbying to stop the state legislature from outlawing capital punishment, and when it was clear they were going to abolish it anyhow, he and Reagan let some black guy go to the gas chamber *the night before* they voted it out. Right, that's a lot of power. Tell Alice to grab it.'

The elevator jolted to a stop, and my muscles tightened as the doors opened on a man. But standing there was just Sergeant Hiram Davies, his thin white hair pristinely combed, a paper lunch bag neatly rolled at the top in one hand, a gym bag in the other. It was one of those freak August-hot days in June, but his uniform had lost none of its starch.

'Aren't you an hour early, Hiram?'

He looked a little embarrassed, as he lifted the gym bag. 'I'm taking Officer Moore's class, Captain.'

'Brenda's giving a class? What in?'

'Aerobics,' Justin explained. 'We do Jane Fonda in the lounge. On the VCR. Whoever's around.'

'That's news to me.'

Justin grinned. 'Pretty lonesome being boss, huh?'

Hiram showed us the front page of a local evening paper – a small-time outfit with views considerably less conservative than I would have suspected the deacon of harbouring. The headline was 'BROOKSIDE PICKS DEWITT,' but that wasn't what he wanted us to see. It was a small piece at the bottom: 'GRAND DRAGON CANCELS ON CANE.' According to the article, the born-again former KKK leader who'd been scheduled to renounce the Klan this evening on the Carol Cathy Cane show had apparently renounced his renunciation instead; at any rate, he'd cancelled his appearances both on the TV programme today, and the panel discussion at Trinity Church tomorrow. Carol Cathy's substitute guests would be Kirk Niebshon, president of Haver University Gay Activists, and Mrs Brodie Cheek, president of the Christian Family Wives Clubs. I said, 'Umm, sounds lively. Well, I guess some of our Klan boys persuaded the Grand Dragon if he wanted to stay born again long enough to enjoy his new life, he'd better keep it a quiet one.'

The elevator let us out on our floor; I saw Brenda Moore and John Emory in sweat pants, headed for the lounge.

Justin said, 'Brookside is the main speaker at Trinity tomorrow night, and they'll still get the crowd. Alice said Jack Molina talked him into it. She thinks Molina's the one who got her the executive secretary offer, too. And Jack's promised to incorporate some of her ideas into the Cadmean Stadium speech.'

I'd already advised the Brookside campaign against formally kicking off with this huge rally in an outdoor stadium, but they wouldn't listen. Not only had they got the big leftwing movie star to agree to appear, she'd talked three other big movie stars into coming too, *and* the biggest female rock star on the charts today, who'd agreed to do a free concert! The place would be mobbed by people who didn't even know who was running for governor, much less care who won. I'd called Brookside personally to suggest that the whole thing was going to be a security nightmare, and he'd told me, 'Molina's in charge. He'll have it under control.' I said to Justin now, 'Dr Molina seems to have got his Bolshie hands pretty firm on the rudder these days, doesn't he? Quite the kingmaker.'

Justin frowned. 'I don't like Molina.'

'Aww. You just don't like his clothes.'

'I don't like *your* clothes.' He patted my shirt front (okay, so it was only 50 per cent cotton), then he socked me on the shoulder. 'But I love *you*. Take it easy. Hiram, hope your sister's feeling better.'

'Justin's a nice man.' Hiram nodded thoughtfully, as we watched Savile the Five hurry down the hall, swinging his father's old briefcase from hand to hand. 'I never understood why somebody like him, you know, with his family background, ever joined the police.'

I said, 'Yeah, I used to think he was slumming among us country copulatives, too, for the low-life thrill, or to rile his folks.

392

But, in fact, he joined because detective was something he knew he'd be real good at.'

'I never said I thought he was "slumming."' Against his tight collar, Hiram's neck twisted like an angry bird's. 'And I'm not a country what-you-said. I'm from Raleigh. Raleigh's a city.'

'But you do copulate, don't you, Hiram?'

'I do not!'

'Well, at least twice. You got two kids.'

His face was so purple, I could almost feel the heat. I apologized.

Walking down the hall, I ran into Carl Yarborough, who wanted to know why the mayor of Hillston had to hear on the radio about Purley Newsome's being in the custody of the Hillston Police. I apologized. I apologized to Lee on the phone for snapping at her because Brookside had dumped Alice. I read a note on my desk in which Mitchell Bazemore said he expected me to apologize to him for all sorts of alphabetized grievances, *a* to *k*. I apologized to Judge Dolores Roche for not recognizing her voice when she telephoned to ask us to assign a social worker to Martin Hall, who'd been expelled from school and needed help. Lee called back and apologized for getting angry at me when I'd snapped at her. By the time Bubba Percy waltzed into my office without a knock, much less an appointment, it was actually a relief that he didn't say he was sorry. Flopping down on my couch, he made a splatting noise with his lips, and ordered me to 'Turn up the air-conditioner. Christ, I hate the South.' He pulled out his pink shirt and fanned it up and down. 'Well, Moonfoot's on his way back to Delaware, and I never got near him. Couldn't get squat about Purley Newsome out of this little bitch of a doctor at intensive care either.' Rolling up his sleeves, he scratched at his reddish arm hair. 'She had a great pair of knocks, though. Next time I'm at UH, I'm gonna ask her for a date.'

'Why bother being so suave? Why not just rip open her dress when you see her in the hall?' I turned from feeding pizza-flavored popcorn to the pigeons on my window ledge – 'Bubba, get your fucking boots off my sofa!'

'Hey, chill out, Captain ... You know, I interviewed your buddy Rosethorn at lunch. That old man's working like a coolie for Hall. Said he hadn't cared this much about anything in a long time. Said it was his last case. You believe it?' I shrugged. 'Me either ... Listen to this. I ask him who his heroes are. He says,

Gandhi, Eleanor Roosevelt, and *you*, Mangum.' A big snorting laugh.

I picked up some popcorn kernels off the rug and ate them. 'Ask Isaac tomorrow, he'll tell you Cicero and Catherine the Great. Go on, Bubba, get out of here.'

He slid his legs out further, so the Italian heels didn't touch the arm rest. 'Mangum, you're a charmer, I guess you hear that a lot, hunh? So, too bad about your pal Alice MacLeod. I'd heard she was on Brookside's short list. But, let's face it, he needs DeWitt's retro bafflegab, the way he's taking these little hike-outs to the left lately. You hear that speech to those women in Charlotte? He's sounded good enough for Gloria Steinem . . .' Bubba's complaisant voice went melodically on, but I wasn't listening. I'd started thinking about Brookside's little hike-outs to the left; thinking about Jack Molina, about his getting his candidate to do all the things Justin had mentioned. Then the idea hit me, and I chuckled out loud: I was already pretty sure that Molina had stolen the videotape from Coop's desk to keep it from falling into the wrong hands. But that meant it was in *his* hands, and that meant, I suddenly realized, *he* could use it against Brookside himself. Use it for political leverage, exactly the way Coop had planned to do. Molina was blackmailing his own candidate, for the Cause.

'What are you snorting about, Mangum?'

I sprinkled the rest of the popcorn on the ledge, and shut the window. I said, 'Utopian socialism.'

'Yeah, it's a laugh riot.' Bubba lifted his hips off the couch, pulled out his pocket comb and worked on a wave in his pompadour. 'Listen, I got some scuttlebutt for you. But you'll owe me.' I suggested that if it hadn't been for me, he wouldn't be city editor, not to mention I'd steered him to Coop Hall and the House of Lords both, and those were the articles getting him national attention. He ran the comb through his eyebrows. 'Believe it, friend. I'm a media star. Pumping for the Pulitzer. So anyhow, wanna hear this or not? Over in Raleigh, I've been sniffing all kinds of doo-doo from my personal and – take my word for it – highly placed team of Deep Throats.' He tapped his nose with the comb.

From my swivel chair, I made a nice basket shot with the popcorn bag. 'Deep throated doo-doo? With that kind of imagery, I'd say don't even mess with the Pulitzer, go straight for the Nobel Prize . . . Okay, okay. Tell me.'

'Numero uno.' His furry arm shot straight up from the couch. 'There was this big pow-wow at the governor's mansion, with Constitution Club money men leaning on Wollston hard to step up his support of Lewis. What I heard was, Dyer Fanshaw and Atwater Randolph foamed at the mouth about the "George Hall mess backfiring," and how if Wollston had listened to Julian Lewis it wouldn't have happened. What do you make of that?'

I said, 'That they're sorry Wollston reprieved Hall. And they're scared Lewis is going to lose to Brookside.'

'My source says they're all pissing blood over the latest polls on Brookside. Word is, ten Constitution Clubbers pledged to funnel a hundred thousand dollars each into the campaign. I got the names. Eight are ole House of Lords alumni. Dyer Fanshaw's one of them. Man, you think if I had a hundred thou, I'd blow it on bumper stickers for some other guy?'

'You would if getting that other guy in office meant you could hang on to the millions you already had, plus maybe make a few more.' I asked if Bubba's source had said why Wollston had to be *pressed* to support Lewis, and was told that the governor had noticeably cooled on his lieutenant governor, if in fact he'd ever been warm towards him – which was both unknown and irrelevant, since the hand-picking of Lewis had been done by the same money men that had years ago picked Wollston.

'I'm with Edwina on politicians,' Bubba added. 'She says to me, "I never vote. It just encourages them."' He lifted one buttock with his hand, and nonchalantly farted. 'Anyhow, that's numero uno. Duo is, I heard some heavy-duty chains were yanked to fly that Moonfoot clown here from Delaware to testify against Hall. I'm talking AG level. Lot of phone calls.'

I nodded slowly, I said that the current attorney general had been Julian Lewis's assistant when Lewis was AG. That, in addition, Hillston's assistant district attorney, Neil Sadler (the man who'd gone up to interview Butler in Delaware), had been on the staff of the current AG's office before coming to work with Mitch Bazemore. Okay, so maybe they'd sidestepped Mitch entirely. But when Isaac Rosethorn's request for Arthur Butler had gone up the red-tape line in Delaware, somebody at the top there had called somebody at the top here in Raleigh, and the Raleigh somebody had explained what was wanted. What was wanted was George Hall back on Death Row fast.

Bubba, combing his sideburns and his eyebrows, wondered why the Lewis people should give 'a flying fuck' about Hall. I told him, 'Because if you don't keep shit covered up, it can get loose and hit the cooling system.'

'Don't get poetic on me. You're just a cop. Cover up what?'

I pulled out the piece of paper Zack Carpenter had given me. 'Bubba, what do you want out of life?'

He gave a good pantomime of serious thought. 'A bigger click. A Porsche and a Pulitzer. A rich smart woman who looks like Marilyn Monroe, thinks like Dr Ruth, and cooks like my mother.'

I laughed. 'Except for the looks and the cooking, Edwina's got it all . . . What about *impact*? How'd you like to play a role in the future of your state? Topple a junta?'

'Can I still have the car and the woman?'

'Look at Woodward and Bernstein. They made a mint.' I told him to go ask Julian Lewis if the reason why'd he'd so strenuously opposed the Hall stay of execution had anything to do with two close friends of his, Otis Newsome and Dyer Fanshaw. I told him to go ask Dyer Fanshaw why his friend Otis had bothered to visit Winston Russell in Dollard Prison, and ask Fanshaw why he'd let his trucks be used to smuggle guns to the Carolina Patriots; and while he was at it, ask Fanshaw if he'd destroyed a suicide note when he'd been the first person to find Otis Newsome hanging from a ceiling pipe in his office.

Bubba's nostrils opened – an intense display of journalistic curiosity from him. Then he swung his long legs off the couch and stood up, adjusting his crotch. 'You and me both, Captain Pig, we could get our butts burned if Brookside blows this election. And the rumour is, the Lewis boys have got hold of something they're planning to drop on him eleventh-hour that's gonna take him out good and fast. 'Course, nobody knows what it is, and it could be total bullshit. I've heard every rumour about Randy Andy in the book: He was never a POW, but stooged for the Commies in Nam. He boffed half the students at Haver. He took kickbacks from all the Haver contractors. I've heard everything from his sister's a junkie, to his wife has affairs. Now I don't care if it's *all* true, still, better him that that—'

I stood up. 'If any of it were true, it would have been leaked by now. Just like Bunny Randolph leaked that House of Lords Club membership list to you.' Opening my door, I motioned him out of my office. 'By the way, that club ever do anything anyhow, besides draw up constitutions saying they didn't want blacks at Haver University, and snubbing them when they did get in?'

Bubba took the hint, and stepped into the hall. 'Yeah, that club did a lot. They helped each other buy the state of North Carolina.'

'That's not a crime, Bubba. That's the way of the world.'

He shook his head, smiling. 'Mangum, don't try to out-cynic a pro. You'll lose. Listen to you. You still think if you dig down deep enough in the shit, you're gonna find that pony. But you uncover one shitty junta, there's another one under it waiting their chance. Me, I'm just interested in shit's infinite variety. You believe in *organized* evil, man. That takes a lot of faith. Call me, you want to shoot some baskets Saturday. Catch you later.'

It's a new world. That's one thought I had when I passed through the lounge where half my off-duty patrolmen were bouncing around in Nikes and pastel wrist weights, panting to keep up with Jane Fonda's grapevine steps and sunshine arms. The other thought I had watching them exercise sent me hurrying downstairs to Etham Foster's lab. He was where he usually was; his long bony back hunched over his microscope.

'Dr D.? A question: You remember that suitcase we pulled out of Willie Slidell's station wagon? Had the presents for his ex in it, one of them was a Jane Fonda aerobics video? Did you ever actually open that tape and play it?'

He swivelled around, frowning. 'Told Summers to. Why?'

'Just an idea. Find out if he did, okay? Call me at home.'

When Foster phoned me an hour later, he was as close as he comes to apologizing. Yes, Augustine Summers had opened the tape, and had played it. But not all of it; after a spot check of the opening of the exercises, he'd put the thing back in its box, and it had been returned, with the other property found in the station wagon, to Slidell's sister, Lana Pym. I told Foster to have someone get a warrant, go to her house and pick up the tape, if she still had it. I told him to tell Mrs Pym, too, that Purley Newsome was in University Hospital, and might appreciate a visit.

It was 9:30 when Etham himself showed up in River Rise with the videotape. Lana Pym had never taken it out of the suitcase, much less played it, or mailed it to Willie's ex in Kentucky. Not that she hadn't violently objected to having it impounded by the police. Eitham arrived in shorts and a HPD T-shirt, and said he'd jogged over. (He lived three miles away, but I suppose when you've been a star athlete, it's hard to break the habit of a healthy body.) When he got there, Justin was in my kitchen cleaning up the cooking utensils he'd brought over to make our 'Cajun' dinner with; he treated his equipment like surgical instruments, and no doubt they'd cost as much. He and I had just managed to pull Alice out of my low leather chair, and a minute before Etham rang the bell, she'd waddled across the hall to talk with Nora and Nora's more-or-less permanent roommate, Isaac Rosethorn. As it turned out, I was glad Alice was gone, because I wouldn't have wanted her to see the sight that popped on to my TV screen after I'd fast-forwarded what had looked, not from just its box and its label but from its first half hour too, like any other one of the millions of Miss Fonda's healthy workout packages. Then all of a sudden, Jane was no longer demonstrating an arm-pumping cha-cha. Instead, two people, white male, black female, both naked except he wore a gold Rolex watch, and she wore what looked like a real emerald ring, were doing a different kind of dance on a big pile of sheepskin rugs. Hamilton Walker had certainly been right about Jamaica Touraine; she was not only amazingly good-looking; she was amazingly a lot of things – things that appeared to be quite lucrative, judging-from the furniture in her apartment.

'Jesus Christ!' said Justin. Then he said, 'Jesus Christ, it's Brookside, okay.' Then he said, 'Jesus Christ!' again. I turned down the sound; it had been about what you'd expect. A few minutes later Jane Fonda was back, saying to keep breathing during the monkey plies. Then Brookside and Touraine returned to the screen; then we were back at the workout, and so on, back and forth, as far as I fast-forwarded. Shutting off my VCR, I locked the tape in my desk drawer 'Well,' I sighed. 'What do you think?'

Etham Foster scowled. 'I think my wife's been campaigning for a rich honkie asshole. Who made this tape?'

Justin said, 'The rich honkie assholes that this asshole's running against.'

I went to the refrigerator. 'Yep, the two-party honkie-asshole system we call American democracy. Ain't it grand? I'm going to fix myself a bourbon. Dr D., you want one?'

'Bourbon?' Justin asked. Like all reformed alcoholics, he was fascinated by other people's drinking. 'You don't drink bourbon, Cuddy. I never knew you to drink anything but beer.'

I finally found the old bottle somebody'd given me for

Christmas. 'There's a lot of things you don't know about me, Savile.'

After we briefed Etham on the background to the video, he stretched his bare dark arms along the back of my denim couch – they reached from end to end – and stared at the ceiling. He said, 'Okay. Cooper Hall got the Touraine woman's copy of the tape. Brookside offers to deal with him. But Otis Newsome doesn't want to deal. Instead, Otis quick calls his brother's buddy, Winston, and tells him to go kill Cooper Hall.'

Justin said, 'Well, if you put it that way, your wife ought to keep on campaigning for Brookside. Comparatively speaking.'

'Probably.' Politics didn't interest Foster much. 'Okay, if you're right, now this guy Jack Molina's got Hall's copy. Purley told you Slidell hid the original. He duped it on to this Fonda tape. Now did he also make a dupe for Otis Newsome? Did he make a dupe for *Julian Lewis*? Did he make a *hundred* dupes—'

I toed off my shoes, and rubbed my feet against each other. 'Julian Lewis has got to be real sorry he let his pal Otis get one hundred per cent behind this campaign. Because now he's tied to the whole thing. And conceivably accessory-after-the-fact on the Hall death. Right after the fact, however, I bet the Lewis crew dumped our city comptroller like a lice-riddled leper with festering boils. Even if they'd told Otis to use his own initiative, I'm sure they had something a little more subtle in mind than racketeering, porno films, and murder. Even Nixon's plumbers didn't go around shooting the vocal opposition.'

'Far as we know,' mumbled Foster.

Justin came back in from the open balcony, where I made him stand to smoke. He said, 'So they turned on Otis, and he hanged himself. It's like the knights that killed Beckett for Henry the Second, and then instead of getting thanked, they're called murderers.'

'You feeling sorry for Otis Newsome? Beckett was murdered, wasn't he? Cooper is *dead*, isn't he?!'

My phone rang. I thought it was going to be Lee, and I was panicking about how was I going to talk to her with Justin and Etham in the room, or excuse myself and take the phone upstairs without them wondering why. But it wasn't Lee. And it wasn't a long conversation. It was a male voice, a low rumbling twang. It said, 'That you, Mangum?'

'Yep, who's this?'

'You're dead, you fuck. I'm gonna take you out. I want you to sweat it, 'cause it's coming. You got that?'

I said, 'I got it, Winston.' But by then I was talking to a dial tone.

Chapter 22

We had to go on the assumption that Winston Russell was in Hillston, and that he meant what he said. It enraged me (and the word's mild) to have to go on this assumption, particularly after Justin and Etham pressured me into moving right then and there into my office, where I'd be surrounded, of course, by police protection. 'Just till we find him,' Justin pointed out in a misguided attempt to calm me down. At the moment, what I wanted was to run to my car, tear off looking for that sick SOB, and keep looking till I found him and beat him to death. Instead, I went to my office. I had Purley Newsome moved into a private room at UH, with two guards. I persuaded Nora to take her children to her brother's, on the chance that Winston knew by now that she was George Hall's co-counsel and lived across the hall from me.

Isaac, on the other hand, wouldn't budge from the Piedmont, remarking blandly, 'He's expressed no interest in killing *me*. Let me know when you catch him. I want him subpoenaed.' Isaac's disinterest in the fact that Winston was trying to kill me made me a little snappish when he showed up at the department at midnight with a bucket of spareribs and a barrage of questions about Dyer Fanshaw, and what I'd heard at Dollard from Zachery Carpenter. Listening, he helped himself to my beer and my blackboard – erasing my work like a teacher impatient with a slow learner. I threw him out at two A.M. and went annoyed to sleep on the couch, with Martha, equally peevish, squirming for room at my feet.

Meanwhile, Justin had roused his favourite informant Preston Pope out of bed and kept him as well as a dozen policemen out all night looking for Russell. They didn't find him. But at four in the morning, they raided a tacky stucco duplex in West Hillston, and caught fifteen Carolina Patriots playing with guns and wearing combat fatigues around the kitchen table, in the middle of what was obviously not a social meeting. Among the group was the man Justin had heard lecture months ago at that survivalist talk, ex-Sergeant Charlie Mennehy (currently out on bail on federal charges). The duplex belonged to his little brother. Also there was the brother's good friend, Willis Tate, the young hood who'd harassed the vigilants at Dollard Prison the night of George Hall's reprieve.

When Justin surprised these boys, they were clearly laying plans to attack the anti-Klan conference scheduled at Trinity Church this coming evening – posters for which were lying around the house, along with a few axe handles, 9mm handguns, and homemade kerosene bombs. Lying around as well was a considerable pile of marijuana. Justin arrested them for illegal possession of narcotics and weapons, then called in the FBI and the Federal Bureau of Alcohol, Tobacco and Firearms, who tore the place apart. The booty included recruitment literature from the White Aryan Resistance and the Southern White Knights, a brochure urging teenagers 'To Get on the Klan Van,' a tactics manual on how to pollute water supplies, a newsletter from a Great Titan of the Invisible Empire offering honour points to any holy hero who'd assassinate the Antichrist Jesse Jackson, an MAC-10 machine gun, two sawed-off shotguns, and four US Army-issue grenades.

After two hours of me personally tearing the Carolina Patriots apart (verbally speaking), Willis Tate broke down and admitted not only that the Patriots had planned to 'drive by' the Trinity Church gathering, but that Winston Russell was 'one of them,' and that Russell had actually shown up at the duplex earlier that day. Under the circumstances (every cop in the state was looking for him), they'd told him he couldn't stay; so much for esprit de corps. Tate had no idea where Russell was now, and neither did his fellow Patriots. Believe me, they would have told me if they'd known. I made very vivid that the alternative was a conviction for conspiracy to commit the first-degree murders of – among others – Cooper Hall and William Slidell. Despite their vows to die stoically for the Cause, the only member of this sorry crew of scum who wasn't by then in a panic of blubbering evasions and self-justification was ex-Sergeant Mennehy, a big, lank, stringy man with a grey crew-cut and a leathery face. And he was so violently disgusted by his troops, whom he called 'fuckin' pussies,' that he spat at one, knocked one out cold, and broke the nose of another, before we pulled him from the holding cell at seven A.M., and sent him across the street to the county jail. As it happened, Isaac Rosethorn was already at the jail, in early conference with George about the day's legal strategy. The decision to move Mennehy over there was to prove, Isaac later said, 'the fluke of fate even I could not have anticipated, and which I am therefore willing to ascribe – theoretically – to Call-it-what-you-will, and why not God?' Naturally, the old lawyer did not fill me in at the time on the particulars of the 'fluke'; he simply had Charlie Mennehy added to the list of witnesses he wanted subpoenaed.

At noon, in Superior Court, the State rested its case against George Hall. Mitch Bazemore never called Lana Pym to the stand, and he pulled no more Moonfoot Butlerish surprises. He didn't even examine his last witnesses himself, but turned them over to the assistant DA, Neil Sadler, who led Bobby Pym's former next-door neighbour to testify that in the months before Pym's death, he had been acting 'funny and nervous,' and had bought an attack dog because 'he was scared somebody was out to get him.' Since Mitch had sent in the second string, Isaac turned his cross-examination over to Nora. She led the neighbour to admit that he'd never seen George Hall around Pym's house, nor heard Pym say that it was George Hall he was scared of. That, on the other hand, he *had* often seen Winston Russell around the Pym house, on one occasion seen him in the middle of the night helping Pym carry large heavy wooden crates inside the garage.

The assistant DA then put 'Fattie' McCramer (current owner of Smoke's) on the stand to corroborate the old story that George had started the bar fight. Fattie also claimed he'd once heard George say he intended to kill Pym, but under Nora's cross-examination contradicted his recollections of when, where, and in what words George had announced this premeditation. Nora also asked Fattie if he wasn't on parole after a conviction for running a numbers game in a public bar. Fattie didn't deny it. He appeared mainly interested in promoting Smoke's attractions to the large audience of spectators. Because of the publicity of the trial, business at Smoke's was already good, but as he said, you can't have too much of a good thing; except, and he slapped his girth, maybe ice cream and fried chicken. Isaac stood and patted his own girth in friendly agreement.

All in all, as I heard from Nora, it was a quiet finish for the State. Seated at the prosecutor's table, his arms folded, Mitch Bazemore was subdued; so unlike himself that Isaac started nibbling on the erasers of his pencil-teepee, no doubt tensely waiting for the sudden leaping charge that never came. But Mitch had a lot on his mind. I'd hit him with most of it at eight this morning when I'd met him in his office, and, among other unwelcome news, played him Justin's interrogation of Purley Newsome. He'd heard it out, without putting his fist through the wall. He'd just squeezed his biceps until his fingers turned as red, white, and blue as the flag he loved. When I'd finished, all he'd done was pull on his suit jacket and say, 'I'm going to the hospital.' I told him that Justin was already at UH, with two state troopers from Boone, trying to get Purley to pinpoint exactly where in the Pisgah Forest Winston had supposedly buried that hiker.

The DA walked out without a single comment on anything I'd said.

Justin told me later that the grilling Bazemore had given Purley Newsome made the Inquisition look like a love-in. When Purley had started a coughing spasm under the attack, and the ICU doctor had tried to evict Bazemore, the DA had physically shoved him out the door, and told Wes Pendergraph that he'd have him suspended if he let anyone else in. Mitch showed up back at the Municipal Building, just in time for court to open, five years older than when he'd left. So one possibility why he was so subdued all day was that the truth about his friend Otis Newsome had finally got to him. The other possibility, of course, was that the truth about the Julian Lewis people (and Neil Sadler was obviously their point man) had finally got to him. Or he'd finally put both truths together. In any case, when I checked in on the trial at noon, Mitch was moving as if somebody had kicked him in the stomach. He stood up slowly, after Fattie left the stand, stared at the seal above Judge Hilliardson's head for a good minute, then said flatly, 'Your Honour, the State rests.'

Isaac looked surprised. But he quickly bowed to Mitch, then turned towards the bench and asked Hilliardson for an immediate ruling in favour of the defence. 'I submit, Your Honour, that the State has made no prima facie case requiring jury action,

404

because the State has offered no evidence, in proof beyond a reasonable doubt, that an act of premeditated murder was ever committed by George Hall against Robert Pym. And I therefore move that a directed verdict be entered for the defendant.' Isaac then limped earnestly forward, and held out his arms to the bench as if the judge might hand him down the favourable verdict like a baby. All Hilliardson did was rub his nose, and adjourn the court until after lunch, at which time he promised to announce his decision.

I took Isaac and Nora across the street for a quick bite at Pogo's, next door to the county jail. I should say Officers John Emory, Nancy White, and I took them there, because I was now stuck with those two obsessive bodyguards preceding me with their hands on their holsters, wherever I went, like I was Caesar or Huey Long. Unfortuitous analogies, I suppose. So the three of us had to wait outside in the June heat, while John and Nancy checked out Pogo's, as if Winston might be witless enough to sit nibbling guacamole at a table for one in the most popular journalists', law-enforcers', and lawyers' restaurant in town.

As I finally pushed us in through the noisy noon crowd, Isaac scared me by getting the shakes, then suddenly losing his balance and falling against the coat counter.

'I'm fine, leave me alone,' he growled while Nora and I led him to a corner table, and got him seated. Loosening his tie, he struggled back into the seersucker jacket he'd taken off walking over. 'Damn air-conditioning gave me a chill. I'm fine.' His face was grey, his brow beaded with unhealthy-looking sweat. A glance in a mirror told me I didn't look much better; I'm too old or too young to get by on three hours of sleep.

'He's not fine; he's a wreck,' Nora argued, handing Isaac a glass of water. 'He's killing himself over this case. He never goes to bed, he's living on bourbon and cigarettes—'

'Well, that's been true for fifty years,' I pointed out as Isaac grabbed a waiter by his jacket and cajoled him into bringing over a Jack Daniels as fast as he could. 'Health is not a priority of his.'

'The *trial at hand* is the first and only priority. Always.' He waggled a finger at Nora to underscore this lesson from the Book of Isaac.

'No, not always,' she told him, softening the news with a rub of his shoulder. Nora appeared to be taking in stride the stares she was getting, as the best-looking of the two women in the place, which was, as usual, a jammed hubbub of Hillston males

405

talking business bull and civic slanders. I knew at least half the customers around me, including an unlikely trio in an intense tête-à-tête at a back table: Bubba Percy, Jack Molina, and Mayor Carl Yarborough. I waved, and in a minute Carl came over to our table to tell me he was 'very pleased' (high praise from him) about the arrests of the Carolina Patriots. As he headed back to the corner, I asked Isaac, 'What the hell you think those three're doing together? Not one of them can stand the other two.'

Isaac sadly sipped his bourbon. 'Interesting,' he said, then stopped and stared at the tablecloth until the waiter took our orders with the surly rudeness on which Pogo's appeared to pride itself.

'What's interesting?' I finally asked Isaac, who was stuck in his visionary trance. 'Bubba's new pals? Your health? The decor?'

'I was thinking of poor Otis Newsome.'

'You mean the fact that he and a goodly number of the leading citizens of this town appear to have been up to their noses in a manure pile of graft, bribery, homicide cover-ups, arms-peddling to paramilitary extremists—'

The old lawyer sighed. 'No, I meant – if my deductions are right – it's interesting that an ostensible virtue, *loyalty*, was Otis's downfall. Loyally toadying up to Julian Lewis and Dyer Fanshaw since their college club days when he was hazing Negroes to impress them. Loyally funnelling to Fanshaw all the city's paper contracts. Loyally protecting his brother Purley by asking Fanshaw to turn a blind eye to the illegal use of his trucks.'

I sawed up my steak. 'Right. Loyally planning blackmail and murder—'

'My point was only that I imagine Otis's motivations were personal, rather than political. Thus his suicide. Whereas I imagine Mr Fanshaw's motives have been neither personal nor political, but financial.'

'Frankly, Isaac, I don't give a good goddamn what their motivations were!'

Nora gave me a look. 'You know, you're a very grouchy person.'

'I've got a killer on the loose, okay? It puts me a little on edge.'

Isaac shrugged. 'He's been on the loose for eight months. Why take it out on us?'

'Don't exaggerate.'

We both finally grumbled to a halt, then talked about Mitch a while. Over coffee, Nora asked her partner what he thought Shirley Hilliardson was going to do when court reopened thirty minutes from now, and he said, 'He's going to overrule my motion for a directed verdict, and instruct us to put on our defence. Now, my dear,' he patted her hand, 'the irony there, of course, is that had the *State itself* not brought up the issue of George's involvement in the smuggling, I suspect Hilliardson might just have stopped this whole mess right now. It's the implication of prior relationship between George and Bobby Pym that makes premeditated murder feasible, and, despite my—' He paused to relish the word. '—dismantlement of Moonfoot Butler, old Shirley will not be able to discount the possibility that George and Pym fell out over the spoils.'

I said, 'Isn't that exactly the possibility the State went to a lot of trouble to raise? What's so ironical?'

'I rather think' – Isaac smiled smugly – 'they regret their enthusiasm.'

Nora noticed me eyeing her uneaten home fries, and tilted them on to my plate. Then she said she thought they should head back to court, if the waiter could be prevailed upon to accept our money, but Isaac told her to sit down again, and have some more coffee. He kept glancing at the door, and mumbled, 'All right, all right, all right, where are they?'

Naturally, I got no answer to 'Where's *who*?'

When the waiter did slouch over, it was not with the bill but a note on scratch paper for 'Captain Mangum.' It said, 'Come to the john. Bubba.' A look showed me that indeed Carl and Molina were now alone at their table. So I excused myself. 'An assignation in the toilet with Bubba Percy.'

'You care so little for motivations.' Isaac smiled. 'I won't ask you to speculate on Mr Percy's. We'll see you later, then. Take care of yourself, Slim.'

'Get some sleep,' advised Nora.

In the men's room, Bubba was reading graffiti on a stall door. I snarled at him. 'What are you looking for, Bubba, a free blow job?'

'Yeah, that's why I asked you to come back here. Listen, Mangum, thanks for telling me about Savile's fucking Klan raid last night.'

'It was a surprise raid. Who did tell you?'

'Savile. He loves to get his picture in the paper.' Percy unzipped his fashionable pants and headed for the urinal, fishing for his dick. 'Can we get serious for a second?'

'Can we wait till you finish taking a leak? . . . Bubba, why the hell are we meeting in here? Also while we're at it, why the hell are you meeting out *there* with the mayor and Brookside's Socialist prime minister?'

'You told me, play a role in the future of the state. Topple a junta. So, that's what I'm doing my bit for, friend.' Zipping up, he grinned at me. 'Love of country. I got a couple of questions, for your ears only.'

'You couldn't drop by the office?'

'This won't wait. Okay, I took your questions to Julian Lewis: He turns green, and denies trying to stop the gov from reprieving Hall. But I've got sources, off the record, singing a whole different song. I took your questions to Fanshaw, and he turns green. So I sat down and did some hard addition—'

'I hate to think I pushed you into taxing yourself, Bubba—'

Two lawyers I knew slammed into the bathroom, stepped around us to the urinals side-by-side, and agreed, while peeing, to settle a malpractice suit out of court.

When they left, Bubba put his foot up on the sink and thoughtfully brushed his suede shoe. 'Mangum, I'd say, offhand, the sum total is, Julian D. Lewis is up to his balls in quicksand, and for a man who's supposed to be walking on the water with Jesus and Brodie Cheek, that's—'

'Problematic.' I leaned on the sink, watched him pull out his comb and stroke it through his hair. 'Is that what you and Carl and Jack Molina are discussing over burritos? Saving the state for Andy Brookside?'

'Damn right. I'm giving them as much shit to throw as I can shovel out, as fast as I can dig.'

I looked at him a while. 'You never "gave" anything away in your life. You wouldn't "give" Mother Theresa your seat on a crowded bus.'

He patted his hair, stuck his comb in his linen jacket. 'Captain Cop, why don't you let God divide the sheep from the goats? You've got a tendency to oversimplify. You're not as pure as you think. I'm not as vacuous as I claim.' Pulling out a long sleek wallet, he found an old snapshot of his youthful self, a genuine hippie with auburn curls down to his shoulders, a peace symbol on his headband, his bare arm around a bosomy flower child in her shift who was shaking a 'Stop the Bombing' sign in the midst of what looked like a confused campus demonstration. 'Gorgeous hair,' I said. 'Yours, I mean.'

'I cut it off for Eugene McCarthy. I was at the Chicago convention in 'sixty-eight. I was a believer, Mangum. Now, that surprises you.'

I allowed that it did. 'Myself, I always had the feeling Hubert Humphrey would make a better president than Richard Nixon. But at the time, standing up for Hubert wasn't a popular notion. Who's the girl? Your first love?'

He sighed. 'Sandy? Yeah. Teaches economics at Stanford now. I never did get in her pants.'

'Doesn't look to me like she's wearing any.'

'Hey, don't be so crude.' He snatched back the photo.

'"Don't be so *crude*?"' I threw up my arms. 'Bubba, I'm impressed. I'm serious. If you'll defend a lady's modesty, if you'd cut off your hair for your politics, maybe you *would* put God and country before Porsche and Pulitzer.'

Grinning, he slipped the wallet back in his linen jacket. 'Why not both? Listen, I help put Brookside in office, he'll owe me. Okay, let me pick your brain.'

'Help yourself.'

The Lewis people, Bubba said, had apparently asked for a 'confab' tomorrow with the Brookside people, at which time both sides were going to lay on the table a peek at their big guns. 'They're making noises that they've got napalm on Andy. They may think they've got enough to make him pull out. We may have more on them than they're aware of. Negotiations. That's what détente is all about. So, look, Mangum, here's the deal.'

'Ah, the deal. I was sort of wondering why we were in the john. But why aren't the mayor and Jack Molina in here with us?'

'Carl's an idealist' was his answer. It wasn't true, but I thought it was kind of sweet that he thought so. Well, the deal was that Bubba and Jack had done a lot of talking in the last week: with Bubba shovelling into the Brookside camp as much Lewis compost as he could find; including the scuttlebutt that the Lewis people had hold of something nasty they were saving up to use against Andy. And with Jack, well, Jack giving Bubba the old 'I'm going to bare my throat to your teeth' line, by telling him he bet he knew what that 'something nasty' was – a videotape in which Andrew Theodore Brookside, 'A New Leader for a New South,' was not wearing so much as his Medal of Honour as he

409

led the New South into places it might not be ready to follow him. Bubba fluttered his long eyelashes parodically. 'According to Molina, some Lewis people secretly filmed Andy humping a black hooker. You know, emulating JFK has led to some serious Liberal image problems.'

Laughing, I asked him if he believed there was such a tape.

'From the right source, I'd believe the Pope was boffing Mitterrand. Now, Jack says that he thought he had the problem contained, but that you've told him otherwise. True? You know about this?'

I nodded. 'True, I know about it. True, the problem may not be contained. And if you know about it, they could be showing clips on "Phil Donahue" tomorrow.'

'Man, I just told you, I've *picked* my side of the bread to butter. Jack knows I'm not only going to sit on Randy Andy's folly, I'm going to sit on anybody I hear's got wind of it. And the lid's still on. 'Cause I would have heard some steam blowing around if it wasn't. Nobody knows. Carl Yarborough in there, now, *he* doesn't know.'

I said they were certainly right to assume a family man like Carl shouldn't find out, either; though his upset might have less to do with idealism than not wanting to put all his eggs in a basket with a time bomb. And I asked if Jack Molina had also told him why he'd thought he had 'the problem contained.'

'Molina said it was up to you to tell me or not, or how much to tell me. Said whatever you told me would be the way it was.' Bubba patted my sternum. 'It amazes me, how so many people seem to have a lot of respect for you, Mangum. Just amazes me. So, (a) what's the background? And, (b), is there a copy of this fuck film loose?'

I thought about it, then told him I knew where two copies were, but it was of course possible that Lewis had access to a copy, which could mean they'd run off a thousand more. Though it seemed to me, if Lewis *did* have a copy, a little more steam would have leaked out by now. So they could be bluffing. But if Bubba wanted to see this film, he could ask Jack Molina to play it for him, because Jack had one of the copies. He'd taken it from Cooper Hall's files after Cooper's death. Bubba whistled through his teeth. 'Cooper Hall?! Hold it. I may be jaded, but I don't *believe* Cooper Hall made this movie!'

I said he hadn't. Then I decided something. I knew Bubba Percy wasn't going to leak anything I told him not to. He was too

410

dependent on me for information. What was more interesting was I realized that – pompadour, crass grin and all – I *trusted* Bubba. I mean, I wouldn't trust him with my sister or my dog or my car or my personal feelings, but I did trust him with the *news*. So I gave him some background on the making and trading of that videotape. While I talked, he kept forgetting to breathe, and had to suck in sudden gulps of air. I said that if I could prove a direct connection between Lewis and the people who'd had that tape made, then Lewis would have more things to worry about than slippage in the polls. Bubba shrugged this off. 'You'll never prove a connection. If he does have a copy, his mucky-mucks'll say it arrived through the mail in a brown wrapper. And Julian'll say he didn't know squat about it, and how he's shocked out of the few wits he has.'

I shrugged. 'On the other hand, he may tell his muckymucks to drop the whole show-and-tell rather than risk the exposure of *his* fanny, as well as Brookside's. Frankly, Bubba, where's Adlai Stevenson?'

'You've gotta have *hair* to win now. The camera's gotta love you.' He glanced at his own hair in the mirror, and gave it a caress. 'Okay, thanks, Mangum. You gave me more than I was figuring on.'

'So you'll owe *me* one. And you're welcome. Just don't print anything without checking with me.'

'You got it. By the way, how much of this flying faeces has Rosethorn got his patty-paws on?'

'Probably more than you. He thinks faster.'

'Gonna be wild in that courtroom then. Let me go grab a good seat. Catch you later.' Shaking a crease in his trousers free, he headed for the door, then turned around. 'Hey, you said two copies of "Debbie Does Andy." You know who's got the other one?'

'Yeah, I do. Me.'

'You?' Bubba's eyebrow went up. 'Just for bedside viewing? Or what should I tell Brookside's boys *you* want? Commissioner of police? Soybean monopoly? Would you settle for the Biltmore Mansion?'

I grinned. 'You know what I want. I want a state of equal opportunity, liberty and justice for all.'

Bubba shook his head at me. 'You don't ask much, do you, el Capitan?'

Walking back to my table, with a friendly wave at Yarborough and Molina, I found Nora seated there alone, drinking a glass of wine in an exhilarated state. She smiled at me. 'What was that, a drug bust?'

'You heard of Yalta. The Council of Trent. The Treaty of Versailles. Well, that was the Treaty of Pogo's Urinal. Where's the Fat Man?'

The green tilt up of her eyes lifted even more. 'Cuddy. Isaac Rosethorn's amazing. You know who just walked in here, and asked to talk? Neil Sadler and the attorney general. The attorney general! They want to discuss a nolo contendere plea from George. To second degree. They'll drop murder one right now. *If* we don't put on a defence.'

I sat down.

'Right!' she said. 'And the thing is, Isaac knew it was coming. He was *waiting* for them.'

'What about Mitch Bazemore?'

'He wasn't with them.'

'Right . . . So much for a pure conservative heart.'

When I asked Nora if the State had given any reason for its sudden generosity, she said they'd given a lot of reasons. 'But right now I bet Isaac's in the DA's office making them eat dirt over the *real* reason.' With a downright violent gleam of victory in her eyes, she pulled a sheaf of papers from her new briefcase. The top one was a list of witnesses subpoenaed by Isaac Rosethorn for the defence in S. vs. Hall 2179 NC. It was a long list. It included Purley Newsome, Lana Pym, Sergeant Charles Mennehy, Assistant DA Neil Sadler, Mr Dyer Fanshaw, Warden Zackery Carpenter of Dollard Prison, and the lieutenant governor of the state of North Carolina, Julian Dollard Lewis.

She laughed from pleasure. '*God, I love him.* So, what do you think he's going to do? Bargain them down to voluntary manslaughter for a nolo contendere?'

John Emory strode inside Pogo's, and tapped his watch at me. I pulled out Nora's chair, and handed her her briefcase. 'Honey, nothing on God's occasionally green earth is going to make that old man give up a chance to make a speech to that jury.'

Chapter 23

'Ladies and gentlemen of the jury. It's late, and it's Friday, and we're all hot and tired, and we're all ready to go stretch out somewhere with a glass of something cool. I need to sit down, and get off this bad leg. And I know you twelve good people would love to *stand up*. And get off those hard chairs!

'So I'm going to keep my opening remarks as short and lean as a fat old Southern lawyer can manage. Not as short as the prosecution would have liked. Because they didn't want me to make any opening remarks *at all*! They didn't want you to hear any defence *at all*! They wanted George Hall to come back in here this afternoon, throw up his arms, and say, "All right. I'm not going to argue with you. As long as it's not *death*, give me whatever you folks decide on in a back room, and I'll go along." Well, by God, they don't know George Hall, and by God, they don't know me!'

The thunder of Isaac Rosethorn's baritone rumbled up through the sixteen handsome chandeliers hanging from the forty-foot ceiling of the court. At the sound, people stirred in the long tiered rows of seats. This was what they'd come for. The grand old man, putting on – according to today's *Hillston Star* – 'his last defence.' Hands in his rumpled jacket, his dark, deep eyes glittering, slowly he walked from George's side, across to the table where District Attorney Mitchell Bazemore sat stiff as a rod, his cheeks flushed, and where Assistant DA Neil Sadler sat with the same bland smile that was on the face of the assistant attorney general, who now sat beside him.

'No, sir. They don't.' Isaac leaned over Mitch, shook his head sorrowfully, then slowly limped, the shoe on his weak leg scuffing the floor, all the way back – past Nomi Hall motionless in black, past the press table where Bubba Percy grinned as he wrote, past Miss Bee Turner at her desk, and old Mr Walkington at his recorder, past a whole row of rapt Haver law students – all the way back to the jury box, where he quietly placed his hands on the rail. Isaac looked at each face in the box. Gave each a solemn nod. Women. Men. Blacks. Whites. Lindquist, the school principal, who was foreman. The elderly farm widow, who'd stopped turning her shoulder on the black man seated beside her. Mrs Boren, who never let go of the purse in her lap. Isaac sighed. 'And, ladies and gentlemen, if the prosecution thinks that, they don't know *you*! If they think you have sat here these long weeks, sacrificing time and convenience and money, sat here and not *cared* whether you heard George's side of the story or not, then they have sadly misjudged the citizens of Haver County. Haven't they? I've been with you day by day for weeks now, and I've seen the earnest, hard-thinking diligence with which you have accepted the sacred duty placed upon you by this great state. The duty to well and truly try this case, to seek the truth, to find it, and to judge it!'

'The old hypocrite,' I whispered to Alice MacLeod, beside me in a side row. 'It was just noon today when *he* asked the judge to render a directed verdict, and throw out the case.'

'The jury probably doesn't know what a directed verdict is,' Alice whispered back, as she struggled in vain for a comfortable position. She was eight months pregnant now, and didn't like sitting anywhere except in the motorized La-Z-Boy recliner she'd forced Justin to buy. A few more minutes here, and she gave up, mumbling as she left, 'This little bastard is kicking the shit out of me. I'll see you at Trinity tonight.'

I sat there deciding the baby must be a boy; would anyone call a *girl* baby a 'little bastard'? So I missed the next few Rosethorn sentences. I doubt anybody else did. Every seat in the huge courtroom was filled, and silent, although it *was* late – quarter to four – and afternoon summer sun streamed in hot yellow light through the western windows. Court hadn't even reconvened until three-thirty, because until then all the counsels had been sequestered first in the DA's office, then in the judge's chambers. What they'd been doing in there was anybody's guess. I sure couldn't figure it out, and hadn't had a chance to ask. One thing was clear. The trial wasn't over. As far as Isaac was concerned, it was probably just beginning.

Zeke Caleb had stepped into my office half an hour ago, and said, 'You wanted me to let you know – well, Miss Bee's downstairs now, calling court to order.' I'd been talking all afternoon with agents from the FBI and the BATF, while off in the holding cell the Carolina Patriots and their lawyer screamed about the exorbitant bail set by Judge Dolores Roche. His argument that she'd used 'reverse discrimination' against those heavily armed white supremacists hadn't gone down too well with a black female New Deal Democrat like old Dolores.

When I'd slipped through the side door into the first row of the courtroom, Shirley Hilliardson was already giving a lecture to the jury, the details of which, as Alice had deduced, they didn't seem to be following too closely. He explained to them sternly that he was overruling the motion that a directed verdict be entered for the defence. At that point, Isaac stood, and calmly took exception to the ruling. 'So noted,' said the judge. Then he stroked the side of his hawk's nose a while, then he announced with no more affect than if he were reading a phone book, that counsel for the State had instructed the bench that, at this juncture, on the basis of the evidence, the prosecution no longer wished to seek the death penalty against the defendant, but was prepared to accept a verdict of guilty of murder in the *second* degree.

The news ricocheted around the room like the loud frantic flutter of birds trying to escape. Some spectators cheered, some hissed. Reporters ran outside for phones. I thought, well, damn, Isaac did agree to the nolo contendere, and I was surprised by how much the fact disappointed me. But then, slow as molasses, the old man strolled up to the bench, and Sadler, the assistant DA, ran up there after him. While they talked, Judge Hilliardson nodded a few times, the twist on his blade of a mouth undecipherable. After both sides returned to their respective tables, Hilliardson rapped his gavel to quiet the fluttering. 'I take it then, Counsellor,' he said to Rosethorn, each word sliced through that sharp mouth. 'The defence does not rest?'

With his hand on George Hall's shoulder, Isaac shook his white mane of hair. 'Your Honour, that is correct. The defence will offer evidence against the charge of murder in the second degree. Or indeed, in *any* degree.'

My breath rushed out. He was going to fight.

But what had happened then at the bargaining table? Last I'd heard from Nora, the AG's deal was 'second degree' in exchange for *no* defence.

'Are you prepared now to make an opening statement, Counsellor?'

'Yes, Your Honour, if the Court pleases. The defence is ready.'

So that's how it had started. And while Isaac was true to his promise, and kept it short (for him, that is – I'd heard one opening statement of his that lasted two hours), he managed to say quite a lot, without my being able to figure out what the hell he was up to.

Right now he was embracing all twelve of those jurors in the warm hug of his low rich voice. 'Now, folks. The defence doesn't have to offer a bit of evidence, doesn't have to say a word. The defence doesn't have to *prove* George innocent. A man walks into this court innocent, and he *stays* innocent until and unless the prosecution *proves* him guilty. So I could tell you, go on back in the jury room right now, and ask yourselves, "Do I have an abiding conviction amounting to a moral certainty that George Hall committed intentional murder?" Ask yourselves, "Do I believe beyond any reasonable doubt that the evidence presented in this courtroom *proves* that George Hall committed an intentional murder?' Think back on what you've heard here, and ask yourselves, "Have I been offered any evidence that George *planned* to murder Pym, *except* for the mumbled-scumbled, inconsistent, contradictory, and blatantly fabricated testimony of a bartender, Mr Fattie McCramer, who is a far better witness for the good eats at his establishment than for the truth about this case? And the testimony of Mr Moonfoot Butler, who came in here claiming to be George's best friend, and didn't know the first thing about him!? Is that-proof?" The self-serving claims of a shameful scoundrel, a convicted felon whose staggering arrest record I wouldn't ask our clerk Miss Turner to attempt to *lift* for fear it would do damage to her back!'

The tiny Miss Bee gave Isaac a steely look, as if to say she could easily lift Moonfoot's arrest record in one hand and Rose-thorn in the other. He smiled at her.

Then he walked to the witness chair, and from it pointed his finger at the prosecution table. 'Ask yourselves, "Have they proved their case?" No, they haven't! Of course they haven't. You know it, and I know it. And what's more, *they* know it. Seven

416

years ago, they came in here hollering for the death penalty. That conviction was overturned. Thank God, in time! Thrown out. They came in here, a month ago, hollering for the death penalty again. Now, oh yes, now, they're willing to give up first-degree murder. Why? Because they know they didn't prove it! Why didn't they prove it?' Isaac's voice, building with each sentence, roared down the length of the room. '*Because it isn't true!*'

His hands stroked sadly down his face, and he spoke quietly. 'Because it's hard to prove a lie. Not impossible, as the sad book of history tells us. But it's hard. You can hide Truth, gag her, smother her, offer her bribes, lock her in darkness. *But* Truth has a way of slipping through the lock, of whispering through the crack until she's heard.' His hand lifted towards the bright windows, as if to pull Truth through them. 'You will hear her now.'

'Amen,' some woman shouted.

Rap, went Hilliardson's gavel.

Isaac didn't take his eyes from the jury. 'The defence will prove that George Hall is not guilty of murder in any degree. Not guilty by reason of self-defence. We will prove it, even though we are not required to do so, because this courtroom, this temple of truth, where I have spent my *life* in the service of the law, has been defiled by the lies set loose here. *And I want it cleansed!*'

'Right on!' yelled, of all people, young G. G. Walker, seated with half the Canaan Twelve. Their loud claps were picked up by other spectators. The long black swoop of Hilliardson's arm slammed down the gavel so hard it flew out of his hand, and Miss Bee Turner had to retrieve it. Standing, he arched over the bench like the grim reaper.'Once more!' he seethed,'and I will clear this court. And Mr Rosethorn, I will ask you to restrict yourself more rigorously to the perimeters of opening remarks, as opposed to closing statements.'

'Yes, Your Honour.' Moving towards the jury again, Isaac's left hand hit the palm of his right in rhythm with his words. 'Members of the jury, what is the truth? Was there malice aforethought? Yes, there was. But not by George Hall. By Robert Pym! It wasn't George who brought a gun to Smoke's. It was Pym! Was there gross and reckless provocation by Robert Pym? Yes, there was! Was there not only an *attempt* to inflict serious bodily harm on George Hall, but the grievous *infliction* of bodily harm? Look at George's face! *Seven years* later, he still carries the scar on his nostril! Did the defendant believe his life was in danger? Why, everyone in Smoke's Bar believed it! Even the long stream of witnesses for the prosecution believed it! Even the arresting officer C. R. Mangum believed it!'

Several jurors nodded, and Isaac joined them. 'Of course they believed it. Because it was *true*.' His arm waved contemptuously at Bazemore's table. 'All this stuff from the district attorney about "Don't let Isaac Rosethorn convince you that George was over-come by irresistible impulse." about the "policeman at the elbow" rule, and how if one had been there, George wouldn't have done what he did.'

Turning around, Isaac's fist slammed the table in front of Miss Bee, who remarkably didn't jump out of her chair. 'Well, *a policeman was there at George's elbow*. He was there jamming this thirty-eight revolver into George's nose!' He grabbed up the gun from the exhibits labelled as evidence, and brought it to the jury. 'Look at this ugly thing. It's scary, isn't it? How scared would you be if a belligerent drunk shoved this thing in your nostril, and said, "Buddy, your ass is grass." Well, I'll tell you how scared I'd be! I'd be scared I was going to die!'

He returned the revolver to Miss Bee, as he said, 'I never had the slightest intention in the world of talking about irresistible impulses . . . Not unless we can agree that *self-preservation* is an irresistible impulse.' He paused, shook loose a handkerchief and tapped his forehead. 'Cicero,' he said, as if the name had just occurred to him. 'Some of you remember him from high school Latin? Old Roman lawyer, back in Caesar's time?' The jury foreman smiled at him.

'Well, Cicero summed up the law of self-defence as it's been upheld by society from time immemorial. Cicero said, "This law we do not learn from books, for it is embodied in each of us: that if our life is in danger, *any* means of escape is honourable. *This is the first law of nature.*"'

His hand stroked along the jury rail reassuringly. 'And that law of nature is also upheld by the laws of this state. All you have to believe is that, to George, at that time, in those circum-stances, there was a reasonable appearance of the necessity of deadly force to prevent his own immediate death, *or* serious injury. If so, the shooting of Robert Pym was an act of self-defence, and the defendant is not guilty of murder . . . Now!' Isaac patted the rail, and stepped away. 'The State brought in its own psychiatrist to tell you – after, by the way, one interview of forty-three minutes – that George is a violent man with dangerous impulses. Well, first of all, in this country we don't put people in prison for having dangerous impulses, but for committing crimes. Second of all, what did these dangerous impulses turn out to be?' Isaac counted them off on his fingers. 'One, George tried to protect himself from a racist thug throwing beer on him at the ballpark. Two, he tried to stop Officer Robert Pym from slamming a handcuffed suspect against a concrete wall. A suspect, by the way, later released for lack of evidence. Three, he tried to stop Robert Pym from killing *him*. As we will prove, all he's ever done is try to protect himself. And protect others. Which, by the law of nature, and the law of this state, he had a right to do!'

The assistant DA was whispering to the assistant AG. Isaac stopped and stared at them. 'Gentlemen, excuse me. I believe I have the floor. Besides, the State has already rested. It's a little too late to start figuring out a case for the prosecution now.'

Over the loud general laugh, I could hear Bubba Percy's guffaw.

Isaac strolled on. 'Oh, we could bring in our own psychiatrist who'd tell you George would no more slap a fly than Albert Schweitzer would. But I'm not going to mess with it. I don't need to.' He shook his handkerchief at the State's table, then stuffed it in his seersucker jacket. 'Instead, I'm going to let you hear from George's commanding officer in Vietnam, who will tell you George was a good and valiant soldier, wounded in battle protecting this country. I'm going to let you hear from the minister of George's church, who, believe me, knows him better than Moonfoot Butler ever did. And hear from the warden of Dollard Prison, who will tell you that even under the savage stress of an *unjust death sentence* – even under the inhuman torture of *seven years* on Death Row, and *four separate nights* set for his execution, even *hours* before he was to be strapped to a metal chair and gassed to death for the heinous crime of protecting his own life from a barbaric assault – even then, George Hall *never* displayed a single instance of these so-called violent tendencies of his. All the violence has been on the other side ... On the other side.'

His head bowed for a moment, and when he looked up, there were actually tears welling in his eyes. If it was a trick, it was one I'd never seen him use before. Quietly, he said, 'I am going to prove to you that George Hall is no killer. Far, far from it. George

419

Hall is a man noble enough to be willing to lay down his life to protect others from being killed.' Isaac let his glance move across the court to rest on Nomi Hall, down whose face a single tear ran. The whole room rustled as people turned questioning faces to each other.

Leaning towards the jury, moving step by step along the rail, Isaac ended his statement with a softly delivered hand grenade. 'Ladies and gentlemen, the defence contends, and the defence will prove, by affirmative evidence, by expert opinion, by deposition, and by *eyewitnesses*, that George Hall had no plan to kill, no intent to kill, did not mean to kill, and had no reason to think he *would* kill Robert Pym when he shot that gun. The defence contends, rather, members of the jury, that *Robert Pym* – accompanied by his companion in crime, one Winston Russell, a killer now at large, wanted on three counts of murder, including the murder of George's only brother, Cooper Hall – that Robert Pym and Winston Russell *did* plan and *did* intend to kill the defendant. That Pym came into Smoke's Bar expressly for that purpose, that he provoked an altercation expressly for that purpose, and that he failed in that purpose only by mischance. Or by the grace of God. Just as the attempt of the State to kill George Hall has failed only by mischance. Or by the grace of God. George Hall has been a victim, sacrificed – as so many of his race have been sacrificed in the long bloody chronicle of this nation's history to prejudice, to politics, and to power. That's the truth.' Isaac's chest heaved in a slow, tired sigh. 'That's the truth . . . And that's why the defence does not rest.'

Nobody moved until Isaac had limped back to his seat. Then together three of the Haver law students stood up and applauded. Here and there throughout the court, others joined in. Among them, Jordan West and Father Paul Madison. Judge Hilliardson banged his gavel, and above the noise announced that he was adjourning the court until Monday morning. Then shouting down that he wanted the defence counsel in his chambers, he stalked off the bench. George waved good-bye to his mother with his raised cuffed hands as the sheriff led him out the side door. Everyone left the prosecutor's table except for Mitchell Bazemore, whose frozen back never altered in the whole long time it took the crowded room to empty.

I watched him for a while before I walked over. He looked up, turned away. 'What's going on, Mitch?' No answer. I saw he'd bitten down on his lower lip hard enough to leave his teeth

420

marks. Pulling up a chair, I put my foot on it. 'I never figured you'd give up murder one, even for a guilty plea. Much less for what looks like nothing. If Rosethorn wouldn't deal with you, why—'

He laughed. I suppose it was laughter. 'Oh, Rosethorn dealt. He dealt. But not with me. So take your gloating somewhere else, Mangum. Take it to the AG. I'm not in on the game.'

'. . . I had that feeling.' The next sentence wasn't easy, but it was fair. 'Look, I'm sorry I ever said you were.'

'Go to hell.' He stood up, stuffing papers in his shiny briefcase. 'Have you found Winston Russell?'

'Not yet.'

'Then why are you sitting around watching this farce?' His face got angry again, which was a peculiar comfort. 'I want you in my office in ten minutes.'

'The FBI's waiting in mine, about those Carolina Patriots.'

His neck pulsed against his buttoned-down collar. 'The FBI can have them. I want you in my office in ten minutes with a warrant for the arrest of Dyer Fanshaw.'

Leaning on my knee, I stared at him. 'My, my, Mitch . . . My, my, my. You wouldn't listen to me. But you listened to Purley Newsome . . . Just tell me this, will you? Did Otis leave a suicide note?'

He slammed shut the briefcase, locking it. 'Mangum, I despise you.'

'Mitch, I'm not the one who shut you out of this case to save my butt. I'm not the one suborning witnesses, covering up rackets, arms-smuggling, and murder. Those are your pals.'

The briefcase swung as he shook it so close to my face, I had to tilt away. 'Just go get that warrant. Understand? Suppression of evidence in a felony; illegal use of the interstate highway—'

Opening my jacket, I pulled out one of the warrants I'd had there since three this afternoon. A warrant for the arrest of Dyer Fanshaw. I gave it to Bazemore. 'Here you go, Counsellor. I've got a little more in there than that. How about seditious conspiracy? Accessory after the fact to murder?'

No comment on my producing the warrant in a lot less than the ten minutes he'd given me. Just a shove against my chair as he bulldozed by. 'You can't prove any of that. So drop it.'

'Mitch, hold up. The same folks that were dealing with Rosethorn don't want Mr Fanshaw arrested for so much as tossing a candy wrapper out the car window. If you've still got any plans on being Lewis's new attorney general, I don't think this is the way to do it.'

'I don't care what you think.' He rammed his way through the doors with his briefcase.

'Right,' I said to the swinging door. 'You just care about crime. Looks like that really is the truth.'

Chapter 24

'So what's the point, Cuddy? What are we doing?' Lee's voice was resigned, angry, and hopeful all at the same time. 'There're three messages from me on your machine. You're never home. And now you can't come to the cabin either?'

'Lee, hey, please! . . . Oh, hell. Just a second.'

Zeke Caleb had opened my office door. 'Captain. That priest friend of yours – Father Madison – can they have more police protection at the Trinity Church thing tonight? Says, 'cause of Andrew Brookside being there, his committee's worried about crowds. Plus all the stuff on the radio about us 'rresting the Klan. He's on line five.'

'Transfer him to Ralph Fisher. He's in charge of that. Isn't Ralph here?'

'Yeah. But Father Madison wanted to talk to you.'

'Well, tell him I'm busy, Zeke!' I pointed at the phone receiver, and waved him back out with my free hand. Martha Mitchell barked when I yelled, then trotted out after Zeke, who naturally didn't bother to close my door. 'Lee? I'm sorry, I'm living in a Saigon intersection here. Look, I explained why I haven't been home. River Rise is under twenty-four-hour surveillance. But sure, I can come to the cabin if you want Officers Emory and White crowded around the fire playing pinochle with us. These kids got themselves orders straight from Carl Yarborough to sit in the bathtub with me! And for the record, you're never home either.'

'I'm home now . . . I thought we could spend the night in the cabin. That's all. I'm disappointed.'

'Where will he be?' Both of us avoided using Brookside's name.

'He's leaving straight from his Trinity speech to fly to New York.'

'I'll be at Trinity. Why don't you come there? We could at least refresh our memories about what we look like. What do you *look* like, Lee? What do *I* look like?'

Actually, I could see Lee clearer and realer than anything around me in my office. Right then, I saw her in the Pine Hills Lake cabin, my old blue wool shirt on over her slip, her hair white with plaster, holding my legs steady on the ladder while I patched holes in the mess we'd found after we'd pulled out the dropped ceiling. I saw her standing in the kitchen at the wobbly wood table, placing, one by one, ridiculously expensive yellow roses in a tin, blue-speckled coffeepot. 'Lee? You trying to place me?'

She made a humming noise. 'Let's see . . . Are you the man with hair the colour of bright-leaf tobacco, and Carolina blue eyes?'

'Sounds like an ad for Haver cigarettes. Is that why you like me? I look like the family business? . . . Well, damn. You're free, and I'm under armed guards.' I spun my chair around, put my feet on the window ledge.

'Okay, not exactly free. I have the board of the North Carolina Arts Society coming for dinner. *But* they'll be gone by ten. I was going to meet you at the cabin afterwards.' She laughed. '*But*, since you can't come at *all*, I thought I'd grab the opportunity to bitch about *your* schedule for a change.'

I laughed too. 'Well, no wonder it's the young who fall in love. They're the only ones with the free time.'

A knock, then Justin stuck his head inside. 'Need to talk to you.'

I nodded. He sauntered through, went into my bathroom, so I said into the phone, 'Listen, I better go. I've got Lieutenant Savile in here.'

'Well, I'd say tell him hello, but he was extremely cool at the Hunt Club this morning. I guess about the nomination. I don't suppose it matters to him that Andy does need DeWitt. Justin comes from a political family; he should understand.'

'Leave me out of this, darlin'. You two can fight it out on horseback some morning at the Club. Slap each other around with rolled-up family trees.'

Her laugh was warm against my ear. 'Oh, I love you, Cuddy.'

Justin came back in the room, wiping his hands on a paper towel.

I said, 'Ditto.'

Lee's voice went playfully husky. 'You don't suppose it's just sex, do you?'

'Not *just*. Well, nice talking to you, Sheriff. Keep your pants on.'

She chuckled. 'At least till I see you. If I ever do.'

'Oh, you will. It's all I think about, night and day.'

'That's not true, Captain Mangum. And I bet I wouldn't love you if it were. Bye.'

I swung my chair back around from Elvis's smile to Justin's. He said, 'What's all you ever think about, night and day?'

'Winston Russell,' I told him.

'No sign of him yet around River Rise. DiMallo just called from your apartment; told Nancy he loved subbing for you; he's playing all your compact discs, turning on all your lights, drinking your beer, just having a ball. Said you lived like a king.

'Tell Nancy to tell DiMallo to keep his hands off my stereo.'

'How come you got Nancy body-guarding? I mean, I don't consider myself a sexist but—'

'I didn't. She went over my head to the mayor. Got herself and Emory assigned to pester me to death. What'd you want to see me about? I've got the FBI meeting me in Mitch's office in ten minutes.'

He tossed the towel in the trash. 'Boone Homicide just found the hiker's body. White male Caucasian. Shot in the back. Purley wasn't lying.'

In addition to this ugly news about the hiker, Justin told me a Patriot had admitted under questioning that Winston took a thirty-aught-six rifle with a telescopic lens from their stockpile yesterday. And a tip had come in: Pete Zaslo thought he'd seen a man who looked 'a little' like Winston leave a phone booth outside the Silver Comet Bar. The grey T-shirt and jeans fit the description the Patriots had given us of Russell's clothes. Plus, Pete said, he'd put on a web-top baseball hat, sunglasses, and was carrying a duffel bag.

Justin pulled an HPD bulletproof-vest from a plastic wrapper, and threw it at me. 'If you leave this building, use this.' Stepping to the door, he slapped the gun holster hanging there. 'And put this on! And I don't mean just wear it. I mean *load* it, and wear it.'

I tossed the vest on to the couch. 'Do we know who Winston was calling?'

'Phone company couldn't help. Amazing anybody in the state *would* talk to him.' Justin was looking at the map of the Trinity Church area, with Ralph Fisher's surveillance positions pinpointed. 'Listen, Cuddy, you really think any pals of these Patriots are going to stage a protest for them at Trinity tonight?'

I sipped at my can of Pepsi. 'I don't think they've got any pals. If they do, I don't think the pals are gonna be eager to claim the relationship just now. If they are, they're gonna walk into a solid wall of cops. Ralph's got ten of ours, four of the sheriff's, and four from the state patrols, two of them mounted. I almost hope they do show up.'

He ran his finger along the map, around the side of the church to the old cemetery. 'My great-great-grandfather's buried here. Eustace Dollard. You know, the governor.'

'I know his prison.'

'Oh, he wasn't so bad ... What's your guess? Is Julian going to use that videotape against Brookside?'

I shrugged. 'I don't know that "Julian" has a copy.'

His hand moved along the map, measuring distances. 'How 'bout the copy *we've* got? Think about it. The man who commissioned the thing killed himself. The man who filmed it was murdered. The woman who was in it left the country. If you give it to Mitch – well, what's the point?'

'The point is, it's evidence in a homicide. I want it to be there when Winston Russell comes to trial.' The meatball sub I'd ordered for dinner didn't look very appetizing. 'Besides, I thought you hated Brookside?'

Justin smiled. 'Would you rather have my cousin Julian as governor of this state? Alice sure wouldn't.' Then he tapped the map, turned, and changed the subject. 'Listen, I talked to Lana Pym. She came in, with a crying kid. She's scared. Demanded police protection. After a visit to Purley at the hospital, Mrs Pym finally believes Winston killed her brother Willie. So she admits he *might* have done all the other things we've been saying he's done. And might do something to her.'

'Could she help us to get to Russell?'

'She doesn't know where he is. She's in a total panic. Of

426

course, she still denies that *Bobby* did anything wrong. She's also enraged that Isaac "*Rosen*thorn" should have subpoenaed her, when he's "working for the nigger" who killed her husband. She said, "I just don't see how this all happened. We were just regular people. Willie wasn't a bad man. Bobby wasn't a bad man."'

'Yeah. Nobody's bad but blacks, Jews, Commies, and queers.'

'And the rich. Let's not leave my people out.'

'Friend, your cousin Julian may be *in*, up to his tennis elbow. So, how much does Lana Pym know about her husband and Winston's scams?'

'I don't think all that much. Obviously, she didn't know about the suitcase full of money, or the videotape. But she admitted she'd lied to me. Brother Willie was *not* with her the afternoon of the Cooper Hall shooting. She said she'd stuck to the alibi even after we'd found Willie in the river because she'd had a call from Russell, and he'd scared her.' Justin went to the window ledge, leaned out to smoke. 'She said, she hoped Winston fried in hell for all eternity, and she'd be glad to pull the switch with her own hand.'

'Probably would.' I threw my meatball grinder in the waste-basket. 'Probably Lana was the one out in that crowd at Dollard with a sign saying "Gas George Hall." Probably already made her kids their own little combat fatigues, and in ten years they'll be marching around with martyred Papa's white-trash Patriots.'

Justin ran his thumb under the leather strap of his shoulder holster. 'White trash, as my grandmother often said, is far trashier than any other shade.'

Angry, I punched the intercom, and told Zeke to tell Mitch I'd be right down. Then I said to Justin, 'Frankly, General Lee, I've never seen much difference between your Confederate heroes galloping around in grey and gold, and white-trash heroes night-riding in sheets and hoods. Go put Mrs Pym under house arrest as a material witness. Send two officers home with her. And get a tap on her phone. Now!'

'Jesus, what are you so pissed at me for?'

'Your "people" are getting on my nerves.'

Justin grinned. 'Imagine how it got on my nerves when they had me put in a loony bin?' Then tossing his cigarette, he squinted into the sun, out over the Hillston skyline. 'Winston's either skulking around outside your apartment, or he's on the roof of that bank right now, getting ready to take a shot through

427

your window. He's not going to be bothering with Lana Pym. All right. I'm off. Alice said you were coming to Trinity tonight. Do me a favour. Don't walk there.'

'I'm not.'

'Alice wrote the last paragraph of Brookside's speech. Tell her if you like it. So long.' Patting the poster of Elvis in the stomach, he left the room.

I glanced out the window. The sun, immense and fiery red, looked like it was resting a moment on the shoulders of the Haver Tobacco Company warehouses, and like the Haver buildings were strong enough to hold it up.

I rode to Trinity in the mayor's limousine, with the vest on, with the holster on, with Nancy and John in a squad car behind us, and with a motorcycle cop in front of us. We left in absolute privacy from the garage under the Municipal Building, which HPD now kept under constant surveillance, and as lit up as a homecoming game.

Leaning back in his seat, sunlight rich on his warm brown profile, Carl smoked peacefully at his Cuban cigar, because his car was one of the few places he felt he had left to do it in.

'How's Dina?' I asked him.

'She's fine. Speaking tonight at the Bush College graduation. Wonders when you're going to ask her dancing again.'

'Well, tell her next time let's make it some place besides the Hillston Club's Confederacy Ball.'

He laughed, then he looked out the car window as we sped down Cadmean Street.

'But you know, Cuddy, I have a deep affection for this city. I like to look at every building in it. Despite the old problems. And the new. And maybe it's not as pretty, or artsy, or high-falutin as some Carolina towns, but it works hard. And it *tries* hard to be decent.'

I nodded. 'Sometimes. Electing you mayor was one of them.'

'That's what I mean.' He rubbed at his bald head. 'I'm mayor. My father loaded tobacco at Haver, and his father worked a tenant farm. And his father was the son of a slave.'

I said, 'I can't trace my folks back that far. Just through the factory and the tenant farm.'

He smiled at me. 'But you can make a pretty good guess, can't you, that they weren't slaves.' We stopped at an intersection in front of the Randolph Office Building, where a bustle of people, white and black, leaving work, were waiting for the light. They stared at our little caravan, and Carl rolled down his tinted window to wave. 'Hello there, folks. Thank God it's Friday, right? Looks like it's going to be a nice sunny weekend.'

Most of them smiled and waved and said, 'Hello, Mr Mayor.' 'How're you doing?' 'Take it easy.'

As we drove on, Carl said, 'That's Hillston. Those people. And I don't want the damn media saying scum like the Carolina Patriots are what Hillston's all about. Or that all the crap in this trial is what Hillston's all about. I want everybody thrown in jail that's supposed to be there, and everybody else free to get on with things.'

I said, 'We're doing our best ... About the trial, I guess you heard – there was a lot of fancy manoeuvreing going on today, and going on *over* Mitch's head.'

The mayor stubbed out the cigar. 'Are you surprised? Mitchell Bazemore manoeuvres with the subtlety of a dinosaur. He's too self-righteous, too inflexible, and too—'

'Honest?'

'I was going to say "innocent" – for high office. So it's just as well. His politics are abominable anyhow. Now, Rosethorn, on the other hand—' Carl chuckled, scratching his moustache. 'Well, if they ever try to impeach me, get me Rosethorn.'

'I don't know the details, just that the AG himself showed up to work some deal with Isaac. You hear anything?'

'I heard they wanted Rosethorn not to put on a defence, and he told them he'd do it if they'd drop *all* the charges. They went as far as voluntary manslaughter.'

'Whooee! And he turned it down?'

'Yep. But I guess in the end they made some kind of trade about something, and let it go at second degree.' He looked at his cigar. 'Miss Bee thinks it's got to do with calling witnesses.'

To my right, the redstone spire of Trinity Church's bell tower floated above the peak of the hill. 'Is Miss Bee your source, Carl?'

'No comment.' He grinned. 'Now. Besides your urine – what were you and Bubba Percy manoeuvreing in the john at Pogo's today?'

'You're asking? It looked to me like you, Bubba, and Jack Molina were all for one as Brookside's main-man musketeers. Bubba said y'all were gonna have a little heart-to-heart with the Lewis side about, well, let's call it mutual damage control.'

He took off his glasses to look at me. 'That's right. We are. Dirty campaigns have a way of obscuring the real issues. Sometimes the voters can get more upset about some personal things, than the things they *should* get upset about.' He put the glasses back on. 'You know what I mean?'

'I think so. . . . Between us, Carl—' I turned towards him, blinking at the sun-glitter on his glasses. '—what do you really think of Andrew Brookside?'

The mayor patted the typed speech on the seat between us. 'What I really think is that the man could be president someday.'

'But what do you think of him personally?'

'I don't.'

Trinity Church was built in the Gilded Age, when they built big, because it hadn't crossed the builders' minds that the country could ever run short of rock, wood, glass, metal, labour, or money; much less short of well-to-do Christians to fill the pews and pay the upkeep. Now, of course, Paul Madison spends half his time trying to scrape together enough raffle tickets to repair the glass, and mortar the rocks, and replace the wood; he spends the other half of his time trying to scrape together more of a congregation than could all sit in the choir stalls. In winter, Trinity was unheatable. Tonight, despite all the whirring fans, and the opening of the stained-glass rows of double-windows – Trinity was uncoolable. But not just because of the summer weather. And not just because it was jam-packed with two hundred concerned citizens of the left and the right, and two hundred Haver students, plus the speakers, plus reporters, plus a fourth of HPD's night shift. It was uncoolable because of the subject matter under discussion. 'The Klan in Carolina: Pawns of Power?'

The Communist Party Workers (who at the last minute had been declined permission to speak – I heard Brookside had nixed them) were picketing outside on the steps, and pulled no punches. Their signs said, 'Kill the Klan!' When our group arrived, there was no one else out there to argue with them. The two mounted patrolmen chatted with each other while their horses shook their heads. Ralph had two more cops in the vestibule and the rest ostentatiously in evidence in the chapel itself – the bulk of them between the speakers and the audience.

An exhibit of hundreds of large photographs in the vaulted

vestibule pulled no punches either. Among them were pictures of bloody Freedom Riders beside a firebombed bus, 1961. White men, women, and children grinning up at the body of a lynched black man, 1935. Twelve thousand hooded Klansmen marching through Raleigh, 1966. A white mob burning a black man to death, 1919. Confederate Knights and neo-Nazis celebrating Hitler's birthday at a Piedmont military training camp, 1983. The Greensboro police watching Klansmen gun down CPW organizers a few years ago. The body of Cooper Hall being loaded into a Hillston ambulance a few months ago. Below, displayed in cases, were exhibits of evidence supplied by the FBI – whips, billy clubs, incendiary bombs.

When we walked past the photographs, John Emory's jaw locked. Nancy swallowed hard, said, 'Oh God. Those are little *kids* watching them burn that man!,' and she headed off to the bathroom. Alice and Justin were there looking at the exhibit too. We talked a while, and made plans to meet afterwards. As it happened, everybody's plans were radically changed.

The conference had begun at five with 'studies seminars' led by local professors, and lawyers from the ACLU and the NAACP. But this evening at seven the big public event began, with speeches by a black state legislator and the widow of a well-known civil rights worker murdered by the Klan. Plus, Professor J. T. Molina of the Hall Committee moderating a panel of three representatives from anti-Klan organizations (the Centre for Constitutional Rights, Klanwatch, and the Anti-Defamation League of B'nai B'rith), along with three representatives from 'white rights' organizations (WAPA – the White American Political Organization; NAAWP – the National Association for the Advancement of White People; and a 'religious order' calling itself 'The Aryan Nations'). Plus Brodie Cheek. Plus Mayor Yarborough. Plus Andrew Brookside, the keynote speaker, who wasn't due to speak until eight-thirty, and still hadn't arrived at seven-forty-five. Brodie Cheek was talking now about how there were a lot more dangerous Communists in America than dangerous Klansmen.

I'd already heard enough of the reverend's views, and stepped out to the church vestibule, where Nancy White grabbed my arm. 'Chief, I wish you'd just go sit down and keep still.'

John Emory crossed his arms over his perfectly pressed uniform. I noticed a thin chain of gold around his wrist; no doubt his new partner's influence. She meanwhile had both her tie and her hat on; also a first. John shook his head at her. 'I wish *you'd* go sit down, Nancy. Or go home. If you hadn't lied to the mayor, to horn in on *my* request anyhow, you wouldn't even be here.'

'Roid, get out of my face, you chauvinist pig. The mayor *never asked* me if I was pregnant, and it's none of his business to boot. Besides, I'm not even showing.'

'Really? Then if I were you, I'd go on a diet.'

'Yeah, well, if I was you, I'd stop starching my shorts.'

My protective shadows kept this going as they paced the stone floor with me. Through the enormous open doors I could see the length of the crowded aisle to the platform set up in front of an ornate rood screen. Above the speakers' heads hung a bronze crucifix bigger than life-size. On either side of Christ hung a life-sized photograph – one of the Jewish storekeeper Leo Frank being lynched near Atlanta in 1915, and one of George Hall being led into Superior Court in chains last month.

I'd said to Paul Madison when I'd arrived that I thought all these pictures were a little rough, and his answer was, 'Too many people think the Klan is just a tasteless joke. These pictures aren't funny.' Looking like a blond choirboy, Paul stood off to the side next to the vestry door now, listening to the speakers. On the dais, the black legislator was shaking his arm at the WAPA official, as he snapped, 'Don't you dare sit here and tell us you don't believe in violence! On the Brodie Cheek show, on *television*, you said, quote, "I keep the Good Book in one hand, and a good gun in the other!" Deny that you said that! You're a *Nazi*!'

Yells from the audience, pro and con.

The WAPA guy, who was wearing a business suit instead of his usual combat outfit, shouted back, 'Our Founding Fathers gave me the right to bear arms! And all you liberal wimps selling this country down the river can't take my rights away!'

More yells from the audience. Jack Molina jumped to his feet, in shirt sleeves and tie. His thin body quivering, he shouted everybody down. 'Quiet! Could we please get back to order! Thank you! We're getting away from the question. The question Mr Smithley was supposed to be addressing is: Is the power establishment in this state still using racism to drive a wedge between poor whites and blacks – just as they stopped the populist movement and the labour movement – in order to keep their political and economic control? *That's* what we're here to discuss.'

Mr Smithley of the NAAWP bellowed, 'The power establishment in this whole country is nothing but a bunch of socialists, atheists, and New York Jews!'

'Oh, Jesus,' I said to Emory. 'I'm going across the street and get a cup of coffee at the doughnut shop.'

'I'll go,' he and Nancy said simultaneously.

'We'll all go,' I compromised.

It was beautiful outside, and cooler. Even this late, the sun had just set; the sky streaked with orange and purple. Janet Malley, Communist candidate for the City Council fifteen years running now, was a broad-beamed, wild-haired woman my age, with a smile much sweeter than her language. From Trinity's stone steps she was haranguing a small group of curious bystanders down below her on the sidewalk, while a dozen of her fellow party members shook their signs at them. Janet stopped talking when she saw me. Flanked by John and Nancy, I gave her a wave, and she yelled, '*Sellout!*' at me. 'Why don't you line those fucking Nazis up against a wall, Cuddy Mangum, instead of trying to *talk* to them?!'

'Evening, Janet. I'm not trying to talk to them. I'm getting a doughnut.'

'*And tell Jack Molina from me; he's a fucking Judas to the Cause!*'

I waved again. 'I'll pass it along.'

Looking back at her from the other sidewalk, I noticed a green van go slowly down the street. I didn't think much of it until five minutes later, it went by again, while Nancy, John and I were drinking our coffee by the window of the doughnut shop. Then I saw the long grey Jaguar pull up in front of the church. I could see Brookside's bright hair in the back seat. His chauffeur was hurrying around to open his door when I heard the van again. It tore around the corner fast, tyres squealing.

'*Goddamn it!*' I yelled.

I was out of the shop and halfway back across the street before John and Nancy could move. The rear doors of the van burst open. Flaring objects arced out towards the picketers, and seconds later there was smoke everywhere. Men in camouflage fatigues were leaping down from the back of the van. Swinging sticks, they charged up the steps towards Janet's group. Behind me, Nancy and John were pounding across the street. The mounted patrolmen were fighting to get their horses through the moil of screaming bystanders, while acrid smoke fumed all over the place so that it was impossible to see.

Brookside was out of the Jaguar now. Standing there. I ran

past the chauffeur, knocking him down. Just as I reached Brook-side, I felt a hard, sharp blow at my chest, and stumbled forward. Then I heard the *powww* of a gunshot.

'WATCH OUT!' Brookside yelled. He turned, flinging his arm out at me.

Nancy and John were all over us now.

I heard more shots. And saw Brookside jerk upwards, then fall twisting, half his body back inside the car. His chest was bright red. I was scrambling towards Nancy. 'GET DOWN! GET DOWN!'

I saw her head slam back against the side of the Jaguar; her hands jerked to her side, blood poured through her fingers.

John had his gun out, and was firing almost straight up. '*Up there!*' he screamed.

I threw myself on top of Nancy, pulling her head under my arms. Both the mounted patrols were now firing up at the opened window in the tower. I could hear the bells up there clanging together. The church doors flew open, two cops ran out into the chaos, one yanked out his walkie-talkie and shouted into it.

I took off, running up the steps to the church. John made a grab for me but missed. '*Chief, stop! Come back! Dammit, Chief!*'

Bodies were flailing at each other blindly in the smoke, most of them running down towards the sidewalk. I hurled people aside, pushing my way into the building. The door to the bell-tower stairs was in the rear of the chapel, by the confessional. I couldn't get it open. I kicked at it, then picked up an iron candelabrum almost as tall as I was, and used the heavy base to ram the door open. In my side vision, I saw people shoving their way out of the pews, some of them shrieking. Ralph Fisher and his men pressed back at them. I saw Justin running down the centre aisle. Already racing up the stairs, I could hear Jack Molina's voice. '*Sit back down. Everybody, please keep your seats.*' I could hear sirens coming.

The steep stone steps of the tower circled up in a gyre. I figured I'd hear him coming down before I met him. I never doubted for an instant who he was.

By the time I made it to the top, I was gagging. The square landing was empty, but the bells still shook. He wasn't there. The duffel bag was. The baseball cap. Empty beer cans. I looked up over my head. In the dark, above the bells, was a small open window on the back wall. A coil of bell rope was lashed to an iron rail, then dropped over the window's side. I crawled up through the scaffolding, shoved myself out the opening. The roof was immense, and now that the sunset was fading, it was shadowy. But I saw Russell. Saw him just as he slipped, inching down the slanted slate. The rifle slid off his shoulder and clattered crazily away, flipping over the edge to the ground below.

Clutching for it, Winston howled, 'Fuck!,' then jumped to his feet, and ran along the length of the rain gutter.

I lost sight of him. I dropped from the rope, fell flat on to the spine of the roof, got up, straddled the spine, and ran, arms out for balance, as fast as I could. If I hadn't been wearing sneakers, I probably would have died.

Sliding down the steep slant, with the old slate tiles cracking beneath me, I worked my way along the edge till I saw a fire-escape landing five feet below. I jumped on to it, scrambled down the ladder to a large stained-glass window that was completely smashed in. Yanking my gun from its holster, I crashed through the opening.

I was in the Trinity vestry, a small room beside the altar where the priests put on their vestments and store the implements of the mass.

Winston Russell stood by the long table in the middle of the room. He had a switchblade in his right hand, and his left arm around Paul Madison's neck.

Chapter 25

He was tall, as tall as me, but built heavier, although since I'd seen him last, prison and hiding had trimmed away the bulk and turned the rest to muscle. His arms were sweaty, sunburnt, and scraped raw, his jeans smeared with dirt and dust; sweat trickled from his scalp through his close-cropped reddish hair into his eyes. The eyes were round, large, white-blue as a shark's. When he saw me, he lurched back with a grunt, the tendons of his arms tightening against Paul's neck. The top of Paul's head barely reached Winston's shoulder.

'Okay, Winston. Step away, and let him go!' I braced the .38 revolver on my forearm.

'Mangum!' Winston jerked Paul tight against him, then growled in his low twang. 'I shot you.'

'You missed.'

(Later, Etham Foster was to pull the slug from the 30.06 out of the metal padding of the vest, an eighth of an inch from my heart.)

He sneered, 'I didn't miss the cunt you're calling a cop.'

Hate raced up me so fast and hot my skin burned. I never *wanted* to kill before. Everything in me wanted to kill him. I made myself breathe. 'I said, let him go.'

His face purplish, Paul rasped in a choked whisper. 'Get out, Cuddy. He doesn't know what he's doing.'

I said, 'Stand still, Paul. This is the man that killed Cooper. And Willie Slidell. This is Winston Russell. His partner Purley's made a full confession.'

A spasm shook through Winston's body. Then he smiled; he

had small even white teeth, and the scariest smile I've ever seen. 'That blubberhead moron came crying home to you, hunh, Mangum?'

'That's right. We've got Purley, and we've got the money too. Put down the knife. You're under arrest. You have the right to remain silent—'

He laughed out loud.

I was thinking: Paul must have heard the window crash, and rushed in to see what was wrong. Winston had grabbed him, then probably locked the door. So I couldn't count on anybody else knowing we were in here. Out in the chapel, I could hear shouts, sirens, the noise of running footsteps, but not towards us.

I stepped forward, steadying the gun.

Paul's eyes were much calmer than Winston's, or mine either. He said, 'Cuddy, don't shoot him.'

Winston laughed again. He locked his arm under Paul's chin, then quickly slashed a deep line down his cheek, and another sideways, cutting a cross in the flesh. Blood splattered all over Paul's face, and dripped down Winston's hand.

I yelled, 'You fucking shit!'

Paul's mouth opened wide from the pain, then he tightened it, breathing through his nose. His hands stayed motionless at his sides. His eyes stayed on mine, clear and light. 'Cuddy, don't,' he said quietly. 'Let him give himself up.'

'Shut up, faggot!' Winston turned the knife sideways, and slowly slid it across the surface of Paul's throat. A bright red curve of blood followed the blade. Paul panted, but he still didn't cry out.

Winston kept smiling. 'You get the picture, Mangum? Drop the gun right now, or I slit this asshole's throat.' We stared at each other, as he raised the switchblade again, his hand spasming, '*I mean it, prick!* Don't fuck with me!'

I nodded. 'Okay, Winston.' Without taking my eyes from his, I slowly held out my arm, then tossed the gun on the floor, where he'd have to come around the vestry table to get it. Very fast, he grabbed Paul by the hair, slamming his head down on the table hard, then he sprang for the gun.

In a smear of blood, Paul slid off the table, dragging with him a red stole with a gold cross. He crumpled to the floor under it.

With the steel muzzle pointed at my head, Winston pocketed the knife while he backed across the room to the broken window. He stepped through it on to the fire-escape landing. 'This time I won't miss,' he snarled, flicking sweat from his eyes. 'Right where Bobby got it. Rot in hell, Captain.'

He smiled, and pulled the trigger.

It clicked.

Frantic, he squeezed the trigger again, over and over as fast as he could. His eyes whitened.

'Don't you remember?' I smiled as I moved forward. 'I don't like loaded guns.'

When I lunged for him, he hurled the gun; the butt hit me right above the eye. The pain knocked me down. Scrambling to my feet, I wiped the blood out of my eye, and went after him. Halfway down the fire escape, he jumped to the ground. I jumped straight from the landing. I was about thirty feet behind him through the Trinity cloister, around the soup kitchen, across the long parking lot. I could see him vaulting over the stone wall into the old cemetery. The damn bulletproof vest felt like a heavy lead slab plastered by sweat to my chest. I'd carried heavier, hotter weight farther and faster in the Mekong, but that – it struck me, as I fought for breath – had been twenty years ago.

At dusk, the moon was at the horizon, immense and orange as the sun it replaced. But the graveyard was so thick with old trees I couldn't see where he'd gone. Still, even when I couldn't spot him through the waxy magnolias or tilted gravestones, I could hear him. How to listen because you can't see; *that*, you never forget from the jungle. How not to make a sound; that you don't forget either. So I heard him crouch to get his breath back. I heard him slither from stone to stone. Finally, scurrying up a little incline, he tripped on a flat tomb marker, cursed, fell. That's when I hit him from behind, coming at him in midair. His shirt ripped off in my hand, but I got him by the neck and flipped him. His first kick caught me in the knee; when I buckled, he kicked me again, in the chest, where I couldn't feel it at all. Grabbing, I twisted his foot, and we tumbled sideways back down the slope. His breath was hot and beery. I felt his fists figure out the bulletproof vest, and dig behind it for my kidneys. I pushed my thumbs into his throat.

Clawing my face, he broke loose, but I tackled him again. Now he was backed against the low iron railing around a large tombstone. The carved stone glowed in the orange moon. In a crouch, Winston panted at me through his bared teeth. 'Come on, Mangum.'

Crouching too, I gestured at him with both hands cupped. *'YOU come on, you fuck! Come on. I've been waiting for this!'*

When I ran at him, he jerked the switchblade from his pocket, slashing out with it. I felt its blade rip open the sleeve of my jacket and tear across my arm. The knife flashed again, burning down the side of my face. *'Yeah*, Mangum,' he gasped, spraying spit. 'Come get some more!'

The inside of my head burst open. I sprang straight at the knife, so fast and crazy it scared him for a second. Long enough for me to get his wrist. The knife stabbed across my thigh while I swung his body over the iron points of the grave railing. My fingers felt his wrist snap, shaking the knife loose. We both went down. Rolling over on him, I cracked my elbow into his nose until I could feel cartilage give way, crushing under my bone. When he kicked free, screaming, I kneed him in the groin, then pulled him back on his feet, and punched my fists into his head. I kept on hitting and hitting, till my hands got so slippery with blood they were sliding off his skin. When I let go, he sank slowly into the grass, pink foam bubbling from his lips.

Quivering, I kicked him in the side of the head. 'STAND UP, YOU PIECE OF SHIT!'

He fought to one knee, snarling at me. I yanked him up by the front of his belt. Swaying, he squinted through his bloody eyes to find me, then he spit red gristle at my face. I slugged him again on the side of the head. The pain in my hand shot all the way up to my teeth. Scraping down my legs, he dropped at my feet, and rolled on to his back.

Like water, my legs gave way, and I fell, crawling from him. It felt like something dangerous was happening inside me. Each suck of breath was like another knife stab. I couldn't get one eye to open, or keep the blood out of the other one. Blinded, slippery with my own blood, I tried to pull myself up to my feet. I couldn't. I knew I had to stop the blood spurting from my arm and leg. I couldn't. I gave up, let my face slide into the grass. The insides of my eyelids saw brighter and brighter red. Then the dangerous thing soared fast and too strong to stop into my head. Everything was black.

A minute or an hour passed. Suddenly loud sirens drilled through my ear. With one hand, I crawled on to my knees. Over the stone wall bordering the cemetery, I saw, in the squint of one eye, a big dark blur flying towards me. It came thrashing under

439

tree branches, rumbling the ground. The blur was a horse. Someone on it shouted, '*Cudddddy!*' He reined in hard, twisting sideways in the saddle. It looked like one of the patrolmen's horses, but the rider was Justin. Behind me, I heard a gurgling grunt, the thud of fast motion. I saw Winston, staggering in a weave, the knife back in his hand.

Light spat out of Justin's gun. The *kerpoww* of the shot cracked all around me. I scrambled to my feet, and saw Winston drop to the ground, his back arching as if he were in a seizure. His hands dug at his stomach. Justin swung himself off the horse, walked past me, his arm straight out. I could see smoke at the long muzzle. He stood over Winston's flailing body. I heard people far away, by the cemetery gates, running towards us, flashlights waving.

My throat burned with the words. 'Is he dead?'

Justin looked down, lowered the Smith & Wesson. Then he fired it again. Winston's jaw smashed in. His chest jumped, and was still.

Justin said, 'He is now.'

I lurched over to him, and stared at Winston's body. When I could breathe, I coughed out, 'You're . . . *goddamn you, Savile!* You goddamn stupid asshole. You killed him!'

'I don't care,' he said, and caught me as I swung my fist at his face and fell.

They had trouble holding me down in the ambulance, because they hadn't let me go find out what had happened at Trinity. Justin crouched near the stretcher. I kept telling him to get away from me. He kept trying to tell me Ralph had everything under control. He told me that Nancy and Brookside had already been rushed off to University Hospital. He didn't know if they were alive. He'd found Paul Madison when he'd run after me, and seen the vestry window smashed. Paul would be all right; they'd taken him to the hospital too. The ambulance attendants fighting me on to the stretcher couldn't tell me anything about Nancy either. Or about how many other people were hurt, or how badly. Or let me use their CB to find out for myself. I heard one of them say, 'This fucker's a maniac. Christ! You cops do this to him?'

'He's the Hillston police chief,' Justin said.

'Don't shit me, man. That's a desk job! This man's a mess!'

I tried to stop them from gassing me then, but they did it, and stuck a needle in me. Later I realized it was oxygen and a transfusion they'd given me. I was told I'd gone into shock from blood loss, with heart fibrillations. At any rate, I came to – fog-headed, lying on a table in the UH emergency room, with blood pumping into me from an IV rack. My right hand was in a cast. I managed to force one eye open. A Vietnamese face was leaning over mine. My body jerked upwards. 'Take it easy,' the man murmured; then I saw his white coat. And next to him I saw Justin, still splotched with my blood.

'Nancy's alive,' Justin said. He put his hand on my shoulder. I hurt too much to move away. 'She's all right . . . But she lost the baby.'

'. . . Aww, God.' I closed my eye. '. . . Is . . . Brookside . . .?'

'He's still in OR. It looks really bad.'

Winston's first shot had hit my vest. Brookside was turning – to shield me – when the second bullet entered his body from the left side, right under the heart. The slug was intact, lodged in the pericardial sac, and they were now performing open-heart surgery, trying to repair the damaged tissue and get the slug out before the heart tore. A team of doctors had already been in there with him for over an hour.

The third bullet had grazed through the skin of Brookside's neck as he fell; the fourth hit Nancy's thick gun belt; deflected, the flank shot struck her in the side, just above the hip crest. The deflection had saved her life, but not that of the fetus. When I came to, Nancy'd just been moved from OR to the recovery room. She was still unconscious.

Justin said, 'One of the OR nurses told me about Brookside. It's a real long shot.' He stood back while the doctor wound tape around my thigh. 'They haven't given up. He's strong, and he's always been a fighter . . . You know, everybody thinks it was an assassination attempt on *him*.'

It hurt a lot to talk. 'He thought so . . . too.'

How could he not think he was the target? But '*Watch out*,' he'd said, at the sound of the first shot. By instinct, thrown his arm in front of me. You can't stage what you'll do. A hero – even by instinct.

Justin was talking. 'Well, from what John Emory described, it looks like Andy had faced round to you, and if he hadn't, that shot would have got him dead front.'

A nurse came from behind a screen, and called the Vietnamese doctor over. He told me, 'Don't move. I'll be right back.'

441

After he left, I asked Justin, '. . . Where's Lee?'

He looked at me, puzzled. 'Lee? She's here.'

'Where?'

'In the director's office. There's too much press out in the waiting room. Alice is with her. And Paul Madison. Jesus Christ! What that sick SOB did to Paul's face . . .'

'Paul's okay though?'

'Yeah. Not pretty, but okay. And no concussion. He must have a hard head.'

I tried to nod. 'Kept telling me to leave . . . like he was going to *reason* Winston out of it.'

His arms crossed over the stained jacket. 'You walk in with an empty gun, right? And it saves your life. The sort of irony I know appeals to you.'

I was thinking – if I had taken the bullets from my pocket, and loaded the gun, would Winston be alive now, or would Paul be dead?

'Zeke's upstairs. I want to go see how he's doing, okay?' Justin started to put his hand on my shoulder, but pulled it away. His eyes darkened to a deeper blue. 'Then I'll come back so you can say what you want to say, Captain.'

I squinted up at him. '. . . You know what I want to say, Lieutenant. He was already down. Disarmed, and down.'

'He was three feet from your back with that knife.'

'Not the second time. Why the fuck did you do it?!'

Justin looked straight at me, his eyes still, then he took a quiet breath. 'The second time was for Nancy. For her baby. He fired on a woman, a pregnant woman.'

'That's your reason.'

'I consider it a good enough one.'

'I know you do. But it isn't a good enough reason.'

'. . . So what are you going to do?'

'I don't know. But as of now, you're relieved of your duties.'

'Okay.' He touched my shoulder, then left.

Justin didn't say a lot of things that I figured he was thinking, because I was thinking them. But I didn't say a lot of things either. He didn't say this was the second time he'd saved my life. He didn't say that Winston had murdered Cooper Hall, and at least three more people, including an unborn baby, and had tried to murder others, who might still die. He didn't say that – whatever her desires – Nancy White should have never been allowed to get herself put on a detail with the slightest risk of danger. He didn't say I should have *really* believed Winston was going to come for me, instead of half *not* believing it, and half hoping he would try, so I could finally get him, because what I obviously couldn't think at all was that he could get me. Not after 525 days in Vietnam couldn't get me. Not a pig like Winston.

Two young doctors appeared to 'do a little more sewing' on me. I let them, and went on thinking.

In a while, Wes Pendergraph came in with a report from Ralph on the attack at the church. Janet Malley had a concussion from a club swung by one of the dozen thugs who'd shown up in the green van. Four of the other picketers had been badly beaten, and a bystander had a separated collarbone. The mounted patrolmen had cracked open the skull of one thug, and fractured the ribs of another. Ten other people had been treated for smoke inhalation or minor injuries. Three assailants, who'd fled in the van, had suffered lacerations when – under pursuit – they'd smashed into a median rail. All twelve of them were now in custody; all proved to have connections to the Carolina Patriots. So, Winston had either known they were planning the attack, or he'd *persuaded* them to do it, as a cover. I thought, the latter.

As for my own injuries – as Etham Foster grumbled, when he stalked into the emergency room an hour and a half later, with our medical examiner, Dick Cohn, slouching behind him – I was luckier than I deserved.

'It was distance saved you, babe, even with that vest.' Etham pressed his large thumb lightly on my breast. 'Good as Winston was, he was just a little too far away. And that's the first time in your life you ever wore a vest, isn't it? Out getting a doughnut!' He studied my arm, then my leg. 'You dumb hillbilly. Man throws kerosene on you, puts cyanide in your car, smart as you are, you think you'd pay attention.'

I mumbled, 'Like always, you're right, Dr D.'

'You look like somebody test-drove a sewing machine all over you.'

Dick Cohn gave his credentials, and asked the Vietnamese doctor what the 'damage was.' The worst had been blood loss from the three knife wounds; I now had seven pints donated by strangers in me. Plus the residents had put fourteen stitches along my hairline, three under my lip, five above my eye, and thirty-some more on my forearm and thigh. Several bones were broken in my right hand. The rest was only 'contusions, bruises, lacerations, some possible permanent loss of muscle tone in the left arm, and possible minor impairment of the left eardrum.'

'Doesn't sound too bad,' said Etham. 'He's got the weekend off anyhow.'

Cohn scratched his neck. 'Bare knuckles against a psycho with a switchblade, *cheesh*! Next time, Mangum, why don't you wait for a backup? Like you tell everybody else to.'

Etham's immense hand turned my head gently as he looked at the sutures. 'Ralph said to tell you he feels, as he put it, "like shit," about not checking that steeple. What I want to know is who told Russell you were going to be there. I figure he'd been waiting up on that landing two, three hours.'

Justin walked back into the room then. 'Nancy came round. But she broke up pretty badly when Zeke told her.'

Dick Cohn made a spitting noise. 'Yeah, I heard the kids lost their baby. That's a tough one . . .'

Justin frowned. 'They tried to make Zeke leave the room before they'd sedate her. They found out that was a mistake, with a six-foot-seven Indian.'

We were quiet for a while, then Cohn asked Justin, 'You hear anything about Andrew Brookside?'

'One of the surgeons just made a statement. He's still in OR. But the bullet's out. There're over a hundred reporters and television cameras out in the lobby. The mayor's out there. Jack Molina—'

I said, 'Who's talking for us?'

'Nobody yet.'

I asked, 'Can I get up?'

The Vietnamese doctor said, 'We're going to move you to a room in a minute. In the morning, you can get up.'

'Can I leave?'

'If you can walk, you can leave,' was his answer.

I told Etham Foster I'd like him to make a statement for HPD, to stress all the precautions we'd taken, and that all the assailants had been arrested, and – He stopped me, and snapped, 'I know what to say.'

Dick Cohn was rubbing his knuckles in his eyes. 'You grits are too much for me. I gotta get back to Brooklyn, where you don't like somebody, you just dump 'em in the river. Nice and simple. But you people! Buffalo Bill here riding up on his fuckin' horse? A fuckin' horse.'

Justin said quietly, 'I knew the layout. A car couldn't get through. It was the fastest way to get to them.'

Cohn lifted both shoulders. 'Of course. What else.'

Etham glanced at Justin, then at me. 'I guess we're all lucky that Savile was as fast as he was. And as accurate. That *was* your three fifty-seven, wasn't it, Savile, not Mangum's?' He slid a revolver from his Windbreaker pocket, racked it open. 'I found this one on the floor in the church.' He spun the chamber. 'This one hasn't been fired. In fact, hasn't been loaded. Which is careless.' Walking over to the sodden red mound of my clothes on the counter, where they'd been stacked after the nurse cut them off me, Etham picked up my shoulder holster, and slipped the revolver in it. Then he lifted the bloody vest, looked at it carefully, pinched out the crushed bullet. 'Close,' he said.

Pulling out his black notebook, Cohn shook it open, and flipped through the pages. 'Yours truly and Foster here were down at the morgue, checked the prelim autopsy on the Russell stiff. Setting aside one three fifty-seven slug in the abdomen, and the same through his jugular, the man had been beaten to a frigging pulp. Major subdural hematoma. I'm talking *critically* ruptured blood vessels in his fuckin' head! Must have been a *bull*. To come back at you with a knife, after *that*! Got a couple of ribs splintering his lung! Incredible. Cheesh, Mangum, what'd you do, run a semi over him?'

Etham was looking at me. 'For a fellow usually too peaceful to carry a gun, you're a man of pretty violent impulses. Not easy to kill a man with your bare hands. Ugly too.'

Cohn yawned. 'So that's Winston Russell, hunh? Well, it's no surprise he managed to take out as many as he did. Sort of inhuman. A walking corpse, torn up like that, and still it takes two from a three fifty-seven to stop him. Un-fuckin'-believable.' He picked up his black bag. 'So, Chief, how do we write this thing up?'

I looked away from Etham. Looked past Justin. Looked at the fluorescent circle of light above my head. Nobody said anything. Cohn cleared his throat, and waited.

I said, '. . . Write it up that the suspect was slain while resisting arrest.'

Cohn pushed the notebook into his jacket pocket. 'By the officer in pursuit?'

'. . . Yes.'

445

Chapter 26

Hair in a white tangle, Isaac Rosethorn came lumbering at a lopsided trot around the corner of the corridor where an orderly was wheeling me to my room. Isaac's distraught eyes were fixed straight ahead as he ran right past us. When I called out to him, he spun around, and with horrible wheezing snorts leaned over my wheelchair, tripping against it as it kept moving. His collar points poked sideways, his shirt flopped out of his wrinkled pants, his socks bunched around his ankles. 'Ah, ah, ah, my dear Slim!' He glanced over me quickly, stared at my eyes, then – to the amused surprise of the young black orderly – he kissed me on the top of the head. 'Look at you, look at you. I could weep.'

'*You* could weep?' I whispered. Isaac's deep sighs caromed down the long sterile hall while he patted my hair at a stumbling jog.

Talking, the old lawyer sat by the bed in the dark, talking, until I fell asleep. Alice had called him at the Piedmont, so he'd been told what had happened at Trinity. And he'd heard more details from Bubba Percy in the lobby. I wasn't surprised that one of the first things he said after the nurse gave up trying to make him leave was that he was deeply upset to hear that Winston Russell was dead.

'You damn old man,' I muttered, groggy. 'All you care about is your damn subpoenas.'

'No.' I felt the breath of his sigh pass near my hand. 'No. I care because I don't believe in killing. Anyone. For any reason. And I feel very sad for . . . anyone who has to carry that.'

'. . . Everybody carries something.'

He patted my leg. 'Ah. God knows . . . It wasn't you who shot him, was it? It was Savile.'

'. . . Yeah.'

'Want to talk about it?'

'I don't know . . .'

He sat back, waiting. After a while, I asked him how badly he'd needed whatever he could have forced out of Winston at the trial. He said, not much; that between us, he really didn't believe he needed much of anybody but George himself.

'So why subpoena half the state?'

As in the past, he advised me to use my noggin. 'At least what little remains undamaged. I did it to scare the bejesus out of them.'

'I heard you did.'

'I did.'

'Heard they dropped to a manslaughter plea.' I pulled my broken hand to a new position on my chest. 'You turned them down. So why'd they let go of first degree? If they didn't want witnesses to—'

I could hear the shuffle of his search through his pockets. 'Oh, there was only one witness who ultimately mattered. That's the one I negotiated; reluctantly felt I had to negotiate, given my client's history. To get the death penalty out of the picture then and there. To take away one day of that horror from George. So a name came off the list, and I will keep that name out of the testimony.'

'Julian Lewis.'

'Exactly. A name in exchange for the threat of the gas chamber.' His chair scraped closer to me. 'Ah, Cuddy. The world. "Those who think, laugh; those who feel, cry." And this old man, well, he goes back and forth . . . I'm told Mr Brookside is still critical. What a miserable thing. Such a vibrant man . . . My assumption is that he was caught in the crossfire of *your* vendetta.'

'Not mine, Winston's.'

'Ummm . . . But apparently, everyone else has taken the shooting for an assassination attempt on Andrew Brookside.'

'Let them.'

'Why not? More thrilling. Possibly more useful.' He was quiet for a moment. Then he asked, 'How is Mrs Brookside?'

'I don't know.'

'. . . Would you like me to find her? Tell her anything?' His

447

hand touched mine. 'Let her know you're all right? She must be here at UH.'

'That's okay. Alice probably told her ... But thank you.' Outside the window, a plane flashed across the sky of summer stars.

'I was recalling you to the stand Monday. Think you can make it Wednesday?'

'To ask me what?'

He chuckled. 'I suspect, what I ask you will matter less than what you *look* like, and why.'

'... Isaac, let me ask *you* something? Why didn't you take the manslaughter plea for George?'

A match flared in the dark, then my nostrils twitched at the sharp familiar smell of his cigarette. 'Why should I? More to the point, why should George?'

I said because manslaughter is a much shorter sentence than second-degree murder, and if the jury should find against them, he'd be sending George back to prison for too long, and besides not even George would deny that he'd killed Pym.

By my side, the small red flame brightened, dimmed. Isaac's mellow, low-pitched voice was calm as the sky outside. 'According to the law, "killing" isn't necessarily a crime, is it? Depends on the killer's state of mind, on his intent, on his alternatives. In George's case, as I will demonstrate to the jury on Monday, his intent was to save his own life.'

I was sliding off into sleep. I mumbled. 'Deep down, we know George also had alternatives.'

Isaac's hand stroked against mine. 'Deep down, we all have alternatives. We can't always reach them.'

Pulling myself up, I told him that yes, after all, I did want to 'talk about it,' about Russell, and I explained what had happened in the cemetery. Quietly nodding, he listened, then he said, 'So how do you feel besides angry, and guilty, and ambivalent?'

'That's a good start.'

'All right. The bureaucratic solution would be to fire Justin. The pure solution would be arrest him for murder; although his purpose was to protect your life, technically, he intended to kill Russell, and he did.'

'How about arresting myself for murder? I was out of control. I beat the man to death.'

'No, you didn't. That's medical speculation.'

448

'I tried to.'

'Ah, intent. Didn't Russell intend to kill you, and in that mutual combat weren't you trying to save your own life?'

'No, I was trying to kill him. I went crazy.'

Moonlight caught Isaac's hands as he rubbed them over his face. 'Crazy . . . I'm going to tell you something. When I was a youngster, Slim, a public defender, fresh out of law school, I had this case. A girl named Edith Keene. A mulatto – as they called her. She shot a white man who she said had sexually attacked her little sister. She shot him six times. She intended to kill him. I didn't want to use an insanity plea, or plead her guilty. I was conceited, and I thought I could get her off on a smart legal loophole I'd come up with. The truth is, I didn't give a damn about Edith Keene herself. Deep down, I think I didn't really even believe she wasn't guilty. In the purity of the law, guilty.

'. . . At any rate, I lost that case, and they put Edith on Death Row. And if she hadn't been before, after a few months in that place, well, everybody who saw her agreed she was insane. So, of course, that stopped the execution, and she was sent to the state asylum . . . She died there. Another inmate beat her over the head . . .'

'What I'm trying to say, Slim, is that the letter of the law is pure – like your arrest record as chief was pure until this happened. But the spirit of the law is as muddy as water with living things growing in it. Right and wrong all snarled together, truth and lie sometimes so entangled at the root you have to be very careful you don't kill one, trying to pull out the other . . . Well, you think about it.' He leaned over the bed and brushed his hand against my hair. 'But later. Now, go to sleep, Slim.'

Around midnight, I inched myself out of the high cool hospital bed, managed to get my eyes open enough to see through, and found that I could move my arms. I could stand up. I could walk. At least limp. My clothes had been thrown away, but someone had brought me one of my uniforms from the office; left it folded on the bureau. Pulling on the HPD khaki pants and the starched short-sleeve shirt took ten slow, tiring minutes. I looked at myself in the bathroom mirror. What looked back wasn't familiar.

When I made it out to the eerily quiet, fluorescent-white corridor, I saw Justin outside my door, bent over in a plastic chair, reading FBI files. He looked up. 'Hiram brought the captain's outfit. He's always thought you ought to wear it. You want your sneakers? They're on the shelf in your closet.'

I followed him back into the room, and he laced the shoes on my feet. 'You don't look good.' He straightened up. '"*At ingenium ingens inculto latet hoc sub corpore.*" According to Horace.'

'Yeah? By which he meant to say what?'

'"But hidden under that wreck of a redneck exterior is the mind of minds."' Justin's smile was full of gladness that I was alive. He didn't think I owed him a thing for saving me. Just as he didn't seem to think he done a thing wrong firing that second shot. Hell, I don't know what that is. An amazing carelessness, born of what? – maybe just born of birthright.

I said, 'Well, tell Horace from me it's always been my good fortune that looks aren't everything.' I started down the hall.

'Don't go down that way.' Justin followed after me. 'If the nurse's station doesn't stop you, you'll run smack into Bubba Percy and a whole litter of nocturnal newshounds.' He returned to his chair in the hall. 'Here's another irony you'll like. You're the hero of the hour. Horatio at the bridge. Coriolanus at the gates. If you think that's purple prose, you should have heard Carol Cathy Cane on the Late News. You've single-handedly made the streets safe for democracy.'

I turned around. 'I guess that makes you the man who shot Liberty Valence.' We stared at each other a while.

He said, 'Cuddy, the truth is, you don't think I was right—'

'You're damn straight. And I'm angry as hell.'

'I know. But if you're going to stay like this, I tell you, I think I'd rather you just charge me, and let me stand my trial, instead of you being witness, judge, and jury.' He opened the typed report. 'I just hope one of these days you'll forgive me for forcing you to make the decision to write up the report that way. Don't think I don't know what it cost you.' Not looking up, he gave me a salute.

I said, 'Don't kid yourself. What forced me to make the decision was what Dick said I'd already done to Winston. Purity – that's what it cost me.'

'Do you want me to resign?'

'. . . No . . . I want you to realize you had no right to do what you did. And I think, Justin, if you imagine yourself telling Alice about it, you'll figure out you don't feel as easy as you say. At least I hope so.'

450

Part Three

The Wind and the Rain

Chapter 27

The hospital director's office was in the old wing of the hospital. Paul Madison opened the door when I knocked. At the far end of the large room, by windows that opened out over the pretty fields and Gothic courtyards of Haver University, Lee stood looking out. Behind her, streetlights glowed on the old golden bricks. She wore a black silk dress with a necklace of pearls; I suppose someone had called her here from her dinner party. Her face, frowning, turned towards the door, but she didn't move. Between us was a distance filled with soft covered armchairs, polished woods, lamps, and rugs. Above the small oak mantel was another painting of Justin's father. He'd died in this room, at the desk near the windows.

Paul's hair was shaved off around the bandage over his forehead. Another bandage covered his cheek, and a thin one bound his neck above the black collar. 'Cuddy!' he gaped. 'You shouldn't be walking around, should you?' His arm pulled around me and drew me back into the hall. 'I went upstairs to check on you, but they said you were asleep. Dear God, you're really banged up, aren't you?'

'I'm okay. Mostly cuts and bruises.'

'Thank God. I'm sorry I wasn't much help. *Why* did that man kill Cooper? Was he insane?'

'I guess – if you think evil's insane. The Russell type makes a useful hired hand though, doesn't it? For the people who were paying him.' There was still blood spotted on Paul's black clerical jacket. I put my hand on his small shoulder. 'I'm sorry you had to get messed up in it, Paul. But, I want you to know, you got a

453

lot of guts. Not the kind of thing they prepare you for in the seminary, is it?'

'Well, Cuddy, in fact it's *exactly* what they're supposed to prepare you for. I mean, death.' His hand touched the gauze on his cheek, felt it tentatively, as if for reassurance. Then, shaking his head softly, he gestured towards the room. 'I was just sitting in here with Lee Brookside. We're still waiting for word on Andy. "Critical but stable" was the last report.'

Following him inside, I looked over his head across the room at Lee. I said to him, 'But Brookside made it through the operation all right. The bullet's out.'

Paul nodded. ' "A miracle of modern surgery," this doctor tells me. I told *him*, "I would debate the authorship of the miracle." The man *laughs*. He thought I was making a joke. But they're very encouraged. *Now*, they tell us how small a chance they really thought Andy had. That the odds were about a thousand to one.'

Moving softly around the desk, towards us, Lee murmured, 'I think those are the kinds of odds Andy prefers.' Reaching the centre of the room, she paused and held out her hand. 'Cuddy . . .'

I stepped towards her, and took the offered hand. 'Lee, . . . I'm sorry.' Her face was drained, pinched; there were lines under the grey eyes I hadn't seen before. Her other hand touched my cast at the wrist. We stood like that for a second before she moved back, her fingers lifting gently from mine, then holding her arm to her chest.

'I want to thank you, Cuddy. We all do. Paul said you're the one who chased down the man who shot Andy.'

I said, 'The man's dead.'

Paul walked over to us. 'And *faced* him down too. Cuddy saved my life.' Indignant, he pointed at my injuries. 'That kind of savagery. He had to be insane. Cuddy, do you know yet? Was he hired by some group like the Klan? The reporters are saying—'

I stopped him. 'Paul, excuse me. Would you mind? I'd like to speak to Lee for a moment?'

The rector stepped quickly back. 'Oh, I'm sorry. I'll go check at ICU again. Fine. And I'll get us some coffee.'

The room was as still as snowfall after he closed the door. We just stood, looking at each other, unguarded, bone-weary. Then she said quietly, 'You're alive . . .'

'Yes . . . What I wanted you to know is – I was right beside him when the shot was fired. His first impulse was to, to shield

454

me. I don't mean because it was me. I mean, because I was next to him.'

She nodded. 'Yes. He is brave.'

I shook my head. 'That's not bravery. That's ... virtue.' She nodded again, but didn't speak. Finally I said, 'Are you all right?'

Her chin lifted as she swallowed. '... A while ago, I didn't think he would make it. They, well, they told me he wouldn't. But now I'm sure he'll ...' She tried to smile. '... win.'

'Are *you* all right?'

Tears welled so slowly in her eyes the first two caught in the lashes, like drops of rain. Then she turned away, and sat in the armchair near the mantel.

She stared into the empty fireplace as she said, 'I was very much in love with my first husband.' I felt first surprise, then an abyss of pain split inside me. I waited for her to go on. The light on her smooth dark gold hair hurt my eyes. 'After the fire,' she said, 'they took me to Nice to ... identify the body.' She had not once talked to me about this young Frenchman, the professional climber, who'd died, trapped in a burning hotel, at twenty-seven. I must have known I hadn't wanted to ask about him. Her eyes lifted to mine. 'I never want to feel that pain again. I never will let that happen to me again.'

I stood there, holding on to the winged back of a chair. My voice was hoarse. 'But you said they think Andy is going to make it.'

Tears fell on tears in her lashes. 'Oh, Cuddy ... I'm not talking about Andy. I'm talking about us.'

I came to her; she reached up both her hands, and grabbed mine. And I said what I'd always told myself I wouldn't ask her. 'You'll never leave him, will you?'

'God ...' Her hands tightened on mine.

'Because of what's just happened.'

Her face tilted up to mine. '... No. You've known the answer to that from the beginning.'

Slowly I pulled my hand away and stepped back.

She said, 'I can't.'

I looked down at her, thought before I said it, then went ahead. 'You could. You won't.'

Her hands fell to her lap. The rings gleamed, beautiful and old. 'No, I won't.' She spoke very clearly.

'... Because you love him? I'd honour that. Because he needs you? You need him? For a commitment to a marriage? I'd honour

455

all of it.' My fist squeezed on the mantel ledge; pain shook my arm. 'But not for his political career.'

Silk rustled as she stood quickly, her eyes bright and wet. 'It isn't only his. It isn't only "politics." And to me, it isn't a "career."'

'Then you tell me what it is.'

She looked at me. 'I don't know if I can make you understand what I mean. I feel very deeply . . . that I've inherited obligations . . . no matter what my . . . personal feelings are.'

'Jesus Christ.' I moved too fast, and, dizzy, I grabbed at the chair back, carefully breathing until my head cleared.

'Can't you understand that?'

I nodded at her; flushing, my voice rising. 'Yes, I can understand it . . . It's *noblesse oblige* bullshit. What you "inherited," Lee, was a shitload of money. Because your great-great-grandpa figured out an easy way for a hell of a lot of stupid people to suck smoke. That's what you inherited! The rest is fucking bullshit.'

'Cuddy, stop it!'

Making my way back through the room of furnishings, I turned at the door. 'Look, I've been through this before, remember? Once before, you asked me to "try to understand." A long time ago. And you came back a year later, *a year too late*, and said you were wrong. Well, you're still wrong.' My face was as burning as hers.

She pressed her hand against her throat. 'Why are you being so coarse?!'

I forced the words through the clamp in my throat. 'Because I'm mad and hurt! Because we're losing each other. *Because I love you.*'

Her hands moved up into her hair and tightened. 'I love you too . . .'

'Then why are we doing this?'

Her face wet now, she stared across the room at me. Finally she said, 'I guess, we got a little too close to death tonight not to be honest.'

The door closed quietly in my hand; the knob was brass.

Chapter 28

Three days had passed since, on Monday morning, Isaac Rosethorn began calling his witnesses for the defence. The press table was now half-empty. Reporters had abandoned the trial for the newer news of Andrew Brookside's 'fight for life' after the 'Terror at Trinity.' The candidate was still in intensive care, and University Hospital's lobby looked like a battle camp, with tripods for tent poles, and raincoats for bedrolls. As I'd tried to sneak out of the place Saturday evening, I was myself assaulted by journalists, their electronic cameras whirring like frenzied hornets. Probably as a result of my emotional numbness after the talk with Lee, I stood there under their grilling, noble as a statue, and came off, Bubba told me, 'prime-time calibre. Gary Cooper in *High Noon*. Loved the bit when you said, "The real heroes at Trinity Church were Andrew Brookside, whose first impulse under fire was to save others. And Father Paul Madison, whose first impulse was to save the life of the man trying to kill him." Good stuff, *paisan*.'

As I walked out of the hospital, I saw Lee in the lobby talking with Mrs Dyer Fanshaw, who was crying. Lee and I looked at each other across the large crowded room for a long moment. Then I turned away and left.

In this go-round with Lady Fame, a picture of me that somebody had snapped as I was being helped into the ambulance at the cemetery made *Newsweek* and *Time* both – in a sidebar to the Brookside story. Edwina Sunderland mailed me the clippings, and I stuck them under the pineapple magnet on my refrigerator. (She also enclosed a blue monogrammed note: 'Cuthbert, You have taken Excitement farther down the road than my envy wants to travel. Come play bridge. Yours, E. N-R. S.') Some newspapers applauded my heroic action ('CAPTAIN KLAN-BUSTER' one dubbed me); others called for my resignation: Under the headline, 'MAKE MY DAY,' a leftist weekly referred to me as a 'rural Rambo.' I cancelled my subscription. The Carol Cathy Cane show telephoned Nancy White in the hospital; apparently Zeke wasn't very friendly to the caller. But by the end of the week, the locusts had flown over us, and were gone; rather, were all hovering above the bed of Andy Brookside, waiting.

So, on Monday, Rosethorn had been forced to begin without a full house 'to tear down the tawdry set that the State has hammered together in this courtroom.' The State's table, on the other hand, was more crowded than ever. There were now four prosecutors – the assistant DA, a state's attorney, and the assistant attorney general – all of whom kept a watchful eye on the DA, Mitchell Bazemore. Judge Hilliardson had instructed this group that only one of them could question any given witness, but Isaac still made much of the defence's outnumbered, underdog position. 'Don't rush me, Mr Bazemore. I'm old and I'm crippled, and I don't have a battalion of reinforcements to relieve *me*!' It did look like an unequal battle: at one table, a well-dressed row of male WASPs; at the other, a young italian woman, an elderly Jew, and a black man accused of murder.

The prosecution proved quite content to throw Winston Russell's corpse to Isaac Rosethorn's dogs, as long as there was no suggestion that Russell had had any more friends while alive – and certainly none in high places – than he had six days after his death, when there wasn't a soul in the state who didn't claim to have despised him. The Carolina Patriots, for example, were eager to confess Russell's sins, years of them – even that they'd known he was getting inside information (of, for example, my whereabouts on Friday) from a deputy in the sheriff's office. The only reason they hadn't told us sooner about all this was that they'd been 'scared to death' of him. Winston was Hitler, and everyone else was a good German.

Purley Newsome – only slightly calmed down by a Channel 7 news shot of Winston's casket – had told Justin (the one person on the force he'd talk to) that the man had Satanic powers, and might easily rise from the grave. At Purley's hospital bedside, Justin had heard hour after hour of ugly confessions, which cast all blame for everything solely on the former idol. Parenthetically, Purley implicated a great many others – his brother Otis, his friend Pym, Fanshaw Paper Company, the Carolina Patriots, and himself. Emptied of knowledge, Purley had then thrown himself on the hard rock of Mitch Bazemore's mercy, and been charged with first-degree murder in the death of William Slidell.

Also a frequent visitor to Purley's bedside, Isaac, too, was a beneficiary of his 'full cooperation,' and had recorded Purley's deposition on a videotape, which he planned to play in court – or as much of it as the judge would allow. According to Nora Howard, all six trial lawyers, along with Purley's attorney, had spent hours huddled around the TV screen in Hilliardson's chambers, fighting over sentences like a panel of censors from the Legion of Decency. Although Hilliardson finally ruled that the tape itself was admissible, since by testifying voluntarily, the witness had waived his rights against self-incrimination, the judge had, on the other hand, sustained many specific objections by the State, and insisted on deletions of his own. Whether because he found them immaterial, or simply tediously maudlin, I don't know. What was left, Nora told me, was good enough. 'If they believe Purley about Winston, then they ought to believe him about Pym. And, let's face it, after one look at you, who wouldn't believe *anything* about Winston?'

So all week, the defence kept the name of Winston Russell, linked to the name Bobby Pym, on the lips of witnesses. And like an old pool sharp, Isaac moved with smooth, relentless speed around the story of what lay behind the incident at Smoke's. Some of his witnesses were on the stand very briefly, and if their purpose wasn't clear to the jury, Isaac's *purposefulness* had all the clarity of an enormous crystal ball; indeed, most of the jurors kept watching him as if he were one. In a short appearance, Zackery Carpenter testified not only to George's quiet character while in prison, but got in as much as he could (over the constant objections of the assistant AG) about Winston Russell's very different prison career, as well as the names of a few of Winston's visitors. While the State literally held its breath – Neil Sadler's face looked blue – nothing at all was asked, or said, regarding the warden's conversation with Julian Lewis the night of Hallis reprieve.

Next, an elderly VA optometrist was called; all he did was state the dates of the eye exams he'd given George Hall, and the prescription of George's glasses. Next, under protest, Neil Sadler, the assistant DA, took the stand. All he did was look huffy when asked to state through whose arrangements, and how often, he'd interrogated Moonfoot Butler. He looked even huffier when Isaac asked him to take off his glasses. Picking up the .38 revolver from the exhibits table, and waving it under Sadler's nose, the old lawyer then walked across the room, turned his back, suddenly spun around, raised his arm, and yelled, 'What am I holding, Mr Sadler?'

Sadler snapped, 'A gun!'

'Look again.' Isaac had slipped the gun inside his jacket while walking away from the witness, and had nothing at all in his hand, which he was waggling back and forth. Sadler squinched up his eyes, then shoved his glasses back on. Isaac said, 'Thank you. That's all.'

Sadler sat down, but kept his buttocks half out of his chair, while Isaac questioned the white-supremacy survivalist, Charles Mennehy, whose leathery tan had greyed during his stint in the county jail. The ex-sergeant admitted by monosyllable that he was now under indictment for gun-smuggling, and seditious activities connected with his leadership in a group called the Carolina Patriots. Mennehy clearly thought of himself as the strong silent type. Asked if he'd ever unloaded a shipment of guns from a truck in a town called Cyrusville, Georgia, he said, 'Nope.' Was he sure? 'Yeah.' All right, had he ever been in a room with the accused, George Hall, apart from this courtroom? 'Nope.'

'Never walked in on a conversation between George Hall and his employer, Mr Dyer Fanshaw, in the offices of Fanshaw Paper Company?'

'Nope.'

'Are you sure?'

Neil Sadler popped up. 'The witness has answered the question!'

Isaac shrugged at the jury, and after a few more questions to which the same 'nope' was the only answer, he abruptly dismissed Sergeant Mennehy. There was interestingly little cross-examination.

Next, Mr Dyer Fanshaw himself was called. Walking briskly down the aisle while stroking his tie, he looked very wealthy, and very indignant. The assistant AG stood up, twitching his thumbs together, while Isaac stared mournfully at the witness. The old lawyer said that he had only a few questions. The first two were easy: Was Mr Fanshaw the president of Fanshaw Paper Company? Yes, he was. Two: Had George Hall been in his employ as a driver? He 'believed so'.

The next question came fast: Seven years ago, had George Hall come to Fanshaw's office and told him he'd seen rifles being unloaded from a damaged crate that had fallen out of the truck Hall had just driven to Cyrusville, Georgia? Waxen-faced, Fanshaw said he could not recall such a conversation. Could he recall ever having been in his office with George Hall when Charles Mennehy entered the room? Fanshaw shook his head.

'Is your response "no"?'

No reply, and Isaac turned to the bench. 'I ask that the witness be required to answer the question.'

Instead, Fanshaw stared at the assistant AG. The assistant AG bounced up, demanding to approach the bench. He sprinted there, Isaac met him, and they began whispering emphatically at each other. Fanshaw – legs crossed, buffed shoe twitching – watched them with a scowl of heavy patience.

Hilliardson told both lawyers to be quiet. He then sent out the jury, who took it ill. The judge rubbed his beak a while, as he studied Dyer Fanshaw. He then said he would hear arguments about whether Fanshaw, now under indictment on charges related to these issues, might be put in a position of prejudicing his own upcoming trial. Twenty minutes later, the judge shook his head. '. . . I am satisfied that to compel the witness to answer might imperil his Fifth Amendment rights. The State's objection is sustained. The defence will drop this line of questioning.'

When the jury returned, Isaac limped sadly back to the witness stand, and mildly asked Dyer Fanshaw, 'Seven years ago were you made aware of a plan devised by the late city comptroller Otis Newsome, together with Robert Pym, Winston Russell, and Charles Mennehy, to bring about the death of George Hall?'

'Absolutely not!' blurted Fanshaw even before the assistant AG, a shrill little man, could shout out, *Objection! Objection!* This is completely beyond the pale, Your Honour! Mr Rosethorn has summonsed a leading citizen of this community as a witness *for* the defence, and here he is accusing the man of plotting to *murder* the defendant himself!'

Neil Sadler bounded to his feet in support of his superior. 'Your Honour! Mr Rosethorn is doing his best to drown us all in a sea of red herrings! Who's on trial here anyhow?! What in the world has this got to do with the defendant's shooting of Robert Pym?'

'Sit down, Mr Sadler,' snapped the judge.

Isaac shrugged. 'All Mr Fanshaw has to do is say, "No."'

Hilliardson leaned over the bench. 'The witness will not answer. The objection is sustained. Strike the question.'

Staggering to the jury rail with his arms in the air, Isaac moaned. 'I give up!'

'Mr Rosethorn!' Hilliardson shook the gavel at him.

And so Dyer Fanshaw was excused without admitting anything, but thoroughly satisfying at least some of the jury (to judge from their expressions) that he had an awful lot to hide, which was exactly what Isaac wanted them to think.

After dramatically brooding in his chair until Hilliardson grew testy, Isaac stood up to call to the stand one Denise Mabry, an attractive black woman very demurely dressed. She was the prostitute I'd sent Wes Pendergraph to interrogate in Washington, DC, the one whose name Hamilton Walker had given me. She swore that on the night of the Pym shooting, Winston Russell had called her over to his parked car – a blue Ford – and forced her to take him to her room in the Montgomery Hotel, where he'd made her perform oral sex on him. That while there, they'd both heard a gun fired on the street below; that he'd rushed to the window to look, then had quickly pulled on his clothes and run out of the room.

Isaac Rosethorn: 'Your windows in that hotel faced where?'

Denise Mabry: 'Down on Smoke's Bar. When I looked out myself, I saw the man lying on the sidewalk. And a cop car. And a crowd.'

Isaac: 'Did you see Winston Russell down there on the street?'

Denise: 'No. I never saw him again. Except a couple of years later, here in this court.'

'He was here on trial for assaulting a female friend of yours, was he not?'

Mitchell Bazemore stood up. 'Objection. Irrelevant.'

'Sustained,' agreed Hilliardson.

Isaac: 'I withdraw the question. One more thing. Did Winston Russell show you a gun when he came to your room that night?'

'Yes.' She glared out at the court. 'He told me to suck on it.'

On cross-examination, Mitchell Bazemore lambasted 'Ms Mabry's' reputation as an 'honest woman,' by asking whether we should believe anyone who at the time of what Mitch kept on calling 'the murder,' had been in the employ of one Hamilton Walker, 'a notorious Hillston pimp.'

Ham Walker, seated in the courtroom in a pale green linen suit, laughed out loud when Denise replied, 'I don't call you a liar just 'cause you're a lawyer. Don't call me one, just 'cause I'm a hooker.'

Mitch then accused her of making this whole story up in revenge for the injuries inflicted by Russell five years ago on her 'fellow prostitute.'

She denied it. 'I'd wanted revenge on Russell, I already got that, reading my newspaper on Saturday.'

Disgusted, Mitch shouted, 'How could you even have known who your ... customer was? Are you telling me this man, under the criminal circumstances you described, *identified* himself to you?'

She looked at Mitch as if he was crawling with maggots. 'I knew who Winston Russell was. We all did. We had cause to know his name. And his face. And to be some place else from wherever he was.'

Mitch went doggedly on. 'Being preoccupied at the Montgomery, you, however, were not a witness to the shooting on the street below?'

'No.'

'Then you really have nothing to tell us about it. No more questions.'

A plump woman in her sixties, a former waitress at Smoke's, was called; she testified that a good hour before George Hall had come into the bar that night, Moonfoot Butler had arrived there alone, and that he had made a 'bunch of' phone calls from the pay phone by the toilets. He'd borrowed the change for them from her, and had never paid her back. On cross-examination, Mitchell Bazemore wondered with some of his old sarcasm how she could possibly remember details from so long ago. On recross, Isaac demonstrated with a quiz show of random questions that the woman had a truly remarkable memory, 'and certainly one manifestly superior to Mr Butler's.'

Isaac's next witness was hostile. So obviously hostile that Judge Hilliardson was quickly persuaded to declare her as such. But Lana Pym was ambivalently hostile. She wanted to protect Bobby and Willie; she wanted to blame Winston and George. The contradictory pull of these desires confused her; a vulnerable position in which to be, with Isaac around. She sat there, bitter and nervous, a small, wiry young woman wearing too much cheap makeup, with her hair dyed a brittle brass, and sheathed in a pathetic black outfit that the State had obviously told her to wear as a sign of her prolonged widowhood. Isaac kept her on the stand over an hour, and the State only came to her rescue whenever the questions appeared to be straying from a simple story of rotten cops on the take, to a tale with political leanings. Not that Lana Pym knew a thing about who might have been covering up what for whom, or why. But she did know more than she'd ever admitted to us, and by a rapidly mixed bombardment of sympathy, traps, and accusations, Isaac forced her to flee, with most of her cache of facts, out into the open.

'I wish I didn't have to ask you to remember, Mrs Pym. God knows, I feel for you deeply. Your only brother brutally murdered! . . . Well, so was George Hall's only brother brutally murdered. And by the same man! But if Winston Russell so tragically led your *brother* astray, isn't it possible he cast the same evil spell over your *husband*, Bobby?'

'. . . Now, Mrs Pym, if you think Winston might have been storing stolen goods in your garage, are you saying that Bobby *didn't* know what was in those crates? Or that he *did* know, but allowed it to happen out of *fear*? I really must advise you to choose one or the other.'

'. . . Mrs Pym, I ask you, does that make sense? Seven years ago you told the police you'd thought your husband was out bowling that night. Now you've said that he was home with Winston Russell, eating dinner. That Winston made several phone calls. That he *received* several phone calls, and that to your knowledge one of them was from Otis Newsome. Now – subsequently, Russell and your husband, both *armed*, arrived in separate cars, at the same time, at the same place: Smoke's Bar in Canaan, which I assure you is not a bowling alley. Yet you're telling me they hadn't made any *plans* while at your home?! Where was Bobby during all these phone calls? Off watching that twenty-four-inch television set you didn't know was stolen from the Hillston Police Impoundment Facility when Winston gave it to you for Christmas?'

'. . . All right, Mrs Pym. Say we accept your sworn testimony that Bobby did not drink, did not go to bars, was never physically violent, had no acquaintances in Canaan, did not know Moonfoot Butler, and had no reason to be seeking out George Hall. Well then! Please come up with some explanation – other than mine – as to why Bobby was *in* Canaan, *in* a bar, acting drunk, and *violently provoking a fight with George Hall?*'

'. . . Ah, my dear woman. My heart aches when I think what you've suffered at the hands of this brute, Russell. Who, in the very hour of your husband's death, rushed to the hospital to *tell you to lie*! Didn't he tell you to lie? Didn't he tell you to keep quiet about his being with Bobby that night?! *Didn't he??'*

By the time Isaac walked from the weeping Mrs Pym over to the prosecutor's table and told them, 'You may take the witness,' they didn't want anything to do with her. Well, Mitch Bazemore did ask her if Robert Pym had ever said he planned to kill the defendant. She said, no, he had no reason to kill him. None. All she knew was that man sitting over there (George Hall) had shot Bobby, and Bobby was dead, and that man was still alive. Mitch said all he could do was offer her his apologies for 'Mr Rosethorn's shabby, contemptible, heartless, and inhuman treatment of a widow.'

Isaac demanded that the remark be struck from the record as 'warrantless, if not indeed *actionable*,' and he demanded an apology from Bazemore. While the two counsellors were arguing, Judge Hilliardson excused Mrs Pym, struck the remark, and called a recess until the next morning. I still hadn't testified. Nor had George. Nora'd said that in chambers Hilliardson had asked Isaac if he could 'expedite matters,' since he very much hoped the trial would not run into next week. At which, the assistant AG had made the mistake of assuming a companionable and jocular tone with Hilliardson, even patting the judge's shoulder, while saying, 'I couldn't be more in agreement, Shirl. I'm set to fly the wife to St Kitts Sunday.' Nora said that Hilliardson gave the man a stare that made hawks look namby-pamby.

Actually, I didn't mind sitting in court. It gave me an excuse to hang around the Municipal Building to check on HPD. I needed an excuse because Carl Yarborough and the City Council had ordered me, with a supporting letter from Dr Thanh at UH Emergency, to take a sick leave. In the meanwhile, Carl had wanted my recommendation for an acting captain; I'd recommended Etham Foster, who said if he saw me near my office he'd have it padlocked. Some people wondered why I hadn't appointed Justin acting captain; his mother even asked me why. Alice didn't. And I decided Justin had had that talk with her. He and I were quiet around each other.

I'd expected I'd be the first witness called Friday. I wasn't. When court convened, there was a big TV monitor set up on a table, angled towards the jury box. Isaac explained that he was going to show them a taped deposition by a witness too ill to appear. Bazemore put in a pro-forma objection, was overruled, and took exception; the deputies pulled down venetian blinds in the tall windows; Nora inserted a black video cassette, and Purley Newsome, his gaunt face propped up on hospital pillows, sulkily identified himself. It seemed to me the jurors were more riveted to his testimony than they'd been to anybody else's – maybe because televised dramas are realer to us now than live ones, maybe because of the story the sick man was telling. This was just some of it:

'. . . So Winston and Bobby leaned on Hall pretty hard, 'cause they needed a driver who was making that North Georgia run. Bobby'd already busted Hall a couple of times, and they told him they'd do it again, get him in worse trouble, if he didn't go along. They got Moonfoot to work on him too . . . Nah, Hall never knew Slidell and Koontz were in on it . . . All Hall had to do was park the truck at the drop-off point in Cyrusville, and, you know, take a hike for a little while . . . Cigarettes. They told him it was just crates of cigarettes. Anyhow, he only made a couple of runs . . . Well, what I heard was, Hall freaked out and the whole mess blew up.'

What Purley said about the source of Hall's 'freak-out' had been deleted as 'hearsay.' There was a blip, then off-camera, Isaac Rosethorn's voice purred, 'By "Otis," you are referring to your brother, the late Otis Newsome?'

Purley's eyes teared up. 'Yes, I am.'

'And you were present that afternoon of the Saturday in question, when your brother Otis had a discussion about George Hall?'

'I sure was.'

'Who else?'

'Bobby. Winston. And Charlie.'

'By "Charlie," you're referring to Charles Mennehy?'

Purley had a coughing spasm, then he nodded. 'That's right.'

'What was said? That you yourself heard, now.'

Wiping his eyes, Purley muttered, 'It was Winston did the talking. Not Otis. And not me. I was just eating my lunch. But Winston said George Hall could mess us up good. How he'd seen the guns when the crate fell out and busted. Then Charlie said he was pretty damn sure Hall could identify him. So Winston says, let's just get rid of him right now.'

'Who is "him"?'

'Hall. George Hall. So Bobby says, well, that's no problem. So Winston says, we'll fix up a plan, you know, so Hall gets it resisting arrest.'

466

'Gets it?' asked Isaac's voice.

'They figured they could, you know, get Hall into a fight, act like they were trying to arrest him. Chase him out in the open somewhere. Then they could shoot him, like they *had* to. You know what I mean,' Purley whined, squirming higher on to the hospital pillow.

'Ah . . . But this . . . plan went astray, did it not?'

'Yeah, it sure did. Winston blew it. Thought he was so smart, too.' Purley nodded with a revolting smile. Then his face resumed its usual self-pitying pout. 'Winston was crazy, Mr Rosethorn. He *laughed* when he told me he'd shot Willie. I said, nobody was supposed to *die*, that wasn't the idea. And he laughed. So you'll say how I had to go along, won't you? I had to.'

Chapter 29

While the jury, sequestered at the Holiday Inn, was not supposed to be reading or listening to anything about the case, no one (except possibly Hilliardson) really believed that all twelve of them had completely abstained for two weeks from one of the few things there was to do in their motel rooms – which was to watch television. Certainly, Isaac and Nora assumed that at least some news about the Trinity ambush had reached them. With my swollen face, my cast and bandages, I provided, as Isaac had planned, a vivid illustration of what they might have heard about the incident. Coming right after Purley's deposition, which had left some jurors slack-jawed, and others with clenched teeth, I was a testament to what Winston Russell was capable of. So when Nora Howard rose in a quiet flow of white cotton, and said, 'The defence recalls C. R. Mangum,' and I carefully limped forward, she gave me a look somewhere between horror and grief. 'Captain Mangum, would you like assistance? We apologize for asking you to come here in your precarious condition.' I eased myself into the chair, and she sighed, 'The news of Winston Russell's savage attack on you—'

'Objection!!' Mitch Bazemore had found his old voice again; the one like a German siren.

'Sustained,' said Hilliardson. 'Ask questions, Miss Howard.'

Nora shook her head at the jury, apologized to the judge, and asked me to please tell her if at any point I was in too much pain to continue. I said I thought I could manage.

'We're very grateful, Captain Mangum. Now . . . you've heard

Mr Newsome's deposition. The Hillston police have conducted an intensive, thorough investigation into the matters he brought forth. Are the facts volunteered by Mr Newsome in this deposition consistent with the evidence produced by your exhaustive, six-month investigation?'

'Yes, they are.'

'In every detail?'

'Yes.'

'Prior to his death, was Winston Russell charged with the murder of William Slidell?'

Bazemore was up again, jingling his pocketful of dimes and quarters. 'Your Honour, I don't know where Miss Howard thinks she's headed. Irrelevant and immaterial.'

Nora asked the judge if she could approach the bench to explain where she was headed. She stayed there long enough to give the jury ample time to study my injuries, which they did with interest. When she returned, Hilliardson told Bazemore he was overruling his objection.

I said, yes, Russell had been charged with Slidell's murder.

'Captain Mangum,' Nora continued crisply, pausing only long enough for me to get in the word *yes*, 'the bullet-riddled body of William Slidell was recovered from a car in the Shocco River by your Homicide Division, was it not? And that car was a Ford on which an attempt had been made to destroy the identification number, and hide the original colour? And after research, it proved to be a blue Ford that had disappeared from the police impoundment facility seven years ago, at the time when Winston Russell had access to that facility. Is that true?'

I said, 'Yes, ma'am. That's true.'

'So it's possible that the blue Ford that Arthur Butler said Russell drove, and that Denise Mabry said Russell was sitting in, near Smoke's Bar, was the car you dragged from the river with William Slidell's body in it?'

'I think it highly probable.'

'And it's possible that this is the same blue Ford that George Hall told the police he'd seen Robert Pym running towards , on the sidewalk outside Smoke's Bar?'

'I'd say so, yes.'

She promised she wouldn't tax my precarious condition any longer, but had one final question. Walking to the posterboard map of the street outside Smoke's, she pointed at a circled spot on the drawing. 'Captain Mangum. When you apprehended

George Hall, seated here on the sidewalk, was he wearing his glasses?'

I'd thought about this all day, trying to see George's face staring up at me from that sidewalk. I said, 'I don't think so. To the best of my recollection, he was not.'

She thanked me, and told Mitch Bazemore I was his. Mitch didn't want me. We hadn't spoken since he'd told me I should be fired because of the Trinity 'disaster,' and had added that if Brookside died he wouldn't rest until I was fired. Now he didn't bother to look in my direction as he asked perfunctorily, 'Captain, you don't remember for certain if the accused was wearing glasses or not, do you?'

'No, not for certain.'

Mitch's hostility got away from him, and he chased it with his usual lead-footed sarcasm. 'For all you know, Captain Mangum, he might have been wearing *three* pairs of glasses, three pairs of glasses, and carrying binoculars! Right?'

I gave him a serious look. 'No, sir. Even with his face all covered with blood from where Pym assaulted him, I think I would have noticed *three* pairs of glasses.'

Nora beamed at me as she offered me her arm to help me out of the witness chair.

After the lunch recess, Isaac Rosethorn pushed himself to his feet carefully, and said, 'We now call the defendant George Hall.'

The tiers of spectators hushed as George took his hand from the Bible and quietly settled into the witness chair. It was a shock to people, I think, to see his hair grizzled, his skin the colour of soot, his eyes sunken behind the glasses – and to compare that with the hard black shine of the young man who'd sat coiled in this chair only seven years ago. The contrast said to everybody looking at him, 'You don't ever want to go to prison under sentence of death.'

George answered every question in the same steady unhurried voice. Talking about himself didn't seem to come easily to him, but he never fumbled for words. He just chose them slowly. He wasn't choosing them to please, or to hide, or to justify himself, or to conform in any way to what might be expected to serve his interest. It wasn't that he was withheld, he was simply self-contained. His world in those seven years had contracted, inside that small barred room, to a terrible solitude without privacy. Somehow within it, he'd found a centre.

Isaac stayed back by the defence table, his hands quietly

pressed against its corner. He let the long silence fill the room before he spoke. 'Would you state your full name and address, please?'

'Timothy George Hall, Jr One twenty Mill Street, in Hillston.'

'And, Mr Hall, when was the last time you were in your home on Mill Street?'

George said it matter-of-factly. 'Seven years, two months, and twelve days ago.'

'And since then?'

'Dollard Prison, except for here, and at the jail.' He gestured with his head at the window facing the county jail.

'Why have you been in prison all that time?'

'I was scheduled for execution on a first-degree murder charge.'

'The murder of Robert Pym?'

'Yes.'

'George, do you believe you are guilty of the crime of murder?'

'No, sir, I don't.'

Isaac looked at him for a moment, then he sighed. 'I don't either . . . George, seven years, two months, and *thirteen* days ago, did you go at night to a bar in Canaan called Smoke's?'

'Yes, sir.'

'Did you go alone?'

'Yes, sir.'

'You did not go there with Arthur "Moonfoot" Butler?'

'I went by myself. Butler was already in there. After a while he came over and talked at me a while.'

'Did you go into that bar planning to kill Robert Pym?'

'No.'

'Did you tell Moonfoot Butler at any time in any words that you planned to kill Robert Pym?'

George shook his head. 'The man lied. I don't know why he did it, but he lied. I never said what he claimed.'

'Why did you go to Smoke's that night?'

'To get a beer. I was troubled about something. It had happened earlier on. I couldn't think it through. My mother didn't allow alcohol in her house – so I walked over to Smoke's to get a beer.'

'Would you tell us in your own words, George, what you felt so troubled about?'

Quietly, steadily, looking only at Isaac, George told the story of how the two policemen had pressured him into making special

471

stops on his Fanshaw trucking route, and into 'looking the other way.' He did not know they'd been stealing. He'd been told by Moonfoot that they were buying large quantities of cigarettes in North Carolina, and selling them at a profit out of state, that other drivers were doing the dropoffs too. Yes, he knew it wasn't right, but they were white policemen, and they said they'd make things hard on him if he didn't cooperate. He'd lost several jobs since returning from Vietnam, and he feared losing another one – or even being jailed on some trumped-up charge.

'You couldn't afford to be out of work because you supported your mother and your younger brother?' asked Isaac.

'We all worked,' George said. 'But Cooper was in high school, and I didn't want him to take on any more . . . He was the class president.' He added this suddenly, as if it were something he'd forgotten to tell Rosethorn, and thought the lawyer would want to know.

He said he'd made only two runs before that summer night in Cyrusville, Georgia, when he'd returned from his 'walk,' and seen at the rear of his truck, three men flinging M-16 rifles from a broken crate into a car trunk. He'd backed off, and they hadn't noticed him. The whole way home to Hillston, he'd thought about what the guns meant. And all he could think of was the articles and reports that Cooper brought home from his political meetings, and kept making him look at. Articles about the Carolina Klan, about their paramilitary camps, about what they'd done in the Piedmont, about how policemen were known to be involved. Cooper talked about it often. Whenever George would say something positive about one of his white platoon leaders in Vietnam, how he'd been a decent guy, or easy on the men, Cooper would explode. He'd show George the articles on the Klan and say, '*This* is what white people are like! *This!*'

Isaac asked, 'Did you think of talking to Cooper about what you'd seen in Cyrusville?'

'I couldn't talk to Cooper back then. We were both hard-headed, and we tangled lots . . . But, yes, I did think about telling him.' Now George turned towards his mother. 'I thought about telling Mama, too . . .' He looked down at his hands. 'The truth is, Mr Rosethorn, I was ashamed for them to know I'd let myself get mixed up in it . . .' The cheap fabric of the black suit stretched under his muscles as he straightened in the chair. 'But, the same time, I felt like I couldn't just let it go. That's what I kept on thinking, when I brought the truck back into the garage, I can't just let it go. These other drivers Moonfoot had talked about. I didn't know which ones they were, and he wouldn't tell me. I got him on the phone, and he just kept on yelling, "Don't you say a word to anybody."'

'Did you think of going to the police, George?'

His mouth twitched. 'No.'

'Why?'

'To listen to me accusing some of their own?'

'. . . So you returned the truck to the Fanshaw Company, and . . .?'

'I kept on standing there by the truck, and I thought, well, I could talk to my dispatcher. So I looked for him, but he wasn't around. Then I saw Mr Fanshaw get out of his car, and head for his office. He'd treated me all right, few times I'd had cause to see him. And I said, well, it's his company, and he could go to the police himself.'

'And did you approach Mr Fanshaw, and tell him?'

An objection from the assistant AG was overruled by Hilliard-son, who told him that if he wished to challenge this direct testimony, he could do so in cross-examination. Isaac repeated the question, and George said that yes, he had. At first, Mr Fanshaw had acted shocked, and said he would 'look into it.' But then his face had got very upset when another man had walked into the office. A man George recognized as one of the men he'd seen unloading the guns in Cyrusville.

'Is that man in the courtroom now?'

'Yes.' And George pointed to Charles Mennehy.

Fanshaw had then brushed George off in a hurry, told him to forget the whole thing, that he'd take care of it. 'I looked in his eyes, Mr Fanshaw's eyes, and I felt like he was lying. It was a real strong feeling. So I just went home. Nobody was there. Later I went on over to Smoke's. And Moonfoot came, sat down, kept at me about don't be crazy, don't cross these white cops anyway anyhow.'

Their talk ended, sometime before midnight, when Robert Pym had walked into Smoke's, and 'begun to hassle people about the jukebox and all.'

Isaac asked, 'Were you surprised to see Pym in there?'

'Yes, I was. He'd never been before. But I didn't think right off, it was due to me. He was loud, acting up, like he was drunk. I went over to him, said how I was shutting off the jukebox 'cause this man was trying to play his music up there. I said why didn't he get out right now. He give me a shove, said, something like, "Nigger, you don't ever talk to a white man like that—"' George squeezed his hand around his fist.

Isaac nodded. 'That's when the fight began? And then he pulled the gun out from his belt, and rammed it into your nostril, and said, "Buddy, your ass is grass"?'

George shook his head. 'I can't say I remember those exact words.'

'All right . . . Now, when you managed to get the gun away from him, and Pym ran, and you followed him, did you run out on to that sidewalk intending to kill him?'

'No. I just saw him running off, and I went after him. But then I saw him sort of scrambling around at that blue car, and I knew how Winston Russell had a blue Ford, and I'd been around Russell enough times to know the kind he was, and it hit me, just like that, maybe they were *coming* for me, 'cause of what I'd seen. So when Pym wheeled back, I thought he had a gun. I just fired at him. Just fired.' George stopped suddenly with an intake of breath, and lowered his head.

Now Isaac moved around the table towards George. 'You said, you *thought* Robert Pym had a gun. You didn't see he had a gun?'

George pointed at his glasses, took them off. 'It was pretty dark. And my glasses must have come off in the fight. I couldn't see too good.'

Isaac limped nearer the witness stand. 'Why didn't you pick your glasses up, put them back on, before you gave chase to Pym?'

'I didn't think to.'

'Then you simply fired blind, hoping to stop him from killing you?'

The State objected to this, as leading the witness, and was sustained. Isaac offered to rephrase. 'When you fired the shot, did you think your own life was in danger?'

George carefully replaced his glasses. 'I can't say I *thought*, like you said. You do it quicker than thinking. And you still maybe aren't quick enough. Over in Vietnam, I knew a lot weren't quick enough.'

'You knew soldiers who didn't act quickly enough in their own defence and so lost their lives?'

'. . . Yes, I did. But I meant, I knew a lot of men where quickness didn't do them any good.'

Isaac's hand touched the arm of the chair beside the defendant's. 'George, why didn't you tell the court at your first trial the story you've now told us? Why did you never mention the smuggling?'

George's face tightened. 'Winston Russell came to me here at the jail that night. He said if I let his name come up, or about the Fanshaw trucks, well, it'd just make things harder on me in the trial. He said they'd never ask for murder one, not if they figured Pym and I didn't know each other. He said since I'd already told them about the Ford, just say I thought it was Pym's.'

Nodding, Isaac asked, 'And you agreed because you were persuaded by his reasoning that his approach would best serve your defence?'

'No.' A deep rush of breath pushed through George's chest. 'He said if I told any of it, he said, I'd wish my family dead and buried, compare it to what he'd do to them. He said he'd use a knife, and it'd take them a long time to die.'

'Those were his exact words?'

'. . . Those words I know for sure.'

'By your family, he meant your mother and your younger brother?'

'Yes.' George looked over at his mother; her hands covered her face.

'He said their names to you?'

'Yes.'

'Did you believe he would carry out this threat to use a knife to mutilate and murder your family?'

'Yes.'

'Why?'

'. . . From looking in his eyes.'

'. . . Was this threat ever repeated?'

George said that after his death-penalty conviction, Winston visited him again at the county jail and told him that he now also knew where George's sister lived with her two small children in Greensboro, and that the same 'promise' held for them. Still later, when George was already on Death Row, he was approached by a lifer-trusty named Gary Fisk. Fisk told him he had a message for him from Winston Russell. The message was 'I keep my promises. You keep yours.'

'And you believed this message.' Isaac was facing the jury now. 'And you never told anyone?' The answer was no. 'And the night before your scheduled execution, when they had shaved you, and given you the clothes you were to wear to your death, and moved you to the cell beside the gas chamber, and brought you your minister, *you never told anyone?*'

George looked up quietly. 'I just said, Mr Rosethorn. I believed the man would do it what he said . . . And I believed if I didn't talk . . . he wouldn't.' He took off his glasses, and stared down at them in his hand. 'But Cooper's dead.'

The assistant AG could not badger George into changing his story; I don't think he tried as hard or as long as Mitch would have. Of course, now, Mitch had nothing to lose. But they didn't let Mitch try.

Some people assumed George Hall would be the last witness. But Isaac Rosethorn often said that at the end of a trial, it was effective to bring in somebody nobody'd ever heard mentioned so far, and to make it clear that they'd come from a long way off, driven by an overwhelming impulse to see justice done. Friday morning, he brought in three such mysterious travelers. The first, a young red-haired woman, introduced herself as Mandy Schwerner, née Katz, of St Louis, Missouri. She sat in a pretty pink suit, handbag on her lap, and told the jury that seven years ago she'd been employed by the city comptroller, Otis Newsome, as his secretary. She said that on the Monday after the shooting of Pym – she recalled quite clearly having the newspaper with the story about it on her desk – that Winston Russell (a frequent visitor) had stormed past her into Mr Newsome's office, while Mr Dyer Fanshaw was in there, and that while there, the men had yelled at each other for some time. She distinctly remembered being curious about why Mr Newsome was so angry with Mr Russell, and why Mr Russell kept yelling, 'He's not going to talk!,' and telling Mr Newsome things like 'calm down' and 'keep your mouth shut, and your friends' too.' Then Mr Russell had left, slamming the door so hard, a print fell off the wall, and the glass smashed.

Somewhat at a loss, Neil Sadler (who'd obviously never heard of Mrs Schwerner before now) asked her whether she still worked as a secretary. She said she didn't. Why, because she'd been fired from her job? She pleasantly replied that no, she'd quit to marry Reverend Schwerner, now assistant minister of the United Lutheran Church in St Louis.

The second of the out-of-owners wasn't really from that far

away. Gary Fisk was an inmate at Dollard Prison. He was very happy to be out of there, even for a morning. Apparently Mr Fisk had damaged his vocal cords while behind bars, because he spoke in a rattling whisper, and Hilliardson had to ask him twice to repeat the message Winston Russell had told him to pass along to George Hall. Fisk added that he'd never had any idea that 'I keep my promises' was a death threat, or naturally he would have said something about it to the warden.

Isaac's final witness was a very old man, frail of limb but very rosy in the cheeks, and perky in manner. He said his name was Lem Trelease, and that he lived in St Petersburg at the Merrymount Retirement Centre, which he endorsed, on the record, as quite merry indeed.

Isaac laughed, promising to send for a brochure immediately. 'Now, Mister Trelease – I should say, Sergeant Trelease – you served with the Hillston police for forty-three years, retiring nearly seven years ago. Is that correct?'

'Yes, it is. They made me quit.'

'Um hum. And seven years ago, at one A.M. on Sunday, July twelfth, were you on duty at the headquarters of the Hillston Police, here in this building?'

Trelease looked around, just to check to be sure he was in the right place. 'Yep. I was night-shift desk sergeant right here at HPD. I was at the desk.'

'And on that night, the night when George Hall was arrested for the shooting of Robert Pym, did anyone come into the station and speak to you at the desk, and ask you to give something to George Hall?'

'Yes, sir.' Trelease sat up straighter, smoothing his unfashionably wide tie. 'A black teenaged boy came in that A.M., asked me if he could talk to George Hall. Said he was his brother. Well, I said I was sorry, but Hall was in the holding cell, and, well, I couldn't let him go back there. So then he wanted to know if I'd take Mr Hall this little thing he had wrapped up in a plain handkerchief, and well, of course, I said I'd have to check it.' Trelease spotted Miss Bee and smiled at her.

'And did you?'

'Yep, yes, sir, I did.'

'And what was in the handkerchief?'

'Just a regular pair of eyeglasses. The boy said, he'd gone to this bar where the shooting was, to find out what had happened, and somebody there said they'd found these glasses under a table, and the boy'd recognized them. He said his brother needed these glasses to see by. And so, well, would I please take them back to the suspect.'

Isaac nodded. 'And the boy was George Hall's brother, Cooper?'

'He said he was. I wrote it down. You could look in the log if they still have it around.'

Isaac said, 'I did look in the log . . . What did you do then?'

'Took the glasses back to the cell, gave them to the suspect.'

'And what did George Hall do?'

'Said thank you. Put'em on.'

'Thank *you*, Sergeant Trelease. No further questions.'

When the judge asked Mitch Bazemore if he had any questions, he rubbed his wedding ring for a moment, then shook his head.

Isaac Rosethorn walked slowly back to his chair. 'Now,' he said quietly. 'Now the defence rests.'

The assistant attorney general had obviously decided that Mitchell Bazemore could deliver his summation without any prompting, because during the break, he left the courtroom and didn't return.

Mitch stood by the jury box, like he always did. He rocked back and forth on the heels of his polished shoes, like he always did. But he didn't begin the way he always began – by calling the defendant a liar, and his lawyer a charlatan. He clamped his hand over his mouth, then suddenly ripped it away, and said, 'The great British jurist Blackstone wrote long ago that all the principles of civilized law could be summed up in one simple code. One simple code. That we should live honestly. That we should hurt no one. And that we should render to everyone his due.

'Remember that, and forget everything else you've heard in this courtroom. Remember that, and forget me.' He jabbed his fist in his breastbone, then shook it at the defence table. 'Forget Mr Rosethorn. He's a brilliant man. A brilliant man and a magnificent lawyer. But he is utterly and absolutely irrelevant now. I am utterly and absolutely irrelevant now. Set us aside. Set aside sympathy. And prejudice. And personalities. Set aside *politics and politicians*. They are, as the Good Book says, "dragons in their pleasant palaces." They have no power here.' Mitch waved both arms in all directions, as if there were no telling where the dragons might be lurking. Isaac put down his pencil and stared at him.

His arms tensed, the DA leaned over the jury rail. 'Cast out of your mind *everything* but that simple code. And *ask yourselves*, ladies and gentlemen of the jury, ask yourselves, do you believe that George Hall lived honestly? Did he hurt no one? Did he render to Robert Pym his due? Whatever Robert's sins may have been, did he deserve to bleed to death on a sidewalk, shot through the *eye*?! Ask yourselves, "Do I really believe this preposterous tale told by Mr Newsome, a delirious invalid, under indictment himself, and desperate to shift blame on dead associates unable to protest?" And even if his tale were true, it does not alter the fact of the crime you sit here to judge. If you secretly planned to kill me, but before you did so, I separately determined to kill you, and I *did* kill you, then I would be guilty of murder. If I killed you because I *found out* about your plan to kill me, and it so enraged me I decided I had a *right* to kill you, then I would be guilty of murder. If I said "well, I wasn't wearing my glasses, so it was just *luck* I shot you in the eye instead of someplace else," I'd still be guilty of murder!' By now, Mitch's face was so dark with blood, he looked as if he *might* have murdered someone.

He began his old military pacing, from one end of the jury box to the other. 'Would a man governed by Blackstone's simple code act as George Hall undeniably acted when he ran out to that sidewalk, *after* the fight had ended, and shot and killed Robert Pym? If we all felt free to act as George Hall did, what kind of America would we be living in? The America of gunslingers and gangsters. A howling wilderness. And what would *we* be? Animals of will and appetite recklessly preying on one another. "Whatsoever a man soweth, that shall he also reap."' Mitch paused, then rubbed his signet ring into his chin as he stalked the length of the bar rail, circling the table where the assistant AG had sat.

'If we do not punish George Hall's act of murder, if we do not see it as our civic duty to punish his act, what are we saying both to this nation's law*breakers* and law*makers*? Are we not saying that nothing holds firm, nothing holds true? What are we saying to our children? Are we not saying there is no right and wrong? And what are we saying to *ourselves*? We are not a nation of thrones or armies. Our throne is our Constitution. Our armies are our laws. And they can protect us only if we *enforce* them.'

Without a glance, the DA strode past his ostensible assistant, Neil Sadler, seated at the prosecutor's table, and paused in front of Isaac.

'I have heard Mr Rosethorn on many occasions speak eloquently to juries of "mercy." He may do so today. Remember this. The State is not the enemy of mercy. Justice is not the enemy of mercy. Without *justice*, mercy has no meaning. We punish crime not for vengeance, but to preserve that fragile bond of civilized men, a democratic society. It is the moral right of a society to purge itself of all who would destroy it. To deter those who infect it with disease. To *reform*. To *restrain*.' Mitch wheeled around, shaking his finger at Isaac. 'And, yes – and this is no cause for apology, and let no one persuade you otherwise – it is our right and duty *to enact retribution.* "Righteousness exalteth a nation!"' His arm was trembling; he dropped it quickly, and took a deep breath, slowly calming himself. Then he shook his head. 'To punish crime is not cruel, is not selfish, is not primitive. The laws of this noble state, the laws of this noble nation, are not "cruel and unusual." They are the envy of other countries, the hope of the oppressed. They are a burning and a shining light around the world. As jurors, it is your sacred duty to guard the flame of that light, to guard it so that America is never left in darkness. George Hall took a life unlawfully. He is guilty. It is your duty to say so. Your oath binds you to that duty. Justice demands it. And in the name of justice, I ask it of each and every one of you.'

Some of the spectators applauded. I don't think Mitch heard them. Shaking, he strode back to his chair, yanked it out and flung himself into it. Slowly, Hilliardson's white long neck twisted to glance at the clock President McKinley had sent via Boss Hanna to Cadmean's father. Swivelling back, he announced that as it was nearly twelve, he thought we should take this opportunity to luncheon; he was therefore calling an hour's recess, after which we would proceed with the defence's closing remarks. Isaac Rosethorn sat slumped in his chair, tapping the pads of his forefingers against the sides of his nose.

Chapter 30

Isaac was in the lobby, bent over, his back against the wall by the portrait of Cadmean; he was staring at the marble floor. When I asked him to come have some lunch, he said he wasn't hungry, that he'd told Nora to go on without him.

'You worried, Isaac?'

With a sigh, he straightened up. 'I'm always worried . . . But Mitchell isn't always that good. He had them listening. I'm afraid he did.'

'What are you going to say?'

'I haven't quite decided, Slim.' He brushed at his hair with his fingers. 'Can you drive with one hand? Drive me to the cemetery?'

I knew which one he meant; I'd been with him there before. Often. And this time, like before, I waited on the path below while he limped across the North Hills grass to the grave of Edith Keene. For ten minutes, he sat leaning against that stone marker whose mysterious message used to puzzle me as a child. 'GONE TO A BETTER PLACE.' Behind him, the marble of the Haver obelisk glittered in the hot June sun.

I watched Isaac's lips moving as his hand soothed the grass with slow constant strokes. Finally he struggled to his feet, patted the crest of Edith Keene's tombstone, and fanning himself with his straw hat, he made his shambling way down the path again. I opened the car door for him. 'You okay now?'

'Better,' he nodded.

'After this is over,' I said, starting the motor, 'you ought to go away someplace nice. You always wanted to go to Rome.'

481

A mild snort. 'When I want to go to Rome, I read Gibbon.' He straightened a crushed cigarette, blowing tobacco shreds from his speckled fingers. 'Besides, I have to get to work. That confession you people wormed out of that poor brainwashed Purley Newsome – probably without fully advising him of his rights—'

I slowed the car. 'Isaac, *no*. Purley's already got a lawyer.'

'He's got a rotten lawyer.'

'Does he deserve any better?'

'Oh, Slim, don't even pretend to think that. The man was mentally coerced. Physically intimidated – How do you open this window?'

I smacked the power button. 'Well, let Nora defend Purley Newsome. She can do it alone. You *retired*. You're old. You're in miserable shape. You're—'

He stared at me, shaking his head. 'It's you who's in miserable shape, and I don't mean your broken bones. And here's Nora—'

'Don't start in, Isaac.'

'She's in love with you.' He said it flatly, simply. 'It breaks my heart.'

I told him I had my own broken heart to worry about. He patted my knee, and stared out at the passing graves. 'What do we know?' he said finally. 'Who are we to talk about broken hearts? . . . Nomi Hall's never told me hers was.' Sighing, he closed his eyes. 'Ah, dear God . . . let me do this right.'

'Mr Rosethorn? Are you with us? I asked if you cared to make a closing statement?' Judge Hilliardson stared down at the defence table where the old lawyer slumped, his head bowed, his eyes shut. 'Counsellor? Do you care to—'

'Thank you, Your Honour. Yes.' Opening his eyes, Isaac pushed himself up from the table, and, as he spoke, took off his seersucker jacket, and draped it carefully over the back of his chair. 'This morning,' he began, tucking in the back of his billowy white shirt, 'Mr Bazemore was kind enough to praise my eloquence. Allow me to praise his. I must say he surprised me. I have many times over the years heard our district attorney address this very jurors' box on the subject of crime, when he'd' – and Isaac's lungs swelled, his cheeks filled – '*huff and puff* about the grand old flag, and he'd shake those forty death-penalty convictions he wears on his scalp belt, and he'd tell us that if we didn't give him one more head on a stake, one more eye for an eye, why vermin would run wild in the streets, and the Founding Fathers would weep in their graves! *As if* the very first meeting *against* capital punishment hadn't been held at Ben Franklin's house!'

He paused, solemnly shaking his head. '. . . But, today, Mr Bazemore didn't do that . . . Never, never before, have I heard him speak so well. I was moved by his deep, unquestionable belief in what he said.' Walking across the court to where Mitch sat, frowning, Isaac stood before him in silence, then gave a slight bow. 'I am genuinely moved.'

Mitch glanced up, then lowered his head again.

Slowly Isaac turned, and both arms rose in the open-handed gesture that court illustrators loved, as his voice lifted and quickened. 'I am moved, *because* the prosecutor has given a powerful speech *in favour of the defendant*. He asks you to set aside prejudice and politics. *Yes! Do it!*

'He asks you to act in the name of justice. *Yes, I ask it too.* I am not here to plead for mercy for George Hall. If he had wanted mercy only, we wouldn't even *be here now*! George would have taken "the deal" offered before his first trial. He would have taken the deal, midway through *this* trial. He would have bargained away justice in exchange for mercy, as *confessed killers* have done, who have spent less time in prison than George has already served; who have spent *no time* on Death Row, where George has *lived alone* in a metal cage, far smaller than your jury box, for seven relentless soul-aching years. With no companion but Death! Think of it! Try to imagine one day, one twenty-four hour day, in that cell. Now, try to imagine *sixty-two thousand* of those hours.'

Isaac waited, staring at the jurors, then he pointed back at the defence table. 'Imagine the courage to keep silence, *but* refuse to plead guilty to a lesser charge. Now try to imagine how much George Hall wants *justice*.'

He waited again, pulling loose the knot of his tie. 'Not because he has earned justice by his suffering. Though that is true. Not because seven years ago he was treated unjustly. Though God knows *that* is true. But because, as a citizen of this nation, he was *born* with the right to justice. He was *born* with it!'

George's eyes followed Isaac, as the old man limped towards him, on his way to the prosecutor's table.

'Yes, Mr Bazemore, it is our moral responsibility in a free society to ensure justice. But for *all*! To do so, we lift our eyes, yes, not to the power of kings and armies, but to the power of *words*, to our Constitution, to our Bill of Rights.' The old stout arm was flung like a spear at the gilded seal above Judge Hilliardson's head. 'A Bill of Rights *first insisted upon* by the delegates from North Carolina as an absolute prerequisite to their signing of the Constitution. A Bill of Rights that takes its power from a great Anglo-American principle – the principle of *equal protection under the law.*'

Returning to the jury rail, Isaac spoke as if what he was telling them was the most important thing they would ever hear. And the truth is, I think he believed that. *'If ever and when ever*, a law is used disproportionately, that principle of equal protection under the law is violated. *If ever, and when ever*, punishment is meted out unequally – to the poor, to the foreign-born, to the black, to the friendless and the unlettered – that punishment is cruel and unusual. And ladies and gentlemen of the jury, if ever that great principle was violated, it was violated by the charges twice brought against George Hall. If ever a punishment was cruel ... it was George Hall's seven years on Death Row ... waiting to die in silence ... to save the lives of those he loved.'

Isaac's back was stooped, the shirt, wettened, clung to it. His head dropped forward, the white hair almost touching the rail, and he was quiet for so long, my heart began to race. But then slowly his back straightened, his head lifted, and his hands clasped at his breast.

'Counsel for the State is right. Law must be a burning and a shining light. But it must be that for *all*. It must burn past power and wealth and position. It must shine through the colour of a man's skin. Laws used against this one for his creed and that one for her sex, laws that are not deaf to accents and blind to origins – those laws make a mockery of our courts and our conscience. Justice grieves.'

Walking back to his chair, he picked up two of the thick law books lying open there, and held one out in each hand. 'No matter if the *letter* of the law be fulfiled, if its *spirit* is violated then it is null and void. Then, as Mr Bazemore's Good Book says, it is broken words in a valley of bones.' His hands tilted and the books slid with a frightening crash on to the table. The sound echoed down the room, as he turned to the jury. 'The spirit of this nation's greatest law lives in one simple sentence. It starts, "We hold these truths to be self-evident." You know the one I mean?'

The jurors looked at him. I saw the farm widow unconsciously nod. 'That's right,' Isaac told her. '*Self-evident* that George Hall was created equal to you and to me, and to Judge Hilliardson there on the bench, and to Governor Wollston over in Raleigh, and to the president up in Washington. *Self-evident* that, as our equal, George Hall has a right not to be intimidated and harassed and threatened because he's black. George stopped believing he had those rights. And two hundred years of history stand as witness to why he should doubt! Doubt he has a right to expect that if he goes to the law about the crimes of the powerful, it will listen. Doubt that if he goes to the law about murderous threats, it will protect him and his loved ones.

'He had the right not to fear that an arresting officer would as soon shoot him as not. The right not to be a sacrifice in a disgusting cover-up of the tangled greed and misguided personal and political allegiances of powerful people! The right not to be rushed through a shabby trial because he was poor and black, and not to be condemned to death for an act that no white man who'd shot a black in self-defence would *ever* even have been *charged* with. *The right to be treated equally.* That *inalienable* right is the real shining torch you jurors are guarding! Because if it can be taken away from George, it can be taken away from anyone – even someday from you, from your neighbour, even someday be taken away from your child.'

Breathing fast, Isaac moved along the rail and stood directly in front of Mrs Boren; his dark sad eyes gazed straight into hers. 'By that light, look at George Hall . . . Look at the courage it took to go to his employer. The decency it took to believe – sadly enough, *unwisely* believe – his employer would do the right thing. You know George has told you the truth. Just as you know Moonfoot Butler is a liar, and the cowardly Judas who telephoned Pym and Russell to tell them where they could find George that night. You know *why* those two "policemen" went to Smoke's that night to seek George out. To goad him into a fight, and then pretend he was resisting arrest so they could kill him!' Mrs Boren stared back at him until finally he bowed his head, and patted the rail as if it were her hand.

'But George didn't intend to kill Robert Pym, even after Robert Pym assaulted him. *Reason* tells you, he would have felt around under that table for his glasses, and put them on so he could *see* to shoot to kill, if that had been his intent! It was a fated, misfortunate shot that Pym was killed. All George was trying to do was save his own life. And you've heard from witness after witness after witness that George *was* right to believe his life was in danger! That is the God's truth.'

Isaac stepped back, raising his arms in a sweep at the jury. 'In the strength of that truth, stand up together. Stand up and break the shackles of prejudice, and lies, that have bound this prisoner to Death for seven long dark years. The key is yours to turn at last. Use it to open the doors. Set George Hall free.'

His wrists crashed together as if they too were manacled, then his arms fell to his sides, motionless. There was no sound but the soaring of his old, hoarsened, beautiful voice. 'Set George free. And when you do, I promise you this. You will hear the mighty wings of Truth set free. You will hear the song of justice in this land. And your hearts will be glad and proud that you twelve men and women of North Carolina have once more sent out the word like a dove across this nation: "We hold this truth to be self-evident. We are all created equal."'

No one clapped. No one cheered. No one moved.

Finally Judge Hilliardson asked if the defence had finished and Isaac nodded that he had. The State's rebuttal was brief. Mitch simply said that the 'handicap' under which George Hall had shot Robert Pym made it no less murder, and that Robert Pym, even in death, had equal rights to justice too. After Mitch returned to his chair, the judge folded his hands together, and told the jury there remained only his instructions. They lasted half an hour. They were, however, according to Isaac, the most lucid instructions he'd heard in twenty years. First, Hilliardson told the jury that they were not the judge. *He* was there to interpret the law, and would take every care to do so justly. Nor were they the police. It was not their function to investigate. It was their function to come to a reasonable conclusion, based on the facts offered in evidence, as to whether or not the defendant had committed the crime with which he'd been charged.

Taking a sip of water, Hilliardson next glanced through the notebook he'd kept during the trial. He would now, he said, instruct them as to the law. And he closed the book. Then he explained murder and manslaughter in all degrees, the perimeters of self-defence and premeditation, the relevance of intent and motive. He told them that the verdict handed down by the first trial should have no bearing on their decision; nor should any suffering the defendant might have endured as a result have any bearing. That circumstantial evidence presented by the State was sufficient to convict if they believed beyond a reasonable doubt that such evidence, viewed in the light most favourable to the defendant, proved instead his guilt. That the credibility of witnesses was for them to decide and that if they believed witnesses unworthy of belief, they should discount their testimony. That the burden of proof rested on the State, and if they *doubted* that proof, then the State had not made its case.

Still, in essence, what it came down to was this: if the jury believed George Hall was telling them the truth, then they were free to return a verdict of not guilty by reason of self-defence, and if they didn't believe him, then they were free to find him guilty. When Hilliardson asked if they had any questions, they looked at each other, already a group, bonded apart from the rest of us. No, they didn't have any questions. Judge Hilliardson's cold hooded eyes met each of theirs. 'Weigh carefully your responsibility,' he said, tightening his hard mouth. 'It is not a light one. I expect and require you to act accordingly.' And at two-twenty-five P.M., he sent them out.

'God, can you believe that Shirley Hilliardson?' groaned Bubba Percy, scraping over a chair to join me in the Municipal Building basement's 'snack bar,' an overlit corridor lined with vending machines. 'I bet he sleeps in a freezer. I bet he pees sleet.' Bubba bit into a greyish hot dog, grimacing as he chewed. There were nine or ten other reporters sprawled at tables around us. Like me, they were waiting for word. The jury was still out. They'd only been heard from once – when they'd sent word at four-thirty that they'd like a transcript of Arthur Butler's testimony. Isaac and Nora were upstairs waiting in the bailiff's office with George. Mitch Bazemore was no doubt in his own office, planning his prosecutions of Purley Newsome and Dyer Fanshaw. My watch said it was two minutes later than it was the last time I looked. Poking at my stale slice of cake, I said, 'What's your guess, Bubba?'

He glanced at his own watch, then chugged half a can of root beer. 'If they'd come back in fifteen minutes – I'd of said, clear-shot, guilty. Back in forty-five minutes, I'd have said, innocent. Now . . .' He burped. 'You got me. Even money. He's got the black vote solid. And the whites, well, let's say the Caucasians on the stand didn't come across like the sort you'd want to see marry your sister.' Bubba tore open a bag of peanuts and dropped them one by one into the root beer. 'But let's face it,

Mangum, nobody *forced* old George to chase the SOB down the block and plug him. And if that's the way he shoots *without* his glasses, I'd hate to have him aiming at me with them *on*. But he had some real good bits in his testimony. Faithful to the end. That's how folks like their blacks.' He took a swig from his can.

'Bubba, it's a real moral uplift being around a guy like you.'

'Any time.' He grinned. 'One thing I am sure of, the pressure's on in there. Get it over with. It's five-to-five on *Friday*, man. That jury doesn't want *another* weekend fucked. Supposed to be great weather too. We could have shot some baskets if you hadn't fed yourself through your paper shredder. You look as bad as this food, Mangum. Is that cake edible?'

I said it wasn't. I added that the cake was merely there as a symbol anyhow. I was, in fact (although I hadn't mentioned it to anyone, and no one had mentioned it to me), celebrating my birthday today.

'No shit,' Bubba said, fairly congenially. 'Well, have a good one. Man, I wish they'd hurry up. I got a dinner date.'

'Who with, Edwina Sunderland?'

'Nah. Cindy . . . something or other.'

A professional colleague of Percy's, a youngster in running shoes, clanked down the pay phone on the wall next to our table. Already trotting backwards, he announced that Andrew Brookside had been taken off the critical list. He was in his own room at UH, and in half an hour he'd be making a statement. Bubba and the rest of the men in the room took off after the youngster as if he'd made a clean sweep of their wallets.

Alone, I went back to the courtroom and walked quietly down the sloped aisle towards the bar rail. Here and there throughout the large silent room, a few people were still waiting, but not many. In the first row, behind the defence table, Nomi Hall sat with her sister and her minister. A deputy chatted with Mr Walkington, the court recorder. I climbed the steps to the bench, where Miss Bee Turner stood briskly tapping the judge's papers into neat stacks.

'What do you think, Miss Bee? Are we on hold till Monday?'

Her small, wrinkled face pursed up at me as she crossed her arms tightly under her breasts. 'No,' she decided. 'I asked the foreman if they wanted to order dinner, and he declined. I suspect they're close.'

Miss Bee, as usual, was right about the goings-on in 'her' Superior Court. And at five-forty-two, she ordered those of us who were in there to rise, as 'the Honourable Shirley W. Hilliardson presiding' stalked to his high leather chair and perched motionless while the jury filed back in. Behind her son, Nomi Hall's hands locked together against her mouth. Mitch sat at the far end of his table, away from his assistant, Neil Sadler. Across the room, Isaac had one hand on George's arm, the other on Nora's hand. But his eyes stayed on the jury. I looked at them too, but I couldn't tell. Their faces were carefully frozen, their heads turned towards their foreman, the school principal. Mrs Boren still squeezed her purse the way she always had.

'Members of the jury, have you reached a verdict?'

Gerd Lindquist, the foreman, stood up, an ordinary-looking man in his late fifties, a little overweight, a little out of shape, a little bald. He coughed, then said loudly, 'Yes, Your Honour, we have.' He held out the folded piece of paper to Miss Bee, who scuddled over, took it from him, and after an expressionless glance at the contents, stretched up on her toes to hand it to Hilliardson.

'The defendant will rise.'

Together George, Isaac, and Nora stood behind their table.

The judge swivelled his chair towards the foreman. 'What say you, members of the jury? Do you find the defendant – guilty or not guilty?'

The foreman glanced back at his fellow jurors. Some nodded at him. Then he turned towards George Hall, and looked at him. Isaac knew. His hand was already raised to hug the black man's shoulder, as the words 'Not guilty, Your Honour' rang out like the clang of bells.

When he said the words, Lindquist smiled, and in an odd gesture, as if they'd just met, he lifted his hand slightly and waved at George.

All the voices sounded together. Martin Hall's shout of 'Yes!' Nomi Hall's sister's sobbing 'Praise God!' Other cheers and words and claps, while Hilliardson waited patiently above the noise. George was still standing. Then I saw his head nod twice towards the jury box. At the accountant, the farmer's widow, the housewives, the bus driver, the flower-shop clerk. The twelve men and women were already beginning to rustle, look at the room, at the weather outside the windows, at their watches; going back to their ordinary lives, shedding their solemnity as if they were a little embarrassed by the sacredness they'd felt themselves. George turned from them, shook Nora's hand, shook

Isaac's hand. And only after that did I see him move for the first time as if he weren't twenty years older than he was. Whirling round, he reached over the wooden bar and pulled his mother up into his arms.

Chapter 31

The day George Hall walked out of Superior Court, and into whatever life he could find, Andy Brookside walked into a lounge at University Hospital, and into the embrace of a mass of new supporters whom all the polls had said would vote against him. These were Lana Pym's 'just regular people,' people jealous of privilege, and suspicious of brains. But they turned out also to be people who couldn't resist a man with enough guts to get shot in the heart, and enough magic to stand up and walk away from it.

I was a year older today, and nobody but Bubba Percy seemed to know it. I was home, alone. Drinking a beer, sorting with my good hand through a box of old papers and letters (a few from my ex-wife, Cheryl, who'd dotted her 'i's with hearts; a few from Lee, whose stationery had the faint scent of her perfume), I sat on my living room carpet and watched Andrew Brookside's impromptu press conference on the evening news. Pale and handsome, he stood behind the jumble of microphones, his arm around Lee, and said very appealing, witty things about the fact that he'd almost died. He said that all along he'd been telling the voters he was the candidate with a heart, and now he had pictures to prove it. He told funny little jokes Lee had supposedly made as he was being wheeled from the recovery room. Lee laughed at them, and kissed him for the cameras.

Martha Mitchell stayed away from me; she'd seen me in this kind of mood before, and maybe figured I was going to have her put to sleep for running up the vet bills in her old age. When I flung the beer can in the trash with the letters, she barked angrily, then hobbled in a hurry all the way upstairs.

I couldn't stand the way I felt either. Not just the itch of my sutures and the pinch of my cast; I couldn't stand any of the objects in the room. Couldn't stand my apartment, my job, or Hillston, or Brookside's arm around Lee, or myself. So I left a note on my door, went out to my car, got in it, and drove. I drove Airport Road twice as fast as anybody ought to. I put on a tape of Jerry Lee Lewis, put it on loud, and I listened mile after mile to the pounding of his hard high white-trash speed, gritty as the country and mean as a knife. I listened to him until I got tired of his noise and his anger, until I wore out my own. I outdrove Jerry Lee – 'the Killer' – and that's hard driving.

Then I turned down the road to Dollard Prison. Parked in the gravel lot, I sat a long while, looking up at the dark brick turrets. George Hall wasn't in there. That was something. Zack Carpenter was still in there, doing the best he could. That was something. Finally, I turned the Olds around, and headed back to Hillston. The lights of the small skyline twinkled, indistinguishable from the lights of the stars. I knew all the buildings by heart. The people in them were reasonably safe. That was something too.

I put on Aretha Franklin, and told her, 'Let's go home.'

The note had been for Justin and Alice. She'd called and asked would it be all right if they came over to watch television. It was a first step we all needed to take. So in the note I'd told them to look for the key where I always left it for them. But from the hall now, I heard rock-'n'-roll music. And when I opened my door, I walked under a canopy of blue and gold balloons, into the chatter of at least twenty people, all of whom worked at HPD, and all of whom spun around and yelled, 'HAPPY BIRTHDAY!' at me. The same message was spray-painted with shaving cream on my balcony sliders. In the middle of the carpet, with a blue bow on top, was a television screen as big as my wall mural, the ultra-modern thin Japanese style, a black square with Dolby speakers. Brenda Moore and Wes Pendergraph ran forward with a life-sized cardboard cutout, taken from a news photo, of me in my raincoat on the steps of the Municipal Building. There was a card taped to my hand: 'The Force Is With You,' it read, and it was signed by the one hundred thirty-eight members of the Hillston Police Department.

'Isn't it disgusting?' shouted Ralph Fisher from my kitchen.

'That's a *sixty*-inch screen! DiMallo and Baker brought it over in the wagon.'

Shouting through the music, I asked the circle of faces, 'Y'all didn't put this on my Visa, did you?'

Etham Foster stood by a plastic tub floating with bottles and cans; overhand he threw John Emory a beer to give me. Then Etham tapped his watch. 'Two hours, thirty-one minutes late, man, to your own party.'

I toasted the Force, and thanked them.

In the kitchen, bacon-fat spat bubbling as Justin dumped a huge bowl of home-fries into my cast-iron frying pan. On my counter, boxes from Hot Hat Barbecue were heaped with greasy bones. Justin looked over at me, and raised his hand. He nodded at me. I nodded back. And then he smiled. 'Well, the party's almost over,' he said. ' "Make yourselves at home." What's that supposed to mean? It's usually considered a little nicer to hang around when you're expecting company—'

'I wasn't expecting this much company.'

Alice waddled in from the bathroom, her sun dress floating out a good foot in front of her. She said, 'I'm glad you were born,' and tried to kiss me, but couldn't reach until I bent from the waist. She rolled her eyes, 'And when somebody else I know gets born, I can't *tell* you how glad I'll be.'

'Hey, grits, come and get your grease,' Justin called. 'Hold these buns smack in the middle, or the hamburgers will slide right out.'

By ten-thirty, everyone but Alice and Justin had gone home, or back to work. John Emory was driving to the hospital, to see how Nancy was doing, and to sit a while with Zeke, who never left the place. Justin and Alice, who'd ridden over with Etharri, stayed to clean up, and I was going to drive them back to Bush Street.

A little after eleven, Nora Howard knocked on the door, carrying a package and a platter of Italian pastries with candles stuck in them. Alice whistled at her. "God, you look beautiful! And you're so tan!" Running her hands over her own stomach, she added, 'I have to hold on to that thought. *You* had children. *You* looked like this. And now you look like *that*. Where'd you guys and the Halls celebrate?'

'The Pine Hills Inn. And I don't think any of us will go back. Their attitude, like their food, was ... don't take this personally, Justin ... a little waspy.' Nora handed him the pastries, then pulled the thin white strap back up on her bare shoulder. 'Isaac went over to the Halls' house. He sent this.' In the package was a thousand-page anthology of love poetry.

'That's an odd present from him,' Alice said.

Nora said, 'My God, look at that TV! They said it'd be *big*, but—'

Rolling the console towards the wall, Justin called over his shoulder, 'Quick, plug it in. *Casablanca*'s on Channel Seven at eleven-thirty. Or are you feeling tired, Cuddy?'

'No, actually I feel a lot better.'

'*Casablanca*'s what we were going to say we came over to watch.'

I said, 'Fine, but I've seen it.'

Justin started yanking jacks out of my old TV set. 'Oh, you love *Casablanca*. You always cry at the noble stuff. "It's a far far better place I'm going than you can follow. What I've got to do, you can't be any part of. Here's mud in your eye, kid."'

'Oh, Jesus!' I plugged the VCR unit into the new model. '"Here's looking at you, kid. *Here's looking at you, kid!*"'

'See!' Justin grinned. 'He loves that movie.'

A thought occurred to me, and on consideration, I decided I liked it. I said, 'Okay, you're right. In fact, I'm going to make a tape of it, if I can find a blank one.' So I opened my drawer of videotapes, reached behind them and found the one I'd hidden there after Etham Foster had brought it to me, the one labelled 'Jane Fonda's Workout,' the one Bubba had joked that I could trade for the Biltmore Mansion. I shook the cassette from its case, then I closed the drawer.

Alice was hauling over my leather sling chair, and Nora was tossing my couch cushions on to the floor. I ate one of the pastries, and watched them. Alice and Nora grinned at each other, like they had a secret.

After a dozen commericals, the black-and-white globe of the wartime world filled the huge bright screen. The earnest narrator's voice said, "... But not everybody could get to Lisbon directly ..."'

I slid the 'Workout' cassette into the VCR, and punched Record.

*

494

After I took Justin and Alice home, I drove across town, up Cadmean Street to the Municipal Building. Hiram Davies was there at the desk, reading his Bible. 'I hope you had a nice party. Everything's fine here,' he told me quietly. 'Everything's under control. You should go to bed, Cuddy.'

I said, '. . . All right.' I patted his hand on the Bible. 'Remember me in your prayers, Hiram, okay?'

The old sergeant pulled his glasses down on his nose to look at me. He shook his head. 'I always do,' he said. 'Go home.'

But first I drove into East Hillston. On Maplewood, there were Andrew Brookside posters in some of the store windows. I stopped at a kerb to look at one of them. '*Your* Candidate. *Your* State. *Your* Choice.'

Cardboard covered the front of the duplex I'd grown up in. There were cracks and holes in the driveway where my father had bent scrubbing for hours at his car, trying to make at least one thing perfect in his life. Farther east, most of Canaan was sleeping, but on Mill Street, lights shone from every window of Nomi Hall's house. Nearby, music still bounced out of Smoke's into the night.

At the top of the hill across the street from Smoke's, the mural painted to honour Cooper Hall was lit from below, so that everyone in Canaan could see it. Cooper's hand reached up, right under the painted sun, as if he'd just lifted it into place. And all along the mural's base, small blood-red brambled roses grew out of the bright grass, climbing up the broken wall, into the colours of the painting.

Epilogue

'A great while ago the world begun,
With hey, ho, the wind and the rain;
But that's all one . . .'

Twelfth Night

Over thirty thousand people appeared at Cadmean Stadium on the last evening in June to attend the 'Night of Stars' Brookside rally. Maybe some of the spectators had really come to see the rock singer, or the Hollywood celebrities, or had come just because they'd heard everybody else was coming. But they all cheered when Andy Brookside stood in the swirling spotlights, and told them that the old power brokers didn't own the state of North Carolina, that *they* owned it. And they all stood up and cheered when he told them that maybe the old power brokers had begun to realize that they couldn't vote Andy Brookside out of the race, or buy him out of the race, or *shoot* him out of the race either!

Then he talked about a lot of things that Governor Wollston had done wrong. He didn't include as one of them the fact that the governor had no plans to stop the execution of Joe Bonder, who was scheduled to die at Dollard Prison in two more days. In a speech interrupted thirty times by applause, Brookside did not say one word about the fact that a twenty-year-old black man – who'd always claimed it was his partner who'd shot the liquor store owner, and who didn't seem to be able to grasp the idea of his own imminent death – was going to the gas chamber.

There were only a dozen protestors outside the gates of the prison the night Joe Bonder died; among them, George Hall stood in silent vigil with his mother, Nomi, and his cousin, Martin. Holding a candle, Paul Madison read aloud from the prayer book. Myself, I was there because I was waiting for Isaac and Nora. They were inside now, seated on benches arranged so that witnesses could look through the glass to see the man strapped into the metal chair. The old lawyer had told Nora he had a single requirement of any partner who might ever be asked to defend someone against a capital charge: The requirement was that she should witness with her own eyes what would happen to her client if she lost.

Near me by the guardhouse, Jordan West kept watch quietly, arm in arm with the young psychiatrist she'd just married. And I recognized faces from the old Hall vigil group moving in a slow circle, with their candles and their signs that said, 'STOP THE KILLING.' But there weren't as many as there had been for George, or the time before George, or the time before that. As Jack Molina told the solitary reporter who drove by to interview them, 'We know we're not in the majority. But then neither were those other irritating little groups of cranks who made pests of themselves, being the first to say, "Stop! Look at what we're doing. Stop this slavery. Stop this genocide. Stop this war."'

The young woman reporter didn't think it was at all fair to compare an execution to genocide; and besides, the condemned man had been given a fair trial.

The candle flame burned in Molina's old wire-rimmed glasses. 'This nation's whole social system is on trial here tonight.' Then resting his hand on the top of his sign, he gave her some figures about who was scheduled for execution across this country, and where in this country, and why. But the reporter didn't write it down, and she left a few minutes later.

'It's not even news anymore,' he said to me, as we watched her drive off. And raising the handle of the picket sign, he walked back to take his place in the circle.

Zackery Carpenter told me later that Joe Bonder 'went in quietly.'

The doctor's execution log told me that at 9:02:45, the chamber was locked. At 9:04:33, sodium cyanide eggs entered the vat of sulphuric acid, releasing gas vapours; 9:05:51, prisoner inhaled gas; 9:09, prisoner in distress. At 9:21:10, heart stopped. At 9:35, exhaust valve opened and drained; at 9:58 – prisoner removed, declared dead.

When I looked at Nora's eyes as I helped her into the car, she didn't need to tell me anything.

Sluggish and blowsy, summer hung on as long as it could, till maple leaves drooped big and limp as dusty rags from the sagging boughs. Downtown, hot empty streets were sticky with melted tar. Lives changed, if they did change, behind air-conditioned doors. The news changed, of course. It quickly forgot George Hall, and ran to Dyer Fanshaw. During summer's long dull days, questions hummed like a lazy fly through the North Hillston homes of the inner circle: Would a man of Fanshaw's stature ever really have to go to jail, or would his fancy quartet of lawyers get him off? Atwater Randolph thought they would; the bank and the towel company weren't so sure. Or so I heard from Peggy Savile. After Fanshaw's arrest, Atwater and his friends had apparently decided I wasn't one of them, and I didn't get invited to the Club's summer dance.

The Club's other favourite subject of gossip turned out to be Briggs Mary Cadmean, who'd apparently at some point forked over millions of dollars to Haver University for the construction of a planetarium; the scaffolding for it was now, ironically, rising right across the greensward from her papa's new textiles laboratory. So, despite old Cadmean's codicil, 'Baby' had figured out a way to have her stars, and her inheritance too. I suspect he might have admired her chicanery. On Jordan West's advice, Briggs had long ago turned over to the journal *With Liberty and Justice* her father's $25,000 bequest to Cooper Hall. Last I heard, G. G. Walker, who was running the office between classes, had talked her into matching the old man's donation.

Speaking of thousands in donated dollars, Paul Madison called me one day with 'great news.' Bill Gilchrist had lied to us. He had not put nearly as much as he'd claimed of the stolen forty thousand into the collection plates at Trinity Church. 'You know, Cuddy,' confessed the rector, 'I *thought*, even in little dribbles and drabbles, I would have *noticed* that sort of rise in our cash take.' Instead of contributing the money to God as he'd told us, Billy had hidden a good two-thirds inside the crypt of a Mr T. C. W. Polk, the church founder, an act which seemed, even to Paul, 'a little much.' Still, Billy's pastor was thoroughly delighted to learn

498

that his lost sheep was alive. For Paul had received a letter from Miami, where Billy had fled with the money – despite his professed eagerness to testify for Jesus, not to mention for Isaac Rosethorn. He'd gone there to escape what he described as 'the heat' – by which I assume he meant that Winston Russell was looking to kill him in some pretty unpleasant way. All things considered, as Paul said, we could hardly blame Billy for taking that plane south.

As for not getting in touch all these months, well, he'd read in the papers that 'things worked out ok for John [sic] Hall anyhow,' and that 'some cop took out Rusel [sic], which to tell you the truth, Father Paul, after comming across the inclosed [a newspaper clipping describing Madison's knife wounds], I say good riddance.' Honesty compelled Billy also to acknowledge that his old Nemesis, a pint a day, had snagged him in February, and hustled him off the straight-and-narrow, down a detour. A detour that wound around Florida's dog tracks and horse tracks. A detour where, as Billy bluntly put it, he'd 'blown his wad to zip.' Which was why (in addition to once again having the ears to hear the call of salvation) he was writing this letter. Could Father Paul mail him, c/o General Delivery, a hundred bucks so that he might take a bus home to Trinity? Paul could. And did. And still expects Billy Gilchrist to appear one day at mass to hoist the banner of St Michael. I said, 'That's nuts.' He said, 'That's faith.'

Perhaps on its time-tested guideline of 'To those who have, more shall be given,' Fortune awarded first prize in Paul's Trinity Church Porsche Raffle to Mrs Marion Sunderland. I was surprised Edwina didn't keep the car herself; it was about her speed. Bubba, on the other hand, was crushed that she didn't slap a ribbon on the hood, and leave it outside the *Hillston Star* for him. But, of course, family blood is thicker than even the pulse of geriatric infatuation, and Eddie gave the Porsche to her grand-nephew, whose new wife, the voluptuous Blue Randolph Sunderland, totalled it a few months later while driving under the influence and over the speed limit. 'The bitch didn't get a scratch on her,' exclaimed Bubba, presumably outraged that Fortune was as cavalier as he was. He didn't win the Pulitzer either.

I don't see Bubba much anymore. He quit the *Star* to become Andrew Brookside's press secretary. 'Give us ten years,' he predicted. 'We'll be rolling Easter eggs on the White House lawn. DC, here I come! Now *that* town is swimming in loose pussy! Catch you later, Mangum. Keep the peace in Boonieville.'

Alice MacLeod, a woman of strong will as well as political fervour, gave birth exactly as she had planned, during the legislature's recess, and while she didn't make the Fourth of July, she did manage Bastille Day. Three more minutes, and she would have missed that holiday too. They didn't even arrive at UH until 11:30 P.M., but the baby was so fast that Justin never had a chance to use all the Lamaze techniques he'd memorized.

'That's the way we do it in the mountains,' Alice whispered with a dopey grin that wasn't like her at all. The next morning she told the 'Features' editor from the *Star* that she planned to finish her term in the state legislature, where she'd be chairing two new committees. After that, she was thinking of running for Congress. Justin's mother and I shared a Thermos of what tasted like pure gin, under the portrait of Justin's father, J.B.S. IV, and we toasted all seven pounds, two ounces, of Cuthbert MacLeod Savile the First.

'Bertie' was what his parents had been calling him before they saw him, but when he slid yelling in the world burning like the sun, his fuzzy head shiny and the colour of Alice's nutmeg hair, they dubbed him 'Copper' on the spot. And 'Copper' he is to all his honorary godparents on the force at HPD, which he tours regularly, first from an L. L. Bean pouch on Justin's chest, then from a hand-carved wooden stroller that had been in the Dollard family since the primordial mud. 'I don't like plastic,' Justin says. But Copper and I have an understanding. He secretly admires the plastic board of buzzing, whirring gizmos I gave him, and the musical robot and the Swing-a-matic I bring out when my godson comes to visit me, and we're already whispering together about computer basketball, maybe an electron microscope.

Justin and I never talk about Winston Russell. But sometimes I dream of that orange moon and the crooked gravestones. And I think of Winston's empty eyes whenever Nancy looks sad. I was best man at her and Zeke's wedding.

As for my life, I do my job, read my books, do my job. I was a witness for the prosecution at Purley Newsome's pretrial hearing, where Isaac (Dr Rosethorn, now that he's been awarded an honourary degree by Haver University) drove Mitch Bazemore into such a bulging rage he popped his collar button. Dr Rosethorn says Nora and he plan to 'tear me to shreds' when I take the stand against Purley, in what will be the old lawyer's 'absolutely last case' before turning the business over to his partner. Sometimes I think he and Martha both will survive me, and live

500

on midnight snacks forever, snarling at each other in that cluttered, smoking room at the Piedmont. Isaac visits the Halls once a week, and Edith Keene once a week, and I visit him more regularly than I used to.

In October, fall finally blew through Hillston, and in a three-day spree painted the town red with falling leaves. People could breathe again; they came out from behind their air-conditioners, took to the sidewalks, carried on vigorous conversations about football and politics. One day the sky was so crisp that on the spur of the moment I bought an Italian bicycle, and rode it home to River Rise. For the last blocks, I followed behind a bouncy school bus, and when Laura and Brian Howard got off it in a plaid tumble of children, I raced over, violently squeezing my horn.

'He really is the police chief,' Laura told her friend.

For about two weeks, health enthusiasts – like my new sergeant, John Emory – had great hopes for me. Every day I pedalled downtown and back, and even twice sped across the Shocco Bridge fifteen miles out to my little cabin on Pine Hills Lake. Then I locked up the bicycle, and went back to travelling by Oldsmobile, like before. I'll probably sell the cabin, although everybody tells me I was smart to invest in waterfront property, and ought to hang on to it. But, of course, I can't explain I invested too much in the place besides money, and suffered a loss.

On the first Tuesday in November, a day of cold grey drizzle, Andrew Theodore Brookside was elected governor of the state of North Carolina. Nora came over that night, offering a bottle of champagne in exchange for a chance to watch the election returns on my huge Mitsubishi screen. The gubernatorial race turned out to be a close one; much closer than Carl Yarborough's victorious bid against Brodie Cheek's candidate for his second term as Hillston's mayor. Communist candidate Janet Malley, who also ran against Carl, gave her old 'the fire next time' concession speech twenty minutes after the polls closed. Julian Lewis didn't concede to Brookside until almost midnight, but then he conceded with that pleasant, tanned, ingratiating Dollard charm that was the family's best-cultivated stock. His followers cried when he thanked them, and he got an appealing lump in his throat as he told them to be of good cheer, 'because after all, as someone said, tomorrow *is* another day!' Meanwhile, he planned to take a rest in Bermuda, then come home and – affable chuckle – look for a job.

The closeness of the race had nothing to do with last-minute revelations about Lewis's personal involvement in a cover-up of his cronies' crimes, or last-minute exposes of Brookside's – in Molina's phrase – imprudence. Neither of those stories ever made it to Channel 7's 'Action News,' or to the *Star*, or any other major paper. Whether because the two camps had come to an understanding about mutual deescalation, or because the media had reached a gentlemen's agreement, or even because Edwina Sunderland (who owned most of the shares of most of the news in the state) had helped Bubba keep the lid on – I really couldn't say for sure. Like I told Andrew Brookside when Lee introduced us, I'm not tight with the powers that be.

As Lewis began his concession speech, Nora and I shot the champagne cork out the balcony sliders into the night rain. We toasted four years of a hero, even a wounded one, instead of more of what he'd called the 'same smug dumb thieves.' As Carol Cathy Cane took us live to Brookside's celebration at the Sir Walter Raleigh Hotel, the ballroom looked like VE-day in Times Square. Even Jack Molina was hugging people, though not his wife, Debbie, who was nowhere in evidence. Nora, kneeling close to the screen, pointed out Justin and Alice in the crowd: Justin, wearing a tuxedo, in a circle of North Hillstonians; Alice near the podium, chatting to a couple of slimeball ward bosses. (Her support of Andy Brookside had stayed as intense as ever, even if she hadn't wanted to be his 'executive secretary.') Father Paul Madison was in the crowd too; still resembling, despite the ugly blaze of his scar, a cherubim beaming down from the frescoed ceiling of some aristocrat's palazzo.

As soon as the band struck up the Brookside theme song, 'Carolina in the Morning,' and the governor-elect stepped, like a star through clouds, out between the dark drapes behind the podium, his campaign workers rushed towards him, so antic with joy that excitement overwhelmed even Carol Cathy, who shouted over the bedlam, 'This is really, oh, it's *wonderful*!'

With eyes glowing, with arms stretched out to all the hands reaching for him, with his bright hair, his lover's smile, Andy Brookside was radiant. He shone. I don't know another word for the way the man wore glory. The whole room lightened as he stepped to the microphone. 'Tonight . . . tonight, "you few, you

502

happy few" have won a great victory for the state of North Carolina! *Tonight the Past died! Tomorrow, with the sun, the phoenix of the Future rises! We will be there, together, on its wings!'*

Lee stood beside him, applauding with the others. She was very beautiful. She seemed happy for him.

I noticed Nora glance at me, then back at the screen; then with a deep slow breath that lifted her shoulders, she clicked the set off, swivelled on the knees of her jeans, all the way around to face the couch, where I was lying, my champagne glass resting on my HPD sweatshirt, Martha's chin on my bare feet. Outside, the rain kept falling. It tapped on my windows, steady as time.

'Listen,' Nora said, and smiled, her head tilting. 'Why don't you give me a chance? Come on, don't you bet if I had, oh, five hundred million dollars or so, I could look pretty good too?'

On the screen behind her, the Brooksides shrank to a bright diamond, and went out.

I laughed, and she nodded at me. 'Good,' she said. 'You're laughing. Laughter's a very good sign.'

Champagne spilled on my hand; I brought it to my mouth, cool and sweet. 'Oh, honey, laughter's our one hope in hell. And the only one.'

Nora said, 'If you could spare me the next thirty or forty years, Cudberth, I think I can prove beyond a reasonable doubt that you don't believe that at all.'

Rain leapt dancing down from my balcony, keeping warm the winter earth.